CROSSED

ALSO BY NICOLE GALLAND

Revenge of the Rose

The Fool's Tale

CROSSED

A Tale of the Fourth Crusade

NICOLE GALLAND

HARPER

NEW YORK · LONDON · TORONTO · SYDNEY

HARPER

This book is a work of fiction. The characters, incidents, and dialogue are drawn from the author's imagination and are not to be construed as real. Any resemblance to actual events or persons, living or dead, is entirely coincidental.

HarperCollins books may be purchased for educational, business, or sales promotional use. For information please write: Special Markets Department, HarperCollins Publishers, 10 East 53rd Street, New York, NY 10022.

FIRST EDITION

Maps designed by Jeffrey Korn/www.jeffreykorn.com

Designed by Cassandra J. Pappas

Library of Congress Cataloging-in-Publication Data

Galland, Nicole.
   Crossed : tale of the Fourth Crusade / Nicole Galland.—1st Harper paperbacks.
      p. cm.
   ISBN: 978-0-06-084180-5
      1. Crusades—Fourth, 1202–1204—Fiction. 2. Knights and knighthood—Fiction. 3. Princesses—Fiction. 4. Impostors and imposture—Fiction. 5. Istanbul (Turkey)—History—Siege, 1203–1204—Fiction. I. Title.

PS3607.A4154C76 2007
813'.54—dc22

2006047082

08 09 10 11 12 OV/RRD 10 9 8 7 6 5 4 3 2 1

For my parents

Contents

Acknowledgments

First to thank are my professional patron saints: Liz Darhansoff, Marc Glick, and Rich Green, and my team at Harper, including but not limited to Jennifer Brehl, Katherine Nintzel, Juliette Shapland, Carrie Kania, Jennifer Hart, Nicole Reardon, and Katherine Baker.

The many others to whom I am grateful fall into three categories, roughly:

The saviors: Alan and Maureen Crumpler, Bill and Rachel Galland, Nick Walker.

The sages: Tom Dunlop, Dr. Michael Angold, Dr. Jonathan Phillips, Dr. Stephen Bowman, Shira Kammen, Dr. Claudio lo Monaco, Jess Taylor.

The incredibly helpful everyone-elses: Steve Lewis, Philip and Becky Resnik, my folks (Karen & Mike Colaneri and Leo Galland), Thomas Hale, Laurence Bouvard, Ruth Levitch, Dr. Peter Noble, Marc Newell, Captains Bob and Morgan Douglas and First Mate Ryan Dickerson, Jeff Korn and Lori Glaser, Lindsay Smith, Mari Morgan, Catrin Brace, Mark Judson, the three blokes from Northern Ireland, the water engineer Allan Bronsro, Amy Utstein, Eowyn Mader, Jeff Sahadi—and Orhan.

My apologies for anyone I have left out by mistake. I take full responsibility for the misapplication of others' expertise.

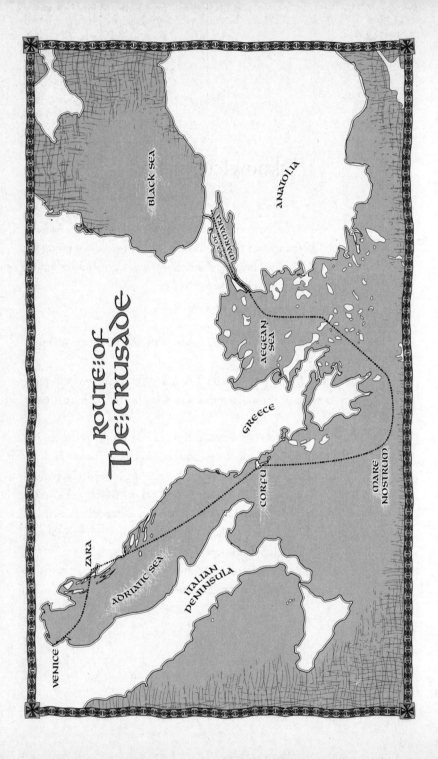

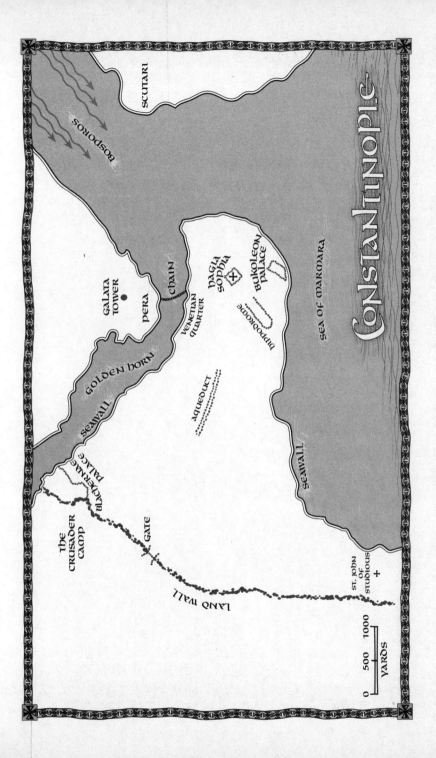

Act I

VENICE

Here let me tell you of one of the most remarkable and
extraordinary events you have ever heard of.

—GEOFFREY OF VILLEHARDOUIN,
Chronicle of the Fourth Crusade

1

FROM SAN NICOLO, that sweltering sandbar of an island off the coast of Venice, rose a strange tent city milling with ten thousand unwashed soldiers and their unwashed squires, whores, cooks, priests, horses, heralds, armorers, and smiths. They called themselves pilgrims, having taken the cross, having sworn to carry out the pope's wishes. This meant they were going to an unknown desert, to wrest an unknown city from its unknown inhabitants.

Their transports and warships, waiting in the lagoon—heavy, strong, capacious, lethal—had been built by the Venetians, would be sailed by the Venetians, and at this moment were being stocked with food and water by the Venetians. In two days, the army and its fleet would finally—*finally*—set sail, after a season of political and financial delays, to do great good for Christendom.

But before they decamped, this would be the site of a gruesome murder-suicide, of such ferocity men would speak of it in fearful whispers, crossing themselves, for years to come.

At least, that was my plan.

As with so many things in this life, I was mistaken.

I LEAPT FROM Barzizza's boat when the water was ankle-deep, trudging angrily through the oily green until I had splashed myself to dry land and the edge of the army camp. Venice was mostly paving stone and water; this was the first time in a month I'd been on living soil. Earth felt comforting under my bare wet feet, but I didn't want comfort—I wanted death, and was panicked at the thought of being cheated of it. I'd learned half a dozen languages, taught myself to play music I did not like, and eaten food I could barely stomach, grown my beard and my hair, and woken up every day forcing myself to go on, for three years, to prepare for my exquisite, redemptive death—a death I now feared I'd been robbed of.

I had no weapon, just a spit of iron small enough to fold my hand around: a spike with a hook on one end, stolen from Barzizza's house, some sort of fishing spear. I don't remember how I learned which pavilion was the high commander's or what trick I used to distract the guards at the door, but the trick was fast accomplished; I was still seething as I scrambled inside, I could still hear my heartbeat pulsing in my temples as my eyes adjusted to the darkness.

There were only two men in this cool, open space: the army commander himself and a large young knight kneeling to his right, presumably his bodyguard. Both wore tunics decorated with broad gold braids. They were whispering together. Neither was the man I wanted.

"*Where are the English?*" I shouted.

The two men started, stared at me; the knight lumbered to his feet, grabbing for the dagger in his belt, as the leader responded, in a droll voice, "They are in England, I imagine."

So it was true, what Barzizza had told me; this final trek had been for nothing. A howl of humiliated rage escaped me. Across my mind flashed the journey back to Britain. I would never survive that. My one chance for revenge had been illusory; my intended victim had never even been in reach. With the warped logic of despair and rage, I decided then that I would still forfeit the one life that was yet mine to take: my own.

Both of the men staring at me now were armed. This would be simple, then: I had only to hurl myself upon the leader, and the bodyguard would kill me instantly.

When you know this one is your final heartbeat, time slows for a final savoring of the senses. In less than a blink I noticed more about my surroundings than I had in years: the feel of the woven-grass mats under my feet; the elaborate, bright decorations on the tent walls; the smell of rose water and woolly must that pervaded the pavilion; the commander's aristocratic handsomeness; the likable face of the young man who was about to skewer me. He had both sword and dagger in his belt; I wondered which he would use.

I also noticed, in that flicker, that I was interrupting something significant. Although the knight had been kneeling, there was an informality between them, as if they were kin. The lord looked oddly *relieved* by my interruption—until I raised the spike above my head and threw myself at him.

The young man was quick for one so large, but he was nowhere near as quick as I was, and I realized that I could accidentally kill the lord. The lord cringed, but he did not move to protect himself, trusting his knight. I myself did not trust his knight, and as my hands descended, I shirked, pulled back a hair, so that the hooked point of the spike just missed the lord's skull and only my knuckles glanced off his bald brow; by then the knight had me, huge left paw grabbing me around the throat, huge right one shoving the dagger point against my liver. So this was it: I was over now, finally and despite everything. Suddenly I was flooded with euphoria, and involuntarily, I grinned at him—my executioner, my liberator. His hair and beard gave his face a golden glow. I literally loved him more than my own life.

Our eyes locked; all my weight rested in his clenched left fist around my throat, the knife at my gut, as I waited for him to plunge it in.

He didn't.

He yanked the blade away and shoved me hard to the matted ground, where I choked on a mouthful of straw.

Something had gone horribly wrong: I wasn't dead.

The knight said something in a garbled language to the lord, who answered similarly. There was a brief debate, which to this day I cannot remember understanding. Listening in stunned outrage, I gradually recognized it as a Lombard dialect I was familiar with; at that point they could have been speaking in my native tongue and it would have sounded like so much nonsense. I was removed from my own skin, too dazed to understand what was happening.

By the time I registered that I was not only not dead but—a far worse affair—completely *alive*, the young man had returned his attention to me. "You're not a murderer," he declared. "You're a suicide. Suicide is a sin, and by St. John, I will not assist you in it."

I gawked. "I just tried to kill your master!" I protested. "Look, you stupid ass, I'll do it again!" I scrambled to my feet, light-headed, fighting back the urge to scream and laugh hysterically at once, and unsteadily I raised the spike. This time I wouldn't hesitate, I'd show the whoreson I meant business. He'd have no choice but to cut me down.

But everything seemed to slow. He grabbed me again, both of those meaty mitts reaching for my right hand, and again he heaved me down effortlessly. By the time I hit the floor of the tent, *he* held my spike. He tossed it away. "You pulled back," he announced. "We both saw it. You made sure not to hurt His Lordship the marquis. You are goading me to kill you, and I won't do it. Nor will anybody else."

He called out, "Richard," and a sweet-faced boy with a colorless wisp of facial down trotted into the tent. The knight gave him an order, and Richard moved toward me, matter-of-factly began to tie my hands in front of me.

"What are you *doing?*" I shouted, horrified.

"You are now my captive," the knight informed me—as if I should consider myself lucky. "No more of this nonsense." Inexplicably, although I no longer liked him, he still seemed to have a warm, earnest *glow* to him, as if this were his normal state.

"I'm a *criminal*," I protested. "*Execute* me, idiot, do the world a favor."

He grimaced disapprovingly and shook his head. And then, as if he were my loving older brother trying to teach me a lesson, he said, "From what I've seen, you are a sinner, not a criminal, and the burden of a sinner is to repent."

This could not really be happening. "You want me to *repent?*" I repeated weakly.

He nodded. The elegant marquis, watching us, looked almost amused now. "You will repent the impulse toward self-murder," announced the knight. "And whatever blackness is in your soul that drove you to such despair in the first place, you must also repent of that."

"And *then* you'll execute me?" I insisted, desperate.

The marquis laughed. The knight did not. The knight seemed to have nothing resembling a sense of humor at all. He was, it now seemed obvious, German.

Ordinarily I would not have sat there passively, letting some boy child tie me in knots insufficient to keep a tree from running off. But I'd just tossed myself into the arms of Death . . . and Death had tossed me back. I was in a state of shock. So when the boy pulled me to standing, I stood. Then, almost as an afterthought, I struggled against his grip. Only because I dimly remembered that I probably should.

"Bind his wrists, but don't hurt his hands," the knight said to the boy. "Look at those hands. I think he's a musician."

I stopped struggling, startled. I followed the boy out of the tent, blinking stupidly in the brilliant haze of the Venetian afternoon.

2

A dead man, or a prisoner, lacks both family and friends.

—RICHARD COEUR DE LION,
"Song from Prison"

THE THREE OF US trudged through nearly a mile of camp city in the late afternoon light. The sand was soft, almost powdery under my feet; it had rained a lot over the past month, but the last few days had been dry. The spark and smell of cooking fires caused my stomach to growl audibly. I had hardly eaten in several days, preparing for my great—in hindsight, ludicrous—moment of delivery, so I was weak as well as stunned. A mélange of languages and dialects made the encampment into a tower of Babel, although by now most had bled together into a patois, a lingua franca, almost everyone could speak: the rhythms and cadences of French, Occitan, Gascon, Piedmontese, Gacilian, Provençal, all of them passing familiar to me and similar to one another; words of tongues I did not yet know; the dialect of Venice; and occasionally, formally, Latin. There were a variety of pitches too—the mass of men making up the quiet baritone drone, and the louder voices, tenor like bells or bass like demigods, issuing commands.

I paid attention to none of it, but I knew what it was: After months of sweltering summer heat on this sandbar, the entire army of Christian pilgrims was preparing to embark, by boat, for the Holy Land. The camp was bustling with activity, everyone relieved that finally there would be some movement, some action, some *accomplishment*. Tomorrow the tents would be disassembled and packed away within the transports waiting in the lagoon; the following morning, with a good wind permitting, they would all set sail to do God's work. With a sinking feeling I suspected I was now to be among them. Beyond that I could not think at all, appalled to find myself alive. I was still dazed, as if I'd been half-woken from a deep sleep and wanted nothing but to return to slumber permanently.

The one thing I did notice was that scores and scores and *scores* of men recognized my captor and waved, bowed, or saluted as we passed. He nodded and smiled in response, the smallest gap between his two front teeth making him all the more likable-looking. He was generous with his attention and seemed to know half the army by name.

At last we reached a cluster of stately but undecorated canvas lodgings inhabited by men of the German Empire, or so I guessed by the change to guttural and unfamiliar language that assaulted my ears. Here, my captor was greeted as reverentially as if he were a count. He grandly flung back the flap and, in the same Lombardy form of Italian (so I would understand the situation), he ordered his squire to tether me, rope around one arm, to the center pole.

The tent was roomy. A curtain was pulled back at either side in the middle, creating one open area. Another young blond man (dressed well) and an attractive woman (in a tight-fitting linen thing) were bustling about in the diffused daylight, packing and folding and shoving things into chests and bags. There was also an older servant. They all paused, startled by our arrival. "Otto, Liliana, Richard," my captor announced. "And you are?"

"They're in worse shape than I am," I snapped, although they weren't. "Are you collecting specimens of human wretchedness?" And gesturing at Liliana: "A whiff of that would drive me to abstinence." She was, in fact, distressingly attractive, especially to one desperate to be dead to the world. Her mouth alone was worth a week of fantasies.

The young man, Otto, looked at me with contempt. Objectively speaking, he was better-looking than my captor, but he lacked my captor's easy, un-self-conscious charisma. "You will not speak of a lady that way," he informed me.

I gave him a disbelieving look. "What, that?" I asked, jerking my head toward her. "You can't fool me, that's a whore."

He grabbed at his dagger as Liliana said, comfortably, "Milord, I *am* a whore."

"He will not call you that," Otto steamed. "Unless he wants his throat cut." He pulled the dagger out to show he meant it. It looked good and sharp, and I still wanted to be dead.

"She's a whore," I repeated at once. "Probably diseased and certainly repellent."

Young Otto took an enraged step in my direction. I pivoted so the whole of my front was within easy reach of his blade—but he was stopped by the knight, who smacked his wrist so hard the blade clattered to the ground.

"Don't touch him," the knight ordered and pushed a surprised Otto out of the tent, chucking the dagger out after him before I could reach it myself. "Liliana, Richard, Richard, leave us." He added something in German.

Alone now, the knight and I looked at each other in the soft light. I was dressed like a servant, and he probably expected me to behave like one. Instead, I took the only remaining camp stool from near the door, dragged it to the middle of the nearly empty tent, by the pole, unfolded it, and plopped down on it, legs splayed, like a puppet without a puppeteer. He now had nowhere to sit, since the chests were all piled on top of one another. He looked a bit aggravated. Good; if I irritated him enough, perhaps he'd change his mind and run me through after all. But without the rush of mad energy I'd had earlier, the thought of goading him to kill me seemed, more than anything, exhausting.

He was a large, fit man. Middling handsome, a face suggesting good character more than good lineage, and perhaps a few years past twenty. He could not have been a knight long; unless he'd been in border skirmishes, this was probably the first time he was going off to war.

"Your accent is unfamiliar," he observed, standing by the door and folding his large arms across his large chest. "What is your language?"

"I speak in tongues."

"Did I hear you playing music in the whores' camp last night?"

It was the second reference he'd made to my being a musician. I shrugged. "I've no idea if you heard me or not. How would I know what you hear?"

"I'll feed you," he announced, suddenly changing tactics. Sweeping open the tent flap, he reached out, and I saw the squire hand him a loaf of bread. He held it up. I couldn't help myself; my eyes followed the movement as if they were lashed to the loaf. "White bread," he said, holding it high in the air. "The food of royalty. All yours."

"What's the price?" I licked dry lips with a parched tongue. Dammit, if I were dead I wouldn't be worrying about hunger anymore, or thirst.

"Tell me what your language is."

"I'm speaking your accursed Piedmontese," I said.

"Not *my* accursed Piedmontese," he corrected. "My mother tongue is German, my second language French."

"Then let's speak in French," I said, switching. "It's more unpleasant to the ear and this is an unpleasant conversation."

"What is *your* tongue?"

I stuck out my tongue and wagged it.

He shrugged. "Don't tell me, then. It's probably offensive to the ear anyhow." He bit into the loaf of bread and made a little sound of satisfaction as the crust crunched in his teeth. "Delicious."

"It is not offensive!" I snapped indignantly. "And how can you talk when all your wretched continental languages hit the ears like stones!"

"Continental?" he said and smiled. "Then you must be from England."

"*Britain*," I corrected quickly and leapt to my feet. I had to end
this. I had to end *me*.

"What city?"

"No *city*!" I scoffed. "It's a *nation*. I won't say it in your language."

"You probably *can't* say it in *my* language," the knight reminded
me patiently. He looked thoughtful. "So you are one of those native
Britons?"

I tried to imagine an answer that might compel him to murder
me, but failed. "*Britannicus Gentes*," I clarified, with a tired sigh, giving in to human appetite. I held my hand out. "Now I want bread for
that."

He tore off a large piece and tossed it at me as if he were throwing raw meat to a captive wolf. I caught it, turned away on the stool
hovering over it, crammed it into my mouth, and started chewing,
then stopped, distressed. "Dry mouth?" he asked and handed out a
wineskin from a peg by the door flap. I stood, approached, grabbed it
awkwardly between my bound hands, downed nearly everything in
it at one go, then chucked the empty skin at his feet with a defiant
smirk.

But the knight just shrugged and picked up the skin. "That's convenient, we needed to empty this anyhow, to pack it. So, to review:
you're a Briton, and you are under the illusion that you're important
enough to keep that a secret." He took a step into the middle of the
tent, snatched up the stool, moved it closer to the door, and sat on
it. Wordlessly, I sat down on the dirt floor of the tent. "What is your
name?" he demanded. "I wish to speak you properly, as a Christian."

"Oh, no, are you one of *those*? You're the third one I've met this
month. Is there an epidemic? I pray to Jesus it's not catching. Every
Christian I've met this year has been a real bastard."

"That will get you killed sooner than your attack on the marquis,"
he warned. "Insult me all you like, but leave my mother out of it."

"It wasn't an insult, it was an expression of fraternity, as I am almost certainly a bastard myself," I said. "You know, it's been three years and I still cannot get a taste for that repellent wheat bread of yours."

There was a longer silence. He was clearly not going to kill me. Or do anything else except wait for me to explain myself, which I had no intention of doing. I certainly wouldn't tell him my name, which I had shed when I left home.

"My name is Gregor of Mainz," he finally announced, perhaps intending to set a good example.

I stared at him in amazement for a moment and then burst into pained laughter.

He looked quizzical but continued. "I am a knight and landowner in the Holy Roman Empire—"

"I know who you are!" I nearly shouted. "I sing *songs* about you!" In my attempts to acquire a continental repertoire, I had learned a tiresome collection of songs about great romantic heroes of chivalry, with their perfect souls, perfect families, perfect ladies, and perfect deeds. To keep myself sane, I'd invented parodies of these popular chansons, and on reflex I recited a few lines of one regarding the Herculean man before me: "Gregor of Mainz, dumb as a pebble! Has no balls, so he's a treble. To pursue his sanctimonious ambitions, he gobbles the pope's nocturnal emissions."

Surely that would push him to vivisect me.

But he just shrugged. "Is *that* as obscene as your imagination goes? I've heard far worse in my time." And then he sang to the same tune, although the rhythm of the line did not scan well: "Gregor runs a brothel full of leprous scut, and the devil daily fucks him up the butt."

It was confounding to hear these words uttered earnestly yet humorlessly, with a trace of a German accent, in a baritone as soothing as warm milk. "Of course, the details aren't quite accurate," he continued, as if I might actually think they were. "In real life, I have the honor—as of a fortnight ago—to be married to Marguerite, the natural daughter of the marquis Boniface of Montferrat, the leader of this crusade and the man you just pretended to try to kill. But we have now examined my life with more attention than circumstances call for. It is your turn. Who are you?"

"A villain," I said promptly. "There is blood on the hands you so kindly spared." In response to Gregor's uncomprehending stare, I went on, hoarsely, "I want more bread; this business of not being dead is exhausting."

Gregor tossed me the entire loaf, and I bit into it directly.

"Why are you a villain?"

"It cannot be encapsulated for your anecdotal interest," I said, chewing.

He was getting impatient. "Did you murder someone?"

"Are those songs about you accurate?" I said. "Are you all gallantry and sanctimoniousness?"

"We're talking about you now."

"Why won't you answer me? Do you have something to hide?"

"No," he said. "But you do, and you're going to tell me what it is."

"For the love of God, surely I've earned the right to hear *some* gossip. Tell me *something*. Impress me. Intrigue me. Mortify me. Just don't *bore* me. If you *insist* on keeping me alive, make it worth my *while*. You owe me that. Start by telling me what all this martial nonsense around us is about." I already knew, of course.

Gregor looked annoyed, even shocked, that an inferior was speaking to him this way. Good, I thought, If I keep it up, perhaps you'll at least kick me out of the tent. But instead, he gestured reverentially to a post near the tent flap, where a small wooden disk hung on a peg. Pressed into the disk in wax was an image of an unadorned shield with antlers and a dagger-wielding arm coming out of it. "That is the seal of the head of this army, Marquis Boniface."

"Your father-in-law," I said with mock grandness.

"Yes, although that has limited legal meaning, as I am married to his daughter out of wedlock," Gregor said comfortably. "But we

cherish each other, and I was a squire in his court. The seal allows me
ready access to him. You know, his troubadour Raimbaut sometimes
refers to him in song and tale as N'Engles, the Englishman—perhaps
that caused your confusion. Anyhow, he is a great man, overseeing
an unprecedented pilgrimage."

"Unprecedented? Nobody has ever gone to Jerusalem to smite infidels before? Funny, I could have sworn there've been at least three
major campaigns in the last century or so—"

"That's not what I mean," he said. "Consider this: he is from
Montferrat in Piedmont, west of here, but the army is largely French
or Flemish, while others like myself are from the German Empire,
and we are now working with Venetians—"

"And apparently your leader is secretly English—that's the real
problem."

"Do you hear the point I'm making?" Gregor asked reasonably.
Clearly reciting something biblical: "My heart goes out to the captains of Israel, who are answering the call among the people, praise
the Lord!"

"This is a Jewish crusade?"

He gave me a sour look. "This *one man*—not even an anointed
king!—is uniting all of these different peoples under a single
banner—the Holy Father's—to work for the greater good of Christendom." He spoke as if even I, by simply appreciating Boniface's
task, was made a better person.

"He must be an ambitious prick," I said philosophically.

He shook his head and tried again. "*They* came to *him*, on bended
knee, and *begged* him to lead them! He had no thought for his own
advancement in it. He answered the summons of Christians in need,
doing his duty as a soldier of Christ."

"He has a good troubadour, if that's the story being bandied about.
Although why any troubadour worth his salt would call his lord an
Englishman as *praise*—"

Gregor made a sound of agitation. "You're wasting my time. Tell

me who you are, *now*, or I'll turn you over to someone . . ." He paused.
"Someone who gets results."

That sounded promising. I am, although hardy, a smallish man,
and if I were subjected to torture, there was a very good possibility
I would not survive it. I'd've far rather just been skewered and had
done with it, but anything would do.

So I said nothing.

Irritated, Gregor moved to the tent flap, where he stood silhouetted, the sun setting behind him, his shadow falling over me. He
stepped halfway outside the tent, called to somebody just out of my
view, and delivered a lengthy monologue in German. He gave me a
final warning glance, but even that had a brotherliness to it, as if he
knew he'd get what he wanted because he *meant well*. Then he exited, and I prepared again to meet my Maker.

3

Lady, I cannot defend myself from you, I must rather die, for I
am weak and heartsick.

—HEINRICH VON MORUNGEN

MY NEW INTERROGATOR WAS merely the woman, Liliana. She carried a wooden cup of something steaming, and
she sashayed into the tent with an expectant smile on her
face, as if she had been waiting for a chance to be alone with me. I
knew that wasn't true, but I couldn't convince my body of that, and I
sagged a little as I felt my blood warm.

"Hello, little British vagabond-assassin," she sang and squatted down on the ground near me. I was still tethered to the tent post. Silky hair hung loose, trailing on the ground once she sat; it was a hue of burnished gold, not quite brown and not quite blond. Her eyes were equally indistinct, the kind of hazel that shifts between brown and green almost unceasingly. The effect of these indeterminate qualities made her incredibly full mouth all the more notable— especially as it hovered a mere hand span over well-shaped breasts that may as well have been naked, they were so barely covered. Her shift was so thin I could almost see her belly button. "You resemble John the Baptist just a bit, but I bet you'll clean up well. Look at those big dark eyes."

"How sadly unoriginal," I said sullenly. "I suppose you're to seduce me into talking about myself? For the love of ale, your precious Gregor lacks imagination."

Ignoring this, she offered me the wooden cup. "Mulled wine," she explained pleasantly. I took it but sniffed at it suspiciously. Damn, it smelled good. "I've got water heating on the fire for your bath, and we'll cut those matted locks and trim the beard. And Milord Gregor has made it my responsibility merely to *educate* you, not to question you." She had an irritatingly lovely smile, and a tone that was at once amused and sympathetic, as if she already knew everything was going to go exactly as she wanted. "Let us begin with a recitation of characters."

I gestured toward her with my head. "Character one—the whore," I said and took a quick swallow of wine. It was very good, which enraged me. I refused to reacquaint myself with the pleasures of being alive. "The whore appears throughout history, wherever there are collections of men, such as, for example, armies. Or cities. Or monasteries. In armies, whores often pretend to be cooks or bakers or . . ." I made a tired gesture, inviting her contribution.

"I'm only here to scrub the armor," she said, mock-defensively.

"Oil the lances," I said, with a bored nod.

"Trim the candlewicks."

"Suckle the babes." I jerked my thumb toward the flap. "Especially the pretty fellow."

"Otto," she said and grinned. "He adores me. He saved me from a hellhole, and he is a bit . . . protective."

She was so much more attractive than I wanted to allow, although she was hardly a sapling; she must been at least a decade older than her protector. "That could be a problem. Protectiveness tends to spawn possessiveness, and you don't look . . . Well, I was going to say you don't look like the sort who's likely to be possessed, but really it's just the opposite, isn't it? That's the problem, right?"

She smiled confidingly. "How rare—a man with insight," she said. She lowered her voice, and without wanting to, I leaned in slightly toward her. "I have ways of navigating the shoals of possessiveness."

"I'm sure you do. I'm sure your vessel sails all the time, with a full hold."

She chuckled delicately and shrugged her shoulders with girlish delight. She was good at this. "Ooo, innuendos in a foreign language. I wish there were more such wit in this tent." She paused for exactly the right length of time and then said, with exactly the right soupçon of hopefulness, "Are you staying with us for a while?"

I shifted my weight slightly away from her—that took real effort—and shrugged. "No. I came to Venice to get myself killed off, but your master seems intent on preventing it."

Liliana looked convincingly shocked. "Why killed off?" she demanded, as if it were entirely her own desire for my well-being that inspired the question.

And despite myself, I almost answered her. "This vessel of yours," I said instead, waving toward her lap. "What's its preferred cargo? I suppose you like them meaty?"

"I like them smart, when I can get them," Liliana said, meaningfully. Why didn't knowing it was an act make it less attractive? I hadn't been this close to a woman in too long. She added quietly, confidingly, "It's *boring*, what I do. I crave a conversation of substance." I knew, I *knew*, this was merely how she was playing me, but still I told myself that she was also, really and truly, putting aside her business for a moment and confiding to a fellow underdog. "I could tell you about all of us, as Milord Gregor ordered me to," she said, "and that would be the most substantial chat I've had in days—isn't that pathetic? So tell me your story, however dark or heavy it is. Tell me and give me *something* more interesting than fellatio to contemplate for a day or two." She lowered her voice. "Unless you'd rather I contemplate it right now." She glanced straight at my crotch and then away. And then she actually blushed.

"You almost had me," I said. "Until that final bit. That was too much."

She looked me right in the face with a disarming grin, as if we were now coconspirators. "Oh, I have you well and good, and you know it. You're *aching* to put your hand up my skirt to see if I want you as much as you want me."

Now it was I who blushed. "No, because I know you don't, it's just an act."

She was still grinning, with a frank, open expression on her face. "And you don't think it affects me, that you can see through my pretense? I'm not used to that. It makes me quite aflutter."

"There are antiflutter tinctures you can take to help with that."

"So you know something about medicines?" she asked. Then grimaced sheepishly at her own clumsy attempt to probe.

"As much as your average hermit-monk," I offered.

"You're not a monk," she said with a knowing smile. She grabbed my left hand and ran her fingertips over mine; the intimacy of it jolted me. "These are a musician's calluses, although—" She took the cup from me and used both of her hands to stretch my right hand wide, palm up. This was unexpectedly erotic. She ran the backs of her fingers up and down my palm, and I actually groaned. "This *is* the hand of a scribe, so perhaps you are a cleric after all?" She leaned in and whispered, amused, "Perhaps you tickled a monk to death, you naughty little cleric. Show me how you tickled him."

I shook my hand out of hers brusquely. She'd struck a nerve; I did not want to play her game anymore, and I no longer cared what anyone knew about me. I just wanted the harassment of interrogation over quickly now. "There was a monk, but I nursed him back to *health*. It was an Englishman wounded him. The Englishman is the one to kill."

"Because he tickled your monk?"

Her amusement infuriated me. "Because he murdered my king."

Liliana stopped laughing abruptly.

"Many, many years ago. But he's done worse since then—he's conquered the whole kingdom. So I had to kill him."

She'd not been expecting this turn. "I see," she stammered. "Kill him how?"

"He doesn't know me by sight. I was going to get into his court in a position of trust, kill him in his own bed, and then be speedily dispatched myself, by his guards."

The interest on her face was no longer an act. "Why . . . get yourself killed?"

"I'm as guilty as he is. He could conquer the kingdom only because *I* brought it to perdition."

For a moment she was flummoxed. Then she said, shaking her head, "How did you do it? Kill him, I mean."

"I *didn't*, that's the problem. But I *prepared* for it, and that's what brought me here." She gestured me to go on, eyes wide. "The hermit I'd nursed back to health, Wulfstan, helped me prepare. He brought me over to the continent and we stayed with his brethren in a monastery while I learned Latin and French and other things that would be necessary to the plot."

Her astonishment was increasing. "An entire monastic community helped you prepare a murder-suicide?"

"Wulfstan was always eccentric. He had his own ideas of Christ,

I think. He never told the brothers why I was really there; they thought I wanted to be a novice, and Christians are just mad for saving souls. Plus I could write, so I earned my keep copying the most inane drivel about loving your neighbor unless your neighbor doesn't eat his little wafer the way you do, in which case you should burn him to death. After a few years, I'd grown a Norman-style beard, and my hair was long like this, I could speak and play music as if I were a native of the continent, and I felt ready to go back to England and attack my enemy."

"So . . . what happened then?" Liliana demanded, still wide-eyed. The fingers of one hand descended gently onto my leg just above the knee, destroying any internal alarm that might have warned me I was being played. I wanted to impress this woman.

"The most damnable thing. At the monastery, we heard that the English had signed on with the army of pilgrims going to the Holy Land—and that my nemesis, my intended victim, was leading them. So I headed here to Venice, where they were all assembling. I arrived a few weeks ago, but this camp is the most confounding thing I've ever encountered, people packed in together like arrows in a quiver. So I decided, for anonymity's sake, to get information from the Venetians. Today I finally found a Venetian familiar with the whole layout of the army camp. I asked about the English. And do you know what?"

"There are no English," Liliana said softly.

"Yes, apparently everyone knew that except me."

Liliana gave me a knowing nod. "Boniface's troubadour calls him the Englishman as a joke; perhaps you heard that, and there was a confusion."

"All that matters is that *my* Englishman is not among the pilgrims. He is not here. I cannot kill him." My throat clenched. "This one task I set for myself, this one attempt at vengeance, this deed for which, should any of my people ever hear of it, they might forgive me my sins perhaps a little, I failed it. And so." I made myself shrug, as if I made these sorts of decisions all the time. "I thought, if God is so perverse as to protect that whoreson, let me at least dispatch *one* of us quickly. I have no weapon, but now I can goad ten thousand armed men to speed me to my Maker. And I would have succeeded at that, at least, but for your accursed Gregor of Mainz."

The knight reentered at that moment, ignoring me. "Well done, Liliana, and you were right—that was more efficient than an actual seduction."

I felt myself redden and pulled away from her. "I knew that was a setup, of course," I said, with such peevishness I embarrassed myself, and reddened further.

"I know you did," she said, with apologetic amusement. "I hope you enjoyed it a little anyhow." She placed her hand even farther up my thigh. I pulled my thigh away.

"You're shrewder than you look," I accused Gregor.

"I'm not actually," Gregor assured me. "But I've learned how to fake shrewdness when I need to. You're under my charge now, and I'm responsible for you. Any murder, even self-murder, is a sin, and I'll be responsible if you—"

"Nobody will care," I said in a flinty voice.

"God will care," Gregor said evenly.

I groaned and smacked my head against Liliana's arm. "Oh no, he really is a Christian."

"Well, as long as you're stuck with us, you may as well tell us your name," she said, smoothing my temple with her hand. Her touch felt so good it was painful. "Calling you the little British vagabond-assassin is a bit of a mouthful."

My eyes rolled in her direction. It was so hard to refuse her, but my name was the only thing I had managed to escape, and I needed to keep it that way. "Chwifiwr-Llofruddiwr," I said in a voice of bland capitulation. Vagabond-Assassin.

Liliana and Gregor each blinked and then made some unintentionally hilarious attempts to repeat this. "It's, mm, beautiful, but is there a shorter version?" Gregor asked, after one attempt in which he seemed to sprain his tongue.

"No," I said solemnly and sat up straighter. "It would be an insult to my family and my honor to diminutize the name."

I think Gregor believed this; Liliana obviously knew it was rubbish but played along. "Well, then," she said with friendly sympathy, "Let us say merely the Briton."

"The Briton," echoed Gregor, as if honored by the chance to call me so.

Liliana cut my hair, nails, and beard, then stood over me in a wooden tub and made me bathe. I didn't take this personally—every man in the army seemed to be cutting his hair and paring his nails this evening, although I needed it far worse than any of them, even the lowest infantry. We all slept that night in the emptied tent, only sheets for bedrolls on the soft, dusty ground. Richard was one of two servants—the other was the older man, his grandfather, who was also named Richard. These two traded off watch responsibilities over me.

They needn't have bothered. Escape was the furthest thing from my mind that night. I sank into defeated lethargy. The mix of frustration, depression, and pure *embarrassment* at my foiled plan made me desperate to be gone, and yet too glum to do anything about it. I was in a state of shock.

4

The Lord is a Warrior—Lord is his name!
—FROM "Exodus, Song of the Sea"

Eve of Feast of St. Jerome, 29 September A.D. 1202

By the head of St. John, it is the earnest desire of this humble knight,
Gregor, son of Gerhard of Mainz, to con and master the art of writing in my humble native vernacular, that I may uplift that language
by using it to help record the radiant glories of our undertakings in the
name of Jesus Christ the Son of God amen. To that end I am obeying
the wise suggestion of His Eminence Conrad, Bishop of Halberstadt,
that I must chronicle certain things. Not the mundane deeds of daily
life, or the great political and military triumphs awaiting the esteemed
Boniface, Marquis of Montferrat, who leads this glorious army and
has in his tremendous wisdom caused me, humble knight that I am, to
be married to his natural daughter Marguerite. Nor shall I endeavor to
capture in a poetic light the glory of the battle and the hardships of the
journey. My chronicling needs be only an inventory of my own humble
attempts as a servant of our Lord and the Holy Father in Rome, to add
glory to my efforts as a pilgrim.

Perhaps until I am more comfortable with the mechanics of the
quill, I will wax with greater brevity, as that took me a duration exceeding that of morning mass, and I have recorded nothing at all yet.

I have added one pilgrim to our ranks. This is good news. He is a

Briton. *If all men of his land are like him, then I pray I am delivered from ever setting foot there.*

His Eminence Bishop Conrad of Halberstadt did me the great honor of coming to my humble tent this morning, when I sent my servant with a message. I explained to His Eminence Bishop Conrad that the Briton's soul is afflicted with demons and he rails against me, and I asked His Eminence's advice. His Eminence believes that the Briton must be delivered to Jerusalem, and that the journey there shall cure him of whatever afflicts him. I have sworn to His Eminence Bishop Conrad to accomplish this, and His Eminence assures me this will be a great boon to the Briton's soul as well as mine.

My brother Otto stood with us near the Briton as the Briton slept, and Otto seemed much amused as I took this oath. As His Eminence was informing me of my obligations—that I must pay the new pilgrim's passage and keep him fed and clothed and must impress upon him the need to take the cross—the man awoke and stared up at us as if we were the very demons that afflict him. He demanded to know if we were speaking about him and railed against us not to do so but to let him be. Otto found unseemly amusement in this. I introduced the Briton to His Eminence Bishop Conrad as my spiritual shepherd, at which point the Briton postulated that my tent reeked as it did because Otto and I are fornicating rams and other such things of an ungracious nature that I will not repeat. Nor did he attempt in any way to show respect to His Eminence the Bishop, although it is an extraordinary thing for a bishop to condescend to visit a mere knight in his tent.

So I lifted the Briton by the wrist to a standing position and pressed him on the back of the head hard enough to effect the appearance of a bow. I did this without malice but because I could see no other way to encourage correct behavior from him.

"I have explained your situation to His Eminence, and His Eminence has declared that a pilgrimage like the one we are about to embark on is exactly what you need in order to cure yourself of whatever disease eats at your soul," said I.

Whereupon the Briton amazed us by saying in perfect Latin, "My soul is not in need of curing, only of returning to its Maker."

"My son," said His Eminence Bishop Conrad, "in the name of the Holy Father in Rome, I must insist you keep with us on this campaign."

"The Holy Father is not here to make me do so," replied the Briton. "I appreciate your advice, but you are not in a position to enforce it." Then he yawned right in the face of His Eminence and began to kneel, as if he would return to his recumbent position. Whereupon I grabbed his arm above the elbow and kept him standing upright, for to slouch before a bishop is the very embodiment of rudeness.

"That is why I have charged Gregor with the burden," His Eminence Bishop Conrad replied to the surly man. "He has sworn upon his sword to see you delivered through the gates of Jerusalem."

The Briton groaned mightily at this and tried, unsuccessfully, to pull himself out of my grasp. My brother Otto laughed harshly at all of this, which I found most unfriendly of him.

"It is for the good of your soul," His Eminence assured the Briton.

"You know nothing about my soul," the Briton complained.

"God does," His Eminence returned.

"God is no more likely to ease my soul in the desert than he is to ease it in this accursed swamp," said the Briton.

"You cannot speak of marvels about which you do not yet know," His Eminence said, which is a speech of great wisdom.

"Now that is a convenient way to end a conversation," the Briton responded, and tugged his arm again, as if he would escape me. Not wanting him to injure himself, I released him. "Why did you agree to this stupidity?" he demanded irritably.

I bowed toward His Eminence the bishop. "I have taken on this assignment because I am a son of the Church. It is a testament to His Eminence's faith in me that he would trust me with the well-being of another soul, especially one so tormented."

Whereupon the Briton resorted to a stream of insults and comments which I believe he mistakenly considered humorous. But he lost interest in arguing with us, and stood quietly until we finished explaining what was required of him. He refused to take the cross; beyond that, he did not respond. I have put him into the care of my servants Richard (son of Richard) and his grandfather Richard (son of Richard) for the day. He finds their names comical and calls them the Richardim. They appear strangely flattered by the ekename.

It is a grave responsibility to have another soul entrusted to my care. I am honored and humbled that His Eminence considers me such a stalwart pilgrim to have faith enough for two men, whatever lies ahead of us. It is my honor to record this, my first accomplishment as a pilgrim, before we have even set sail.

I must now uncramp my fingers and take myself to Boniface's tent, to continue a disturbing conference we had been having yesterday before the Briton interrupted us.

ONCE THE BISHOP had departed, the sheets were packed away, the tents were struck, and all was put onto the ships. The horses (Gregor's destrier Summa, Otto's Oro, and two packhorses) were blindfolded and led on broad wooden gangways into the belly of the horse transports; the horses were put into slings to keep them from hurting themselves during the voyage, and then the hatches on the side of the ships were tarred closed. These vessels were an experiment of sorts, designed specifically to accommodate the largest equine transport Venice had ever attempted.

Gregor, like many of his fellow Germans, had a berth on a ship called the *Innocent*, in honor of the undertaking's patron, the ambitious young pope. Over the course of the day I was trundled around between the Richardim, grandson and grandfather; although I had no German, my other languages were good enough for me to learn a few things. Men were complaining as they worked—about a courier with money who hadn't arrived from Lyon; about someplace called Zara; about being overcharged by a salted-fish merchant. Gregor's name came up, but never in complaint. Among the knights of the Empire, France, Flanders, and Italy, the man who'd saved me from myself was revered as high nobility. Yet he was berthed in the *Innocent*'s between decks—better lodgings than the infantry or carpenters or smiths or caulkers or sailors but very much a common dormitory.

I observed to my captors that the commander's son-in-law required better lodgings. At this, the elder Richard betrayed more savvy than I'd have guessed: He explained that, at Marquis Boniface's request, Gregor had agreed to set off on the journey not as a member of Boniface's entourage but as a common German knight, loosely associated with Bishop Conrad's party. Gregor was willing to be deprived of the right of hobnobbing with the noble class he'd married into, willing to remain "with the men," because this made him more useful to his commander. Boniface had fashioned Gregor's persona into a hero from a chanson de geste: his loyalty and valor had been rewarded (hence the marriage), and yet he remained the very epitome of the undemanding soldier who wanted only to serve his lord. Because of the association with Boniface, Gregor had high status among all; because he was pitching his tents with the knights, he was adored by them as one of their own. The elder Richard saw this more clearly than Gregor did.

Many of the transport vessels had towers built fore and aft on the decks; these would be added to later on and used—the Richardim explained—to besiege the high harbor walls of infidel cities. In the meantime, the cabins within these "castles" were partitioned off into minuscule closets for the highest ranking pilgrims onboard; belowdecks was divided into several long, cramped dormitories, each of which reeked of vinegar and each of which housed a dozen knights, their squires, and chests full of their arms and armor; others, including Otto, would travel on the horse transports, watching the mounts; infantry were crammed in even more tightly on other vessels. Upon appropriating me, Gregor had bargained at a high price to have a little extra room.

"Don't make me do this," I said wretchedly to Gregor, staring about the claustrophobic space. Only the open hatchway above let in light. The others in the cabin ignored us. "Crossing over from Britain was the worst experience of my life. Don't make me go all the way to Jerusalem this way. Slitting my throat would be a *kindness*."

"Jerusalem isn't on the coast," Gregor said, in the tones of a reassuring father. He might not have been happy about his role as my spiritual chaperone, but he was taking it very seriously. (Gregor, it turned out, was constitutionally incapable of taking things any other way.) "We'll be back on dry land long before then. Anyhow, we're going to Egypt first."

This confused me. "Are we? Have they moved Jerusalem?" I knew nothing of geography, but Wulfstan the hermit had been preoccupied with stories of the Old Testament, and after all the time I'd spent with him, I knew it did not make sense for Jerusalem to be in Egypt.

"There is talk of conquering Alexandria, that's in Egypt, before we go to the Holy Land itself. It is a detail that doesn't concern you."

"If it's a detail that prolongs my captivity, then I must disagree."

"Then pester someone else," said Gregor peaceably.

So I returned to pestering the Richardim, but with little satisfaction. On Gregor's orders, they took me via gondola to the main island, the buzzing Rialto, and purchased things for me that I protested I would never need: extra clothes, a quilt, a water skin, bedding, charms to ward off seasickness and bad luck. They also purchased a cage of half a dozen hens, grapes and wild mushrooms (in abundance), and vile-looking dried herbs with poetic names such as common fumitory and toadflax, which they explained would make it possible to shit at sea.

I had spent much time over the past month in this astounding market square fronting on the Grand Canal. Like every first-timer to Venice, I'd been amazed by the riches of the clothing, foods, spices, wares, houses, the multiplicity of language, customs, dress. I, from the wilds of a landlocked, hilly country, had also been struck by how flat, overcrowded, and claustrophobic the place was, how stale all the smells, how fractured the light off the water, and above all, how sound carried and echoed so bizarrely and confusingly in a place of water and rock. But none of that, today, got my attention. I was still in shock because I thought I was supposed to be dead. I did not even try to escape from the Richardim; that would have taken too much imagination.

Tasks accomplished, we returned by gondola and sat on the deck of the ship, bored beyond tears, breathing in the swampy lagoon air, which was so thick one could almost lean against it. Naïve and suspicious but fascinated by me, the Richardim were easily coaxed into telling me almost everything they knew. They knew nothing about any plan to divert to Alexandria. However, they did know—and were happy to talk about—the only other thing of interest to me in all of Venice: their whore.

Liliana, a poor knight's youngest daughter, was destined from birth to become either a nun or a concubine. (The younger Richard explained this to me as he practiced tying and untying knots on the deck. His grandfather, with a very small knife, was carving a block of wood into what appeared to be a chess rook.) When her father's lord first saw Liliana's pretty smile, her future was secured for her, and she was schooled for her new position—or positions, Richard said with a snicker. His Lordship was genial and doting. The arrangement suited everyone—until His Lordship died and his son took over everything, including his father's sundry women. Liliana, who'd been treasured and indulged by the father, did not like the son's tendency to treat his chattel as if it were, well, chattel, and so she ran off to a faraway city, where trying to promote and protect the only skill she had, she suddenly realized just how easy things had been for her as a concubine. She spent two miserable years as a common whore (young Richard, who did not really believe a whore could be miserable, did not provide details of this part of her biography). One night, she had just finished servicing a youth named Otto of Frankfurt, a fellow (according to Richard's authorized account) she found rather cute, when she was rudely set upon by a pack of drunks, none of whom were cute at all. Otto of Frankfurt was still in the area, musing with great longing (according to Richard) on the woman who had just beguiled him. He heard her calls, came to her aid, dispatched her attackers single-handedly, hired a woman to tend to her wounds, and invited her back to Germany when he headed home from the day's tournament, where he'd served as squire to his famous half brother Gregor of Mainz.

This raised Otto's esteem in my eyes. A little. Enough to listen to Richard blather on about him as I tried to figure out how to stop existing, here on deck, in the late afternoon sun. I had given up the hope of getting anyone to kill me off; Gregor had advertised I was not to be hurt. The elder Richard had a tight grip on his little whittling knife, and he was agile for a man his age; wrestling the knife from him was unlikely. I would have had to take a more involved role in my own demise than I really had the energy for. The rigging of the sails would take me to the crow's nest; if there were rope up there (and there was rope *everywhere*), I could rig a noose . . . "They have the same father," Richard was explaining. "Otto is the younger by a few years, and more than ready to be knighted, but he wants to be knighted as reward for some dramatic enterprise—"

"—like smiting infidels in the Holy Land," I guessed. Maybe there was a small coil that I could carry up the rigging with me, to use to hang myself. I glanced about. The coils down here were all too large, and usually attached to something already.

"Exactly," the older Richard said. He had finished the little chess piece, if that was what it was; he stuck the knife into the back of his belt out of my reach and took the rope from his grandson for his turn at practicing a knot. The younger Richard idly threw a wood chip at a grey heron that had landed on the rail; it flew off with an ease I envied. "So Otto wants to travel with the army and fight, but he doesn't want to *arrive* there as a knight, because he wants to be knighted *there*. Early on, of course, so that he gets a knight's share of the spoils when the spoiling starts. So he proposed to Milord Gregor that he come along as part of Gregor's household, like a mounted sergeant, only of course he's actually heir of no small estate on his mother's side. So Otto's paying his own way and covering much of Milord Gregor's costs, plus he's providing a whore."

"But why Liliana?" I asked and casually held my hand out for a turn with the rope. Over the course of the afternoon we had already established that I knew four times as many knots as the two of them together; I'd learned most of them in my cloistered assassin training under Wulfstan. "Liliana is years his senior. Why doesn't he have some nubile waif?"

Old Richard shrugged and handed me the coil. "Claims she's the best he's ever known. He goes with others now and then for variety, but I've never seen a youth that age cleave so to one woman."

"I'm surprised he would be willing to share her, then," I said, eyes on the rope. Yes, it would be long enough—barely. I hitched the coil over my head and shoulder and began to wind a hangman's knot, as if I were aimlessly fidgeting with it.

"Well, he doesn't *like* it." Young Richard laughed, almost apologetically. He was obviously new to fornication but didn't want to appear so.

"But he sees the advantages," the elder said. "He'd rather have his favorite fuck with him on the greatest adventure of his life than pay money to lie with ugly strangers. But bringing her along in close quarters would cause tensions if he weren't willing to share her. So we have certain, y'know, protocols."

"We like the protocols," the younger said, turning pink.

"Discretion will be practiced," the older explained.

"Will be? Hasn't yet?" I stood up as if to stretch my back, then reached out with one arm to grab onto a stretch of rigging that I'd heard a mariner refer to as a ratline—a spidery ladder straight to the basket near the top of the mainmast. I tested it for tautness. It would hold my weight. I was barefoot, like most of the mariners; I'd already figured out that the best way to stay stuck to the boat deck was to grab the tacky stuff between the narrow planks with my toes.

"Oh, *we've* been practicing discretion," the elder bragged, trying hard to show how blasé he was about unlimited access to a beautiful woman's nether regions. "But Gregor's bride came to Venice with us—they were just wed, in fact—and he's been plowing her regularly to get an heir before he sails off. She left yesterday. So the need for *him* to practice discretion has not yet arisen."

"*Arisen*," said the younger squire, with an illustrative gesture, and guffawed idiotically.

"*Shit*," his grandfather cried and grabbed desperately for my foot, but I was already too high up the ratline. The two of them began to shout at me, terrified about their own negligence, and within moments there were three Venetian sailors on the rigging. One was just below me and already nearly overtaking me; the other two were coming from the other side of the ship, and looked ready to leap through the air on top of me. All three of them were armed.

"Don't hurt him!" Gregor's voice sounded angrily from below. I glanced down, cursing. Gregor was holding the older Richard by the ear, looking enraged. "Bring him back down and give him to Otto if these peasants cannot handle him."

"Sorry, milord," Richard said, stricken.

"*Me?*" cried Otto from the steer-board side of the deck, in protest. "I was just about to row over to see if Liliana is comfortably settled in."

"I'm sure Liliana is as uncomfortable as the rest of us," Gregor said. He released Richard and strode toward Otto, but only to gesture to the longboat in the water below them. "I must find Boniface before sunset. You're on duty."

5

And such celebration did they make that night, none was too poor to add great illumination to it.

—ROBERT OF CLARI's *Chronicle of the Fourth Crusade*

AND SO OTTO WAS made my guardian that evening. A young man with a martial single-mindedness, he bored me to nausea explaining the difference between the rules of Covert War (no plunder, spoiling, or ransoming allowed), Ordinary Warfare (in which plunder, spoiling, and ransoming are all the fashion but there must be no harm done to civilians), and his favorite, only a fantasy until this very campaign: Mortal War, or, War Without Limit.

"I'm familiar with that one," I said wearily.

By the time all the ships were freighted and settled in, the casks of biscuits, dried cheese, dried peas and legumes, salted fish (for feast days), onions, butter, wine and water all put in the fore and aft compartments of the hold, the sun was beginning to set over the lagoon. I had assumed we'd make an early, wretched night of it in our cramped and smelly quarters on the *Innocent*. I doubt there was ever a knot tied by human hand that I cannot undo, so I had full confidence that I could get away. But all aspirations to vengeance had withered with humiliation; I did not deserve the dignity. It would be far more fitting to have an inglorious and unremarkable death. I'd escape before midnight, find a knife, and fall on it. Just get the damned thing over with.

So I was frustrated to discover that, in fact, we were not settling in for the night. Enrico Dandolo, the blind, octogenarian Doge of Venice, had other plans for us. In a canny diplomatic move, he had coaxed certain rich Venetian denizens to invite certain pilgrims (as the crusading warriors were called) to spend the final evening in the city as their guests. This was to prove that there was no ill will despite the six-month delay in setting out, and to encourage them to return to Venice to spend the piles of plunder they were sure to earn in the next year.

One of the wealthiest men of the lot was an aristocrat and merchant (in Venice these two were not mutually exclusive), and a veteran of the Emperor's Crusade in the Holy Land five years earlier. He had offered to feed a small group of Boniface's knights, including Gregor (he'd specified that he liked Germans), and to share his wisdom before they set out on their own adventures. Gregor was eager for a real meal before weeks cooped up on a ship, but he was unsure what to do with me. He didn't trust the squires to keep me contained, and Otto balked at the order to stay behind guarding a captive.

"I've heard about the feasts this Barzizza throws," Otto said. "I want to go."

I almost yelped at the coincidence. When I'd first arrived in Venice, I'd wanted a local who would know the layout of the foreigners' camp. Through much of the warm, spitting rains of September, I'd scoured the Rialto. Then, two days ago, lounging near the newly risen campanile, I'd found Barzizza the dried-fish mogul. Barzizza was a gregarious but almost comically stupid man. I claimed to be a musician to the French king's court, and although I looked like a wild man, he believed me. He decided we must become friends, so that I could introduce him to my patrons back in France, whose society (he assured me) he would soon be worthy of. Before breaking the news that there were no English on San Nicolo, he had shown me much of his home, a palazzo on the Grand Canal; I had a clear diagram of the main hall and ground floor in my head. Escape from there would be easier than from the ships, and I could swipe a sharp knife from his kitchens on the way out. "I'll go along as if I were your servant," I offered. Gregor gave me a suspicious glance. I held my hands up in a yielding gesture.

Gregor and Otto looked at each other. "He'd be under your direct supervision," Gregor said, as a warning.

Otto shrugged. "I can handle him. As long as I'm not deprived of my meal."

We were ferried in a slender, tarred-black gondola from the *Innocent* to the marble water gate of Ca' Barzizza, decorated with images of leaves and palm trees.

Barzizza's face lit up when he saw me. "Ah, my favorite goliard!" he said, taking me warmly by the hand and kissing me on either cheek as we all stepped out of the gondola into his storehouse. Gregor and Otto both blinked in surprise. "I treasure this coincidence! But you left all your instruments here yesterday, do you know that? I will have the boy retrieve them for you so you may continue to seek your Englishman."

That hit me like a slap: another reminder of the plan that had failed. "Thank you, milord," I said, forcing a polite smile. This meant that I might yet accomplish it . . . but the thought of that journey back to Britain was impossibly arduous, even given the years I had prepared for it. Dripping with self-loathing, I decided to stick with offing myself here in Venice. Otto was hardly cunning; if I behaved myself for an hour or so, his guard might be down, and then I could slip away.

Barzizza led us through his high-ceilinged showroom, which like so much of Venice was elaborately decorated with flowing curves; water, their source of wealth, also provided their aesthetic here. (I admit I liked this better than the pointy, prickly style everyone else was so mad about, which just made me feel exhausted for the stoneworkers.) The room reeked of dried fish "from the heathen, barbarian, frozen shores of the Black Sea!" Barzizza apologized. He led us, surrounded by light-bearing servants, up a set of broad marble stairs to the next level of his enormous house. Here was a long, flat-ceilinged hall, with marble panels on the wall and large arched windows looking onto the Grand Canal. The trestle tables were knee-high, and instead of benches, there were cushions strewn on the floor. The cushions had silk covers on them, with rich dyes and elaborate floral designs, obviously worth a fortune—but they were still on the floor. The knights, all in ceremonial splendor, glanced uncertainly at one another.

"This is your introduction to the comforts of the East!" Barzizza said grandly, enjoying their confusion. "Your own brethren, after living there awhile, take their meals this way. Remember me when you dine with your lord Boniface in just this fashion, once he is crowned king of Jerusalem!"

The knights glanced at one another again. "Perhaps you misunderstand the purpose of the pilgrimage, milord," said one of the knights, cautiously. "There already is a king of Jerusalem, King Aimery. We go to free the city so that he may return to it."

Barzizza gave him a knowing grin. "What's in it for Boniface, then?"

"He's making a pilgrimage, milord," Gregor said. "No doubt His Majesty will reward the marquis with lands and titles, but the marquis goes as a servant of Christ."

Barzizza laughed. "Ah, yes, that's what they all say," he said with a friendly nod. "I think *I* even said that."

"The marquis is an exceptional man," one of the other knights said, managing to sound both polite and rebuking.

"Of *course* he is, of *course* he is," Barzizza said amiably. "I did not mean to cause insult. If he can accomplish this campaign, I'll bow to him myself. As you see, I am a very devout man." And then he began an exercise to which he'd subjected me the day before, namely: explaining the religious significance of all the paintings on his walls. There was some complicated icono-cryptology that I found ridiculous—an eagle represented some archangel, and the implied archangel in turn implied some specific aspect of God; therefore, viewing the eagle was meant to evoke a very specific religious sensation. I don't like someone having to *explain* to me why a thing is significant or moving for me to be moved by it. That's why I like music—all you have to do is experience it and you know all by yourself whether you've been moved or not.

A middling musician played a husky-sounding psaltery in a corner, mostly the sort of troubadour music I myself had been studying. He began with "Kalenda Maya" (that annoying May Day song, the most ubiquitous, overplayed tune in the troubadour canon), then moved on to rather simplistic German *Minnelieder* in honor of Gregor's homeland. After Barzizza's chaplain intoned a blessing, the meal was served with as much ceremony as a high feast back home. The food was brilliant colors and smelled even better than what I had been served at dinner here the day before, but, as yesterday, I took only a small mouthful—I knew from experience how debilitating all those bright spices could be to a system unfamiliar with them. I was glad I wouldn't be anywhere near these men's berths tonight.

Barzizza spent much of the meal preaching the dangers and discomforts of sea travel, of which he had decades of experience. He warned us at least seven times to take plenty of laxatives (he recommended pennyroyal, smeared onto the body with oil and vinegar), for constipation was a discomfort nobody could escape from. He told us to avoid local fish, poultry, and soft cheeses, but to trust hard cheeses, and heavily spiced sweetmeats; he hoped we had all thought to write out wills before departing, and he could get them notarized for us at a discount in San Marco Square; he warned us that, once you get salt water on you, you never dry out but remain forever sticky; he advised us to adopt a sailor's stance, knees bent and legs wide apart; he warned against seasickness and said the best cure for it was to stay abovedeck, stand in the middle of the ship (where it rocked less), and stare at the horizon; he told us the mariners had a strange lingo of their own that we'd do well to learn if ever we hoped to understand them. He also alerted us to the superstitions of sailors the world over, so that we would do nothing to cause dismay and get ourselves thrown overboard as harbingers of bad luck. We must not step onto the boat with our left foot; nor throw stones overboard; nor look back at the port after once setting out on the journey; nor kill any dolphins (whatever those were), albatrosses (ditto), or gulls (gulls I remembered from the Channel crossing); nor cut our hair or nails while at sea; nor utter the word *drowned*; nor whistle; nor have women or priests onboard (although obviously some adjustments would have to be made in that regard); and above all, we must not throw the sailors' cats overboard, for nothing could be more certain of inciting the displeasure of the gods, cats being the luckiest things one could have onboard (as well as the only way to control the mice and rats). And these injunctions were for us who were merely pas-sengers; for the mariners themselves there was an entire unwritten testament of shalts and shalt-nots, regarding rigging, fixing, mend-ing, charting courses . . .

After this helpful if dismaying monologue, the man continued holding court over the final dishes, as if he had himself once liberated Jerusalem, although Jerusalem had not been liberated since before the birth of any of those present. I tried at this point to excuse myself to the privy (and my mortal escape), but Otto growled, munching, that I could wait until he needed relief himself. I'd no other pretext to get away from him.

When he was queried—especially by Gregor—it became clear that Barzizza had not himself seen much fighting when he was in the Levant five years earlier (on an aborted crusade proclaimed by Gregor's own king). He had been with those whose task it was to find a material benefit, whatever the military outcome was. He knew how to profit from loss as well as victory. And profit, he told us with a twinkle in his eye, took many forms.

"For an example," he said, smiling cherubically, "I will show you my greatest treasure." He signaled to a servant, as if sharing some

private joke. I knew this man from my visit here the day before; supposedly he was a eunuch, but somehow I doubted it (for starters, he
was mustachioed). The servant, looking bored, bowed stiffly and left
the room through a disguised door in the wall.

The door had been completely invisible until he opened it. It was
directly across the hall from where Otto and I sat; perhaps there was
another such disguised door right behind us? I adjusted myself on the
cushions and began to finger the plaster behind me.

Barzizza turned back to his captive audience. "Mind your manners
now, for you are about to meet a princess." This caught everyone's
attention, even mine—he'd mentioned no princess when I was his
guest. "Oh, yes." He grinned in response to our collective reaction.
"This is why, my lads, you must all be on the alert for unexpected opportunities. Our last engagement on the Emperor's Crusade, before a
truce was called, was in a small but very wealthy town on the Egyptian coast, ruled over by an infidel lord who would make the Doge of
Venice himself seem a pauper. These infidels had refused to convert
to the path of Christ, and so they had been killed—"

"Thus demonstrating Christ's love for the world," I muttered.
Before I had gotten even the second word out, Otto elbowed my
bony torso. I elbowed him back, hard, and Otto, on reflex, grabbed
at my head to yank my hair. I ducked my head away. "*That's* why you
haven't been knighted," I hissed in his ear. "Because you still act like
a *toddler*."

Then I cursed silently. That had been inexcusably stupid. Now
Otto would be paying close attention to me—and my fingers had just
found the hidden door that was, in fact, directly behind us. I men-
tally surveyed what I remembered of the place. We were above the
kitchen. This would be perfect; I could back out of the door, down
the steps, through the kitchen, grab a knife, and just *do it* before I had
time to think much about it.

Barzizza had not noticed our tussle. "Not everyone was killed,"
he was saying, grandly. "Among the survivors was the infidel lord's

daughter—no angelic virgin, of course, as she had children of her own, although they had been slaughtered, I think, by then. But still fetching and fecund. I was owed a great deal, but my boats were full to bursting, so I claimed her and brought her back with me. Do you know why?" he asked in a smarmy tone. My fingers had found the outline of the door; it opened out toward the stairs. I pressed against it and it moved; it was unlatched. All I'd have to do was push it. Once everyone's attention was on the approaching princess, slipping out would be easy. "Not for the ransom, no, because of course, there is nobody left alive to pay it," Barzizza was continuing. "And she had no riches about her, except her clothes and jewels, which were opulent, but what is the worth of one lady's attire when there is an entire palace to pillage? She's a handsome woman, but hardly a rosebud, and they're never quite as fuckable after they've had children. No, no, I took her because I have vision. Venice is a great center of commerce, but only because we trade—wool from Britain goes east, silk from Asia goes west, and so on. We ourselves *produce* very little, only glass and some brocade. For most of us, it's a dreadful slog. I myself am a rich man because I work very hard at an unpleasant business. My fish comes from the land of barbarians above the Black Sea, by Novorossiisk and Kerch, so I have spent too much time dealing with barbarians—some of whom practice human sacrifice! There are better things to sow and reap from barbarians, and in fact—ha ha!— there are better barbarians to sow and reap. There are, if I may speak plainly, certain products you can only make yourself. If you have a vision." There was a sound from the hidden doorway across the hall. Barzizza smiled smugly. "Speaking of a vision, here is my own Princess Jamila." He gestured grandly, and the supposed eunuch pushed a veiled woman into the room. Otto sat up straighter to look, and I might have slipped out then, but my own curiosity held me back.

There was an instant murmur of appreciation, not for her beauty—the veil covered her face from the nose down—but for her bearing. She was wearing a long silk robe with arabesque designs of an extraordinary blue-green, and even as she stumbled from having been shoved by the eunuch, she moved with graceful dignity. There was none of the pale, girlish shyness that constituted femininity in the West; her age was hard to determine from her eyes, but she was unafraid of and unapologetic about her womanliness. Having regained her balance, she took a few more steps into the room and glanced at her captor with such extreme disdain I could physically feel it despite the veil hiding her face. I should go now, I thought—but I didn't go. I could go in a moment.

"Yes," Barzizza said, with satisfaction, looking at our collective responses. "You can *feel* one of the reasons that I wanted her. Heathen women are more notoriously primitive in bed than even Jewesses. She does not disappoint that way, although after five years I grow bored even with that." This provoked catcalls from around the room, which the woman pretended not to hear. I had a brief fantasy of punching Barzizza in the face.

"But it's better than that, lads," Barzizza said confidingly. "She is the only surviving member of the ruling line . . . until she has a child." A dramatic pause. "My child. My *son*. Even as a bastard, the child will have royal bloodlines in the Holy Land. When we take back that land, as God wills, a child of her body will have a claim to rule that city. Not bad for a mere fish merchant, eh? To refound an infidel dynasty with Christian seed?"

Whether it was drunkenness, politeness, or stupidity, most of the young men around the high table huzzahed his reasoning; only Gregor looked appalled and unconvinced. "But it's been five years, and no child?" he asked cautiously. "Are you sure she's fertile?"

"Oh yes," Barzizza said, with a brief glare in her direction. "Fertile and diabolically clever. Seven times she's brought on her monthly flux, when all the signs said she should be growing with my seed. It's some kind of Saracen magic, but I have a doctor from the Salerno school looking into antidotes. If I have to keep her tied to my bed for a year, with a guard over her night and day, I'll do it."

The woman appeared to have understood none of this. But then: "Come here," Barzizza ordered. She crossed to stand beside him, with a sudden air of resignation, and clasped her hands before her, poised and waiting.

"I wait upon your every whim, sir," she said stiffly in the Venetian dialect, with an accent I'd never heard before. Her voice was low and soft, almost like a leonine growl. She sounded as if she was speaking through clenched teeth.

"You displeased me last night," Barzizza informed her loudly, performing. "You require humiliation." He glanced around the room with a leer. "Anyone ever patted a princess before?"

"For the love of St. John," I heard Gregor mutter in resigned disgust, before he was drowned out by his fellow diners heartily agreeing to Barzizza's caveat that they restrict themselves to what was above her belt. The horde rose swaying to its feet to form a chortling line in front of the woman, who with eyes averted and face still veiled, began to shrug her loose gown off one shoulder. Otto chuckled and rose to move into the queue for whatever was to follow. Now was my opportunity to disappear forever.

I did not take it. I wanted to stop Otto. In fact, I wanted to stop all of them.

No—I wanted to do even more than that. I wanted to help the woman.

That was a dangerous feeling: wanting something. It meant I was back among the living. It meant I cared. It was only a specific flicker of caring, no great love for life, just a gut impulse to look out for someone other than myself. But it was enough to snap me back to clarity, because I had to work out a plan immediately. I am bad at plans, but I realized dashing out the secret doorway wouldn't get me what I needed.

I caught Gregor's gaze and, once I had it, reached as if for Otto's dagger. Over the hubbub, Gregor whistled; Otto, recognizing some code between them, turned with irritation toward his brother and, in pivoting, moved his dagger out of my reach.

Gregor glanced meaningfully over the heads of the other knights, from Otto to me; Otto realized what was expected of him. As much as he wanted to return to Germany someday with a list of exploits that included groping a Saracen princess's breast, he would not have the opportunity tonight. He grabbed my elbow and dragged me toward the stairs; our departure was unnoticed in the thrill of the captive's disrobing.

The primary portal was the water door, opening onto the Grand Canal, but none of the gondoliers were here to take us back yet. Otto, irritated, asked to be let out the servants' entrance, into the torchlit courtyard where the well was. From here we went into a tiny, barely moonlit alleyway, then right into another, then left into another.

"Spoiler," he growled. "You got us thrown out, just for spite."

"Yes," I said, as if apologizing. "I felt bad for the woman."

"She's infidel war booty living a life of leisure in one of the nicest homes in Venice, and you feel *bad* for her?" Otto said incredulously. "She should get down on her heathen knees and thank her heathen gods for her *luck*."

I slowed as we came to the end of yet another blind little alleyway. "I think in her case it is a single heathen god, but yes, you're right," I said. "Now you've put it that way, I regret my behavior. Shall we go back? I won't make a fuss."

He shot me a suspicious look, but he slowed as well. "Truly?"

"Of course. But I *am* sorry about this."

"Sorry about wha—" Otto began, then stopped with a strangled sound as I stepped slightly ahead of him and thrust my elbow back and up straight into his midriff. He struggled painfully to breathe, whining like a pulley in need of oil; I shoved him, and as he stumbled, I kicked him hard behind the knee, which knocked him to the cold pavement. He scraped his face along the side of a building on the way down.

"Sorry about losing this lovely belt," I said and untied the leather band from around my waist. I snatched Otto's hands as he lay face down in the muck and used the belt to bind his thick wrists together behind his back. He groaned breathlessly and tried to turn over; obligingly, I rolled him onto his back and then plopped myself down, with zest, straight onto his midriff; he wheezed again in pain, his hands pinned defenselessly under our combined weight. I straddled him, facing his feet, and untied his own belt, slipping off his purse and knife, and setting them down. With his belt in hand, I stood, rolled him onto his stomach again, and now began to bind his feet with his belt so that they were cinched, behind his back, to his bound hands.

In the moonlight, Otto's face—that part not smeared in street offal—was almost as dark as his red tunic. He began to curse, voicelessly and close to furious tears. He could not collect enough breath to fortify himself for a struggle, and I worked quickly. I satisfied myself that the ties would hold, then gave Otto an affectionate smack on the cheek. "Don't take it personally, lad. You've got spirit, and in other circumstances we might have been the best of friends. May the good Lord watch over you in these dangerous streets." I picked up his purse and his dagger, and trotted off into darkness, back the way we'd come.

6

Tell me lady, are you grateful for my becoming your servant?
Knowing you, I think not. Indeed, you find me a burden.

—CHRÉTIEN DE TROYES,
"Love Song"

THE SMALL L-SHAPED ROOM on the top floor of Ca' Barzizza was not lit, or warmed. Some light came in through a single small window from the courtyard. This had to be the room: it was empty except for a small sleeping mat and a prie-dieu in the corner, which conveniently was in a spot not visible from the doorway. My eyes adjusted to the dimness as I waited. Downstairs, the music had changed to something twangy, and the knights were making obscene noises as they patted the Saracen princess.

Five years imprisoned in this small empty room; the thought made my skin crawl.

Finally the music stopped, the voices quieted to guffaws. Later, footsteps approached from below. The bored-looking servant opened the door and gestured to the woman to enter before him. She was dressed and veiled again but looked disheveled. He shoved the door closed behind himself; his back was to me. She looked away from him, hands folded together, her stance dignified and grim.

"Did you enjoy that?" he asked, in what might have been a leer if it had not sounded so lazy. He reached toward his own groin. "I sure did. Come on, skirt up."

I *knew* he wasn't a eunuch. Barzizza was even dumber than I thought.

From my precarious perch on the prie-dieu, I threw myself at the man's shoulders and wrapped one arm around his throat, pulling him down and back with my weight. He reached up to pull my arm away, but I grabbed my own tunic, locking my arm bent around his throat. For an eternity, as I remained semi-airborne, the two of us hovered in a slow-motion tug-of-war over his windpipe. He gurgled; I grunted with the effort of holding on, praying I wouldn't have to use the dagger on him; she stood watching, silent and bemused—it must have been a sight, for the man was a head or two taller than I and easily twice the mass.

Just when I thought I was in trouble, my victim finally passed out, collapsing backward to the wooden floor almost on top of me. I leapt away at the last moment, then turned my attention to her.

She'd stepped back with one slippered foot; otherwise, no reaction. "What do you want?" she demanded in her strange, throaty accent, sounding scornful behind the veil.

I smiled reassuringly. "I'm returning you to your people."

Her eyes widened. "How?"

"There's an entire navy in the harbor, first stop Alexandria in Egypt. They are undersubscribed, so they have some empty berths." I held out my hand with a flourish.

She shook her head once. "Why? Who are you?"

This was not the response I'd anticipated. "I owe the world, among other things, the well-being of one royal lady. Will you come quietly, or must I bind and gag you?"

She folded her hands neatly in front of herself and considered me. "Why should I leave the devil I know for the devil I don't?" she asked.

I made a very ungentlemanly grunt and then demanded, "*What?*"

"You might be another Barzizza—or worse yet, you might mean well but be incompetent, and get us both killed."

An incredulous moment, then: "I'm here to rescue you, and you're questioning my credentials. Are you perhaps expecting a *better offer?*"

Behind me, my victim huffed a little, although he was still out. Princess Jamila took a step to the side and pushed the blanket off her cot, then pulled the sheet off. "Here, bind him with this; he'll come to in a moment. Did you bring rope?" I shook my head. She tossed the sheet in my direction. "Then how do you expect to get me out of here?"

"I climbed up the wall. Climbing down's a little harder, but not much—"

"—Not much for those who know how to scale walls. I am not among that population. Was that your only plan?" I could feel her dark eyes staring at me appraisingly in the light through the window. I wondered if she could see me turning red.

"We'll use the sheet, I'll lower you out the window on it," I said—triumphantly, as if this were some clever retort. "Then I'll climb down myself."

"Then how shall we tie him up?" she asked, in a tone of retort not unlike mine.

"Your bedding consists of just one sheet?" I asked sarcastically. I gestured toward the blanket. "That will hold your weight just as well."

"*Vous n'ête pas français?*" She was trying to place my accent.

"I speak French, but I am not a Frenchman," I said in French as I returned to my victim. I used a small tear already in the sheet to rip it and stuffed a wad of it in the fellow's mouth. She tried more languages, some of which I admitted I knew, none of which was native to me; some were completely alien. During this linguistic inquisition, I used Otto's dagger to butcher the rest of the sheet, and tied up the inert body; it was harder to lug his deadweight than it had been to wrestle with him. She did not look like she would budge until she figured out who or what I was. So when I finished binding the man,

I stood up and interrupted her to recite the last stanza of a bardic lament in my own tongue. Her head tipped to one side, like a dog's does when it hears a strange sound.

"Confused you, didn't I?" I said with a brief grin, switching to French. "I win a lot of drinking bets with that one at all the damsel-rescuing festivals. Speaking of which, there's one beginning right now— Shall we *go*, milady?"

She was silent for a moment.

"If we are going on the boats," she said after a moment, "we must bring supplies."

I made an exasperated sound, after a final tug at the servant's ties. "Your Highness—"

"There is no sense in escaping if we die on the way," she said reasonably. "And you, *clearly*, have not thought this out. I've made the voyage before, you haven't." She slipped past the guard, who was coming to and moaning, and went to the prie-dieu in the corner. She tugged at the top, where one's praying hands rest, until the board came off. She reached into the shallow box below and pulled out a small sack. Seeing the surprise on my face, she said, "Do you think I have not made my own preparations, these past five years? Do you think I have simply sat in this room feeling sorry for myself whenever that buffoon spreads my legs? I don't think such a woman would be worth the rescue." She glanced at the sack. "I must ask you frankly if you will be expecting carnal favors as a condition of rescue, because if you are, then I must bring—"

"Absolutely not," I said, appalled. "I swear on all I hold holy, my only intention is to see you safely to your homeland. I pledge my very life on it. I will see you home, unharmed."

"Very well, one less thing to worry about." She tossed the bag back into the hollow and continued more loudly in her businesslike tone, "Since you are unshod, take this man's shoes. They'll be too big for you, but perhaps we can trade them for a smaller pair onboard. You will want them in the desert."

I am sure I looked stunned. "You're awfully nonchalant about this," I said.

She blinked. I could not see the rest of her face, but the blink was expressive enough: she thought I was an idiot. "Do you *wish* me to be hysterical?" she asked. "Will that make it easier to steal me away?"

"No," I admitted.

"Will you feel more *heroic* if I behave as if I'm a traumatized child or an excited pet?" she asked in the same terse voice.

"I don't know," I admitted, then added, peevishly, "*Perhaps.*"

"And is the point of this exercise to make you will feel heroic?"

"Well, if you must put it like *that*," I said, "shut up, and come with me."

7

When they came forth upon the sea, and hoisted their sails and pennants upon the forecastles, then truly it appeared as if the whole sea was aswarm.

—ROBERT OF CLARI's *Chronicle of the Fourth Crusade*

Dawn of the following morning, i.e., Feast of St. Jerome, 30 September

It is to my great sorrow and shame that I must amend the earlier entry, to say that the Briton will not be going with us in pilgrimage to Jerusalem. I was sleeping in the cabin of the Innocent, which is cramped and smells of something wet and stale. It is hard to sleep, but finally God was good enough to grant me slumber. My brother Otto, sopping wet

and shivering, has just woken me as the sun begins to rise, to report
the most villainous story I believe I have ever heard. Upon leaving the
home of the noble Barzizza, the Briton pulled a mace from his breeches
and threatened Otto with it. The Briton then debated with several
barbarian brigands—Otto began the story remembering two, but as he
continued to explain what happened, he recalled a third. All of these
men had been hired by the Briton to help him escape. They were debating whether to sever Otto's limbs or bind and toss him whole into the
Grand Canal. He valiantly fought off the four villains with nothing but
his bare hands, ripping half the Briton's hair out and, with the artful
use of his knee and the grace of God, ending the progenitorial potential
of two of the brigands. He was lucky to have escaped with his life, and
I thank God for it. The Briton's various instruments (for he was a
renowned musician in his own land) I brought back from Barzizza's.
We will sell them and donate the proceeds to the cost of the pilgrimage,
the debt of which injures our momentum.

THE THOUSAND-ODD loose women were collected together into
two ships, which had been given the predictable names of the *Venus*
and the *Aphrodite*. I knew Liliana had a berth in the former. Nobody,
not even the priests, pretended for one moment that these ships
would not be crawling with men from the moment they set anchor at
night. Every night.

I'd traded Otto's purse for passage on the *Venus*, hoping Liliana
might be willing to help me with Princess Jamila. Our arrival, in the
middle of the night, caused no stir at all, but my heart sank when I
realized what a dung heap I had brought Her Highness to. The *Venus*
was purgatory. On the deck were women who truly were camp followers, who would take casual comers for scrip, food, or barter; the
cramped space below, out of the weather, was reserved for those like
Liliana whose "patrons" entertained the vain hope of a little privacy

at sea. I was terrified that Jamila would somehow be recognized by the mariners; I didn't know how many Venetians had had a chance to pat her. Barzizza would sound the alarm, and only one gondolier had been hired in the middle of the night to take a pair of fugitives out to the fleet; as Her Highness had pointed out a few more times than necessary, we could be tracked down easily.

At least she did not stand out on the ship—a woman veiled, like many things Eastern, was popular in Venice. It was very late, and there were lamps at stern, stem, and amidships, but they did not throw enough light to show off the worn finery of her dress. We skirted through sleeping women, made our way down a ladder in a hatchway—and I heard Her Highness make a small, unhappy noise as the thickness of the air below hit her nostrils. The hold did not stink as badly as its male-filled equivalent, since most of these women had an investment in smelling nice, but it was not pleasant. Like the *Innocent*, like any ship newly washed down for a long voyage, it also reeked of vinegar, so severely it made the entire inside of one's face feel inflamed.

Unlike the knightly quarters on the *Innocent*, the sleeping arrangements were completely haphazard, with not the slightest thought for comfort. There were no cabins or berths, just a large, open hold. Since the women's ships would be the sites of more nocturnal quaffing than any others in the fleet, the lowest deck of each was filled entirely with tuns of wine and ale. Hammocks were strung up so close together on the between decks that nobody could turn in her sleep without waking those above and below; a central aisle and small side aisles for getting in and out were the only open space. It was further crowded by two large water casks on either side; a few women had staked out the areas beneath the curve of the barrels, and slept against the sides of them rather than in hammocks—still cramped but providing an illusion of privacy. Remembering a comment Otto had made, I slipped through the hammocks toward the nearer cask, to see if Liliana was one of these women.

She was. Not knowing I had mistreated her master and then fled, she was not surprised to see me; however, she was surprised that I had company, especially so well-dressed. There was no room for either of us, but Liliana managed to find some anyhow. I ended up stick-straight, pinned between the cask and the hull, listening to the water trickling down into the bilge all night, like a little creek; she and the princess, without even a proper introduction, lay spooned together against the cask, in a space barely big enough for Liliana herself. The circumstances were hardly humane, but the princess made no complaint at all. In fact, she slept soundly, which neither Liliana nor I managed to do.

The morning came bright and sunny, with a favorable wind. This relieved the mariners, for we'd already missed the northwesterly melteme wind farther east; they were worried we'd also lose the bora, the wind from the Dolomites that made eastward passage easier this time of year. To a ridiculous amount of fanfare, Enrico Dandolo, the ancient, blind Doge of Venice—who had dramatically taken the cross himself a few weeks earlier, just as I was arriving in Venice—was ferried out to his ship, meandering through the moored fleet so that we all could get a glimpse of him. From the raucous cheering of the sailors, it appeared this man was adored by his people at least as much as Gregor of Mainz was by his fellow knights. I'd heard as much from Barzizza too—in fact, Barzizza had gone on and *on* about the piety, prudence, and civic attentiveness of this great doge. Dandolo held public court almost every day of the year; what king or emperor could say as much? Granted, he lacked the power of such anointed rulers, since every decision he made had to be ratified and approved by committees that blossomed out of a vast oligarchy of Venice's rich citizens. But he was a forceful presence, and Barzizza particularly liked him because he'd devoted much of his life to fostering peaceful relations with someplace called Byzantium, which Barzizza had to cross to reach his fishing waters.

Dandolo was formidable, despite his age. He was not large, but he was tough as dried meat, lean and seared by decades of salt water and sun. He was no bureaucratic quill pusher; he had put in his time traversing the great sea before being elected doge. And the blindness, mariners whispered reverentially, was relatively recent, an accident in a far-off place called Constantinople; before that, he had put in years as a soldier too. Three decades older than the elegant courtier commanding the army—Boniface of Montferrat—Dandolo looked as if he might have wrestled him to a draw. He wore long, bright robes with swirls on them, like Jamila's, and a sash rather than a belt; also, a gold cap almost like a crown. His was the largest galley, with three hundred rowers, the hull painted bright vermilion, the red sails topped with silk decorations. Although the last to be boarded, it would be the first to leave the harbor, the winged lion of St. Mark fluttering from the flags at the tops of both masts, trumpets and timbrels playing loudly on the deck.

Once the sails were up, there was a surfeit of rope lying on the deck, which the sailors would soon spend hours laying straight, untwisting, and coiling up again. Cooking fires were stoked; depending on the ship, these were either in the hold or up on the raised deck in the stern (the mariners for some reason called this the poop deck). Wine was splashed liberally across the deck of every ship, a symbolic offering to ancient sea gods—which struck me as, first, a desperate waste of wine, and second, a decidedly queer way to begin a Christian pilgrimage. The master of each ship shouted at his crews, and not quite in concert, all burst into a queasy rendition of *Veni Creator Spiritus*. Ship after ship after ship sailed or rowed out; the sea looked like a bobbing city when all the vessels were out—the rowed galleys, the transports, the horse transports, some pulling barges and longboats behind. On the foredeck of every ship was an array of crossbowmen, well-heeled Venetian youths. Fifty of the galleys were Venice's contribution; each other ship (or collection thereof) carried a noble lord and his followers. Bishop Conrad of Halberstadt was high lord of the *Innocent*, but the *Venus* lacked such patronage. Somebody told me the fleet would make a chain three miles long. As we sailed from the lagoon, sails caught the wind and unfurled with a noise so thunderous I was afraid I might go deaf. It was a stupefying sight, all those sails—enough hemp canvas and silk to drape over all of Venice.

In the midst of the hubbub, the celebration, the percussive music, and the general excitement, Marquis Boniface of Montferrat—Gregor's father-in-law, the devout pilgrim-leader of the expedition, the man I'd almost murdered—disappeared.

BEING OUT ON the open sea was riotously loud in a way I did not remember from my daylong passage to the continent, three years earlier. Every imaginable pitch of creaking surrounded us relentlessly: sometimes it was timber against timber, or tarred gunk (*oakum*, to those in the know) shrieking as it was pinched and pierced between the boards (*planks*) of the hull, or rope (*line*) straining within wooden pulleys (*blocks*); sails shivered so loudly they seemed to be speaking to the gods, especially when they went briefly slack; the drums that set a tempo for the galley rowers rumbled in everyone's ears; rigging made all sorts of ghastly noises I'd never've guessed simple line could make. Even the birds (for there were always birds, those scavengers) were screechers.

The wind was fresh but cold, and unrelenting, and ripped words out of our mouths before Liliana and I could share them with each other, so we quickly gave up trying to discuss Jamila, who'd remained below. The mariners spoke, but always with few words, as if a phrase contained a paragraph: "this wind," "Zara," "Byzantium," "the other line"—these were treated as engrossing monologues.

The sway of the boat was like nothing I had experienced before, except for that dismal crossing of "the sleeve"—the water ineffectually protecting Britain from the barbarian hordes. Those who compare being shipboard to riding a leisurely cantering horse are sorely wrong; it would have to be a lame horse with legs a dozen yards long that never stops for breath and bucks every few moments for good measure. The sensation of what ought to be solid forever moving under one's feet—this is not an experience the gods ever intended mortals to endure. For most of the day, the sun was of a staggering strength, its reflection glaring up from below almost as badly as the real thing glared from above. Princess Jamila seemed completely immune to the trauma of it and spent most of her time below, where the wind and sun did not trouble her, although the listing (*heeling*) of the boat seemed even worse in the dark and stink.

For the first several hours, almost all of the women abovedeck were falling over on top of one another on the curved deck, grabbing at whatever they could for balance—heavy coils of line, rigging (*shrouds*), masts, trunks lashed down along the sides (*bulwarks*)—and being ordered by shouting mariners to stay put. I settled down in the middle of the deck (*amidships*), for Barzizza was right: things rocked less here. I thought about the warhorses in the transports and wondered how they would manage. Otto had explained they were each supported in a sling, so the worst of the rolling would not lame them . . . still it must be hell for them. Once they let the animals out for grazing, whenever they made land, they'd never get them back into the ships. Now that I had my own reason to reach Egypt quickly—Princess Jamila's safe return—this concerned me in a way it wouldn't have before.

The mariners themselves were a wonder to behold. Unlike us landsmen, they related to the ship the way a knight does to his horse, or I to my harp: intuitively, intimately, subtly. All were sunburned, and I could never tell their ages, for there were young men with old faces and old men with bodies limber as that of any youth. The master of the ship stood on the poop deck and spent the entire day, it seemed, just gazing about us. He had two boys posted to either side. If he felt we were moving too close to another ship (it really was like a city under sail), he'd call out to the boys, who in turn would shout down to the helmsman, who in turn would pull on lines to steer the rudders that stuck out to either side of the ship like oversize oars.

Meanwhile the sailors would await instruction, then leap with the uniformity of a school of fish when orders were barked at them. They pulled some ropes (*halyards*) together, four or five men on one line, moving like acrobats. It entertained me (for a while) that they would pull on things in one place and a lateen sail would rise in some other part of the boat, tied to beams (*yards*) that were in turn attached to the towering masts.

We'd be always within sight of land, because the Venetians would need to spend a good part of every third day refilling the galley rowers' water supply. At such stops, temporary crewmen, who knew the local hazards, would be hired. It took time to negotiate with these men. The days were growing shorter, and because of the shoals in the Adriatic, it was not safe to travel except in good daylight. It would be a long trip south.

A few hours into the ordeal, I misjudged a step and nearly fell into the sea; we were going at such a fast clip I doubt they'd have stopped for me, and suddenly I was acutely aware of my own mortality as something that I needed—even wanted—to avoid. A day earlier I never could have imagined that. Despite myself, I had to live a little longer: I had to get Her Highness home.

I learned, this first day, that sailors don't like having women on their boats because of some fear involving mermaids. (This makes no sense to me: if the danger of a mermaid is that she'll lure a man into the water, why not keep pretty women around to entice you to remain onboard? I tried this argument with many of the sailors, but they maintained their fear, almost as if they were *proud* of it.) The most superstitious of the sailors had refused to crew the whore ships; and so the mariners on the *Venus* were of two types: the ones who were not at all superstitious and the ones who had decided they could get over their fears if a high enough price was paid, in either flesh or money. The former group quickly saw the benefit of pretending to belong to the latter group. The whores—who were the savviest unit in the army—had anticipated all of this and planned accordingly. Ours was possibly the most convivial vessel on the whole of the Adriatic.

Once the ships turned in to the wind to drop anchor that first night, there was across the entire fleet a mad rush for the longboats that trailed behind the galleys and transports, as men charged to be the first for relief. There was still no rest for the mariners themselves, of course: they had to scrape the hulls free from barnacles and algae; they had to make sure their lines remained unkinked; they had to oil and patch the forward part of the masts, which sailing into the weather got most battered; they had to check the sail seams, for these were most susceptible to sun damage.

But for the army, evening meant carousing. The women, just to make sure the men knew where to come, had festooned the sides of the *Venus* and the *Aphrodite* with their undergarments, much as the sides of the other transports boasted the knights' family pennants. This boat was just as sloppy and vinegary as others—but the spell of female laughter transformed it, in the collective imagination, into a palace with sails. It had more lanterns, musicians, and wine than other transports, all of which helped with the illusion.

When Otto first arrived at Liliana's sleeping mat and recognized the blue-green veil of Barzizza's princess, it took him a moment to realize this was a very large problem. "What's she doing here?" he demanded, confused.

Liliana, kneeling over her, lowered her eyes to avoid his look; Jamila herself was deep asleep and did not stir. There was a brief, awkward silence. It was made more awkward, but somewhat less silent, when I stuck my head out from behind the water cask. "I brought her," I said.

In hindsight, I'd say it was at this moment Otto realized he'd have to revise his story of our last encounter.

This realization did not put him in a good mood.

In fact, I suspect he would have gone ahead and killed me then, left to his own impulses. But Liliana reached up and pressed the flat of her hand against his knee. He looked down, steaming. "*Don't draw attention*," she whispered fiercely, glancing at the rowdy crowd that was pressing in on him from three sides.

For a moment, Otto's eyes glanced among the three of us, trying to figure out exactly what had happened and how he could take control of it. "Did you collude in this?" he asked Liliana angrily.

I answered first: "No, it was all me."

Slightly mollified, Otto hissed, "This was a stupid place to bring her."

"Yes, it was," I agreed. "Every other option proved even stupider."

Otto took a breath in and opened his mouth to speak again, then hesitated.

"Yes," I said. "Lots to contemplate here. I've been contemplating it all day myself. I recommend you take me back to the *Innocent* and leave her here."

"Then that's precisely what I shall *not* do," Otto retorted.

I shrugged. "Please yourself. Any other option is even stupider."

Otto glanced about the loud, tumbling collection of undressing bodies. Some were attempting things in the cramped and close-set hammocks; others were swarming up on deck. Lamps swayed wildly as the boat rocked in the sea, throwing dizzying shadows across all of us; the mass of bodies warmed the space by the moment. There was no air down here, and there could be no privacy either. "Once we get to the *Innocent* I'm going to pound you," Otto warned.

"I assumed you'd pound me in the longboat on the way over."

"The pounding I'm going to give you would capsize the damn longboat," Otto assured me. He looked back down at the sleeping form.

Liliana shrugged. "She's not going anywhere."

Otto grimaced thoughtfully. "Maybe I should bring her to the *Innocent*, too."

Liliana shook her head. "Nobody's noticed her yet. Don't go parading her about through the fleet, somebody might pinch her from you."

"So what? Gets her off our hands," Otto said, but he didn't sound convinced.

"I bet there's profit to be had in holding on to her," Liliana coaxed, understanding the look on his face. "I'll keep an eye on her if she stays here."

Not sure if Liliana was actually conspiring with Otto or with me, I gratefully kept my mouth shut.

8

I ARRIVED AT Gregor's berth with a black eye and a swollen lip, but Otto had not thrashed me much beyond that; he believed in a fair fight, and there's small satisfaction in socking an opponent who will not defend himself.

Upon our lamplit reintroduction, Gregor sleepily voiced a few choice oaths in German. There were several utterances of what I think was "John the Baptist," which I took to be a reference to what he'd like done to my head. After a moment he pulled himself out of the cramped little berth, threw a cloak over his shoulders, and then dragged me up on deck, through the dark, to the Bishop of Halberstadt's cabin back on the poop deck. His Eminence was roused from his own bed and briefed by candlelight. None of us was surprised—or especially delighted—when he announced that Gregor now had *two* souls to shepherd to Jerusalem.

"Her Highness and I are only going as far as Alexandria in Egypt," I corrected him, sitting down and leaning back against the bulkhead, pretending to clean my fingernails. "But we very much appreciate the transportation."

Gregor grabbed my collar and hauled me up to standing.

"I hope and believe," said the bishop gravely, his jowls exaggerated gruesomely in the candle flame, "that by the time you reach

Egypt, you will have so blossomed under the influence of this good knight, it will be your most ardent wish to go on to Jerusalem."

"If that gives us free passage to Alexandria, then I think it is a grand prediction. Do we get fed as well? I wouldn't mind some boots either; we couldn't get them off the servant's feet." I glanced down at my unkempt state. "Perhaps a new belt—"

"We must collect this princess," the bishop said to Gregor, ignoring me. "She should be under my direct influence."

"Direct influence," I echoed. "So that's what they're calling ecclesiastical undergarments these days."

"A noblewoman of that stature must not be subjected to a ship full of whores—"

I opened my mouth, but Gregor squeezed his hand around my elbow, a signal for silence, and for some reason, I obeyed him.

"Your Grace," said Gregor. "Consider her position. She is a princess of Egypt."

"Exactly! As well as converting her, we should be able to ransom her when we get there, but that means keeping her healthy—"

"She's even more valuable than that," Gregor said evenly. "Did I not explain that she has offered to help us negotiate a surrender with the lords of Alexandria?"

"She—" I began an incredulous protest, but he squeezed my elbow again. Suddenly I realized, with perverse delight, that Gregor— the humorlessly earnest Christian sheep—was lying to his shepherd.

The bishop looked as if he'd just learned his own shit was worth its weight in gold. It was the best news he had heard in a decade. "Then she is *extremely* valuable and must *certainly* be under my guard, until we can give her to Fazio himself, come Zara."

"Who's Fazio?" I demanded anxiously. "She's not going to any Fazio."

"His intimates and peers call the marquis Boniface, Fazio," Gregor said.

"I thought they called him the Englishman."

"A well-loved man has many epithets," said Gregor peaceably.

"Oh!" I said, looking pleased. "And all these years I thought I was having abuse heaped upon me. Which I certainly understood, considering—"

Gregor had returned his attention to the bishop. "Your Grace, I share your desire to turn her over to the marquis, but naturally, because she is a Saracen princess, she cannot stay among us on the *Innocent*."

The bishop hadn't been expecting that and frowned. "Why not? A princess—"

"A *Saracen* princess," Gregor repeated, apologetically, conciliatory. "Have you not heard tales of the customs there? She is used to living only among women. For now, the only equivalent we can offer her is to stay aboard the *Venus*. We certainly cannot ask her to share a small room and bed with a high-ranking man of the cloth. It would be most distressing for her, and it would insult her sense of propriety so deeply that she might grow unwilling to assist our cause."

In the swaying candlelight, I could see Conrad trying to work out a countermand that would not make him look too flagrantly like a self-serving hypocrite. But there really wasn't one, so he finally acknowledged the wisdom of Gregor's argument—then announced he would need to interview Her Highness the next day himself. He sent us away and went back to bed.

Neither of us spoke until we were back on deck by the ladder going down to Gregor's berth. The moon was full, and it was a clear night, so we could see each other's faces easily.

"Thank you," I whispered.

He shook his head. "That was not a favor to you." Gregor pointed to the cross that spanned the back of his tunic, shoulder to shoulder. "Do you see this? I have sworn an oath to liberate the Holy Land. I am of course naturally inclined to care for the well-being of a lady, but this"—the cross again—"comes first. I am interested in her because she might be of use to Marquis Boniface, that's all."

"What does Conrad have to do with that?"

Gregor reached for a bit of rigging to steady himself, as if he already knew we would lock horns. "Boniface and Bishop Conrad are natural allies, because they're both in the Holy Roman Emperor's inner court. But lately I've sensed tension between them, and until Boniface is back with the fleet, I want to keep her—"

"Back with the fleet?" I interrupted. "Hold on, are you speaking of Boniface, the man I nearly killed? He's not with the army? The army he's *commanding*?"

"That's right," Gregor said, looking almost defensive in the moonlight. "He had personal business to attend to back in Montferrat, that had to be handled before he left on this great and very long enterprise. Until he's back and I can turn the princess over to him directly, I don't want anyone else laying claim to her, not even Conrad."

"When will he be back?"

"I don't know," Gregor said—always he spoke to me as if to a younger sibling who was trying his patience. "He left too abruptly for me to have a final audience with him."

I found that odd. And odder yet that Gregor himself—Boniface's beloved, useful son-in-law—had not been taken along. "Boniface was avoiding you," I guessed.

Gregor grimaced. "Perhaps he was avoiding me," he conceded.

"Why?" I remembered that my attack on Boniface had interrupted a private conference between the two of them.

Gregor eyed me suspiciously and said nothing.

"I just watched you lie to your own bishop, Gregor, we're practically colleagues now."

He grimaced again. But then he spoke. "I never question milord's judgment, but I'd heard something that discouraged me, and I had been in the middle of asking him about it when we were interrupted by a certain suicidal Briton. Boniface decamped before I had another chance for an audience with him."

"So he *was* avoiding you. What were you asking him about?"

He shook his head. "It has no bearing on this matter."

"If you're planning to turn my princess over to him, I want to know what's wrong with him."

"She's not your princess, she's stolen property and—"

"She was a prisoner of war!" I said, forgetting to whisper.

"She was among the *spoils* of war," Gregor countered quietly and glanced cautiously about the deck in the moonlight. "Barzizza has a right to demand her back."

Dammit, I'd been afraid he'd get legalistic about it. "Then why turn her over to your precious marquis?" I snapped nervously. "Why not do the *right* thing and just send her back to that stupid fart in Venice?"

He gestured sharply for me to lower my voice, glancing in the direction of the Venetian mariners awake on watch. "Boniface commands me on this expedition. If he says hand her over to the bishop, I will, and gladly. If he says use her as a bargaining chip when we get to Alexandria, I will. But if he says return her to Barzizza— I will."

I get itchy in the presence of people who are so dispassionate and stalwart about their duty, in part because my own failure in that arena has been known to have catastrophic results. "Well in that case, why did you even *mention* her to the bishop, if the bishop is subservient to Boniface?"

Gregor sighed heavily. "Mostly because I wasn't thinking clearly, because it is the middle of the night and you surprised me. But the hierarchy is not so simple as one being subservient to another. Boniface commands us as soldiers, but the bishops command us as pilgrims."

I snorted. "That leaves a lot of grey area."

He gave me a tired, confiding look. "Grey is too serene a color to describe it. In the past, these major expeditions to the Holy Land had a king, or a collection of kings, leading them. This one doesn't. Boniface is the commander, but only because three other commanders sought him out and *begged* him to *become* the leader, when the original leader died. He's not the first person they asked, and he didn't leap at the chance, because he knew what a monumental challenge it would be, and an utterly thankless task. Few of the men he's commanding speak the same language he does, almost *none* owe loyalty to the same sovereign, and then, of course, the bishops—"

"Yes, yes, we've been over this," I said. "I didn't care the first time and I don't care now. I just want to make sure the princess gets back to Egypt. With as little interference as possible from the marquis *or* the bishop. Or you."

"Unless we can negotiate with the rulers of Egypt, we will attack them. They are—presumably—somehow connected to your princess. Since your desire is to restore her to her family members, wouldn't you rather we don't kill off what's left of them?"

I allowed that this would be a good thing.

"Well then, *cooperate* with me. Stay alive, stay out of trouble, and help me keep her out of anybody else's clutches until Boniface rejoins us."

I finally saw the bigger picture. "Ah. You are keeping *her* under *my* thumb to make it easier to keep *me* under *your* thumb."

"Do you have a problem with that?" he asked.

I thought about it. "No," I admitted. "But I'm only staying under your thumb until she's home. None of this going-on-to-Jerusalem. We disembark in Egypt, and then all bets are off."

"We disembark in Egypt, and then we see what God has in store for us," Gregor corrected.

"Same thing," I said agreeably and held out my hand for him to shake.

9

I WAS ROWED BACK to the *Venus*, where the orgy was still raging. Immediately I went belowdecks to check on Jamila, who was—to my amazement—still sleeping, pressed up against the water cask, with a thin wool blanket between her and the chill wood. Liliana's skirt was being lifted by the elder Richard as his grandson watched, rapt; I found myself alone in the melee of laughter, sweat, and fornication.

Life's reclamation of my soul was not complete; there was nothing attractive about any of the gaiety or any of the women. I was among the living, but only as a shell; I had my own crusade, my duty to uphold, my damsel in distress to save, and *that was all*. I knew nothing about her and did not care to; it was not personal, it was only a feeble attempt to show whatever gods cared enough to judge me that I was capable of a good deed. Then I would return to my previous intention. I was guiltily glad now to delay that final satisfaction, but in the meantime I had no need for the normal distractions of a real human life. I did not need companionship, or laughter, or a woman.

But I needed music. Any music—if not my own galloping Celtic harp pieces, then the intricate formality of trouvère songs, or the simpler rhymes of the troubadours, or the accent-heavy German tunes, or even (as a last resort) that stupid May Day song "Kalenda Maya." Gregor had retrieved my instruments from Barzizza but was keeping them stowed on the *Innocent* as surety for my good behavior. My main instrument, from childhood, was the harp, but I knew the pipe, had learned the gittern on the continent, played a good fiddle, although I find bowed instruments fussy. I don't need an audience, but I desperately need the activity. So what I noticed on the whores' ship that night was not how many women there were with upraised skirts but how many psalteries and fiddles were not being played, or were being played badly by men who thought they could impress the women. I got my hands on something bowed that I had never seen before, a long, skinny teardrop with a flat face and only three strings, tuned *ut-sol-ut*. I fooled with it for a bit and discovered that, if I held it near my shoulder, and sounded it high up the neck with its short and tight-strung bow, I could play individual strings, which was excellent for dance tunes. The sound was scrawny and shrill—it sounded like an old woman screeching—but it carried well and was easy to play fast. It was a good distraction; it and I were the official entertainment of the boat before the moon had set. I had a dozen ersatz minstrels trying to keep up with me, and I was afraid the deck might collapse under the estampie dances. I doubt a fellow has ever been propositioned by so many pretty women so often in one night, with so little interest in accepting even one.

Shortly before dawn, I finally collapsed belowdecks, in the main passage between all the hammocks. But about an hour later, I was yanked from sleep by a new commotion above. As always, that first flicker of consciousness came with leaden pain, the realization that, dammit, I was still alive.

It now smelled really awful down here, with stale ale and sweat and semen added to the vinegar and overripe floral bouquet of womenly perfumes. As I watched, the bottom hem of an elegant black and purple tunic began to descend the ladder to the lower sleeping area, swirling around the ankles of elaborately tooled leather boots.

"Come to begin the conversions?" I called out wearily. "You are eager to your task, eh, Your Eminence?"

"Shut up!" and "Fuck off!" and other friendly comments were shot at me from a score of female voices among the many hundred sleepers.

Bishop Conrad made an unpleasant sound as the stale stench of the hold hit his nostrils. "Bring her above," he ordered. "I'd retch down there."

I pulled myself up from the floor and staggered along the narrow walkway to the water tun. Liliana looked weary, but her eyes were open. Amazingly, the princess was still sleeping peacefully. "She's not awake," I called up to Conrad.

"Shut your mouth, you whoreson!" grunted a melodic host of female voices.

"Then *wake* her," Conrad called. The women recognized his voice, or at least intuited his status. "She's a hostage here, not a princess." His boots ascended out of sight.

"I'm not convinced she's a princess anywhere, actually," Liliana whispered groggily. "I don't think a princess could sleep through what she's slept through."

"I thought you'd drugged her," I whispered back.

"Are you kidding? If I had drugs that worked so well, I'd be taking them myself."

A few moments later, I was on deck with my rescuee, both of us squinting into the dawn. Liliana had given her a belted overtunic, which did not fit her well: It was low-cut to reveal as much of Liliana as possible, thus meant to be worn over an equally low-cut shift, but Jamila's shift was modestly high at the neck. The mix of slinky overtunic with not so slinky shift bunched up under it was not flattering; also, she was shorter than Liliana by nearly a head and her proportions were different, so nothing about it sat right on her. With an ill-fitting dress, dusky skin tone, and no glittering face veil, Princess Jamila looked almost dowdy, but her comportment was still regal—and intimidating.

We stepped gingerly over the throngs of women who were waking on the slanted deck, stretching sore, stiff limbs. Most of them had barely slept and did not roll their mats up now, intending to nap during the day once the sailing was under way. The mariners, not wanting their decks cluttered up with sleeping bodies, were snap-ping at them to put the mats away. The women mostly ignored them. The mariners were even more unhappy about Conrad's arrival, for of course, all sailors know that it's bad luck to have priests onboard your ship—and unlike whores, priests are unlikely to recompense you for the danger of their presence.

Bishop Conrad was perched on an enormous coil of line near the bow, two servants sitting cross-legged at his feet. Gregor was with him. There was also a third gentleman, about Conrad's age and very aristocratic, standing on the far side of the rope coil, arms crossed, leaning against the bulwark.

"My daughter, I greet you," Conrad said in patois to the princess as we approached. He held out his hand for her to kiss his ring; she looked at it impassively.

This was the first time I'd seen her face in daylight. She was about Liliana's age—a few years my junior—but in no way resembled her. Liliana looked innately, permanently cheerful; Jamila must have been a stern beauty when she was twenty, and even now she had a striking handsomeness, but you could not call her chipper. Her face was broad, her eyes and eyebrows very dark; the hair on her head was hidden beneath a long scarf but was either wavy or severely tousled, because the veil did not lie smooth. Her complexion was dark. In a proprietary way (she was *my* princess), I found her attractive, al-though she lacked the conventions of feminine beauty.

She turned to Conrad, and in the patois that we all intuitively used—a mix of Italian, French, and other languages—she replied sternly, as if chastising him, "I assume you wish to convert me to the religion of St. Paul."

"It is the religion of Jesus Christ I intend to share with you, mi-lady," he corrected, as if to an amusingly ignorant child.

She looked confused. "You wish to convert me to the Jewish faith?"

I liked that. Maybe she had a sense of humor after all.

Conrad did not realize he was being baited. "Milady, I am saddened to see that, after five years among us, you are ignorant of our
beliefs. Let us begin at the beginning."

"In the beginning was the Word," she recited promptly. Conrad's
eyes widened.

"You know the Bible?"

"From Genesis onward. Alpha to Omega, as they say in Byzantium."

Conrad smiled. "Wonderful. Then you have already received the
Word of God."

"Where I come from, the Word of God is usually called the
Qur'an. But I very much enjoyed hearing the little stories in your
book. Especially the Old Testament. No offense, Your Eminence, but
after Jesus died, it is all dull and preachy."

The aristocratic stranger huffed indignantly; I laughed aloud;
Conrad glared at me. "Forgive me." I coughed. "Continue."

Conrad examined the princess's face. "So you have read the Word
of God but it did not fill you with his radiance."

"I don't know what you mean," she said after a thoughtful moment. "Does this radiance . . ." She tried to think of just the right
word. "Would it make me want to live my life a certain way, or would
it merely inspire me to pray to God a certain way?"

Conrad blinked. "A subtle question. You are of a higher intelligence than most women." He glanced at Gregor. "Not just a soul to
save but perhaps a mind to nurture."

"Yes, she might be another Hildegard of Bingen," said the unknown man sardonically, in French. He had a tenor voice that carried across the deck. A number of the women glanced over, then
glanced away again without further interest.

"I know Hildegard von Bingen, from her writing," Princess
Jamila said offhandedly to the nobleman—in perfect French. "She
had a decent grasp of medicine, particularly regarding the behavior
of blood in the human body, but she is not nearly as sophisticated

as the learned of my race. Her music is quite beautiful, given the confines of the modes in which she composed. I would not much care to be an abbess, however. This religion of St. Paul, it does not appeal to my aesthetic sensibility."

"*Why* do you call it the religion of St. Paul?" asked the tenor, ignoring the rest of her commentary (which had left Gregor and me agog).

"Because there was no Christianity before Paul," she replied mat-ter-of-factly. "Your Jesus was merely trying to reform Judaism, not un-like the Karaite sect more recently, or the Shi'a within Islam. His final supper was the Jewish Passover feast, was it not? It was not a separate faith until the fellow named Saul spent too much time out in the sun and suffered hallucinations. He was so disturbed he even got his own name wrong."

Her questioner was disquieted by this answer; the bishop looked mortified. "Where did you hear such a thing?" Conrad demanded.

"Barzizza's priest tried to educate me," she said. "He didn't say it that way, of course, but it did not take much insight to realize that your religion was founded by somebody with sunstroke. This is per-haps why he said crazy things like you must not copulate if you can possibly avoid it. Even Maimonides the Jew does not preach such nonsense." She glanced with amused contempt about the deck. "I find it strange that this boat exists only for copulation, although we are on it specifically to promote an epidemic of Christian doctrine. I find it even stranger that you are going to *kill* people to promote Christian doctrine—I don't recall where Christ asked anyone to do that."

"Christ would never suffer his holy city to be overtaken by blood-thirsty infidels," the bishop insisted.

"It was in the hands of bloodthirsty infidels when he was cruci-fied," she retorted. "They were called Romans. But I'm sure he would be glad to know it was eventually returned to his fellow Jews. Shall *you* give it back to his fellow Jews after you have slaughtered all the Moslem women and children within the gates?"

"We would never slaughter women and children," Gregor said, in a tone that was at once insulted and placating.

"No? When did they change the custom?" she asked. "When you first came to us, more than a century ago, you slaughtered everyone, in a city that had not even tried to prevent your entrance. Tens of thousands of Moslems and Jews you killed, and tore the corpses apart to search for swallowed gold, and danced over the rivers of blood running through the streets. Then you went into your church and sang praises to your own holiness. We are still waiting for an explanation."

"The explanation is that, for centuries before that, your people did the same to us in Christendom!" Conrad exploded.

"Ah yes, an eye for an eye, I've heard about that," she said. "That is a Jewish doctrine, of course, and it means something different in its original context, . . . but how interesting that you emulate the Hebrew nation even as you seek to exterminate it. But then, of course, Paul never quotes from the Hebrew translations of the Bible, only the Greek ones. Personally, from reading his Epistles, I think he was a heathen who wanted to use the Jewish state to spread his pagan beliefs."

"Pagan beliefs?" Conrad echoed, stunned.

"Pagan *belief*," she corrected herself. "A *Roman* belief, in fact. This notion of a divine being and his sacrificial death. This is, of course, Bacchus, who was worshiped by the Roman heathens, who *oppressed* the Jews. The belief is *not* a fulfillment of *any* Jewish law, as Paul said. Nobody before Paul contemplated Jesus in such a heathen manner—including Jesus himself, for he was a good rabbi. He did not claim to die for anyone's sins—that would strike all of his followers as meaningless or worse, heretical."

"He was not a mere rabbi," Conrad said, incensed. "He transformed the world with new words and thoughts—"

"What was new?" she asked. "Love thy neighbor as thyself? That was central to Pharisee thought. Sabbath was made for man and not man for the Sabbath? That's written in the Pharisee law books. So is belief in the resurrection of the dead. So is that parable about a camel going through the eye of a needle. Your Jesus was an excellent Jew, and based on his teachings, an excellent Pharisee—"

"Jesus Christ was not a Pharisee!" Conrad wheezed.

She serenely ignored the interjection—"but your Paul was just an excellent political collaborator with Roman tyrants. He *was* very *effective* at what he did, which brings us back to your butchery and all that: you *keep doing* it, even though you are no longer *ever effective*. Now of course it is obvious that mostly you do it for greed—"

"That's not true!" said Gregor, back in the game now that it was at a level he could understand again. "Most men who go on crusade return poorer than they went. And they know that going out. We do it because it strengthens our faith."

"Slaughtering people strengthens your *faith?*" she said, flabbergasted. "I *certainly* do not remember Jesus suggesting any such thing." She turned to Conrad. "Do *you* remember Jesus suggesting such a thing?"

"Going on *pilgrimage* strengthens our faith," Gregor clarified, using that big-brother tone I'd already heard too often. "We only kill people who would prevent us."

She gave him a look as if he were a child who had disappointed her. "First of all, your early Church fathers scoffed at this obsession for traveling to sacred places, for to a true believer, God is everywhere. Beyond *that*, however, when Salah ad-Din held Jerusalem—that is Saladin to you," she clarified, seeing all her listeners look confused— "he allowed you in to make pilgrimage, and you tried to kill us all anyhow. This is *not* about access to the holy places. You are being disingenuous. I will not be lied to. This interview is over." She turned and walked away from us, steering carefully through the stretching throng of women and lashed-down wooden chests; she descended back into the hold. We all watched her go. Gregor, the golden boy, looked like he'd been slapped; Conrad just looked confused.

"She will take much work—" the bishop said at last.

"You'll never get the chance if I can help it," I interrupted. I looked over at the stranger with the ringing voice, who'd made the comment about Hildegard von Bingen. "Who are you? Are you try-ing to lay claim to her as well?" To Gregor I muttered, "What about keeping her hidden until Boniface's return?" I wagged a warning fin-ger at the nobleman and said, "No touch, you!"

The man gave me a sour look. "I am Simon of Montfort," he in-formed me soberly in French, clearly assuming his name alone would make an impression. It did not. "I came to this ship to speak with you, not with your infidel female." He made a commanding gesture to Gregor and Conrad; the two of them, suddenly mild as lambs, moved away across the deck, out of earshot, followed by Conrad's scampering servants.

Simon had an aristocratic grandness that reminded me of Boni-face, although it sat more comfortably on Boniface. He gestured for me to come around the coil of line. I didn't. So he spoke over it. "I am berthed on the *Innocent*. Gregor's brother Otto had some rather astonishing stories to tell about you yesterday."

Thus it was from Simon of Montfort that I came to learn about my hired brigands and the details of our sensational, if fictional, at-tack on Otto. The story delighted me, and warmed my appreciation of the burly young German dolt.

" . . . Then this morning, before mass," Simon concluded, "I heard that you had returned to the fleet of your own volition. That seemed decidedly peculiar. I was further struck by the interest Gregor seems already to have developed in you—"

"It's not reciprocated," I assured the baron. "I have no nefarious designs on him."

"*Your* designs are not the point," Simon said. Not quite hiding how irked he was that I wasn't moving closer to him, he strolled around the coil of rope, then sat on it on the nearer side. He closed his eyes a moment and appeared to be basking in the morning sun, to justify his move. Then he gestured me closer, and even though I did not respond to the summons, he lowered his voice as if I had. "The danger, little heretic, is that people can be led astray even by those who do not *mean* to lead them. The Devil—or his agents— may be using you to get at Gregor, without your even knowing." Simon suddenly lowered his voice still further. "He's one of the most important knights in the army. Not just as a soldier, and not just as Boniface's son-in-law, but as a true believer who lives his beliefs. He has a power to move men. You should see the adoration he receives at tournaments—"

"I know, I have to sing about it all the time."

"It's a quality he himself is still unaware of. I'd hate to see anybody manipulate that quality in him."

I felt an unexpected surge of protectiveness toward Gregor. "You really mean you would hate to see anybody *else—other than you—* manipulate it."

"If it is to be manipulated, I would rather it be in God's interest than the Devil's."

"And you claim to have the wisdom to know God's interests?"

"Not I," he said, with a soupçon of sanctimony. "That honor belongs to the Holy Father in Rome. I am merely His Holiness's champion and soldier."

"And in regard to what, exactly, are you concerned about Gregor's being manipulated?" I asked. "I assume that is the point of this interview."

"*Zara*," he said and gave me a searching look.

I shrugged. I'd heard the word, but it meant nothing to me.

"Are you aware," he pressed on, "that the Holy Father and Boniface of Montferrat are not on friendly terms?" I had not been aware of this, and my face must have revealed surprise. "Yes. The pope and the leader of the pope's army despise each other." He nodded at Gregor. "And that good young man believes he can, and must, be loyal to them both. He has a fantasy that all his fathers are as one.

When he learns how wrong he is, when we reach Zara and he has to choose between God and . . . *whatever* it is the marquis stands for, I will not hesitate to steer him toward God. I hope you will agree with me."

"Am I a heretic if I don't?" I asked. "Or does heresy, per se, only consist of errors about really important things, like which teeth to use to chew the Eucharist?"

Simon frowned impatiently and demanded, "What's your intention toward him?"

I batted my lashes at him, gave him my best girlish smile, and rested the tips of two fingers against the collar of his tunic. "I don't like to kiss and tell," I chirped. "But I will say he's the jealous type, so I shouldn't be standing this close to you." I shrugged coquettishly and wrinkled my nose at him, grinning. Simon grabbed me by the elbow and yanked my face so close to his that I could feel his breath on my eyelashes. "You had fish for breakfast," I told him. "With mustard. Isn't that hard on the digestion?"

"What are you up to?" he demanded.

"Oh, about . . . three at a time, usually Venetians. But it was a slow night. The women are teaching me tongue exercises, and I expect the turnover will go a lot faster soon." I ran my tongue extravagantly over my top lip and winked at him again.

"Are you an agent of Boniface's?" he demanded, urgent. So that was what he'd been afraid of.

I rolled my eyes and made a face of contempt. "I don't do business with men named after saints." I raised the edge of my lip in disgust. "They're far too kinky for me."

Simon looked at me humorlessly. "I see you are merely a joker," he said, almost to himself. He nodded with grim satisfaction. "You cannot do much harm."

I wish with all my soul that Simon had been right.

10

OVER THE COMING DAYS, then weeks, an equilibrium was reached aboard the *Venus*. I was glad that Liliana and Princess Jamila, although they had nothing in common but womanhood, took to each other with understated ease—not as if they were passionate friends but as if they had been comfortable acquaintances all their lives. Sleeping curled up together no doubt contributed to this, but at least they *could* sleep in that position; I spent a week without a full night's slumber. The mistresses quickly realized their quarters were inferior to the common whores', and after a little catfight, the two castes of loose ladies switched places. I was glad of it, for I much preferred sleeping on the deck. I'd spent most of my life confined within a small, damp castle, so the hold of a ship held no terror to me, but I liked to see the stars. I'd only learned to read them under Wulfstan's tutelage, and it was a good game to recognize them in an unfamiliar clime.

The hardest thing to adjust to was the sound of people's voices. There were so many dialects and languages, of such different rhythms and tonalities, that I would listen to them more for their music than for their meaning, especially since I was so indifferent to what was going on around me. Mine is the most beautiful language spoken on earth. The dialect of Venice *sings* (like mine), and German has interesting *sounds* (like mine)—but only mine can boast of both. French, or at least a patois based on it, which unfortunately became the most common, has nothing to recommend it at *all*.

The princess hardly ever spoke to me—not out of coldness, sim-

ply because this was not the place, and she was not the person, for
chitchat. But she became Liliana's quiet, dignified shadow; she was
not above helping with the quotidian chores of the boat; she had
uncanny knowledge of herbs and medicines, which often came in
useful; her impressive linguistic abilities helped her mediate the arguments that inevitably break out when different cultures are thrown
together in a crucible. If any of the women or mariners knew what she
was, they kept quiet about it; if she felt any distaste at being crammed
together with prostitutes, it never showed. Each evening when the
ships dropped anchor, she would disappear beneath the curve of the
water cask; in a setting where most women were *trying* to catch male
attention, nobody noticed or disturbed her. Still, I spent every night
scampering up and down the ladder to cast the occasional protective
eye on her.

I was expected to play music on deck for as long as the common
women were entertaining visitors (I refused to play Kalenda Maya
more than thrice a night). For this service, it was established without
anything ever being said, I was given a little more room to sleep, and
sustenance, and invited to make myself familiar with the women.

I was indifferent to this final benefit. Sometimes I'd watch Liliana with dispassionate nostalgia, remembering my body responding
to her nearness in the tent on San Nicolo, but she just seemed part
of the hubbub now. And seeing how exhausted she was each dawn,
it was hard to pretend there could be anything remotely erotic about
it. Otto came to the ship every night for her; usually, one of the Richardim found transport over to the *Venus* for a round with her (the
younger one was so newly initiated into carnal indulgence that these
rounds lasted about as long as a sneezing fit). Then Otto, almost
without exception, requested a final tumble before leaving. Gregor
came to the ship too, but only a few times a week, and when Liliana
betrayed too much fatigue, he'd pay to go with somebody else. It was
endearing, how apologetic Gregor was about whoring. St. Paul would
have approved.

Boredom was by far everybody's worst enemy, as days stretched into weeks. The mariners wanted us all cooped up below while sailing; we rebelled and found ways to take the air—but still boredom flourished. Besides eating (which happened in shifts, near the stern, in meals consisting of salt meat for the sailors and watered legumes for the rest of us), and of course sleeping and fucking, most of the *Venus*'s denizens played childhood games, told one another stories, read one another's palms, invented betting games, tried to learn new musical instruments (so they could play Kalenda Maya), and spent no small amount of time on personal hygiene: crushing vermin, mending ripped tunics, sitting hopefully in the wicker baskets intended for defecation, and swallowing some of the most disgusting laxatives ever devised. Once the sailors realized how comfortable I was in the rigging, especially the ratlines, they let me perform clumsy acrobatics, which I enjoyed and which won me many flirty looks from all the prostitutes but only long-suffering, motherly amusement from Princess Jamila. It was, at least, a way to pass the time. Daily—although this was no respite from boredom—there would be mass, performed on deck facing east. For fear that those with seasickness might vomit up the body and blood of Christ (raising interesting theological issues), a special "dry mass" was observed, which consisted of swallowing nothing but priests' verbiage. More distracting, but even less pleasant to endure, was the cramping down below during rainstorms, or when we were becalmed. These periods were infrequent, but even a fog on the open sea is not an experience I care to dwell on—sailors grow even *more* superstitious then, and there was always the unspoken fear we'd lost our way. We all felt wet, and often sticky. Some of the prostitutes with poetic pretensions compared the cool clamminess to certain parts of a dead whore's anatomy.

Sometimes the bishop, when visiting the boat on whatever pretext, would interview me, and he came to the conclusion that I was an irritating but harmless eccentric. This was not nearly as amusing as His Eminence's continued attempts to interrogate the princess.

She and Conrad got into several debates that left him baffled and her
complacent. Once, Conrad pleaded with her to convert, grieved and
confused as he was that so few Saracens ever did so. The princess told
him that there was no mystery to the lack of such converts, and that
it was entirely the fault of certain Christians who called themselves
the Knights Templar.

These knights ruled an area of the Holy Land where dwelt the
mysterious and feared Assassin sect, and the Assassins had decided to
convert, en masse, to Christianity. The Assassins as Christians would
have been (literally) a coup for the spread of Christendom, for this
reason: each man prepared to give his life to assassinate (hence the
word, a newish one to Western ears) an enemy of whatever cause
they espoused. Had the Assassins indeed become Christians, Jamila
explained, Islam would quickly have been rendered impotent. Christianity by now would have been the dominant force throughout the
Holy Land. But had the Assassins become Christians—she further
explained—they would also no longer have been subjected to the
Knights Templar's tax on infidels. Therein lay the rub. The Templars
were not prepared to give up the income from taxing the Assassins;
they wanted the Assassins' money more than their eternal souls,
more even than their astonishing martial prowess. So when the
Assassins showed up to convert, the Knights Templar attacked them,
and continued attacking them until they agreed to remain infidels
(at which point, the knights *continued* to attack them, because they
were infidels).

On another occasion Jamila corrected Conrad's tale of the crucifixion, insisting all Moslems knew the *real* story: Jesus had only *seemed*
to be crucified, for God loved his only son too much to subject him
to torture, and if Christians didn't know that, then they were sorely
ignorant about their own religion. When Conrad insisted that no,
Jesus was very much crucified, she calmly cited the Acts of John, in
which Jesus proclaimed that only a phantom was crucified, and not
he himself. "And if he wasn't *actually* crucified, then I'm afraid I'm

not quite sure what the point of your faith is," she concluded sympathetically, and that was the end of the interview. To me, she walked on water.

ABOUT A MONTH OUT, I finally adjusted to the fact that I was still alive, and likely to remain so for a while. It happened without fanfare one morning. I awoke without an internal stab of pain for the first time in years. I was not *happy* to waken, but I accepted it. I still could not think beyond getting Princess Jamila back to Egypt, but this was no longer "the thing to do before dying," it was now just "the thing to do next." And that, to be honest, was less exhausting.

I began, that day, to pay occasional attention to things around me. This was a mistake, because by nightfall I had already been drawn into the confusion of the world.

11

You have failed to honor your side of the treaty. But let us make the best of it (said the Doge). There is a city near at hand: Zara is the name of it.

—ROBERT OF CLARI'S *Chronicle of the Fourth Crusade*

WHEN MY BEING DRAWN BACK into the world began, Gregor and I were standing amidships after dark; Jamila, who seldom left her little hiding place while the ship was anchored, had come up to join us for fresh air. The deck was always loud and boisterous, but at least we were not quite surrounded, and there was a crisp autumn breeze to clear the air. Although it was crowded, I kept nearly an arm's length between myself and Her Highness, so that, should the boat lurch suddenly, or I find myself jostled by passing revelers, I would not be pressed against her.

Gregor had been trying to explain something to me. I hadn't been listening when he began, so I wasn't quite sure what it was, and I didn't care. I was much more interested in watching a whore near the stern as she lightened the belt purses of three admirers in a row without any of them noticing.

"Before the army was massed," Gregor was saying, in his golden-boy, big-brother tone, "before Boniface was even involved yet, the leaders of this campaign made a deal with the Venetians, through the Doge of Venice, Dandolo."

"That's the tough old blind fellow with the big fancy ship?" I asked absently. The whore's fourth victim caught her in the act of opening his purse; she convinced him it was just a harmless prank.

"And the shrill voice. The army signed a contract with him—that we would have from the Venetians a certain number of ships and, with them, the services of their seamen for a year. We would pay, for this arrangement, eighty-five thousand marks of silver."

"What's a mark of silver?" I asked distractedly.

Gregor looked insulted. "As a knight, I don't concern myself with such matters."

"If you are familiar with the English coin called sterling, created about two decades back, a silver mark is worth more than one hundred fifty of those," said the princess in an aside to me, as if she were amused at Gregor's ignorance.

I whistled. "I bet that's more money than the King of England has at his disposal," I said, still distractedly. The woman I was watching handed her ill-gotten gains to a companion, who moved off through the throng toward an open hatchway. I knew the companion; she played a good pipe, and we performed together sometimes when she was between customers. She was the only whore on the boat I had fleetingly contemplated rubbing hips with over the past month.

"It's more money than Philip of France has too, which is why it's so unfortunate that neither of Their Majesties would join this endeavor," Gregor said. "They're too busy fighting each other. So the crusade has become a project for a group of nobles, and sadly they made a promise they couldn't deliver on."

I have always liked stories involving incompetent nobles. I decided to really listen and removed my attention from the piper's hips. "What was the promise?"

"That there would be nearly thirty-five thousand soldiers. Less than a third that many actually showed up in Venice—and that's including those of us from the Empire, who came belatedly when we heard that there was need. Each man pays his own way on a pilgrimage, but even when each man paid his share—even when the richer lords dug into their treasuries to try to make up the difference—the army was short by nearly half. We should have paid all of it by April last, but not one mark had exchanged hands. The fleet was supposed to set off this past summer, but they all just sat in the sand and heat, half-starved and skirting the plague, waiting for enough of us to join them, to have the money to pay the terms of the treaty." He gave me a look of sympathy. "Your Englishman was probably among those who pledged but never showed up."

I'd had the same thought. "And of course," I reasoned, "once other men heard about the problem in Venice, they were not much inclined to go to such a place and get ensnarled in the problem themselves."

"Exactly," Gregor said. "Many pilgrims went to Marseille or other ports and sailed by their own arrangements. Some—like your Englishman—didn't show up at all."

"Won't they be punished for betraying the contract?" I asked, wondering if "my Englishman" might meet his grisly just rewards even without my assistance.

Gregor shook his head. "As with everything about this campaign, it's not so straightforward. When the contract was signed with the Venetians, the army did not yet exist. The contract signers were *hoping* that thirty-thousand-odd men would do what they'd sworn thirty-thousand-odd men would do. They had no legal right to *make* that many men do any such thing. They *trusted* that their fellow pilgrims would cooperate with them, they *expected* all men of the cross would collude, and they were disappointed."

I was delighted by this detail. "Well, that was idiotic, wasn't it? And these are the same men leading you into battle? Can you trust their judgment?"

"It wasn't the leaders who signed the treaty, it was envoys they sent to Venice."

This was bordering on farce. "So a bunch of *messengers* are the ones whose bad judgment led to this? Who are these envoys? How do they get this sort of power?"

"One of them is Geoffrey of Villehardouin, the marshal of Champagne—"

It was getting more ludicrous with every sentence! "Shouldn't a marshal know a little something about raising a military host?" I hooted. "Isn't that—not to put too fine a point on it—what marshals *do?*"

Gregor made a placating expression, as if he knew I was right but it would be rude of him to admit so publicly. "He blames all the knights who did not appear as he had said they would," he said. "If they were here, then we wouldn't have this problem."

"If *he* hadn't *stupidly promised* that they would be here, *then* you wouldn't have this problem."

"And we wouldn't have this fleet."

"Yes, you'd have a smaller one that you could actually *afford*. Where does your darling Boniface fit into all of this?"

He gave me a long-suffering look. "That's what I was *explaining*."

"Excellent, carry on."

"After weeks and weeks and weeks, it became obvious that, no matter how deeply we dug into our purses, we did not have enough to pay the Venetians. But the whole Republic of Venice sank a year's labor into making this fleet—half the men of the Republic are on this campaign, and nearly all of her sea power has gone into it. Venice will be completely ruined if we don't pay them for it. So the doge, Dandolo, made an offer to Boniface: We'll sail you out after all, on credit, with two caveats: first, that you pay us as soon as you've won booty from fighting, and second, that along the way . . . we may use this fleet to, let us say, *make an impression* on our neighbors in the Adriatic."

I nodded. "I see."

"The leaders, including Boniface, agreed. I am disturbed by this. So are the clergy, especially Bishop Conrad, and many of the nobles, like Simon of Montfort."

"You have no cause to be," said the princess.

We both cringed slightly, certain she was about to make Gregor look stupid.

"The Venetians are just showing off their own might, aren't they?" she continued. "That is, yes, the ships are full of armed soldiers, but the truly impressive thing is the size and magnificence of the fleet itself, and Venice gets full credit for that. Your army is not actually going to attack people with whom you have no argument—you're Christ's warriors, not Venice's hired thugs. Yes, the knights' pennants and shields make a terrifying impression, but they're just lying on the sides of the ships. The actual labor involved in intimidating these port cities is all that of Venice, which built the ships and sails them. The knights and nobles could sleep through the entire trip, and the effect would be the same. You are not being asked to do anything but, literally, go along for the ride."

"That would be true," Gregor said, "were it not for one wretched detail."

"That being?"

Gregor glanced around the deck carefully. Everywhere in the swaying light of swaying lanterns, men and women were laughing, embracing, kissing, singing, dancing, fornicating, drinking. Nobody was paying attention to us, but Gregor was constitutionally uncomfortable with gossip. He took a step toward her and gestured me to step closer too, then said quietly, "There's a rumor going around since just before we set sail. Simon of Montfort is enraged about it. On the Dalmatian coast is a city called Zara—"

"Ah, *Zara*," she said. "Barzizza was always going on about Zara and its pirates."

"What about it?" I asked. I'd noticed the name cropping up with increasing frequency among men gossiping on the deck at nights, but that was when I'd been determined not to take an interest in anything important going on around me.

Before Gregor could answer, the princess explained over her shoulder, to me, "Zara was a rival of Venice's within the Byzantine Empire and submitted to Venice about a century ago. Then, some two decades back, she rebelled and asked for protection from the King of Hungary. Venice keeps trying to resubjugate her but always fails."

"Dandolo wants to try again," said Gregor. "With our help." Jamila's eyes widened. "Or so goes the rumor."

I made a disgusted sound under my breath and would have launched into a diatribe, but I was interrupted by Liliana's laughter behind me. She and Otto, arm in arm, had approached without my noticing. "That stupid Zara rumor again," said Otto. "Everyone's so disturbed about it, you'd think we were being asked to desecrate the Holy Sepulchre."

Jamila shook her head. "This rumor must be nonsense. The pope's army cannot attack a Catholic city unprovoked. The King of Hungary has taken the cross, so the city's under papal protection. Your entire army would be excommunicated if you attacked."

"I know that!" Gregor said, upset.

"How do you know so much about all these Christians?" I demanded of Jamila.

"I've been living among them for five years. What is your excuse for *not* knowing?" She turned back to Gregor. "You can't think there is truth to the rumor?"

"I didn't at first," he said. "But when I asked Boniface to deny it formally, he . . . hedged."

Finally I understood why Gregor had been giving me this lecture. "That's what I interrupted," I said. "The moment we met—I interrupted him mid-hedge."

Gregor nodded grimly. "And then he disappeared."

"Without taking you with him. What does your Bishop Conrad say about it?"

"Conrad always deflects the topic," said Gregor, after a flicker of hesitation. I doubted Gregor had fought very hard against the deflection.

"Such leaders you have," I said. "One's mute, one's absent—"

"We prefer them that way," Otto said cheerfully. "It keeps them out of our hair."

"I don't prefer them that way," Gregor said, addressing his brother sharply. "I want to know what's really going on, and what the proper course of action is. Excommunication is worse than death, Otto."

"If you're so concerned about it, approach your bishop," I urged Gregor. "And don't *let* him avoid the topic. He's here tonight hearing confession. Don't let him leave the ship until he's answered you."

Gregor looked uncomfortable. "If he's avoiding the topic, there's probably a good reason for it, and it would be disrespectful of me to—"

"Oh, for the love of God—literally, milord, *for your love of God*—confront him!" I insisted. (In retrospect, this was probably the moment I really got myself entwined into the confounding web of Gregor's moral compass. As with every Rubicon I've ever crossed, I took the decisive step mostly just to entertain myself in the moment.) "Find out if we're really being diverted to Zara and, if so, what you can do to prevent it. What could be a greater crusade than that? Than safeguarding the mission of the pope's army?"

Gregor mulled over this a moment, chewing on his lower lip. I was finally starting to understand the young man's character: he was the nonpareil of obedient sons, but he had no earthly idea how to *lead*. The golden glow that suffused his being when he was doing what he knew was expected of him congealed into a tepid, grey fog of indecision when he had to mint his own moral coins. This was ironic, given the influence he unwittingly held over other men. I had seen myself, on the *Venus*, how other knights regularly adjusted their tone of speech, their manner of dress, and the style of their hair to emulate Gregor; he was oblivious. He did only what he thought was expected of him, and he assumed other knights were doing likewise. He really had no experience of making up his own mind about anything. So when a look of determination *finally* came across his face now, I felt like a proud parent. "Very well," he said. "I'll talk to him at once." He turned and moved away from us toward the bow.

"Why do *you* care if the army is diverted from its divine purpose?" Liliana asked me.

I made a face. "This army *has* no divine purpose. I just want to get to Alexandria as quickly as possible to get Her Highness home safely."

"For which she thanks you," said Her Highness without expression. Her eyes flickered, almost anxiously, after Gregor.

"And I admit," I added, because I couldn't help myself, "I have a native resentment toward any group trying to conquer any other group. If it's not yours already, leave it alone, give it back, or give something mutually acceptable in return, and we'll all get along grandly, thanks."

"But what you have is yours only because you or your people took it from somebody else," Otto countered smugly.

I gave him a superior snort. "That's not true. My people were on our land from the beginning of the world."

"I doubt that," Otto said. "*Somebody* had to be there first."

"Yes, *we* were there first!" I snapped, loudly. Couples near us paused in their exertions and glanced over.

"As I said, I doubt that," Otto laughed.

"But naturally you'd be raised to *believe* it," Jamila said. I think she meant to pacify me, but the effect was condescending. Retorts ricocheted through my mind, but I did not indulge in them. I would wait until I could fashion an equally condescending rebuttal, and then *I'd* embarrass *her* in front of everybody else.

"Well, even if we weren't the first," I said for now, "I can't undo the past, and I'm not claiming anybody else should try to. My people lived through centuries of vengeance, and it profited us nothing. Vengeance as a way of life is highly overrated."

"You're a hypocrite," Otto announced, still amused. "You came to Venice expressly to throw your life away on vengeance."

"As a way of *life* it is absurd. As a way of *death* it's effective and seductive," I shot back. "If there'd been anything inside of me that wanted to stay alive, I'd have taken a different course."

The princess looked startled. "What are you talking about?" she demanded.

"He's a would-be suicide, didn't Your Highness know?" Otto laughed. "Gregor took charge of him to prevent him. The blockhead couldn't manage to accomplish it, but he was hell-bent on self-extermination, until he stole you from Barzizza." He was about to elaborate, but Liliana saw the dismay on Jamila's face and signaled him to shush.

Jamila stared at me. I tried to look away but couldn't. I tried to mouth some witticism, but I couldn't do that either.

Despite the boisterous noises around us, a loud silence suddenly filled the space directly among the four of us.

I looked down at the grimy deck and tensed, waiting for the princess to say something in her superior tone so that I would feel justified in lashing out at her to hide my shame. She said nothing. The awkwardness lasted for what seemed several weeks.

"Well, I'm heading back to the horse transport," Otto finally said, uncomfortably. He gave Liliana a kiss, bowed briefly to Her Highness, and signaled to a longboat alongside the ship.

The three of us remained in awkward silence.

"Come on," I said, brusque. "I could use a drink." I gestured to the hatchway.

They followed me without speaking. Liliana rubbed my forearm in a comforting gesture, but I pulled away with such force that my hand brushed across Jamila's shoulder. A shock went through me at the touch, and I leapt back sharply; a drunken couple staggered by and lurched into me; I lost my balance, and I fell directly against Jamila. "I'm sorry, milady," I stammered in a panicked voice, pulling away from her by grabbing a nearby bit of rigging. "An accident."

Liliana snorted with nervous laughter, and the princess gave me a funny look. "I realize that," she said gently. "I have never met a man so preoccupied with not touching me. Even Gregor is less decorous than you."

"Gregor's been molesting you?"

Now Liliana and the princess laughed almost in one voice—in that way women laugh together about a private joke. "That's not what she said," Liliana retorted. "Your mind is very eager to leap to her nether regions, isn't it?"

I was appalled that this was the subject of their merriment; of all the women on that ship, the princess was the last one I would have fondled. "She's in my care," I stammered. "She's been severely abused by a man who had no right to touch her. I can't bear to see her subjected to even the most casual abuse again."

Liliana gave Jamila a there-he-goes-again look, but Jamila held out a hand.

"We've been pressed together for many days now," she said to me, "and you have made sure, at your own extreme discomfort, not to touch me. You have not laid a finger on me since you trundled me onto the ship, and while I appreciate your intention, I think it is causing the most appalling stiffness."

"And not the kind of stiffness I can help you with," Liliana clarified. I glared at her as I felt even my ears turn red: obviously, the women had been talking about me for days, maybe weeks.

"So." The princess reached down and took one of my hands in both of hers. I drew in a sharp breath and tried to pull my hand away. She laced her fingers around mine and held it. "For the love of all gods, just let yourself sleep with your back pressing against mine tonight, without contorting yourself. You are falling apart for want of sleep."

I looked at my hand in both of hers. Her fingers were soft and felt distractingly pleasant. Something about this moment was off. I realized what it was, and voiced the thought at once: "A princess would never speak this way to a man of my station."

"I know you only as the man who saved me from hell and continues to protect me, and I shall treat you accordingly," she said, not flustered by my implied accusation.

"Don't romanticize it," I said in a surly tone. "As you pointed out bluntly at the time, I hadn't thought out what I was doing, and I was not properly equipped."

"Forgive me. I was frightened, and so I was harsh," she said. "You improvised very well with what you had, which takes a special kind of wit. Your plan was successful, that's all that matters."

"It was only successful because you improved upon it."

"True—ergo, refrain from solo subversive activities in the future. Always get help. But take heart: I would not have gone with you if I did not intuitively trust that you were capable. My trust has proven well-founded, and with you as my shepherd, I lack nothing. To me you are swifter than eagles and stronger than lions."

"That's quite Old Testament of you," Liliana observed softly.

"As I have always said, that is the part of your Christian Bible I find most attractive," the princess replied.

Liliana moved away from us—she had sensed, before I did, that Jamila wanted a word alone with me. And it was literally that, one word:

"Why?"

I shook my head. "I have a history of not thinking out my actions. It is not a history I can live with any longer. Please don't ask me to say more, milady."

She went to join Liliana when she understood I would not speak. Jamila, more than anyone I'd met since Wulfstan, would have made a worthy confidante . . . but as I was realizing, slowly, how big and mad the world was, my own suicide struck me as the peevish impulse of a pathetic weakling. This woman had seen her children and husband slaughtered in front of her, then spent five years locked in an empty room, expectant brood mare to a nincompoop. She had the fortitude to stick around to see what happened next; how could I not do likewise?

Feast of St. Elizabeth, 5 November

> If what I do is against my will, it means I support the law and
> hold it to be admirable.
>
> —Romans 7:16

I, Gregor, son of Gerhard of Mainz, have been deeply remiss in chronicling events relevant to my development as a good pilgrim. While I do not seek to excuse my laxity, I will explain it by two causes, those being: first, that the movement of the ships, even when anchored, makes writing very difficult, as my penmanship herein no doubt evidences; second, that there have been many conflicting rumors and arguments about, and I feel it is my duty as a soldier, as a pilgrim, and as a son by marriage to our leader Marquis Boniface, to let these things rush over me as water over a drake's back. And so I have tried to stand aloof. But I find it increasingly difficult to remain thus, owing in part to the influence of the Briton, who is now less melancholic than once he was but no less bilious. I shudder to contemplate how the hot, dry desert will affect his humors. This evening I have finally taken it upon myself to speak in conference with His Eminence Bishop Conrad, and I find my own inner balance much restored. I will put the memory to parchment now, that I may refer to it in future days should I ever find again that my resolve threatens to grow weak or confused. The matter had to do with Zara.

I had crossed to the bow of the ship to speak with His Eminence. His Eminence was offering penance to the common women, and so I waited until he had completed his task, marveling to myself that I have now passed more hours in the company of some of these women than I have with my own wife, such are the strange and sad ways of holy war. When the common women moved away from us, I asked His Eminence if His Holiness Pope Innocent III approves of this defilement of our cause (meaning the diversion to Zara at the insistence of Dandolo of Venice).

His Eminence was sorrowful to hear my question. He answered, "Of course His Holiness would never approve of any defilement of our holy cause, but he knew this diversion might happen anyhow, for the Venetians are so relentless for their money. The Holy Father's legate, Peter Capuano, admitted to me back in Venice that His Holiness did not approve of such a diversion but said also that His Holiness wanted above all to keep the army intact. Capuano interpreted this to mean all the clergy should tacitly condone the diversion, just to make sure the fleet sailed intact out of the Venetian lagoon."

At this moment we were interrupted by none other than the Briton, who made a monstrous, swaying silhouette in the lantern light. He announced that the words of Legate Peter Capuano were "staggeringly cynical" and other unflattering comments. It distressed me to find that I was pleased by his arrival, for he spoke sour words to a good man, and I should not take pleasure in such a thing. Yet he had voiced a thought I shared. The Briton then asked His Eminence what might happen when we reached Zara. Emboldened by the Briton speaking so frankly to His Eminence, I admitted I would like to know the answer to this too. "Given that the pope is against it," I asked, "can you condone an actual attack, Your Eminence? Can the army?"

His Eminence held up his hands in resignation. "In truth, this has been tormenting me for days, Gregor," he lamented, and my heart was heavy to see even this servant of Christ besieged by doubt. "I begged the legate for advice. He hemmed, and hawed, and finally said that I should do what conscience dictates when the time comes."

The Briton interrupted here with words spoken in sarcasm, but we paid him no attention and he ceased to heckle. Conrad continued:

"I have meditated upon every possible outcome. In truth, there is none that sits comfortably with me. But you, Gregor, you are different. You need not worry yourself as I do, my son. Your way is clear. You are a soldier. The leaders—all of the leaders, the pope, the marquis, and the doge—all want the army held together. Your only responsibility is to act accordingly."

"By the head of St. John, I do not believe Boniface would condone an attack if he knew the pope were against it," I said, for sure I know the marquis to be the best and most obedient son in the Holy Father's dominion.

"Boniface is not here trying to prevent the siege," His Eminence reminded me. "If he felt it crucial to prevent the siege, he would be here to prevent it."

To which I argued: "He cannot be here, he had urgent business back home."

"What urgent business would that be?" the Briton demanded of me.

To which I had to admit that I did not know the details of such business but surely it was urgent all the same.

"Maybe," the Briton said, "it is simply the need to absent himself from an attack he finds abhorrent."

"Abhorrent but necessary," His Eminence amended. "He knows the diversion, at least, is necessary. And Gregor, my son, though I prize my role as your spiritual adviser, you and I both know that you must follow your commander's wishes first."

"I do not know what his wishes are! He is not here!" I complained, for I was sorely cross and perplexed by now. Then at once I mastered my anger and apologized for raising my voice to my esteemed superior.

"Boniface's wish will always be to keep the army together," His Eminence Conrad repeated.

"By fighting, or by refusing to fight?" I begged him answer.

"We cannot know that until we are actually there," Bishop Conrad answered, and surely nothing truer than this could be said in the circumstances, for His Eminence is a wise man. "This is merely a trial we must survive, my son, to then go on to our real destination in the Holy Land. If you have to make a choice, remember that His Holiness desires you to keep the army intact too."

It soothes my heart to be reminded that my duty is in fact straightforward.

ONE NIGHT LATER, when the moon was half-spent, a growing sense of crisis loomed over the fleet. Men were speaking in hushed tones of being manipulated by the Venetians, of being diverted from their holy undertaking, and finally, even of deserting.

Men were speaking in hushed tones of Zara.

One of the men whose tone was not so hushed was me. If you'd told me a month earlier that I'd ever take the pope's side on any issue, I'd have laughed derisively, but he and I were in accordance now. Hating on principle anyone beating up on anyone else, I was enraged by confirmation of the intended attack and had provoked debate with a few of the *Venus* mariners—who, all being Venetians, hated Zara. For my efforts I now had matching black eyes and a few bruised ribs. Simon of Montfort, my Boniface-wary interrogator from our first day sailing, was also an outspoken opponent of the Zara plan. Having heard from Gregor that I'd gotten into fisticuffs on the subject, he came over to the *Venus* to commend me. This was almost more annoying than suffering bruised ribs.

Otto and Gregor spent two days trying to calm me down. I doubt they felt solicitous toward my bodily well-being; it was, merely, a matter of not wanting me to make a nuisance of myself, since Gregor was accountable for me. Princess Jamila, more attentive to me than I deserved, reminded me with quiet firmness against composing another subversive plan because I was statistically likely to fail at it. I reminded *her* she had merely advised me against planning such a thing *alone* and asked her to help me with some plan to help the Zarans. She replied with a most Jamila-like gesture, a small, subtle flourish of her fingers that referred both to herself and to everything around her. "I am not in a position to do that," she said with finality.

The most popular theory being bandied about was that the fleet would approach the coast looking so intimidating that the Zarans would instantly surrender and there wouldn't even be a battle. I became verbally violent when I realized Gregor was among the many hoping for this outcome. When the fleet was just a day from the Zaran harbor, he and Otto both made one last attempt to reason with me, during an evening visit to the *Venus*.

"If the Zarans surrender without a fight," Gregor was explaining, "the army will be able to move into the city, giving us shelter through the winter without the sin of using military force against fellow Christians."

"The threat of force *is* the use of force," I retorted. "The Zarans will die of cold and starvation instead of by your swords or arrows, but it will be your doing just the same. If that's such a *sinless* scenario, why did Simon of Montfort try to shun it by bribing the captain of the *Innocent* to leave the fleet and sail straight on to Egypt?"

"That was just a rumor," Gregor said. "Simon won't break up the army."

"And more important," Otto said, "once the Zarans surrender, they'll be surrendering their goods too, so we can take it all, and finally pay the Venetians back. So calm yourself, Brit; their surrendering would be the best of all possible outcomes."

"Not for the Zarans!" I said.

Otto looked bemused. "Why should we care about the Zarans?"

I stamped my feet and announced, "I will not stand by and watch a people intimidated into giving up their sovereignty. Where in the Bible does Christ tell his disciples they should do such a thing?"

The two brothers stared at me. "I think there is something personal in this response," Otto taunted, cautiously. "There is also something ignorant. The Zarans are not above piracy in their efforts to stay free."

"Maybe if they weren't being persecuted by *bullies*, they would behave more *politely*," I snapped back.

"Oh, that's no excuse, everybody bullies someone," Otto said with a shrug. "That's the way of the world."

"Whom did Christ bully?" I demanded. I thought that was clever and wished Jamila was within hearing distance.

But Otto deflated me. "He bullied all of his followers," he said promptly, with a stubborn blankness that I knew I would never penetrate.

Giving up on him entirely, I turned to Gregor with a final entreaty: "*At least* admit it's a perversion of your mission to go through with an attack. You're letting Venice manipulate the army of Christ for her own mercantile ends."

Gregor nodded unhappily. "I understand that, but if we *don't* go through with the attack, the Venetians won't take us where we need to go, and we'll be forsworn in our holy vows."

"Damned if we do, damned if we don't," Otto said pragmatically, unconcerned. "So it may as well be 'do,' because the choices are damnation in cold wet tents all winter or damnation in nice warm buildings with lots of loot. It's not a difficult decision."

I made myself ignore him and focused instead on Gregor. "If you do this," I warned, "you are betraying your own undertaking. It's more than a perversion. It's a *sin*."

Otto made an impatient gesture and turned away, but Gregor— rather oddly—looked *pleased*, in his elder-brother way, that I had said this, and clapped me on the shoulder. "While it grieves me that you may be right," he said, "I'm at least glad to hear you finally thinking like a son of the Church."

That was about the last response I was expecting. "Excuse me?" I said.

"It's a sin to attack," he said, "because they're Catholic."

"It's a sin to attack," I corrected, "because they are weak and you are strong."

Gregor was dumbfounded.

"Am I the only man on this ship who's read the gospels?" I hollered and walked off in a huff, dodging prostitutes and soldiers in various degrees of undress. Clearly, if the righteous thing were to be done here, I would have to do it on my own.

Act II

ZARA

Now the men of Zara were well aware that the men of
Venice hated them.

—ROBERT OF CLARI'S *Chronicle of the Fourth Crusade*

12

IN TIMES OF DANGER, an enormous iron chain was fastened across the mouth of Zara's harbor, its weight dispersed along a train of barges. By the time the *Venus* approached, this chain had been broken by the Venetian iron-prowed galleys ramming it.

The Zarans, although making a show of force from their towers, had retreated within the city's walls. Having heard rumors of the approaching fleet for weeks now, they'd draped bolts of white cloth, with enormous golden crosses sewn to them, over the walls and rooftops in plain view. The meaning was clear: *We are children of the Holy Father in whose name you make your pilgrimage.* Under their horrified eyes, our enormous flotilla anchored. The city was built on a peninsula, a spit of land running parallel to the mainland, surrounded almost entirely by water. It was not as low or flat as Venice, but it was much smaller, and despite the walls surrounding it, it hardly looked impregnable.

The first ships to arrive had clogged the harbor after expelling the Zarans' own vessels into the royal blue Adriatic. The Venetian ships were moored so tightly together that sailors were walking between them without planks. The army began the exhausting task of disembarking and set up camp on the gently sloping mainland to the east. The war galleys circled the city, crossbowmen on the foredecks with weapons trained at the walls and towers—towers that flew flags emblazoned with images of peacocks, heralding Zara's defiant new affiliation with King Emeric of Hungary.

The ships had arrived in clusters on two successive November mornings, but each cluster had more than a hundred vessels, and these could not be unloaded all at once. Need and privilege dictated order: the horses were brought to land first for exercise; they were followed by the highest barons; then the knights; after this the foot soldiers and workers who could start quickest into collecting stones for the catapults and other menial tasks that would make it very clear to the Zarans how imminent an attack was. As each ship was emptied, it would pull out of the harbor to make room for a new one to unload.

Eventually, when everyone and everything important was on land, the passengers of the whore ships would be given leave to disembark. But for a long, dull stretch of hours, Jamila, Liliana, and I lolled with a crowd of common women and concubines on the deck of the *Venus*, our attention on the camp that was blossoming up the slope from the rocky beach. The water, even with the turbulence of horses and men slopping about in it, remained impossibly clear. The sea here was an extraordinary color, like a fabric woven of green and purple trying to make blue. British seas were grey in comparison. The air was crisp and moist, like a fall day in Britain, but with fierce sunshine everywhere, except far inland, where a bank of clouds hovered above a white mountain range.

I was restless, from a combination of boredom and disgust. I'd already thought of a dozen ways to undermine this attack on Zara, but most of them were faulty (as Jamila kindly pointed out) and all required me to get onshore, to the camp. I doubted I could trust Gregor with any plan; I *knew* I could not trust Otto, which meant I doubted I could even trust Liliana. Only one thing I knew: Simon of Montfort would be an asset, if I could work him right.

I strolled across the deck to look at the broad swath of water between Zara and the labyrinth of islands that protected it from the open sea. This bay was about as large as the Venetian lagoon, but besides the difference in color, this water looked cleaner, clearer, colder, and the air was breezier. Also, these islands, in sharp contrast to the Venetian bogs and sandbars, jutted out of the sea like the tips of steep submarine mountains.

Hearing a drumbeat across the water, I turned to see a small galley flying a red flag with two keys crossed, gold and silver. I called out to the women, who came to join me on the steer-board side of the boat. "Look at that. Somebody's in a hurry."

"I've seen that flag," Jamila said. "The crossed keys are the pope's, I think."

"Things are about to get interesting," said Liliana, looking amused.

The vessel skimmed over the bay straight toward us, since the *Venus* was the farthest outlying ship in the flotilla. Somebody onboard the smaller vessel waved. A *Venus* mariner waved back and called out, "Cargo?"

"Papal legate!" hollered back a mariner from the smaller boat. "Very urgent!" The rhythm of the drums changed, the oars reversed one stroke, then cut into the water without moving, and the smaller boat stopped with a heave alongside us. "Where's the best place to moor without getting trounced?"

Exultant, I looked over my shoulder at the women. "Papal legate! What extraordinary timing! He's here to forbid the attack."

"I'll bet you your harp they won't listen to him," Liliana replied.

I grinned. "I'll bet you your pudendum I can *make* them listen to him."

"*You?*" Liliana said, as Jamila groaned and began to admonish: "*No*—"

"You didn't see me do this," I said.

And jumped overboard into the peacock blue water.

Wulfstan had insisted that I learn to swim; it was his one request at which I failed utterly. It always confounded him that a man so deftly acrobatic could be such an incompetent lug in liquid, but it made sense to me: my agility lies in the tension between empty air

and solid matter, as a fiddle creates music. It's all about playing with
opposites. But water is an indeterminate, self-contained between-
ness, and swimming in it provides no opposite to play against. Therefore, I cannot master it. Or at least, that's my excuse.

So, I was counting on being rescued. More specifically, I was
counting on being rescued by the papal legate's boat, not the *Venus*.
I was successful in this scheme—a line was thrown down from the
larger vessel, but almost as quickly, a longboat was released from the
smaller one and a crewman leapt into it. The man, looking bored,
paddled the short distance over calm water toward me, but I had already begun to panic.

I yelled, limbs thrashing, until the inhaled sea cut off my voice.
The water was repulsively salty, so salty it was almost sweet. I thought
we were in shallows, so I stupidly reached down with a bare foot
to touch the seafloor; each time I did it I submerged myself, and my
efforts to surface felt as if I was trying to slither up an oil-coated rope.
My bruised ribs felt like they would snap. Because the water was
so salty, it was very buoyant, but not enough to hold me up. The
water in my eyes confused me, and I couldn't see straight, couldn't
figure out where the line had been thrown. *This was a mistake,* I
thought angrily. Drowning itself did not disturb me—Jamila would
almost certainly get to Egypt safely without me now, which was my
only excuse for remaining . . . but drowning without first accom-
plishing this new task was infuriating. The fury energized me enough
to try reaching out of the water once again, and this time, a hand
that felt like unplaned wood grabbed the back of my neck and lifted
me into the air.

By the time I was out of the water, shivering and gagging, the
pounding of the drum had resumed and the legate's galley pulled
away again, skimming over the water directly for the shore.

"Why would you jump out of a boat full of whores?" asked the
rower who had rescued me, laughing hoarsely. His accent was melodious Venetian but everything else about this fellow was rough and

hoarse. "You an idiot?" He pointed. Liliana and Jamila had grabbed the rail, and a crowd of otherwise bored prostitutes, hearing the splash, had gathered shouting to one side of the deck, enough to make the boat heel. "There's the master—shall he throw down another rope for you?"

"All heading to shore soon," I sputtered, retching brine. "I'll go with you. Fun for a fortnight or so, but after a while it's enough to make a body wish for monastic orders!"

He shook his head. "That's a problem I'd like to have," he grunted.

The tongue of land that was Zara was higher than Venice by the height of a man; the mainland was low at the shore, then rose into a wooded slope a bowshot in. Miles back, enormous, grey-white cliffs erupted into the horizon, as dramatic as the Alps, and towered abruptly heavenward. The skeletal layout of the camp was similar to the set up on San Nicolo, back at Venice, although it lay on the slope: predictably, the army leaders' tents were on the highland. The doge's pavilion was close to the water. It did not take long to figure out where Gregor's tent might be.

The sand was stony here. On dry land for the first time in six weeks, I could hardly stand up. My legs felt as if the bones had turned to liquid, as if all of me had turned to jelly; the land lurched beneath me far worse than the sea ever had. I staggered, still soggy, through narrow lanes of half-erected pavilions, half-dug latrines and wells, and soldiers halfheartedly preparing for battle. I almost fell into one of the wells, I was so wobbly. My plan was unformed yet, but I knew I had to get—and remain—as close to the papal legate as possible, and that meant obtaining credentials. Since I had none myself, I decided to borrow Gregor's: Marquis Boniface of Montferrat's wax seal.

When I reached the German section of the camp, Gregor's red-and-white tent had already been staked but appeared deserted. I approached it from behind, pressed my ear to the cloth wall, heard nothing. I sidled around the edge, still wobbling on my jelly legs, stuck my head into it . . . empty. The Richardim must have been exercising the horses. A few of the German infantry looked at me strangely, but only because I was wet; half the army recognized me as a man of no importance from the *Venus*. I assumed the attitude of one who belonged here; they had more important things to attend to; nobody interfered.

The tent contained three wooden chests closed with iron, unlocked and waiting to be unpacked. I tried to remember what articles had gone into which chests. Six weeks earlier, on my first full day as Gregor's captive, I'd been too far sunk in self-destructive stupor to pay attention to what was going on around me. But now I recognized the chest that held the portable altar, and the larger one that held the sleeping rolls . . . the small, ornate one was logical for packing important things Gregor wanted close at hand, such as Boniface's seal. This chest was on top of the altar chest, and already open. I scampered over to it to rifle through it.

I didn't have to rifle. The wooden disk sporting the wax imprint of Boniface's seal was lying just on the top. I grabbed the seal, almost shoved it into my damp tunic, thought better of it. I turned to leave.

The younger Richard was standing in the doorway, gaping at me. Damn.

"What happened to your *eyes?*" Richard demanded; he hadn't seen me since I'd had the scuffle with the sailors.

"What would it take for you to agree that you did not see me here just now?"

The boy was flattered when he realized he was being bribed. "For how long will I have to not see you?"

"I don't know yet," I said. "I think I'll be back later, but even then you're not to say you saw me here. Tell me your price."

"You've got no means to buy me off!" The boy laughed. "And I'm honor-bound to my master Gregor anyhow."

"Lad, I'm telling you the truth: this is in Gregor's interest, what I'm doing."

"What are you doing?"

"I can't tell you that," I said, without finishing the thought, which was, because I'm not sure yet. "But trust me. I am looking after Gregor's soul. In fact" —I lowered my voice— "I'm acting in the interest of the Holy Father." The boy's eyes rounded. So he was a good son of the Church, even if his favorite thing about this excursion so far was Liliana's fanny. Useful information. "Yes, lad. So please, don't botch it for us. I promise you when the time comes that you will be proud of having assisted. You don't see me here. If anything is missing, you know nothing about it. If they want to know whose wet footprints these are, say you trod in mud and they are yours. If you get into serious trouble as a result, then you may squeal—I don't want you coming to a bad end, nor would His Holiness. Otherwise, keep your tongue quiet in your mouth. Understand?"

Being part of a benign conspiracy in league with the pope was even more thrilling than merely being bribed. Richard nodded, wide-eyed, awed. "Would you like dry clothes for whatever you're about?" he asked, now eager to assist. "My dress livery should fit you, they cut it large for me." Moments later I was in a dry white linen tunic, with Gregor's family emblem emblazoned on my chest.

The leader of the army, Gregor's hero and father-in-law, the marquis Boniface of Montferrat, had still not rejoined the campaign since mysteriously slipping away before the first day of sailing. His second in command was the virtuous young Count Baldwin of Flanders. Baldwin's happy marriage was the stuff of song: his wife was waiting for him in the Holy Land, and he was the only nobleman who'd never summoned common women to his cabin. He was also the most notoriously pious of all the counts; Baldwin really was the *ideal* crusading leader. But in Boniface's absence, and especially here and now, the Doge of Venice had become the de facto head of the campaign. I'd gathered this from gossip on the *Venus*. So, I guessed, if a conference were to be held following the papal legate's arrival, it would be in Dandolo's pavilion. It took little subterfuge for a small, dark-haired man dressed like a squire to huddle just outside the postern opening, at everybody's backs.

There was a meeting, but a very small one. There were at most a score of lords, a few with servants and retainers. There were also several clerics, including Conrad, Bishop of Halberstadt, who looked miserable; to avoid him, I stayed in the shadows and watched some bewildered salamanders try to figure out what a pavilion was. A young man I figured must be Baldwin of Flanders was present. Enrico Dandolo, Doge of Venice—ancient, overdressed, blind, and yet radiating a ruthless charisma—sat beside the speaker. There was something about Dandolo I'd intuitively liked from the moment I'd caught a glimpse of him before sailing; I was his secret enemy now, but if we'd met in other circumstances, I think we'd have taken to each other. For one thing, I'd heard he appreciated good music; it was his consolation for loss of sight. In Venice, music wafted from his palace almost continually; while sailing, more ambitious men than I had vied for the honor of playing on his galley, where (it was rumored) he liked a gentle tune to be sounded day and night.

The speaker, when I entered, was an imposing figure with the crossed keys on the front of his long red tunic: this must be Peter Capuano, the pope's representative. He looked exhausted, but more than that, for someone of his eaglelike bearing, he looked strangely . . . sheepish.

"In Venice, you agreed that we would do this," Dandolo said, unseeing eyes glaring. "You spoke as the Holy Father's agent, and you condoned this act of reclamation. You have no right to unsay it now, or tell us that His Holiness has."

My reaction to hearing this was relief: if the pope forbade his own army to attack, then obviously his army couldn't attack. The fleet would then have no choice but to press on toward Egypt before winter, and my princess problem would be resolved quickly.

Capuano mumbled something indistinct and held up a scroll. "His Holiness's word is indisputable. And he is absolutely clear in this missive. I will read it again, milord." He unrolled the scroll from the bottom and held it up, his hands shaking with anger. He read the Latin: "To the counts, barons, and other crusaders, without greetings. I, Pope Innocent III, father of the Christian Church, strictly prohibit all who hear or read this missive from the evil of invading lands of fellow Christians unless they imperil your pilgrimage. Any man who raises arms against the Catholics of Zara for any reason but self-defense shall lie under sentence of excommunication, and all papal indulgences withdrawn, including remission of sin. If you die while committing or assisting violence against Catholics, your souls shall burn in everlasting damnation." The men eyed one another; he lowered the scroll, knowing he'd made an impression. "You must not do it, milords."

"You shall not listen to him!" Dandolo snapped. His voice, tenor with age and tension, reminded me of the yapping of a small, ferocious lapdog. "The pope oversees spiritual matters, not the problems of this world. The problems of this world include your army's debt to us, and the only way—the *only* way—to solve that problem is through the submission of Zara. You may attend the well-being of your souls after you have attended the well-being of your earthly affairs, and chief among those is your obligation to the state of Venice. We were scrupulous in honoring our side of the treaty, and you failed to honor yours. You had paid us *nothing* by the time you should have paid us *all*, and *still* we made this fleet for you, for we trusted you to honor your promise. You *must* take responsibility for that. His Holiness is an idealistic young man who knows nothing of the world."

Eyes turned briefly to Count Baldwin of Flanders, who looked troubled. "I must side with the great doge," he said grimly. "With no great joy in my heart, of course, for there can be no joy in drawing blades on fellow Christians. But because of the false pilgrims who did not answer the call, we are in a delicate position, and if we do not keep the army united, we will never achieve our true goal of liberating the Holy Land."

"We make a mockery of liberating the Holy Land if we do so with stained souls," Bishop Conrad said from the other side of the tent. "All who would not suffer excommunication must abstain from this act." *About time you took a stance, Conrad!* I thought. I hoped he was either liked enough or feared enough that he'd be listened to. Maybe I could count on him to help me with a scheme if a scheme was still needed.

"Thank you for recalling that concern," said a man I recognized from his *Venus* visits as Geoffrey, the marshal of Champagne. Now that I knew he was the envoy whose bad judgment had gotten the army into this scenario to start with, I was hopeful to see him make a fool of himself. He spoke with grating complacency. "Legate Peter, please once more reread the opening phrase, from strictly prohibit."

Peter Capuano held up the scroll and scanned the opening line. ". . . strictly prohibit all who hear or read this missive from the evil of invading—"

"Thank you." Geoffrey dismissed him. "Including Venetians, we are an army of some twenty thousand, of whom fewer than two dozen have heard or read this missive. Technically, all those who do not hear or read it are in no spiritual danger whatsoever if they honor the terms the esteemed doge has asked of us and attack the city."

"That is unconscionably duplicitous," Conrad said angrily.

"And who are you to speak of duplicity, Bishop?" Dandolo shot back. "You urged the pilgrims to agree to this so that we would carry you out of Venice—and now, once we're under way, once it is too late for us to refuse you, *now* you tell them not to act as they agreed to? You knew about this back in Venice . . . Why didn't you speak out then?"

The bishop, chastened, did not answer. I dismissed him as a possible coconspirator; I had no time for wafflers.

"I beg you, milords," Baldwin of Flanders said soothingly. "I charge all of us here to take the pope's admonition into our hearts, reflect upon it in our prayers tonight, and let us see where we stand as a group a day from now. We all took the cross in the Holy Father's name; Their Eminences are right that we cannot simply disregard his wishes. At the same time, we are of course in debt to Venice, and grateful that she is willing to carry us, although we have many times over failed to honor our side of the treaty. Give us until tomorrow to meditate on this, and we will speak again. In the meantime, let us not breathe a word of the papal condemnation to anyone. It would cause deep distress among the men. Your Eminence"—he turned to the legate—"may I entreat you to suppress the writ, until tomorrow, when we will try to agree on how to proceed?"

Capuano scowled. "I agree to suppress the writ until it's clear how to proclaim it."

Since realizing that preventing this attack was up to me, I'd more than made up for my lack in interest: I had sounded out everyone I could on the *Venus*, and I was now familiar with all gossip regarding the politics of the upper echelons. So when the Bishop of Soissons offered, "You may lodge with me, brother," I knew that Capuano's acceptance was reluctant; Soissons was—often literally—in Dandolo's camp.

"But come to *my* tent to dine, brother," said the Bishop of Troyes, who was chums with Geoffrey, marshal of Champagne. Beholden to the pope though they were, both these bishops would see to it that the writ was never publicized. Capuano knew that.

The meeting was dispersed, lords muttering to one another as they all wobbled out, having as much trouble regaining their land legs as I was. The doge signaled that he wished to proceed to his private tent, and so the Venetians too went out—none of them wobbling as badly as the lords but all a little uncertain on their feet. Capuano was left alone with his aides, staring in frustration at the papal writ he still held in his hand.

I approached him, from the shadowy end of the tent, and bowed deeply to get his attention. I was glad it was dim enough that my blackened eyes might not be noticed. "Your Eminence," I said, with my best Lombard accent, and began to present the seal of the campaign's highest commander. Then I clutched my hand over it, hesitating: if Marquis Boniface and the pope disliked each other, my masquerading as the marquis's man would not win me the trust of the pope's man. Capuano gave me a studying look as I straightened from the bow. "Are you with Gregor of Mainz?" he asked in a hopeful voice.

For a moment I was nearly frightened, until I realized he was looking at Gregor's livery, the St. John's wort on my chest. Now I was *really* impressed with Gregor: the papal legate knew his emblem on sight!

"Yes, milord. He is grateful, and considers it close to miraculous that you arrived at Zara the same day we did. My master Gregor instructed me to present myself to you as your servant. He would want to assist in the safekeeping of the papal writ, so no factions may get at it to use it nefariously."

I knew this was a dangerous gambit, for if the man knew what Gregor's symbol was, he must surely know who Gregor's master was.

Apparently, he did not. Or if he did, his regard for Gregor's piety outweighed it.

Because a moment later I was holding the pope's letter. And I knew exactly what to do with it.

13

HAVING SLIPPED INTO the section of the camp sporting the red crosses of the French, I found it no challenge at all to position myself right in front of Simon of Montfort in the clouding afternoon. I was, unfortunately, being held very uncomfortably between two soldiers, my feet a good hand's span off the rocky ground, because I had gotten this close by caterwauling parodies of Christian hymns. But I had Simon's full attention.

"It is the British heretic," Simon said with pleasant dryness. "I commend your livery, but I see you still have not taken the cross."

"No, I do not take things that are not mine, except the occasional princess. Oh, and this," I amended blithely and presented the papal writ. "Milord Gregor of Mainz wanted me to show you this."

"How did you get this?" Simon breathed, wide-eyed, recognizing the seal.

"Milord Gregor gave it to me, I'm just following his orders. I'm not sure what it is, I only know that the doge wanted to keep it suppressed. Milord Gregor felt that you could do more with it than he could, since you're a baron and he's just a knight."

Simon of Montfort blinked at the parchment as he read over the pope's enraged injunction against conquering Zara. "This is momentous. If Gregor of Mainz procured this so that I may publicize it, then I assume he will side with me publicly against the attack?" I nodded, knowing I could guarantee no such thing. I understood why that detail mattered to Simon: if Gregor of Mainz did something, at least half the soldiers and most of the knights would assume that it was the right thing to do, regardless of where their own lords stood on the matter. "And the rest of the knights of the Empire?" Simon pressed.

He was actually taking the bait. His eyes glowed as if he were slowly becoming possessed. My mind raced through all the ways to handle this, and I decided that, for this question at least, honesty was probably the safest choice. "He has no official power over any of the Germans, but all of them regard him most highly. If he refrains from fighting, it is *likely* they will follow suit."

Whatever was possessing Simon's eyes spread to the rest of his face. "This changes everything." He glanced over his shoulder, at his considerable entourage of family and friends. He handed the letter to an abbot and returned his attention to me with barely contained excitement. "Very well, my little heretic. Let me meditate on this overnight, and tomorrow I shall summon Gregor. In the meantime, do not speak of this, and I will keep the Holy Father's letter."

"Of course, milord," I said, nodding, and grunted a little as the two guards dropped me to the ground.

THE GODS OF TIMING had favored me today. I returned to the tent and finished changing back into my stiffening wet clothes just as Liliana and the princess were finally wobbling in from the *Venus*; Gregor and Otto were still out with the squires and the horses getting exercise. Liliana saw that my tunic was covered with crystallized salt from the bay and brushed me off vigorously—the most physical contact I'd had with another human being for a year. It felt good. "You missed a bit," I said hopefully, lifting my tunic.

She grinned. "Whatever you're up to, it seems to've put you back among the living," she said, approvingly.

"What *are* you up to?" asked Jamila sternly, *not* approvingly. "I thought we had established that you're trying something on your own—"

"Not on my own," I said, a smile broadening my face. "Milady, I have taken your advice to heart, and I am working with the best of the best."

When the men returned to the tent in late afternoon, it appeared as if I had been with the women all day; neither they nor the younger Richard said anything to contradict the impression. I decided not to work on Gregor until I heard something from Simon of Montfort; I had a feeling I would have only one chance to sway Gregor toward a plan of action, so I wanted to be absolutely specific about what the plan was before he even suspected that there was one.

Jamila had assisted Liliana in preparing an evening meal just outside the tent; the camp kitchens were not set up yet. It felt *so good* to be off the ships, on solid ground—even if the solid ground still insisted on swaying like the sea. It was a luxury to have a meal in the tent, despite it being all hard tack and dried pork, the latter of which Her Highness ate nothing. There were seven of us in a tent intended for five: Gregor, Otto, the two servant-squires, the two women, and myself. We were a strange and motley assortment, with little in common to us all except our relief at being off the boats, so most of the dinner conversation was confined to that, ranging from delight at using real privies to gratitude for the smell of fresh-dug earth and autumn leaves.

I was so used to keeping a protective eye on Jamila when she was up and about that on reflex I tailed her after dinner, as she helped Liliana to wash up. "Dietary restrictions, milady?" Liliana asked in a pointed voice, as I was helping them scrape the wooden dishes into a communal scrap heap. I heard the words but hardly registered them, my focus up the slope toward Simon of Montfort's camp.

"It is against Moslem custom to eat pork," Jamila answered.

"Not just Moslem custom, I think," Liliana whispered.

There was a pause. I thought I saw a light from Simon's camp moving in our direction, but I was wrong. It was getting cold—the clouds that had hovered over the inland mountains had pulled down over us, and I wondered if they might bring rain.

"Am I in danger?" Jamila whispered behind me, with apparent disinterest.

"You're in a camp full of armed crusaders," Liliana said. "So I would have to answer yes."

Was that a lantern shining on Simon's flag up the slope? . . . No. Well, of course he wouldn't *advertise* his coming, he'd come covertly. Wait . . . who was that? Nobody, just a servant. The two women had continued to speak, in tense, terse whispers; the first thing I heard clearly was Liliana's voice again, saying something about "be attacking Zara soon—"

"Oh, no, darling," I hummed, turning to face them. I dropped my voice to a whisper too. "We will *not* be attacking Zara. I've seen to it. In fact, stretch your legs while you can, both of you, because we'll be back onboard within a day, sailing straight for your homeland, Your Highness."

The expressions on their faces were satisfying; I took the dishes and headed off toward the newly dug well, pleased with myself. Only much later did it occur to me to think about their whispered conversation.

THE NEXT MORNING was grey and drizzling. The camp was settled into, and men began the grimmer task of sharpening weapons and piling boulders for the catapults. They all knew what was coming, and all from foot soldiers to barons were preparing, although most of them either grumbled about it or expressed utter perplexity. It gave me smug satisfaction to know that they were all toiling for nothing, that soon they would call off this insanity—and that they would be glad of it. I hovered at the opening of the tent, trying not to glance toward Simon's camp, trying not to look like I was anticipating anything at all.

Jamila had been watching me like a hawk and asked, sotto voce, what exactly I was up to. She was suspicious of my levity.

"Your Highness," I whispered back, "once I was responsible, somewhat indirectly, for my people falling under the yoke of our conquering neighbors. Today, I shall prevent the same thing from happening to another people. I am about to redeem myself, a little bit."

"Does that mean you are no longer required to kill yourself?" she asked.

"Quite possibly," I allowed, embarrassed she'd brought it up. "But don't worry, milady; even if I remain of the terminal inclination, I shall first return you home."

She gave me a sharp look. "If returning me home is all that's keeping you from removing yourself from the face of the earth, then I shall feel morally obliged to delay your attaining the goal."

Shortly after breakfast, the drizzle having softened to a heavy mist, a somber procession approached the camp from Zara's land gate: men dressed entirely in long white tunics and over them cloaks closed with huge brooches at the chest, sporting the longest beards I'd ever seen. The doge's tents were closer to the harbor mouth, and so the delegation had to cross through all of the Venetian tents and much of the army camp to reach their destination, attracting fascinated stares and a growing train of gawkers as they went. Among the gawkers were Gregor and Otto; to keep an eye on Gregor, I went too, still waiting for word from Simon of Montfort.

The doge received the Zarans privately in his pavilion, the cloth sides of which were staked down against the November chill. The two Germans and I were among hundreds, maybe thousands, who milled about outside in the damp, hoping anxiously for confirmation that the parley would lead to a surrender. Many of them, including Gregor, were actually turning east and praying aloud for this. Despite my temptation to dismiss Otto as a bloodthirsty lout, he too seemed relieved that the issue might be resolved without armed conflict. I said nothing, but I was almost hopping from impatience on the sparse, wet grass. Where was Simon? How could I prepare Gregor if I didn't even know what to prepare him *for*? I was nervous about being in collusion with somebody I hardly knew and didn't like. If Simon didn't do *something* soon, it would be too late.

After a short time, there was a small fanfare, and Enrico Dandolo, surrounded by his guide and guards, was led out from his receiving pavilion, leaving the Zarans alone inside. His entourage waddled like ducks across a small open space to his much larger private tent. A moment later a flock of couriers erupted from this structure, sprinting along the harborside and up the hill, toward the lodgings of the army's leaders. Gentle viol music began to emanate from the doge's tent, as if its chief resident hadn't a care in the world; in the smaller pavilion, meanwhile, the Zarans hunched together in miserable silence.

The thousands of men watching shifted slightly, but nobody dispersed. It was obvious what was happening: the Zarans had offered to surrender to Dandolo; Dandolo was playing the grand showman. He was stretching out the sweet moment of diplomatic victory by making the Zaran contingent wait unattended in his pavilion while he conferred in his private tent with the army leaders, whose approval he did not actually need and whose opinion he did not actually care about. He was summoning them purely to prolong the Zarans' humiliation. He was in for a rude surprise, I thought—and that gave those of us saving the Zarans a little more time to undermine him . . . But where was Simon? Time was running out. In moments, it would all be over, and Simon's possession of the papal commandment would be a meaningless technicality, because Zara would have already turned herself over to the doge.

The mist reasserted itself into drizzle. Soon, from all corners of the camp, the leaders began to appear in a rush and crowded into Dandolo's private tent, responding to the couriers' summons. *Where was Simon?* I glanced at Gregor, wondering if I should just break down and tell him what I'd done, but I doubted he would help me to salvage the situation. He was a soldier, he obeyed authority; I had none with me, having given up the papal writ.

Chuckles of victorious relief began to rise up from Dandolo's tent. Dandolo's voice, ringing out with smug jubilance, was already proposing how to divide the riches of Zara that would be theirs as soon as they accepted the surrender. I caught a glimpse of the Zaran delegates within the smaller pavilion; listening to Dandolo's voice, a couple of them had broken into humiliated sobs.

Finally, from the far end of the army village, Simon of Montfort strode briskly toward the doge's camp, a large and growing group of high-ranking soldiers following. He was beaming. I tried to act nonchalant. I'd never found myself in this position—having personally started something I now had no control of. Please, I thought, *please* let Simon of Montfort not foul this up.

"He's not going to Dandolo's tent," Gregor said, sounding uneasy about this realization. I was a little uneasy about it myself.

"Why is he waving at you, Gregor?" Otto asked, watching the swift approach.

"I have no idea," Gregor responded, in a mutter.

I'd have no chance to prepare him—or even myself. Dammit, I should have kept a closer eye on Simon. I hoped he knew what he was doing and Gregor would get carried along in his current. "Go with him," I whispered, just as Simon approached. "He's expecting it."

And then Simon was upon us.

14

For though the will to do good is there, the deed is not.
—Romans 7:15

The Day After the Feast of St. Martin, 12 November A.D. 1202

I must write now without the artifice of style, for what has happened requires chronicling. By the head of St. John, I swear that what I write here is the truth. But there is so much to say and I am still so clumsy with the quill, it could take me days were I to attempt anything like proper form. I shall have to present this to the marquis Boniface when he rejoins the campaign, else my name shall suffer undue humiliation and abuse.

I begin on the shore across from Zara. The Zarans had come to surrender to Dandolo, the honorable Doge of Venice. This surrender would have excused the pilgrim army from having to raise arms against fellow Catholics, so I was glad of it on that account, but truly none of us were happy to be here. I am a good pilgrim and, like the other good pilgrims, want only to get to the Holy Land to secure it from the infidels.

Like other good pilgrims, I was waiting to hear Milord Dandolo accept the surrender, but he left the Zarans alone and summoned the lords of the army to him in his other tent. However, Milord Simon of Montfort went not to Dandolo's but rather to where the Zarans were, and where I and others were waiting near the threshold.

I was astonished when Simon of Montfort threw his arms around me in a warm embrace; I was so confounded by this gesture I allowed myself to be shepherded inside the receiving pavilion with no sense whatsoever of what was to happen next.

Milord Simon hailed the waiting Zarans. The Zarans looked up with the eyes of the vanquished. One man was in tears. Simon said: "My lords! My fellow Christians! I bring you words to make your hearts happy: Do not surrender to Enrico Dandolo!"

The Zarans were as shocked by this greeting as I was myself. They looked about at one another and Simon in confusion. "Do you mock us, milord?" one of them asked.

Milord Simon gestured to an abbot in his entourage, who held up a piece of parchment I'd never seen before. Then he spoke a lie that I now understand he believed to be the truth. No phrase exists strong enough to express my complete stupefaction when he said: "The abbot Guy is holding a letter from the Holy Father himself, which just arrived here yesterday and has come to us through the noble efforts of this worthy knight Gregor of Mainz, son of the high leader of this campaign. It forbids the faithful in our army to attack you, upon pain of excommunication."

I do not know what was more astonishing to me, the news of the letter's existence or my publicized affiliation with it, for truly I had never seen nor heard of the thing before that instant. I was about to cry out in protest, but I realized that would accomplish nothing useful in the crisis of the moment, so I refrained from speech until I could better glean what would happen. My ward the Briton was grinning at me from the door like an amoral child who thinks it has accomplished a clever trick. He is to blame for this, and I shall tell Milord Boniface so when he returns to the army, else I shall be forever blamed for the fellow's mischief. However, I must state that I believe the Briton did this in a misguided attempt either to please me or to goad me into action he truly believed proper. It is an expression of how twisted his soul is that he would have to stoop to villainy to achieve what he considers good.

"The Franks have no argument with you, milords!" Simon continued. "We did not take the cross to harm any fellow Catholics, and we will not do it!" The Zarans stared at him in astonishment. "Believe me when I tell you this. No soldier in this army desires to shed Christian blood. Only the Venetians have a grudge against you. Yes, the Venetians might attack you, but I swear to you, in the name of Innocent III, they will do it without the participation of a single soldier. You can surely withstand the attack of a few godless sailors! Don't you know if you surrender now, you lose everything but your lives?"

"If we don't surrender, we may lose even those," a Zaran said.

"We will not attack you," Milord Simon of Montfort repeated, slowly and clearly. He took the Papal letter from Abbot Guy and read it aloud, pausing after each sentence. One of the Zarans had no Latin, and another translated to him quietly in a language that was harsh to my ears and seemed to consist entirely of consonants.

The Zarans turned to one another in amazement and murmured in their own language. "It is easy to promise things in private," one said, after Simon had returned the letter to the abbot. "But will you promise this openly to our people? To the whole city?"

"It has already been done, milords," Milord Simon insisted. "My man Robert of Boves has already gone to your city's gate to reassure your fellow citizens that the pilgrims will not harm you." Milord Simon smiled with great love at the Zarans. "Will you be gone from here? Return to your city and prepare to meet the Venetians, if they

are so unwise as to pursue this. You can withstand their attack with
far less long-term loss than if you surrender to them. I shall read this
letter to the assembly of barons who are collecting with the doge now,
and I promise you, its existence will prevent any harm to you from the
army." Simon smiled beatifically at me, for he believed I had initiated
all of this, although I swear upon my duty as a soldier, nothing could be
further from the truth. I felt exactly as I did when a tree fell on my head
once, in the moment before I lost consciousness. I must have looked
troubled, but Milord Simon did not notice.

The Zarans seemed finally to see that Milord Simon was serious.
They fell on their knees in gratitude, uttered great thanks, and then,
hurriedly, collected themselves and left the pavilion. Outside, rain
began to fall but could not dull anyone's spirits.

Milord Simon looked around at his supporters and smiled magnani-
mously as they all cheered him. He has a ringing voice, quite beautiful,
and I have sometimes thought that he is much gladdened to hear it fill
a room. He said: "It warms my heart to know that the true Christian
spirit shall prevail after all. It gives me hope for our campaign's future.
Gregor of Mainz especially—I thank you for spiriting the letter away
from those who would suppress it. Let us salute this blessed turn of
events." He made a gesture toward a corner of the pavilion, where a
cask of Milord Dandolo's wine sat.

I did not drink. I stood in the center of the tent as the cheering went
on around me, trying to determine how sorry or glad I should be for
the events that had just happened. Knights came up and bowed or even
took my hand to kiss, and did me honor by expressing admiration for
my deeds on the tournament circuit. They said they were honored to be
involved in this great deed with me now. A few had been my captives,
taken on the field in sport. Thinking of captives, I glanced to the fly for
my ward the Briton.

He looked happier than I have seen him in the six weeks of our ac-
quaintance. I didn't know his face could express such pleasure. He had
done a heinous wrong, but truly he believed himself angelic for it. And

at that moment, I confess, even I believed he was some impish angel come to bolster my reputation. I swear on my own honor, I would never have instigated any such undertaking with Milord Simon, but I felt I was participating in righteous action now that it had begun. To defend the pope's wishes against those who would undermine them strikes me even now as the act of a true pilgrim. Despite all that followed, I believe Milord Boniface will be pleased with me for attempting to honor His Holiness's orders.

However, the situation did not go well for us.

Almost immediately, Milord the doge of Venice, Enrico Dandolo, was escorted back into the tent between his guards, followed by a relieved and happy crowd of two hundred noble barons. Milord Dandolo's face was bright with triumph, for he believed the city was about to be delivered to him without a single arrow being loosed.

His triumph lasted a flicker longer than anyone else's, for it took the changing sounds around him to make him realize something was wrong.

"What has happened?" he demanded into the sudden silence. "Where are our Zaran supplicants?"

Milord Simon of Montfort waited until the entire ensemble had entered the pavilion, making it very crowded. Then he spoke thus, which was ungentle: "They are not your supplicants, and they are not here, Dandolo. They've been informed of the true situation, and they have returned to their city to defend it against the godless Venetians who would attack it. The pilgrims will not attack, and the Zarans know that now."

Dandolo's face went pink with anger. "What madness is this? Of course the pilgrims will attack; it has been agreed to. What evil are you working, Simon?"

Simon's face became as pink as Dandolo's. "What evil am I working? What evil are you working, when you would suppress the Holy Father's will to serve your own greed! Guy!" He turned toward the abbot holding the letter, and pointed to the trestle table. "Up there! Read the papal writ to all these lords!"

The abbot climbed onto the table and held up the Holy Father's let-ter. He said: "In the name of the pope, I forbid you to attack this city, the inhabitants are Catholic and you are pilgrims!" He unrolled the scroll, looking for the heart of His Holiness's message. Before he found it, Dandolo shrieked with rage, and his bodyguard, misconstruing his master's anger, leapt onto the table with a dagger. He snatched the letter from Guy and tossed it down, then grabbed Guy's collar and raised his dagger as if to stab the abbot.

Immediately I pushed through the tightly packed room, elbowing hysterical men out of the way until I was beside the table. I grabbed the Venetian around the knees and jerked at him until he toppled over my back, smacking others in the crowded space as he fell. As he hit the ground, I spun to face him and straddled him; it was easy to take the dagger from his distracted grip and hold it to his own throat. Simon of Montfort had jumped onto the table behind Abbot Guy to protect him from another attack, but there was none. All were so startled by what I had done, they froze and stared.

"You shall not shed the blood of a holy man," I shouted.

"Who is that?" demanded Milord the doge. "I do not know that voice."

"But you have heard of him. We have all heard of Gregor of Mainz," Milord Simon de Montfort said. "He is the marquis Boniface's son-in-law and acolyte, the envy and hero of most every soldier in the army. If you inspire him to raise steel against you, ten thousand men will hear about it and assume that you are wicked." Men nodded, as if to grimly acknowledge this. I had a strange reaction to this praise, for I was proud to hear it but it gave me a heavy burden of responsibility now.

I released the Venetian into Simon's hands and straightened, shov-ing the dagger into my belt. All men's eyes were upon me. My eyes, in turn, were upon the Briton at the fly. He nodded once, for he under-stood how sore I was with him for putting me in this position, but then he smiled too. I almost told them that it was his doing and that I was no policy-maker at all. But I was ashamed to have been tricked by such a lowly villain, and anyhow, that course of action would not mend the situation now.

I decided to offer no policy but simply my own humble credo: "I did not come with this campaign to destroy Christians, milords."

"You don't need to destroy them!" Dandolo shouted. "They are surrendering. Your moral dilemma has been averted."

I could have argued with him that the greater moral dilemma was disregarding the pope's orders. But he had about him the attitude that soldiers do in battle, namely, that what matters is not principles but pragmatism. So I spoke of pragmatism too: "The Zarans will not surrender now, milords, because they trust us to obey the pope's edict not to attack. So the moral dilemma is still very much here—"

"But it's not a dilemma when the solution is obvious!" Milord Simon called out. "Whoever among you is willing to disregard His Holiness's orders, help the Venetians with their vendetta against a Catholic people who never harmed you. But you will not succeed, the Zaran walls will stand, and this campaign will have only SUFFERED by your misguided efforts. The army must hold together in the wishes of the pope—and obey his orders." (And indeed I must agree with this.)

Milord Dandolo uttered curses and then said, "Lords, this is not an opportunity to prove your spiritual fulsomeness! It is a crisis with immediate, practical repercussions that preempt even your most heartfelt vows. I had this city at my mercy, and your people have deprived me of it! Are you not men who honor your sworn word? Well, you swore to assist me to conquer Zara, and now I summon you to do so!"

There was a hesitation. I understood this situation, but I prayed the lords would honor His Holiness. I prayed that, at the crucial moment, they would not agree to attack the city.

But they did agree.

The tent erupted with expressions of angry concession. The anger was aimed at both Milord Dandolo and Milord Simon, but especially at Milord Simon, for he is one of their own and has embarrassed them.

Milord Simon was shocked when he realized his fellow barons had gone against him. "I will not fight, nor will my men!" he shouted.

"Nor mine!" one of his vassals shouted out, perhaps redundantly.

Milord Simon called to Milord Peter of Amiens, one of his staunchest allies. Milord Peter shook his head against Milord Simon, for he would not break up the army. "Gregor of Mainz?" Milord Simon cried out, half a plea and half a challenge.

By the head of St. John, it was wrong of Milord Simon to call me out thus, as I command no company myself. I looked at the Briton standing near the door of the tent. He was sore unhappy now, and I feared he might do something even more drastic than his accomplished interference and make my situation even more uncomfortable. "Milord," I shouted over the din and prostrated myself at Milord Dandolo's feet. The crowd of men contained itself, and I rose again to standing. "Is it true these barons will fight at your order? And will order their men to do so?" I looked around the tent, and two hundred voices assured me that they would. It was clear that they did not want to; it was equally clear that they would not now be talked out of it. What mattered most to me, as an obedient soldier, was that the army as a whole would attack if ordered. I would not break up the army, but I felt desperate to avoid outright battle, for it was the fault of my own ward the Briton that we had lost the opportunity for victory without a struggle.

"We may still avoid bloodshed," I said. "Send an ambassador to the Zarans. Warn them that they were misled. Warn them that, if they do not surrender, the army will indeed attack, and they'll be destroyed. If they understand the danger they are in, perhaps they'll surrender after all. They will not keep their liberty, but at least they'll keep their lives."

This was greeted by a cry of agreement and relief. But Milord Dandolo silenced the crowd with a single wave of his hand and scoffed thus: "Who will they trust? I will not send Robert of Boves or Simon, or even you—nobody who participated in this debacle can be trusted. But if I or my representatives go, they will think I am trying to trick them."

I said: "Bishop Conrad of Halberstadt, milord. He is a man of the cloth."

Dandolo agreed to this, and His Eminence Conrad went out at once. Tempers were still high, and the doge dismissed the congregation, promising that heralds would spread news around the camp as soon as the Zarans had responded.

I ran out of the tent, for the Briton had disappeared and I feared the worst. And indeed, as I exited, I saw him perhaps ten paces away, looking as if he were about to vomit. As he knelt there, a group of young soldiers walked by, and he reached out toward them. With the dexterity of a villain, he managed somehow to steal a dagger from one's belt. I ran at him, but my brother Otto had been watching too and reached him first. He grabbed the Briton's wrist so hard the Briton dropped the dagger.

"Oh, no," said Otto. "You are going to live through this with the rest of us."

15

THEY ALL THOUGHT it was Simon's doing, but I'd begun it; if a single Zaran died who would not have died in a simple surrender, blood would be on my hands now. This was almost worse than the sins I had committed back home, where at least we were all members of the same tribe; here I was a meddling outsider even among the meddling outsiders. I shuddered to think of how Jamila would respond to the news.

I'd spent my rage against Otto on the haul back to the tent. Now I was as animated as a damp rag. He trundled me before him and shoved me to my knees on the unrolled bed mats. The rain made whispering sounds on the tent roof. "Tie him to the pole. Keep a sharp eye on him and sharp objects away from him," a grim Gregor said to the elder Richard. Richard had been whittling a little chess piece, his usual hobby when he had a free moment. He stuck the knife hilt-deep into the earth, far from me, and offered Otto and Gregor cloths to dry their faces. Gregor looked around the tent. Then he blinked and looked again. "Where's the boy?" he asked.

"And the *princess?*" asked Otto, turning the question to Liliana, who was chopping the supper ration of dried pork into six unequal parts.

Neither of them answered. There was a pause.

"One of you say," Gregor ordered. "Where are they?"

"She's gone, milord." Liliana pushed the wooden tray with the pork rations away. Out of a woven bag she pulled a fungus-looking object and began to chop it.

"What?" I said hoarsely, looking up.

"She's gone," Liliana repeated. "Took Richard with her, but he'll be back."

"Gone where?"

"Town." She pushed the chopped fungus to the side. She pointed with the knife—out of the tent, across the harbor, toward the walls of Zara. "That town."

"When?" I demanded, horrified. I pulled myself up to rest on my elbows. "*Why?*"

"When the Zaran surrendering party was on its merry way back inside, no longer a surrendering party. She and Richard slipped inside with them."

"You let him go?" Gregor demanded angrily. He turned on the old man. "You let your own grandson go into enemy territory?"

Liliana answered quickly, "As Simon of Montfort's men were making very clear throughout the camp, the Zarans *are not our enemies*. At least they weren't for about a thumb's span of the day. Jamila wanted the boy to go with her so that he could bring back a reward to thank you for her escape from Barzizza."

"Bring back a reward from *where?*" I demanded. "Where has she gone?"

With a huff of exasperation, Liliana shoved the point of the small knife into the wooden tray. She looked up at us, especially at me, impatiently. "She knows people here. The family of an Egyptian trader. She decided it was safer to deliver herself up to him and return to Egypt with one of her own people than with Christians who are heading east to *kill* her people. Or rather, to kill the people she is willing to let us *think* are her people."

"What does that mean?" I demanded.

"Come now," Liliana said with exaggerated patience. "You know as well as I do that Jamila's not a princess."

"I *suspected* she wasn't, I didn't *know* it," I huffed.

"You say that as if her identity is obvious, Liliana," Gregor interjected, calmer than I was. "I don't know what she is, other than Barzizza's chattel. What do you know?"

Liliana gave us all an incredulous look, and then started laughing. "Do you really not know? I assumed I was the last to grasp it, because what am I but an ignorant whore? I thought we had a tacit understanding not to comment on it." She looked at our puzzled expressions and nodded, the usual mix of amusement and sympathy returning to her face. "All right, then," she said. "I suppose the ignorant whore is not doing so badly. Think about this. She is well-educated, she speaks many languages and knows about the laws and ways and even *money* of many cultures. She holds her own in discussions of philosophy and theology. She won't bow her head in submission to any earthly power—"

"That doesn't prove she's not a princess," Gregor interrupted impatiently.

"She's not a *princess*, milord," Liliana shook her head. "Her family never had estates. She has a lifetime's worth of being an outsider who knows how to blend in, even disappear when necessary, without self-pity and without shedding a bit of dignity."

"Just like you!" Otto said, kneeing me in the back. I smacked at his leg; he cuffed me hard in the back of the head. I didn't have the energy to keep up the fight.

Liliana rolled her eyes. "You're still not seeing it. Perhaps I recognize it because her kind of people lived near me in town. Don't you see that she's a Jew?"

There was a moment of shocked silence, and then I started laughing painfully.

"What was she doing in an Egyptian palace?" Otto demanded.

Liliana shrugged. "My guess is her husband worked for the lord. I think the Jews are more accepted there than they are in Christendom."

"So she's gone to the house of a fellow Jew here in Zara?" Gregor said, trying to make sense of this.

"I don't know if he's a Jew, but he's Egyptian. He's someone she knew, and for whatever reason, he has a family here. She took young Richard with her to send us back a token of thanks." She looked directly at me. "And she especially said you're not to kill yourself." She returned to chopping the mysterious fungus.

As we sat there in stupefied silence, there was a sound from the flap, and young Richard entered, wet with rain but cheerful, carrying a leather bag the size of his head. He placed this at my feet with a combination of self-important pomp and boyish glee.

"For you, from the princess," he announced, grinning.

"We know she's not a princess," Gregor said.

"Why don't you let him open the bag, milord?" he said, smug beyond his rank.

I sat there stupidly, but Otto was happy to comply—and let out a cry of amazement. He reached into the bag and pulled out two bulging handfuls of silver coins. He looked up at Gregor, eyes glowing.

"And there is more of this inside the walls." He nodded toward young Richard. "And with the lad's help, we know *exactly* where it is."

"Don't even *think* that," I said in a surly voice.

"What's wrong, milords?" asked the boy, taken aback.

"While you were on your errand, things took a few mad turns," Gregor said hurriedly. "It now appears that we are going to attack the city after all."

"Which means," Otto continued chummily, "that eventually we'll ransack the place. So tell me carefully, lad, exactly where lies the house with all this treasure."

FROM THERE, things went badly. Simon of Montfort and Robert of Boves had been so confident of their assurances that now nobody in Zara could imagine the Frankish army actually attacking them, and they dismissed Bishop Conrad as a pawn of the Venetians. The Zarans, with a gleeful defiance that was my fault, prepared the city for an attack that they were absolutely certain would consist, at most, of a few hundred sailors.

But it was more than ten thousand soldiers and nearly as many mariners who spent the rest of that wet day preparing to assault them. The only exception was Simon of Montfort, who withdrew his men from the encampment and restaked his tents miles away, out of sight from what would follow. Then, as the sun was setting behind clouds, Simon sent a procession to our tent, loudly, publicly asking Gregor of Mainz to lead an official withdrawal of the German knights from camp. Hundreds of German knights gathered to see what Gregor would do.

Gregor, his face rigid with his own indecision, excused himself inside and drew closed the flap. The men surrounded the tent, with a low rumble of speculation that cloistered us from the world as if we were in deep snow.

Gregor sat on the floor with Otto and me, debating with himself about what to do. Neither of us would-be counselors was any use to him. To Otto, it was simple: the army had decided to attack, and Gregor was part of the army, so attack he must. To me, still tethered and wretched, it was equally simple: this attack was a heinous sin, all the more heinous because our (very well, *my*) own bumbled attempts to protect the Zarans had in fact put the Zarans in greater danger. Gregor would be nothing but hypocrisy in muscled form if he did anything less than withdraw from the campaign in protest.

"I wasn't the one trying to stop them from surrendering!" Gregor snapped. He buried his face in his hands. Metaphors and poetic imagery aside, Gregor truly did seem to glow grey and gold by turn, depending on his moral clarity at any moment—it was a genuine physical phenomenon, as if he were his own religious artwork. Now he was wreathed in fog. "If I withdraw, I'm guilty of tearing the army apart. If the army falls apart, we will never free the Holy Land, and I have *pledged my life* to free the Holy Land."

"And remember the Song of Deborah," Otto said. "'Why sit you idly by the bonfire listening to the *whistling* of the *shepherd?*'" (This, emphasized by his smacking my shoulder—I guess I was the shepherd.) "'The kings came, they fought—'"

"They didn't fight Catholics, Otto," said Gregor.

There was a commotion at the entrance, a squall disturbing our snowdrift, and somebody opened the flap. Gregor gestured sharply to the older Richard to pull it closed again, but before Richard could reach it, the Bishop of Halberstadt's damp head appeared in the opening. Gregor and Otto scrambled to their feet to welcome Conrad. I did not.

But I felt a glimmer of hope. I knew that Conrad was against this attack, even though he'd been appallingly passive in the face of it.

"Your Eminence," Gregor said, relieved. "That crowd—"

"That crowd is Simon's fault, not yours," Conrad said reassuringly. He looked as if he had aged a decade.

"It doesn't matter who *caused* the crowd, Your Eminence," Gregor said. "Only that it is waiting for me to speak to it." And then, to my disappointment, he said, like an adoring acolyte, "Tell me what to do."

"Tell him to fight, I beg you, Your Eminence! Otherwise he looks like a bad soldier," Otto insisted. "And that reflects on everyone who's serving with him."

Conrad frowned at Otto. "Son," he said, "you are not just a soldier, you are a soldier in Christ."

"I'll be a soldier in six feet of clay if there's no food and shelter all winter, Your Eminence," Otto countered. "And thanks to this idiot"—and here he kneed me in the back—"there's no peaceful way to get that now."

"Shut up," I begged miserably and curled up on my side on the floor mats.

"Not fighting doesn't accomplish anything, does it, Your Eminence?" Otto argued. "Simon of Montfort will have nothing to show for his grand retreat."

"Simon is deserting the army and going straight to Syria," Conrad announced. "He will not attack Zara, or accept shelter at the expense of the Zarans, or allow winter to prevent him from pushing forward. He is being an exemplary pilgrim."

"Except for the fact that he is weakening the army," Gregor said.

Conrad nodded sadly.

"And you don't want me to do that," Gregor said.

Conrad nodded sadly. "That's right."

I sat up. "You can't be telling him you *want* him to attack Catholics," I insisted.

"I want him to stay with the army," the bishop said. He turned back to Gregor. "But the Briton is correct, I hope you will not fight."

"You want us to sit in the tent?" Otto said harshly. "Forgive me, Your Eminence, but that doesn't make us good Christians, that makes us women!"

"There's a little more involved in being a woman," contributed his laundress-scullery-cook-mistress-laborer under her breath as she prepared the evening meal.

Gregor looked at Conrad in distress. I felt for Gregor; his puppeteers were doing a wretched job all around: I'd failed my attempts; Boniface had disappeared completely; and Conrad was, once again, equivocating.

"There is no satisfactory answer to this problem," Conrad said—equivocating. "There is only an array of moral compromises."

"I'm not compromising if I fight," Otto announced.

"If Gregor abstains from fighting, you must too," the bishop said.

"That's hogwash, Your Eminence," Otto said. "He's not my superior. He's my half brother, and *my* mother was the nobler. I'm not his vassal, and I'm *certainly* not his inferior."

"I'm a knight and you're not," Gregor pointed out. "And I'm your elder."

"I'm paying most of our expenses," Otto shot back. "I'm fighting if I choose to, and there is no compromise in that."

Conrad gave him a sour look and corrected him. "Your compromise, my son, is that you'd be allowing the Venetians to turn you into their mercenary. If you don't see how that's a compromise, then you and I have much work ahead of us regarding your spiritual acuity. On the other hand, Simon compromises by weakening the army for further engagements, in removing his men and encouraging others to leave. Gregor doesn't want to compromise at *all*, and so in these circumstances, he risks being cornered into inaction." He turned to Gregor. "A fair assessment?"

Gregor grimaced thoughtfully. "Yes, Your Eminence," he said.

Conrad turned back to Otto. "So the decision for Gregor will be what allows the least evil. If that means staying with the army but refusing to actually raise arms against the Zarans, so be it. It is a decent compromise, and if you had any real dignity as a soldier, even if you lacked Christian compassion, you would take a similar course, rather than being a toady of the Venetians."

Having finally received orders, what he was waiting for, Gregor was lifted out of his grey fog, which was replaced by the golden glow. Immediately, he went outside to address the men of Germany, torch held high but emitting less light than he himself seemed to be, and announced that he would not leave but neither would he participate in battle. He did not need to ask them to follow suit. The golden glow pretty much guaranteed they would. One of us, at least, was soothed.

16

 WHEN WE AWOKE the next morning, Otto had disappeared from the tent.

This required dexterity on his part. The tent was large, but for warmth, we all huddled together beneath overlapping blankets: Liliana on one end, then Otto, Gregor, and the squires watchfully to either side of me, closer to the door. There was nothing titillating about this intimacy, not even when Otto warmed his hands by putting them up Liliana's skirts and describing what he found there.

Somehow, in the damp chill of dawn, our young man had managed to disentangle himself from the blankets, waking none of us—including his mistress and his brother, to either side of him—and then exit the tent with all his armor and his sword. Not even I, the lightest sleeper, had stirred. Liliana woke first, realized what had happened, and said, sounding almost amused, "Oh dear," which woke the rest of us.

We all sat up and looked around, instantly wide awake.

Then all of us turned to look at Gregor, who looked like he did not want to be looked at.

There was a brief, loud flare of trumpets and drums outside.

Then there was an awful silence, and then a far more awful sound: a few hundred paces away in the harbor, giant rock catapults had been whiningly loosed from a galley, whipping stones over the walls of Zara. Even larger siege machines would soon be hurtling boulders toward the bulk of the walls themselves. The forbidden attack on Zara had begun, and somewhere out there on the water, Otto was assisting in it.

For a moment none of us said anything; we just sat there shoulder to shoulder, feeling with each thud the irreversibility of what was happening. The attack was prosecuted entirely from the boats, which nearly surrounded the city; the boom of galley drums and the splash of oars filled the pauses between volleys of rocks. Gregor was so tense that the air around him felt like I could pluck it and draw sound: as much as the pilgrim in him refused to fight, the soldier was deeply galled to know that there was action he could not participate in. He was like a horny priest witnessing an orgy.

Finally Gregor nudged the younger Richard. "Get dressed, go out there, and find Otto. Tell him to return to the tent."

"Let me go instead, milord," the elder Richard said.

"I can do it," the younger one said churlishly.

"I'd not have the boy on a battlefield, milord," the elder said to Gregor. "That's how we lost his father, rest his soul."

"As you will," Gregor said peaceably. The elder Richard nodded solemnly in thanks and, gestured to his grandson to stay inside. He dressed and left the tent in silence.

In the clammy dawn outside, Liliana stirred the fire and heated ale in which to soak and soften the dry biscuits that were our main food. The boy and I rolled up the bedding and tucked it away into a chest; then I curled up on the floor matting, willing my soul to depart to purgatory. It didn't do as it was told. Nobody spoke.

When the biscuit gruel was ready, the others sat huddled around the fire outside. I huddled on my own in the tent, feeling my body heat seep into the earth. I heard Gregor utter a brief blessing. They ate in silence; I ate nothing. Sounds of the attack tumbled into the tent. The beat of the drums in the war galleys and men screaming, distantly, added to the echoing rumble of the catapulted stones. There would have been no such screaming if I'd just let them surrender. The tent was surrounded by the pounding of men and boys running past us from other parts of the camp to help with the attack.

The others finished eating and sat there for a moment.

"Richard, see to Summa and Oro," I heard Gregor say quietly. "Liliana, firewood. But keep an eye on the Briton. And don't let him near your cook knife."

Sounds of the attack grew more intense as men hurled rocks at walls draped with the very cross they'd taken an oath to protect and serve. People were probably dying. They would not have been dying if I had minded my own business and left all of this to the experts.

It was dinnertime when the elder Richard returned to the tent. He had no news of Otto; he had not been able to find him anywhere, on any of the ships in the harbor.

We spent the whole of that first day around the tent. I wanted my heart to stop beating. I think this time Gregor didn't fault me much for it. He himself was in a foul mood, trapped into inactivity. I thought Conrad had done a shoddy job of counseling him; I was glad he wasn't fighting, but I wished he'd been exhorted to uproot and walk away entirely. My feeble attempts to champion such a move were a waste of breath.

It was a dull day; the Richardim were the least bored, for the grandfather continued his whittling and tried to teach his grandson a few woodworking skills. Gregor never once relaxed; like a hound, he was so trained to respond to certain stimuli that the effort *not* to join the battle was exhausting him. Over the course of the day, German knights, pressured by the counts in whose households they served, came to the tent seeking forgiveness from Gregor for their impending soldierly efforts. Most other Germans—including sev-

eral barons—refused to fight, and all day, streams of them stopped by
to reassure Gregor of their position, and to thank him for setting a
precedent. Count Berthold of Katzenellenbogen (a name I could not
have invented even if I'd needed to) made a personal appearance,
filling the tent with his retainers and servants, all of them smelling
of mustard. He came with Conrad, both of them to salute the young
knight who had created—by his fortuitous combination of personal
integrity and family ties—an honorable solution to "the Zara problem" that none else could have: sitting in passive protest. If any lord
found fault with Gregor's position, they were too preoccupied to
scold him for it.

Sunset was early so close to winter, and as it grew dusky, Otto
finally returned, as if he had stepped out of some other world. The
intermittent rain had stopped an hour earlier. He was covered in dust
and debris, exhausted in the satisfied way one is after a day of cheerful exercise, and seemed to have found the events exhilarating rather
than disturbing.

I'd never seen a man in full mail armor before—we used leather
back home—and he was intimidating, even with the helmet tucked
under one arm. He was in chain literally from head to foot, only his
face and boots bare. "Did you see those *petraries*, the rock throwers?"
he said, pulling at his mitten laces with his teeth. Liliana brought
her hands to her face in a reflexive gesture of relief, and he ran to
her, grabbing her in his dusty iron arms and dragging her away from
where she'd been peeling tonight's ration of mysterious root vegetables. "You were worried?" He laughed and buried his dirt-streaked
face against her bare cleavage. "Mmmm, show me how worried you
were, sweethearts."

Liliana forced herself to laugh, trying to make it sound offhand or
even harsh. "Nobody present is interested in watching you take your
pleasure at anything at this moment. I don't think they even care to
feed you supper."

"Ha!" Otto scoffed. "I'm the only one here who did his soldierly duty today, I'm more deserving than the lot of you put together! If the matter's privacy, we can throw the rest of them out of the tent!"

"It's my tent, Otto, and you will not insult me in it," Gregor said with a flash of anger. I realized, with mixed feelings, that he was jealous of Otto for having spent the day in action. "If you lack the discipline to control yourself, you may take a blanket and go mount Liliana up in the hills somewhere."

Otto, pulling off his mittens, looked around at the relieved but unsmiling faces. "Well that sounds much more satisfying than anything going on in here. God's balls, is he dead?" he asked, pointing at me. Without waiting for an answer, he continued, "Come, Liliana." Grinning, he gestured for her to retrieve a blanket from the chest.

Gregor stretched an arm across the tent flap. "Tell me first what happened today. I'm glad you are unharmed," he added and looked as if he hadn't wanted to admit it.

Otto shrugged and moved to the chest since Liliana had remained still. "We went out on the war galleys, set up the rock throwers, and threw rocks at them to clear them from the walls. Didn't accomplish much. They threw rocks back at us. Didn't accomplish much either. Sort of boring, actually. Those galleys can move! Those rowers are made of solid muscle, and they're the most disciplined lot I've seen in my life. Y'see," he went on, suddenly conversational, one soldier to another, excited, "the goal's just like in land warfare, to get close enough that we can throw over grappling hooks and get onto their towers. You'd think it'd be easy, their walls aren't so tall, but they have half a mountain's worth of stones inside, and they chase us off with the catapults pretty efficiently. Nobody was hurt that I know of. We stopped when it got dark. We'll do it again tomorrow, and the next day, until we smash the walls down or starve them out."

"And then?" I demanded from where I lay curled.

Otto, having collected the blanket, shut the chest and stood up again, reaching for Liliana's arm. "And then we do what soldiers do when they conquer a city," he said with satisfaction. "Pillage and loot—"

"And rape and slaughter." Liliana breathed in disgust and walked with resignation toward the entrance flap. "Come along, milord pilgrim, let's go defy St. Paul."

Gregor stepped aside; Liliana, looking grim, led a beaming Otto out of the tent.

I sat bolt upright, appalled with myself for taking an entire day to realize, through the haze of my moroseness: "I have to get Jamila out of there!"

"She's not a princess," Gregor said in a tired voice.

"She's a *person*," I retorted. "I swore to see her safely home, and you're still sworn to take her as a convert to the Holy Land. If we just sit back and wait for her to be among the raped and slaughtered, we are the greatest sinners in this entire army."

He mulled this over. I tried to read his color; he hovered between grey and gold.

"And it's something to *do*," I said, feeling desperate.

"I agree with your impulse," Gregor said after a moment. "But since I've met you, every plan you've made has gone afoul somehow."

"Then *you* make a plan," I said quickly. I sat up and wiped my hands expectantly. "I'll do whatever you suggest, as long as it keeps her safe."

Gregor, from his heralded exploits as a tournament champion, was a great believer in carefully assessing circumstances, especially one's environment, before planning how to save one's princess, unhorse one's opponent, or engage in one's sundry other chivalrous undertakings. So the next morning at dawn, before the trumpets had sounded a resumption of the siege, the two of us walked down to the harbor and past it for reconnaissance, to the little stretch of land where the spit of Zara was attached to the mainland. Around most of the city, the walls descended directly into the water; here, for the couple bowshots of dirt that connected it to the Dalmatian coast, the wall was protected from attackers only by a ditch filled with the city's garbage. There was one land gate to the city; it had been barricaded within by the Zarans, to keep the army out, and barricaded without by the army, to keep the Zarans in.

There were no siege machines set up along the land wall. An attempt had been made to ram the gate, but the Zarans had dangled chains from above, which entangled the head of the ram. Now the land wall was merely being guarded, to keep the Zarans from fleeing; there was no action near it, and it took no subterfuge or risk for Gregor and me to examine it on our own for a passage in. We spent three days, dawn to dusk, scouring for it, without any guard questioning our intention. On the fourth day, we doused cloths with Liliana's perfume, wrapped them over our mouths and noses, and descended into the dry moat below the wall, filled with rotting garbage. Damp from a week of drizzle, it was extremely ripe.

Gregor, with his soldier's eye, immediately discovered the Achilles' heel of Zara: a segment of the dry moat had a natural rock overhang, which would have protected any attackers trying to mine a tunnel there. Tunneling under a wall and blowing it up—undermining—was the surest way to bring down a city, he explained. That would have guaranteed victory, and led to a violent pillage of the town, and if he'd felt this was a justified attack, he'd have gone straight to the doge or Baldwin of Flanders to point it out.

But he did not want the responsibility of bringing about the fall of a Catholic city he had been forbidden to harm.

But he knew it was his soldierly duty to report what he had learned.

But he did not want the responsibility of bringing about the fall of a Catholic city he had been forbidden to harm.

Grey, grey, grey.

I listened to him bellyache as we continued to scour that same small segment of moat, picking our way through rubbish heaps.

"I'm going to write a new song about you," I finally warned, to shut him up. "'The Whinging Cavalier.' Listen: Oh, the whinging cavalier, he's hung like a lavaliere—"

"Is that the Briton?" said a familiar voice from above.

Gregor grimaced as his brother's head appeared over the edge of the moat. Otto stared down at us, puzzled. "What are you doing down there?" he asked.

"What are you doing up there?" I shot back.

Otto shrugged. "I was rotated to guard duty after I got into a fist-fight with some mariners. Boring as screwing a nun. Are you just stretching your legs, or have you finally decided to do your soldierly duty, Brother? Wait a moment! Look at that!"

Gregor and I glanced at each other, similar balls of lead landing hard in our respective guts: Otto had seen the segment of the ditch that would be easy to mine.

"We could mine that!" he declared eagerly over his shoulder. "Hugh! Call the count, show him this!" He glanced back down at us and grinned. "You're my good luck charm! Stick around!"

We scrambled out of the moat, lest we bring down the walls ourselves.

In less time than it takes to sing *The Song of Roland*, men were working on the tunnel, under the protection not only of the natural overhang but of a wooden roof covered in vinegar-soaked hides, which the Zarans' flaming arrows could not burn. By a perverse stroke of fate, the stony overhang protected a natural break in the bedrock that seemed to have been constructed by God for the sole purpose of making it easy to undermine and blow up the walls of Zara. The Zarans, watching from the towers and listening to the miners' shouts of satisfaction, realized they had no chance and immediately sent a delegation to offer surrender, once again, to the Doge of Venice. We heard all of this back in the tent, in relay from the Richardim, who were delighted to have some activity to engage in beyond whittling blocks of wood into chess pieces.

This time, Dandolo received the Zarans in the company of Baldwin of Flanders, Boniface's young deputy. Baldwin was markedly less sanguine than was Dandolo himself. The two men had already established terms, which the Zarans accepted instantly and with great relief: the city would be turned over in an orderly fashion to the Venetians; the Zarans' worldly goods were to become the common loot of the army, but the Zarans themselves would not be harmed. Gregor, present for these talks, reported this to me with grim satisfaction. A besieged city, upon forced surrender, has no reason to hope for any quarter—but Baldwin and the clergy had insisted that mercy be shown, to limit further damage to the campaign's reputation. There was to be no bloodshed, no vengeance exacted by the Venetians against the "pirates" they had just defeated. It was unlikely that these terms would be fully honored, but the hope was to minimize the chaos.

Baldwin of Flanders asked Gregor to play a constabulary role during the actual surrender, which would begin the next morning. Gregor accepted the office with gratitude. It was unglamorous but would allow him to be chivalrous—gentle with the vanquished yet doing the duty of a soldier. He explained all of this to me and left the best news for last: "It means that, once they surrender, I will be allowed into the city *before the rest of the army*."

In other words, before anyone else could get to Jamila.

"Then I'm your man, milord," I said. So I couldn't help the city, but I could help one soul.

Or so I thought.

Before dusk that night, a Venetian messenger arrived at the camp, hired by a private citizen (at huge expense) to issue a proclamation around the Adriatic. The citizen was a wealthy merchant named Barzizza. The proclamation was that a slave of his, a well-dressed Levantine woman of nearing thirty years, had gone missing some seven weeks back.

There was an enormous reward for her capture and safe return.

17

DOZENS OF MEN came to our tent on feeble pretexts to see if Liliana's quiet companion from the *Venus* was still with her. Otto posted the Richardim at either side of the tent to explain that the princess had already been captured and returned to Venice.

His impulse was not philanthropic. He just wanted to nab Jamila himself so he could claim the reward as soon as the city capitulated. We were the only ones who knew where to find her once the gates were thrown open.

"That is practically *cannibalism*!" I shrieked and threw myself at him in the middle of the tent. I grabbed his throat with both hands and tried to shake him. "She became a virtual member of your clan while we were sailing—you should be planning to *save* her, not to profit from her suffering!"

Otto pried my hands away, pushed me off almost effortlessly, and pressed me onto the floor of the tent, one booted foot on my throat. "I'm not a monster," he retorted calmly. "Face the truth, Brit, she's going to be caught. And *since* she's going to be caught, then let it be us who profit from it—we were the ones through whom she had a little taste of freedom, after all."

I made a sound of enraged disagreement that he thought meant I was choking. He removed his foot, and I sat up, glaring.

"In fact, here's a thought," Otto continued, coaxingly. He offered me a hand up. I did not accept it. "Maybe you should come with me to fetch her."

"Do you really think I'd do that?" I demanded angrily.

"She trusts you; it will be less traumatizing for her if she's taken back into custody accompanied by a familiar face."

"Stop speaking of her as if she were cattle," I said in disgust and got to my feet, wiping the sand from his boot off of my throat.

"How should I speak of her? She's not a princess. She's not even a lady. She's just a Jew."

"Lower your voice." This was Gregor, whispering sharply, as he looked up from the portable altar where he had spent much of this, and every, evening. "There are enough rumors circulating about the population of this tent without any of us offering more information to eavesdroppers."

I poked Otto's shoulder to get his attention. Faster than a blink he had grabbed my hand and twisted it hard within his own, so that I had to throw myself against him to keep my wrist from snapping. "Don't *poke* the nobles, minion," he warned cheerfully and released me.

"You can't turn her in if I get to her first," I said, rubbing my wrist.

He grinned. "Is that a wager?"

"It's a *fact*."

"Let's make it a wager," he said, cocky. "If I find her first, I turn her in and I keep all the reward, and you don't make a fuss about it. If *you* find her first—"

"She and I run off together and *you don't track us*," I said. "We obviously can't stay with the fleet any longer with a reward on her head."

"Done," Otto said cheerfully and held out his hand to shake. I took it.

IT WAS HAUNTING to arrive with Gregor at the land gate in the dark of the morning. There were perhaps two hundred constables of his rank, all armed with sword, dagger, and upright ash lance, and all in padded cloth armor of bright red, so that they could be recognized by both Zarans and victors during the turnover. He'd given me a red surcoat to wear to pass as his squire; nobody questioned us. It was cold and still, but the city was already awake and nervous. There was no wailing or caterwauling because the Zarans were a hard, proud people, but frightened children sometimes squawked and frightened brides sometimes sobbed quietly, and there was damp sorrow in the air. It reminded me of my homeland when the English had finally conquered us three years earlier. No, it had been worse then: the smell of burning wood, burning hair and flesh and bones, the sweet stench of blood, and the screams . . . I rubbed my face to try to rub away the memory.

The walls of Zara were not so high, but they were deep—a good ten paces, with storage chambers built into them for goods to be unloaded from the water gates or for shipbuilding supplies. Once inside, we faced a dense mass of Zarans who had already lined up at the land gate. They waited with their carts, families, livestock, and earthly goods. The soldiers at the gate would not let them out for another hour yet, and so the entire southern end of town was solid with the stalled traffic of nervous couples, crying children, and muttering old people.

We followed the slight upward slant of the street, working our way awkwardly through the about-to-be refugees. I could feel their hate. It made me heartsick; I'd been in their boots too recently. Once at the gate, their wagons would be checked for valuables, which they wouldn't be allowed to take out with them. Then they would be free to vanish into the approaching winter. That was kinder treatment than we had received at the hands of the English. They'd wanted to annihilate the lot of us.

This road from the land gate was a high street, one of two thoroughfares running south to north, the length of the town. Based on young Richard's description from his errand with Jamila, it was the other such road, closer to the harbor, that we wanted: there huddled the merchants' houses. We zigzagged through cold, narrow, muddy alleys, crossed one market square that smelled like rotting meat; beyond that, a narrow diagonal alley between pale limestone buildings led to another square; at the far side of this was the street we sought. It too was choked with wagons, horses, and terrified families on foot.

Many of the merchants kept their storerooms at the front of the ground floor. One of these would be the Egyptian trader's. We turned left onto the street, now far enough north that the crowd had thinned. We counted the wooden gates until we came to one on our left that, according to young Richard, was the place we wanted.

This gate, wide enough for a small cart, was slightly ajar. It opened into a passageway as broad as a room, a sheltered vestibule neither inside nor outside, which in turn opened into a courtyard. From the courtyard, I heard Jamila's voice.

Then I saw her, in a long dark tunic with arabesque designs. She was with a dark-complexioned older woman and two teenage girls, all of whom were holding a donkey by the halter and all of whom began to scream as soon as my grim, vermilion-clothed companion stepped into their yard. The donkey pulled free and disappeared into the shadows of a courtyard stall. Jamila looked alarmed, but I made a reassuring gesture. She began to shout over the feminine screaming, in a language I had never heard before, both guttural and musical; she was trying to calm them down. I had never seen her so engaged in movement. She had a grounded fluidity to her gestures, and she was very hands-on with them, taking them by the chin to get their attention, stroking their arms and faces, pushing them to sit quietly together on the wagon in the corner stall.

"Please let them leave," she said to Gregor, sounding nervous—it was the first time I had ever heard her nervous. "They're terrified, and they're putting all their trust in me. Please assure me I am not betraying them."

Gregor looked miserable.

"Better do something quick, Otto will make a beeline for this place," I warned. "He'll try to turn her in for the bounty."

"What bounty?" Jamila demanded.

"Barzizza has caught up with us," I said.

She went pale. Sensing her unease, the older of the two girls started crying, and her mother looked as if she'd join her in a moment. Jamila snapped her attention back to them, convinced them to sit again. "Let me guess," she said to me in a withering tone. "You have a plan."

"Better than that," I retorted. "I have Otto's word of honor that if I find you before he does, I can take you . . . away . . . without . . . his . . . pursuing . . ." My words slowed like honey in winter and then stopped altogether as Gregor, with a wretched expression, took a step toward Jamila and slowly, almost apologetically, closed one large red glove around her arm. She had never looked so small or fragile to me.

"You're not going anywhere," he said. "You're in my custody until I can deliver you to the marquis Boniface."

"*What?*" I shrieked and leapt at him, my hands clamping closed over the hilt of his sword. His free hand easily fit over both of mine and prevented me from drawing the sword.

"Don't do that," he warned me. "I have no choice. This is my sworn duty."

I tugged my hands free from his grasp and began to wallop him on the chest, which—after a satisfying initial grunt—he mostly ignored. I let loose a stream of curses in every language I knew.

Jamila, by contrast, had completely recovered herself. "Get them to safety first," she said. "Then we'll talk about what happens to me."

There was a loud, long blare of a trumpet from the land gate, silencing me. It was followed by another, and another, and another, from all over the city. From outside the city walls as well. And from the Venetian ships.

Zara had just officially surrendered.

The plunder was about to begin.

At that moment, we heard the gate outside swing open. Booted feet scrambled through the entryway—and then Otto appeared, breathless, with an expectant glee on his face that transformed to disappointed disgruntlement. He shouted something unrepeatable in German by way of greeting me; he acknowledged neither his brother nor Jamila. "I was the first soldier through the gate! How the devil did you get here first? You'll never get her out safely, y'know, one of those other whoresons out there will steal her from you, so you might as well let me have her. Dammit!"

"He's not taking her anywhere, Otto," Gregor said.

Otto saw Gregor's hand on Jamila's arm. His eyes widened, and then he grinned. "Brother!" he cried approvingly, humor restored. "Well done! I'd no idea you knew how to connive. Staying out of our wager so you could be my backup without him suspecting you! Clever man! Come on then, let's get her to Barzizza's envoy."

"She's not going to Barzizza, she's going to Marquis Boniface," said Gregor.

Ever mercurial, Otto instantly glowered. "Why? Boniface won't reward us like Barzizza would, and we need that reward! The *army* needs that reward, to help pay the *debt*. She's worth nothing to Boniface if she's not really a princess." A strange look flashed across Gregor's face; I think he felt both foolish and relieved to be reminded of Jamila's political worthlessness.

"She's also worth nothing to *Barzizza* if she's not a princess," I said.

"Barzizza doesn't *realize* she's not a princess," Otto said, as if I were thick. "We have to exchange her for the reward before he figures that out."

"While you are discussing this, may I at least help my friends prepare their retreat into the wilderness?" Jamila asked in a tight voice.

Gregor glanced at her. "Will you give me your word of honor not to flee?"

"My word of honor is more valuable than my identity?" she asked drily. "I advise you to trust my common sense, sir: I guarantee not to flee because the attempt would be foolish." When she pulled her arm away from him, he let her go. She signaled the older girl, who grabbed the ass's halter, but the animal began trotting around the yard stubbornly, changing direction with a jerk every few steps trying to throw her off, as we all watched.

"You can't turn her in for a reward you know she is unworthy of," Gregor scolded Otto. "That's fraud, it's dishonorable."

"But it's not dishonorable to treat an innocent woman like a piece of property?" I demanded.

"She's not an innocent woman, she's a captive of war," Otto retorted.

The younger sister grabbed the ass's ear and pulled; the beast squealed with outrage, snapped out to bite her, and broke from the older girl's grasp. It trotted away, shaking its head indignantly. The girls chased it into the vestibule.

"She's only a captive because she was believed to be royal," I objected.

"She's only *alive* because she was believed to be royal," Otto corrected.

"It follows, then, since I am not royal, I should be dead," Jamila said conclusively. She took a step closer to Otto and held her arms out in an undefended gesture. "Why don't you follow your own moral algebra and see to it yourself, sir?"

Otto looked disturbed. "What moral algae?"

She gave him a contemptuous glance and turned to me. "Where did you find these people?" she demanded. I was flattered.

"In a swamp," I replied, making a mental note to learn what algebra was as soon as possible. "Come on, let's get you to safety."

"All three of you are wasting your time on me. You should concern yourself with the others in this yard." The ass came trotting back into the courtyard, fleeing the girls, who were in tears of frustration and fear. The sounds of exodus from the road were already fading; the distant row of looting soldiers was less distant. There was a scream from a couple of houses over, echoing in the stone street, and angry voices shouting threats. Jamila shifted uncomfortably. "There is silver well-hidden in this house, and I'll lead you to it if you help this mother and her children get to safety."

"So you're not fleeing with him?" Otto asked, brows raised hopefully, pointing at me.

"That's correct," she said.

He took a step toward her, with an eagerness I didn't like, and I darted between them, glaring at him. "You gave your word," I reminded him. "I got to her first."

Otto's hand was already on his sword belt. "Our wager only holds if you're fleeing with her," he declared with the legalistic promptness of an attentive Catholic. "If she's not fleeing, that's outside the scope of our wager, so our wager is forfeit, and I can turn her over to Barzizza's men for the reward."

"You are such an ass!" I shrieked and lunged at him. With astounding speed, he wrapped his arm around my throat, kicked my legs out from under me, and had me pinned supine on the damp ground, his knee pressing hard against my sternum. I tried to cry out, but my breath was knocked out of me; he released me, spun and grabbed Jamila, and had his arm around her throat. The mother and daughters screamed and ran into the cellar under the kitchen.

Before I was even back on my feet, Gregor had drawn his sword and was standing between Otto and the passageway to the street. "Otto, you will not defraud a Venetian merchant who never did you harm," he announced. "If you turn her over to his men, I myself will tell them she is not a princess."

"Fool!" Otto hissed.

"Knight," Gregor corrected.

There was a long pause, punctuated by Jamila trying to breathe without wimpering. Finally Otto released her, pushing her harshly away from him. She stumbled, and I rushed to steady her.

"I can get the Egyptians out," Otto huffed in a disgusted voice, to his brother. "I know someone at the gate. We worked together during the siege—I dragged him out of the way when a catapult collapsed, so he owes me a favor. If I take the woman and her girls to the gate, I can ask him to look the other way while they go through with a little money on them."

"Can you get Jamila out too?" I asked, struggling to get my breath back.

"Of course not," Jamila said herself, shakily. "It's one thing to ask someone to turn a blind eye as a widow and her daughters sneak out a few marks, it's another to ask him to keep mum about someone with a large bounty on her head. I'm staying here." She pulled away from my steadying grip, embarrassed that I could feel her tremble. "Apparently," she said, struggling to sound calm, even droll, "the good Lord has decided you need somebody sensible to keep an eye on you awhile longer."

18

WE FINALLY GOT the ass harnessed. Gregor went to attend to his constabulary duties. Otto and I, having attained a grudging truce, left to help the Egyptians out of the city.

As routs go, the day was calm and contained, but it was not bloodless. Shutters were torn off windows, wooden outbuildings were reduced to cinders, furniture was strewn about the street as if God had chucked it there at random. There were smells of things burning that should not have been burning. A few dead, mutilated bodies lay like tossed dolls around one market square; a woman sobbed hysterically in the street, unable to move because both of her legs were broken. I plucked Otto's sleeve; with a grimace, he followed me to the poor woman, hoisted her up, and put her onto the wagon; the Egyptian family looked at her in alarm but did not protest. A few children clung to one another in a wide-eyed, desperate pack, shrieking for their parents, running aimlessly like confused chickens, then clutching one another again. I gestured them to come to me; they ran off screaming. There were no animals around, because everything edible had been used to flee, or if left behind, had already been slaughtered for consumption by the hungry army; plumes of dark smoke from emerging bonfires dotted the city. A couple of squires were fighting with each other, fists and daggers flying, over the silver their masters had told them to smuggle, stolen from the official booty that was to be divided at the main church.

By late afternoon, every Zaran was a refugee and every member of the army was settled within the city walls. In fact, our little tribe had settled into the very house to which Jamila had fled. I argued against this, but she pointed out that for us to leave the house for others to vandalize was to add to the crime already suffered by its owners. I finally yielded to this logic, after much heckling from Otto, who found the need for such justification far too precious to bother with.

I also had to suffer through various understated rebukes from Jamila about my extreme misjudgment regarding my attempts to avert an attack on Zara. "I asked for your contribution, but you declined to give it," I reminded her. "And then you simply *left* us."

Working in shifts, with Jamila hiding upstairs, we brought the belongings over from the camp. The main chamber was above the front passageway, and although it would be a tight fit for seven people through the winter, we saw that we could manage it. And we would have more space than most; an army of nearly twenty thousand was squeezing into a town built for fewer than a third that number.

Gregor, of course, could've simply presented himself at the largest palace in the city, which was being held for his father-in-law, the marquis Boniface. He did not do this. Since I wanted to keep Jamila away from lordly attention, I gratefully accepted his choice without seeking to examine it.

Liliana oversaw the domestication of the space: The bedding would be spread the length of the room, to be rolled up and put to the side by day for seating; to one end was annexed a smaller room, forming an L; at the joining of the two rooms was a fire pit and in the smaller room a large, heavy table for food preparation, with space beneath it for storage and some small canisters of exotic-smelling spices and seasonings. Jamila, who knew the house, showed us where the privy was, the winter vegetables in the small garden, where staples for humans and horses were stored, and firewood, and storage spaces, and medical supplies in a cupboard, and a few musical instruments, including one large stringed one I had never seen before, somewhat resembling a pot-bellied gittern.

"And that's everything you need to know, sirs," she said at last, when we had completed the tour and were back in the main room.

Six sets of eyes examined her with various degrees of disbelief.

"Ah," she said, understanding. "Yes, I suppose there is one more thing." A pause. "As has been pointed out, I am not a princess."

"You need to tell us more than that," said Gregor.

"Of course." She gestured to the beds, already unrolled for the night. When we had all sat, she nodded and took a shaky breath. "I am a Jewess."

"We know that. More." The attitude that had struck me as brotherly when Gregor had tried to wring information from me back in Venice seemed more menacing now, but he was being gentle with her, considering.

"My father was from an Egyptian merchant family. He was a merchant himself, and a rabbi—our priests are not removed from the world like yours, they are like us, but very learned. He married my mother and moved to Constantinople, the center of Byzantium and one of the great cities in the world. I was born there." She paused.

"Why are you not there now?" Gregor asked.

"When I was young there was a huge uprising against foreigners. I've even heard that Dandolo, before he became doge, was visiting Constantinople at the time and was blinded in the midst of all the violence. The whole thing did not affect us so much directly, because the Jews lived outside the city walls, across the harbor. But it frightened my parents, and we fled to Genoa with friends, Genoese Christians."

"Then why aren't you in *Genoa* now?" Gregor pressed, as if she had left Genoa just to vex him personally and he expected recompense.

"Because that's how it often is when you're a Jewish merchant. My father did not specialize but dealt mostly in wools and textiles. We moved as we had to. We learned the language of every place we went to, and the laws, so that we would do nothing wrong. There were no other children, so my father shared his learning with me. The learning included languages and scriptures, and sundry random things—"

"But why did that fool in Venice think you were an Egyptian princess?" Gregor demanded, losing patience as each response failed to make everything plain.

She held her hand up calmly. "I am explaining. In France I was married to a physician, who was from a family we'd known in Constantinople. Then he was summoned to serve a Moslem lord near Alexandria, and I went with him. I learned a lot by necessity, I know as much as any doctor—"

"I don't care about your professional credentials," Gregor said. "I want to know how you came to fool Barzizza."

She gave him a look. "I am *telling* you, sir. I had children, the same age as the lord's, so I became trusted to care for them all. The lady was fond of me and made me an attendant. It was beautiful there, although we were in the hinterlands. I learned that I would rather be with Moslems than with Christians. And from Western merchants visiting, I learned that Christians would be kinder to me if they believed me to be Moslem, and less kind if they believed me Jewish. You do not need to know *how* I came to learn these things. You do not need to know anything else, except that five years ago, some pilgrims like you came with the cross on their shoulders and attacked us without any explanation. There was no dispute, so there could be no resolution; there was nothing but massacre. My husband was killed in front of me, my children were disemboweled before my eyes and left for carrion to eat. By pilgrims exactly like you." Her voice held no accusation or rancor; its very matter-of-factness was devastating.

"Not exactly like us," Gregor said, holding up a pedantic finger.

"Exactly like you. They were German."

Gregor lowered the pedantic finger. "I remember that campaign," he said quietly to Otto.

"We wanted to go on it as squires!" Otto said, less quietly. "When they came back early because of the emperor's death, I was jealous hearing all the stories. They won someplace called Beirut—"

"Beirut, Saidin, yes. There was also a small splinter group that made a sortie south toward Egypt. They discovered us. I don't know what they were thinking, perhaps we would be a toehold into Egypt. Barzizza was with them for reasons of his own. I had been put into the real princess's gowns as a decoy, and he fell for it. I did not see the point in enlightening him. I did not see the point in much of anything, by then."

There was a long silence. My eyes smarted.

"I . . . cannot speak on behalf of those who came before me," Gregor said, almost conciliatory. "I can promise you only that I come to this calling from a pure heart and would never offend God with such behavior."

"Then when you reach Egypt, go to our home and make sure my son's bones are finally buried properly, like the good Christian that you are." Her voice sounded a little strangled. Despite her dispassion, this was a strain for her.

Gregor turned on me brusquely. "Well?" he demanded.

"Well what? Are you upset she's not a princess? You're only interested in damsels in distress? I didn't realize you were merely chivalrous—I thought you were actually *good*."

Gregor gave me one of his tiresome all-seeing-elder-brother looks. "That's not what I meant. We're about to invade Egypt, so obviously it's significant if she's an Egyptian princess. I must determine what to do with her, given that she's not one."

"Your bishop still wants her for her soul," I reminded him. "So you are bound to shelter her as far as Jerusalem."

"I am Castor to your Pollux," Jamila said to me wryly.

"Romulus to my Remus," I corrected. "The bishop fancies himself the mother wolf."

"I think even the bishop would agree we can't be expected to keep her," Otto said to his brother, without malice. Jamila grimaced but nodded a little, having expected this. "She's just another mouth to feed now, and winter's coming on."

"That's a specious argument," I said. "She was already an infidel; I don't see how the details of her infidelity make a difference."

"St. John's head, it makes an enormous difference! The Moslems are simply nonbelievers, but the Jews killed Christ," Otto objected.

"As if you give a—" I began to object, but Jamila gestured me to silence.

"We didn't, actually, but since you believe that we did, sir, . . . what would have happened if we hadn't? If your Lord had never suffered on the cross, what would you then be worshiping?"

"That's not the point!" he huffed. "We're not a hospice, we're an army. We've already taken in one stray heretic, because my brother is a fool. We cannot absorb the needs of another mouth to feed, especially one whose presence gives us no benefit at all."

"I'm not sure that's true," Gregor countered. He turned to her with an air of generosity. "Jamila, do you speak the language of the coast of Egypt?"

"It's my native tongue," she said, looking between the two Germans warily.

"She could be lying about that," Otto argued.

"She could be lying about all of it," I said. "She could be lying about *not* being a princess."

"When Boniface arrives here, you will offer your services as a translator and guide to him," Gregor announced—truly believing he was doing her a favor.

Jamila thought about this. "If, once he is here, you still wish me to do that, sir, then I will do it." It was a particular way to phrase it, but nobody else noticed.

"So we'll just continue as we were, shall we?" Liliana asked with perverse cheer, rosebud lips parting in a smile. "Because it's been pure joy and harmony so far."

BY SUNSET, everyone was settled, and Otto went to the church-clustered square up the street to learn what was happening with the loot. Gregor had no interest or claim in the plunder of the town, but Otto had a right to his share of the spoils. He had even convinced himself that, between having been the man to discover where to undermine the town and being heir to a large estate back home, he deserved at least as much booty as a knight.

But he returned later that evening empty-handed and frustrated. He spent most of the following day hovering about the wide square outside St. Donatius in pouring rain, with Liliana for company, while Gregor made the Richardim join him in church to pray for forgiveness for what the army had accomplished.

Jamila and I spent several hours alone in the house as she tried to coax from me the story of my own past. I told her that I had escaped the English invasion of my kingdom, and that I was to blame for that invasion. But I would not tell her *why* I was to blame, because I couldn't bear the thought of her despising me. I told her how, in my flight, I'd saved the hermit Wulfstan from the Englishman, the same lord who'd conquered my kingdom, how I'd nursed Wulfstan back to health, and how he'd helped me prepare to assassinate the Englishman, in such a way that I myself would die.

"No man of God would help with such a thing," she said.

"He was no ordinary man, and so he worshiped no ordinary god," I said awkwardly and was relieved to have our conversation broken off by Otto's and Liliana's sudden, sodden entrance.

Otto had returned this time with a pittance: no silver, no precious stones, just a carved wooden cross and one enameled candlestick.

"Not even a *pair* of candlesticks," he huffed later, when Gregor had come back. "Nothing so handsome as a matched set, just a virtual lump of clay. And after all the silver I gave them from this house! I'd've kept it for myself, if I'd known I'd be so cheated."

"You'd've been hanged for stealing," Gregor replied patiently. The elder Richard removed his master's sopping mantle and spread it near the hissing fire pit, pushing Liliana's farther from the heat.

"I'm not the only one who feels unrewarded," Otto said, as if this justified his larcenous impulses. He gestured Richard out of the way and rearranged Liliana's cloak so that it was as close as possible to the drying flames—it was these small, peculiar protective gestures he made toward her that kept me from despising him. "A lot of the younger knights, and almost all the infantry, are nearly up in arms. All of the good stuff went straight onto the doge's transports. I wouldn't be surprised if the army turned on the Venetians and beat them all to death. Why the devil do the *Venetians* get all the loot?"

"Perhaps because you still owe them nine tons of silver money," Jamila said.

* * *

THE NEXT DAY was sunny, and so dry not even the earth stayed damp; Otto went a third time to the church of St. Donatius, to protest the distribution of the booty.

By late afternoon, he had not returned.

At dusk, we heard shouting out in the streets, and soon heralds were running down the thoroughfares warning that a fight had broken out at some place called the Forum, between Venetians and some foot soldiers. Within minutes, the sounds of shouting had increased tenfold and seemed to be coming from all corners of the city. Heralds came by screaming helpfully that the fighting had spread everywhere. Then the heralds stopped, because the brawls were announcing themselves.

"I'd best retrieve my brother," Gregor said, the long-suffering elder sibling.

Because of the violence, he went out armored, and his squires hastily began to put him into his full chain mail, an extremely cumbersome undertaking: over his shirt, a quilted tunic; on his head, a thickly quilted cap; thick cloth stockings on his legs. Over all of this, the same thing again in heavy, draping iron chain mail. After this was all in place, at elbows, shoulders, and knees was added rounded plate armor for more protection. And then, above all that, a white tunic with the pilgrim cross on the back and Gregor's own insignia—a St. John's wort flower—on the front. Chain mittens were tied onto his hands (a Byzantine innovation brought back to Boniface's court by the marquis's brother, Gregor explained, as if I'd find this remotely interesting); an enormous bucket with holes punched out of it went over his head as a helmet. The elder Richard handed him a flat-topped shield made of leather-covered wood, also with the St. John's wort emblem; the younger Richard buckled on the sword belt and then knelt before him and handed Gregor his sword, hilt upright, like a cross. Jamila pointed out east to him; he turned in that direction and uttered a prayer to St. George as the Richardim wrapped themselves in their own waxed-leather armor. Finally all three of them went out into the street, calling to Liliana to bolt the front gate behind them.

Liliana decided to go up onto the roof of the house to watch the mayhem—not that she'd be able to see much, since most of the houses were of a height. She seemed more amused than disturbed by what was happening. "Nobody innocent is left to be wronged," she pointed out. "Anyone who gets hurt now has got it coming to them. Might as well enjoy the distraction." She left us. Jamila and I, for the second time since I'd stolen her from Venice, were alone together.

She gave me a strange look: for such a humorless face, the expression was almost impish, as if she was a cat that had cornered a mouse and was about to play with it.

"I'm not talking about my past," I informed her.

She shrugged. After a pause, she wordlessly went into the kitchen, opened a chest, and pulled out the unfamiliar stringed instrument that had been left behind. She brought it back to where I sat by the fire, knelt beside me, and placed the fat belly of the thing on her lap. She lifted the peculiar bent neck with her left hand and then, to my surprise, ran the fingers of her right hand across the strings with the casual ease of a seasoned musician.

It was the most seductive thing I had seen a woman do in years. It was so seductive as to be distressing. All that time on the boat she had watched me watching the female musicians; she had to have known the effect that this would have on me.

"I've played since childhood," she explained.

"What is it?" I asked, trying to sound nonchalant.

"We call it *al-ud*, the wood. I think in Europe this has become *a lute*."

"Play something. Just not Kalenda Maya."

Jamila tuned the thing, then began to recite in that strange, liturgical-sounding language from the East and brushed the backs of her fingers over the strings. She played an astonishing, complicated tune that was dark, moody, and wildly ornamented, and she sang in harmony with it, her voice making endless little trills in and around the melody. If wailing could be made beautifully melodious, this was it. It sent chills up and down my back.

"What was that?" I asked in amazement when she put the lute down. Once she stopped, we could hear the fighting outside again, but we both pretended not to. To be honest, I don't know what I wanted to get my hands on more—her, or the instrument.

"A maqama," she said, smiling. "In the Spanish style." With her right hand she stroked the side of the instrument. "This is the first time in five years I've played without Barzizza trying— Well, never mind. It is the first time I've truly played for pleasure."

"What's a maqama?" I asked promptly. I would not admit her playing was arousing if that put me in the same category as Barzizza. I would admit only to a craftsman's interest in her art.

"Just a story with different musical poems interwoven into it. It's very popular these days in Hebrew music."

"So it's religious?"

"Oh, no," she said. "We don't even *have* instrumental music for our services—they did a thousand years ago, but not since the temple was destroyed in Jerusalem. No, this is secular." She smiled confidingly. "Don't tell our armored friends, but the only part of the world where Hebrew poetry is religious is in Germany, and the work from there is considered extremely provincial and dull. The Andalusian school, which is most fashionable, uses Bible passages only for effect—for example, quoting scripture about rape and torture in a song that turns out to be about an energetic flea."

"Your people write panegyrics to *fleas?*"

"To anything that stirs strong emotion," she replied, refusing to be baited. "If you think you can control yourself, I'll sing a *muwash-shah.*" She gave me a coy, sidelong glance that was utterly unlike her and did things to parts of my body I usually forgot about. "A girdle poem," she said teasingly. "The great Maimonides despair that it aroused the spirit of harlotry."

"Oh, we've got Liliana for that, thanks anyhow," I said nervously. I gestured at the lute. "So what other kinds of pieces do you play on it?"

She shrugged. "All sorts. Lamentations, drinking songs —"

"Let's hear a lamentation."

"All right. This is from the Talmud."

"The Talmud! My favorite!" I exclaimed, wondering what a talmud was.

She played a tune that had me almost shuddering with goose bumps; her voice, when she sang, took on such profound grief I thought she must be singing of her own dead children. But then she sang it again in translation, so I could understand: "Do not withhold your compassion from him who cries out to you from the bottom of his soul. Do not despise a miserable wretch who begs your mercy"— and then, in a meaningful voice, looking right at me, "Do not hold against him his earlier sins, buried in his bosom."

"All right, all right, I can take a hint," I said, moving to sit cross-legged near her. "You may as well teach me to play it."

She offered me the instrument, and I took it, the scooped belly resting in my lap, my left hand trying awkwardly to close around the broad neck. Cautiously, I sounded the open strings all four in a row. They were tuned in intervals of fourths and fifths.

She rested her hand on the neck of the lute, to still the vibrations from my striking them. I closed my other hand over hers on the neck of the lute and before I could stop myself I heard myself say, "If this were a romantic poem, now would be the moment when I'd take you in my arms and ravish you."

"Mmm," Jamila mused noncommittally, without moving toward or away from me. "Let me show you how to use the plectrum."

She held out her hand for the instrument.

She was still coaching me when Liliana came down from the roof much later. We'd not touched each other again, but it felt as if some private part of me was interweaving with some private part of her;

it was more erotic than a kiss would have been. It was unnerving to suddenly be so awake. Unnerving, and uncomfortable, as if I were betraying the woman I'd loved back in Britain. Would she be jealous of this? Had she ever been jealous? I was appalled that I couldn't remember. Jamila saw I was distressed about something and, without probing, turned her attention to Liliana.

"How can you see in the dark out there?" she asked.

"Everyone has torches with them. As men are wounded, they fall back and become torch bearers, and so there is more and more light for the ones who remain fighting. First it was exciting, then it was boring, and now I'm getting worried, because it's been going on for hours, and things are only getting worse."

Jamila grimaced. "Gregor didn't mean to get involved in the skirmishes, he just went out to retrieve Otto, but surely Otto is easy to find in a skirmish."

"Otto in a battle rage is not easy to outmuscle, even for Gregor," Liliana fretted.

I sat up a little. "But he might be easy to outsmart."

"Oh, not again." Jamila sighed. "Do you never learn?"

19

THE PROBLEM WAS NOT finding the fight, it was finding *which* fight, for there were scores of unending brawls forming a cloud of violence throughout Zara. I didn't know the layout of the city, but I noticed I was in a slight dip between two sections of higher ground. I was not the only one belatedly joining the fracas; just up ahead I saw the imposing vermilion-draped escort of the Doge of Venice, hurrying from the harborside, a trumpet heralding his arrival. I doubted Dandolo's presence would soothe anything, but he would probably lead me someplace central, so I followed the entourage.

Two hundred paces from our door, I found myself in a large, open area, important-looking stone buildings around it: the apse ends of two churches and the porch end of another, and to one side a long covered gallery. The square was lit nearly as bright as if it were midday, full of angry, shouting men, most of them with colored crosses on their tunics. I saw Otto almost at once, safely to one side. He had been wounded—how, I could not see, but both squires were kneeling over him. He craned his neck to watch the fighting, his back against a building to my left. The doge, up ahead, stopped at his guide's suggestion, and I nearly walked into his rear guard. I caught myself and stepped to the side, around the doge's entourage, so I could see what they were staring at.

I was astonished by what met my eyes. Astonished, and awed—here was Gregor of Mainz in his full rage and glory as the fighting animal he had been trained to be. I only realized that it was Gregor because an admiring crowd had stopped pummeling one another to form a ring around him and his attackers, and they were chanting his name.

A well-dressed man lay motionless just behind him, near the covered porch, with a lance disappearing into his eye, his face resting in a puddle of blood. His tunic had a green cross on it. Gregor stood in front of the body to protect it, and he was fighting off four Venetians all at once. They were stymied by his armor, especially the helmet. But they'd made their mark on him: there was blood near both ears, his surcoat had been torn off and lay on the ground in tatters around him; worse, the right sleeve of his chain-mail hauberk had been hacked through and his arm was hideously gouged. He had one assailant by the throat with that hand, a second by the throat with his left; a third had clambered onto his back and had wrapped one arm around Gregor's helmet; a fourth was grappling him around the waist. Others had already been fended off, and there were two more waiting to throw their weight on him as soon as they could find a place to do it.

His armor allowed little agility for simple street fighting. He was able, however, to slam the unprotected head of the Venetian he held with his left fist into the unprotected head of the Venetian he held with his right. They both slumped and went still; he dropped them to the stones and tried to grab his other two attackers at the same time, but the wound in his right arm was so bloody everything on that side was slick, and he could not get a fix on the man on his back. So with his left hand, Gregor grabbed the head of the man who had attached himself to his waist, pulled the man away from his own massive torso, and then yanked him in close again so that he broke his nose against Gregor's hauberk; Gregor pushed him away and then tried again to deal with the sailor perched on his back, who still had one arm clutched around the helmet and was slamming the heel of his free hand against it relentlessly. Gregor couldn't get a grip on him. Finally, in desperation, he reached up to his helmet and ripped it off. The attacker fell with it as it went flying off, and for a brief moment Gregor was unbesieged. He staggered to his knees, his bleeding face purple with exertion, his breathing so hard that his armored torso ballooned in size with each labored inhale.

Two more Venetians stepped up, and the mob, Venetian and Franks alike, screamed with excitement. But these two noticed something else and immediately darted back into the crowd, which suddenly turned almost like a school of fish.

Another Venetian across the open space had signaled them— with a lance. From such a close distance, on foot, the lance could not pierce armor, but it certainly could puncture Gregor's throat, which was now exposed and steaming with sweat in the cold, torchlit night. Gregor was too exhausted to notice he was about to be attacked again, and even his supporters were too caught up in the drama of the moment to be articulate enough to warn him—they shouted, but to his ears it was a roar of congratulation. He clutched his wounded sword arm and craned his head to the right to try to see the damage.

I sprinted into the middle of the circle and, bent over, to present myself as an unexpected obstacle. I and the Venetian, and the lance, became a gasping, grappling mass of tangled, confused extremities, and Gregor, alerted, ducked to safety in front of us. At once he was surrounded protectively by fellow knights, shamed out of their spectator state by a crazy little Briton.

The Venetian had fast reflexes, and before I could recover from what I'd done, he was on his feet and dragging me to my knees. I looked up, disoriented, the wind knocked out of me, as the Venetian released me, brought his fists together, and slammed them down straight onto my left collarbone. I heard myself shriek, and I blacked out from the pain.

20

SO OTTO FINALLY KILLED HIS MAN," was the first thing I remember hearing. It was Jamila's voice, but it was unusually conversational for her.

"His *men*, actually," Liliana's voice replied, in an equally gossipy tone. "Three of them. All Venetians who were ganging up on him."

"A hundred men died in that brawl," said Gregor's voice from slightly farther off, disapprovingly. "So far every casualty on this campaign has been of should-be allies."

I made a sound so they would know I was awake. The scene before me was incongruously domestic, oddly homey: the two women were chopping mallow root on the cutting table in the kitchen, while

Gregor stretched out on a mat staring at the ceiling near the fire, upon which strips of meat—*fresh meat*—roasted on a spit. A boiling pot of something hung from a chain over the flames too. Lamps, or rush lights, had been fastened all along the walls. I guessed it was night outside; it was very quiet. I was covered with woolen blankets, and when I tried to move, I discovered my left arm had been immobilized—the upper arm bound at a particular angle to my side, and the forearm held bent in a bandage tied around my neck.

"The little one's awake," Liliana said, popping a piece of the root into her mouth and sucking delicately on her fingers a moment. "Shall we give him some chicken stew?" She ran her tongue over her thumb one final time, which (with those lips of hers as backdrop) looked obscene. "I do like these seasonings," she told Jamila.

"Our cooking is underappreciated because the Franj eat so much pork," Jamila replied. "Pork has too much water in it, and lard is hard on human digestion, it should be reserved for torch fuel."

It was disorienting to hear such domestic chitchat, especially from these two women. I tried to look over more directly at them but could not quite turn myself that far. "The little one would love some chicken stew," I announced.

"You're awake," Jamila said. I could tell a rebuke was coming. "I must say, you did a brilliant job outsmarting Otto. That was *truly* clever. Keep up the good work."

"Be a little kinder, he's still weak." This was Liliana, who wiped her hands on her skirt and grabbed a small wooden bowl from under the cutting table. From the ladle in the pot, she served me a helping of something that smelled very good.

As I shifted uncomfortably trying to get the bowl to my mouth, Jamila turned to me. "Stop fidgeting. You have a broken collarbone. You may not move it from that position for a month."

"I can't move my left arm for a *month?*"

"Actually three," she said sympathetically. "There is dried mandrake for the pain, but it will make you sleepy."

I moved my neck back and forth. "Can I move my fingers?" I asked, panicked.

"Fingers and wrist," Jamila said. "That's all you need to practice the lute, at least beginners' tunes. That's about all you'll be doing this winter, so you're likely to get quite good at it. You'll have to hold it at an angle, but that will give you a distinctive style."

"There are worse ways to pass the time," I conceded.

"One of those being *listening* to you learn to play the lute." Liliana laughed. "You were lucky, with only your left side wounded. Gregor nearly lost his sword arm. Otto came out all right, although he got walloped pretty hard, but then, he had it coming. Jamila is a gifted healer; you wouldn't believe the concoctions she came up with from the dregs of the medical chest here."

Jamila made a casual, dismissive gesture. "Agrimony and yarrow," she said, as if their properties were common knowledge. "Feverfew for the bones. Fennel for the wound on Gregor's eye, luckily it flowers late here." She winked at me. "But you should know that, you were a nurse yourself once."

"Gregor would be dead by now without her," Liliana insisted, "and I'm not sure Otto would still be with us either. It's good we didn't throw her out! The surgeon had no idea what he was doing—Gregor was in *worse* shape after he attended to him."

"Really?" I said, eager for reassurance that Jamila was secure, even if she did take a little too much pleasure in humiliating me.

Gregor nodded from across the fire. "The wound got infected—"

"It was *poisoned*, sir," Jamila clarified, chopping. "So was Otto's. Somebody was fighting very dirty."

"I still have fever," Gregor said to me, as if embarrassed to admit it. "I'd have lost my arm, bled to death. I asked Conrad to hold a private mass in Jamila's honor—"

"I'm sure that means a lot to you," I said to her with a harsh laugh.

"Now Bishop Conrad thinks she's his mistress." Liliana said with a giggle.

"And I've taken an oath to protect her all the way to Egypt," Gregor continued—almost smugly, as if he had expected my heckling and knew this would quiet me. And then the most remarkable revelation of all: "And so has Otto."

This, indeed, caught me short. "Where *is* Otto?" I asked.

"Otto's on his feet already; he's a young buck and heals faster," Liliana said. "He's with the horses in the courtyard. Bored to tears now that the excitement's over."

"What did I miss, then?" I asked. The area around my left collarbone pulsated with pain. I took a deep breath and wished I hadn't.

"You saved Gregor's life, sounds like," Liliana said. "He'd stepped in to keep the body of some Flemish lord from being torn to bits and kept some other Flemish lord, Baldwin or something, from getting his head bashed in when he tried to intervene—"

"Baldwin?" I echoed. "Baldwin of *Flanders?* The *count?* Liliana, he's second in command of the entire army!"

"Well, he and the Flems were so grateful to Milord Gregor, they gave us, let's see . . ." She pointed to the inventory, piled against the far wall of the room. "Wine, beef, and chicken, and pork, all first-rate meat from the palace they took over. And some nice cooking knives, and extra blankets, and lamps and lamp oil, and wool and yarn and a standing loom, and they'll pay for new cloth and a new hauberk for Milord Gregor. Baldwin threw a *parade* for him this afternoon! They had to carry him on a litter because he's too weak to walk, and the litter was painted *gold!* And the German counts melted down trinkets they'd gotten in the spoils, and made a *medal* for him!"

"All that for protecting a Flemish corpse?" I said. I was distracted, my eyes on the piles of goods against the wall. I thought of all the bereft Zarans waiting to exit the gate. Jamila eyed me as I eyed the goods; she understood.

"No, for protecting *Baldwin*, but that was only part of it," Liliana continued, enjoying the chance to gossip. "Right after you went down, Dandolo and Baldwin demanded an end to the brawling. Gregor was about to vivisect the fellow who hurt you, but as soon as he heard Dandolo's order, he was the first to lay down his weapon and offer a hand in peace, so now he's even a favorite with the Venetians."

"But the army and the Venetians are still seething at each other," Gregor interjected glumly. "And I don't think it's likely to change. And now, even within the army, the lower ranks are enraged because all the plunder went to the barons. The knights and infantry got *nothing*. There's bad feeling everywhere."

"And everyone is excommunicated, I take it," I said, slurping at the stew.

"But most of them still don't *know* they are excommunicated," Gregor amended, still lying on his back. "You've been drugged on mandrake for days. You've missed a lot: Baldwin and the other leaders sent an embassy to the pope to ask forgiveness for the attack. The Venetians didn't send anyone, because they claim they did nothing wrong. And—thank God—Milord Boniface has sent a harbinger to announce he'll finally reappear in the next day or so and resume command."

"Now that the attack on Zara has happened without him," Jamila said. "Sir, I don't think he really had pressing business back at home. I think he merely wanted to avoid being excommunicated with the rest of the army. He can appear as the white knight and make all things well again."

Gregor raised his head off the bedroll, but only to make a gesture of disagreement. "I cannot believe such a thing of Milord Marquis. He's a pilgrim, and more than that, he is a knight. He's spent his life following the chivalric ethos. Such cynical strategizing would be anathema to him, especially in his role as a pilgrim."

"If you say so, sir," Jamila said, obviously completely unconvinced.

21

Valiant Marquis, Lord of Montferrat . . . I praise God for exalt-
ing me enough to find such a generous liege lord as you, who
turns me from a nobody into a valued knight.

—RAIMBAUT OF VAQUEIRAS,
      "The Epic Letter (to Marquis Boniface of Montferrat)"

BONIFACE, the handsome Marquis of Montferrat, did indeed appear within the week on his ship, the *San Giorgio*. An army-wide celebration was declared, with casks of
wines and piles of cakes distributed liberally; Dandolo the doge made
many public displays of respect toward him, which calmed the army
even as it irritated the Venetians. As soon as he was in residence
within the largest palace, Boniface very publicly summoned his favorite, his son-in-law, Gregor of Mainz, the man of the hour.

Jamila had become a tyrant about Gregor's healing properly. She
allowed him to eat less than he wanted to and drink only when he
was actually parched. He could not eat for three hours before sleeping and had to eat food she spiced according to how warm or cold
or wet or dry the day was. She would allow certain foods to be eaten
only in certain combinations and plied him with figs, which grew on
trees in "our" garden. Likewise, pomegranates, with which he had to
conclude each meal.

Gregor was still very weak, but he could now walk unassisted. He
wore his only undamaged tunic to meet his wife's father; it bulged

on the right sleeve, from the bandage beneath it. He was nervous and slightly overwhelmed: he was anxious to see Boniface, whom he admired deeply but who had abandoned him in Venice without an explanation. Further, his head was spinning from the relentless commentary he'd been subjected to: from myself (I wanted Boniface to return Zara to its inhabitants and push off at once for Egypt) and from Otto (who wanted all the soldiers to receive restitution from the siege)—and from Jamila, who repeated her theory that the marquis's absence during the siege had been calculated and urged Gregor to find out why.

Feast of St. John of Damascus, 4 December

I begin to doubt the wisdom of keeping such a chronicle as this (besides that my arm is so sore), for two reasons. The first is that there are so few opportunities to write the uplifting sentiments and developments that I had anticipated would be the main substance of the entries. The second is that I begin to harbor uncomfortable thoughts on certain topics and it might indeed be unwise for me to express them freely.

But to the matter:

My esteemed father-in-law met me in private, in the presence of only his guard Claudio. I was honored that Milord Boniface embraced me with such warmth. We made brief discourse as family should. Milord brought affectionate greetings from my wife, Marguerite (who I am so honored to have wedded, although truly I hardly know her, having married her at Milord Boniface's request in Venice, mere weeks before the campaign set sail). I offered greetings from Otto, who was once a page in the marquis's court. Milord Boniface insisted that I and my "lance" (this being the newest term for a knight's entourage) move into the palace compound immediately; a suite of rooms was already prepared for me. Milord personally poured a mug of warmed wine for me, and bade me sit on one of the many elegant Zaran settles lining the walls of the main hall.

Then Milord Marquis changed his tone, for he had grievous things to discourse upon. He began: "First I must apologize for departing so hastily in Venice. Personal business compelled me." I wanted to query him on that, but Milord Marquis leapt at once to even sterner matters and said to me, "I am delighted to hear of your recent glory, but I require you to explain your behavior regarding the siege of Zara."

In truth I had suspected he might query me on this and had spent no small amount of time contemplating how to answer. The Briton, my brother, and the Jewess had all expressed their views to me. They were not quite all in agreement with one another, but all of them spoke eloquently (or in Otto's case, loudly). Now, in the moment when it mattered, I found myself taken by confusion. The whir of all their voices in my head made it hard to hear my own thoughts. In my weakened state, I was rendered almost inarticulate, especially insofar as Milord Boniface had managed to ask the question without revealing his own feelings about the attack.

I began several times to respond to him and then hesitated, unsure if the words I spoke were truly my own. Finally, feeling very weak and foolish, I merely said, "It seemed to be more than a coincidence, that you disappeared as the decision was made to attack Zara, and then you reappeared just after the damage was done."

"Is my courage being impugned?" Milord Boniface asked, without rancor. "I, who introduced chivalry to Italy, who rescued heiresses in my youth with no thought of personal reward, who was as great a tournament champion as is my noble son-in-law? Is my courage being impugned . . . by one who would not even come out of his tent to fight?"

"It is not about your courage, milord, it is about your absence," I corrected. "It seemed deliberate. Nobody would question your willingness to go into battle if the battle was the right one. So some wondered if your absence meant this battle was not the right one."

Milord Boniface seemed amazed at this. "Is that why you attempted to interfere as you did, with that villainous Simon of Montfort?

You thought my absence meant I disapproved of the attack? Or was ashamed by the need of it? Were you trying to act on my behalf?" But then the marquis laughed bitterly and said, "That is ironic."

"Are you saying you approved of the attack?" I asked, shocked.

"Lad, what choice was there?" Milord Boniface said. "We were shamefully in debt to Dandolo, and entirely dependent on his fleet. If we had not agreed to conquer Zara, the campaign would have dissolved. It was regrettable, but there was no way around it. I realize how difficult it was for the men, and especially for someone like you."

I was flooded with confusion and even a sense of betrayal when I heard this, but I could not have expressed it in words. I kept my voice calm and said, "But, milord, if you knew how difficult it was for us, how could you not be here to lead us? How can you abandon your followers in a crisis that tries their souls as well as their lives? I spent half my time on the voyage explaining why you weren't with us, struggling to find a way that would not make you sound like a coward or a hypocrite." (In truth, this last claim is misleading, for it was only the Briton and the Jewess to whom I tried to explain these things. Nobody else seemed much concerned.)

Milord Boniface made an unhappy face. "You are right, of course," he said. "You are absolutely right, and I am sorry for it. But my absence at that moment was unavoidable."

"Then we should have waited until you were no longer absent, milord," I said. "Once we were on the shores of Zara, we should have waited until you arrived. If you'd shown yourself to your men and reassured us this was the right thing to do, Simon of Montfort would never have had a chance to intervene, and we would have fought with you leading every charge."

To which Milord Boniface answered: "And then I too would be excommunicated, and what sort of example would I make for the rest of the campaign?" Truly I was shocked to hear him say this, but Milord Boniface, not noticing my shock, elaborated: "'Come, my fellow sinners, I am the chief sinner, do as I do!' No, lad, that would never do.

As it stands now, the army has a leader still in good graces with His Holiness, a leader who can serve as a shining example for the much more important task ahead of us, which is reclaiming the Holy Land."

I thought then of Jamila, who had claimed all along that this was the explanation for Milord Boniface's absence. I had defended him against her words, which I considered faithless cynicism. I was stunned to learn not only that she was correct but that Milord Boniface himself so openly admitted it. I said: "So your absence was deliberate."

Boniface looked exasperated. "Of course it was deliberate. For the good of the army and its morale—for you—it had to be."

I felt grieved now toward him whom I have never before been grieved by. "So you had no pressing business at home. That was a lie. Even now, today, when you greeted me moments ago in this room, you were lying to me, milord."

To which Boniface answered, in a peaceful voice, "No, son, I really did have urgent business to attend to, which you will hear more of soon. Happily, I was able to do it while avoiding the siege of Zara. And now I must request that you, as one of my dearest, assist me in making the best use of all that has happened since. May I discuss with you the project by which I propose we do that, or do you need time to wallow in the realization that prayers alone can't get us to Jerusalem?"

I truly did not know what to say. Milord Boniface is my father by marriage, the man who trained me to knighthood, the man whose courtly exploits I memorized at a young age and carried within me as a model for my own behavior. And now he is telling me, casually, that he is just as capable of deceitful stratagem as any other lord. Worse than that, that he will employ stratagem even in his relationship with the Holy Father! What does this say of me, if I have been using him as my model?

He was waiting for an answer to his question. Finally, because I could not think clearly to say anything else, I said, "I am just a knight, milord."

"You're more than a knight, you are a popular hero," Milord

Boniface corrected me, with familiar affection, as if this were the sort of conversation we engaged in all the time. He did not realize that, from my perspective, we had never had any conversation like this. "And deservedly so. That means, in the onerous process of keeping this army functional, you are a useful game piece. May I tell you how I want to play that piece?"

Myself: "Milord, I'm only a soldier—"

Milord Boniface: "—whom other soldiers think of as their model. That is a helpful detail. May I tell you how I want to employ it?"

I was confused that he, my lord and father, sought my permission to proceed. I said, "You may tell me whatever you like, milord."

"Are we in accord?" Milord Boniface pressed me. "Do we agree both that you are favored by the men and that I may use you accordingly?"

I was somewhat unnerved by Milord Boniface's behavior in seeking my permission. Normally when I am unnerved, and craving counsel, I try to imagine what Milord Boniface would say if he were there. But now he was the cause of my need for counsel. When I turned inward, I found the loudest voice therein was my brother Otto's. And so I spoke as Otto might have counseled: "If you want the soldiers' regard for me to be helpful to you, milord, they must see that you will let me act in their interest."

Milord Boniface nodded. "An excellent point. How might we do that, lad?"

I said, "The men feel cheated by the Venetians taking all the spoils—"

Milord Boniface: "That is because we owe the Venetians so much money."

Myself: "I know that, milord, but it is hard to do a soldier's duty and not receive a soldier's recompense. If I might convince you to grant them something, even if it is a token reward or a mere gesture of respect—"

Milord Boniface: "Of course. I'll take it up with Baldwin this evening."

I was surprised by how easy that had been, considering the lethal brawls that had broken out over this very issue. "Is it presumptuous of me to ask your word on that, milord? Given the woes the campaign has faced on this matter?"

"It is my pleasure, lad." Milord Boniface smiled at me. "I swear on the head of St. John. And I'll make sure they all know it was at your insistence. Any other suggestions on shoring up your popularity?"

Because of the great confusion that came upon me during this interview, I was now hesitant to speak to milord of certain things, particularly matters involving the Briton and the Jewess. So I decided to keep my own counsel on those things for now, and instead, I said: "I am deeply grateful that you would restore me to your entourage, but I think, milord, that I should not move into this compound with you. At least, not at the moment. The perception of me within the ranks may alter in a way that isn't useful to you. As was true when we first set out, I should be seen as belonging with the men—not as belonging with you while merely condescending to speak to the men."

Milord Boniface exclaimed, "That is astute, lad! But are you willing to continue to make such a sacrifice? To turn down a place at your leader's side and live in squalid merchants' quarters for the long-term good of the campaign?"

Myself: "For now, milord."

Milord Boniface: "Do you have acceptable lodgings, at least?"

Myself: "Yes, milord."

Milord Boniface: "If you want for anything, send word and I'll provide it." He grimaced, happily and thoughtfully. "Between this and your already legendary behavior the night of the fight, you will be considered a veritable patron saint of the army. And once we've convinced the men, Gregor, I have an extraordinary project arising that will make excellent use of you." He smiled a paternal smile at me. "Surely this is why God created you. You will keep my army whole and happy."

22

MOST EXCELLENT FELLOW!" Otto said with satisfaction when Gregor finished telling us about his interview with Boniface. "It's a pity not to move into the palace, but I'm proud to have you as a brother. I'm going to brag about you."

"Nothing's done yet, Otto," Gregor warned. "And it may not involve material reward, it may be something as simple as a formal thank-you."

By the following evening, a rumor had spread around the camp that Gregor of Mainz had stood up to Marquis Boniface, demanding that the knights, sergeants, and infantry be rewarded for their efforts in taking Zara. The rumor grew, and over supper the next day Otto and the squires were comparing claims of Gregor grabbing Boniface around the throat and shaking him or swearing on the spirit of St. George that he would not set foot from Zara until the men had been rewarded.

Gregor was agog. "It was nothing like that! How do such rumors get started?"

"I bragged about you to a few comrades," Otto admitted offhandedly.

Liliana rolled her eyes and held out a trencher with chicken on it, but Gregor was too distracted to notice it. She handed it to Otto, who took it.

"Otto, you shouldn't have mentioned anything," Gregor said crossly. "We don't really know what he's willing to do."

Otto munched down heartily on a thigh. "I said nothing at all like the crazy stories that were circulating later in the day!" he protested, chewing. "I only told them *exactly* what you told me."

"Including my emphasis that he might not have meant material reward?" Gregor demanded. "Do you realize how dangerous it is to raise false expectations?"

"I didn't say he promised anything specific!" Otto insisted.

"Rumors have a way of expanding on their own, sir," Jamila said and set a second trencher between herself and me. She placed a biscuit in front of Gregor.

"Well, I don't see how the harm's done," Otto countered, taking another bite. "The worst that can happen is that Boniface will be pressured into coughing up *something*."

"And what if he can't do that, Otto?" Gregor demanded, as if he were reviewing a logic exercise with a lazy pupil.

"Eat something, milord," Liliana urged and handed another trencher with a whole chicken on it to him. Distractedly, he put it down in front of himself.

Otto slapped Gregor on his good arm. "Of course he can do it, Brother, he's a *marquis*! I'll bet you my Cologne sword, we're finally going to get some gold!"

"Your Cologne sword is your *only* sword," Gregor said, in a tone suggesting Otto often made this wager illadvisedly.

"Or silver at least," Otto continued. "Or a worst-case scenario—he can't give us any money now, so he has to win back our respect by being extra-generous to us when we get to the Holy Land. We benefit now, or we benefit later. Either way, nothing bad can come from this."

Jamila and I exchanged glances over the low table. She gave me a warning look.

OVER THE NEXT FEW DAYS, rumors of Gregor's insubordinate behavior toward Boniface exploded in volume and intensity. I designed these rumors to be blown out of proportion with each telling. Eventually it was reported that if the entire Frankish army presented itself in the open-air forum three days hence, Boniface would appear and give each soldier there a piece of silver, from his own hand, to thank them for taking Zara. Boniface, it was emphasized, had *only* agreed to do this because the great Gregor of Mainz had forced him to, and Gregor of Mainz—everyone knew—had staked his reputation on getting satisfaction from Boniface on behalf of the men.

Jamila herded me into a corner while Liliana was washing up from dinner; the rest of them were out with the horses, since the afternoon was clear and mild. Astonishingly, *only* Jamila had figured out I was behind all of the rumors. "Have you thought through what you're doing?" she demanded.

"Yes."

"Would you please explain yourself?"

"No," I said. "You can't affect the outcome anyhow, so why do you care?"

"Human curiosity. Not just about the outcome but about how your mind works."

I grinned, flattered that she was paying attention to me. But I told her nothing. If she disapproved, she might do something to sabotage me, and I couldn't risk that.

"I'll smash the lute. And all the instruments you brought from France."

"That's hitting below the belt," I cried. She gave me a look: she meant it. "All right," I said peevishly, still flattered that she was paying attention. "It's just this. I don't know what Boniface's 'project' is, but I'm sure it's not benign, so Gregor shouldn't be a part of it. So he must be made unuseful to Boniface. He must lose his reputation."

She gave me a searching look. But there was something about one corner of her mouth that suggested she approved of the idea. "The last time you played with Gregor's reputation, Zara was sacked. If you continue, you may bring all Christendom to its knees."

"Does the Jewess have an objection to that?" I asked smartly.

"Not especially," she admitted, after the briefest pause.

THE WINTER SO FAR had been damp but very mild—nobody needed to wear cloaks when the sun was out. But the day of the supposed hand-out, the weather suddenly fell chill. The open-air forum was not large enough, so men were standing, crowded, sitting on one another's shoulders, leaning out windows of the surrounding buildings. They didn't mind the press; they were a rowdy, cheerful, eager throng. They knew they would be walking away from the place with money in their fists. And they knew their beloved Gregor of Mainz was the clever fellow who'd pressured Boniface to give it to them.

Boniface of Montferrat—Fazio to his friends, marquis to his subjects, the Englishman to confused would-be assassins—did not, of course, appear. He'd heard the rumors; everybody had. He was not stupid enough to show up before thousands of armed soldiers who believed they were getting something he could not give them. I'm sure he'd spent the last few days trying to find a way out of this fix. There wasn't one. That's the beauty of a simple plan.

An hour went by. Another. I studied the limestone paving stones that had been quarried from inland mountains, and passed the time by counting seashells trapped there from the days of Noah and the flood. The men were called to prayers but didn't go. The mood shifted, grew listless, then agitated. Boniface knew just how long to wait before sending a runner to the square to announce that he was laid up with fever but would welcome one man, and one man only—Gregor of Mainz—to his bedside to discuss the situation. Gregor, his bandaged right arm bulging slightly out the side of his surcoat, was sent off with hearty buffeting of his good shoulder and cries along the lines of "Give him a piece of your mind, German!" or "Don't let us down now, Gregor!"

Otto and I watched him walk down the thoroughfare with Boniface's page boy.

Otto looked at me narrowly, dawning comprehension on his face. "We're not getting any recompense, are we?" he said.

"Of course not," I said.

And then it hit him:

"Did you do this?" he demanded.

I nodded.

"Why?"

"I don't like to give away the ending," I said with an apologetic smile.

Feast of St. Daniel, 11 December

I record the following conference as a private penance. I am grieved by the marquis but far more grieved at myself, for I have failed everyone.

I was let into Milord Marquis's residential palace, where the marquis, in perfect health, was waiting for me beside a roaring fire. This time there were no embraces or familiar niceties, and Milord Boniface told me frankly that we are both in a severe bind because of the rumor. A rumor that is my fault. It began with me speaking too freely and boastfully to the infantry, and it will destroy us both unless we together think of what to say so that the men will not perceive themselves as being cheated.

I know that it was my fault, but still I thought (and think) the best way to keep the men from feeling cheated was to make sure that they are not, in fact, cheated. So I said: "You ought to give them something, milord. You gave your word to do so."

Milord Boniface: "What can I do at this point? They're expecting something material, and I cannot pay ten thousand men out of my own coffers."

Myself: "Do something, milord, I beg you, or you'll make liars of us both."

   Milord Boniface: "They want money, I have no money. Anything
else I do, no matter how much I humble or extend myself, will not
satisfy them now, so I will not degrade myself by trying."

   Myself: "So you will do nothing."

   Milord Boniface: "Gregor, there is nothing I can do. What can you
do? How may we turn this to our advantage, so that we do not upset
the men?"

   There was a very awkward pause, for I knew that what I must next
say was not an answer to his question. Finally I said: "Forgive me for
saying so, milord, but you have misled me. I have in turn misled the
men. I am responsible for the rumors, that is true. I allowed the men to
think that they would be thanked as they deserved. If you will not even
thank them, then I have surely failed them, and I shall have to tell them
so directly."

I'D ANTICIPATED Gregor would fall on his own figurative sword.
Boniface—as I'd anticipated—did not object to his intention. And
when Gregor returned to the broad open square, to tell thousands of
his admirers that he could not secure for them what they all believed
him capable of, he was booed and even cursed. As I'd anticipated.

   Boniface remained snug in his palace, a thousand paces away.
Yes, it was terribly sad to lose such a convenient pawn, but not nearly
as sad as losing one's own reputation. He understood the peculiar
mechanism of the body politic: although he was the one failing to
reward them, they would be enraged at Gregor, not at him. He had
merely disappointed them, as leaders always disappoint their people.
Gregor, however, had betrayed them, by falling from a pedestal he
hardly knew the height of. This had been my intention all along, and
I do not apologize for it. In fact, I recommend it. If you meet a good
man and see him getting pulled into politics, do him a favor and ruin
his reputation early on.

Gregor, to his credit and to my dismay, immediately set about to reclaim the army's confidence in him, at least as a soldier. He was good at this. He was still battered and bruised and could hardly lift his sword arm, but he convinced a group of fellow German knights to join him for training exercises for the horses outside the city walls; then, with the mild December weather cooperating, he organized them in a mini-tourney against some Flemish soldiers, although he wasn't well enough to participate yet himself. The rank and file would never forget (I hoped) that he had fallen off their pedestal, and was merely human, and could not be expected to influence the leadership—but they were grudgingly impressed by his relentless attempts to regain their confidence.

Boniface obviously heard all this through intelligence. He must have realized, with guarded relief, that Gregor would remain a popular hero. Some of his minions tried to dissuade him from planning to use that popular hero as a strategic tool for his great "project," but he was not to be dissuaded. Yet.

23

AS THE YEAR OF our Lord 1202 gave way to the year of our Lord 1203, our household began to coalesce into a tribe. Gregor, when not throwing himself into martial exercises and otherwise reestablishing his role among his fellow knights, found himself the unlikely father figure of an unlikely menagerie.

Otto had an amazing knack for overextending himself during training, and his endless reliance on Jamila's ministrations warmed the coolest of the relationships between us all. Meanwhile, the rest of us got on remarkably well (that is, once I'd accepted the fact that nobody was traveling to Egypt, or anywhere else, until spring). I spent a lot of time out of the house during those weeks, on matters I would not discuss, but while at home, I felt increasingly *at home*. I taught the Richardim how to *play* chess, since they had between them already carved two full sets of pieces; with Otto I attempted scintillating moral debate, which invariably devolved into an unequal wrestling match (my arm being in a sling, and he outweighing me by several stone), at the conclusion of which Otto always considered us the best of friends; the women continued to bond in that peculiar way women do, attending to most of the domestic concerns, weaving and spinning while chitchatting for hours on topics I truly thought each of them too intelligent to bother with; Jamila and I would discuss worthier matters, such as poetry or the tension between guilt and vengeance—and we would play music together every day, and almost flirt, but never quite. I was an apt pupil of her musical style, and I loved the way she looked at me when I was playing well.

Jamila had begun to practice some small bits of her native customs, which disturbed the pilgrims in the house a great deal until she translated her incantations into the lingua franca and they were rendered so inoffensive as to be downright dull: "Blessed are You, Lord our God, King of the Universe, who weighs down my eyes with sleep, and my eyelids with slumber. May it be Your will, Lord my God and God of my fathers, that I lay me down in peace and rise up in peace."

The younger Richard, upon hearing this, eyed her warily and then demanded, "What happened to the part about eating Christian babies?"

Gregor was lord of the manor, the one for whom we played music, with whom we played chess, and against whom we played one another for affection. There was something about that man—despite his humorlessness and occasional dithering—that made people want to know he loved them, or at least approved of them.

But more important than such domestic matters: as the year of

our Lord 1202 gave way to the year of our Lord 1203, Marquis Boniface of Montferrat was visited, with great fanfare, by envoys from the
court of his ally and kinsman Philip of Swabia, King of Germany and
destined Holy Roman Emperor.

Gregor knew King Philip, of course. He had never been a member of Philip's court, but as squire to Boniface he had spent much
time there in his youth. But he and Boniface had grown cool with
each other since the unfortunate Affair of the Rumors, and he assumed he would not be among the elite circle called to meet His
Majesty's envoys.

He was astonished to learn that he was wrong.

Feast of St. Genevieve, 3 January A.D. 1203

*It is difficult for me to believe that I am capable of expressing even
greater astonishment each time I open this scroll to write something
new upon it, but my amazement increases tenfold with each passing
development of this campaign.*

*I was yesterday summoned to the great palace that is Dandolo of
Venice's for the winter and ushered into a small private room where
Milord Boniface awaited me and embraced me as warmly as ever he did
before we departed Venice. Milord Boniface began the conversation by
calling me "son" many times over. "The messengers from the German
court, in addition to their formal embassy, brought a private message
for our family, son," Milord Boniface said. "I am to be a grandfather
this coming spring."*

Myself: "Congratulations, milord. This is not your first, is it?"

Milord Boniface: "No, son. But I believe it's yours."

*I found myself unable to breathe for a moment. Milord Boniface
smiled and continued: "We hear that Marguerite is doing well. She is
dividing her time between her mother's home and yours. I hope that
this happy family news will induce you to heal the rift between us. Of
course I would not call it a rift." He corrected himself with an eager-*

ness that is not his usual comportment. "At worst a bump. Would you agree, son?"

I nodded without speaking, for I was still stunned by the weirdness of impending fatherhood, especially because I hardly know the mother. To be honest—and I do penance for this regularly—I have now lain with Liliana more often than with my own wife, and I admit I have more of a thought for random women around the camp than I do for my own bride. (I know also, for she confessed this, that Marguerite's heart is bound up with another, of whom I am not jealous. All in all, it is a strange business and in no way matches my childhood reveries of how parents are made.)

Finally, I asked, "Thank you for this news. Is that the only reason I've been summoned here?"

Milord Boniface: "No, no, my son. To show that you are welcome back to the heart of things, I wanted you to be present for the historic meeting that is about to take place in the next room."

I confess I was pleasantly surprised by this and put aside my confused thoughts about parentage for the moment. "Indeed?"

"Indeed." Milord Marquis gave me a meaningful smile. "We have dynastic ties now, Gregor. I will respect that if you will."

I found this comment vaguely unsettling without quite knowing why. (Later the Briton insisted I found it unsettling because I intuited it was a threat, but I do not believe that.) Without comment, I followed Milord Boniface into the doge's hall. I believe I may have gasped aloud when I entered, for nothing could have prepared me for this gathering. There are things about it I will not even write here.

There were only a handful of men present: Milord Dandolo with his attendants and a musician strumming quietly in a corner, but there is nothing remarkable about this, for Milord Dandolo is known to like musicians and keeps a great assortment and has them playing near him all the time; also present were Boniface's immediate subordinates, such as the honorable Count Baldwin of Flanders, et cetera; and present too were the German envoys. No other men were there, not even the bishops, who would normally be present for confidential meetings. I soon understood why they had been excluded.

The embassy addressed itself primarily to Milord Dandolo, and so I guessed that everyone else in this room had already been told about the matter.

"Milords," began the elder German envoy, after polite introductions all around. "Do you know the name of Prince Alexios, rightful heir to the throne of Byzantium?"

Milord Dandolo: "Yes."

Milord Boniface and the German envoy looked at me, and I realized I was expected to speak, which amazed me, as I was so severely outranked by all in the room. I said: "The name is familiar, milords," for this was true, but I could not recall why.

The German envoy began a recitation: "The Byzantine Empire lies between here and the land of the infidels."

"Not directly between," Milord Dandolo corrected. "Considering we are traveling by water, one must hardly describe it as being 'en route.'"

German envoy: "It is a Christian nation, although lamentably it does not follow the Church in Rome, but—"

Dandolo: "I do know a bit about the Byzantine Empire, sir, since it held Venice in thrall for centuries. It puts your own pseudo-Roman imperial conglomerate to shame. Its capital, Constantinople, has no equal in all Christendom, and certainly not in your so-called Holy Roman Empire."

The envoy ignored the interruption, for I believe he had not expected to be heckled. "Byzantium's emperor, or basileus, is one Isaac Angelos, who some eight years ago was blinded by his brother, a loathsome usurper, and thrown into prison. Isaac's son Prince Alexios was imprisoned with him. But a year ago, through the most extraordinary bravery and valor, this Prince Alexios escaped from Constantinople and made his way to Germany, to join his sister Irene. She is married to Philip of Swabia, King of Germany."

I must add here a note of my own: Philip of Swabia is more than

King of Germany and claimant to the throne of Holy Roman
Emperor. Far more important to the matter here, he is close kinsman to
my esteemed father-in-law, the Marquis of Montferrat. I understand now
that this is why Milord Boniface had not sailed with us to Zara. He was
not merely avoiding excommunication—his "urgent business" must have
been with Prince Alexios! Whatever we were about to hear had been part
of Milord Boniface's plans from before we even departed Venice.

"We all know about the boy Alexios," said Milord Baldwin, looking
tense. "He has petitioned the Holy Father on at least two occasions,
asking Innocent to step in and restore him by holy decree to the Byzantine throne. This is quite inappropriate, as Constantinople—indeed, all
of Byzantium—is lamentably heretical, and not under the pope's sway,
being the kind of Christians called in the East Orthodox."

German envoy: "Indeed. Prince Alexios realizes this. He also realizes you are an army requiring riches to fulfill your destiny. He is the
rightful monarch of a very rich empire . . . but he requires an army to
fulfill his own destiny."

I believe Baldwin and the other counts had anticipated this, for
they merely grimaced; Dandolo looked as astonished as I felt myself.
I opened my mouth, but Milord Boniface's hand gripped hard on my
arm, and I contained myself. I felt as if suddenly we were in some
preposterous goliard's tale.

The German envoy had a rehearsed speech to continue: "It is a
logical, profitable, and rightful equation, my lords: help the prince to
attain what pleases God, and he will help you to attain what pleases
God in turn. Not only the money and manpower to pay your debts and
continue on to the Holy Land but something of even deeper satisfaction
to the Holy Father in Rome."

Count Baldwin was displeased and said: "As I have already said
to the marquis, I fail to see how going off our course again, to sack yet
another Christian city, could possibly be pleasing to the Holy Father."

"It would not be a sack," the envoy said. "And it would return
Constantinople—indeed, all of Byzantium—to the pope's bosom. All of

Christendom would be reunited under the Church of Rome. You will
find there is almost nothing more pleasing to the pope than this prospect. And on a more practical level, Prince Alexios offers two hundred
thousand silver marks for your assistance, and far more beyond that. I
have an official proposal with everything he will provide, if you will only
allow him to provide it, by helping him to his throne."

The counts had no reaction to this extraordinary sum, but Milord
Dandolo voiced a strange sound. Boniface signaled to the envoy, who
offered the letter to one of Milord Dandolo's guards, who quietly read it
aloud. It was clear that all the French counts were already familiar with
its contents. None of them looked pleased about it.

As Dandolo listened to the letter, Milord Marquis turned to me, his
face extremely solemn, and said: "Gregor, my son, this is your opportunity to have your voice heard by your superiors. In light of the damage
done by your gossip when I first arrived here, you must confine your
comments to this room. But I welcome you to speak frankly. What is
your response to this offer?"

I was astonished to be asked this, and even more astonished that
all the barons were waiting to hear my answer. As with the efforts of
Simon of Montfort, I felt as if I were being polled for policy, which is
not my calling. As if my esteemed father-in-law could read my very
thoughts, he said in a soothing voice, "I am not giving you the burden
of deciding what to do, I ask only for your immediate and personal
response."

I began: "I consider all detours repellent, milord—" Whereupon
Milord Dandolo, hearing my voice, signaled his guard to stop reading
the letter so that he too could listen to me. I was now even more intimidated, and in truth I stammered a moment, then continued: "Because
of the diversion here to Zara, we are now the only pilgrim army in
history to have been excommunicated by the very pope in whose name
we set out. Most of my fellow soldiers don't know that, and I will not
tell them, because telling them would only lead to further rioting, which
would divide the army even more."

Boniface said: "The army is divided over money, Gregor. If we accept this offer, money will no longer be an issue."

I said: "It hurt my soul to contemplate attacking Christians when the issue of Zara first arose. I cannot bring myself to contemplate it again."

"Nor should you," Boniface said soothingly. "It need never be a real attack, except against the Varangians, the Usurper's mercenary guards. It is most emphatically not an attack against the city or its citizens, as Zara was. This has nothing to do with the excellent people of the city. Constantinople has endured enough regime changes to be blasé about them—and its people do not like the Usurper. We will be engaging in a show of arms against a single man, who has sinned against his brother and his lord—a man who has wronged all the people of his empire. You, as a Christian knight, would be hard-pressed to find a more perfect villain. Even if there were no compensation, you should want to undertake this because it is right action. A loyal son would oust the tyrant who attacked his father. He wants our aid. How can such duty be repellent to you?"

Myself: "Because it is not what I have sworn to do for the pope. There may be other worthy causes to attend to, but our vows to the Holy Father must come first."

Milord Boniface: "Of course they must. So we must do whatever we can to fulfill them. We are presently unable to fulfill them. If we do this, we can fulfill them."

There followed a moment of silence, as I thought about this, and my esteemed superiors watched me thinking about it. This made me uneasy. It was odd that a group of counts should so care what one mere knight was thinking.

At last, I said: "The pope did not approve of attacking Zara, even though that was a necessity too. Will he approve of this?"

Milord Boniface: "He has not forbidden it."

I said: "Milord, has he been asked? The bishops are excluded from this meeting. That suggests this is being decided outside the knowledge of the Church."

Milord Boniface: "His Holiness has been alerted to it."

Milord Baldwin coughed softly, as if prompting a child to speak.

Milord Boniface: "And if His Holiness forbids it, obviously, we must not go. Given he does not forbid it, what is your response? Again, this is your one chance to speak openly on the matter, and I will ask you to stand by whatever you say."

Myself: "Milord, I must tell you frankly, I do not like it, and I hope that you do not elect to do it. If the decision is yet to be made, I beg you to reject the offer."

Milord Boniface: "But if we do accept it? Consider your witnesses. Whatever you say now, you will be held to account by every leader of this army."

I wished dearly then that I could have asked the Briton's counsel. Every voice that had opined to me, about anything, in the last three months now echoed round my head so loudly it made me dizzy. But finally, the voice I heeded was the one that been branded into me longest ago.

So: "Milord, I am soldier," I said at last. "I will obey my commander. If you decide we must go, then we go."

Milord Boniface looked relieved, and pleased. "You give me your word of honor?"

Myself: "I do, as long as His Holiness does not forbid it. I will not disobey a direct order from the pope."

Milord Boniface smiled. "Thank you, my son," he said. "I am sure you will not have to." He gave Baldwin a meaningful look. Milord Baldwin grimaced thoughtfully in response, and suddenly I realized that all of this had been as a chess move: Milord Boniface was demonstrating to Milord Baldwin that even Gregor of Mainz could be brought to heel . . . and that, by extension, the entire rank and file could be too. For although my standing among the men is not what it was before the Affair of the Rumors, many still seem to look to me for inspiration.

"This means it is possible, milord," said Baldwin, as if all of these unspoken understandings had been spoken. "Its being possible doesn't mean it is right."

"If we don't accept the offer, we won't get to Jerusalem," Boniface said. I think these two lords had already spent time arguing about this. "We must get to Jerusalem. We must make the best of a bad situation." He stood and paced the palace room, a little agitated. "The men will not understand that on their own. We must, all of us, help them to understand it. Make it palatable. It will not be well-received. They'll think it is some new plot of the Venetians—"

And here, Milord Dandolo the doge interrupted him to say:"Which it certainly is not. I have not even agreed to it yet."

The leaders looked at each other, surprised.

Milord Boniface: "I assumed you would be a willing partner."

Dandolo: "Why? I've spent most of my life healing trade relations between Venice and Byzantium."

Milord Boniface: "But surely you hate this usurper. He's been horrible to the Venetians. In 'ninety-five he encouraged Pisans to attack Venetians. He taxes Venetian goods unfairly—"

Dandolo: "I know these things. I do not like the man. But there are thousands of Venetians living within Constantinople; they'd be in danger if this coup you are proposing proves unpopular; so would all of our trading contracts. Do not assume I am with you."

There was an awkward pause.

Milord Boniface: "What might entice you to be with us?"

Dandolo's answer was so quick that I knew he had been working this out since the moment he understood where the conversation was leading. "First we must negotiate exactly how to evaluate the payment, for a mark of silver is worth four times a Byzantine hyperpyra. We cannot be rewarded with hyperpyra, it must be pure silver."

"Understood," said the German envoy.

"More important," continued Dandolo, "we would need to make it absolutely clear—to our own men, as much as to the city—that we had no argument with the city, but only with its ruler. Alexios must be welcomed, his return and accession must be seen as good for the city. They are wild for regicide in Byzantium; if he is installed by force, as a new tyrant, he will not last the afternoon, and then he will never be able to pay us what he's promised and all trading enterprises will be imperiled. It must be handled in such a manner that the citizens think of us as their deliverers, not their conquerors."

I felt a warmth within me when I heard that. I said, "I like that well, milord. If that were our mission, it would be not only my duty to see it through but my pleasure. And I will willingly tell my fellow soldiers so."

Milord Boniface, truly relieved now, sat down beside me again and grasped my shoulder with affection. "Thank you, my son. In fact, in anticipation of your cooperation, I have already arranged a token of my gratitude."

Myself: "I don't need to be bribed to do my duty, milord."

Milord Boniface: "Of course you don't. But don't deprive me of the pleasure of indulging you. If I may proceed as we discussed, Dandolo?"

A look of comprehension slid across Dandolo's wrinkled face. "So it is for this you asked my intercession? If I had known to bribe Gregor thus myself—"

Milord Boniface: "It is not a bribe!"

"Of course it's not," Dandolo said, but I think he was sarcastic. "It's merely an indulgence. Pray then, milord, be indulgent now and deliver it to him."

Milord Boniface took a moment to recover from Milord Dandolo's rudeness and then said to me. "Gregor, your friend is free."

I was perplexed, so he repeated it with emphasis: "Your friend. With the Doge's intercession, Barzizza's claim on the princess has been revoked."

I felt as if I had inhaled something much larger than my lungs. Boniface smiled compassionately. Suddenly I noticed the musician had stopped playing.

Boniface said: "Don't worry, Gregor, you are not in danger for having taken her, nor for hiding her. Bishop Conrad told me about her. I admit I'm hurt you didn't confide in me directly, but never mind, I am your wife's father after all. The matter is settled. Your mistress is free from Barzizza and out of danger."

* * *

"WAIT, WAIT, WAIT, who are the *Greeks?*" Otto asked. "I thought we were talking about the *Byzantines*."

It was a rare sunny afternoon, incredibly mild for January, and the door up to the kitchen was open to let in light and air. We were all resting after the midday meal—except for Gregor, who had dined with the German envoys. Jamila and Liliana were cleaning up the kitchen area; the squires were polishing the silver statues in Gregor's travel altar; Otto was mending something on his leather training armor; I was lying back against my rolled-up bed mat and practicing the lute. My arm was still in a sling; I used my fingers instead of a plectrum, but I was pretty good for less than two months at it. Good enough to be hired as an occasional musician by Boniface's steward, in fact—and, of course, to play in the palace of the doge.

"Greeks, Byzantines, Constantinopolitans—all the same," Jamila repeated.

"Are you sure? Maybe Boniface wants us to attack the Greeks but he's trying to trick us into *thinking* they're the Byzantines. It's the sort of thing he would do," said Otto.

"It is common parlance to say Greeks or Byzantines to mean the same people," Jamila explained yet again.

"So we are going to Greece?" I asked, strumming a Greek-sounding chord.

"No, we're going to Constantinople, which is the capital of Byzantium."

"Which is full of *Greeks?*" I said with impish incredulity.

"That's what we *call* them," Otto said, suddenly an expert.

"They consider that a slur, by the way," Jamila said, wrapping the kitchen knives and setting them aside. "Although I don't see why it would be an insult, to be called after the second greatest civilization of the ancient world."

"Second greatest to whom?" I asked.

"The Romans, of course," said Otto.

"*No*," the Jewess said with a superior smile and began to hum a tune we all recognized as the melody she used to sing the Song of Songs.

"Ah, her secret bigotry!" I announced and strummed a harmonizing flourish on the lute. "And what do they—the Greek-Byzantine-Constantpissers—call *us* then?"

"From what I remember of my childhood there, you don't want to know what they call Westerners," said Jamila. "They don't like you very much."

"It hardly matters what they call us," Liliana said. "We call ourselves so many things already, I can't keep track if we're talking about ourselves or someone else. We're pilgrims, soldiers, crusaders, people of the cross, sometimes we're the army or the fleet. But we're also French, Franks, and Latins, despite the fact that nobody in this house is any of those things, and almost half the army is actually Flemish!"

"I think we're French and Frank—and pilgrims and soldiers—to set us apart from the *Venetians*," Otto said from where he sat working by an open window. "We, together *with* the Venetians, are the Latins, to set us apart from the Greeks and the Saracens."

"Who are actually the Byzantines and the Syrians," I said conclusively.

"But half the Syrians are actually Turks," Jamila added, almost apologetically.

"Oh, let's face it, as long as it is clearly *us* and *them*, it doesn't matter what names we use," I said. And then I sat up very straight, very fast, for Gregor had come into the kitchen without any of us noticing. "Speaking of us and them," I said soberly and strummed an ominous chord. The others bowed almost guiltily in Gregor's direction.

Gregor looked at me as he unbuckled his sword belt and handed it off to the older Richard, who had moved to the stairs to take his cloak. "You are insane," he said.

"Your father-in-law is ever so much handsomer than I remember," I said.

Gregor looked around at all the others. "Do you know what he's done?"

"Yes," Otto said, but Gregor was so upset he just kept talking: "He's gotten himself into Dandolo's palace as a minstrel. He was *sitting in the room* during a confidential—"

"He's already told us the whole thing," said Otto.

"Of course he did," Gregor muttered.

"I've been playing for Boniface all week," I admitted cheerfully.

Gregor was alarmed. "He doesn't recognize you?"

"What, from a brief encounter three months ago in dim light, when I looked and smelled like John the Baptist? Strangely, no."

Gregor blinked. "What do you think you're *doing*?"

"Keeping an eye on things," I said, sounding somewhat more blithe than I actually felt. "I don't trust him. But then, on principle, I don't trust anyone in power, so it's not personal."

Gregor looked around the room as if it might contain some object that he could use to force me to desist. He thought he found it: Jamila. "Couldn't you have counseled him out of this?" he asked her, as if they were my parents and I a difficult child.

"Actually, sir, I think it's a grand idea," she said.

Gregor voiced exasperation.

"I think Boniface is determined to go to Constantinople, even if the pope forbids it," I announced. "I'd like to see if I'm right about that. He'll figure me out eventually, I'm hardly subtle. But in the meantime, I can get a measure of the man."

"What do you *care* where we go?" Gregor asked, as if I were being unreasonable.

"I don't want my means of transport to be diverted to Byzantium when I have to get Jamila to Egypt," I said, as if I were being reasonable. "I have a peculiar tendency to honor my vows."

The knight sat down on his bedroll, and the younger Richard

scampered over to him to unlace his boots. "Boniface really thinks Jamila is a princess," he said. "Have we never told Bishop Conrad the truth about her?"

"I didn't notice that," I admitted sharply. "I was more preoccupied with the fact that Boniface was threatening you with her welfare and you were too dense to realize it."

"What?"

"Oh, Brother, please, don't be stupid," Otto said impatiently. "He was letting you know, officially, that he knows about her. He can come and get her any time. She's not *free*, she's in a walled city in the middle of winter surrounded by soldiers, for the love of God! What kind of naïve simpleton are you? He was saying: do what I want or I'll appropriate your princess."

Jamila made a tired sound and leaned her head back against the wall. "They're right, sir. He's misjudged my worth, to you and to the world."

"Not your worth to me," Gregor corrected. He patted his right arm, which now had only a single layer of bandage on it. "I owe you my life and well-being, Jamila, and I "—this said with a glance in my direction—"I honor my vows too."

24

THERE WERE THREE MEETINGS on three successive days at the doge's palace, each one larger than the day before, but all held in secret (with musical accompaniment). Rumors were flying around the camp by now that Something Very Big was being decided, without the men having had a chance to even hear about it. Out of hundreds of lords whose cooperation Boniface needed, he only ever found a dozen men to sign the covenant swearing to restore Alexios to his throne. The rest (including, it was rumored, his second in command, Baldwin of Flanders) refused. That should have meant that we would press on directly toward Egypt.

And yet somehow, in the labyrinthine way that these things happen, there was a grudging, growing consensus among the army leaders that, upon leaving Zara in the spring, the fleet would sail not straight to Egypt but first to Constantinople, in order to restore it to Alexios. If the pope had an objection, he was apparently in no rush to let us hear it, although this may have had something to do with the state of the Adriatic in deep winter. Or perhaps with the fact that (as we learned much later) His Holiness was somewhat preoccupied with fleeing into the hills because of a clash with the Roman senate.

Soon after the German envoys left with their happy news, an attractive, if no longer youthful, woman appeared at the postern gate to Boniface's palace. Other women there gave her surly looks and did not want to admit her to his private rooms. She ignored them and spoke directly to Claudio, Boniface's guard. "I from Gregor von Mainz, have message for marquis," she said with a thick German accent.

She was lying, of course. Gregor hadn't asked her to come here. I had.

But feeling protective, I was there myself to keep an eye on her, this first visit.

Liliana had never seen Boniface in person before she was escorted into the room that day. The attendant left, but the chamber remained populated by two guards and a trio of viol players (one with a bandaged arm), playing Kalenda Maya, Boniface's favorite troubadour tune. She had interrupted a game of chess between the marquis and a guard.

Boniface smiled at her, slightly bemused. His eyes—like those of nearly every man who'd ever met her—went straight to her mouth, with its pouting lips which looked like they were craving mischief.

"I heard there was a woman come from Gregor, and I thought perhaps it was his precious princess. But you have the wrong coloring."

She looked at him the way a dog does upon hearing a strange sound. "Princess no," she said hesitantly, with the heavy accent. "Woman of brother. Lordship can German?"

"Well enough," Boniface said and changed from the patois. At this point I could no longer understand what was said, but I grasped the essentials, and Liliana gave me details later. "You said his brother?"

"His half brother, Otto of Frankfurt, the handsome blond man that goes with him everywhere and is so good with horses," Liliana gushed, suddenly very articulate in her supposed native tongue. "To be honest, milord marquis, I come here for his sake, not Gregor's." She fell to a kneel at his feet, her cleavage quite exposed to him. The guard at the chessboard leapt to his feet, prepared to pull a hysterical woman away from the marquis, but she kept her composure. "Otto is a remarkable soldier, but he is always in his brother's shadow, and I'm afraid Gregor's rises and falls will affect Otto unduly. Please, milord, consider Otto for advancement independent of his brother."

Boniface looked confused. "I don't understand what you're asking, woman."

She looked up at him pleadingly. "Please be aware of Otto of Frankfurt for the extraordinary soldier that he is. Please consider his fortune independent of his brother's."

Boniface frowned. "Is Gregor planning something nefarious, that you feel the need to distance Otto from him?"

"Oh no, milord, it's nothing like that. I don't understand what Gregor's doing and I don't really care. I just know that he goes to see you and comes back sulking, and tells all the foot soldiers and knights to obey you, but he's always in a bad mood. That's no way to get on in the world, I think. I only care about Otto's fortune. Please allow him to establish it on his own, and not only in relation to his brother. That's all. He's too demure to ask for such a thing himself, so I am asking for him."

Boniface relaxed, smiled sarcastically. "Are you indeed? And that is the sole purpose of your coming here? To ask this little favor of me? I am supposed to believe that?"

She nodded, looking doting and heartfelt. If I hadn't known her, I'd have thought this woman had nothing but cabbage between her ears. "My fortune lies with Otto, my lord" —she giggled at her feeble pun—, "and I guard it very jealously."

"And that's the only reason you've come?" Boniface pressed, still amused and disbelieving.

Liliana pursed her lips, an expression more sultry than confused. "Is there some other reason I should come?" As if she couldn't help herself, her eyes flitted over the marquis's athletic form—and then she looked away hurriedly and blushed the tiniest bit. She'd used that blushing bit on me when I'd first met her; it was effective.

Boniface gestured around the opulent palace. "Most whores who worm their way into a chamber like this come with the aim of remaining here. Especially in wintertime."

She smiled her bewitching, amused smile. "Oh, *that's* why all the women outside looked so hostile!" she said, as if it had just dawned on her. "No, milord, I am not here to advance myself." She beamed innocently at him. "I am here only in Otto's interests."

He looked her up and down, and made a circling gesture with his finger; she looked surprised; slowly, as if she weren't sure why he was commanding it, she turned in place. He gestured her to come closer to him, which she did with a bemused expression; he leaned in close to where her neck met her shoulder, closed his eyes, and took a deep sniff in. "Very nice," he said, opening his eyes again. "Are your breasts firm enough to bother with disrobing, or shall we just have you lift your skirts?"

Liliana did an astounding job of appearing to hide how flattered she was. "Oh!" she gasped, with a startled, fetching laugh. "If milord wants an old cow like me! I saw what you have waiting for you just outside, they're much fresher than what I offer."

"But not as seasoned," Boniface replied pleasantly. "Occasionally one likes a bit of seasoning." He gave her a studied glance. "But if you thought I wouldn't want you, what were you planning to offer me in exchange for Otto's advancement?"

She shrugged, looking beautifully stupid. "I heard that you were kind to women in need, and I hoped your natural sympathy—" She cut herself off and looked, convincingly, like she was too addlepated to even finish the thought. I wanted to hug her.

Boniface was delighted, which relieved me. "I am indeed kind, but I'm also a little curious. I'd be much obliged if you could quench my curiosity about something."

"I'll . . . quench anything you like, milord," she said with an uncertain smile, as if she wasn't sure if they weren't perhaps talking in code about something obscene.

"Tell me about Gregor's princess."

I knew the German for *princess*; this bit of dialogue was the real reason Liliana was here. I simplified my playing to a chord progression so that I could try to gauge her success by watching their body language.

Liliana did a brief dance of internal equivocation, expertly alerting Boniface that she had a secret she could barely contain. He cooed at her, invoking Otto's name; she dithered and finally whispered, as if she were frightened to admit it: "I don't think she's really a princess, milord."

Boniface looked interested but hardly stunned. "Oh? What do you think she is?"

Liliana ran her tongue distractedly over her lower lip, which probably gave every man watching her an immediate erection. She stared hard at a decoration in the middle of Boniface's chest. "I hope it doesn't reflect badly on you and your daughter if it came out that Gregor's taken on a common whore from Genoa as his mistress."

I heard the word *Genoa* and tried not to stare too obviously at Boniface, to see if he would believe it. (I admit it was not the best of schemes, but I was determined to render Jamila uninteresting and unuseful to him without revealing her race, lest that endanger her.) He snorted and released Liliana. "A Genoese whore? Why do you think that? The woman has convinced a number of intelligent men—including the Bishop of Halberstadt and a well-traveled Venetian—that she is an Egyptian princess."

"Are they so experienced at comparing Genoese whores and Egyptian princesses, to know the difference?" Liliana asked, sounding confused and fascinated.

"Are *you*?" Boniface demanded.

Liliana's innocently stupid expression did not waver. "Well, I'm not, of course," she said with a slightly sheepish laugh. "But we're in a house that was owned by Genoese merchants, whom she says she knew 'from back home.' Does it matter? You don't really care if she's an Egyptian princess, do you? Because she's not one."

Boniface frowned at her. He turned to one of his attendants and said sharply in Piedmontese, "Learn the original residents of Gregor's lodgings, then find out where they've fled and track them. Bring them back to me for questioning." The attendant bowed and left the room at once, as I felt all of the blood drain from my face.

My reverence for Liliana's performance abilities quadrupled: her expression remained absolutely stupid and untroubled. "Have I said something wrong?" she asked in German. "I'm so sorry I don't understand your language."

"Don't worry yourself, lovely," Boniface said and began to untie his belt. "But as you have no useful intelligence to offer me, I must insist on the conventional payment for showing favor to your sweetheart."

"We can make it unconventional if you like," she offered, as if there could not possibly be anything else on her mind. "Do you want me on the bed?" She glanced around, but there was not one in here. She looked questioningly at the guards and page boys, who carried on with their activities indifferently. She might have glanced at the musician with his arm in a sling, but he was studiously avoiding her, trying desperately to think of how to undo what she'd accidentally set in motion.

"Let's start standing," Boniface said. "My favors don't come cheaply. You'll be here awhile."

I HAD GOTTEN MYSELF hired on by the canonical hour and was dismissed at the next ringing of the church bells. But supper was long over by the time Liliana herself returned. The household was settling into bed, but Otto kept glancing down into the courtyard; he saw Liliana as she began to climb the stairs. She looked exhausted.

"Glad you're back safely," Jamila said, then returned her attention to the lute.

Otto glared at Liliana. He didn't speak at first, but the intensity of his stare kept her rooted in the doorway, unable to move. The rest of us, seeing there would be an argument, buried our attention in our evening routine—washing faces, dimming fires, saying prayers at the altar.

"Where've you been all evening?" Otto growled.

"Looking after all our interests," she said simply.

"Richard says you left toward Boniface's palace. What mischief are you up to? What truck do you have with Boniface or any of his men? He's misused Gregor *and* he's misused me, the way he's misused every man in the army."

"Otto, mind how you speak of the marquis," Gregor said uncomfortably.

Liliana looked down at the threshold and said nothing.

"What are you up to?" Otto demanded angrily and grabbed her wrist, twisting it. She took in a sharp breath and winced; I stood up to intervene, but Gregor was already there, one meaty paw shoving his brother away from her.

"Be gentler, Otto," Gregor warned. "But tell us what you've been doing, Liliana, and put his mind at rest."

"I thought that if I could cozy myself into Boniface's circle, I might learn the pope's response to the Byzantium diversion," she said, as prompted. She gestured toward me with her chin. "I know he's there too, spying, but he always fouls things up."

Gregor and Otto exchanged glances. They believed her. It helps to sprinkle your lies with just enough truth to make them viable: I did, indeed, tend to foul things up.

"Well, for heaven's sake, *don't* tell us what the pope says," Otto ordered. "We're going even if the pope forbids it—"

"No we're not," said Gregor.

"Gregor, you know we will! We came to Zara without his consent, we'll do this without his consent. I don't like it either, but we've got no *choice*!" He turned back to Liliana. "That's why you shouldn't tell us: if Gregor knows we're displeasing His Holiness, he'll sulk all the way there."

"Well, never mind, then," Liliana said, with a casual shrug. "I won't pursue it. Boniface's pestle is too large for my mortar anyhow— a nice stretch once or twice, but I wouldn't want to make a regular exercise of it."

Otto gave her an angry look. "Don't talk like a slut," he said.

"I am a slut," she said, with finality.

He raised his arm, and for a moment I thought he would hit her; Gregor moved to step between them but Otto pushed his brother away with his other elbow and slammed the heel of his upraised hand against the doorjamb, making the whole wall shake. He shoved Liliana roughly out of the way and stormed down the stairs into the darkness.

"He wants to marry me and he can't." This, as if apologizing for Otto's behavior. "C'mon, Brit," Liliana went on, lacking energy for a more artful segue. "Bring a blanket. I'm barely up for one more, and you're the smallest of the lot."

I had never been with Liliana, so whatever excuse she could concoct to go off alone with me would have been a lie, but I didn't appreciate that one. I heard Jamila make a little voiceless sound in her throat as I started to get up; I didn't dare look over at her.

Otto usually stormed off to the stables when he was angry, so we did not go there. Instead we went up onto the roof and lay down closely side by side in a blanket, so that we would be mistaken for fornicators if any of the others came looking for us.

I lay on my right side. Because my left arm was still in the sling, I could not pull her closer to me, but my body pressed against hers. I pretended to sniff her as Boniface had, and she laughed a little, sounding tired. "Yummy," I said with a bad German accent. She smelled like sex. "I'm going to end up wanting to get under your skirt," I warned, casually apologetic.

"I won't take it personally," she said, yawning in my face. "What do we do next?"

"Turn Jamila into a convincing Genoese whore."

"I meant what do we do about Boniface going after the Egyptians?"

I shook my head. "They fled two months ago with plenty of money on them; they're safely back in Egypt by now. But don't tell Jamila about any of this or she'll fret that she's endangering people, and she'll run off again."

"We can't have *that*," Liliana said. "You wouldn't have anything to *live* for."

In the darkness I felt the blood rush to my face. "I don't think we should tell anyone, actually," I said. "Otto's just too volatile, and Gregor might feel duty-bound to report to his leader that we're playing with him."

"I doubt it," she said. "I think he's developing a healthy disillusion with his leader."

"Not healthy enough," I insisted. "Not if he's still a soldier in Boniface's army."

25

DEEP WINTER SETTLED onto Zara. It was milder than anyone was expecting; it felt to most of us like early spring. The warmth was so exceptional by British standards, I kept forgetting it was still winter at all and argued with Jamila about loosening my splint. Gregor and Otto put in their time guarding hunts and foraging parties, which did an admirable job of bringing in boar, rabbit, hare, beaver, and various kinds of deer. Jamila hesitated to eat this meat, calling it a Hebrew word that she translated variously as "torn" and "forbidden." But she was just as hesitant to eat the shellfish that were so easy to harvest. She got tired of subsisting on squid; however, she had nobody to blame but herself—and, of course, Jehovah.

Not satisfied with the Italian tunes I usually needed for my occasional sessions for Dandolo or Boniface, I practiced the lute for hours a day and offered to teach Jamila the most beautiful language in the world in exchange for her mentorship. She picked up a few phrases and soon had me muttering nursery rhymes to myself in Judeo-Arabic and even Greek. Boniface thought I was a numskull, but he liked my playing and invited me to become a member of his household if I wanted full-time employment that would include running messages and collecting firewood (I declined), and even gave me a cast-off tunic of his red-and-white household livery (I accepted). I was glad to have access to him, but I grew heartily sick of playing Kalenda Maya, that overrated circle dance he and most of the army loved. My greater concern, however, was that Bishop Conrad—a longtime colleague of Boniface's—might warn the marquis that there was more to his new stupid lute player than met the eye. That had not happened yet; perhaps the prospect of being useful to *anyone* gave Conrad hives.

Liliana continued to visit Boniface, sharing the occasional giggly gossip with him about the useless Genoese whore who passed herself off as an Egyptian princess. Otto, at peace about sharing her with the four other males in the household, sensed an extracurricular rival and almost lost his mind with jealousy. We all suffered for it; few males make less agreeable company than a horny youth waiting for his lover to return from an assignation with somebody grander than himself.

I finally took a tumble with Liliana myself, a detail I include here only because, at the critical moment, I realized how desperately I wished I was having that critical moment with someone else. Liliana, of course, already knew that, and in her charming, sympathetic way, found my distress amusing. She urged me to simply proposition Jamila and see what happened.

I couldn't. Partly it was the strangling power of guilt and grief, remembering another woman I'd loved. Partly it was Jamila herself. I could (and did) talk her ear off regarding matters musical, linguistic, or philosophical, but I became ludicrously tongue-tied whenever the opportunity arose to speak on a personal note. Which wasn't often: privacy was at a premium with seven people living in a single room. But more than that, I'd've felt I was taking advantage of her dependence on me. That, in hindsight, was both naïve and cocky, but the problem with hindsight is that you never have it until after you need it.

Jamila would not leave the house all winter; Boniface's clemency notwithstanding, she was afraid of attracting attention and being spirited back to Barzizza. She, more than any of us, was waiting, saving her strength, as if she intuitively knew the trials that lay ahead and wanted to be rested for them.

But she continued to wield a heavy hand in health matters, citing the great Maimonides whenever we challenged her. None of us had heard of Maimonides, but when she explained he had been doctor to the great Saladin, the fiercest warrior Islam ever had, Otto and Gregor meekly followed her instructions. Each morning she corralled us all to enough exercise to break a sweat; then a brief rest (or a warm bath once a week, which was an enormous novelty to the Richardim), then breakfast. Morning mass—Gregor's greatest priority—was an afterthought to her.

Her gentle prodding elicited from me a few oblique truths about my history I never thought I'd say aloud. She (but only she) came to know that I'd once fallen hard for a married woman who was, most regrettably, a queen; this had destroyed not only the woman, but her husband, and by extension the kingdom he had ruled: once rendered leaderless, it had fallen immediately to the hated Englishman—

"—whom you would then have assassinated, at the cost of your own life," she concluded, the night she'd finally put all the pieces together. She had a careful firmness to her tone, as if she were a physician palpating a wounded limb.

I nodded.

"From the little I know of your people's sagas and traditions, I will concede it sounds quite *Celtic*," she allowed. "But it does not strike me as a very *useful* application of either your life or your death."

"Your god is a vengeful god himself," I retorted sourly.

"I do not waste much time trying to *emulate* my God. Are you trying to emulate your own? If so, I believe you have it wrong—he died for *others'* sins. There is nothing especially heroic in dying for your *own* sins."

"I was not after heroism," I said, red-faced. "I was after justice."

"The only person to benefit from your plan would be your enemy's heir, who would inherit all the sooner. Forgive me, but I fail to see the justice of that."

That I relished these humiliating conversations says something about my state of mind that winter: I wanted to be talked out of my own beliefs but was not sure what to replace them with.

Gregor's arm and other injuries healed under Jamila's care; soon he was sparring and grappling with Otto. He heard there were military schools throughout Byzantium and wanted the pilgrim army, to a man, to get some training too. So he led close combat sessions in the forum and sent Otto outside the walls to do equestrian drills with the mounted sergeants, to experiment with rumored Saracen tricks like riding bent-kneed with their stirrups directly under them. Otto scoffed at this—riding so short was no way to absorb the blow of a lance. Ah, said Gregor, but it allowed great mobility for archery—and so the next thing to do was either encourage knights to shoot better or teach archers to ride. Otto considered both of these ideas ridiculous.

By now, Gregor was firmly back on the pedestal he'd once fallen off of. He was adored by everyone all over again; we hardly ever saw him, he was so frequently being invited to quaff or spar or pray with various sectors of knightly society.

But generally, the tone of the army was bleak. They had been told now of the diversion to Constantinople, the location of which almost none of them understood. Gregor would remind them that loyal knights and soldiers obey their lords—something he believed enough to speak with suasion. But he also reminded them that they were still awaiting a required blessing from His Holiness in Rome. With his golden halo misting moral certainty upon them, they agreed.

I was playing for Boniface the day one of the French bishops came storming unannounced into the marquis's private room, the bodyguard Claudio at his heels. Several of His Eminence's attendants followed, scurrying and almost sheepish, as if they could not keep pace. The bishop was red-faced and breathless, and held a piece of vellum in his hand, waving it in the marquis's direction.

"He forbids it!" he shouted, anguished. "For God's sake, milord, this is pure condemnation, every word of it."

Boniface sat up abruptly and gestured me to stop playing. "Who knows?" he asked. The bishop shook his head: nobody. Boniface relaxed. "Then don't tell anyone," he said with finality and gestured me to continue playing, as if that were the end of it.

"Milord!" the bishop said, horrified. "The *Holy Father*—"

Boniface stopped him, then signaled me to leave the room at once.

"Complete privacy," he said to Claudio, who ushered me out.

I had long since spied out the palace grounds and knew I'd never be able to listen in on their discussion. So I took the lute back to the house, then rushed to the misty forum to find Gregor. Besides pens for boxing and wrestling and blunt-weapons duels, Gregor had ordered a scaffold built from which descended a rope; knights weighed down with sixty pounds of chain mail would crawl up this using only upper-body strength. This was where I found him, about to climb. It was always noisy in the forum, with sound bouncing around the stone walls; I whistled to get his attention and gave him a very, *very* serious look; he released the rope and walked over to me.

I was almost trembling with anticipation. "The pope has forbidden the Byzantine diversion, but Boniface is going to suppress that fact," I whispered.

Gregor stared at me. He blinked once. Swallowed. Ran his tongue over his front teeth behind closed lips. Grimaced. Wiped the moisture off his face. All the time staring at me. Behind those eyes, an entire universe lurched.

"You are mistaken," he finally said.

"I was in the room when the bishop came with the news. Ask Boniface yourself!"

"And where will I say I heard about it?" he asked. "Not from Boniface's men. Not from the bishop's. If you were present for such an encounter, you will be the obvious leak. You'll be found out."

I shrugged. "I'm surprised I've lasted this long. I've only been hanging around there to see what he's capable of, and now I know. I needn't continue. Confront him!"

Gregor crossed his arms over his chest and continued to stare at me. I was starting to feel slightly chastised, but I didn't know why. "So I tell him I know, and then what? He denies it. It's my word against his, and until I see the writ myself, I'm not even convinced that my word is correct."

"*I* saw it!" I insisted. "My eyes are as good as yours!"

"Unless others see the writ with *their* own eyes—"

"I can get my hands on the writ!" I said, wagging my head with excitement. "Eventually! Somehow! We'll reveal him for the schemer that he is!"

Gregor nodded slowly. "According to you and Otto both, if we do that, or anything close to it, he'll take Jamila."

I stopped wagging my head.

"Think about what happened last time you publicized a papal writ," Gregor went on. "In the end, it did not make a difference. It didn't stop the army. So there's no guarantee it would stop the army this time. Do you want to jeopardize Jamila for the sake of trying a tactic that's already been proven not to work? As a military man, I don't condone that sort of risk." He continued to give me the appraising stare.

"So you're going to *ignore* the pope's forbidding this?" I demanded. "After preaching the need to have the pope's permission?"

"I assumed Boniface would obey His Holiness's word. Now you are trying to tell me that's not so." That, of course, had been his universe lurching. I was enraged but not surprised by his conclusion: "As I said, you are mistaken." A knowing pause. "Or lying."

"*Gregor*—" I hissed through clenched teeth.

"You don't want this diversion, because you are in a hurry to get Jamila to Egypt," he announced, with all-seeing dispassion. "You want me to prevent the diversion for your own selfish ends, and you know this is the only way to convince me to do so."

I felt my mouth and tongue pulling downward into an expression of self-righteous nausea. "You're accusing *me* of trying to play you?"

Gregor gave me a small smile. "Briton, you try to play me all the time."

"So does the marquis!" I snapped.

"I've known you a matter of months, and I wonder if I can *list* the damage you've done, the headaches you've caused. I've known Boniface most of my life, he gave me knighthood and a wife, and the few times he has duped me, it was a necessary evil in service to a greater good."

I turned away and shouted wordlessly, briefly, with frustration. I stamped around in a small circle on the wet limestone paving. "*You are maddening*," I cried.

"And you are mad," he said.

He excused himself to return to the rope, but he was not emanating his usual golden glow.

"I SHOULD ASSASSINATE *Boniface*," I declared angrily to Jamila, an hour later, as I stormed around the common room. "I could even use my original plan."

She had the lute now and was coaxing from it soft, complicated decorations of sound still beyond my abilities. "I thought you had relinquished your murderous impulses," she said, looking down at the sound hole as she played, to spare me having to make eye contact. "You elected not to pursue your Englishman."

"That would merely have been vengeance," I said. "This would be *preventative*, to stop Boniface from doing further harm."

Jamila said nothing for a moment, just finished the melodic line she was in the middle of. Then she stopped the strings but kept looking down at the lute. "As with your original plan, you'd be killed. Is that agreeable to you? As it once was?"

"Don't worry, I'll get you to Alexandria first."

She looked up from the lute. "I was thinking of your mentor, the hermit."

"Wulfstan? He'd agree with me. He spent three years helping me prepare for something like this. Every skill and art I learned at his suggestion would be utilized."

"Would it?" Jamila asked, in a tone that instantly robbed me of my certainty.

"Yes," I said, slightly huffy and held out one fist, to uncurl my fingers as I listed: "Foreign language skills, already useful. Musical abilities, likewise. Patience and timing and the discipline to keep my mouth shut when I must—"

"*Only* when you *must*," Jamila commented, as I continued: "How to use a knife in hand-to-hand combat. And above all," I said, unfurling my pinkie finger triumphantly, "acting for the sake of something bigger and more important than myself."

"But he mentored you at much more than that," Jamila said. "You've told me. He wanted you to learn to swim, encouraged your agility—how you can climb and balance and tie complicated knots and do acrobatics. How to read the stars, the seasons, the clouds. And he *tried* to interest you in the Bible. I don't see any of that as training for a minstrel-assassin."

"All of that was just to mask our real intentions from the brothers," I explained.

"Oh, really? You faked the role of novice monk by performing rope tricks and scaling walls?" Jamila said. "Were you convincing?"

"It doesn't matter," I said impatiently. "What matters is what it's brought me to. There's an obvious villain doing obvious wrong, and I've the means to stop it."

"No," Jamila said, "you've the means to stop *him*. Someone else will take his place, but you'll be dead by then, so you won't be there to stop *them*. If you've a sudden investment in seeing this army be righteous, don't squander yourself on the leader. Save yourself for the led."

"*The led* has no use for me, he thinks I'm lying to him!" I shouted, turning on her sharply. "He thinks I'm trying to gull him!"

Jamila gave me a motherly nod. "*That's* what you're upset about," she said. "So rectify it. It's not *quite* as simple as murdering the leader of the army, but it's a start."

"I don't know how," I said and scowled.

"There is an ancient, mysterious concept that we in the ancient, mysterious East call cause and effect," she said, her tone pushing past irony to sarcasm. "I recommend it. If you don't want someone to think you're a trickster, don't play tricks."

"It's not a trick!" I said, defensively. "I'm telling the truth!"

"Good," she said. "Keep doing so. Eventually he'll trust you. And if by then you're still convinced Boniface's evil, *then* you'll be in a position to make a difference."

"So what do I do until then?" I demanded.

She held out the lute toward me. "Practice the maqama I taught you yesterday."

I reached out for the lute but then at the last moment pulled my hands away. "I have a much better idea," I said.

BISHOP CONRAD'S LODGINGS were almost as grand as Boniface's—a small palace built for visiting church dignitaries, reassuringly Catholic and oppressive. I'd been admitted claiming to be a confidential emissary from Gregor, then enlightened Conrad to my real purpose once in his presence.

"Naturally all the higher clergy have discussed the writ," he said to the tip of his shoe, which he was using to nudge a bear pelt closer to the fire pit. He was not an old man, or a fat man, but he had splendid jowls most men take a lifetime to get; they almost swayed when he shook his head, as now. "You are not entitled to an explanation."

"I beg you, Your Eminence, I can't bear Gregor—my chaperone to the Holy Land—thinking me a liar," I complained. To demonstrate my eagerness to be allied with him, I nudged the bear pelt with my own (newer but less decorated) shoe. "I'm *begging* you to tell him that I'm not lying about this, Your Eminence. That's *all*."

He nudged the pelt once more, then finally made himself look directly at me. I'd always thought of him as hearty but now he looked permanently dyspeptic. Perhaps it was the jowls. "To tell Gregor that you are honest means to tell him that His Holiness has indeed forbidden the diversion."

I shrugged. "So? Why wouldn't you want him to know the truth?"

With eyes back to the bear pelt: "This situation is complex and subtle, my son—"

"The Holy Trinity is subtle and complex, Your Eminence. If you expect me to grasp that someday, let's practice by testing my intellect on this."

"The Byzantine diversion is sadly necessary. That is all you need to know."

"So you won't help me prove my truthfulness to Gregor."

"*Are* you truthful? Idiot lute player?"

It seemed a threat; I felt my eyes narrow. "Have you told Boniface who I am?"

"What would it accomplish?" he asked. "Telling him would have consequences, but I do not know what those consequences are, or in whose interest they would be. I'm not even sure, at this point, in whose interest I should *want* them to be." He sighed with a combination of complacency and sheepishness—as if he were complacent *about* being sheepish. "Perhaps by now you have noticed that I am unlikely to commit actions whose outcomes are not clear to me."

"Now that you mention it, I *had* noticed that on occasion, Your Eminence," I said, in a voice so soggy with sarcasm it sounded sincere. "I'm grateful to have a chance to profit by it. But I'd be more grateful if you could prove to Gregor that I'm honest."

"But you are *not* honest, little lute man."

"So you'll endorse my dishonesty toward Boniface while *not* endorsing my honesty toward Gregor. In what way does this demonstrate the Christian values I am supposed to embrace?"

Conrad signaled with irritation to one of his bodyguards. "I have no time for your catechism," he informed me. "Especially as you have no intention of taking my response to heart."

And by then the guard was physically removing me from His Eminence's presence.

26

Fare well rain, the time of showers is over and gone, the winter
is past, and everything is created to be beautiful again.

—ANONYMOUS HEBREW *piyut*

Feast of St. Joseph of Arimathea, 17 March

*I return to this chronicle after long weeks away from it, for there has
been absolutely nothing worthy of recording. Around the occupied city,
rumors circulate that news from Rome is good—that His Holiness Pope
Innocent has forgiven us all our sins, even the Venetians, and that he
supports whatever action the army needs take to put Alexios upon his
father's throne.*

In truth I do not know if I should believe this.

*And to be honest—even believing the pope had given Alexios his
blessing, the great majority of the soldiers remain unhappy about the
diversion. They want to fulfill their vows and get back home, as I do.*

I have some small estates to maintain, and a wife to become acquainted with, and soon a child for whom I must serve as an example.

On several occasions recently, furtive messengers have come to my tent from some of the powerful barons—Peter of Amiens, Otto of Champlitte, once even a vassal of Baldwin of Flanders—to ask me if I will side with them, should they desert and go directly to the Holy Land by whatever means they might scrape together. I confess that I am sorely tempted to do so. But each time, I send back word that I cannot break up the army. I think the Briton would interfere with my declining messages if he could, and so I cause Otto to sit on top of him until my squires have returned to say my refusal is delivered safely. Otto finds it great sport.

Even without my involvement, however, fully a thousand men collected together for permission to leave the host and go directly to the Holy Land. It was reluctantly granted them. The Briton lamented angrily when he heard this: "If I knew or trusted any of them, I'd have gone with them and taken Jamila with me!" This distressed me more than I would have guessed. Although he is a thorn in my side often enough, still I grow attached to him, and Jamila is the most admirable and capable of women.

Milord Boniface sent for me a few weeks ago, to comment that I am not doing much to deserve the reward of my "infidel mistress's" freedom and requested me to give rallying speeches at the martial exercises each morning. I try to do so. The Briton watched a few times and said, mysteriously, "Your gold is gone," as if I would know what that meant. I believe I kept up a good face, but for those who know real conviction when they see it—such men, I do not think I convinced. This has been a time of great confusion for me. I think about the Briton's claim that Milord Boniface is suppressing the Holy Father's injunction about the diversion. I begin to wonder, might he have spoken truth?

Feast Day of St. Rupert of Salzburg, 27 March

*Bad feelings grow worse. Another thousand disgruntled decamped for
the Holy Land eight days back. Just after this, Milord Boniface again
chastised me—in a fatherly, concerned way—for not doing more in
behalf of the army. Now he has also posted his man Claudio just
outside the gate, a reminder that he knows exactly where "the princess"
is. (Therefore a certain other member of the household enters and exits
the house over the neighboring roof, so as not to be affiliated with me in
Claudio's eyes.)*

*Yet more recently, another group of soldiers tried to desert on foot,
only to be chased by our enraged victims—the Zarans—back to the city.*

*"I am failing in my duty, milord," I said this time when I was called
to account. "For your sake and the sake of the army, give me some
other duty."*

*That time when I was summoned, it was to report to Milord
Dandolo and the marquis together, although the two noblemen, in all
honesty, do not like each other and hardly ever speak. Dandolo has
come to believe that his own Venetians are deserting at the urging of
some piously honey-tongued pilgrim, and he has decided it must be me.*

"You're encouraging them to leave," he insisted.

*Anxious with frustration, I said, "Milord, by St. John's head, I
swear I'm not. I'm less likely to encourage them to desert than . . .
than would that lute player be." And here I pointed at the man with a
bandaged arm playing for Dandolo, for Dandolo always has musicians
around him.*

*That musician affected extreme puzzlement. "Why would I tell
anyone to desert, milords?" he asked. It was one of the few times this
man, of whom I absolutely have no personal knowledge, had ever spoken aloud in Boniface's presence, and contributed to the already-solid
impression that he is a complete idiot. Then he added, in a sly voice,
"D'y' mean because of that time the pope forbade it?"*

Of course it was clear from my reaction that I was hearing this for the first time ever, from anywhere. "What is that, milord?" I demanded in a shocked voice.

Either Dandolo had already figured out that the pope had protested or he genuinely didn't care. Milord Boniface glared at the stupid musician, who looked briefly distraught, a chastened child who didn't quite understand what he'd done wrong. But the marquis's energy turned instantly to me, and he said in a reassuring voice, "It's true Innocent was disturbed at first by the suggestion."

"Then we mustn't do it!" I insisted and began silently to fashion an apology to a certain friend of mine.

Milord Boniface, however, was calm and said further, "I have corresponded with His Holiness since, my son, explaining the benefits to the Church, and he has changed his mind. He now supports the diversion." He gave the musician a sour look. "That happened when our little lute man here was not present."

Naturally I wanted with all my heart to believe this, and so I said, "I am delighted to hear it. Might I have the honor of seeing his letter?"

"It is with the Bishop of Soissons," said Boniface. "I believe he may have already sent it back to Soissons for safekeeping."

I said, now uncertain of his truthfulness: "So I must take your word for it."

Milord Boniface said: "Is there some reason my word would not suffice?"

I hesitated, for I would not speak harsh words with a lord and kinsman in front of anyone from Venice. But he demanded an answer, and so I said uncomfortably, "You've broken your word before, milord."

"Gregor," Milord Boniface, the stern patriarch now, upbraided me. "Every day this winter I have honored it. Every day it is within my power to see your lady friend seized, by thousands of men who know where she is and what she's worth, bounty or no bounty. Every day, I see to it that she isn't seized. My word is good enough."

A few nights ago, in the rain, five hundred soldiers and their

servants stowed off on a small cargo transport and tried to sneak away
under cover of dark. It foundered on the shallow rocks outside the har-
bor and sank; all five hundred drowned in moments. It has taken three
days to dig their graves and commemorate the dead.

Finally men have stopped trying to desert.

AT THE BEGINNING of April, with the sun far warmer than any of
us were used to in early spring, and my accursed splint finally off, the
army began to pack up belongings to carry into the ships. There were
fewer men now, but there were fewer boats too, for boats had taken
the deserters away. The day of sailing, per Boniface's request, had
originally been the seventh, but we had to delay a day, for that was a
Monday, and as *everyone* knows, the first Monday in April is the day
Cain killed Abel and, therefore, *clearly* an unpropitious day to begin
a sea voyage. (It is a wonder to me that anyone ever manages to accomplish anything maritime at all.)

When the women were called back aboard the *Venus*, I went with
them. But first the three of us, with the Richardim, spent half a day
preparing the house for the return of its rightful residents. While the
rest of the army did a final thorough pillage of its winter quarters,
the Richardim cleaned the stable and laid down fresh straw for the
anticipated return of the recalcitrant Egyptian donkey; Jamila and I
had already started the kitchen garden with seeds she'd found stored
from last fall's harvest, and I sowed the warm-weather plants as the
women scrubbed, swept, and tidied. We left behind a chess set the
Richardim had carved together during long winter evenings; I left
money I'd made playing for Dandolo (Boniface did not like to pay in
money); we left behind three more cloaks, neatly hung on pegs. But
we took along the lute, for that had been their gift to Jamila.

When finally the three of us closed the gate behind us, we were
departing the best-stocked, best-attended building in all Zara. We

were beaming with satisfaction, imagining what the Egyptians, having survived their plight, would at last come home to. With the arm of a beautiful woman tucked under my elbow to each side, I led them down the street, the lute case hanging on my back.

Jamila had not left the household compound since the day we moved in last November; she grew nervous as we approached the closest public square, so Liliana pulled off her own veil and draped it over Jamila's face; we put Jamila between us, where she felt more protected, and guided her, as she was now sightless. To distract her—and to distract myself from the warmth of her body bumping against mine—I grew silly, deliberately walking us into walls, through puddles, round in circles, until I had them both laughing. The laughter of each of them, for very different reasons, was seductive—Liliana's because it came so freely, Jamila's because it was so rare. Giddy with pleasure, we made our way down to the harbor and waited until a boat could row us out to the *Venus*. We assumed we'd be on the high Adriatic within hours.

But hours later, we had not left. Dozens of plumes of black smoke were beginning to rise from the city. Jamila pointed to the war galleys: the enormous catapults that had once failed to tear down the walls were being set up again by the Venetians in the harbor. This time there would be no defense of those walls, and they would fall, just as surely as the buildings within were falling to the flame.

Within days, the city of Zara had been razed.

27

The first of May! No leaf of bay, nor birdie's air, nor flower gay
Could ever sway (O lady gay) I who would dare to hear your say.
Lady Fair, I beg your praise
That you'll care for me always.
I'm in your fray, I'm here to stay, believe me, pray,
I'd sooner slay a rival, ay, than ever stray.
— "Kalenda Maya" (*May Day*) (*a very loose translation*)

OUR FIRST FEW WEEKS on the island of Kérkyra, at the westernmost edge of the Byzantine Empire, would be remembered by many with something approaching nostalgia. It was the deceptive calm before the longest, most trying storm of all our lives.

Despite shoals, it had been an easy trip down the coast. The mountains to our east had moved nearer to the shore, until they seemed to rise straight out of the sea. The old smells, sounds, and physical encumbrances of being on shipboard had been a welcome distraction from those final, dismal days of watching Zara disappear under the wrath of Venice. The water grew even more astonishing in color—green where it was too shallow to sail, velvety royal blue in depths, a color so saturated it looked edible. Pines flourished on the mountainsides, brilliant green from the limestone, looking like spring shoots back home. Travel by boat is never pleasant, but it was easier the second time around. I passed much of the trip teaching

Jamila my bowing technique (it's hard to remember to breathe while the bow is in motion—the natural tendency is to wait until the end of a long stroke), mostly because it was an excellent excuse to touch her wrists.

Nobody knew at first why we had even stopped here, or where exactly we were going next. Boniface, the doge, and the highest-ranking counts had all stayed behind, outside of the smoking ruins of Zara, awaiting Prince Alexios's arrival from Germany.

The island of Kérkyra, also called Corfu, is a long strip of land, fatter to the north and then tapering to the southeast, a minuscule Italian peninsula—or, as on certain maps, a lamb chop. The huge half-circle harbor, with a fortress-town perched on the lower lip, is on the eastern side, within sight of mainland Greece. The good people of this town, having heard of Zara's fate, greeted us with boulders, so violently catapulted that the ships had to flee the harbor on first attempt at anchoring. Actually, our reception was not entirely due to our reputation. The world-famous Genoese pirate Leon Vetrano (no, I'd never heard of him either) had conquered the island a few years back, and used it to stage raids on someplace called the Peloponnesus. He had finally disappeared into the mists, but the locals still didn't like unexpected visitors. We tried entering again, now to the north of a little harbor island, too far from the powerful raised catapults of the fort. It was treacherous here because of submerged sandbars, but finally the entire fleet achieved safe harbor. Once the Venetians had ravaged several outlying villages and horrified the eastern half of the island into angry submission, we were all allowed to disembark, and we encamped on the plain.

It was beautiful and endlessly sunny here—the mountains were softer than those near Zara, the air even milder. It was wonderful to be someplace that did not feel confined by ship hull or city wall. There were extraordinary songbirds and birds of prey, some of which—kestrels, falcons, larks—I recognized. There was more benign wildlife than I could remember since I'd been in Britain—

geckos, herons, hedgehogs, geckos, egrets, squirrels, geckos, all sorts of little scurrying things you're not likely to find in paved cities or on boats. I especially liked the geckos; they struck me as reptilian versions of myself.

There were occasional rocks catapulted from the two high fortressed peaks within the town walls, occasional small and reckless adolescent sorties, but generally we were left alone. Conrad and the other bishops were even invited into the walled city to dine with the local clergy, who were not Catholic but Orthodox. They argued theology and politics (in particular, the Orthodox were horrified that the Church should ever be involved in warfare) and left on polite terms.

Rumors had begun to spread (as rumors do) that Gregor of Mainz was going to Constantinople without a quarrel—although, just as he had done outside Zara, he would refuse to fight. I can't imagine who spread these rumors, but they made a salutatory impression, especially on the German and Flemish knights. Even if one didn't want to fight in support of Prince Alexios, there was no reason not to go along. *Going* to Constantinople—said the new rumor—was itself unobjectionable, just a new leg of the greater pilgrimage. Constantinople was, after all, one of the five holiest cities of the Christian world, with so many relics within its walls their very proximity could heal all illness and remove all stain of sin. It was rumored that the fabled head of John the Baptist—widely known to be Gregor of Mainz's family saint—was there. A diversion to Constantinople would be good for everybody's soul.

Especially mine.

For it had occurred to me that Jamila probably had more family still alive there than she had in Egypt. Hence my willingness to manufacture Gregor's willingness to go.

Actually, it was not manufactured. Gregor was not *happy* about the diversion, and he was half (but only half) convinced it was the wrong thing to do. He was beginning to suspect that I'd spoken true when I claimed Pope Innocent had forbidden it. On the other hand, he still had his one straw to grasp: his leader said they were going, so they were. It confused him, but eased his mind, when I changed my tune and supported the idea.

Many men, however, wanted nothing more than to see their oaths fulfilled in the Holy Land so they could return to their families, homes, and personal affairs. They did not *want* to go astray, or get involved even peripherally with other nations' politics, even if doing so meant they could see the fabled city of the Byzantines. Besides, the army had contracted with the Venetians for a year, and that year was more than half over. Only a dozen leaders had ever signed the pact to assist Alexios; surely (it was grumbled in the alleys between the sergeants' tents) that oath could not bind the entire army.

Gregor, aware of the growing undercurrent of dissension, fretted about it, and now, ironically, I did as well. Who would've thought I'd care that an army I detested was diverted from a mission I detested, to carry out another mission I detested even more?

We were not the only ones who fretted. Otto had no philosophical investment for or against the diversion; he wanted only to make sure the army stayed intact as an effective fighting (or at least pillaging) force, *wherever* it was headed, and a dissenting movement threatened that cohesion.

And then, of course, there was Jamila. Jamila, who blossomed out of confinement, spent hours in grateful semisolitude on the outskirts of camp, basked in the bright sun and gathered the flowers and stems of local medicinal herbs. Jamila, who smiled at my acrobatic antics, who laughed at my puerile humor not because she found it funny but because it delighted her that I tried so hard to make her laugh.

But Jamila, also, who chided Gregor when she thought I couldn't hear her, behind the tent one sunny afternoon: "Sir, you are avoiding an examination of your moral dilemma because you're worried about me. If you believe the pope forbids the Byzantine diversion, then you feel you'll have to do something that puts me at risk. So I become your excuse for not looking at the situation very hard."

I never heard Gregor's response to this, because Liliana, with whom I was eavesdropping, pulled me out of hearing, sensing I was about to interrupt.

The doge's red galley was spotted on the horizon in the late afternoon, and the entire army erupted into wild speculation about who would disembark. All across the sun-drenched plain, men were flocking toward the harbor to see the notorious Prince Alexios finally appear. I went down there with Gregor because, despite myself, I was intrigued. Now that I had my own reason for wanting this diversion to take place, I was willing to entertain the possibility—in fact, the hope—that there might somehow be merit in it. I knew that Alexios was barely twenty, but I remembered my own king at twenty, and he had been a charismatic leader of men by then, the nonpareil of noble underdogs. Perhaps Alexios was a noble underdog himself, and the Usurper as much a villain as my execrable Englishman. Perhaps Alexios *deserved* both Gregor and me to be his wholehearted champions. Perhaps assisting him to topple his uncle the Usurper could be a sort of parallel redemption for me. I was willing to consider it.

The harborside was lined with barons and their households wanting to see what they would be consigning themselves to if indeed the army went on to Constantinople. Prince Alexios stepped out of the cabin on the doge's galley, and we all finally caught a glimpse of the youth whose circumstances were altering the fate of the campaign.

He looked unremarkable, and nearly pleasant. Dark brown hair and eyes, skin of an aristocratic paleness, but somewhat sallow. The apples of his cheeks were high and round; he was not quite gangly, but not far from it, and he did not move like a master of either broadsword or lance. He wore an air more of tired petulance than of martial dignity. He also wore a lot of pearls—not as jewelry but on his *tunic*, which I found preposterous.

Nobody was impressed. One could sense the disappointment; one could hear it in the pause before the dutiful cheering and applause.

The youth himself, on his own merits as a man, would win no converts and might even lose a few before he was on solid land.

"My lords!" the handsome, charismatic, martially impressive, battle-seasoned Marquis Boniface called out beside him. "Behold the future emperor of Byzantium!"

Again there was polite huzzahing, but not the roar of excitement that would have convinced me they stood any chance at all.

"Ah," was all that Gregor said beside me. There wasn't really much else to say.

"All you need to do is get him on the throne." I was trying to be helpful. "You're not responsible for his earning a place in song as a great leader."

Gregor had no response to that. After a moment, he gestured down toward the shore, almost sheepishly. "Boniface will expect me—"

"Go bow and scrape in person," I said. "I'll start composing verses about the snot-nosed boy's handsome brow. I suspect they'll want me at Boniface's soon myself."

I returned to the tent.

And my heart sank.

Liliana was perched—alone—before the cutting tray, where she and Jamila by habit kept each other company. On a panicked instinct, I counted the bedrolls and saw that one was missing. Liliana glanced up sharply; her eyes were glistening, although she was trying to recover herself.

"She's gone," she said, cleared her throat, and went back to cutting up dinner. "For real, this time. You knew it would happen eventually."

"How could you let her?" I shouted.

"I couldn't stop her!" Liliana said, her voice breaking.

"Where did she go?" I demanded. "How long ago did she leave?"

"She left while everyone was down at the harbor, but I don't know where she went," Liliana said stiffly. "Perhaps to town. I think

there are Jews there. I gave her as much food as we could spare, and a
bedroll and a blanket."

"Well, she's obviously not heading to the *town* with all that, she
wouldn't need any of it in *town*," I said, feeling frantic. "She'll probably try to find a merchant ship heading east." I leapt toward the cloak
pile and reached for a wrap. "Nothing's going in or out of the harbor
right now because of Alexios's arrival, so maybe I can still stop her."

Liliana made a suspicious little sound, and I dropped the cloak.

"Tell me what you know," I demanded.

"I don't *know* anything," she said. "But . . . she figured the harbor
would be closed to regular traffic, and I think she simply wanted to
get as far as away as possible, as quickly as possible, so you couldn't
find her. So, actually, I'd say head inland."

I snorted. "She's just, what, gone off into the wilderness alone, to
hide for a few days? That's reckless and risky in a way that's *completely*
unlike her."

"Well, yes," said Liliana. "But if she needed to evade you, would
she really go someplace you'd *anticipate?*"

I grabbed the cloak and ran out of the tent.

I knew nothing of tracking someone in the wilderness; I spoke
no Greek; I did not know the geography of the place and had a limited view from the crowded plain. To the north, this plain curved
around the harbor bay before rising toward gentle mountains; to the
south, from what I could see, the island stretched on generally flat; to
the west, perhaps an hour's walk away, was what appeared to be the
island's massif, a spine of mountain—the one place nobody with any
sense would head alone on foot. I chose that.

At the edge of the army camp, there were about seven ways to
continue toward the mountains. Having nothing to go by, I chose
the broadest. I wouldn't call it a road—it was wide enough to see
that carts used it occasionally, and herds of sheep or goats, but it was
not paved or marked in any official way. It meandered through the

plain and then up the side of a steep mountain, with many tributaries branching off. From these I chose a trail at such random I could not have followed my own way back down. I cursed under my breath every step, knowing I was exerting myself for nothing useful.

If I ever needed proof that God exists, I found it in the confounding fact that Jamila and I had taken exactly the same way. She was laden down and I was not; still, it was almost dark before I overtook her. Violent storm clouds had suddenly materialized over the mountain mass ahead; the air was so heavy with the expectation of rain that every noise sounded louder than it should have. There was a grayish purple glaze over everything.

I was just as surprised as she was. I turned a sharp bend, and there she was, sitting cross-legged beneath an olive tree, its trunk so gnarled it looked like lacework fashioned out of rope.

I said, "Ah." I was out of breath; she, having been resting for a while, wasn't. "There you are, then," I said with exceedingly forced nonchalance. Suddenly nervous, I passed her at the tree and then began to pace, self-consciously, in a large circle in the path. "Wondered where you'd gotten to. You know you left your lute behind?"

Jamila looked down into her lap abruptly. I thought she laughed; her body shook, and she made a sound like laughter, but when she looked up there were tears in her eyes. "You see," she said in a shaky voice, "I wanted this. I would never have allowed you to come with me, but secretly I wanted this so desperately."

"That's good," I said gruffly. "Because you're not getting rid of me. I took an oath to see you safely home."

"I don't have a home," she said.

Shaking with emotion, and feeling quite absurdly gallant, I held out my arms. "Yes, you do," I said. "Right here."

At which point, without fanfare, it began to rain so hellishly, I expected to see geckos heading two by two for higher ground.

Feast of St. Theodosía, 29 May

*I write again while on a boat, although I will speak now of matters that
happened back on land, on Kérkyra. It grieves me to recollect this.
Indeed, I did not even want to write it at all, but the Briton knows now
that I keep this chronicle, and he begs me to write the truth, so that
it exists somewhere, although we both know that truth will never be
heralded beyond this roll of parchment. He hovers over me as I mark
down these words, and would take the quill out of my hand to write it
himself, had he any German.*

*I begin this story in the camp, shortly after Alexios arrived. Upon
meeting Alexios, the barons were so universally dismayed to discover
they were shepherding a mere boy to the throne of the most powerful
empire in Christendom that most of them developed strong reservations.
Their dissatisfaction was so pronounced, Alexios could surely sense it
plainly. When a group of lords followed him to his tent to question his
abilities, he fell to his knees before them, imploring them for aid.*

*This did not help the unheroic impression he'd made when first
he had arrived. They began to shout at him—and at Milord Boniface—that the covenant would not be adhered to. They had not signed
the treaty with the German envoys back in January, they had never
endorsed it, they had never had cause to support it—and they would
not support it now. In short, they would not go to Constantinople.*

*Milord Boniface sent for me, hoping I could do something to sway
even my superiors the barons, believing me to be a unifying force.
What I did next was unifying, certainly, but not the way Milord Boniface intended it to be. In retrospect, I would I had not done it.*

*For you see, the most important thing is to keep the army together
in the Holy Land. To go via Constantinople is fine—but only if the
army as a whole commits to it. "The army as a whole" is most vital
because, eventually, we will get to the Holy Land, but if we are not the
entire army, then we stand no chance against the infidels. The army*

was about to be permanently split asunder by an honorable but short-sighted group of noble officers, and I was desperate to prevent that split.

This cabal had been wooing me in my tent at the very moment Boniface summoned me. I must add here an important domestic detail: the Jewess and the Briton had both departed from my tent, with the intention of never returning. Although it has nothing to do with the politics of the lords, this is an important detail.

Led by Peter of Amiens and other barons I also respect, the dissenters told me that they would desert Milord Boniface altogether and throw in their lot with a lord named Walter of Apulia. They wanted me to join them, for if I did so (they honored me by saying), many of the soldiers would follow me, even if doing so meant forswearing their own lords. Indeed, they flattered me enough to say the lords themselves might change their plans if Gregor of Mainz so willed it.

Milord Walter was sailing soon from Brindisi, on the Italian peninsula, and was sailing right past Kérkyra on his way to the Holy Land—directly to the Holy Land. No Byzantine diversion for him; only the pope's mission and then swiftly home again. In truth, I understood the lords' desire to sail with Walter; I myself would just as soon have done so. But I was trying to think as I do when I am leading men on the tourney field. What would this splitting of the army achieve? Two things: a group of deserters too small to be effective in their project, and a group of nondeserters also too small to be effective in their project. The choice, I argued, was not Walter versus Boniface, Constantinople versus the Holy Land, Alexios's desires versus the pope's, a longer expedition versus a shorter one; no, the only choice that mattered was an army that could hold together versus one that couldn't, and that was an easy choice. What was not quite so easy was how to attain it.

If I stood up in defense of Alexios (especially when Alexios himself was on his knees, the Briton begs me to emphasize), that would only further alienate those with doubts about the ~~snot-nosed boy~~ young prince, and that alienation would weaken the army. But to forswear Alexios was to forswear Boniface, and my forswearing my own leader

and father, besides being unthinkable itself, might engender utter chaos,
which would weaken the army.

So I chose a middle way, a variant of what the Briton calls my
"maddening tendency to sit in the tent and do nothing." Within three
hours of Alexios's supplication, thousands of men (more than half the
land army) had, under my direction, pulled up stakes and moved to the
far southern edge of the plain in drenching rain. I conceived of this exodus merely as a stalling tactic, although it looked more dramatic than
that. Here is why it was a good thing: by appearing to split the army,
it actually kept the army from fracturing, for it created a union of two
otherwise disaffected factions: those who claimed they were ready to
plunge out to Milord Walter of Apulia's passing boats and those who
merely demanded reassurance that, whatever happened to Prince
Alexios, the army would go on to Jerusalem, and promptly. Although
these two groups had different intentions, they were united in their need
to show Milord Boniface that they would not be trifled with. I felt a
similar need myself.

And so, of course, Boniface trifled with us all.

28

Continuation of entry from Feast of St. Theodosia

Once settled into our "dissenters' camp," a group of us held conference. I had Otto beside me. I was proud of my brother, to stand by
me in this action despite that he is, first, not one to entangle himself in
the confusion of leaders' issues and, second, unlikely ever to give up a
chance for adventure, which he thought he was doing by supporting me.

I remain astonished that I could have such sway, so easily, over such an enormous segment of the army. Once they calmed themselves, most of the lords admitted they did not really want to defect; the force that Milord Boniface led was the force to which they'd pledged themselves, and however enraged they were with him, he was still the leader of something they were loath to quit. But this being the second time that they were diverted from their course, they wanted to bring the leadership to heel somehow.

And yet, because they were lords of men themselves, they did not want to make too public a show of resisting leadership, lest their own vassals take that as a model. They wanted the result without the risk. It is often this way among the lords. (I refrain here from several comments the Briton would have me make regarding such men. I write these sentences only so that he thinks I am translating his dictation into German. Shitheads He peers over my shoulder so I must Cowardly Arseholes include some improper words he has picked up from my servants, for I shall never Hypocritical Bastards hear the end of it, if I simply refuse to mark his Whoreson words down.)

So. As soon as the cloudburst had settled to a drizzle, I mounted and rode back to the scanty remains of the mother army to coax the few lords who had not yet elected to leave. I hoped that if the entire army could be in concert around one grievance—Prince Alexios—then Milord Boniface would have to bend, so that the army would not break.

Every day for the rest of my life, I shall look back at that drizzly afternoon on Kérkyra with astonishment; how did I become a man who could even try to thwart my lord? My lord was wondering the same thing. But more than that, my lord was working out how best to thwart the thwarting.

Four armed horsemen in Boniface's livery had waited until I was within calling distance of his compound. Then they surrounded me, lances pointed, shouting. One of them dismounted and grabbed Summa's reins with violence. I was dragged from my mount, bound and gagged, and carried into Milord Boniface's tent.

* * *

THE RAIN HAD LESSENED down in the plain. For Jamila and me, higher up the mountainside, it hadn't, although it might have been worse if we'd crested the ridge. We passed a miserable night. The olive tree had boughs wide-spaced enough to spread her blanket over them; we put her sleeping mat on the already sodden ground beneath it and huddled there together, unable to make a fire for warmth or light. We ate some of the food she'd brought, mostly biscuits; I had run out with nothing but my cloak. We were both completely wet, and although it wasn't cold, it certainly wasn't warm, or comfortable. It had not rained much here in a couple of months, and the water pooled for the first few hours, the topsoil resisting it. About an hour after sunset, presumably the moon rose, but we got no useful light from it through the pouring rain.

"Well, this is certainly cozy," Jamila said through chattering teeth, when I sat behind her and wrapped my arms around her for mutual warmth. "*This* must be the moment in the romance when you grab me and have your way with me."

I rubbed her arms briskly for warmth and tried humming a tune we both liked by Cercamon ("Asleep or awake, I shiver and quake"— seemed appropriate). We were both soaked through. I was touching the woman I desired, but we were laughably removed from any possible intimacy. I opted for the high road: "I'm not going to have my way with you while you're dependent on me. I don't want to take advantage."

Jamila laughed. "Are you the one who brought the blanket for cover? or the mat for sitting on? or the food for eating? Are you the one who will know how to speak Greek to the locals tomorrow when the rain has cleared and we find proper shelter? *Who* is dependent on *whom?*" She turned her head to grin at me over her shoulder. A grin on that face did terrible things to me, even in the dark. "But don't worry, you're safe with me, I would *never* take advantage of a poor, dependent vagabond."

Somehow, sitting up, with my cloak thrown around us, we slept a little, each dozing on and off in bits until the sun rose on a day that was bright and clear and almost mockingly dry, except for mother earth and the two of us. Jamila woke first and elbowed me gently; I had slunk into my final round of slumber with my head leaning hard against her back. I grunted a little as I pulled myself to consciousness. We were painfully stiff but too cold, in sodden clothes, to throw off the wrap and stretch.

There was no chance that we would find dry kindling, even if we'd had the means to kindle it. The remaining biscuits, despite our best attempts, were soaked. Jamila kept her hair covered, but the veil was so wet now, she pulled it off, wrung it out, and draped it over a branch to dry, although the morning rays were weak still.

"If you won't go to Constantinople," I said, meaning to sound playful, "come back to England with me while I fulfill my mission."

"Why, so I can bury you? I've buried too many in my life already."

That largely put an end to the morning chitchat.

We ate the soggy biscuits, made feeble attempts to groom ourselves, and despaired of what to do with the sleeping mat and blanket, wet from muddied rainwater. We decided to leave them out to dry in a field off the roadside; if we failed to find civilization within a few miles, we could come back to fetch them.

"Where are we going then?" I asked at last. "If not to England?"

She shrugged. "There must be boats on the western side, heading for Italy."

"You are *not* going back to Barzizza," I said.

"Of course not," she said. "I thought perhaps Genoa." A pause. "You are welcome to come with me, but I can't guarantee how you'll be accepted, as a Gentile."

"I'm willing to take that risk," I said. I grabbed her wrist. I saw her take a quick breath, and she smiled, shy and hopeful, and certainly expectant. We took a step closer to each other; our wet clothes brushed together, clung and stuck.

"Are you certain?" she asked. She turned her wrist slightly upward, as if tentatively surrendering herself into my clutches. With her wet hair cascading manically around her shoulders and the damp tunic clinging with indecorous persistence to her breasts and hips and thighs, she suddenly looked like some sort of pagan sex goddess—an uncharacteristic but very attractive addition to the list of things I liked about her.

"Of course I'm certain. I have nothing and nobody waiting for me anywhere else. I have nothing else at all."

Her smile faded; she glanced down at my hand, then pulled her wrist away. "Neither do I," she said. "I'm not burdening you with it."

"I'm not burdening you."

"You're making me the antidote to suicide," she said, "Forgive me, but I find that a burden." She purposefully stepped away from me. "There must be a village along this path before too long, or at least a farm."

I had little left to say. Jamila filled the silence by pointing out to me the amazing mix of plants, herbs, and flowers we walked past: olives, cypress, cyclamens, mastic trees (these full of resin, she added, if I wanted something to chew on), pomegranates, oaks, walnuts, sage, thyme, rosemary, privet, anemone, irises, lilies, oleander, chamomile . . . When she had exhausted these, she moved on to the lizards, geckos, snakes, and fully three dozen different kinds of butterfly.

Around midday, just as it had become very tedious that we had no food left, a horse and rider came tearing over the crest of our most recent rise, where several wider paths converged. The horse splattered mud up to our faces; I shouted in angry protest at the rider, who was red-faced and frowning—and who was Otto. He gawked with relief when he saw us, pulled Oro around sharply, and without preamble reached down an arm toward me. "Gregor's been arrested. I need your help!"

I was so shocked I stood stupidly a moment; Jamila moved past me and reached for Otto's arm, but I pushed her away. "No," I said.

"You can't go down there. It's unsafe for you and it might be unsafe for him."

"If I'm in any way responsible—" she said.

"It's Boniface's doing, not yours," Otto said and spat.

"What does that mean?" Jamila demanded.

Otto didn't answer, just kicked his foot out of the stirrup and held down his arm; I grabbed it, lifted my leg up high enough to get my toe in the stirrup, and he pulled me up as if I were a child. I wrapped my legs around Oro behind the high-backed saddle. Jamila immediately clasped an arm around each of our left legs and leaned her weight upon them, heavily enough that the horse had to adjust its stance beneath us.

"Hey!" Otto snapped and tried to move Oro from her, but she clung to us.

"What is Boniface up to?" she demanded.

Otto grimaced. "Nobody *really* knows what's going on, but he sent a note to the tent saying . . ." As the absurdity of it suddenly hit him, he laughed a little, angrily. "Saying that he would only release Gregor in exchange for the princess."

"There *is* no princess!" Jamila shouted. "Why doesn't Gregor just *tell* them that?"

"Boniface probably doesn't believe him," said Otto.

"Or doesn't *want* to believe him. I'll set it straight; you stay here, safely out of the way," I ordered Jamila.

"You cannot do this for me," she said, leaning harder on my leg. "It's absurd that he still thinks I'm a princess, but if *that's* the trouble, then there's a very simple remedy. He'll have no interest in an impoverished Jewish widow. Let me mount."

"No!" I said, but Otto ignored me. He released his boot from the stirrup again, and as she hopped around trying to get her toe in, he pulled her up in front of him. Oro snorted briefly in protest.

We were back down on the plain two hours later, Oro nearly dead from exertion. Things were in a muddle. In the dissenting camp we paused long enough to change horses and hear the news, which was only that there was no news: Gregor had been taken by Boniface's men yesterday, had disappeared into the marquis's private tents, and had not been seen or heard from since. The dissenting barons had sent a messenger for him, but the messenger had been chased away by Boniface's guards, who said only that if anyone were to return with the princess, Boniface would receive that person.

"*No*," I insisted yet again, as Jamila said at the same moment, "You see? It's good that I came back. I beg you, please take me there at once."

"I said no," I repeated as I climbed up behind Otto, now on a borrowed mare.

"What do you suggest instead? Continue this inane game of hide-and-seek?" she demanded, holding up an arm, imploring a now uncertain Otto to help her. "When the most important thing we're hiding is the fact that there is really nothing of value to hide? I'm tired of being a fugitive. Sir, I *beg* you, take me there."

And so we trotted along that dreadful final mile, with me barking orders at them the entire way to mask my anxiety: Otto was to find out what the situation was before Jamila presented herself; Jamila was to do nothing without my approval. I had no idea what I was saying, it was blathering nerves, and of course once we arrived nothing happened as I'd said it must. We dismounted a few hundred paces from the marquis's tent, and I approached separately from them, as if I were merely one of the marquis's casual entourage curious to know the latest gossip. Trusting her well-being to Otto nearly made me ill, although I knew he genuinely meant well.

Continuation of entry from Feast of St. Theodosia

I return finally to the matter.

I was in my second day of captivity. This consisted of being tied hands and feet to a cushioned stool, three armed guards—young knights I had ridden with for years in tournaments, and all of whom I'd bested—standing over me.

Milord Boniface and I had already exhausted the discursive potential of the situation. I had emphasized that I was not trying to break up the army but rather trying to preserve it intact; I simply was not committed to keeping it intact and Byzantium-bound. I clarified, often, that this reflected not my own regard for Milord Boniface's leadership but merely my observation that most of the army had independently lost its regard for Milord Boniface's leadership (i.e., his endorsement of Alexios) and was about to bolt into pieces as a result. In keeping all dissenters united under the banner of dissension, regardless of their particular complaints, I was keeping most of the army together—which I had been told was my chief responsibility by Milord Boniface himself. Milord Boniface had only to adjust himself to the collective will of the army and he would easily be reunited with it.

Milord did not see matters as I did. He saw that most of his men had bolted with Gregor of Mainz, and so Gregor of Mainz was the key to getting them back.

"Do not be stupid, Gregor," he was saying for perhaps the dozenth time. "This is very simple. Forswear your dissent, and I shall release you. Refuse, and I shall disown my daughter and leave you with nothing but a bastard for a wife."

This disturbed me immensely, for I would not willingly bring a defenseless woman to harm, but I did not admit that. Instead I said, "I hardly know the lady, milord, despite she carries my seed. You love her more than I do, or you would not have given her to your favorite knight. You will not play with your daughter's life that way. I don't care how many times you threaten it. It is an empty threat."

"Very well," he said. "Forget your marriage. As you obviously did when you took up with an infidel and began to practice her vile religion. I must denounce you for it publicly. And if I do, those men out there won't follow you, even if I give you perfect freedom to try leading them."

I began to say: "Milord, I beg you to consider their complaints before you—"

Milord Boniface made a coarse, dismissive gesture. (The Briton believes I should draw a picture of it here, but it is familiar to anyone who knows the dialect.) "You will not tell me what to consider, boy," he snapped. "If I yield now, this army will be rendered rudderless! I am not an anointed king, Gregor. I have enough of a struggle asserting control as it is. If I let a popular uprising sway me from my course, it's over—this army will have no leadership at all. A king or emperor in my position could bend a little, and it would appear to be divine indulgence. I cannot do that. For the love of God, if there were any man in this army I'd ever indulge at this moment, it would be you. I cannot do it, Gregor."

I said, "So I must promise you that I won't lead them to dissent, and then this farce is finished? I walk out of here, don't make trouble for you with the army, and we pretend this never happened?"

"It's not that simple anymore," Boniface said with relief, seeing I might relent. "Unfortunately, you're so damnably good at rallying troops, there are enough of them rallied that they will cause trouble even without you. No, at this point, I require you to ride out publicly with me to dissuade them from the insubordination you originally lured them into. You must bring them back to me."

I asked, "And if I refuse?"

Milord Boniface smiled tightly. "I don't like to do this, Gregor, and even now I hope you will not consider it a personal rift between us, but I must reclaim my army. Therefore, if you do not help me to reclaim it, things will happen to your beloved Jamila that you would not like to see happen to your worst enemy."

I breathed a genuine sigh of relief; I almost laughed. "Go ahead and try," I said. "She is no longer among us. If that is the dagger you're holding to my throat, I'm afraid it isn't very sharp."

Milord Boniface tensed, startled. "You're bluffing. She's in your tent. I've had her watched from the day you left Zara. I've only to send men to your tent and she's mine."

I shook my head and felt now a great weight lift from me. This was Milord Boniface's last gambit, and it was failing. He would not control me now. He would have to bend to the will of the collected lords. "On the head of St. John, I swear it. She ran off yesterday in the confusion of Alexios's arrival," I said. "I have no idea where she is, and I don't expect ever to see her again. It grieves me too, milord, to see you and me asunder, but I won't call off the dissenters simply to protect Jamila." I laughed indeed now, almost apologetically, explaining, "She does not need my protection any longer!"

And then a mud-splattered, dark-haired woman ran into the room ahead of the guards, ahead of Otto and a certain lute player, ahead of my ability to divert disaster. She threw herself onto her knees before the marquis.

"My name is Jamila of Alexandria, sir," she said to his muddy boots. "I am not a princess."

Milord Boniface's face glowed with delight. "I know that, Jewess. I figured that out months ago. But thank you for responding to the lure."

"I'm worth absolutely nothing to either you or Gregor," she said.

Milord Boniface made a thoughtful face. "Oh, I don't know about that," he said.

I shouted in despair, but already the marquis was bending over and pulling a jewel-hilted dagger from his belt. Otto shoved the lute player out of the tent, sensing he was about to lose his wits from horror, as Boniface yanked Jamila up roughly by the hair, threw back her head so that her neck was exposed, and pressed the point of the dagger just above her collarbone. She yelped with shock.

"Shall we ride out together, Gregor my son?" Milord Boniface asked in a voice of perfect courtliness. "And tell the army it is going to Byzantium?"

* * *

THERE FOLLOWED on the soggy plain of Corfu a most emotional reunion of the dissenters and their leaders. Alexios was flanked on either side by his two most expressive supporters: the Marquis Boniface of Montferrat and Gregor of Mainz.

Gregor of Mainz gave an impassioned speech exhorting the dissenters to restore the greatest throne in Christ's kingdom to the man whose God-given right it was to have it. He dissolved into passionate tears at the feet of Peter of Amiens and the other dissenting barons, begging their forgiveness for misleading them. When he could collect himself, he pleaded with them to keep the army whole and told them this was their holy duty. Seeing how deeply moved the troublemakers were by Gregor's tears, Boniface and the others likewise fell to their knees with sobbing prayers of supplication.

The troublemakers, completely flummoxed, relented and stopped making trouble. They returned to the fold.

After a solemn mass was performed to thank God for the army's delivery, the marquis delighted many of his newly returned wayward sheep by revealing to them that the much-rumored infidel princess really did exist and had been retrieved at last. She had been persuaded to offer her expertise on the politics, customs, lands, and ways of the Egyptians, for we would be moving on to Egypt as soon as our work was finished in Byzantium. She was being given, at last, lodgings worthy of her rank: in one of Boniface's own tents. She would, of course, be converting to Christianity.

On the eve of Pentecost, 24 May 1203, the pilgrim army set sail for Constantinople. The princess sailed on Boniface's ship, where it was rumored he treated her with the gallantry her rank deserved.

Act III

RESTORATION

All those who had never seen Constantinople stared
intently at the city, for they had never imagined there
could be so fine a place in all the world.

—GEOFFREY OF VILLEHARDOUIN,
Chronicle of the Fourth Crusade

29

JUNE 23, the Eve of St. John the Baptist, was a beautiful day—sun warm, sky azure, wind with us. The fleet under sail was magnificent, canvas unfurled and knights' pennants whipping along the sides of the boats; stripes and blocks and squares of colors, lions and bears and dragons and angels and stags and eagles, trees, leaves, feathers, birds, boars, keys, wheels, horses, weapons, castles, imaginary creatures, a few symbols that struck me as obscene, and a thousand other images flapped and waved in the breeze, commanding any passing fisherman to contemplate their greatness.

Churchmen demanded that we hold to the canonical hours, but the sailors refused to ring bells while under sail—yet another of those maritime superstitions. Anyhow, nobody lived the day around such artificial demarcations as hours; here, on the water, the pagan powers of sun, moon, and wind reigned. We had a swift and easy journey through the water called Mare Nostrum, the wind at our back much of the time—creating the remarkable experience that there was no wind at all. At the great Y of this great sea, we had gone left and north to Byzantium, where right and south to Alexandria had once been the plan. Now there was no going back. We continued north through the Aegean and then turned eastward through great perils of navigation and into calmer water. As it finally approached dusk, on this endless day of endless sunshine, the ships prepared to drop anchor in the Sea of Marmara, in sight of Constantinople, Byzantium's greatest city.

In a self-serving but canny flourish, Boniface had sent a message to our tent before sailing claiming the princess required her
handmaid's presence for the duration of the sea voyage. Liliana went
without hesitation, and despite Otto's raging. It was obviously his
own comfort, not the princess's, that Boniface wanted, but at least
the women were together. Believing himself to have their respective
mistresses in hand, Boniface did not worry himself overmuch, for the
duration of the journey, about the German brothers. Holding the
women hostage was enough. I'd tried to get myself onto Boniface's
boat as a musician, but even in his livery, I was rebuffed for lacking pedigree. At least for Prince Alexios's first month with the army,
only nobly born troubadours would play him "Kalenda Maya," and
only the sons of noblemen would serve his meals, remove his boots,
scratch his balls, or turn down his bed. So I was rowed back to the
Venus and tried to figure out another way to reach Boniface's captives. But I couldn't swim and was too poor to get away with bribery,
and my efforts were stymied.

Gregor and I spoke carefully and briefly, lest any of the marquis's
men begin to wonder why the marquis's stupid musician was so
chummy with the marquis's troublesome son-in-law. At Gregor's insistence, I had grudgingly agreed that all our efforts—once we could
make any—must be to get the army to Egypt as fast as possible. Since
Gregor had failed to *prevent* a diversion to Constantinople, his new
goal was to see that the diversion was completed *quickly*. Now that I
perceived Jamila's real home as Constantinople and not Egypt, I had
no such personal investment in hurrying on, but you cannot weather
as much together as Gregor and I had weathered without feeling like
family. Even if it meant an alliance with Boniface, getting the army
in and out of Constantinople fast became our shared new goal—after
rescuing the women.

But there could be nothing said or done for the entire month of
the journey there. My hands were tied as surely as Gregor's. I hated
Boniface heartily, but I did admire his dexterity. Gregor would have

to be his lapdog now, indefinitely. It was not that Jamila's and now Liliana's well-being rested on it; despite his heroic softheartedness in the heat of the moment on Corfu, Gregor would sacrifice both women for the sake of his duty to the army, and Boniface knew that—that was why the charge of trafficking with a Hebrew sorceress was so useful. There is no room, on any crusade, for harborers of Jews. As long as he had Jamila in his grasp, Boniface could play that card against Gregor at any moment.

I had to content myself, under sail, with listening to Otto prattle on about the only thing that grabbed his attention more than fornication: the art of war, and its minutiae—especially in matters equestrian, for Otto was a true lover of all Things Horse. Once, I'd sat through the energetic recitation of the history of horses in battle, beginning in Lombardy—Boniface's own land—in the early seventh century. (Otto resented Boniface but was proud to have even a loose affiliation with a land with such a heritage.) As an indirect result of this, Italy had always had the most sophisticated, disciplined infantry of any place in Christendom, because knights and foot soldiers had for so long operated together as an integrated unit. I dozed off for the next five centuries but awoke to a new litany, now of the pedigree of Gregor's great horse, Summa, who at over eighteen hands was surely one of the largest in the army. Then Otto had moved on to explain the latest developments in sword technology (something called steel from someplace called Scandinavia), and I'd drifted off again into my own fretful daydreams.

Now we were at last, at last, *at last* off the shores of the great Byzantium, with an army that was about to commit an illegal act against its Holy Father's express orders, not realizing that was what it was about to do. The Venetians drew the whole of the fleet into a curving line, over a mile long, so that all could gaze together at Constantinople, Queen of Cities, which had risen into view before us golden in the late afternoon light. Along the huge line of ships, an awed silence descended. In the sunset, rigging and gawking pilgrims were silhouetted against the great canvas sails like sketches on vellum.

On the deck of the *San Giorgio*, Boniface of Montferrat probably wondered if he had not misjudged his chances at making an impression upon so great a city. His honored guest—bound at the wrists with an armed youth hovering over her—said, with a knowing look, "That's nothing but a downwind seawall. Wait until we near the Bosporus."

On the *Lady Pilgrim*, the Bishop of Troyes had invited Bishop Conrad and Gregor of Mainz to gaze upon the panorama with him. They agreed that it would be a marvelous thing indeed if the great churches rising up before them, churches of such spiritual wealth, worshiped not by the law of the Byzantine patriarch—a foolish man whose name they could not even remember—but by that of His Holiness Pope Innocent III.

On the *Venus*, I stared dumbfounded, blinking, speechless. I could not make sense of what was before me now: we were still miles offshore from Constantinople, yet its walls stretched out so far I could not see the ends of them as they vanished inland in one direction and curved around the protruding, peninsular nose of the city. There were more towers than I could count—than I could understand the need for—and within, rising higher than the walls, were squat domes like those of churches I'd seen in Venice. One in particular seemed too large to have been made by man. There was a deceptive tranquillity from this distance; stone buildings rose gracefully on verdant slopes behind the walls. I wasn't sure what I'd been expecting, but it wasn't this. The city seemed almost smug from here, and deservedly so.

The next morning at dawn the fleet weighed anchor and sailed directly alongside the walls of the city itself, as the awed silence stayed upon us. When we were in hearing distance, heralds in the vanguard transports sounded trumpets and pounded drums; this cacophony summoned to the walls an enormous flock of turbaned, bearded citizens, who stared at us unenthusiastically as we sailed by, the local fishing vessels scurrying to move out of our way. It was hard for me to believe there could be so many people all in one place. There were some rude gestures from the walls, some clownish waves, but generally, the Constantinopolitans appeared more wary than either welcoming or defiant.

We sailed and rowed past this headland of the city and then tried to continue on, into the broad mouth of a broad river that poured its swift-flowing southbound current directly against us. It was the fluid equivalent of trying to walk into a gale. From this spot of such sailing difficulty, we had an astonishing view of the city to our left. There was that one reddish, squat-domed church, far larger than the rest, around which the metropolis seemed to expand. Near it, just visible, was an enormous stone or metal column, on top of which perched a speck that, when viewed through squinted eyes, turned out to be the statue of a man on horseback, apparently raising a hand to point at the very shore where we were headed. (The *Venus* mariners muttered unhappily about that, but, as I have had occasion to note before, mariners are a determinedly superstitious lot.) Nearer than the church and its ambivalent equestrian, roofs of great anonymous buildings crowded the low hill by the seawall. The walls themselves did not impede the view of what was behind them, but the hills and outlying buildings did. Along a narrow inland harbor, humbler buildings rambled on and on out of sight. There was a string of wooden barges stretched protectively across the mouth of the harbor. The barges themselves could not protect much, but upon them lay the city's great, fabled defense: its harbor chain. Although it was barely visible as a rumpled black line from here, the very fact that we could *see* it from so far away gave evidence of its massive size. I could hardly believe that enough people to build and inhabit such a place could live together without waging internecine war. Surely more people dwelt behind that tower-studded wall than existed in all Britain. What could two hundred ships of soldiers accomplish against all that?

We landed at the site of an imperial summer palace called Scutari; Boniface and his closest cronies moved into this red-and-white stone monstrosity; the rest of the army staked their tents nearby, atop the steep hills that plunged straight down into the river, which was called the Bosporus—and which was not a river, I was informed by a Venetian sailor, but a *strait*. (When I asked him for the definition of a strait, it seemed to me that he was merely describing a specific kind of river. Mariners are so fussy with their terminology.) The sailing transports were towed by the galleys against the current farther up the Bosporus, to a place where the shoreline hills began to soften; here it was easier to unload both horses and heavier objects—armor, storage boxes—for portage to the camp compound.

Upon disgorgement of the equine transports, a shortage of horses was revealed. Many had died en route, from disease or dehydration; we had consumed them, none the wiser until now. Despite pillaging the palace stores, the army was desperately low on supplies, and the infantry was put to foraging. Grains and fruits ripened early here, so the army helped itself to the fields and orchards of local villages. That, I thought, would make a really grand first impression on the local population.

Wobbling as the solid land seemed to roll in waves beneath us, Gregor, Otto, and I pretended to settle into one of the whore pavilions for the afternoon, hoping for interesting gossip, but heard nothing. While Gregor was adamant that we operate by diplomacy, Otto and I agreed we needed to get into the palace for a look-round, to know better how to spring the women out; we agreed also that I could do this most unobtrusively, since nobody knew to associate me with the captives. So I donned Boniface's red-and-white livery and presented myself at the gates of Scutari Palace with lute and fiddle. I had no idea what the plans were for prosecuting this campaign, nor did I know how long we'd linger here. Which meant I did not know how long I'd have to worm my way into the women's presence now that I was in the palace. I didn't even know where they were being kept.

I had thought all palaces alike; I was wrong. This was my first

Byzantine palace. I'd see a far grander one within the month, but this one dazzled me. I was unceremoniously let in through a side door and up several flights of marble stairs, to a large, high-roofed hall with walls that actually glittered gold. Blue and green marble columns held up the huge golden ceiling. The floor was a busy geometrical pattern of polished stone—dark green, maroon, white. (I realized then the Greeks were either mad or stupid; who, given the choice, would choose domestic flooring as hard and cold as marble?) Columns defined a low gallery along one wall, to which I was escorted. I found myself beside a mosaic of rosy peasant children milking goats that were larger than Gregor. Across the hall from me, a row of arched windows faced out over the Bosporus strait, giving us a grand view to the city and its harbor. There was only one chair, where Alexios was sitting; following the Byzantine custom, everybody else, including the musicians, had to stand in his presence. "Everybody else" in this case was an extremely convenient assemblage for my business: the Marquis Boniface of Montferrat; Enrico Dandolo, the Doge of Venice; Boniface's immediate subordinates, mostly counts and barons.

And Gregor of Mainz, who had managed to get himself into the palace, too.

And, at last: Liliana and Jamila.

30

THEY APPEARED well-treated and well-clothed; in fact, ridiculously well-clothed. Palace wardrobes had been ransacked to give them brocade gowns worthy of their supposed stature, with (my heart fluttered) bare shoulders. Jamila wore a headdress like a small crown, with its own earrings dangling from it, which under other circumstances would have made me laugh out loud. It bulged with turquoise and globs of jewels so huge I thought they must be glass.

Of course, the official reason for Jamila's ludicrous costuming, in fact the whole ludicrous charade, was to keep Gregor in line: the princess, beautiful and helpful and on the cusp of conversion to Christianity, was much spoken of, always in connection with Gregor of Mainz—so if she were suddenly revealed as an unrepentant, common Jew, it would destroy his integrity among his peers. (This struck me as very silly, but then, I had not been raised in the world of continental chivalry and its attendant anti-Semitism. Where I came from, Jews were only Bible characters, and since they were a put-upon nation, we admired their ferocity in dealing with their enemies. Thus, Gregor's terror of being associated with one struck me as decidedly unsoldierly, but I finally accepted that he and I navigated by different stars.)

Gregor was on his knees before Alexios, bowing his head. I realized he had been summoned here to reconfirm his willingness to play along with the farce—thus the women's presence too. I stepped into the musicians' box next to the piper, who seemed to have had more to drink than to eat today, at least based on his breath.

"Crazy, it is," he whispered to me. He had to lean against the wall to keep from falling over. "Damn royals, all this silliness. Been bowin' to each other for the past three hours, haven't they? Here's an *ut* so you can tune your strings to me."

Boniface had knelt beside Gregor and began helping him to rise. "My son, you must not debase yourself so, we are all soldiers of Christ and equal in his eyes," he began sonorously. I'd never heard the marquis sound so satisfied.

"As a soldier of Christ, milord, I must emphasize my eagerness to see us accomplish our task here, that we may the sooner press on to the Holy Land and do his intended work," said Gregor. "The sooner we attain victory here, the sooner we may strive for it where the Lord will actually smile upon our efforts."

Boniface frowned, but Alexios did not grasp the nuance of the comment. The prince was looking bored, actually, and excused himself—an exit that took place with a great deal of fanfare from my fellow musician and myself. He demanded that Liliana retire with him. She glanced at Boniface with a look that teetered between boredom and desperation. The marquis made a gesture of regret, blew her a kiss, then signaled a guard to make sure she went along, docile, after the prince. A good thing Otto wasn't present.

"And now, Her Highness will share her knowledge of the environs," Boniface announced, ostensibly to the small assembly of lords but mostly to Jamila.

None of them questioned why an Egyptian princess would know so much about a land three seas removed from her own. Either they had an even worse grasp of geography than I did or they knew what she was but were also playing along with the farce.

The men followed the sweep of Boniface's gesture toward the bank of high, arched windows looking westward, toward the city. At a noise from the marquis, an attendant signaled us to stop playing. I set down the lute and craned my neck—I had an unimpeded view across the width of the hall and out the windows, over the men's heads.

"Milady," Boniface said with a grand gesture and placed Jamila like a preacher before them. We were three flights up in a palace that was perched upon a cliff twice that high again. We were directly across the Bosporus from the chained mouth of the deepest, most protected harbor I've ever seen. It spilled out eastward into the Bosporus just as the Bosporus spilled southward into the Sea of Marmara. Jamila explained to her audience that the city proper, safely behind the massive, towered walls we'd sailed past last week, was a peninsula—not a nearly detached, penile spit of land, as Zara had been, but an insolent protrusion jutting off the mainland, a sort of rounded triangle, like an upturned nose or the curling toe of a fancy shoe. The toe pointed east, toward us, across the Bosporus. The northern shore of the peninsula—the place where the shoe would be laced up—was protected both by the wall and by this deep and narrow harbor, the Golden Horn, the greatest trading port in all the world. The city continued tentatively north beyond the harbor (to our right), in a settlement called Pera; Her Highness's voice caught as she said this word. An enormous tower, Galata, guarded not only Pera but, more important, the harbor mouth, where the Golden Horn flowed out into the Bosporus. Across the calm, safe (but deep) waters of the harbor, ferry service was regular and cheap, Her Highness added, as if she were trying to sell us real estate.

The same was not true for boat service across the turbulent Bosporus, which separated us from all this urbanity. A swarm of tiny craft huddled in the dead center of the channel, facing directly into, and inexplicably resisting, the current while the one or two fishermen in each boat concerned themselves with checking nets. Transport boats sailed nervously and swiftly south down the strait, no doubt with a wary eye on the gargantuan Venetian fleet. We saw no boats trying to cross against the current.

"It is extremely challenging to cross the Bosporus," Jamila explained, speaking again from her distant childhood memories. She made no attempt to play the part of princess, but her native bearing remained as intimidating and graceful as the first time I'd set eyes on her. "It requires boats with special equipment."

"Which is obviously why none of Alexios's supporters managed to get over here to greet our arrival." Boniface smiled at Jamila. "Proceed. Explain what *that* is."

That, to which he gestured, was a swath of reddish orange tents on the slopes below Galata. They were too small from here for us to read the insignias on the pennants.

"That is the army of the *basileus*, His Majesty Alexios the Third, uncle of your prince Alexios," Jamila announced. The men murmured with interest and pressed closer to the windows, as if an extra half pace would give them a clearer view of a man four thousand paces distant. "He is the man whom you refer to as the Usurper."

"Because he *is* the Usurper," Boniface said in a warning voice. "Confine yourself to the geography lesson, Your Highness."

Jamila pointed out the window. "He is there to protect the chain. The tower he's at the foot of, Galata, was built to guard the harbor mouth. You see one side of the hill faces the harbor, and perpendicular to that, one side faces the Bosporus. At the foot of the hill, between them, the harbor chain has been fastened closed. That chain is the largest in the world, each iron link longer than a man and thicker than his arm, and it is attached at the waterside in Pera." Again her voice twinged at the word. "Between the Bosporus current, the archers up in the tower, and the Usurper's army of Varangian guards right there on the hillside, it will be impossible to unfasten the chain, and it is simply impossible to break it—that's been tried many times in the past five hundred years, and never with success."

"Must we get into the harbor?" somebody asked. "Why can't we just attack the city walls directly?"

"Because we are not attacking the city!" Dandolo snapped. "Only its current ruler. Anyhow, attacking the city walls from the water is a futile undertaking. That current makes it impossible. We crafted this fleet specifically to attack in the waters near Alexandria, not in the treacherous current of the Bosporus. We might hurl some rocks at them, but we could not secure the boats to engage in combat. The only way to take the city from here is somehow to get into the harbor. This has been known for centuries but never accomplished."

"So our only choice is to engage directly with the Usurper's men for custody of the chain," Gregor observed, staring out the window. There was a long silence as they stared bereftly out the window at the singular topography. "Milord," Gregor said cautiously, "please consider what that would require: for us to cross against the Bosporus current and then land—still in the current—at the foot of a virtual cliff teeming with armed men. To get to the chain mechanism, we'd have to fight our way *sidewise* around the hill, unprotected from not only the soldiers but the scores of archers in the tower above. That is a *huge* tower," he said, sounding slightly desperate.

"There is a reason the city has never been taken," said Jamila. "It's not because it's never been attacked. It's been attacked by far larger forces than yours."

Gregor was still staring out the window. "Can we bypass the Usurper, bring the boats straight to where the chain is attached— What did you say that cliffside neighborhood overlooking the harbor was called—"

"Pera," Jamila answered quietly. "That is where Constantinople's Jews are."

Ah. Where she'd been born and where members of her extended family probably still resided. Where I'd have to return her, to honor the vow I'd made. The longing on her face as she stared at what she couldn't see broke my heart, and made me jealous.

"If you try to reach the chain from below, you will still have the archers in the tower. That is the genius of Galata Tower; you can shoot clear to the water through a full half-circle arc."

For a while longer the men stared out the window. Several times a baron would open his mouth to make a suggestion, then see the flaw in his plan and stop himself.

"Do you understand now why I did not rush to agree to this?" Dandolo said, like a rebuking father, after a long silence. "I resent this empire, but I respect its few remaining strengths, which consist mostly of Constantinople's flawless defenses."

Gregor stepped back from Jamila, worked his way closer to Boniface. "I will not encourage men to risk their—" he began, but Boniface shushed him with a gesture.

"If need be, yes you will," he announced quietly and walked away.

*　*　*

FOR THE NEXT FEW DAYS, a tense, silent standoff continued. Each evening the sun would set beyond the Golden Horn, the harbor smugly secure behind its great black iron chain. The pilgrims spread out foraging, heading farther and farther inland. Here was largely wilderness, but there were cornfields and orchards nearby; it was a popular area for the summer palaces of the Byzantine court's enormous aristocratic circle. I was astounded by the density of fish in the Bosporus. I watched a peasant stand on the shore, reach into the water, and with his bare hand pull out a bonito. This was a neat trick, so I tried it myself—with similar results. But knights and barons required flesh, and so the foot soldiers and servants spent most of the week seeking it out for them.

In the evenings, we would huddle in the tent and in low tones anxiously discuss—sometimes debate—the situation, while the Richardim played chess beside the lantern. We agreed that impeding Boniface would accomplish nothing now; it would only make him hold the women tighter and might slow down the larger task of reusurpation (as I had taken to calling the treaty with Alexios). Gregor returned to rallying the troops in daily training exercises. His old golden glow was gone—I doubted even then that it would ever return—but he spoke with warmth and earnestness to the men, telling them the only path to salvation lay in concluding their business here quickly and efficiently.

I tried daily to get back into the palace as a musician and was occasionally successful, but I didn't see the women again and was never left alone long enough to try to find them. Otto tried relentlessly as well; he never was a quiet soul, or subtle, and all the guards knew he would be trying to break in anyhow, so he did not make it even through the gate. Not knowing what was going on was maddening.

Following the Feast of the Precious Blood of Our Lord
Jesus Christ, 1 July

*I had thought not to enter anything into these pages so long as we were
in Byzantium, for this was meant to chronicle a pilgrimage only, and as
long as we are diverted, I consider our pilgrimage suspended. However,
on reflection it strikes me that I must chronicle how we intend to return
to our course, and so I shall write after all.*

*I believe that if we act with great precision, speed, and decisiveness,
we may yet make Jerusalem by autumn. Thus, I make myself now a
warrior in all ways, which was hard to do while cooped up in a house
in Zara through the winter, or on a ship for months at a stretch. Finally
I am somewhat in my element, and although I am older, wiser, and
sadder than I was before I saw the canals of Venice, still I am more
content than I have been since then. I have sharpened my sword, whose
name is the Hand of Nicholas (in honor of the bishop who defended
the divinity of Christ by striking Arius in the face at the Council of
Nicaea). I have been leading training sessions and rallying the troops
again. Boniface heard about this and responded well: I am now daily
summoned to Scutari Palace to attend the parliaments in which the
leaders contemplate their next course of action. This has been going
on for a few days. I privately prefer the counsel of Dandolo of Venice,
who (despite his bloodthirstiness in Zara) pleads for diplomatic resolu-
tions, not an actual attack. But I am always gracious to my esteemed
father-in-law, who finally feels that I, like fine leather, have molded
myself to accommodate what pulls most at me. This morning, Milord
Boniface publicized his faith in me so far as to invite me to command a
unit of knights overseeing the foragers assigned to gather fuel. I took my
brother Otto as my second in command. He is more aggrieved about
the situation with the women than am I, and requires as much diversion
as the Briton and I can think to give him, so he was grateful to come
out with me.*

As is normal for such circumstances, we did not bother with our armor (especially because the day was very hot), only our squires following with our shields. We were not expecting to come across troops so far from the city, but in late afternoon, in sweltering, humid heat, we surprised a camp of five hundred Byzantine soldiers, all on horseback. I believe they were a scouting party sent to learn more about us; however, they may have been guarding the empire's eastern flank against incursions from the Seljuk Turks.

Although we have had no experience mounted in arms together yet, the eighty knights of my unit did an impressive job of dividing into four squadrons and charging at the Greeks in their camp—a corps six times our size. The Greeks wore a strange armor I have not seen before: close-fitting but skirted, and looking like horn or shell, in small connected plates making up the hauberk, with iron on the shoulders; it resembles images of ancient Roman soldiers. Milord Boniface had alerted me that Byzantine battle training leans toward group action rather than individual feats of valor, so I expected that a group of them would be something fearsome—but they were, rather, fearful. They were shocked by our great ferocity and fled (with womanly cowardice but admirable coordination), deserting their tents, their provisions, and many mules and horses. We pursued them for a mile, until I realized that the true value of this victory lay in what was still at the camp and returned to claim the booty. In truth it was a small accomplishment, but my soldiers and I were received back at Scutari like conquering heroes. If word of our great abilities reaches the Usurper, perhaps he will surrender to us before there is even the opportunity to meet him in arms. By St. John's head, we might be back in the boats and sailing to Egypt within days! Tomorrow at the midday meal, all of my men and I are to be feted at the palace, given the best of the palace's stores as our meal, and serenaded by a band of musicians. We hope to see the women there as well, but I suspect Boniface will have sequestered them, as he does whenever I am there.

* * *

Alexios liked that I could play his native music on both the fiddle and harp, so it was easy to secure a place on the musicians' dais for the feast. Between tunes I chatted with the other musicians, especially the drunken piper; he had no idea where the women were being kept but made stomach-churning comments about what he assumed Boniface was doing with them both, "especially that dark one, she's Greek fire in a skirt."

I felt my mouth open to make some comment my mind had not formed yet, but I was interrupted by Gregor's gentle baritone coming from the high table. I turned. Prince Alexios was at the center of the table, and in by far the largest chair, yet Marquis Boniface seemed to be the one holding court. Gregor, bulkier than Boniface but not as elegant, was to his right, wearing a ceremonial tunic hastily prepared by Boniface's tailor for this feast: the chest was emblazoned with the upper half of Boniface's coat of arms (an arm wielding a dagger, framed by antlers) and the lower half of Gregor's (a St. John's wort flower), thus demonstrating to all present how closely the hero of the day was allied with his leader. This was to impress the knights as much as the lords: *See*, Boniface was saying to the men, *stick with this fellow and you'll eat at my table*. Otto sat beside his brother, the handsomer of the two, distracted as he tried to spy out where the women might be kept.

It amused me, how ill at ease Gregor was in such a setting. He was as natural as the elements on a training field, with dirt or mud or horse sweat clinging to him; he was casually confident in a war council, where the fate of an army hung on his insight; but put him in a dress tunic and he looked like a boy trying to hide his first erection from his mother. The confiding smile of the soldier suddenly seemed sheepish; the elder-brother confidence of the strategist evaporated like spirits set too near a flame. "Milords," he said, "my men and I thank you for honoring us this evening, but truly we did no more than what our duty called for. And while we found it satisfying and reassuring that we were so efficient in dispatching our enemy, I hope you will join me in my prayer that today was the last of any bloodshed here."

There was a musing, collective *hn* of surprise at this sentiment.

"By that I mean," he pressed on, "let us hope that we are able to place His Highness on the throne as quickly, efficiently, and bloodlessly as possible, and then, enriched, that we may move quickly on to the Holy Land to fulfill our vows, leaving the people and the nation of Byzantium in peace and prosperity."

Leathery Dandolo, the Doge of Venice, applauded, nodding heartily. And a fraction of a heartbeat later, Alexios and Boniface followed suit, at which point the rest of the hall joined in as well. Dandolo seized the moment: he held out a hand for silence and rose from his seat to speak. Agreeing with the wisdom of Gregor of Mainz, he emphasized that, if there were to be any warfare at all, it might, and he hoped should, be limited to taking Galata Tower and releasing the harbor chain. Once the fleet had sailed into the Golden Horn, that should be the end of battle. If the Usurper even survived an attack on Galata, surely he would capitulate then. Or at least his advisers, seeing which way the wind blew, would remove him themselves and come flocking, with the all-important Varangian Guard in tow, to Alexios. The battle for Galata Tower should be all that was ever asked of the fighting forces.

Because Prince Alexios was present, the doge worded his argument carefully, but it seemed obvious that Dandolo did not think much of Alexios's potential. This made him anxious to see that the transition of power happened peacefully. Alexios as a tyrant would never stand a chance; he would fall, and that would interrupt trade. Dandolo, now that I finally understood him, was really very simple: he existed for Venice, and Venice existed for commerce. All of his decisions came back to that. He would be unshakably consistent, unlike the bishops and their annoying spiritual hand-wringing and legalistic Catholic flip-flopping. Dandolo hardly cared that I existed, and he wanted something different from the world than I did, yet I thought of us as accidental allies.

The applause that followed dutifully on his speech (Boniface and Alexios looked *bored*) was cut short by a sound outside the door. Half the soldiers leapt to their feet as the hall received an unexpected visitor.

31

A SMALL, DARK-HAIRED MAN in a long robe like the one Dandolo often wore, his hair and beard very long, entered. A guard patted him down. Carrying a scroll, he crossed the hall to the table where Alexios and the lords awaited their dessert. He bowed deeply and then surprised everyone by announcing in Piedmontese, "I am Niccolo Roux, and I am a native of Lombardy now living within the walls of Constantinople." He offered the scroll. Gregor stood, moved into the open section of the hall, took the scroll, and examined the seal.

"That's who he is," Gregor allowed. "He's been sent by our prince's uncle."

Boniface summoned the man to speak and, at the same moment, signaled his French interpreter to translate for the northern barons. "My lord," Niccolo began smoothly and then went on to show great skill at speaking parenthetically: "My lord the *basileus* Alexios sends greetings to you, the best men alive (except those with crowns, of course) and from the greatest countries in the world (except Byzantium, of course). He marvels at your appearance in his empire, for he (a Christian) knows that you (Christians all) are on your way to save the city of Christ and the Holy Sepulchre, and he cannot fathom what would lead you to these parts instead. If you are in need of food, he is happy to provide for you and help to send you on your way (as his forebears have done for your forebears). He is certain you cannot be here to do him any harm, for (even if you were twenty times the size you are), you would naturally be utterly annihilated if (for some unforeseeable reason) he were given need to wish to harm you."

With a wan smile, he bowed and took a step back, anticipating that there would be considerable discussion before he was responded to.

But Boniface answered instantly and smoothly. "Good sir, how can your lord marvel about our entering his empire, when this empire is not even his? It belongs to his nephew, who honors us in this hall with his presence. If your lord is willing to throw himself upon his nephew's mercy, returning his throne and domain, we will happily intercede with his nephew on his behalf, arguing clemency and provisions enough for him to live comfortably to the end of his days. We have nothing more to say to you. Do not be bold enough to return to us unless it is with a message that your lord wishes to surrender." Casually, he made a gesture suggesting that Niccolo Roux was to leave now.

The emissary looked suddenly dyspeptic. He glanced around the room, at the unsmiling faces waiting to return to their meal. Apparently he needed to reassure himself that there were no Greeks present, and then he threw himself hard at Gregor's knees, grabbing his boots in supplication and almost overcome with emotion.

"Please, my lords," he said, in a lowered voice, as if even unaccompanied he were terrified of being overheard. The Lombard accent suddenly grew stronger. "The emperor is not an evil man, but he is not sound of mind. Since he blinded his brother, Emperor Isaac, a decade back, he has not slept a single night in peace but is so plagued with guilt and desperation for what he has done, he borders on the edge of insanity now. He is not stable, and his wrath, if inflamed, will fall quickest and hardest on the Latins living within the city walls. My people and I will suffer for your enterprise before you have even unsheathed your swords. I beg you, milords, as fellow Catholics, as fellow Romans"—with a supplicating gesture—"and you, milord marquis, as a fellow Lombard, *please* do not meddle in a world you do not understand."

Boniface looked repulsed by the fellow's display and gestured Gregor to shunt him away. "What devilishness is this?" he demanded. "Does your lord consider us such simpletons we would respond to a trick?"

"This is no trick, milord, I beg you," said the Lombard, releasing Gregor but remaining on his knees. "We will be the sacrificial pawns. Why do you think he sent a fellow Lombard to speak to you? He wanted to make sure you understood, in your own language, how important it is for you to mind your own business. I speak as your neighbor, not his, and yet I *beg* you, milord, pack up your ships and sail away."

Boniface gestured toward Gregor, who immediately bent over the nervous emissary. Gregor hoisted him and held him in the air until Niccolo finally relented and lowered his feet to the ground. Gregor released him but stood between him and the marquis so he could not continue his pleading.

"You may leave us," Boniface announced. "And nobody in this room will *ever* refer to that peculiar, ignoble outburst."

"I disagree," said Dandolo, almost amused. "We must *use* this information. I won't gratuitously risk the lives of any of my men— they are the pride, the flower, and the future of my homeland. If the Usurper is personally feeble, and the men around him know that and despair of him—we might try to negotiate with them."

"They won't," Niccolo said miserably. "Everyone is too frightened of—" And Dandolo concluded with him: "The Varangian Guard."

"The what, milord?" asked a count.

"The Varangian Guard," Dandolo said, as if anyone with any education should have known this. "The mercenaries who make up the emperor's personal army. They're famously loyal and famously incorruptible. They are the only reason most recent emperors have lasted as long as they have. If they even suspect this fellow has told us what he has, they'll no doubt kill him as a traitor. But we should at least send a spy. We should consider what is possible before throwing valuable lives away in warfare."

"Hear, hear," Gregor said warmly and opened his mouth to continue.

Boniface stood up so fast his chair shot out behind him, making an unpleasant screech on the marble floor. "Do not gainsay me," he snapped at his son-in-law. "I will speak with Dandolo on the matter, but *you* may not speak against me. It is a delicate truce between us, and you shall not take liberties. Lombard, did you hear? You are *dismissed.*"

I too was dismissed a moment later, with my fellow entertainers, when it became clear that the entertainment, as such, was over for the day.

To exit the palace via the servants' gate, I walked, with lute and fiddle cases both hanging off one shoulder, through a courtyard to a side gate. I was fuming with agitation. A building here had an upstairs balcony; I always glanced up there when I walked through, on the unlikely chance of seeing one of the women, but I never had.

Liliana stood there. She smiled and called out, "Hello, Lute Man," as if we were casual acquaintants whose paths naturally crossed whenever we found ourselves in strange Byzantine palaces. My stomach clenched; I stopped short, but she vanished into a doorway up there. Startled, I continued walking toward the exit, grateful I finally had some information about the women's general location. Now I just had to figure out how to use it.

As I neared the gate, I was greeted by a fellow musician passing me, and as I looked left to greet him, I had the most confounding sensory experience of my life. At the same moment I was accosted by smell, touch, and sound: the smell was human excrement, which wafted unpleasantly by just as my entire right side took the impact of a crashing body: a woman grabbed my elbow and pressed herself into me as if she wanted us to take up the same space; her free hand reached toward my face and, literally jerking my attention from the musician, pulled my face down against hers, cheek to cheek and then, good God, lip to lip. "I suppose you forgot to bring rope again," Jamila murmured, her lips moving against mine. "Luckily I've worked it out so we don't need any this time. What would you do without me?"

My heart jumped. "I'd hoped to do this under other circumstances," I said, kissing her too. I brought my hand across to caress (that is, obscure) her profile as we kept walking briskly, toward the gate. "*What* is that smell? Did you escape through a latrine?" She was wearing Liliana's shift.

"Nearly," she said, grabbing my face with her hands as if she were so in love with me she wanted to eat the skin off my lips. "A little on my hem, my shoes were covered but I kicked 'em off." She waved her hand in my face to obscure her own. "See the ring? I left the other jewelry behind, but this I couldn't bear to lose. Do what you're told."

"What about Liliana?" I asked. We were ten paces from the exit.

"Safe," she said. "Still in here, but safe."

"Otto's half-mad from—"

"He'll survive. We talked it out, and this is best. We have a very specific plan, so do what you're told." She tapped my nose and, grinning for anyone watching, kissed me again. We were at the gate. I saw from the corner of my eye people watching us, smiling: *Ah, love.* Or: *He must have paid her well.* In any case, we made a benign impression.

And then we were outside the palace compound and in the army camp. Stone gave way to soil. The breeze was stronger, the air was fresher, my heart slowed a little. We continued to walk forward in that clumsy way that peasant couples do when they have eyes, and hands, only for each other. She kept grinning. Her grin was not an expression I was used to, but she looked adorable. "You're grand at this rescuing business," she said, planting kisses on my forehead. I wanted another kiss on the mouth, but I was too flustered to remember how to get one.

"I hardly feel heroic," I said.

"We've been *over* this," she said. "Is the purpose of this exercise for you to feel heroic, or for me to get out of here? Someday you'll learn the greatest heroism is in the smallest acts. If you could just learn that, you'd stop causing so much *trouble*. In the meantime, do what you're told." Another grin, and then a kiss on the lips.

"Hey! Lute Man!" a commanding voice called from behind me. Oh, dammit, we would be caught now, now that we were supposed to be out of danger.

I glanced behind me. Dandolo's steward was standing at the threshold of the gate, waving a small bag at me. "Your fee!" he called out, not wanting to actually demean his feet by treading off palace grounds. "Take it now or I won't remember later."

"Ah, yes," I said with satisfaction. Jamila was releasing me, so I released her too but brought my hand around to squeeze her buttock—purely for the benefit of anyone watching, of course. "Wait here, poppet," I brayed. "I'm bringing home the salt; it will buy you a pretty tunic." I turned back and trotted up to him in the gateway.

But once my face was visible from inside the walls, a page boy signaled to me to re-enter the courtyard. "Lute Man!" I resisted the urge to glance back out at Jamila and stepped into the yard. The boy pointed up toward the balcony. "Lute Man!" he said again.

Liliana, like an excited child, began, all aflutter, to prance down the stairs. I took a few steps farther into the yard, confused. "Lute Man!" she said. "I've something for you from my mistress!" Ah, so they had in mind an entire escapade. "My mistress loved your playing 'Kalenda Maya' last week, she's been wanting me to reward you! Just wait . . ." And when she got near the bottom of the stairs, she stumbled and tripped. She managed to land rump first, unhurt, but

I couldn't tell if it were staged. Everything else the two of them had worked up had been so theatrical, this was probably part of it.

I was beside her in a moment, and if it was an act, it was a good one. She'd torn her tunic skirt and skinned part of her shinbone. But she flashed me a quick grin. "Here," she said, handing me a bag. "From my mistress. Help a clumsy woman up."

I helped her rise; we bent over her torn tunic and made a fuss, as if that would help to mend it. "What's *your* plan for getting out of here?" I whispered.

"I'm treated well here, don't worry about me," she whispered back.

"I can't just *leave* you here. If I bring home Jamila and not you, Otto will—"

"It won't be like that. Trust me. Just do what you're told." We stood but kept fussing over her tunic. She raised her voice. "So there you have it, Lute Man! The princess is your biggest admirer, and next time you're here, she begs you play for us."

"It will be my honor," I said, then turned and ran out the gate, nodding to the steward as I went. Jamila's absence would be discovered soon; we had to get as far away as possible, and quickly.

But Jamila wasn't where I'd left her.

I looked around and didn't see her. Below me, the emissary's boat was rowing back across the Bosporus; behind me, the palace went about its business; around me, the camp cleaned up from dinner, horses were exercised, whores were waking up. No Jamila. I felt a brief spasm of panic, but I calmed myself; the two women, however melodramatic, seemed to know what they were doing. I looked at the two little bags clutched in my hand. The red-and-white one was just slivers of money from Dandolo; the purple one was the one that Liliana had handed me. I opened it.

It contained a little rolled-up scroll of parchment, with a few words hastily penned on it, smeared from being rolled up before the ink was dry. They were misspelled, so I had to sound them out a couple of times before I realized she meant to write, in the language I had taught her, *Maddeua i fi. Yr wyf yn y cwch.*

Forgive me. I am on the boat.

I looked up. And saw the Lombard embassy's boat pulling back across the Bosporus, toward the Usurper's camp. Toward Pera.

32

INSTANTLY I DECIDED she was, for the third time, wrong to leave me—which justified pursuing her. I didn't want to prevent her from returning home; I just wanted to make sure she got there safely. Obviously. How very chivalrous of me.

I hid my instruments by a tree, scrambled down to the water, and used the money from Dandolo to try bribing a Venetian to row me across the Bosporus in a longboat after her. I had no takers. I offered then to buy the longboat but lacked the funds.

So I tried to swim across, although I cannot swim; I hoped Christian charity would coerce one of the Venetians to come and save me in a boat, which I'd then commandeer somehow.

This plan failed: Christian charity was not part of today's Venetian diet, and I was whirled around the bend of Scutari, grasping desperately to a branch, before a fortuitous eddy flung me smack against a mooring pole. There was a guide rope tied to the pole, the other end anchored into a rock low in the cliff face. The rope was slimy, but it was firm; hand over hand, drinking a stomachful of seawater, and not infrequently butted by fish, I pulled myself back to solid, stony ground and sat there gasping, retching, sopping, and trying not to feel sorry for myself.

When my heart's thudding had returned to something like normal, I tried to think what to do next. Otto and Gregor were still at the feast, but our tent would be searched as soon as Boniface realized he'd lost Jamila. So my going to the tent was a bad idea.

Come to think of it, my going anywhere at all was a bad idea until I no longer looked like a drowned gecko. The afternoon was very hot; I lay on the rocks and stretched myself out, first on my back and later on my stomach, drying off. When hunger pressed me, I rose and, with no little effort, grabbing at exposed roots and overhanging branches, groped my way up the overgrown slope, to the top of the hill overlooking the Bosporus and the city. Once I was up there, travel was easy, and I made my way back to the outskirts of the army camp in little time.

It seemed best to hide in plain sight and go straight back to Scutari Palace, especially since I needed to know what was going on there. I approached the postern gate with the excuse that I'd left my rebec inside. An extra guard just outside the gate prevented my entry, but he sent a page to fetch the rebec from Dandolo's steward. I was told to wait.

"You weren't here before," I said to the guard, to make conversation.

"High alarm up. Haven't heard? The princess was kidnapped by the Usurper!"

Surely nobody was stupid enough to believe that. I tried to appear duly horrified. "When did *that* happen?" I demanded. "I was just here!"

"Hour back," the fellow said brusquely, knowingly. "As the feast ended. The envoy took her. But we're scouring the camp. Could've had inside assistance."

"Where's Gregor of Mainz?" I asked, to test the waters.

He shook his head. "Wasn't him. He was with the marquis. Maybe his brother, though."

"Wasn't his brother with the marquis too?"

"Brother's been screwing Boniface's mistress," the guard said, as if this explained something.

"She's actually the *brother's* mistress," I said, trying to think of how to get past him. "And anyhow, the brother hasn't had a chance to screw her for a month."

He looked contemptuous. "If he's not screwing her, she's not his mistress, is she?"

"My goodness, you've got a point there," I conceded. "I guess Boniface really wants to find the princess, eh?"

He sneered a little. "Not the most important concern, compared to more important concerns."

Well, he was right about that, anyhow.

Dandolo's steward appeared and curtly informed me that the rebec was not mine to collect. I grumpily retrieved my hidden instruments, then ducked into one of the women's pavilions and spent an hour or so playing and listening to soldiers gossip.

The gossip told me little. Everybody knew the Usurper had sent an emissary who'd been rebuffed by Boniface; Boniface had earned credit with the rank and file for his imperiousness. Everyone also knew the princess has disappeared, but that was now of secondary interest. An attack on Galata Tower was proclaimed unavoidable and was far more urgent news. Some of the soldiers argued to head straight for the city walls; others, savvier, had worked out that would be too difficult in the current of the Bosporus, which meant the harbor chain would have to be broken, which meant the Usurper, who was guarding the chain, would have to be defeated first. None of these rank and file seemed to grasp that the Usurper was a better target than the city because *the argument was only with the Usurper,* and not with the city at all. This distinction, of such moral and legal significance to their leaders, did not exist for them. They just knew they were here to fight villains, triumph, and then move on quickly toward the Holy Land, where yet more villains and triumph awaited them. My various sly attempts to set them straight were completely ignored. They didn't *want* to grapple with complicated nuances; they wanted to triumph over villains.

I was almost asleep that night, frustrated and teetering on hopelessness, and also feeling peevish at having been abandoned by Jamila. A cool gust of wind through the tent suggested someone had just entered.

And there she was—Jamila—bending over me.

Her face was unreadable. "I'm back," she whispered. "Is everyone asleep? I have some information Gregor must take to Boniface."

"I'm up," Gregor said quickly and sat bolt upright. Otto and the servants were awakened too; immediately the elder Richard was sent out to bring fire from the watch's lantern.

We huddled around Jamila, grogginess banished. Young Richard, most pubescent and thus feeling most acutely deprived of female company, leaned closer to her breasts than was appropriate. She gave him a stern motherly look, and he retreated.

"Where's Liliana?" was Otto's first question.

"We could not manage how to get us both out," Jamila said. "And the one who got out had to speak Greek." He looked as if he expected an apology for her leaving Liliana behind. She looked as if she might, in fact, make such an apology.

"You went back to *Pera*," I growled, accusatory. My throat ached.

"No, I didn't. If I had gone to Pera, I would never have come back," she said, eyes averted. "I went to the emperor's camp."

"The Usurper's camp," Otto corrected her, on reflex.

"Usurper is a redundant term for most Byzantine emperors; the emperor he deposed was just another nobleman until the emperor before *him* was deposed," she informed Otto impatiently. "This restoration of the supposed true royal line is ludicrous. Anyhow." A pause. "I saw the chance and just felt compelled to do it—I spent the evening in his tent, presented myself as a servant and they treated me as one. And I learned things I thought you should know. So I came back."

Gregor was astonished. "You could have . . . In the name of St. John . . ."

"I'm impressed!" Otto laughed, looking delighted. Almost too delighted.

"The emperor—the Usurper—is not a well man." Jamila tapped the side of her head meaningfully. "Were he some minor baron in the countryside, he might be a competent lord. But he is not woven of ruling fabric. He took the throne from Isaac—they say he blinded him with his own hands, but truly it's hard to believe it.

"No doubt your leaders will have learned already that the con-scripted army is in appalling condition, the archers can't shoot straight, half the men could not lift a rock over their heads, every-one detests the emperor except the Varangian Guard, and that's only because they're well-paid mercenaries from other lands. The navy is falling apart, there are hardly any ships left, and many of those are worm-eaten."

Otto and Gregor exchanged startled looks. "We knew almost *none* of that," Gregor said, elated. "What else?"

"The emperor is—" She paused. "He's eaten alive by guilt for having blinded his brother. He lives in daily terror of God's wrath for having done it."

"That we heard," I said.

"But Boniface didn't believe it," Gregor amended.

"He should. On the one hand, the man is arrogance itself—he speaks like he believes he has every right to rule not just Byzantium but the entire world—and yet, when he's alone with his closest counselors, he whines fearfully the way my son used to when he had done something dreadful and knew punishment was coming. And his advisers address him with the delicacy of people speaking to the deranged. I spent years in the confidences of a ruler and his family; I know what kind of character it takes to keep a land together, and this man has nothing of it. I was shocked. If you topple the palace, you do so because it's already rotted from within."

Gregor nodded thoughtfully. "Then do you think, if we can take

Galata Tower, that will be the end of it? Even if he's not killed or captured?"

Jamila, to the dismay of the rest of us, immediately shook her head. "Just the opposite, sir. If you take the tower, which is considered untakable, that makes you a mighty force. But if he *escapes* that mighty force, that makes *him* a *mightier* force. That's how his reason works. If you don't take him at Galata, if he gets safely back across the harbor, he'll believe himself invincible. He won't surrender or negotiate, and you'll have to actually attack him in his home. And a siege like that could last . . ." She shrugged. "Indefinitely. I think you should capture him at Galata. Him, personally. His court is about to collapse, and if you control him when it does, you'll have the entire empire at your mercy."

"You came back to tell us that?" I said. "Instead of rejoining your people?"

She nodded.

"Why? Why do you care what happens to all these godless Christians?" I asked this, of course, so she could finally admit she couldn't bear to be away from me.

"If there's bloodshed, the Jews will suffer," she said instead. "Pera is right there, where an attack would be. So if there is any way for me to assist in preventing bloodshed, it's my duty to my people." She looked Otto straight in the face, almost accusatory. "To all of my people. Including the ones in this tent."

Otto looked away.

"You want me to go to Boniface?" Gregor asked. "He'll know I heard this from you, he'll reckon you're back in camp, and he'll hunt you down and take you back into custody to continue his silly charade. Can you get back across the Bosporus to safety?"

"I don't see how, now—the embassy's boat was a rare chance, which is why I scrambled for it when I saw it coming over. I'm stuck here. But if what I'm saying can be used to avoid a battle on the slopes of Pera, then I don't mind being stuck here for a while. If Boniface finds me, he won't misuse me if he still considers me useful. At least he won't misuse me more than he has already, and that was nothing compared to Barzizza."

"Did that whoreson—" I began.

She clapped my mouth shut with her outstretched hand, which still sparkled with the gold and ruby ring she'd worn when she escaped. "He was unpleasant but not violent. I am a *princess*, after all."

I grabbed her hand and stared at the ring. She'd had nothing else with her when she fled. "How did you get back this way across the Bosporus?" I asked.

She stiffened slightly and pulled her hand away. "I bribed a fisherman. There are many on the other shore."

"With what did you bribe him?"

Silence.

"Ah," I said.

In a comforting, dignified voice, she commented, "Don't worry, I am inured to the horrors of the uncircumcised from all my years in Venice."

THE NEXT MORNING I woke to the disagreeable noise of an argument in German. I opened my eyes to see that Otto was fully dressed and Gregor still dressing; Otto was halfway out of the tent and clearly wanting to head off in a hurry. The word "Boniface" kept coming up between them.

Suddenly I understood the problem. Even more than Gregor did.

I leapt away from the blankets and tackled Otto round the knees, knocking him over in the dust outside the tent. "Get off me, vagabond!" he hissed angrily. It was a crowded morning, with infantry and poorer knights moving from the first round of morning mass toward the mess tent. I did not want to call attention to our scuffle, so I grabbed a chunk of his hair just above the ear and dragged him back inside.

"Whoreson," I hissed. "Don't do it."

"Don't do what?" Gregor asked, without getting up from where the older Richard was lacing his boots. Otto and I brawled often enough.

"He's going to turn Jamila in to get Liliana back," I growled. Pulling his hair to keep his head low, I straddled his chest and placed a finger directly on his eyelid, putting just enough pressure that he yelped in alarm. "Stay still and I won't hurt you," I said. He could easily have clobbered me, but we both knew Gregor would come to my aid.

"*You're* the whoreson," Otto growled back at me but didn't struggle.

I looked over my shoulder at a bewildered Gregor. "I think Boniface secretly offered to release Liliana in exchange for Jamila, and conveniently enough, here is Jamila to accomplish it."

Otto turned red, which convinced all of us I was correct. "She said she didn't care what happens to her," he argued crossly. "And it's not just for Liliana, it's for everybody's sake, as Jamila said herself—"

"I did *not* say I didn't care what happens to me, sir," Jamila countered and pushed the blanket off her. "And it's not as if Liliana's suffering."

"She's a captive!" Otto said.

Jamila laughed. "She's a marquis's mistress. She's dressed in silks and furs and gemstones, he treats her very well and she chose to stay behind. I should sacrifice myself so that she can return to living in a tent? Where five different men will paw at her and expect her to look after them? I think not. She'd never forgive me."

"I love her!" said Otto, suddenly a tragic hero.

"Then be happy for her good fortune," Jamila answered. "Even in her finest days as courtesan to a count, her life was not as easy as it is now."

Otto, slightly frantic, declared, "She wants to be with *me*! More than anyone!"

"What you are contemplating is horrifically dishonorable," Gregor scolded. "This woman saved both our lives back in Zara. Get off him," he said to me, in a more companionable voice. I did. Otto scrambled to his feet and faced off angrily against his brother, his stance suggesting he expected to succumb to an onset of fisticuffs. Gregor, unimpressed, crossed his arms and shook his head paternally. "You have two choices. First, you may go to Boniface and tell him you have intelligence that may be helpful in planning our next move—but you require no reward for providing it. He'll know well enough how you came by the intelligence, but you *shall not* contribute to his finding her."

"What if he threatens Liliana?"

"He won't do that," I said impatiently. "He's enjoying her too much."

Otto gave me an infuriated glare. "And second choice?" he demanded.

"Second, you may sit in the corner and allow me to tell him instead."

GREGOR AND OTTO WENT to see Boniface together, to advise him that a friendly local had advised *them* that the Lombard emissary was speaking the truth when he'd collapsed in fear. While they were in his company, a politely smiling Boniface sent two soldiers to examine Gregor's tent for runaway pseudo-princesses and found only the Richardim, playing chess when they should have been cleaning saddles. The soldiers returned empty-handed; nothing was said about Jamila by either side. To Gregor, Boniface expressed his shared hope that Galata would be the end of the affair but declined to entertain Gregor's suggestion of kidnapping the Usurper as a potential alternative to doing battle.

*   *   *

LATER THAT DAY, on the hills of Scutari, the commanders met on
horseback in a wide meadow to organize the army. So far, there'd
been no warfare, only a siege, occasional skirmishes, and foraging;
moving throngs of armed men around a battlefield had not yet been
something to contemplate. Boniface summoned Gregor to this gathering. Neither said a word to the other about Jamila; what they were
doing now was far more important. The leadership decided there
would be seven battalions, with young Baldwin of Flanders leading
the vanguard. Boniface, with all the Lombards, the Tuscans, and the
Germans, would lead the rear guard.

Otto was annoyed to learn that he'd be in the rear guard. To
make himself feel better, he indulged in his favorite new pastime:
trying to enlighten me about the wonders of the military arts. I
was treated to a history of traditional French battalion composi-
tion (each division, under a local baron, being made up of various
squadrons—two dozen knights riding shoulder to shoulder in two
or three ranks, *flanked* by archers), as compared with more modern
developments (in which a group of some ten knights and five dozen
sergeants fought together, with archers *preceding* them). The Northern French were better at cavalry fighting than anyone because their
training was the best; the Southern French, having a less romantic
attachment to knighthood, were closer to the Italians in excelling
at the integration of foot and cavalry. Otto felt much better once he
knew I'd gotten that straight.

How many hours must have passed over that day and the next,
with Jamila and me hiding—sitting in silence, or speaking in soft
voices, close enough to touch but never touching. I still fancied myself responsible for her well-being, and so I still felt (although we'd
spent that drenched night with my arms clasped about her) that I'd
be taking advantage if I laid a hand on her now, or responded to
her laying a hand on me. Which she did twice or thrice. Whenever
she did it, I was physically jolted, as if I'd rubbed my feet too rapidly against wool and then touched metal. I felt it everywhere—my

stomach, my crotch, the soles of my feet, my scalp. I never let myself touch her in response.

The night after the leaders created the battalions, the camp prepared for combat. It would have been normal, in a pilgrim army, to send the women away the night before, but nobody thought to issue that order (perhaps an acknowledgment that what was about to happen was not *really* the work of a pilgrim army). Still, the women were not much engaged that evening, except by a few nervous squires who feared this might be their last night on earth. Everybody else was preoccupied with their souls: the bishops, abbots, and lesser clerics circulated through the camp, hearing last confessions, desperately pretending the pope had not forbidden this attack, and helping those who hadn't done so yet to write up their wills. As happened every night, at various fires around the camp, musicians gathered to play, but the songs tonight were somber, more hymnal than the usual crusader anthems. (Such as, for example, in French, by Conon de Béthune: "Good Lord! We've boasted so much of our courage, now we'll see who's really brave!"—Or, for those who preferred Provençal, a sardonic gem from Peire Bremen lo Tort: "If ever I go back to Syria, may God never let me return home!"—Or, for those who preferred the German rhythms, perhaps some Friedrich von Hausen: "My heart and my body wish to part now, although they've long traveled together." Or, perhaps, for the criminally tasteless, one more round of "Kalenda Maya.")

The bishops reserved their time for the barons, but late in the evening, as the fires were dying to embers, Conrad made an appearance at Gregor's door. A bishop extending himself for a knight was an extraordinary gesture, and publicized just how important this particular knight was. Conrad was too exhausted from doling out penance (and, oh yes, lying about His Holiness's wishes) to indulge in polite formality; he requested that the front half of the tent be cleared for shriving Gregor, that he might then go back to his own tent and sleep. I grumbled mightily but followed Otto and the squires to the small curtained section at the back of the tent, where Jamila had been bundled.

In the ongoing confusion of Who was trusted with What Information, Bishop Conrad had casually fallen out of favor. None of us actively distrusted him, but when we had to limit ourselves to revealing things (like Jamila) to a small circle we absolutely trusted, not even Gregor had thought to include Conrad. So it was understood immediately, with nothing being said, that we would not tell Conrad she was in the tent with us.

We settled behind the curtain to listen to prelate and knight, who sat facing east by Gregor's travel altar.

"Did Boniface send you?" Gregor asked tiredly. "A final checking-in on my goodwill?"

"No," Conrad said. "I came here only to see if you are at peace within your soul."

"I'm not, actually," Gregor said. "Are you? When we are once again about to attack our fellow Christians, to foist upon them a ruler they don't even seem to want?"

"It is a necessary test—" Conrad began, but Gregor cut him off.

"Yes, Father, I know, a necessary test to prepare us for the ordeal God desires for us," he said. "Just like Zara. But Zara brought us no closer to the Holy Land, and I'm not at all sure this will either."

"Because you want for faith, I think," Conrad said. It was, technically, a rebuke, but the tone was mechanical, as if he said it because that was what any Catholic priest hearing such a thing should say in reply, not as if he believed his own words.

"I don't want for faith, I want to be convinced we stand half a chance at victory before we put men's lives at stake!" Gregor retorted. "We cannot rout the enemy. It is virtual suicide."

"You need only take Gal—"

"Galata Tower, yes, I know," Gregor said with barely contained rage. "I'm the one who's been emphasizing that, Your Eminence. Myself, and Dandolo of Venice. Sometimes I think Boniface would be perfectly content to allow us to fall into a complete siege of the city."

"That may indeed be the next test, but we can pray it isn't—"

"Your Eminence," Gregor said between clenched teeth, "we cannot lay siege to a city this size, nor should we try. As Boniface himself said back in Zara, this is most emphatically meant to be an attack not on the city, only on its leader. If we are going to do this, we should do it sensibly. Assailing an unassailable tower is not the way."

"My son," Conrad replied, in a voice teetering on helplessness. "If God wills us to take the day, we shall."

Such a practical source of succor, our good bishop.

33

THE NEXT MORNING, the fifth of July, the crusaders were blessed one final time in a hurried predawn mass, then rushed in the sunrise to their positions: armed knights and sergeants to the horse transports; archers and other infantry to the galleys, which huddled protectively around the horse transports as they worked their way across the streaming Bosporus. They had gone far up-current to help with the crossing.

I wasn't with them; I stayed behind in the tent to watch over Jamila. But I can describe that first brief skirmish; I'm a minstrel, after all, and I heard the story directly from heroes. Frankly, there is little to tell.

The Usurper could see that the mass of ships had been loaded and were finally under sail; he moved into battle formation on the slope. The Byzantines must have been confused now, because the Franks' action was suicidal. The enormous protective chain was across the entrance to the Golden Horn, and no ship had ever broken through it. If the fleet tried to assail the city walls at the mercy of that current, they would be swept harmlessly south into the Sea of Marmara. The ships would have to try to anchor near the shore, below His Imperial Majesty's camp, where His Imperial Majesty's archers would simply pick off the Franks man by man, from the slopes, as the Franks scrambled to secure their boats. The Franks would be sitting ducks. None of them would land alive.

I am sure this whispered assurance was reaching every man present on the hill of Galata when the fleet in the water before them did something nearly inconceivable: the sides of the transport hulls broke open and belched forth thousands of screaming, fully armored knights on horseback, straight into the water, which was up to the horses' nostrils. While the Byzantines gaped in amazement, the archers on the boats let fly their shafts. They spent one round from the boats, then leapt into the water ahead of the horses, bows held over their heads, and splashed their way onto the shore, shooting again as soon as they were in water shallow enough to keep the bowstrings dry.

At this point the Byzantine army, under the command of His Imperial Majesty—also known as the Usurper, Alexios III, and various other names, depending on who spoke them—turned tail and scrambled up the steep hill, to flee over the crest beyond Galata Tower. Baldwin of Flanders and his knights, first out of the transports, followed hard on their tracks; they were followed by Boniface's mounted men. Summa staggered under the extra weight of water sopped into Gregor's armor padding and the large draped saddle cloth. With ten-foot lances clenched under their armpits and steadied across their horses' necks, the knights pursued the fleeing soldiers straight up the steep hill and past the brooding tower, the Jewish settlement of Pera on the falling slope to their left. They chased their enemy at least a mile inland. Then His Majesty's men raced across a wooden bridge that took them to the northwestern tip of the city walls and prudently began to burn the bridge behind them.

The pilgrims halted to regroup. Their horses were exhausted, and many lame, from the abrupt, uphill scramble after a night on the boats. The Usurper was already back at the city walls; they couldn't get him now. So they returned toward Galata, to release the chain across the entrance to the Golden Horn. This, even without the capture of the Usurper, might signal the start of victory.

But not yet. The chain was attached down at the shore to a wall surrounding Pera. The Usurper himself had been routed, but the Galata Tower garrison, with vast stores of arrows, had bolted the tower's gates closed and rained havoc down on the soldiers and mariners trying to get near the mechanism that unlatched the chain. The pilgrim soldiers worked in small groups, several of them holding up protective shields covered with wet hides while others fumbled with the mechanism's casing.

The Galata archers shot arrows sodden with Greek fire, a terrifying glop that exploded when it touched water. The Frankish soldiers shouted in horror and fled. They tried again with vinegar-soaked covers to their shields, but the rain of arrows was so ferocious it was impossible to work.

Boniface signaled to his heralds, who pounded drums calling the soldiers to stop. He wanted to scout the area and plan a sensible attack: they would still somehow have to take the tower. Except for the scouts, the remainder of today would be for rest—and celebrating their routing of the foul Usurper. They would resume hostilities tomorrow. For tonight, the ships would have to anchor unsteadily in the current of the Bosporus.

BY THE TIME Gregor returned to the Usurper's confiscated camp, preparations were being made for an early feast, and rumors about all the booty from the routing had reached exaggerated proportions. This, he now understood, was a bad sign. It meant that soon the infantry would expect there was enough to trickle down to them, and then they'd be disgruntled when it didn't happen. Whenever there was booty, whether from Zara or from taking over a small town somewhere to get staples, it went immediately to the Venetians toward payment of the debt. The soldiers saw this. They saw the Venetian sailors apparently getting richer and richer as they, the army, toiled just as hard, and had nothing to show for it. What did not go to the Venetians went to the army's richest lords, who had loaned the expedition money. Otto still complained about this bitterly several times a week.

But he was not complaining yet today. Today the hillside below Galata resounded with relieved, cockily triumphant fighters who'd barely had to fight as the army moved into the abandoned imperial tents to bivouac. Most of the men wanted to send across the Bosporus for the women, back in the safety of the home camp, but the leaders would not allow it, warning that their real mission was not quite yet completed.

The Galata garrison was composed largely of foreign mercenaries—the famous Varangian Guard, most of them from farther off than the crusaders themselves were and all of them more battle-ready than the average crusading foot soldier. Taking this tower remained the key to winning the city, and every commander in the army knew that. Whatever bloodlust they might have had was satiated by their gleeful routing of His Majesty; now they all just wanted to see things resolved quickly. So huge bribes were offered up in various foreign languages, but they were ignored by the stalwart Varangians. Gregor heard a rumor that most of the Varangians were Englishmen and sent across the Bosporus for me.

"I'm not English," I said with disgust when Gregor explained why he'd summoned me.

"The English were your neighbors. If there are English, mightn't there be some of your sort here too?" To Gregor this was a reasonable assumption.

To me it was not. "That's like saying . . ." I tried to think of a metaphor that was worthy of my scorn. "You may as well say, here is a king and here is a worm. They both sleep wrapped in silk, so are they not the same creature?"

Otto grinned. "So you're finally admitting you're a worm."

Gregor gestured to the tower in frustration. "Please try. Please."

"Am I to offer bribes?" I demanded impatiently. "Am I to ask the nice mercenaries not to shoot at you because you have a British associate? What's the *point* of this? I've left Jamila alone in the tent! I only answered your summons because I assumed it was important!"

"You can talk almost anyone into almost anything," Gregor said. "And that's in a foreign language. I'm sure in your native tongue you can accomplish miracles."

"Catastrophes," I said. "My specialty is catastrophes."

"That would be almost as good," Otto said.

"If we can't convince them to surrender, we'll have to kill them. This is an attempt to minimize bloodshed," Gregor coaxed.

"And we all know how successful I am at *that*," I said. But I crossed to the bottom of the tower and began to yell. I admit I was not helpful, because I was so enraged at Gregor for calling me away from Jamila. *"Oes yna rhywun yno sy'n siarad yr iaith yma?"* I hollered. *"Os felly . . . peidiwch a'i gydnabod. Eisiau i chi fradychu eich dinas fabwysiedig a'u gadael nhw i mewn i'r twr y mae'r ffyliaid yma. Cadwch eich cegau ar gau. Ardderchog! Daliwch ati!"**

There was no immediate answer. I shrugged. "Well, I tried," I said and rubbed my hands together. "How else may I be of service?"

But Gregor and Otto had to meet with Boniface's advisers, to hear what the Seventh Division would do the next day; the squires had to attend to Summa and the other horses.

So I found myself left to my own devices, and I knew exactly how to apply them.

---

* "Does anyone up there understand what I'm saying? If so, don't admit it! These madmen want you to betray your adopted city by letting them into the tower. Just keep your mouths shut! Excellent! Keep it up!"

Starting from Galata, I followed the walls of Pera down the steep slopes until I found Pera Gate. It had, of course, been closed and locked, but it was forged of diagonally crisscrossed iron bars. Very easy to climb.

Before I topped it, however, I realized I was in trouble: every Jew in Pera knew what was happening outside their walls, and all were preparing for what they were certain would become an assault on them directly. Long-robed men, anxiously patrolling the settlement, saw me before I was halfway to the top; they were running toward me, by the dozens, shouting angrily. Perched above their heads, I was an easy target if anyone had stones or arrows to let fly. Nothing was actually thrown at me, but at least fifty knives flashed warningly below. "*Shabbat shalom!*" I hollered without thinking—it was the greeting Jamila whispered to us after she lit candles on Friday nights. Today was Saturday. Was it still the Sabbath? "*Shabbat shalom!*" I tried again.

The crowd was made up of the strangest men: their coloring was as varied as the whole of the pilgrim army, but all of them had long hair and beards and wore long dark gowns or tunics. Each had a little skullcap on his head. They glowered at me in fear and warning, and rattled off questions in a language I could not follow.

"Jamila?" I said desperately. "*Sabah el-'hair?*" I tried, hoping I was saying hello. "*Awafi?*" That one meant "good appetite," I knew, so at least they would understand that I was not here to be belligerent. She had drilled me harder on Greek, and I knew enough to say, haltingly, "Do you know Jamila? Baby, here. Then go to Genoa. Marry physician France, go to Egypt." They all just stared at me. "*Al-ud,*" I pressed on, imitating the playing of a lute. "Two children."

Eyes began to meet around the crowd. Voices muttered.

"Father?" one of the men demanded in a tense voice. I grimaced apologetically and shook my head.

"You?" the old man asked.

I hesitated. "*Franj*," I said apologetically—the Arabic word for all men from the West.

More looks were exchanged. I had to do something to prove I was harmless. The men nearer to the iron gate kept craning their necks to see what the crusading force was doing up the slope. I chewed my lip a moment, then held up a finger, a gesture to say, *I have it, let me show you.* "Come down?" I asked. If I stayed up much longer, the real Franj would notice me and, by extension, notice all of them. The crowd must have had the same collective realization, because they grudgingly gestured that I could descend.

I hoisted myself over the finials topping the gate and climbed down as men continued to peer up the hill, out the gate, their faces fearful. When my feet touched the earth again and I turned to face the group, I found seven knives at my nose. I threw my hands up to show I meant no harm. The oldest man there made a grunting sound, and the armed men retreated slightly, but they glowered warningly and kept the knives held out.

I knelt down in front of the elder and gestured for his hand. After a hesitation, he held it out, palm down. The crowd shuffled in closer, protectively.

I turned the gnarled old hand over, then tapped one callused fingertip in the center of his palm and with a good (I hoped) evocation of Jamila's accent, I recited, "*Bukit maya. Ja afoor sharab shweya.*" I glanced up and saw, with relief, that they were all bemused. This was the first line of a children's poem; the words, in a Hebrew variant of Arabic, were about a birdie drinking a drop of water, or something like that, delivered with a childish lisp. Jamila had taught it to me in the boredom of the Zaran winter.

I had to hurry; they were all anxious. I took the man's pinkie finger. "*Ha'ye tuch'bus,*" I said. This little girl bakes. I released the pinkie and solemnly took the man's ring finger. "*Ha'ye tu'udjin.*" This one kneads the dough. Now, cautious chuckling around the circle. I moved to the man's middle finger and waggled it; he recited with me: "*Ha'ye tut'buch*," this one cooks. And the index finger: "*Ha'ye tik-nuss*," this one sweeps. I moved to the man's thumb and concluded, "*Ha'ye twadee rudwee an Baba*"—this one takes dinner to Papa—and made a gesture as if to run my fingers up his arm. He reflexively winced and grinned, as if expecting to be tickled, and pulled his arm back. Then he stared, amazed.

After a moment, he turned his head into the crowd of men and said something that included the name Samuel ben David.

Men shifted out of the way and a tall, well-dressed man, barely older than I, moved forward until he was standing by the elder, whom he addressed respectfully as something that sounded like "*rabban*." This younger man had a humorlessness that reminded me of Jamila when I'd first met her, but his coloring was very different—lighter, almost Flemish, his hair a reddish color, his eyes sharp and intelligent. The older man gave the younger orders, and the younger turned to me.

"I speak French," he said. "You will tell me where is Jamila. We know her. But a public gathering is not good, and anyhow these men must go back to preparing our defenses for when you attack us."

And so I found myself inside a Jewish home on the afternoon of the Sabbath.

Except for Zara, this was one of the few times in my life I'd been inside an actual house. I'd grown up in a primitive castle; spent three years in an ascetic hermit's cloister and an abbey. I had been in peasant huts, but these tended to be transient. This was the first time I'd seen a comfortable dwelling of commoners that was a real homestead, a place intended to perfect private life and collect domestic memories; I was surprised how intrusive I felt in this small, neat room. I had no idea whose home it was, or why Samuel and the elder had chosen it. Most of the men went away, taking their knives with them, which relieved me; only Samuel and the elder Hebrew remained.

An old woman stuck her head nervously into the front room from

somewhere farther back; the house, like the entire huddled settlement, was quiet but almost shivering with tension. How bizarre that
an entire community was walking and eating and praying and going
about its life as the battle for Galata Tower raged on the other side of
a wall. She came into the room, a bulky satchel in her hands: packing
to leave, to flee before the marauding crusaders could break into Pera.
Perhaps, then, the community was not, exactly, going about its life.

There were no cooking fires, not even any candles lit, although
an empty two-pronged candelabrum sat on a small table. But there
was plenty of light from the street; we were facing south, on a summer afternoon, on a hillside so steep that we could see over the roof
of the neighboring wooden house.

The old woman whose home it was resembled Jamila, but only
in the way all the men outside had seemed to resemble one another.
Like Jamila, she had dark eyes and dusky coloring, with broad hips
and shoulders but a narrow waist. Her face was round, her features
strong. Like Jamila, she had a dignity that bordered on haughtiness,
although she was clearly distraught. My translator seemed to be expressing apologies to her—I thought, at first, that this was for invading her home during the Sabbath. Or more likely, for interrupting
her escape. But whatever he said, it made her drop the satchel with
a clatter and stare at me with such shock that I wondered if I myself
should be apologizing. The old man and the woman exchanged tense
words. Finally, the younger man turned to me.

"How do you know Jamila?"

"I know *a* Jamila. How can I be sure it is *your* Jamila?" I said defensively. Now that I was so close to reuniting her to her community,
I found myself not wanting to succeed. Everything here was too alien
to be a part of her.

Samuel looked at me coldly. "There was a child here, who would
be perhaps thirty now. Her parents were Isaac and Ruth. They left
when she, Jamila, was a child and went to Genoa. In France she married a physician she knew from Pera; they went to Egypt, to the pal-

ace of a Moslem lord there, and had two children, Benjamin and Miriam. We were told of an attack and slaughter five years ago by Germans, and we heard nothing more."

I felt my chest constrict. I was going to lose her to these strangers. "Yes, it is the same woman. The palace was attacked, and her family was killed, but she was taken captive by a Venetian."

Samuel blinked repeatedly. The older woman, intrigued, tugged his arm. He said something softly; the reaction of the two elders was enormous. She turned back to me demanding something loudly and frantically.

Not knowing what to say, I decided to conclude as succinctly as possible: "We sailed out of Venice and brought her with us. She's in the army camp."

Samuel, dazed, repeated this almost under his breath; the elders gasped, and then the woman started sobbing. "Why would you do that?" demanded Samuel.

"Oh, you know." I shrugged. "Just the Christian thing to do." The man did not hear the irony; I made a dismissive gesture. "Never mind. I did it. Because she looked so sad, and it was so wrong, and I wanted to help her. The pilgrims don't know what she is. You don't have to explain that," I added, as Samuel, eyes glued to me in wonderment, began to translate. "She's in the tent of Gregor of Mainz, the best man in the army."

Samuel tensed. "The best soldier, you mean. The best killer. And a German?"

"I haven't seen him fight. He is just a good man. Good here." I pointed awkwardly to my heart.

"No doubt a veritable Judas Maccabee," said Samuel, sardonic. "A second Joshua. Gideon reborn."

"No. In fact he tried to talk the leaders *out* of a fight. She is under his protection."

"I'm sure she is," Samuel said grimly. "I do not know how to say—"

"I swear to you he has not touched her. I want to know if she has family here."

Samuel shook his head impatiently. "Don't you understand why we brought you to this house? This woman, Deborah, is Jamila's grandmother."

Now it was my turn to be amazed. "Milady!" I said on reflex, and bowed deeply to the old woman, who looked at me as if I might be mad. I straightened, realizing this was not the expected etiquette. In fact it seemed idiotic; I'd never once seen Jamila bow, or use the terms *milady* or *milord* to *anyone*. I had no idea what to do instead. I hadn't planned this part. "I'll bring her here! Or . . . She's across the Bosporus right now, in the base camp. Is there other family? I could take them to her."

Samuel tapped at his own chest. "I knew Jamila as a child. She is married—was married—to my brother. The physician who went to Alexandria."

"Then you have already suffered at the hands of the pilgrims," I said quietly.

"*German* pilgrims," he clarified. With venom.

I decided not to respond to that. "So you're essentially family. Will you come with me to get her?" I was ashamed by how acutely I did not want to yield her up to these people, who would make her a stranger to me all over again. My guilt at my own covetousness made me even more determined to see it through; it also made me feel like I might vomit.

"A Jew in a camp of crusaders? As you're preparing to conquer us? It is hardly the battle between Behemoth and Leviathan, but I'm surprised they haven't yet burned down our entire settlement—"

"They don't want to conquer you. They just want to replace the Usurper with Prince Alexios."

He looked at me as if I were speaking nonsense. "The Usurper? Do you mean Emperor Alexios? Who is *Prince* Alexios? For that matter, who are *you*?"

"I'm with Gregor of Mainz. I go where he goes. He goes where the army goes. The army is here because it has the rightful ruler to the empire, or so they say—Prince Alexios, the son of Isaac Angelus."

Samuel, appalled, repeated this to his elders, who shifted uncomfortably. "We think there is no rightful ruler; it is so ridiculous, all the coups," he informed me. "It is unstable. Bad for trade. Bad for us. This is an unusual place, with so many races living together and working together. What causes us problems is the greed and stupidity of the rulers. We don't want another coup. Things will be bad enough left to themselves; having you so-called pilgrims meddle will only make it worse."

"I'm not a pilgrim," I said defensively. I pointed to my shoulder. "See? No cross."

Samuel considered me. "You are an interesting man," he said at last. The old woman said something, then reached for the satchel on the floor and, with an almost grandiose air of defiance, began to unpack it right in front of us. Samuel grimaced, then declared, "When you're done with your battle for Galata Tower, we will send for Jamila from the tent of Gregor of Mainz. Her grandmother has just sworn she will not leave Pera now, and so I shall remain here with her."

"Is that safe?" I asked.

"Is anything safe today?" Samuel retorted.

"Will you send for her discreetly?" I did not want to have to explain why discretion was so necessary.

"We are Jews," Samuel said. "We are made of discretion." I nodded, stood up, and headed for the door. "This is a *mitzvah* you have done," Samuel called out. "I will make them understand that."

I raised a hand to acknowledge this, without looking back. I wondered what a *mitzvah* was.

THAT EVENING, the pilgrim army fell asleep drunk and happy, certain they would take Galata Tower effortlessly first thing in the morning—and that would be the end of the fighting. The French guards watching the harbor were a bit surprised by the amount of traffic ferrying across. But all the boats were civilian, carrying only two or three workers—merchant barges, fishing boats, ferries carrying fuel. Disturbing the daily business of the city would make it harder to win the people to "the cause," so these vessels were allowed to traverse unmolested, even when they continued long after dark.

And so, by the early hours of the morning, thousands of heavily armed Byzantine soldiers—disguised as merchants and fishermen and fuel gatherers—had made their way through the gates of Galata and up into the tower.

34

THE FRANKS, drunk and happy, slept soundly, needful of a good night's sleep before tomorrow's assault on the tower, which they all believed was lightly manned. I myself, not knowing any more than they did, helped to play them to sleep. ("I rejoice to see a lord on his armored horse fearlessly lead his men into battle, for his brave courage fills all their hearts" and all that rot.) I was in a state all evening, in equal parts of peace and agitation, fulfillment and longing. I would lose Jamila tomorrow, to those strangers in Pera. But it was the best achievement—the one wholly good deed—of my entire life.

And yet I'd have traded an eternity of heaven not to have to do it.

AT DAWN the squires strapped Gregor into his armor. The army had lost its chance to grab the emperor directly, but if this attack was successful—if the tower was taken, and therefore the harbor chain loosened, and therefore the fleet able to sail into the harbor, where no invading fleet had ever sailed before—that *should* be enough to make the city, if not its leader, capitulate without further bloodshed. I heard Gregor reminding himself, in grim little mutters, that whatever blood he shed now was to prevent more bloodshed later. The more decisive they were today, the faster everything else would follow, and they might still be in Jerusalem come autumn.

Would I be with them? I had decided no; I would somehow have to make the journey back to England and see my original vows fulfilled. Thousands of lives had been destroyed when the English overran my kingdom; I had to answer for them all, now that my promise to Jamila was about to be fulfilled. Somehow over the course of the past three seasons, my need to end my own life had oozed away. I'd be willing to contemplate another scheme—but the Englishman had to die. What else was there for me to do now, once this trifle of a battle was complete?

Eve of the Feast of St. Pantaenus, 6 July

I indulge here in something rarely written down, the details of a battle as viewed from one man's eyes. Most men who fight in the heat of battle are not the sort given to writing in detail, but I shall try to keep the ink wet long enough to do it here.

The Briton was helping Otto tack up Summa on the slope outside the pavilion where we had slept that night, one of many tents left by the Usurper in his flight. The Venetians were aboard galleys, fastening the rock slingers to the deck, hauling boulders into the cups of catapulting arms. The Richardim were tightening Summa's gear.

As this is my first entry of an armed encounter, and I wish to stress how I am in all ways a pilgrim, here is the symbolism of my armor, . the litany I recite silently to myself whenever I gear up: the greaves upon my legs keep me from straying from the true path of my faith (thus it troubles me that many raucous German infantry fight bare-legged); my hauberk helps me to resist temptation; my helmet reminds me of my fear of shame. Most important, of course, is my sword, the Hand of Nicholas, the shape of which reminds me of the cross on which our Savior made his sacrifice and whose hilt contains the most precious object I possess: a strand of linen from the robe of John the Baptist. Finally I take up my shield, which Otto mocks me for having—he prefers the newer style Milord Boniface has made popular, slightly longer than what I prefer from my childhood games. Anyhow, to the matter:

I was about to mount; Otto and the Briton were debating something foolish; we were interrupted by a wail of surprise. The gates of Galata Tower opened fast, and wild-eyed, long-haired men in that strange, skirted armor flew out, spears, battle-axes, swords, bows at the ready: they were the Varangian Guard, plus thousands of conscripted men from the Greek army. They bore down upon us with such outrageous fury that most pilgrim knights, only half-armored, had no time to get to horse. The unarmed soldiers and servants fled instantly. We were near the edge of the camp, in a lightly wooded area; I saw the Briton approach a tree and scramble up as fast as a terrified cat.

Even as the gate opened below, from the top of the tower a spate of archers shot a wall of fire arrows down at the ships by the shore. A catapult on the roof of the tower hurled boulders that must have taken twenty strong men to carry up. They hit no ship but started waves that capsized some longboats. The fire arrows rained down the hill without a break, as an impossible number of men kept pouring out of the tower gates below.

A group of Flemish footmen near the mouth of the tower had already fallen. As Baldwin of Flanders shrieked formation orders to his battalion, the Flemish knights and barons pulled together and, more protected than the foot soldiers, turned against the oncoming Greeks. The rest of the camp, on the uneven footing of the slope, scrambled to our weapons, and within moments the advantage of surprise was over for the Greeks.

The advantage of altitude, however, was still theirs, since most of us were below them on the hill. Greeks surrounded Jacques of Avesnes, a Flemish lord—perhaps mistaking him for the great Baldwin of Flanders, as their pennants are similar—and slashed him across the face. Bleeding, he was dragged up the hill toward Galata. I believe they meant to hurl him to his death from the tower, in front of us.

There was too much confusion for anyone to help him until he had been dragged nearly to the tower gates. Then, like something out of a chanson de geste, a Flemish knight performed a dazzling act of devotion: having fought his way to his horse, he leapt onto it, drew his sword, and galloped straight up the hill toward the tower, alone and un-protected. He fought off everyone who came at him, and when he got to the Greek soldiers abducting his master, he grandly slashed the heads off two of them, hoisted the wounded baron onto his horse's withers, and raced with him back down the hill to safety. He was not even wounded in the rescue.

We who had not yet been set upon by the Greeks had watched this from lower down the slope as if it were a tournament. We applauded and cheered, thumping one another on the arm as if we'd placed a bet upon the action. The mood shifted immediately: within three heart-beats, half the crusader knights were mounted, our horses scrambling up the slope with the morning sun at their tails, and we began a furious counterattack.

Once we were horsed, the Greek soldiers had no chance. As yesterday, they panicked and many tried to flee. Some raced down the hill and onto the end of the great chain that went across the harbor—as thick as the arms of the blacksmiths that had forged it, it could support a great number of them, but as they began to crawl like ants along it out over the water, they were picked off easily by the crossbowmen on the ships and fell screaming and dying into the water. Others ran down the hill toward the ferries and barges that had villainously brought them over the night before, but here too they were exposed, and many of them collapsed into the harbor to their deaths.

Several hundred of the Varangian Guard, though, headed straight back for the tower, intending to close the gates against the enemy. And all the while, Greek fire still rained down from above, some on arrows, some spat through tubes.

My brother Otto was the first to realize the tower gate was closing, and he cried out to get my attention. We spurred Summa and Oro into a flat-out gallop, struggling up to the base of the tower, and frantically dismounted before the horses had stopped. Each of us stumbled to get his balance from the hard landing, and then, as if we had rehearsed this, we stepped through the threshold and each threw all of his weight against one of the two tower gates as the Varangians rushed to pull them closed. The Varangians struck at us with axes, swords, daggers; the blows glanced off our mail, but by St. John's head, we'd've been doomed had other Franks not rushed immediately to join us.

The gate slowed on its enormous, screeching iron hinges—but it did not stop. Otto and I found ourselves pushed together as the doors swung inward. For a moment we were in danger of being pressed to death against each other between the closing gates.

But other riders threw grappling hooks around the edges of the doors and hauled them open again. Now there was enough space between them for armed crusaders to rush into the tower. Still breathless from exertion, Otto and I ran in with them, drawing our swords with difficulty in the press of bodies.

I was trained to be a fighter; the training is surely more deeply entrenched in me even than my religious fervor, and the outrage of the last ten months was in desperate need of an outlet. I swung two-handed at a Varangian, at the level of the man's throat, and felt a surge of satisfaction as the side of my sword cut straight through windpipe and spine. The guard fell to the floor, where he was trampled by all his fellows, but I had already pivoted, shield before me but to one side, to strike at a second uniform, this one at waist level. The side of the sword sliced into the armor of overlapping plates, and I pushed it straight in like a lance, impaling the man through the stomach and flinging him back against the wall with a sharp, quick jerk. The body slid to the floor, the wall behind smeared with blood. Arrows rained down from the floors above, making a horrible racket on my helmet. My sight was hampered by the helmet, but I turned and saw Otto wrestling with a guard—no, not wrestling now. Otto had his man. He cut straight across the fellow's chest until he was twain. I pivoted again, seeking another target. Most of the Byzantines fled up the stairs to the floors above, followed so thickly by the pilgrims that there was no more room for another knight to follow.

A moment later there was a frantic clarion call from the roof of the tower. It was the Greeks, signaling surrender.

THERE WAS RAUCOUS cheering and celebration around the tower. I—and others like me who had scrabbled up trees and behind buildings for protection—returned to terra firma. The remaining Greek soldiers and Varangians were imprisoned in the cellar.

Ironically, there was such a fire raging all around the small tower where the chain mechanism was housed that *still* nobody could get near it. The whole point of this attack had been to release the damned chain, and still, in victory, they could not accomplish it. So the Venetians took a more direct approach: boarding the *Eagle*, the largest of the ships, they rammed her iron-clad prow right against the famously unbreakable harbor chain—

—and broke it.

The *Eagle* sailed into the harbor, half of the fleet rowing in behind her.

The battle of Galata Tower had been watched by hundreds of thousands of Constantinopolitans across the harbor, from the city walls and the hilltops within them. Galata being taken was surely alarming enough. But nobody in history had ever broken the chain. No invading body had ever forced its way into their harbor. There was a defensive wall between the harbor and the city, but it had never been tested, because nobody had ever gotten this far. Throngs and throngs and throngs of onlookers were hushed, and frightened. And angry at their emperor for allowing this to happen. They watched the Venetian fleet slowly make its way deep into the harbor and moor there. And they watched the inevitable outcome of the rain of arrows: they watched the wooden houses on the hill below the tower catch fire and blaze away to embers.

They watched Pera, the settlement of Jews, burn to the ground.

As soon as I realized what was happening, I ran back to the Pera Gate and tried to climb it. The raging flames within had made the iron unbearably hot, so I ripped pieces of my hose off and wrapped them mittenlike around my hands to get over the gate. But once within the walls, I despaired: Nobody was left to help. All the residents—including Jamila's grandmother, the rabbi, the man called Samuel—either had fled or were already dead and ashes. The acrid, impossibly dry smell of burning bones suggested the latter. Through the whirling cinders, choking smoke, and spitting flames, I could make out nothing familiar from the day before. I couldn't breathe from the heat and the little cyclones of debris that pranced across what had been the Jewish settlement. I finally retreated back over the gate before I myself succumbed, fighting to keep conscious and shrieking blasphemies.

It took until the early afternoon for Gregor and Otto to make it back toward the tent. The squires followed with the horses. The two men were exhausted but exhilarated, bruised but glowing with satisfaction for their efforts.

Until they saw me, black with soot in tattered hose and tunic, staring at them.

Staring hard. Not so much at their faces—they had taken off their helmets—as at their bodies. Their surcoats were covered in blood and gore, much of it dried now but starting to stink fiercely in the afternoon sun. I tried to remind myself that the blood and gore was a good thing: it meant this insane undertaking was a hair's breadth from completion. It meant the city must be amazed by the army, it meant the Usurper had all but lost his throne, it meant we'd crown Alexios, and soon, and then be gone. I saw in Gregor's face the shining hope that all of this would follow from the blood that he'd just shed. But I could not care about or believe any of that now.

"What happened to you?" Otto said sarcastically. "What's wrong, Brit, haven't you seen blood before?"

I glared at Otto. "Yes," I snapped. "I've been drenched in more blood than the two of you put together. Is that somebody's eye?" I went on harshly, plucking at something pink and damp on Gregor's surcoat. "Is Christ smiling down at you for this? Do you become more Christian if you smear yourself in Christian gore?"

ALL EVENING and late into the night there was boisterous, ecstatic celebration all around as I huddled in the dark, mourning people I had met only once, for a moment, people I'd wished didn't exist because I would have lost Jamila to them. Now I wouldn't lose her to them, and that knowledge crushed me. I sobbed.

But the army celebrated its victory bivouacked in the Usurper's camp, whose red-walled tents were decorated everywhere with paintings of fierce animals. Pilgrims who had stood out as especially heroic—the Flemish knight who saved his master, Otto and Gregor for stopping the gates from closing, others for felling the most guards within the tower— were toasted all around the camp. Everywhere was music, wine, and food. They'd done the impossible: they were inside the Golden Horn! Now, surely, Gregor said in several happily drunken toasts and speeches, either the Usurper would capitulate (or catipulate, or cachipulate, as the evening progressed) or the city would throw him over in favor of Alexios. We would see our hopes fulifilled, slurred Gregor, and we would move on to the Holy Land ver-ver-ver-very soon now. Hooray!

Early the next morning, the stable boys, cooks, and women were ferried over the Bosporus in the galleys, and so the entire body of the army was united again. The Richardim had convinced me to bathe myself clean of the soot and grime from Pera; now I waited for Jamila at the shore, damp, depressed, and nervous she'd be recognized in the herd of women from the camp.

Then I realized this was not the place to find her. I climbed back up the short, steep slope and waited just inside the gate to ruined Pera. The awful smell of charred bones made it hard to breathe. There were a few looters rummaging through the ruins; I wanted to scream at them and chase them off, but—with a rare, for me, bit of thinking ahead—I realized it would be a bad idea to call attention to myself while Jamila was likely to be looking for me. I glanced around for Hebrews who might be trying to collect the remnants of their lives, but I saw none. They were all either dead or gone. Dead or gone. All of them. An entire society, with threatening knives and silly children's rhymes and neat houses and empty candelabra. Gone.

I went back to the gate. Jamila appeared within an hour, disguised by cloaks on this warm, glaring morning. She looked exhausted; her face, when I was close enough to see it, was puffy and pale.

We said nothing to each other. For a time we just stood there. Muted sounds of happy reunions were audible between soldiers and their women outside the walls.

I clasped my hands protectively around her arms and realized I was sobbing again. "This happened to my home too," I whispered into her hair. All I could offer was empathy, and empathy felt feeble.

"I want to see what's left," she said.

With one arm protectively, tentatively, around her shoulders, I led her in along the main street and then up the slope, toward the charred skeletons of buildings. The Jewish settlement had been densely built, the wooden houses clustered together, a fragment of them set off from the others by a fence. There had been hundreds of buildings here, all wood; they'd radiated out from what had been a synagogue, with a large courtyard just beside it. It looked nothing like it had just two days before, when I'd already been bewildered by it; the area was small enough that the looting had been largely completed, although a few squires and sergeants were still picking through the smoking rubble of the larger houses. They were armed and I wasn't, so I kept my indignation to myself for fear of drawing attention to Jamila.

"There was a wall there," she mumbled, to herself mostly, as we picked our way through burning ash. I remembered seeing it the day before. "It was to separate the Karaites from the Rabbinites. The Karaites had different customs, so they stayed on their own side of the fence, and we all ignored one another. I always wondered about them, as a little girl. Too late to ask anyone now." She grimaced tearfully as we approached the burned courtyard of the burned synagogue—the only open space in the settlement that had appeared cut to a level surface. "I remember this from childhood," she said. "Every year for the Feast of the Tabernacle, they would erect a very large hut right here—almost like a giant wooden cave—and everyone would eat together all week. In Genoa, when the holidays came, my father would build a little hut like that just for the family, but here it was the whole community, all the families. The rich families, the *hashub*, would feed the *alub*, the poor ones." I listened but I don't think she was actually trying to inform me. It was a reverie. I had never seen her this vulnerable, fragile.

"I have to tell you something," I said. "Two days ago I came here, and I met your grandmother Deborah."

Jamila took in a sharp breath and looked instinctively up the hill. "Oh," she said in a broken voice. "This was the way." She rushed behind what had been the synagogue, along a narrow street of what had been houses. She was heading toward the house where I'd been taken, only she was looking down so that she would not get disoriented by the broken shells of buildings. Her childhood memory of the streets was good: a moment later, as I trotted dolefully behind her, she reached a stone foundation with a few charred bits of lumber protruding from it. Most of it was ashes, ground into dirt by looters; had the wind picked up again, the air would have been unfit to breathe for days. Automatically and nervously, I scanned the area for signs of a human skeleton, but whatever could have burned had burned completely.

"This was her house," she whispered, eyes glassy.

"I know, Jamila," I said, guilty for a reason I couldn't understand. "I was just here. I sat on a stool in this room, and I talked to your grandmother and two men who also remembered you. I was *just here*." I gestured miserably at the wreckage. "It was a *home*."

Jamila nodded, her eyes unfocused. "It was a wonderful home. This is where I learned that nursery rhyme I taught you. I remember teaching it to my daughter in Egypt, and thinking about this room where I had learned it. Did you tell my grandmother I was alive?" I nodded. She smiled a little. Her voice broke. "I'm glad she knew."

"They couldn't all have died," I said. "The whole community? Perhaps they fled together somewhere? Somebody surely helped her. I climbed over the gate yesterday when the fire started, but there was too much smoke, and I couldn't find anyone."

She shrugged. "They're gone."

"I'll find them," I said at once. "Or at least, I'll get you back to Alexandria, as I originally promised. You must still have people there. I'll find a home for you."

She shook her head. At first I thought she was rejecting my offer, but she was once again lost in reverie: "I remember the first moment I saw you, crazy-looking little stranger, choking that awful man, announcing you were rescuing me and using the Christian army to return me to my home. I thought you were out of your wits! Not that you've convinced me otherwise, but look, I . . ." She gestured to the charred house foundations, her eyes wet. "You've done it. Mostly by accident, but still, my God, I'm standing here, you've accomplished it. It's a *mitzvah*."

"What does that mean? Samuel used it too."

"Samuel?"

"A man who knew your family."

She collected herself a little. "Very old man? With thick white hair?"

I shook my head. "Reddish hair, and younger." I hesitated. "Your husband's brother."

She took a slow breath in, a sad smile on her lips. "Oh. I remember him from childhood; he was always very tall," she said, as if height were a behavior. "Their mother was from France and taught me French, so it was easy to learn the language later. I wonder how many others from my childhood remained here. A *mitzvah* is an act of kindness," she concluded. "Especially done in a manner of righteousness."

"Is it a *mitzvah* even if I fail to conclude it?" I gestured to the ruins around us. "I don't know what to do for you now. I don't even know what to do for myself."

Jamila took one of my hands in both of hers, trembling badly. "I think it is best to remain still during chaos. This is chaos now around us, and the next few days are likely to be so. But then things will be calmer, and we can see straight again. You and I must sit quietly and let the explosions come and go, and then, in the calm that follows the storm, we shall each decide from there where our paths will travel. Right now, when so much is about to happen, and so quickly, and we know so little, the best action is no action at all. Let us draw breath and see what happens next."

FOR FOUR DAYS the army stayed encamped outside Galata, waiting for some evidence that the Usurper was capitulating or at least catipulating. No such evidence was forthcoming. Gregor advocated sending envoys or even spies over to the city to learn the state of things. The waiting drove him crazy; summer was wasting, and he would not be tricked into spending another winter off target as an occupying force. A war council was summoned, and Gregor appeared; but ignoring Gregor, the leaders—even a grim, reluctant Dandolo—decided to move on to attack Blachernae Palace, the emperor's fortress on the northern corner of the city walls.

35

THE ARMY PULLED UP stakes and marched inland up the north shore of the harbor, to the bridge over which the Usurper's forces had fled from Galata the week before. On a hot, dry July afternoon, the army settled near a recently deserted monastery on a low hill, from where we could gaze east across the Golden Horn and south down the city. Constantinople, from this angle too—the opposite extreme of where we'd first viewed it from the Sea of Marmara—was astonishing. A gargantuan moated, double wall of rock, with dozens and dozens of towers spaced barely fifty paces apart, stretched *for miles* from the inland extreme of the harbor, where we were, all the way south and west to Marmara, making up the one landward side of the triangular city.

But the point was not to storm the city. This attack was still only intended against the Usurper, not his people, and the Usurper was ensconced in the palace of Blachernae. Blachernae made up the northern corner of Constantinople; somehow, its wall had to be breached, the Usurper taken down, Alexios put up in his place, and all of us reassembled on the ships with time to sail to the Holy Land before winter had set in. (And now I did think of it as *all of us* again, for with the loss of Pera, I was newly determined to take Jamila to Egypt after all.)

The Venetians would make a naval attack up near Blachernae while the army tried its own assault directly on Blachernae's land defenses. The Usurper—so went the theory—would be pinched between the two.

So the Venetians remained on their ships, preparing them: hides dampened by vinegar to prevent fires from catching were nailed to the hulls; vines woven into loose nets draped over the masts and yardarms to soften the impact of catapulted rocks. They built catwalks with grappling hooks on the end; when they sailed their boats aground at the seawall, the catwalks would be thrown out to catch onto the walls so the mariners could storm the towers directly.

Inland with the army, setting up camp took longer than usual: a defensive palisade had to be built around the siege machinery to protect it from the Varangian Guard, who tried to destroy it on short, ferocious sorties from the land gates, sorties that took place sometimes six times a day. The extra time it took to build the palisades drove Gregor nearly wild with aggravation; he wanted whatever was to happen to happen fast, so we could get back in the ships and head toward Egypt. So did I. To make things worse, we were running low on food again, but it was not safe for anyone to wander from the camp in search of sustenance because of the raids. Now even the lowliest of the infantry understood the need to win a battle fast: it meant Alexios could be crowned, *and then he'd feed us*. The seven battalions set up a rotational guard over both the fortifications and the foraging parties, but each battalion found itself besieged within an hour of coming on duty. A few days into this arrangement, nerves were fraying, patience wearing thin, and stomachs rumbling constantly.

Throughout the preparations, Boniface spent much time closeted with Prince Alexios. (Remember him? I forgot about him daily.) Around camp there were no warm feelings for the Pretender (as he was coming to be known, in contrast to the other Alexios, Usurper),

and he was hardly a seasoned military man. Gregor was in atten-
dance on the inner workings of the battle plans and was disturbed
to see that Alexios not only adored but actually fawned on Boniface,
considered the marquis his savior and his closest personal friend and
confidant. Alexios was an ineffectual pup, drooling gratefully but
nervously at his master's knee.

Each day after dinner, Boniface would host a war conference in
his pavilion. Dandolo would come to shore to be present at these parliaments; I was employed to be a lutenist, although nobody—usually
not even Dandolo—ever listened to a note I played. Sometimes I
had the feeling I was a minor pawn in his subtle but relentless games
of one-upmanship with Boniface: he wanted to throw his weight
around gratuitously, however he could, just to demonstrate that he
must be catered to. One simple way to do that was to demand a ridiculous luxury, like a musician nobody paid attention to. However
petty or perverse the reasons were, I was glad of them, for I wanted to
be kept abreast, firsthand, of what was going on.

By Wednesday the sixteenth, all was ready, and the plans were
finally announced: The three larger battalions would make an initial attack, led by Baldwin of Flanders. The four smaller divisions—
including Gregor's—would remain to guard the camp and siege
machinery, under the direction of Boniface.

When informed that they would not be among the vanguard,
Otto was incensed all over again, as if he were learning it for the first
time.

"Do you really want to fight, sir?" Jamila asked him, from her protected corner of the tent, where she quietly mourned the loss of Pera.
"In a battle you can't possibly approve of, if you have any shred of
morality?"

Otto turned on her, eyes raging. "Not fighting is as immoral as
fighting now, because our stupid leaders have made their stupid vows.
There is no good to come from this in the bigger picture, no matter
what position anyone takes. I can't approach this as a pilgrim, so I

may as well approach it as a soldier, and as a soldier, I want to fight. So perhaps when jerks like this fellow"—this with a gesture toward me—"immortalize this day in infamy, a few of us can be regarded as a little better than the rest, because at least we did our job with valor, even if the job itself was not valorous."

As I contemplated all the ways there were to retort to this, Jamila gave him a sympathetic nod. "If it means that much to you, sir, I have a suggestion that I believe can give you what you most desire. It requires only your knife."

Otto needed no convincing; Gregor and I were taken aback at the sight of him and Jamila hovering in the corner over his dagger, conspiring together. Jamila held out a scolding finger when I tried to listen in.

"Very well, then, I'm going to try playing for Boniface," I said.

In the marquis's livery, I was admitted easily enough; I had played three bloodlust songs accompanied by the fiddle and was just beginning that smarmy "Kalenda Maya" for a change of pace when there was a ruckus outside the pavilion, and of all people, Otto was admitted. One had the sense that he was admitted despite the steward's better judgment. One had the sense he was admitted because he did not allow a choice in the matter.

"Milord!" he said and ran into the space, bowing even as he ran. "Milord Boniface!" He threw himself kneeling at Boniface's feet. I almost shouted in alarm because he held a thick hank of wavy black hair.

Somehow, I made myself keep playing.

"Milord," he said and glanced up at Boniface, unsure if he should wait for permission to press forward. "You gave me your word I could have Liliana back if I delivered Jamila to you. I do so here and now, milord." He thrust the hair up at the marquis.

Boniface stared at the tableau of Otto and his offering a moment, bemused. "That is not Jamila," he said after a beat.

"It's all that's left of her," he said. "She perished in the fire at

Pera, milord. I found her burned body and could salvage no more than this. And this." He fidgeted for a moment with his pinkie finger and pushed to the tip of it the very fine gold-and-ruby ring that Jamila had had on when she'd escaped from Scutari Palace. Boniface frowned thoughtfully. Otto held them up higher, bowed his head. "I offer them to you in exchange for Liliana." Boniface gestured Otto to hold up the lock of hair. Without taking it, the marquis sniffed at it. His face showed some surprise, then he nodded—Jamila or Otto must have smoked her hair so it would seem burned.

But then Boniface shook his head. "That exchange will not happen," he said, as if suddenly bored by Otto. "One woman for another was the deal. You're not giving me a woman. You're giving me her artifacts. If you like, I will give you some of Liliana's artifacts—she has many beautiful hair combs, for example, all of which I have given her, and a shift made entirely of lace, which she wears exclusively for my viewing pleasure. But I will not give her to you unless you give me back my princess."

Otto's lower jaw stuck out a little. "Jamila was not a princess."

Boniface smiled a little. "You know what I mean, boy. Bring her to me."

"I have!" Otto said with irritation, holding up the thick tress. "I give you all that exists of her on earth now. I ask you to honor your word and give me Liliana."

Boniface's lip lifted a little on one side, and he shook his head. "No, lad," he said. "I enjoy fucking her far too much to yield her up in exchange for a dead slattern's hair." The curled lip relaxed into a smile; the smile was directed dreamily over Otto's head. "The way she sucks me into her when I mount her, the way she grabs my arse to press me even harder down onto her —" Otto looked as if he might very quietly vomit. Somehow I kept playing. Boniface's smile grew lopsided, and he shifted a little in his chair. "Just thinking about it makes me hard. I'm going to fuck her as soon as you depart from here."

"By St. John, milord, it is not right for you to speak to me that way," Otto said, really sounding as if he might be ill. "She is my woman and you do me great injustice."

Boniface shrugged. "She came to my tent on her own two feet back on Corfu, unescorted, and she is free to leave whenever she so wishes."

"If that is true, let her tell me directly to my face that she doesn't wish to return to me," Otto said, barely avoiding a whine.

Again the slightly curled lip. "She doesn't want to speak to you. She's afraid of your blubbering, which would embarrass her."

Otto paused a moment, to contain himself. I'd never seen him try to contain himself before; I was relieved, and actually impressed. "What might induce a change of heart, milord?" he asked finally, in a low and neutral voice.

Boniface smiled, pleased that Otto understood. "If you brought me Jamila—all of her, in person—Liliana might be so impressed by that, her view of you might change."

Another pause.

Then Otto said, "I have done so," and again held up the hair and ring. "There is nothing of her left but this."

Boniface leaned down and took only the ring from Otto. He held it up and examined it. "Oh, yes, this one. This ring is very valuable, one of the most valuable things in the treasury at Scutari, from whence we dressed Her Highness. Thank you for bringing it back rather than pocketing it yourself. That makes you an honest man, my lad." He slipped the ring onto the tip of his pinkie and lowered his hand. "I think I'll give it to Liliana after I fuck her today."

"*Milord,*" Otto said, his voice ragged. "I've brought you valuable information. Even if you will not honor your word regarding my woman, at least demonstrate that you are a fair and just leader, and reward me for the intelligence I've given you."

Boniface crossed his arms and thought a moment. "She's really dead?"

"Yes, milord," Otto said, between clenched teeth. "You are tormenting me for no gain at all. I *cannot* render to you what God has claimed already for himself. I had to cut that ring from off the swollen finger of a corpse. The body, what was not already burned, has been buried by now with all the other Jews." He glanced up and dared to glare at Boniface. "Don't tell me there is no value in that intelligence."

Boniface nodded. "I agree, lad, it is valuable enough."

"Valuable enough for Liliana?" Otto demanded.

Boniface winked at him and shook his head. "No. And you know that. But you're right, it's helpful, and you deserve some recompense. What else would you ask of me?"

I almost started applauding Otto when I realized. He had known, coming in here, that he would not get Liliana; that hadn't even been his aim. "I want to be in the vanguard, my lord, and fight on the front lines tomorrow at dawn."

Boniface considered this. "Gregor approves?"

"Gregor has washed his hands of me, milord," Otto corrected, fibbing a little. "He has given up hoping that I will behave like a subordinate."

Thus it came to pass that Otto of Frankfurt was most honorably transferred into the vanguard force. Had he not been, the world might not have changed so very much within a year.

36

 THE MEN HAD ALL been barbered and shriven (again) the night before. By the time they were armored and their horses saddled this morning, it was already hot, although the sun was barely above the horizon. All the knights and armored sergeants, regardless of their usual livery, wore loose white surcoats over their armor to prevent it overheating. The Venetians had arranged their fleet in the harbor, but the land force, spread out over the fields between their own palisades and Blachernae Palace, must have appeared to the Greeks as the more formidable force. So the Usurper had sent most of the elite Varangian Guard to the walls of Blachernae; the larger but less expert regular army, made up of conscripted citizens, probably seemed strong enough to fend off the harbor attack.

Each division of the crusading army had just over a thousand men but only a few hundred each on horseback; the rest were knights who had lost their horses, plus sergeants, archers, crossbowmen, and foot soldiers. The very air was so tense I almost felt I could pluck it and draw sounds.

Baldwin of Flanders had the first division at arms, sporting white flags with green crosses; behind him were two more. Gregor waited grimly by the palisades with the remainder of the army, staring at the back of Boniface's head. Now that the moment had come, I knew he was frustrated: it had taken him a long time to accept the need for this attack, and now that he'd committed to it, his soldierly duties would consist of sitting motionless on Summa and doing little for most of the day. This campaign had taken too long to organize and smelled of incompetence now that it was finally to be prosecuted.

There was a blare of horns and trumpets from around the field, and a voice screamed out the order to attack. A swelling thunder shook the earth as the three battalions galloped and ran toward the palace walls, carrying dozens of siege ladders and, at a much slower pace, pushing wheeled towers, catapults, and covered carts.

In the encampment, stable boys, cooks, and common women craned their necks to see what was happening. Most of them ran farther up the hillside, where they could see over the army that was waiting by the siege machines.

I had, at first, slighted even the idea of watching. But when the thundering came to a stop, when I realized the army was actually *there* and the attack would actually *begin*, human curiosity got the better of me, and I came up with a better way to watch, which was imitated by half of the dependents left behind the palisades. Spare segments of siege ladders lay around the camp. These, when righted and leaned against the wall, were high enough to use as perches to view what was happening down the slope. Comfortable with precarious heights, I clambered above the spikes topping the palisade, while on the ladder, Jamila, veiled, peeked over the top.

From here we saw the vanguard struggling to set the ladders against the walls of Blachernae. As the Franks tried to climb the heavy, broad contraptions to get up to the parapets, a hail of arrows greeted them, felling almost anyone who lacked protective chain mail—mostly infantry. Huge vats of burning pitch poured down the wall. More damaging, because they were easier to aim, were the smaller buckets that were full of the entire palace's overnight excrements, combined with things like rotting food, broken dishes, scalding cooking oil, fettle scrapings from the smithies, carcasses of stillborn puppies. Such offerings were hurled upon the soldiers trying to climb the ladders; combined with arrows, they assured that Latins were killed, wounded, or dislodged almost as fast as they swarmed up, but there were enough of them that they kept swarming.

I could see Gregor from where we were. He was not watching the attack. He was staring at the back of Boniface's head and occasionally glancing at Prince Alexios, who sat on a gangly young stallion—his own equine equivalent, really—to the marquis's right. I wondered what this day meant to him. What must it be like to see an entire plain of men—men who owed him nothing, no feudal or Christian obligation—prepared to go to their death on his behalf? Alexios seemed to find this no more than his due.

Boniface uttered a cry of satisfaction, which led to general cheering and pulled my attention down to the plain. The cheers were sparked by the first good sign of the morning: two Frankish soldiers had already gotten to the top of the wall and were fighting off the axes of the Varangian Guard. Surely, as with the tower of Galata, two were enough to start the siege. Surely now the vanguard would sweep up onto the parapets and take the castle; the Usurper would flee again, and victory would be theirs.

This was the collective hope of the watching army. Except for Gregor. Gregor was possessed by the same thought I had: *One of those men is Otto.*

On the wall, Otto and the stranger beside him were efficiently fending off the axes although certainly neither was used to such attacks. They were back-to-back but moved almost in unison, as if a single mind worked both bodies together. Otto swung at an oncoming soldier's armpit and wounded him severely enough for the man to fall away. But at that moment, the other Frankish soldier had less success: three Varangians came at him; his head landed on the blood-splattered stone walkway, then one arm, then the other; then the rest of him. Otto leapt away from the corpse and, in that blink of wavered concentration, failed to sense the heavy flat of an ax descending on him very fast.

"He's not killed!" I said quickly, although I suspected I was lying. I'd helped him gear up for battle this morning; he'd been wearing an iron helmet with lots of quilting under it, so there was a chance he was only unconscious from that blow, not dead. Yet.

Once he fell, he was not set upon with violence. Two Varangians grabbed his limp arms and lifted him; a third retrieved his sword as it fell from his grasp. One of the two holding his arms hoisted him onto his partner's back, and accompanied by cheers, jeers, and catcalls, they carried their burden to the far edge of the broad defensive wall and down steps into the sprawling palace compound.

"He's been taken captive," I announced, feeling calmer. If he were dead, they'd never have bothered with a nicety such as carrying him off the field . . . unless they wanted a body to abuse in public later, as an intimidation tactic. I pushed that possibility from my mind.

"The pilgrims will carry the day," Jamila said with forced confidence. "And he'll be released."

"Will they?" I asked. "When will they begin to carry it?"

With Otto removed and his cohort dispatched, there were no more Franks on the wall, and it looked unlikely the Varangians would let any more make it. They seemed to have an endless supply of archers and arrows, and the pilgrim archers were doing a feeble job of picking any of them off. They also had enormous crossbows and smallish catapults, which sent fire arrows and other flaming projectiles at the siege engines and wheeled towers—half of which burned down in the arid air.

Jamila and I watched from the ladder until the sun was overhead. The pilgrims looked like ants trying to climb up a slippery, sunbaked rock. The air was so hot it shimmered—a rare phenomenon to me. As the heat grew worse, the speed and agility of the men noticeably decreased. The Franks got a few more men—perhaps a dozen—on the walls, but without exception they were killed up there. Baldwin had finally withdrawn, and the other two battalions made a strong attempt, but they never had a chance.

I tried to make a game of seeking out details within the army to distract us both. "Notice the bishops pick their noses more than the lesser clergy," I pointed out, gesturing to the rear guard, some hundred yards ahead. "I wonder what that means."

"Baldwin's flag bearer rotates the standard in little circles when he's nervous," Jamila said, playing along without enthusiasm.

I gave her a dismissive look. "That's hardly interesting," I scoffed and pointed to the section of the Seventh Division where Gregor sat mounted and watching. "Now look at this—the fatter infantry adjust their balls more than the skinny ones."

"And the poorer ones mutter prayers aloud more often than the well-dressed ones," Jamila said. "With Jews it would be just the opposite."

* * *

Eve of the Feast of St. Arnulf of Metz, 17 July

I have been remiss about writing here; it is hard to maintain the mind-set of a warrior and a clerk at the same moment.

There are few things more difficult for a soldier than to be told his job in a battle consists of watching and waiting. There were so many ways I wish I had participated, even if I could not climb the walls myself; even something as humble as safeguarding the wooden blinds from behind which our archers shoot at enemies—this would have been accounted joyful duty. But I did nothing except sit and wait.

The noise of the attack was astoundingly loud even back before the palisades, and we all felt it with every organ in our bodies, even our bones. It made me nearly mad with a desire to spur Summa into the midst of things. As midday approached, however, the cacophony dampened with the army's enthusiasm. Perhaps we were getting used to the intensity; perhaps we were all going deaf from it.

Then a new and different ruckus began from the harbor:

Radiating triumph, a dozen Venetian transports were sailing toward us, the men onboard cheering—literally dancing with delight. They beached the ships as near as possible to the encampment and leapt off onto the soft ground, jubilant about something. Clearly they'd been faring better than the land army. One of the ships was a horse trans-port; sailors rushed out to wedge away the sticky resin holding closed the great hatch. The hatch fell open, forming a gangplank to the beach. For a moment nothing happened. Then, to my astonishment, dozens of beautiful horses and mules—bare-backed, in full Byzantine gear, sporting the torn remains of harnesses—leapt out, down the gangway, and onto the shore, chased by sailors within. They herded the horses toward the palisade as stable boys and squires rushed out of the camp to meet them.

Boniface sent a messenger to speak to the Venetians; the messen-ger returned with extraordinary news: Just out of our view, the doge's flag, the winged lion of St. Mark, flew over the tallest of the protective towers on the upper harbor—and the esteemed doge, plunging into the thick of things, aged and blind, had put it there himself. Such valiant leadership had spurred his devoted fellows to astonishing heroism: the Venetians had taken more than two dozen towers, and the day was barely half over!

The messenger continued, reporting that the inept natives trying to defend the harbor towers were being replaced by Varangian mercenaries, who were far more skilled and dangerous than the conscripted army; the Venetians were starting to feel the crush of an effective counterattack at last. "But the doge has an idea how to handle that," the messenger concluded and pointed to the southeast. "And the wind is in his favor."

A ragged billow of smoke was rising from the harborside. We could not tell from here how large the fire was, but the smoke itself was so dense, the Greeks could not attack into it. Within moments the cloud was not only higher into the sky but broader in several directions, and the Venetians delivering their booty, seeing it, broke into a fresh round of cheering. Since the wind was coming off the harbor, the Venetians were behind the cloud, not choked by it, and they could follow the fire as it forced the defending army back into the city. Doge Dandolo had not wanted warfare—but unable to avoid it, he was proving the most valiant strategist and warrior of the day.

I had an intelligent guess about what would happen next: the Usurper, desperate to distract the Venetians and unable to do it with a frontal attack, would probably direct the Varangian Guard back to Blachernae, perhaps even send a mounted cavalry out of one of the gates to put us into such severe distress that the Venetians, as our allies, would have to divert manpower from their own victorious front to come to our assistance. But there were still four battalions of us completely fresh, not employed in battle, and I knew from experience that the Greeks could not hold their own against us on a battlefield. Also we had, still unused today, a contingent of excellent Genoese crossbow-

men, believed the best in Christendom. I wondered if they were as
eager to see action as I was.

THE GLEE OF THE Venetians had helped spirits within the camp,
but the Venetians were gone back to the harbor, and the mood in
the camp was once again tense. And there was something unnerving
about being here, in a city of tents that housed at least ten thousand,
when it was nearly empty.

Jamila and I, still perched at the top of the palisade wall, stared
bleakly toward Blachernae. From the harbor, the cloud of smoke bil-
lowed. Ahead of us, the Varangian Guard not only doubled on the
top of the walls but began to make short, deadly sorties, lightning-
fast raids out and back before the Franks could even get close to
the open gates. The crusaders would obviously not prevail. Which
meant, among various other disasters, Otto might never be released.

"I'm not a gentleman," I said suddenly.

"Is that the start of a joke?" Jamila asked.

I shook my head, a little shamed, a little apologetic. "I'm not a
gentleman. I'm about to ask something no gentleman would ever
think of asking a woman. And I have no excuse except that I'm just
a crude barbarian." I grimaced one final time and then glanced down
at Jamila. "I have no right to ask you this—"

"Of course I'll go with you, your Greek is appalling, and I made
you promise not to try anything like this without me," she said with
dry impatience. "We'll have to disguise you to get you through. You
hardly even pass as a Frank, let alone a local."

I was shocked at her offhandedness. "Are you so willing? You owe
Otto nothing."

"Otto killed me off to Boniface. Thanks to him, I'm not a fugitive
anymore. Anyhow, I'm not just doing it for Otto. I'm doing it for you.
And Gregor. And even Liliana. For the tribe."

Continuation

Sitting on Summa in the pounding summer sun, lance butt resting on my right stirrup, I stared morosely as my fellow soldiers continued to take a beating. The squadrons of the rear guard took turns trotting our mounts in a wide circle to keep them ready to race, but it was becoming obvious there would be nothing to race to, unless it was in retreat back to the camp. The vanguard was working tirelessly, but they were getting nowhere. I thought about my brother, wounded and no doubt chained or even dead, in the bowels of Blachernae, and shuddered, feeling powerless.

I urged Summa up a few steps, until I was nearly level with Boniface. "Milord," I said softly. "That was my brother—"

"All of these men are your brothers," Boniface said calmly, without looking away from the field. "Return to your place and wait."

WE COULD NOT BELIEVE how easily we'd gotten through the gate. A bowshot farther down the harbor, where the fire raged, the gates were bricked closed; in the other direction, even three hundred paces inland, we could not have gotten close to any gates because of the land attack. But we'd scrambled over slippery rocks to the northwestern reaches of the harbor walls, which doubled as the water gate for Blachernae.

Jamila had been able to convince the guard that we were local women of Genoese birth who'd been trapped outside the city walls, returning from a visit to her brother, an apothecary at the monastery who knew many healing herbs. "We" being, of course, she and her decrepit mother, bent double with age and wearing a most indeterminable, shapeless garment, her face covered by a scarf, which her doting daughter had stolen for her from the French army to hide the dreadful disfiguring brought on by a wasting disease. Jamila was able to rattle off the names of half a dozen local herbs her fictional sibling had given her, and even show samples of several she'd collected up in the hills. The mother appeared to be speaking in tongues, rattling off nonsense as if it were a native language; the daughter patiently took her mother's callused, hairy-knuckled, undelicate hands and stroked them reassuringly, telling her to be quiet now, they were safe, those miserable Franks would not try to rob her of her virtue any longer.

We were unarmed, plausibly female, and obviously distressed; the guard could hardly pay attention to his duties, he was so distracted awaiting news about the fire, the battle, the harbor attack. He let us through. Not into the palace grounds but along a boardwalk stinking of standing water, through a gate that opened onto the broad avenue between the palace walls and the stately homes of visiting aristocrats.

"That should not have worked," Jamila said shakily under her breath, once we were alone on the avenue.

"Well, it *did* work," I growled in falsetto, hobbling along bent over beside her.

Just one street over, the fire raged; it sucked the world into it in a hot, harsh wind, and the smells were horrible. Fancy gardens were falling to the flame; the servants' quarters in all the homes were blazing, but at least the wind was blowing away from us.

The sun was high, slightly ahead, sending our shortened shadows directly behind us as we began to move into the neighborhood. The avenue was deserted—and it had the air of a place that was unused to being deserted. After a few dozen paces, it curved strenuously uphill, and high up, to our right, we could see what must have been the entrance gate to Blachernae Palace. This too looked unaccustomed to its current solitude.

"What do we do from here?" Jamila asked, carefully eyeing the closed doors and shuttered windows of the buildings all around us. It was unnaturally, eerily still, except for the fire wind and the bass roar of the unseen inferno. The racket of each battle—naval behind, land ahead—sounded distantly, dulled by the city walls to either side. "You swore to tell me the whole plan once we were inside."

"Inside the palace," I corrected.

"We may not have a chance then. Why can't you tell me now, so I can tell you what needs improvement?"

"Because until we're inside, I don't know what the plan is," I said.

Jamila came up short. "Are you mad?" she demanded. I assumed it was a rhetorical question, as she was already familiar with my methods. "You said you knew what we were doing!"

"I do know: we're rescuing Otto."

"*How?* You said you knew *how* to do it!"

I shrugged. "By getting him out of prison. So we find the prison, and then we get him out. I can't give you any more details until we're inside. I *told* you it wasn't safe to do this. You *insisted* on coming along."

"You *asked* me to," Jamila snapped back, fear making her peevish. "I said I would as long as you knew what to do."

"And I will know, I promise," I said, to relax her. "I promise you, we'll both be safe." After a pause I added, somewhat imprudently, but for the sake of clarity, "As safe as any two prison breakers can be, who have snuck into an enemy fortress."

"No," Jamila announced. "No unplanned plans. I thought you'd learned." She pushed the basket up to her elbow, crossed her arms, and gave me a look of defiance.

"All right," I said wearily, with a yielding gesture. "Suggest something."

"*I* shouldn't *have* to."

"You don't *have* to," I said. "I told you I'd figure it out when I get inside."

"You're mad," she said crossly and continued to think. "All right, how about this? We're from Pera, and we're here to petition the emperor for funds to rebuild—"

"I think the emperor has more pressing matters to deal with to-day," I said.

"Then . . . we're from the royal dairy, and we're here to give an account of the spring calves being weaned."

I again made a gesture of concession. "If that's what you want to say; you're the one who speaks Greek, after all."

"Is it a good idea?" she demanded, dismayed by my lack of enthusiasm. I was not used to seeing her so unnerved. "Will it work?"

I shrugged. "I'm sure it will," I said, meaning to sound comforting but instead sounding almost condescending. "Let's find out." I took her free elbow and tugged her forward.

37

Continuation

I stared at the walls of Blachernae, hating how incompetent I felt to do anything to help my brother or, indeed, the army. Tension and boredom knotted together were rubbing a hole in my stomach. I assumed the Briton and the Jewess were back in the tent and feeling even more helpless than I was. I wondered if Liliana had heard of Otto's capture. I counted seventy of our siege towers burning or crippled.

Summa stamped a foot against the flies, as bored and discontented as I was. I had sent young Richard down to the walls to collect Oro, Otto's stallion, and bring him safely back to camp. I pray there will be no cause to give him to another rider.

JAMILA GAVE ME the basket of herbs and approached the guard at the side gate of Blachernae. The guard wore the Varangian livery, but he was very young, probably a squire who had been handed an ax and told to watch the gate. All of the seasoned soldiers were up on the walls now, or inland dealing with the fire and the Venetians who came after it. It was strange to me that, in response to an enemy attack, none of the citizens were fleeing here, to their sovereign's fortress, for safety—where I come from, that's the whole *point* of having a sovereign with a well-protected home.

Jamila had discarded the dairy cattle scheme and worked out three new ones, equally unsatisfying, in as many minutes. I had indifferently approved each of them; it did give me a certain satisfaction that, however sharp she was at pointing out the flaws in my schemes, she was not so sharp at inventing her own. Now, by her own decision, she was a newly employed maid of the imperial bedchamber, sent to fetch back this wise woman from the Genoese district (the Genoese hated the Venetians, those dogs!). The wise woman had some herbs that would help His Imperial Majesty's mental clarity and prowess, so that he would be able to determine how best to fend off these accursed devils. We merely needed to be let into the servants' quarters, where a midwife would know how to prepare the herbs. (Jamila's schemes were getting increasingly elaborate, perhaps to make up for their complete lack of intelligence.)

The youth hesitated. He wanted to summon one of the senior officers on the tower. At this point the wise woman (whose face was covered in modesty of the Holy Spirit, which worked through her) burst into a fit of outraged cursing. "She is saying," Jamila translated, "that if you hesitate, these herbs will never reach His Majesty in time. Do you not smell that fire? Do you not hear the fighting on the walls? There is no time to lose, it must be at once. You harm your emperor, whom you have vowed to help, if you don't let us in right now. Don't you know there is a *battle*? Even His Imperial Majesty does not stand on ceremony in a battle!"

"That shouldn't have worked either," she muttered, as a porter lead us directly into the palace grounds. I gestured that she should follow without fuss, although we would have no liberty in here at all. It was hard to believe this was a porter, for his tunic, although extremely short, was tailored to fit him very well, and it had gold thread running along the hems and cuffs.

Within a few minutes it was clear, in fact, that the scheme *hadn't* worked—we were *not* being taken to the servants' quarters. Perhaps there'd been miscommunication, but I doubted it. We were in a gallery all of marble that opened into a hilly courtyard full of fruit trees. The porter handed us off to a civil servant—a long-haired, bearded man in a red cloak over a blue gown who looked at us suspiciously, asked Jamila some questions, and then sent the porter off in another direction.

"We're in trouble," Jamila said, grabbing my fist so hard it hurt my knuckles.

"Breaking my hand isn't going to help matters," I whispered back. She released me. "Thank you. What's happening?"

"You'll see," she whispered back.

"That's not helpful."

"There is nothing I can tell you right now that would be."

The old man led us through an opening, into a yard filled entirely with kitchen herbs; it was on a slope, and we trudged up the hill, slipping occasionally in mud from a recent watering. We went inside to an empty room made of brick with lots of windows; outside and then in again, through a bewildering series of corridors, halls, rooms, and courtyards, until I could not have told you with any certainty whether we were still within the palace grounds or, indeed, even within Byzantium. Everything was striated brick, with lots of windows, lots of light. There were people everywhere, hurrying and anxious, and nobody paid us any attention—Blachernae, although not penetrated, was under attack.

The people were fascinating; they all looked alike to me, but were not at all what I'd expected. All of them, at a glance, had coloring like Jamila's, but many women had dyed their hair brighter, redder—

which was easy to see because so many of them wore their heads un-covered, their tresses piled up in startling confections where crowns would sit. All wore long gowns—purple, red, blue, dark green, with elaborate geometrical designs woven into or printed upon them, and pearls sewn up and down the sleeves.

The men were even more fascinating. To start, all had long hair and long beards, except the ones with no facial hair at all, about whom Jamila whispered, "Eunuchs." Some wore tall dark hats, others white turbans. Some wore long sashed gowns like those of Dandolo and Alexios, but the ones my age or younger wore short tunics that hardly covered their buttocks. These tunics were so tightly tailored, their wearers appeared to have been sewn into them. Their legs—of which you could see literally every inch—had fancy geometrical de-signs woven into the hose. This was a people mad for decoration.

Suddenly we were in a small, high-windowed room, which was deceptively tranquil and taken up almost entirely by scrolls, inky parchments, and a mound of quills waiting to be sharpened into styli. Behind this mound sat a well-dressed, mournful man just be-yond the prime of life. He was dressed entirely in red. Introductions were made, with Jamila arguing timorously with both men, and then this fellow became our new, and grudging, chaperone. He led us up a set of polished wooden stairs behind him (*wooden* meaning four different kinds of inlaid wood in intricate forms); we went through another labyrinth of offices and passageways—and then I realized we really were in trouble.

A robed officer who appeared to have been constructed of dried reeds (not even hair, for he was bald) intercepted us, with our chap-erone, in an antechamber high up in a grand brick building. In the next room, enraged voices were declaiming at one another, all sten-torian—each man being only as polite as he must and at least as loud as he dared.

The reedy bald man, whose collar shimmered with pearls, was tall; his voice was as thin as he was; he wanted to know who we were and what we were doing here. Jamila's tremulous voice made it clear she was lying, even without my knowing what she said. Her increasingly apologetic tone and the man's growing ire suggested that now she was doing something worse than lying: she was telling the truth, or something like it.

"What is going on?" I demanded in a clenched falsetto.

The reedy, man made an impatient sound and snatched the veil away from my face. I tried to snatch it back, but it was too late: I was obviously not a woman. Whatever else Jamila might have been able to convince them of (which wasn't much, by the sound of it), we were obviously trying to trick somebody.

"Hello," I said in Greek.

I blinked at the verbal onslaught that followed and glanced at Jamila. "I'd love to make this a dialogue, but I need your help," I said.

She bit her lower lip, then took in a nervous little gasp and said, "He thinks we're thieves, and he's going to cut our hands off if we don't have a better explanation for our presence here." Then she added hurriedly, almost guiltily, "And if it's helpful, in the next room they are arguing about the emperor. The men in there hate him. They want to get rid of him, but the Varangian Guard—"

"*They* want to get rid of him?" I demanded, flabbergasted. "What is the *problem*, then? Everyone wants the same thing—to get rid of the Usurper!"

"The Varangian Guard," she whispered back. "They're incorruptible, and more dangerous than any native Greek, and he's always surrounded by them."

Before she could continue, the Reed Man started haranguing us again in Greek. Jamila opened her mouth to respond, but I interrupted her, thrilled by our unexpected opportunity. If we were stuck in the thick, we might as well make the most of it: "Tell him we're here to get rid of the emperor."

She blinked once. A pause.

She blinked again, her mouth pursing. "What?" she said. She was enraged at me.

"Tell him we're here to get rid of the emperor. Somebody in there hired us as assassins. Of course they won't own up to it, now that we've been caught, but that's what we're doing here, and we're happy to carry on and get rid of him, if that's the consensus."

"*No,*" she said, in the deepest voice I have ever heard a woman use.

"Not assassins then," I said, placating. "We're here to . . . trick him into abdicating. To convince him. What does the Varangian Guard do if he *abdicates?*"

Jamila blinked. "I . . . I don't know. I assume they swear themselves to whomever is crowned as his replacement."

"And who will replace this fellow if he does abdicate? Who decides that?"

"I have no idea," she said.

I winked at her. "Let's find out."

"My ancestors will haunt you through eternity after this gets us killed," she warned and then began to speak to the Reed Man in Greek.

It is remarkable how fast things can happen when somebody believes you're on his team. In about the time it takes pigs to copulate, we were in front of a group of nobles who were better-dressed, and far more frantic, than any group of humans I'd ever seen. All of them wore rich colors of blues, reds, even purples, with stiff, elaborate bands of gold embroidery on their cuffs, their hems, around their upper arms, at their collars. Their tunics were tied by long, elegant sashes. And I mean no disrespect to the fairer sex, but all of the men were behaving the way I'd think a group of women might, if they found themselves in a dire predicament. However, the actual women in the room (there were several, well-dressed and pearl-studded) were infinitely calmer than the men. The walls were covered with marble panels, with tile mosaics near the top depicting nude nymphs frolicking in a pagan temple; the ceiling was all golden; so was the table.

I explained that we had been hired through a middleman and I did not know who our employer was by name, but it was presumably one of the men present. I was a conjurer and trickster; my assignment was to trick the emperor into believing that he must abdicate.

"You are lying to us, of course," said the man who seemed to be the leader of this particular cabal, or at least the richest—a man wearing so many pearls and pretty rocks sewn into the front of his robe, I was surprised he didn't fall onto his face.

"I might be, but I can still accomplish it," I retorted cockily, through Jamila. "He is notoriously superstitious, is he not? And somewhat paranoid?"

They all exchanged looks. The rock-strewn man demanded, "Who are you, and who *really* sent you, and what were you *really* planning to accomplish?"

"And how would you accomplish *this*, instead?" asked another one. That was a promising detail: it meant at least one of them was contemplating my offer.

"I was sent by nobody, milords," I assured them, knowing they wouldn't believe me. "You've got a friend of mine in your prison cells, and I thought I'd spring him."

"How were you planning to do that?" demanded the Reed Man.

"The obvious way," I said. "I thought I'd get myself intercepted by you, be brought to this conference, offer my services, have them accepted, get rid of the emperor, and have my friend released as my reward." I grinned at him. "It's working so far." By now Jamila could hardly speak to translate; I think she was expecting one of them to decapitate us both at any moment. Without giving any of them a chance to comment, I added, "Allow me to present a proposition, milords. Give me access to the emperor. If I have not convinced him that I'm a sorcerer within a single try, boil me in oil and have your filthy way with my beautiful assistant." (I suspect my beautiful assistant did not translate it quite like that.) "Tell me what you want him to do, and I'll see that he does it, or you can kill us both." Even my voice faltered at this claim.

There was heated discussion around the table. Eventually we were informed that some other faction in the palace (there were many) was trying to convince the emperor to ride out and meet the feeble Frankish barbarians in battle, but "our" faction was against this idea, for this reason: once the Byzantine army won (which was universally presumed), His Majesty would have a mandate to go on being emperor, a hobby at which he had proven himself utterly inept for eight years running. "Our" faction wanted to urge the crisis to its point and use this moment to replace him altogether—replace him with (such a coincidence!) the man with all the rocks on his tunic.

Since the option was having our hands lopped off, I made Jamila promise them that I could prevent the emperor from joining the enemy in battle, a promise I was happy to make as I wanted to see that battle happen no more than they did. If I could keep Gregor from turning himself into mincemeat, I was happy to do it. Otto's capture had been bad enough. Germans and their romanticized martial valor.

We were led into the imperial bedchamber by the Reed Man; by now I'd decided this fellow must be the palace steward. The bed-chamber was an astonishing room, as fancy and almost as large as any of the halls we'd seen. There were lots of windows, lots of gold tiles, lots of marble, a decorative marble floor, and romantic scenes of romantic peasants adorning the upper walls. The bedstead appeared to be made entirely of greenish turquoise. We were told we would be waiting for a while.

"Do you have *any* kind of plan?" Jamila asked, looking at her hands as if she expected to lose them within moments. "Let me remind you that everything you've undertaken since I met you has been a botched job."

"That's not true! I got you out of Venice, I got the Egyptians out of Zara, and—"

"But *this* is by far the most infantile, dangerous, ill-considered, *inane*—"

There had been a rising mumble in another room; it suddenly grew louder and broke into shouts. One voice was loudest of all, and clearly angry or desperate above all the others. "That's him," Jamila whispered. This was the voice that suddenly approached the door, and with a hurried fanfare from a breathless-sounding trumpeter, the door was thrown open. Emperor Alexios III—the Usurper—entered his private apartment.

38

HE HAD A STRING of anxious attendants with him, as well as the Reed Man and the man with stones sewn into his tunic, and he was wearing clothes that looked as expensive as the whole of "our" faction's put together, with five times as many stones sewn into his long purple gown and ten times as much gold thread as well. He wore something on his head more cumbersome than any crown I'd seen, almost more of a gold hat weighed down with pearls and rubies. Anyone would be in a permanently foul mood with all that extra weight on his brain.

The Usurper himself had the same name and the same general look as his young nephew, the Pretender. That is to say, this Alexios too was not an impressive or remarkable-looking man, but he looked like he expected to be pampered. He was past the prime of life, and was passably handsome in a nondescript, round-cheeked sort of way. Like the prince, he was tall and somewhat thin, with dark (in his case, graying) hair; there was a family resemblance in the jaw. He stalked around the room with aggravation, muttering to himself; the door was slammed closed against whoever had been following him, and a few fists pounded on it. His Majesty yelled out a single phrase, with anger and an outstretched fist, and the noises outside silenced at once. Jamila paled and whispered, "Said he'd kill the next man who knocked."

The emperor calmed from his striding and sank down onto the edge of his huge, silk-swathed, turquoise bed, looking around at his attendants as if they were movable statuary. Everyone but him stayed standing. "Move," he said absently to one man who happened to be between the bed and us. The man scattered to the side; the Usurper looked Jamila up and down—and did not recognize her from her afternoon in his tent, a possibility that occurred to us both as soon as he began to examine her. Then he turned his gaze to me. "I have been told you are here," he said, to me. "I did not summon such a creature. Explain yourself."

Jamila translated this nervously, and I responded at once. "I am the Madman of Genoa, of course." I imperiously gestured her to translate, and as she said the word *Genoa*, I bowed elaborately and sank to my knees at the emperor's feet.

He snapped at me angrily, and I leapt up. "Nobody sits in the emperor's presence, not even on their knees," Jamila warned. "At least I think that's what you just did wrong. Keep talking, *fast*."

I began to stroll around the bedchamber, smiling cockily at everyone whose eyes I met, trying to think. "I am a seer, and I'm called the Madman of Genoa, and my services are sought around the world." I signaled to Jamila, and she translated. "Even the pope—no, sorry, say the Archbishop of Corfu—church and crown alike, everywhere," I said. "They come to me for assistance when they are having a hard time hearing the Word of God. I speak to them in his name."

This was translated, haltingly: Jamila probably tried to amend my declaration to make it slightly more plausible. The disbelieving monarch commented slightingly on my appearance.

"It is to appear as Christ did on the fortieth day of his temptation. He'll ask why nobody has heard of me; it's because I am a sort of secret weapon nobody wants to admit to having." I kept striding grandly back and forth across the marble floor, trying to hide my nervousness.

"We're about to die, you know that, don't you?" Jamila asked. "You have one chance to convince him you're a sorcerer, and you're failing."

I snapped my fingers, genuinely grateful for the reminder. "Yes, of course! Tell him I know the name and hometown of the knight they captured today—Otto of Frankfurt, he's from the German Empire—" I said the name directly to His Majesty, then turned away again to continue with my ramble.

But saying the name had an effect. His Majesty had just had paraded before him the Greeks' one captive of war; His Majesty had questioned the captive and knew a little about him. His Majesty grunted now, intrigued, and ordered me, through Jamila, to say more. "He is from a noble family of Frankfurt. Second son to his father, first to his mother, and through a convoluted pedigree, heir to some sizable estates through his mother's brother. He is a sergeant, and very good with horses. He was a member of the Seventh Division under Boniface of Montferrat, who is his brother Gregor's father-in-law, but he was transferred to the vanguard under Count Baldwin. He has a whore named Liliana. She has a fetching little mole on her left shoulder. He lets other men mount her, but there is one position she reserves only for him. I will demonstrate it if His Majesty would kindly bend over and lean against the bed."

This was translated (except perhaps the last bit). The emperor was astounded. I glanced at the reedy palace steward and risked a wink.

"Tell him," I directed Jamila, with flourishing gesticulations, "God gave me this information to impress upon him that he should listen to me, and believe what I tell him." This was translated, and I was given permission to continue. "Tell him God is *very* angry for his blinding his brother Isaac, and he will suffer for it if he doesn't follow my advice."

"No, that is getting far too dangerous," Jamila objected quietly, but when I dramatically glared at her and made a haughty gesture of impatience, she passed it on.

The emperor blanched, and everyone in the room went very still. A famous nerve was being struck.

"Are you saying you can save me from the curse I brought on my own head?" His Imperial Majesty demanded.

"Yes" was my answer. "But you must listen to me very carefully."

The pounding began on the door again, frantic now. Voices begged His Majesty to get on his horse and lead the troops out to confront the invading army, to draw off the Venetians before they could press their advantage from the fire. Reed Man and Rock Man grimaced to themselves; Jamila, although she knew nothing of battle strategy, was able to piece together the basics of the argument and hurriedly passed them on to me as His Imperial Majesty shouted at his lords outside to shut up and leave him alone—he had something far more dire to deal with now, something touching his immortal soul.

Then he gestured for me to speak again, quickly. I had no idea what to say. Before I'd left Venice, my impromptu exploits had usually been mere entertainments; I was still new, and inept, at having to use pranks as strategy.

"Milord," I said, trying to sound confident. "You are blessed with great wisdom, for God had told me to counsel you to do as you are planning anyhow, to take your men out through a northern gate, as many as you can muster. This will draw the Venetians from the harbor to land, to assist their comrades the Franks. More important, it will keep the fighting outside the walls, where the citizenry will not be so affected by it."

"Some of my own men have already told me to do this," His Majesty retorted impatiently. "I don't trust them. Some of them helped me against Isaac, so I already know they are capable of treachery. They were the ones who told me to put the Varangians on Blachernae this morning, instead of on the harbor, and look at the disaster that has caused: the Venetians have taken the harbor. So I will not follow that advice just because it came from *them*." He practically spat out the last word, in the direction of the door, where the suspect advisers were still shouting out frantically from the other side.

"But I am giving you the same advice from God himself," I said reasonably. "However, as a matter of important detail, God told me to add this: you must not actually *attack* the Franks, because you are not safe *from your own men*." With a dramatic flourish, I gestured Jamila to translate this much. The emperor's eyes widened, and he went pale. The man with the rock-riddled tunic (who had his own plan to be the next emperor) was almost as alarmed.

"What?" the emperor demanded.

I went on, "One of the men outside your door is indeed in league with the Frankish army." Rock Man relaxed a little, seeing I was going to ruin not *him* but one of his competitors. "God has not told me who it is yet, but here is the proof." As I grew more confident that His Majesty was swallowing this, my stride became cockier, my gestures more dramatic and clipped. "The leader of the attack is a Flemish count named Baldwin." I took a few steps, paused, turned, and made a summoning gesture toward a window. "He is the key. You must watch him—no, not him, his *flag bearer*." I said the words as if they were an evil incantation. This verbal flourish was lost in Jamila's calm but monotone translation into Greek, which I thought was a shame. Now my hand clasped into a lateral fist, as if I were holding a pole upright. Very slowly, I swiveled it in a tiny circle. "When you are facing them directly, watch this man. If he moves his flag a little, like *this*"—and I gestured broadly with my free hand—"that is his signaling the traitor near you to attack you there on your horse, right in front of your own army, and take your crown for himself." I paused for Jamila to translate.

The emperor stared at me in absolute astonishment. "Tell me what this has to do with Isaac," he begged, not looking nearly as imperial as he had moments earlier.

Isaac. Damn Isaac. Isaac was just supposed to be a ploy to get His Majesty's attention. "God has allowed this threat to come into your court as punishment for your blinding Isaac," I said. "But God in his infinite mercy is willing to test your obedience to him, and if you are obedient, you will be saved." This was translated. "If you see this sign, of the flag, then you *must not attack* but must instead come back into the palace, and *then*—having seen the proof that I am speaking on God's behalf to you—*then* you must do as I say at that time." That would buy me a few hours. "God does not ask you to trust me entirely yet. First, you will be given proof. On the battlefield. Go now, Your Majesty!" I concluded, gesturing toward the door when the pounding began again. "My interpreter and I will be here when you return. We exist only to serve you." I sensed Jamila suppress a groan before she translated that.

Alexios the Usurper looked at me one final time, troubled, and then signaled to the many officers dotting the room like chess pieces; immediately they all scrambled toward the door, dutifully cheering the approaching battle. As they rustled by us in silk and jewels, His Majesty summoned one man to his side and growled an order to him with a gesture toward me. All the blood drained from Jamila's face.

"What?" I asked, as the officer strode toward us with a nasty smile on his face.

"He said, this Madman of Genoa is a sorcerer," Jamila whispered. "He said . . . he said, find out everything he has to tell us, and then hang him."

39

Continuation

It had been a long day, and it was far from over. Squires and cooks
had brought food around to all the waiting battalions, and the three
vanguard divisions had fallen back to regroup. I was growing increasingly restless under Milord Boniface's leadership—the vanguard had
been hard at it all day, and the other four divisions had done nothing.
Around this time, I sent young Richard to the tent to check on the
Briton and the Jewess, but he reported them missing. With bitterness
but understanding, I decided that they had finally fled. I was hovering
between boredom and agitation, as were thousands of my fellow soldiers, when there was a roar down on the field and a procession began
that we will all remember for the rest of our lives.

Beyond a narrow river that ran straight under the wall, a gate
opened, and imperial troops began to pour fast out of it. The emperor
himself was among the vanguard. Because the gate was on the far side
of the river, we could not easily attack the troops as they emerged.
Also, the Greeks had their backs to the sun, while our men, as soon as
they pivoted to watch the flow of troops, were staring almost directly
into it. So there was nothing to do but move into a battle-ready formation, then watch as the entire Byzantine army ran and trotted out the
gate onto the field. Troops marched out. More troops marched out.

More troops marched out.

More troops marched out.

More troops marched out.

It was as if the Queen of Cities was populated entirely by soldiers, and all of them were following their emperor out the gate. The opposing army was soon twice the size of the entire crusading army, vanguard and rear guard together—then three times, four times, five times our size . . . six times our size . . . seven times . . . The sun was slanting sharply now, and soldiers were still riding and running out of the gate. Even when the egress finally died to a trickle and a defensive guard moved before the gate, there was no way to know how many tens of thousands more were waiting within the city, to come to their aid. The Usurper had the sun and the geography of the field both to his advantage—and the numbers.

Halfway through this monstrous procession, Milord Boniface had grown a little pale and signaled all of the divisions to join the vanguard in a broad, shallow formation, so that we created the longest possible front. As Greeks continued to march out, Milord Boniface whispered something to Milord Geoffrey the marshal, who nodded and spurred his horse back toward the palisade. By the time the entire Byzantine force was lodged on the plain, there was a lot of ungodly noise coming from behind the palisade walls.

I turned in confusion to look and saw the noncombatant males of the camp— the stable boys and water boys and grooms and cooks and clerks— all rigged out in a grotesque equivalent of armor: with cooking pots on their heads for helmets and quilts and blankets wrapped around them for protection, they were armed with kitchen knives; long, pointed sticks of wood; and handfuls of small, pointy rocks. In their own grotesque, pathetic way, they were terrifying, and terrified.

Boniface chuckled with nervous approval—this had been his idea—and gestured them to march together to join the far edge of the front. They perambulated, but I cannot say they marched, exactly. In nothing approaching any sort of formation, about a thousand boys and old men—and more than a few women—were turning out to fill the ranks. They were one of the most unusual battalions in the history of Christian armies. Unfortunately, they hardly made a dent in the size

difference between the two forces. By St. John, the Greeks outnumbered us ten or a dozen to one, at least.

The Greeks moved toward the river slowly. At Baldwin's order to
trot, his battalion vanguard moved slightly ahead of the rest to meet the
Greeks, bowmen in the front, then foot soldiers and a corps of knights
who'd lost their horses—then the cavalry, sergeants first. His forces
were nearing exhaustion, but they were grander to look at than the
rows and rows of Greeks. Unfortunately, looking grand would count
for nothing now, facing the endless bulk of Greeks across the valley. It
did not matter if the Greeks were lesser soldiers; there were so many of
them compared with us, there was no doubt what the outcome of the
battle would be. The river still lay between us. Either side would have
to ford it to reach the other, but elevation favored the Usurper, who
would be crossing from higher ground to lower. We waited, terrified,
knowing we were about to be crushed, wondering when he would signal an attack. I shifted in the saddle and quietly urged Summa to turn
in a circle, just to keep his muscles warm. We were massively outnumbered. I was not afraid to die, but I prayed to the Lord to be forgiven
for dying doing something I could not be proud of, dying having failed
to see my vows fulfilled. Dying at the hands of Christians whom my
own army was attacking while we were supposed to be on Christian
pilgrimage.

Arrows were on bows, spurs ready to press against horses' flanks,
hands on axes and swords and knives. Baldwin's standard-bearer irritated me by nervously fidgeting with the flag staff, so that it spiraled in
distracting circles. It was so pronounced I thought at first it might be a
signal of some sort, but nothing happened.

For a long time the two armies stared at each other, every man in
both waiting for the emperor to call the attack. Ten thousand pilgrims
whispered prayers, knowing we were about to be obliterated.

Nothing happened.

Baldwin's standard-bearer fidgeted. I almost shouted with irritation
at the man, my nerves were so tensed for an attack.

The emperor wheeled around abruptly and galloped back into the
city gates. His army, after a confused, stunned moment, slowly began
to follow him.

The pilgrims were left, unmolested and unhurt—and astonished to
find ourselves so—on the giant plain outside the city.

40

No prisoner can tell his tale accurately without complaints.

—RICHARD COEUR DE LION,
"Song from Prison"

THEY DIDN'T HANG ME for a sorcerer, of course.
His Majesty had left us to somebody who in turn left us
to the care of—thank heavens—the reedy palace steward.
He'd removed us to an antechamber, where we'd been interrogated
by the man wearing stones, whose name was Theodore Laskaris. Laskaris was extremely distracted by what was happening down on the
field. Finally, we'd been taken to yet another part of the castle, high
up, with windows that looked out over the battlefield. It was a large
room whose ceiling appeared to be solid gold. The walls had mosaics
depicting frolicking hunters, children playing hide-and-seek, Diony-
sus having his way with a virgin—the usual. This room, which had
the best view onto the plain, was crowded with well-dressed nobility,
male and female, all ages, murmuring anxiously together and peering in turns out the windows. Their clothing, although not as re-
splendent as His Majesty's, still left me agog: even the pages had gold
thread sewn in designs into their cuffs. We spent at least an hour in

here, watching and trying to eavesdrop on various little factions, as the emperor's army formed outside the walls.

Some of the factions were amusing. One group of women, burdened with a preponderance of turquoise and lapis lazuli, carried on a commentary on who might next be emperor, should Alexios (Usurper) fall in battle. For as long as it might take to pluck a hen, their worthies debated the Imperial Question from a unique perspective: what man among the oligarchy showed the greatest taste (i.e., wisdom) regarding gemstones? Jamila managed to translate all of this without a smile, but I could see a sardonic glint in her eyes. Those who valued topaz over peridot were clearly wise. Any man who would adorn himself with lapis lazuli, honey-toned zircon, olivine, emerald, amethyst, or turquoise (especially the green sort) clearly could be trusted. A lover of balas rubies likewise inspired trust. But there were those who favored the unfashionable opal— or worse yet, *alexandrite*. These men should never be allowed near the throne of Byzantium. Those who favored garnet were only fit for secretarial positions, although the purplish almandine would not be out of place on the robes of an imperial adviser. There was dissension within the group regarding the hard, pale diamond— a relative newcomer to the local jewelry world, and most of the women found no appeal in something nearly or completely colorless. They considered it a passing fad with little staying power. One of them was scratched across the face by a dissenting lady in the group.

"I'm so terribly sad you aren't more like these worthies," I whispered to Jamila.

When His Imperial Majesty in the field below suddenly, inexplicably retreated back toward the gate with an air of panic, a cry filled the room. Jamila clutched my hand to keep from screaming in amazement; even *I* was astounded that my scheme had worked. At once, the men and some of the women behind us began to form into new, urgent little clusters, muttering together about what to do next.

Most scuttled out of the room together, many disagreeing with one another.

There were those left here who knew French, and no doubt Italian, so we had to be very careful about what we said. We were, however, able to establish that I thought Jamila was observant (the flag bearer's fidgeting having been her find), nimble-witted, and courageous, while Jamila thought I was devilishly, improbably brilliant—but still a bumbling idiot for not knowing how to get us out of here. "And we have no idea where Otto is," she reminded me under her breath, as we stared out onto the plain, watching the Byzantine forces trot bemusedly back in through the city walls.

"Sorry, I got distracted," I retorted, with a triumphant gesture toward the reprieved Franks.

IT WAS TURNING dusk now, and celebratory campfires were already lit, some wine drunk, some women eyed. There was no feasting, for the stores were still depleted and nobody knew what to expect on the morrow. Gregor later told me that everybody in the army camp was relieved but shocked, and overwrought from the tension and exhaustion of the day. Had the Usurper withdrawn merely to amass a larger army? There must have been half a million people within the city walls; even a quarter of them in arms would double the size of what they'd faced today. Not one soul in that camp closed his eyes all night.

I'D LOVE TO TAKE credit for the Usurper's actual abdication, but of course there were much greater forces at work. Late that night, counseled by the Madman of Genoa and a score of men he'd known for years but still didn't trust, His Imperial Majesty Alexios III took as much money as he could carry from the royal treasury and fled the city with his favorite daughter and his most trusted ministers, looking fearfully over his shoulder. He abandoned the rest of his family, including his famously adulterous wife, Euphrosyne, and their daughter, Eudocea, already showing signs of her mother's sexual mores. I reassured His Majesty that he would merely be ruling in absentia for a while, until things had calmed down and the crusaders had departed for Jerusalem, which they were bound and determined to do as soon as possible. For this final prediction, he rescinded the order to have me hanged, which I thought was very generous of him.

To say the emperor left behind unfinished business would be something of an understatement. And besides the future of the city, and the throne, nobody was quite sure what to do about the bizarre Genoese soothsayer and his interpreter. While they knew I was a fake, many of them were grateful for my contribution and suspected they might want my services again before the whole debacle was over.

For it was a debacle. Not that their emperor had fled in response to a pretender's armed forces—that happened not infrequently. In fact, there was established protocol for such cases: if the emperor fled, the pretender rose to power with little further resistance from the city or its nobles. But this was different, we realized, as we were shuffled among various rooms, always just on the outside of the official hubbub, without being given anything to eat or drink or even leave to sit. Nobody wanted to hand over power to a puppet of the Franks. The empress Euphrosyne claimed that the emperor, although fled, was still in power, and appointed their son-in-law—our well-dressed friend Laskaris—to take the throne as deputy. This was contested by most of the nobility in all of the various rooms, for various reasons that even Jamila could not grasp. Laskaris was then suddenly imprisoned, although Jamila could never figure out by whom, or why.

"This is a hell of a way to run an empire," I said.

There were offers and counter offers being bandied about, and finally a grudging consensus was reached, in a manner neither of us could even track: to *placate* the hated Latins without actually *capitu-*

lating to them, Prince Alexios's direct line would be restored to the throne. But not in the form of Prince Alexios himself. Instead, they would re-crown his father: blind Isaac, now in prison in the depths of Blachernae.

Here reentered into the picture our reed man. He was not, it turned out, the steward of the palace. He was a eunuch, named Constantine Philoxenites—a constellation of syllables I so enjoyed I made a little chant of them. He, we learned, was in charge of the royal treasury. More than that—or more likely, *because* of that—he had the extraordinary distinction of being the only person alive who could, in the absence of an emperor, successfully tell the Varangian Guard what to do. If he had told them that *he* was to be the new emperor, they would have believed him, and with the guard behind him, he suddenly would have been. But—if you'll excuse the term— he lacked the balls for such ambition. Rather he was given the task of convincing the Varangian Guard to return their sworn loyalty to the former emperor Isaac, although by Byzantine custom, blindness disqualified a person from such authority.

"Hasn't much slowed the Doge of Venice, blindness," I mused, when Jamila explained this to me. "Perhaps it will work out well for Emperor Isaac too."

We were in a new antechamber, and somebody had thought to give us nuts and fruit. A new chaperone was hovering about us, but his attention, like everyone's, was distracted, waiting for His Imperial Majesty Isaac Angelos to be brought up from the lower depths of the enormous palace compound. This ascension would be marked by rejoicing, as if he were exactly the fellow they'd wanted for the job all along and his being deposed for the past eight years was just an unfortunate clerical error.

Yet another domestic officer appeared from yet another room, whispered to our chaperone, and left. Our chaperone turned to us and growled something to Jamila. She looked grim. In fact, she looked so thoroughly defeated she was almost smug about it.

"And now, we are being arrested," she informed me, as if she'd been expecting this all along (which, of course, she had been). "I don't know by whom. Until they can determine whose side we're on and if we've done anything treasonous. I am now convinced we will not come out of this alive."

"No! The way things work around this place, we're safer in a prison cell than anywhere else, anyhow," I said, in an awkward attempt to comfort her.

Our guard spent our trek toward the prison level trying to coax me to predict his future; he thought I really was a fortune-teller. He also explained that there had been a spate of arrests this past month, whenever the paranoid Usurper suspected somebody of colluding with the Franks, and so there was a bit of crowding in the cells holding political prisoners, which we were deemed to be.

"Prison," in the most magnificent palace in Christendom, was not what I'd expected. These rooms were of plain brickwork, not marble, and lacked the opulent gold and silver designs and jeweled and stained-wood inlays of the rooms above. There were no billowing purple curtains delineating rooms, no tapestries, no mosaics of nymphs frolicking around, no music. But the rooms had lamps, and beds within, with real blankets, and even bolsters to rest imprisoned heads upon. I repeated to myself that we were probably safer on the inward side of these doors anyhow.

At one door, we were pushed in and left; we heard the lock clang behind us.

We turned to look at the cell. There were two cots, each with a man lying on it faceup. One of them, we knew well enough.

"Imagine meeting you here," I said to Otto.

If Jesus himself had walked through the doors with the keys to the kingdom of Heaven, Otto could not have been more astonished. He jerked himself toward a sitting position, then groaned and sank back down onto the cot, grabbing his head, muttering something in German. His armor had been stripped, and he wore a drab, grey tunic.

His cell mate was dressed in a shabby version of the gowns worn by the rest of the male population of the castle; there was even the odd pearl left clinging to it. He was a barrel-chested man some years my senior, with dramatic eyebrows and an equally dramatic mop of dark red hair. His beard was thick, but he wore no mustache. His face was fiercely intelligent; as we entered, he'd been holding forth to Otto in French.

"Is that really you?" Otto asked, eyes closed against the pain.

"No, we're figments of your fevered imagination," I said.

"How did you get in here?"

"Oh, you know how it is. We got bored with the battle and decided to take a stroll, passing by here, thought we'd say hello."

"Are you here to release me? What's happened?"

The Greek gave us an exaggerated wave, as if we were a quarter mile distant. "*Bonjour!*" he uttered in a loud, sarcastic whisper, letting us know how very rude we were being for not introducing ourselves. This behavior was almost more eccentric, but far more sympathetic, than anything we had experienced so far within Blachernae. Jamila smiled apologetically and began speaking to him; they exchanged a few words in Greek.

"This gentleman is also named Alexios," she said to me.

"He told me his name was Eyebrow," Otto protested.

"*Mourtzouphlos,*" corrected Eyebrow. With a winning blend of self-deprecation and grandiosity, he gestured broadly at the thatch above his eyes, waggled it up and down, and laughed. The laugh was warm and rumbling.

Jamila smiled. "*Mourtzouphlos* means 'bushy-browed.' He was imprisoned under Alexios III—the Usurper."

"Now the ex-Usurper," I clarified in Italian, to Otto. Otto cheered, then collapsed with a brief sob of relief. Mourtzouphlos wanted to know the cause, so Jamila quickly brought him up to date in Greek, as I did the same for Otto.

Mourtzouphlos looked pleased by news of the Usurper's flight but then seemed to grow nauseated. "So again, the Venetians and the Germans are allies?"

"It's not like the last time the pilgrims came, and there are very few Germans this time," Jamila said reassuringly. She switched to Greek for what became a lengthy dialogue. Occasionally, seeing the stupid expression on my face, she would translate enough that I had a vague sense of the matter. Byzantine history was mind-numbingly complicated, but I managed to grasp that, about a decade ago, a crusade had been led here overland by the German emperor Frederick Barbarossa (whose name Otto cheered at almost the way a baby bird chirps when it sees its mother). A century earlier, the very first time a "pilgrim army" had come through, the Greeks had merely thought the Latins madmen. In 1146, they came through again in two waves (German, French) and behaved so abominably that the Greeks now thought them beasts. But the third time, most recently, was the worst: Barbarossa had approached the city as if he would conquer it—a scenario Emperor Isaac had contained by taking Barbarossa's envoys hostage ("That was *my* idea," Eyebrow said. "But Isaac never gives me credit for it!"). The Greeks had ferried Barbarossa's army over the Bosporus to Anatolia, where Barbarossa had been considerate enough to drown, thus ceasing to be a significant threat.

"But the Byzantines and the Germans were also often allies," Jamila reminded Mourtzouphlos, for Otto's sake. "And now your princess is married to the German king."

"Oh, yes, I know," Eyebrow said cheerfully. "Hope springs eternal! To honor the German-Byzantine overtures of friendship, I have clasped hands with my German brother here, and we have sworn a lifelong fraternity. Eh, Otto?" He held out his arms toward Otto, beaming.

Otto grinned feebly despite his pain. Jamila moved to his bedside and began to gently palpate his head and neck, checking to make sure nothing was broken. "After they paraded me around in front of the Usurper, they brought me down here," Otto said, "and Eyebrow was eating his dinner—he shared it with me. Oh, that hurts," he said when Jamila pressed one spot on the side of his head. "They brought supper only for him just now, and he shared that too. And the water. He even offered to share his whore when she came in for her regular visit!" He groaned sadly. "But I was in too much pain to move. They had some old Jewish physician come in to attend me, gave me something to drink, made me feel much better. I thought of you, Jamila. Does Liliana know I'm alive? Does she even know that I was captured?"

He was rambling, relieved to see us; catching himself, he let it drift to silence.

"He's all right, but he'll be sore awhile," Jamila told me as she finished her examination. "He can walk, but probably not run right now without falling over."

"Walk where?" Otto asked eagerly.

"We're assuming they'll release you now," I said. "But we don't actually know."

"You should try to spring Eyebrow too," Otto urged. "He was in Isaac's court, in fact, they've spent most of the past five years together. You know that palace we moved into across the Bosporus when we first got here? Well that's where Isaac and his family and his men were held until Prince Alexios escaped, and then they were all brought over here to keep an eye on."

To get Jamila's attention, Mourtzouphlos reached off his bed and tugged playfully at her veil—for a moment I was annoyed, especially when Jamila smiled at him, as if charmed by the flirtation. He began another lengthy speech; my feeble Greek was enough to grasp that he was listing—in an incredulous tone—the things Prince Alexios had promised to deliver in exchange for the crusading army's assistance with this coup. Whatever the question was, Jamila gave an affirmative answer.

Mourtzouphlos laughed with tired sarcasm. "Little Prince Alexios!" He sighed, and went on in French. "Eh, that boy always was a fool, and the entire empire of Byzantium can never deliver what he has promised you. You have all just labored to put him on the throne, and you will never get your reward for it. Not one penny." He seemed perversely amused by this, in exactly the way I might have been if I were in his place.

"You don't know what you're talking about," Otto said dismissively. "You're a nice fellow, but you're not quite right in the head."

"Fine words from a man of good breeding who by his own admission can barely read or write!" Mourtzouphlos laughed.

"That's *normal*," Otto said. To Jamila and I, he elucidated confidingly, "He's a little mad. He claims his whore is the Usurper's daughter."

"She's not my whore!" Mourtzouphlos corrected, grinning. "I am her gigolo." He grinned and gestured to his eyebrows. "Why do you think these are so bushy? I spend so much time with my face in Her Highness's thighs, it has pushed my mustache all the way up here!" And then to Jamila, with a grin at once avuncular and naughty, "I hope the pretty lady will excuse my rudeness? I do adore my little Eudocea, but her father—" He made a face. "What a pathetic rule that man has had! Isaac was a numskull, but at least he cut a good figure on the battlefield. His brother Alexios, your usurper—he was never more than air surrounded by skin! Everyone else—his wife, his wife's brother-in-law, his wife's brother-in-law's hunting bitch—told him what to do. Michael Stryphonis—that very brother-in-law— when he was made ruler of the imperial fleet, and he needed a little money, what did he do? He sold the ships and kept the money for his own coffers! And he did this just last year, when surely he must have heard rumors that your fleet would be attacking us!" He laughed with pained amusement. "I love Byzantium with all my soul, but sometimes I think Byzantium no longer loves herself, that she suffers these idiots to oversee her."

Over hours in that cell, Mourtzouphlos and I took to each other. We had a similar irreverent humor, a willingness to say whatever we were thinking. He was intelligent and witty; I was touched by how deeply he really loved his city and its people—the actual *people*, the merchants and traders and artisans and bakers and carpenters and butchers. He had dozens of stories featuring such individuals; before he'd been imprisoned by the ex-Usurper, his life, although aristocratic, had kept him in daily touch with real citizens. He was one of the only noblemen I've ever met who spoke as if he understood that high rank brought with it an obligation to care for those less powerful. Compared with the feather-headed twits Jamila and I been subjected to upstairs, he was refreshing. He liked me too; when he heard how Jamila and I had come to be in this place, he crowed with delight; he applauded when Jamila described her rescue from Barzizza.

"You are a good man to know!" he announced with thunderous glee. "And dashing, although you are a pip-squeak. I wish that you will stay in Stanpoli and get yourself some bushy eyebrows too! If the lady will excuse the rudeness," he said again, with such disarming warmth that even an abbess would have excused the rudeness.

By the time anyone remembered about us, Byzantium had a new emperor, neither Usurper nor Pretender.

41

THE PILGRIMS WERE TRUMPED by the very system they'd claimed they were trying to uphold. In the dark of the morning, the blind Isaac and his beautiful young wife, Margaret, were placed upon the throne in full imperial regalia—including (my favorite detail) purple shoes. The entire palace, which had been wide awake all night, prepared to swear their loyalty to Isaac, although only hours earlier they had all been negotiating frantically on behalf of the man who'd robbed Isaac of his eyes and throne.

"But then they seem rather used to this usurpation business here," I commented, when the news of the accomplished recrowning reached our cell. Yes, Mourtzouphlos explained with pained amusement, this was the way of Stanpoli (as the natives affectionately called Constantinople). A man, not a nation, had been bested. The city itself might be attacked—even damaged—but never conquered. Because it was so enormous and populous, there was no sensible *cause* to conquer it but to make oneself its new emperor, and such matters were decided by palace intrigue or on the field, beyond the city wall. ("And always by madmen," he opined. "To want to be *basileus* of this place, what kind of madness does that take? When you can have all of the benefits of the good life with none of the responsibilities, why wear the burden of a crown? Without such a burden on your brow, it is easier to throw back you head with drink or food or dance or a mouthful of a woman's breast.") The citizens themselves, from those in direst poverty to the wealthiest aristocrats, continued their lives with perhaps a few artful rearrangements to please whoever was in power. The people, seeing their lord unthroned, would simply accept whoever came next. Grumble, perhaps, but never rise up as a population to prevent it—the one exception being the legendary Andronikos Comnenus, who rose and fell by common acclamation. But generally, the people were too busy with their own affairs. It was the way of Stanpoli. It was the privilege of a mighty, prosperous people. "We have been the mightiest power in Christendom for hundreds of years despite the frequent changes of power, so clearly we are doing something right, eh?" Mourtzouphlos concluded cheerfully, halfmocking but wholehearted.

I shook my head. "That is so alien to my way of life I can't even think of anything witty to say about it."

"That's all right," he said with gruff affection. "I'm wittier than you are anyhow. You be clever, I'll be witty, we will make quite a splash out in the world! Oh, the eyebrows we will have! If you will excuse my rudeness, lovely lady . . ."

WORD CAME in the night to Prince Alexios's tent that his father, Isaac, had been resurrected. Word came, specifically, in the form of two people. One was a Byzantine messenger who carried a lamp and knew the local landscape well. The other was Otto of Frankfurt—released by the newly recrowned Isaac as proof to the crusading army that he approached them in friendship. The conflict between the throne of Constantinople and the crusaders was over. The sword would be replaced by the olive branch.

"There's just one little problem with that," I pointed out. "*Isaac* never made a deal with the crusaders. Only *Alexios* did. Alexios has to be on the throne to be able to fulfill his part of the treaty. And now Isaac's on the throne, and Isaac really *is* the rightful ruler, so there is no valid reason to replace him with Alexios."

"Being blind," Jamila reminded me. "And frankly rather feeble-minded."

"They could make them coemperors," I suggested playfully. "It's no more illogical than anything else we've seen."

"Believe it or not, that's a common practice here, when the ruler is growing old or weak," Jamila said. "The way your mind works, they should really hire you to help them run the place."

It was late morning, and we were finally expelled from the palace, because nobody knew what else to do with us. Of course, nobody really believed I had any supernatural power at all—except for Emperor Isaac, who having heard the story, asked to meet me, was immediately entranced by my mystical abilities, and invited me to come back any time and tell the imperial fortune, for which I would be handsomely rewarded.

As a final word of wisdom, I'd advised him to release his loyal friend Alexios Doukas, alias Mourtzouphlos, and see he was reinstated to court. This probably would have happened anyhow, but Isaac seemed very fond of me for thinking of it.

And then, finally, we were at liberty.

We were dismissed without ceremony through the ceremonial front gates; in case somebody somewhere was watching us, we walked south along the harbor wall, as if toward the Latin Quarter, and within a hundred paces we were in the charred remnants of the burned segment of the city.

It was massive, and the destruction absolute: acres and acres, up and down three of the largest hills and spreading toward a flatter section farther inland. This had not been a densely populated stretch, since it was mostly aristocratic palaces, but there had been a lot of material available to burn. There is a particular horrific smell that lingers after bodies have been burned alive, a smell one's own body naturally responds to violently, with an impulse to gag, sob, and flee all at once. That had overtaken me at Pera. Here there was none of that; the smells were mostly woodsmoke and the occasional acrid odor of complicated dyes, or alloys, succumbing to the flame. The people who had lived here were well-off, with servants and their families now left homeless too. Hundreds of them were rummaging through the smoking remains, soot-streaked, many sobbing, others shouting with rage, fighting with one another, cursing the Franks, cursing the Usurper. There was no reason they'd associate Jamila with the army outside—but my hair and beard were too short to be convincingly Greek. And we were strangers; these people likely all knew one another; we would stand out. We paused, uncomfortable. I took both of Jamila's hands in one of mine.

This was it.

"Go on without me," I said. "It's absurd to drag you back to the camp. You could disappear into the city and choose whatever identity you like."

"You have a quick ear; you'd be speaking Greek within a season too," she said and pulled her hand away, blushing but not looking at me.

For a moment I was dizzy with fantasies of raising cute Greek children with her in our peaceful, cute Greek home. Mourtzouphlos could be their godfather, and teach them dirty jokes; I could learn the local musical styles, and play at the court; we would be happy, we'd worry about nobody's well-being but our own . . .

No.

I gestured to the hovering survivors and mourners. "There'll be more of this, wherever the army goes next."

"And you think you can stop it by staying with the army?" She still wasn't looking at me. "Instead of coming with me?"

"*I* can't stop it. Gregor can maybe, but only if I'm goading him." *So let's go back to the army camp together,* I wanted to say, but of course I couldn't suggest something so stupid. "This city isn't home to me, but it was home to you once," I insisted dutifully.

"Not the city." She gestured weakly in the direction of the harbor. "Pera. I hardly knew the city itself, seldom came over here. Pera and its people were my home, and they're gone. I have no home now but Gregor's tent, and no people but the lot of you. Even if Boniface discovers I'm not dead, I think he'll finally give up his idiotic masquerade, now that he's gotten what he wants; he won't bother about me anymore."

I wanted this so badly I didn't trust myself to think straight; surely it was a bad idea, and I tried halfheartedly to remember why. "It's dangerous to both you and Gregor for him to harbor a Jewess," I said dutifully.

"If Gregor wishes me to leave, I'll leave," she said. "But first we'll have to ask him." She reached out tentatively and took my hand. "Come along, Galahad."

"*Must* I be Galahad?" I asked. "Galahad never has any *fun.*" She smiled. Her hands were warm. They squeezed mine. We both shivered a little.

We hurried back north, to the gate we'd entered near Blachernae the previous afternoon. Getting out was simple; the camp was in
sight, and easy distance, up the mild incline toward the monastery.

But the camp was so frenzied with activity, it took a while for us
to even find Gregor's tent. We were surprised to discover it nearly
empty, and completely packed up, even the travel altar put away
in its special chest. I was astonished to learn from the one person
present, the older Richard, that my fanciful solution to the imperial dilemma was actually a fact: Alexios would be crowned, and he
would rule beside his father. In fact, Alexios, with an honor guard of
Frankish soldiers, had already moved into the castle to be reunited
with his father and stepmother. Isaac had sworn to honor all the
outrageous terms of the treaty his son had made with the crusaders,
the treaty Eyebrow had laughed at in the prison cell. There really
would be two hundred thousand marks in silver, and other goodies including ten thousand soldiers to aid the campaign, and five
hundred knights guarding Jerusalem in perpetuity. The army was
ecstatic.

"The master is ready to sail for Jerusalem as soon as we're paid,"
Richard continued happily. "He's volunteered us to help pack Boniface's tents, and I'm heading there myself now. And Milord Otto's
using his moment of glory to petition for Liliana's release from Boniface. And then we'll celebrate all day and night. We've earned it!"
He departed, whistling to himself.

This left Jamila and me alone in the tent in the afternoon heat.
Jamila gave me a knowing smile and picked up a blanket from a
chest. She tossed it to the back of the tent. The dividing curtains
were drawn back; with the same smile, her eyes on me, she tugged at
one tie so that it tumbled down across half the width; she sauntered
to the other side and pulled that one too, so that the tent was now
two spaces, the back more private, darker, containing the blanket.
She slipped into it.

I peered into the back half; light flickered in from a rip near the ceiling. I felt my pulse in my throat, just behind my Adam's apple. Jamila was lying on the blanket.

"Join me," she said.

I stepped in. I knelt down and placed a hand on her head, like a parental benediction. I stared into the ceiling of the tent. Then I realized I was scared to look back down from the ceiling, scared to meet her eyes. So I kept staring at the ceiling. Despite the bustle outside, the silence in here was so loud I could almost tell what key it was in.

"This is the part," Jamila said. "At last. You know that." She was looking at me while I looked at the ceiling. I could feel it.

"What part?" I asked, still not looking down.

"The part where you take me in your arms and have your way with me."

"Oh," I said.

"We've both earned it, we both want it, and we finally have an opportunity."

I closed my eyes, took another breath, finally lowered my head to face her, and opened my eyes. "I'm scared of doing anything," I said.

"Why?"

"There's something locked," I said, putting my fist on my heart. "You would unlock it. I need it to stay locked."

"Why?"

I shook my head, looking away from her.

She regarded me. "You know, I loved my husband very much, but still I—"

"It's not that simple," I snapped. "I have blood on my hands."

"You just prevented a battle that might have claimed ten thousand lives," she countered.

"With the result that the greatest empire in Christendom gave up its sovereignty to its French-speaking attackers," I said, disgusted. "That's what happened in my own kingdom. I am not permitted redemption, Jamila. Whatever gesture I make to do right, it only reinforces my old sins. It doesn't matter what I do now."

Instead of soothing me or uttering some superior observation, she just shrugged and asked, "If it doesn't matter anyhow, why stop yourself from doing this?"

I fidgeted. I looked at her. And away. And back. And away. And blushed.

"You're blushing," she said quietly, without emotion; an observation. "Does that mean you want to?"

"There is nothing simple about this," I warned. "This isn't like a tumble with Liliana. This *means* something *huge*, but I don't know what."

"Well, there's only one to find out, and that's to *try* it."

"A moment?" I begged, holding up a hand.

She shrugged again, comfortably. "Take all the time you need. I'll be here in all my splendor, with all the component parts you've already fantasized about, my arms, my legs, my breasts—"

"A *moment*," I repeated, glaring. "A long moment. In silence. And then I'll have my way with you."

Her face lit up. "Good!"

There was a pause. I tried to rearrange my soul.

"You are being terribly melodramatic," Jamila chastised, and I jumped.

"Be *quiet*," I snapped. "Now I have to start the moment all *over* again. We'll be here all *afternoon*."

She laughed—that incredibly rare, rich sound of Jamila's laughter. "This is much more memorable than being serenaded, or given jewelry!" she announced approvingly.

The pleasure on her face was so rare, and made her so beautiful, that for a moment it erased the stain on my soul, and I was free to act. I bent over her while she was still laughing, and pressed my lips against hers. Her laughter was contagious and made me chuckle. Then we could not kiss properly for our hilarity, so we rubbed our noses into each other's cheeks and necks and ears, which tickled and only made us each laugh harder. I hadn't laughed so hard since childhood, I think. I rolled on top of her—every inch of me feeling her beneath me shivered. I reached down for the long skirt of her tunic. Eagerly she helped me hitch it up between our pressed bodies, but just as it was nearly high enough, I rolled off her again.

"No," I said. She stopped laughing. My face was pressed into her neck. I pulled away a little so I could look at her. "I want to do this properly. Let me undress you completely, not just pull up your skirt as if you were a whore. I want to touch you everywhere."

In the dim light, her face warmed with pleasure. "But what if we're intruded on?"

"Who is going to intrude on us this beautiful afternoon, while everyone is celebrating?" I scoffed.

"Hello? Milord?" said a voice from the outside flap.

Jamila almost choked on a giggle as I bolted upright, cursing under my breath. "Excellent timing," she whispered.

I recognized the voice, a German sergeant on guard duty for this section of the camp. As I stood up and reluctantly willed my erection to deflate, she whispered, "Shall I undress while you're out?"

"No," I whispered hurriedly, trying to erase that proffered image from my mind. "I'll see to this person's business, and then I'll come back and undress you myself."

"And have your way with me," she said firmly, as if she wasn't certain she'd convinced me of this yet.

"Well, naturally." I pecked her on the forehead and headed through the dividing curtain, announcing, "Gregor's on guard duty, I'm his servant."

"Man for him," the sergeant said crisply. "Won't speak his business but to him."

"Let him come in, then, I'll attend him." As soon as I was out of close proximity, the thought of being that near to her terrified me with joy, and I was actually glad of a brief distraction. As long as it remained brief.

The sergeant stepped aside, and a familiar figure moved into the tent: a somber, fair, long-bearded man about my age.

"I've come for Jamila," said Samuel.

For a moment, I couldn't even think, let alone speak.

"Yes," I said at last. "Of course you have."

Act IV

CONSTANTINOPLE

The Greeks and Franks are now most friendly with each
other in all ways.

—GEOFFREY DE VILLEHARDOUIN,
Chronicle of the Fourth Crusade

42

Feast of St. Arnulf of Metz, 18 July

My brother Otto and I returned to the tent, cheery with celebrating our glorious and bloodless victory, to find it (the tent) in violent disarray, every chest opened and the contents hurled with furious randomness around the space. The Briton's lute and fiddle are destroyed. The Briton himself is almost as bad. He informed us, in a state of agitation, that Jamila has been collected by the surviving Jews of Pera, who are now living God knows where, and he is the one who led them to her. He spoke as if he were responsible for an abduction, not a reunion.

I ordered him to repack everything exactly as it had been, and I could not leave hovering over him until he'd done it. At which point I finally permitted him to succumb to his old churlishness, which in truth seems to have returned to him in full force. He is more upset about this deprivation than is Otto about Liliana.

At night, the imperial father and son, Isaac and Alexios Angelos, respectfully requested the army move back across the harbor, into the shadow of Galata Tower. An army stationed directly beside the palace walls creates the impression of a forced occupation; Their Majesties need to assure their citizens that such is absolutely not the case. As Dandolo of Venice once specified, we are their champions, not their conquerors.

Our leaders are so relieved by victory, they have agreed to this, especially as the request is accompanied by cartloads of food and casks of wine to ease the transition.

However glad I am of nourishment, I chafe at the news that the army is pulling up its stakes only to restake them elsewhere. The army is supposed to embark the ships and sail off for the Holy Land right away; indeed, I have already seen to it that my belongings are packed away for this reason. Otto, now the seasoned veteran eager for the next battle, has urged me to complain to Milord Boniface. Milord Boniface is not available to complain to, as he is passing the night in Blachernae, in celebratory conference with Alexios and Isaac. I shall speak to him tomorrow.

Feast of St. Arsenius, 19 July

Milord Boniface returned at dawn to the disassembling camp, where he began conducting army business on a tent platform while his actual tents were packed up and ferried across the harbor to Galata. I approached this platform as a meeting was adjourning: milord marquis, counts, army bishops, and a Greek man, very tall and slender, with no beard—in fact, his skin is as hairless as a woman's, and his voice is high. The leaders of the army looked joyful, embracing one another, cheering the names of Emperor Isaac and soon-to-be Emperor Alexios. The Greek eunuch—as I suppose he must be—looked grim and excused himself to head back toward Blachernae, surrounded by as many fearsome bodyguards as an emperor might have. (These are members of the Varangian Guard. At the risk of vanity, I must say that before Constantinople I'd hardly met any soldiers I considered my physical match, be they mercenary or knight; but every Varangian Guard I've seen could probably knock me down.)

The counts and bishops were dispersing as I approached, but His Eminence Bishop Conrad, seeing me, changed course to greet me warmly. "Gregor, my son," he said, very joyful, "God is rewarding us for our intervention! Alexios and his father have already paid the first half of what was promised!" He pointed beyond Boniface's platform, where sat a line of wagons bearing iron-wrapped wooden chests. One

*of these chests, surrounded by armed soldiers, was open for display,
and truly it contained a marvel, for it was filled to the top with silver
money, gleaming coldly in the morning sun. I was struck speechless. I
have never seen so much money in the whole of my life. His Eminence
expressed delight, but seeing I did not share his humor, he excused
himself.*

*Finally I reached the low dais on which sat my esteemed father-
in-law, and although I was plainly in sight, a servant announced my
presence grandly. Milord Boniface smiled, stood, and stepped around
his camp desk to embrace me. He was radiating joy and relief; indeed,
he could hardly sit still.*

*"My son," he cried, "have you heard the happy news?" And he ges-
tured to the carts. "One hundred thousand silver marks!"*

*I did not want to show that I was awed, but it was difficult to con-
tain my response. "He owes us twice that, milord," I managed to say,
for indeed this is the truth.*

Milord Boniface said: "The other half will come soon."

I asked: "Why does he not present it all at once?"

*"They've almost emptied their treasury to give us this," Milord
Boniface replied. "They do not have the money we require. They will
need to obtain more silver first."*

I asked: "May I ask how they plan to obtain it?"

Milord Boniface answered: "Taxes, I imagine. Why?"

*I said: "A hundred thousand silver marks? From taxes? That is
twice as much money as the kingdom of France contains! That will
destroy the city!"*

*Milord Boniface now looked very sober. He sat back in his chair
and gestured sharply for me to be seated on a stool beside him.
"The treaty does not say that they will pay us money whose source
we approve of. It simply says that they will pay us." He smiled again.
"This is excellent news—for one thing, once we give our share to
Dandolo, we've finally fulfilled our debt to those accursed
Venetians."*

"So the Venetians get all of that?" I demanded, as I pointed to the chests without looking at them, lest I reveal how amazed I was to be in the presence of such riches.

"They will get most of it. But . . . when the second half comes to us, which will be soon, we split that right down the middle! Gregor, this is a good thing. Let you and I not celebrate by immediately reverting to our old patterns of squabbling. Why did you want to see me?" Milord Boniface seemed very earnest to change my mood to match his, and tried now to make an unseemly joke: "Do you wish to try outbidding your brother to get Liliana back? Don't tell him this, but I think she fancies you. I know she doesn't fancy him anymore, but I am too kind to tell him frankly."

I said: "I want to know when we're going to Jerusalem."

Milord Boniface chuckled paternally and patted my arm. "My good pilgrim," he said, "first let's take a moment to restore ourselves and bask in our good fortune."

I said: "It's not good fortune, it's a means to get to Jerusalem." And I do not apologize for saying so, for it is true.

Said Milord Boniface: "We're going as soon as we're paid in full."

Myself: "And when will that be?"

Milord Boniface: "Immediately after Alexios's coronation."

Myself: "And when will that be?"

"The first of August," Milord Boniface said, as if he'd won an argument. "A fortnight. And then he'll pay us the rest, Constantine Philoxenites assures me. And then we'll go straight to the Holy Land." He leaned back and clasped his hands on his lap, smiling at me like a doting father. "And then, Gregor of Mainz will make a name for himself as the greatest pilgrim in the history of Christendom. And then he'll return with me and remain a favored member of my court for as long as he likes. Despite his being married to my daughter, he can even have everybody's favorite whore back." He sobered a little. "Speaking of such women, I am sorry to hear about the death of your Jamila."

I said, "How long do you really think it will take Alexios to pay us?"

Milord Boniface sighed. "Gregor, I command you to stop fretting about it. I trust the men we've just put on the throne, or I wouldn't have put them on the throne!"

I said: "We didn't put Isaac on the throne—"

"We removed his brother the Usurper, and we could easily have removed him too if I deemed it necessary," Milord Boniface retorted. "I did not. We are dealing with reputable stock, and I have confidence in them."

"I'm glad to hear it, milord," said I. "In that case I trust we shall soon be getting on with our pilgrimage."

Said Milord Boniface: "If you're so concerned about getting on with your pilgrimage, Gregor, take advantage of where we are now and visit the holy places of this very city. Hagia Sophia, the Church of Holy Wisdom, is the grandest house of worship in the entire world."

Said I: "Grand is not the same as holy."

Said Milord Boniface: "At the far corner of the city, tucked away, is the most extraordinary holy relic in the world: the head of John the Baptist. Go and venerate it."

Despite myself, my eyes glanced down toward the city walls. I share the birthday of John the Baptist, and further, my family emblem is his very flower. I have a minor relic of his—a strand from his robe— encased in the hilt of my sword. I have a close relationship to him. My father-in-law knows this well.

"Indeed," Milord Boniface said, very desirous to change the subject. "In fact, I make that an order. While your squires are relocating your tent, give yourself a day of solitude and visit the city. There are relics and churches and shrines beyond number, waiting to receive you as a pilgrim. Constantinople, the Queen of Cities, the new Rome, waits for you to worship."

43

I HAD NO INTEREST in worshiping the Queen of Cities, but Gregor refused to leave me alone in my morbid humor.

He, taking his role as pilgrim very seriously, left behind not only his weapons and armor but even his regular clothing, and wore only his long white undershirt, belted, with sandals, a wooden pilgrim's staff (which I'd thought was an undersize tent pole all these months), and his purse. I looked positively dashing in comparison, even in my hose still shredded from scaling the burning gates of Pera.

We entered the city on foot, through Blachernae Palace. Gregor had not seen the inside of this astounding compound and was appalled at my indifference as we were ushered through some of the same courtyards I'd been herded through with Jamila just two days before. To justify my attitude, I revealed sullenly exactly how much she and I had accomplished here. He was flabbergasted—and for many weeks, until he saw for himself what I was capable of, he probably did not believe me.

From Blachernae we entered the northern reaches of the city. Approaching the smoking neighborhood incinerated by the Venetians two days earlier, we encountered our first Sacred Site. This was a small, round, domed church, in the style of those I'd seen in Venice. It had once been surrounded by orchards but was now surrounded by smoldering charcoal stumps; the church itself, of stone and brick with a tiled roof, was unhurt but for soot outside.

Here was convened a flock of enterprising young Greek men who

knew just enough French or Italian to present themselves to visiting pilgrims as guides. It was impossible to guess their station, but
they were of the very-short-tunic-and-overdecorated-hose school of
dressing. For less money than I would make in an evening playing
for Dandolo, one of these young men would guide us to the most
important Christian sites. Many knights were spending the day as we
were while their tents were relocated across the harbor; the Greeks
had figured that out already, so there was a crowd of guides to choose
from. They were all smiling and assertive.

Gregor gestured to a young man on the outskirts, who was hanging back, less aggressive at hawking his services than the others. He
was barely more than a boy, short, with a rectangular head and a firm,
squat jawline, a naturally somber face, and intense dark eyes. His hair
was long, but he was still working on the beard; his tunic was of the
short variety but not quite so short or the hose so decorated as those
of his contemporaries. He introduced himself as Ionnis.

"What do you charge, Ionnis?" Gregor asked awkwardly; knights
don't usually sully themselves with mundane things like finances.

"No money, milord," he said solemnly. "I show you good things,
no money."

Gregor glanced at the other guides—those who had found potential customers were haggling with them earnestly, or already leading
them into town. "You charge nothing? Why? These others are charging."

"I show you what a beautiful city we have. Understand me," said
Ionnis, unsmiling. It was hard to tell if this was a command, a request,
or a query. "We have a beautiful city, and you will keep it beautiful.
Understand me?"

"Yes," we said together.

We walked into the church. Nearly the whole interior was visible
at a glance, for the floor plan was square and open. The first thing we
saw was a mural of saints on the walls, staring at us—looking much
friendlier than their Catholic counterparts. Ionnis bowed three times

to them, then touched the ground and made a sign of the cross in their direction. He crossed the space to a separate painting of a specific saint, a woman, and touched it. And then *kissed* it. And then began *talking* to it—not a prayer or a chant but what appeared to be a casual conversation. Gregor and I exchanged looks. To keep from saying something regrettable, I distracted myself with a further look around.

As in Blachernae, much of the decoration was mosaics of minute tile work, the background gold baked into tiny bits of glass and set into the walls. The windows were small and high up, but the light that came through them bounced off these golden tiles and gave the space a warm glow. I'd never seen images of Jesus Christ that made him look so human, so gentle and so loving; it soothed even my crotchety heart a little. In every church I'd ever been in, my eye was drawn at once to the crucifixion on the altar, an image so gruesome it was easy to see why Christians are obsessed with pain and death. Here, in contrast, the altar sported only a squared-off cross and a picture of Mary and her babe above it; Jesus Christ in his full glory smiled (yes, *smiled*) down on us mosaically from the arc of the dome directly overhead, a peaceful expression on his face and one hand raised in benediction. The Catholic Jesus was always far too preoccupied with his own misery to be good for much of anything, except maybe as a role model for how to suffer. Suffering is easy, it's just a response to something that happens to you; Gregor and I, in our disparate ways, each excelled at it. I've never understood why somebody should be deified for it.

But *this* Jesus, up in the dome of the church, impressed me. He was extending patience and compassion—almost good humor—to all below, no apparent thought for himself, even though (if he really were a god) he knew exactly what he was in for, a few verses later. That's not easy, but it is something to aspire to.

I would have aspired to it myself, if I weren't so busy suffering.

Our guide whispered to a priest, whose black gown was decorated with gold braids and a large white collar with black crosses all over it; besides the strangeness of his costume, he had long hair and a long, *long* beard. After some nervous looks from this good elder, and offerings paid out of Gregor's purse, we were allowed to see holy relics, including a piece of cloth supposedly torn from the Virgin Mary's robe. We could not touch this, of course. It was housed in a small gold box, which in turn lived in a large silver box with gold curls welded to it in a complicated geometrical design featuring a fleur-de-lis. Yes, it was enthralling, but its charm was in no way dependent on the tiny bit of cloth within having come from the Virgin's robe. I was briefly amused by Gregor's rapt fascination. Ionnis looked just as rapt as Gregor did—I think he wanted to lead pilgrims on their pilgrimage in part to undertake it himself.

When they had finished their venerations, we went back outside. As soon as we left the cool, golden church, I felt my depression lumber down upon me once again, a physical force every bit as real as the nasty July heat.

"May we see the head of John the Baptist?" Gregor asked next.

Ionnis grimaced slightly. "It is a far journey, out in the woods of the city."

"Not nearly as far as we have come already," said Gregor.

Ionnis made mental calculations. "We do that at the end of the day, if you wish to, but first we go to the closer churches, and then of course the Church of Holy Wisdom."

"I don't care a fig what we do," I said with excessive blandness, not that Gregor had asked me. Ionnis gave me a funny look. "I'm only here under duress," I explained.

"I do not know the word *duress*," Ionnis said unsurely.

Gregor, emanating that compassionate-omniscient-big-brother radiance of his, explained, "It means he is very sad, and he wants to *stay* sad, but *I* don't want him to stay sad, because it is bad for his soul, and also makes him unfit company."

Ionnis *almost* smiled, but I think he was just being polite to Gregor.

Our young guide shepherded us through the burned-out desola-
tion, down a narrow valley that ran parallel to the harbor, a hundred fathoms inland from it. To either side of us loomed steep hills of
smoking ruins. Finally we trudged out of the fire belt, and the density
of the town began to grow, with houses smaller and more pressed
together, and greenery disappearing. Almost everything was of wood,
and many of the homes—even the very modest ones—were several
floors. Constantinople was a well-built town, but it was very flam-
mable: it was a miracle the fire hadn't done even more damage.

We walked south into increasing heat and urban compactness.
There were far more men than women on the streets, as had been
true in Venice, but the women here sometimes walked with hair
or even shoulders uncovered. The women were shy of us, but men
waved, smiled a little too broadly, attempted greetings in broken
French. They were almost obsequious. Gregor took it at face value
and seemed pleased by the attention; it made me cringe.

Streets grew narrower and more crowded, buildings more massive and made of stone now. Ionnis was a fountain of information
as we made our way along, and Gregor encouraged him, which I resented, because it interrupted my sulking. The young man was desperate for us to understand that, despite its smiling men, this city
was leery of Western pilgrims. I only caught a few of his more impassioned speeches (*impassioned* is not really an apt term for Ionnis—he
was an earnest lad but relentlessly solemn). As Eyebrow had complained in the prison cell, all pilgrims had behaved abominably when
they came through in '46, and in the three generations since then,
the stories of their barbarity had increased, as such stories do. While
Ionnis himself realized much of it was rumor (he had been raised,
he said proudly, by a wise man who taught him to think for himself
and to question everything), he'd seen how the city suffered because
of Barbarossa. The Usurper, terrified that the German hordes might
descend again, had paid a yearly tribute to Germany of eight tons
of gold just to prevent that. This tax—the Alamanikon—burdened

seeing our interest, began to fill in anecdotal details, it took on almost mythical proportions:

The aqueduct was part of an engineered waterway nearly a thousand years old and more than a hundred miles long, funneling a northern lake south via rivers, canals, tunnels, and external creations like this one. In a subtle, constantly falling grade, water was channeled down toward the city, then along the aqueduct into a tunnel in the farther hill, and finally into a series of cisterns. If the city was threatened from without, it would never lack for water.

Our guide seemed amused that I would find this so impressive. It had been around forever, after all, and had nothing to do with the glory of God. And we were pilgrims. We did not care for anything, did we, beyond the glory of God? Well, he would show us the glory of God, so we would understand how important it was to keep the city safe. "Understand me," he implored. And we did. Any impulse I had to poke fun at Gregor's excessive piety was squelched; this young man believed such piety was the key to keeping his homeland intact, and I would not cause him anxiety. I played along.

We went to many churches and monasteries that day, stopping for a dinner we could hardly eat because it was so spicy. Everywhere we encountered other members of the pilgrim army, also sightseeing and, like us, drooping in the heat. They, like Gregor, were delighted and amazed by how welcoming the citizens were. The army really was the city's champion! We were the saviors of Constantinople! We had done our Christian duty by them!

Nowhere in any of the cool, golden churches were we forced to gaze upon a crucifix, but we saw any number of relics in their reliquaries (which ranged from delicate to gaudy), beautiful golden mosaics, and a procession of peaceful Christs blessing us from the domes above. Every time I saw one, I thought again that it was admirable, that I should embrace the philosophy of good-natured loving-kindness in the face of suffering and pain . . . then we'd walk out of the church into the oppressive summer heat, and without the image as a everyone in the empire, and Ionnis had personally witnessed tomb of former emperors despoiled to pay for it.

"You are afraid something even worse than that will happen now, because of us, because of what Alexios has promised us," said Gregor gently. The young man nodded once. Gregor put a hand on Ionnis's shoulder as we walked along. "Lad, I have no power to sway these things, but I give you my word of honor to try preventing such a travesty."

When we were about half a mile out of the burned section but still a mile or more away from the tip of the peninsula, the hills to either side paused, as did the urban congestion, and we found ourselves in an open valley of gardens and grazing ground with something amazing in the middle of it: a *huge* stone bridge led from the hill to our right, all the way down the valley floor to a hill at the far end. Its span went from hilltop to hilltop, elevated by a procession of arches, astride another procession of arches. It was easily the height of fifteen men in the middle, where the valley was at its the deepest, and more than a thousand paces long. I supposed it was for carts to cross the valley without having to carry their loads down one steep slope and back up another. But that seemed impractical; I'm at home with heights, but I could not imagine most men being comfortable up there, let alone a donkey, horse, or ox—and it had no railings. Gregor noticed it just as I did (it was impossible not to notice) and voiced appreciation. Our guide paid no attention to it.

"What *is* that?" I demanded. Ionnis looked, and used a word I didn't know. He tried a couple of other words and finally said, "Water bridge. Understand me?"

"An aqueduct," Gregor said. "I thought so, but I've never seen one so big before."

Coming from an underpopulated land where it is always raining, I'd not encountered anything like this. It was extraordinary; it jolted me right out of my churlishness. As Gregor explained to me what it was and what it did, it became even more extraordinary; as Ionnis, visual reminder of benevolence, simple grumpy suffering seemed so much easier.

A few churches either professed to have no relics or did not want to show them to us, even when Gregor made an offering—until he brought out Boniface's wax seal. When he explained he was the army leader's son by marriage, he was invariably allowed to see the goodies. Ionnis hadn't known whom he was guiding, and he was stunned when Gregor first pulled rank this way; then he jabbered away in Greek to everyone we passed, grimly pleased for having been selected by God, or fate, for today's duty.

In fact, to maximize his opportunity to boast, Ionnis decided that we should take a scenic detour toward the harbor en route to the Church of Holy Wisdom. We were not far from the Venetian neighborhood; we had only to pass below a harborside hill, and suddenly it was almost as if we were back in Venice. The buildings were mostly wood, but the architecture was Venetian. It was cool and breezy by the water (unlike in Venice)—yet the sounds, the smells, the Venetian dialect, the sorts of faces, even the details of passing chitchat, were all familiar to me. The Venetian aesthetic, especially in costume, is similar to the Byzantine. But there was a distinctly *Western* feeling here. There was a bustling plaza like the Rialto set up with stalls and shops. The doge had visited here earlier today. I heard people gossiping excitedly about him: Dandolo was revered even by the expatriates of Venice. Some worried that taxes might be raised against resident Latins, to help pay the rest of what was owed to the visiting Latins (i.e., the army). But otherwise the atmosphere seemed positive, and cautiously hopeful. Young unmarried women roamed the marketplace in giggling groups, anticipating an evening visit from the Venetian mariners. I resented their opportunity for romance and smugly told myself that none of them would find anyone who made them happy.

Gregor clapped one heavy hand on my shoulder, turning me toward a small stall that sold fresh cheeses—something we each prized from our respective homelands and had together lamented the absence of while traveling. "There's the place that gets my patronage!" he said happily. "Let's go!"

"There is even better curd in the Genoese Quarter, down toward the point," Ionnis suggested. I think he wanted to make sure we walked through the entire Latin Quarter, so he could show us off. "And you can get Egyptian flax very cheap right now, because it is high summer—there are markets along the wharf, emporia from Russia, Lombardy, Spain, Palestine—"

"We'll go there too," Gregor announced contentedly and strode into the stall. I followed him grumpily, Ionnis trailing after us, continuing to list the lands represented on the wharf and stoically bragging that the city's daily income was the equivalent of twenty thousand gold pieces. "That's excellent news; you can pay us in five days," said Gregor, not listening (or getting his exchange rate right). He bought a very small sampling of cheese (having blithely doled out all his money to the churches we'd entered) and sent Ionnis to the bakery next door for fresh bread.

We stepped out of the stall onto the wide and crowded street. I found myself looking into a face so familiar, it took me a moment to realize how strange it was to see her. Jamila and another Jewess were standing only a few feet away, with baskets tucked into the crooks of their elbows. It had been only yesterday that she'd left, but I felt as if I hadn't seen her for weeks.

"What are you doing here?" I demanded shrilly.

Gregor, suddenly self-conscious, nodded to Jamila; then he smiled nervously, experimentally, at the other female. Jamila hurriedly introduced her as Ruth. Ruth nodded but turned away. Jamila did not look at me.

"Ruth doesn't speak French," Jamila said to Gregor, as an apology.

"And we burned down her house," I added. "But otherwise she thinks we're *grand*." I turned back to Jamila, and asked carefully, "Your grandmother?"

Jamila shook her head, looked down.

I felt a part of myself turn to lead, reached out a hand awkwardly in comfort. She shook her head again, more brusquely, and pushed the hand away. "Jamila—" I whispered.

"Never mind," she said quickly, cutting me off. She wouldn't look at me. The other woman intuited the substance of the conversation and protectively wrapped both hands around Jamila's arm. This, Jamila submitted to—which struck me as grossly unfair, since she had known this woman less than a day.

"Where are you living?" Gregor asked gently.

She gestured to the small building we'd just exited. "We know the family, and they are allowing some of us to sleep in their store for a few days," she said.

"There's not enough room for the two of you to stand up in there, let alone sleep," I objected. I had already made the mental calculation that, if her grandmother was dead, she had no family left in Pera and so she ought to come back to us. To me.

Jamila continued to look nervously at Gregor and completely avoided looking at me, even as I stared at her. "We don't know how much longer we can stay, but there is a Moslem family just a few streets over, near the mosque. I knew their nephew in Alexandria, and they may be able to put us up for a while. The community is planning to rebuild Pera as soon as the . . . as soon as you depart for Egypt."

"If it's just the two of you, stay in the tent with us," I offered immediately. Gregor glanced sidewise at me—a wary German version of the Blessing Christ.

"Thank you, but I think not," Jamila said, *still* not looking at me, even though I edged closer to her. I could easily have reached up and caressed her face. I tried to pay attention to what she was saying. "And it is not only two. There are eight of us staying in the shop."

"That's tighter berth than on the ships," said Gregor. "Is there no other option? Some sort of Jewish nunnery—are you all women?"

"No," said an accented male voice about a foot above and behind Jamila's head. "Mostly men, in fact, because fewer women escaped the inferno you brought on."

We all looked up at the speaker: Samuel, the brother of Jamila's murdered husband, stood there. He had been standing so still and quiet that he blended into the street crowd around us, only his fair coloring and a peculiar cap differentiating him from any other man on the street. Jamila made introductions between Samuel and Gregor, and continued not to look at me. Although childhood friends who'd been reunited only yesterday, she and Samuel already had a rhythm of stern father and obedient daughter—such an airless dynamic, it made me love Gregor for his earnest big-brotherness.

After the introduction, there was an awkward pause.

"When are you leaving to smite the infidels?" Jamila finally asked with a pained attempt at dry humor.

"Once we're paid," Gregor said, fidgeting under Samuel's intense gaze.

"So, never," Samuel said.

"Don't you think they'd make paying us a priority, to get rid of us?" Gregor asked—his own nervous attempt at humor. Gregor wasn't very good at humor even in the best of times; this had all the levity of hematite.

"I wish they would do so," Samuel said. "But there are many things that cannot wait. There is the harborside to rebuild, and damage from the Venetians' fire—"

"And wounded soldiers to care for," said Jamila.

"And Pera to rebuild," said Samuel.

"And Galata Tower to repair," said Jamila.

"And the civil service of an enormous government to keep up, in the midst of all the upheaval and change," said Samuel.

"And of course, the gala coronation feast must needs be provided," said Jamila.

They spoke with the same accent, and a comfortable rhythm, as if they had practiced this. As they rattled off the list of woes, a hint of ironic humor finally crept into Samuel's voice—as if he leeches it from her, I thought.

There was another awkward pause.

"Have you been touring the city?" Jamila asked. "What have you seen?"

"The aqueduct, and a bunch of churches," I said in a sullen voice. "And you."

"You need a guide who can tell you the significance of things," Jamila said quickly, nervously, only making chitchat to keep the awkward pauses at bay. "If I knew more, I would do it. Samuel might know some things?" She directed this up to him.

Samuel, once again humorless, answered, "I am not so familiar with the city itself. The Jews were moved out of the walls and over to Pera years ago, until it was burned down when you attacked and half of us were killed."

Another awkward pause.

It was broken by Ionnis returning with the bread. "Now we go to the great Hagia Sophia, the Church of Holy Wisdom, to finish the pilgrimage," he announced.

"Yes, pilgrims, finish what you've started," said Samuel grimly. He curled one proprietary arm around Jamila and one around the other young woman, and shepherded them deliberately away from us.

44

WE DID NOT GO to Hagia Sophia that day, and certainly we did not go as far as to see the head of John the Baptist. This was partly my fault; I was moping like a pimple-faced boy after we parted from Jamila, and Gregor, still glowing from his proximity to so many sacred relics, did not want his experience of either the greatest church in the world or the most significant relic he could conceive of to be marred by my bad mood. It was also oppressively hot, and we were limp from tromping through the heat for hours. So we bade goodbye to Ionnis, our earnest guide, tried to pay him, were rebuffed, and promised that we understood him—his city truly was a holy center. We headed to the camp, taking a ferry across the harbor, the famous Golden Horn.

In our absence, the camp had been moved back to the hill topped by Galata Tower. As our ferry neared the rocky shore, we saw that the gilded royal barque was docked against this side of the harbor; Alexios was visiting Boniface in the camp compound. Boniface had spent the entire evening and night before in Blachernae. In fact, Alexios had hardly been away from Boniface's side for more than a few hours since he'd first joined the army back on Corfu nearly two months earlier.

"Can't Alexios *breathe* without Boniface's help?" I whispered. "What's that snot-nosed boy going to do when the army departs for Egypt?"

"That is not our concern," Gregor said sharply.

We found the tent; Otto was out exercising the horses with the

Richardim. Gregor was too tired to join them and wanted some moments of silence to reflect on all of the holy glory he'd experienced today. For some reason, he did not wish to do this while shut up in a small, enclosed space with a grouch. So: "Go play for Boniface," he ordered.

"I've lost my instruments," I said, curling up like a hibernating rodent.

"Destroyed them, you mean. I'm sure he has a spare gittern or viol or whatnot."

I shrugged—difficult to do lying curled up. "I don't give a sheep's arse what Boniface and the snot-nosed boy're up to. I don't care what the army's up to. Do your own espionage from now on. Boniface holds no interest for me."

"I thought you'd take interest in Liliana's welfare, that's all," said Gregor pointedly. He grabbed my minstrel livery from a chest and chucked it at me.

It was just his way to make me leave the tent, but after a moment of trying to pretend I hadn't heard him, I cursed and pulled myself off the floor.

It was an unpleasant and useless afternoon for seeking Liliana. But Boniface did have an extra gittern, *and* viol, *and* lute, and when one is wretched, playing music is marginally a better way to pass the time than pretending to be a hibernating rodent.

Within the pavilion it was cool, because a few of Alexios's servants were waving enormous fans woven from tree bark. The fans were so big, it took a grown man to hold each one steady and a boy to pivot it; the fanners themselves had to stand outside the shade of the pavilion, to keep the fans from taking up too much space inside. Earlier, in the worst of the midday heat, one of them had fainted, which Alexios was still complaining about. The prince in general still seemed constitutionally petulant, despite his relative good mood about winning his fifth consecutive dice game against Claudio, Boniface's bodyguard. When I arrived, Claudio had already lost all his money to the emperor-to-be, but the emperor-to-be would not allow him to stop playing, so Claudio had lost his knife, his belt, and a jeweled pin to Alexios as well.

His Highness had brought a cask of wine from Blachernae, from which a servant was distributing a new round to Boniface's sycophants. Alexios was seated on Boniface's thronelike chair, while the marquis sat beside him on a stool. Everyone else either stood or, if they were too drunk to stand, sat on mats that had been laid out.

I'd come just as another musician was due for a break, so I was ushered in to play his lute. "Lute Man!" said Alexios. "Play that tune I like so much!"

"Kalenda Maya?" I asked, trying not to sound appalled.

"No." He laughed.

"The why-does-my-husband-beat-me song?" (Another princely favorite.)

"*No,*" he said. "The *drinking* song."

This narrowed the possibilities hardly at all. "Carmina Burana?" I tried helpfully.

"*No.* The one where *I* sing *with* you."

"Ah yes, Your Highness," I said, squelching the impulse to stick my tongue out. I began to play, and then sang the first verse, which was also the second, third, and coincidentally fifty-seventh verse, of an intricate, hallowed anthem: "Hoard the good wine, chuck out the bad. And then sing along with me: this song calls for booze!"

"*This song calls for booze!*" Alexios echoed off-key, for this was the tricky part, the chorus. He drained his cup, and everyone else in the tent promptly, obediently imitated him. "Another verse!" he decided indulgently, holding his cup out for more.

There was a movement by the entrance. "Ah, Gregor!" Boniface said with relief, and stood up, delighted to interrupt the performance. "Thank you for coming so quickly! Excuse me, Your Highness. How was your pilgrimage, Gregor?" He handed his cup to a page boy, and crossed to the doorposts of the tent. The marquis embraced the knight, who didn't look like he was here by choice. I guessed Boniface just wanted to reassure himself that Gregor, drunk on the sanctity of the New Rome, would be more malleable now. "Please join us. We have the honor of entertaining His Highness."

Gregor let Boniface lead him to the prince, to whom he bowed and said all the congratulatory, grateful things he was expected to say, concluding, "God surely smiles upon our undertakings, that we who have delivered the empire may now safely leave it in your hands. Yours is a beautiful city, and were it not for our eagerness to be off at once to fulfill our vows in the Holy Land, we would surely wish to stay a few weeks more."

Alexios himself was inebriated, and after a distracted nod to acknowledge Gregor, he turned his attention back to the dice game without responding to him. "I'm going to win your sword before we're through here," he informed Claudio, preening.

"Please, Your Majesty, I cannot lose my sword, I am nothing without it," Claudio said unsteadily.

"Don't say such things," Alexios chastised. "Why, not a year ago I was a fugitive without a dagger to my name—and now I'm the Emperor of Byzantium!" He chuckled condescendingly. "So do not be dismayed at the thought of losing a mere sword."

"Gregor!" said Boniface quickly. "Tell us something more of your impression of Constantinople. Did you see the head of John the Baptist?"

Gregor looked regretful. "I did not get that far today, milord. My servant was overcome with amazement at some of the other objects we encountered and had a fit. I had to bring him back to the camp. I'll go again."

"I remember seeing that head, as a child!" Alexios chortled. "Once a year, at the end of August, we always had to trudge out to this godforsaken little part of the city. It's not the *whole* head, you know, just the crown of the skull. When you go, though, on your way you'll go by the old palace." He rolled the die in that sloppy way drunks do. "Make sure to say hello to poor old Euphrosyne!"

"Who is Euphrosyne, milord?" asked Gregor dutifully.

"My aunt by marriage. And until a few days ago, the Empress of Byzantium," Alexios said smugly. "Then Uncle fled and forgot to bring his wife, so when my father was reenthroned, she tried to hide. But Father found out where she was and said he was going to send guards to take all her money to help pay our debt to you all."

"Does she have enough?" Gregor asked bluntly. To Boniface he added, quietly, "That would be a convenient, and justifiable, way for them to pay the debt."

Alexios laughed. "The way she lived? I doubt she's anything left! But there are plenty of others who helped to engineer Father's downfall, so among them, they'll make a nice fat contribution if they want to keep their heads." He licked his lips. "Euphrosyne has a libido the size of my empire. She was my first woman—seduced me right after Father and I were first imprisoned." I had a hard time imagining this puerile fellow fornicating with anyone even now, let alone as a twelve-year-old. Alexios looked extremely satisfied with his memory of it, however. "That woman would hump anything with balls," he said reverentially. "She was a credit to her sex." He raised his cup high. "A toast to Euphrosyne! To filling her crotch and emptying her coffers!" The rest of the men, whether or not they'd been listening, called out in agreement and drained their cups. Immediately, Alexios's servant began to refill the cups from a large clay jar. The young man's attention went back to Claudio. "You're too easy to beat. You're dismissed." The emperor-to-be turned his bleary gaze on Gregor. "Gregor of Mainz, on the other hand, from what I've heard, is a tough man to break. So I'll play Gregor for a while. Gregor, what's your preference?"

"I don't play games of chance, milord," Gregor said with an apologetic bow. Claudio had already scrambled away from the gaming table.

"Very well then, I'll pick the game. I pick five stones," Alexios announced. He gestured imperiously at the dice. "And I want to raise the stakes. In honor of Euphrosyne, loser owes the winner a woman. Have you got a woman?"

Gregor glanced at Boniface with an openly questioning look on his face.

"The lioness," Boniface said after a moment, as if answering Alexios.

Alexios's face lit up. "Liliana? The one who'll only open her lips, not her legs?"

I snorted with laughter; Alexios interpreted this as fawning and condescended to grace me with a tipsy grin.

"She isn't mine," Gregor said mildly. "She is my brother Otto's." And then, pointedly, "Isn't she, milord?"

"Absolutely," said Boniface, draining his wine cup and signaling for more, without quite looking at Gregor. "She's free to return to your stuffy little tent at any time. I can't imagine why she hasn't gone yet. Perhaps she doesn't want to give the furs back."

"Women," lamented the lutenist (me) while retuning the bottom string. "Forever looking after their own interests, milords."

"But it would *be* in Liliana's interest to let me fuck her," Alexios complained, now looking at me as if one of us were an idiot. "Sure, Fazio is good to her, but with me she'd be an emperor's mistress! What more could any woman want?"

"Obviously something the lord marquis has that you don't, milord," I said, with an illustrative gesture and the guffaw of a clod who doesn't know any better. I found that this persona allowed me to get away with an awful lot in Boniface's tent. Delivered in my actual cadences, the line would have resulted in a flogging. Instead, I got off with a reprimand:

"You're such a boor," Alexios said with bored disgust. "Fazio, I don't like this fellow anymore. Keep him for his music, but don't let him speak aloud in my presence."

45

EXCEPT FOR THE MOMENTS I actually had an instrument in hand, I was nearly catatonic the fortnight leading up to Alexios's coronation. It was worse than my three years of obsessive planning for a murder I would never commit, because at least then I'd had a purpose. Now there was no reason to wake up at all. Gregor had no need of my meddling; although he despised Alexios, he was in relative cheer, believing the army really would go on to Jerusalem right after the first of August. Otto, occasionally caterwauling about the evil of Boniface and fickleness of women, was upbeat too. They were soldiers, and their side had been victorious, with a minimum of bloodshed and a maximum of glory. That's what soldiers look for, after all.

My inability to share their satisfaction convinced me it would be disastrous to go with them to the Holy Land, even if I'd had a reason to. I took a respite from Boniface's. Alexios's personality so repulsed me, the lure of earning intelligence or even money paled compared with the pleasure that could be obtained from staying far away from him—and I did not believe Liliana was really all that miserable, or she'd have let me know by now; instead, she avoided me at Boniface's compound. I preferred to curl up in the tent and sulk about how much I missed Jamila.

I certainly had no interest in the coronation, especially of a youth so obviously unfit. But Gregor believed that all I needed to heal my soul was a dose of Hagia Sophia, the famed Church of Holy Wisdom; he insisted that I go with him and Otto as part of Bishop Conrad's entourage, which would consist of a dozen German knights, their squires, and their servants. (This was a conscious choice on the part of the renowned German brother-soldiers—to be publicly affiliated at the coronation not with their martial leader but with their spiritual one. It was a way of reminding everyone who saw them that the real task still lay ahead of them.) I didn't put up a fight about going, because it occurred to me I might run into that Eyebrow fellow, Otto's prison mate. We could make scathing remarks together about the ceremony. That might be entertaining. He would insist that Jamila wanted me to get into her skirt, and then I'd feel further justified in sulking about her.

Even on the journey over to Hagia Sophia for the coronation, it was clear the bloom was off the rose. The crowd of guides by the harbor was smaller than it had been a fortnight earlier, and their attitude was already jaded. They were merely offering a service now; they were no longer warmly welcoming. Conrad gave Gregor the task of hiring one. Gregor was vacillating between a fellow about his own age and build, and a venerable, monklike elder when we both heard a familiar voice a few yards away say, "Understand me?" and we pivoted at the same moment.

"Ionnis!" Gregor called out heartily. The somber young man who had taken us around was in earnest discussion with one of our fellow Franks, a French steward, but he ended the conversation with an uncharacteristically rude (but characteristically somber) gesture of dismissal and trotted urgently toward Gregor as if he were Gregor's long-suffering vassal. "Yes," he said and bowed his head, unsmiling.

"Will you guide us?" Gregor asked. To the bishop, a few paces away, he called out, "Your Eminence, this is the very fellow I told you about! We're in luck. Ionnis, this is His Eminence Bishop Conrad of Halberstadt. If you guide his party to Hagia Sophia, you may sit with us for the coronation and get a most excellent view."

Ionnis gave Gregor a look of disappointment. "I will not stay, but

I can take you there. Two *stamenon* for that, sir—or if you have no local money, one French *denier*."

Gregor blinked. "You . . . I thought . . . last time, you did it freely?"

"To show good things to good pilgrims, I would do it freely," Ionnis said. "This is very different. Understand me?"

"Yes," I said, as Gregor said, "No," with a frown that meant he understood perfectly.

"Not real pilgrims, any of you," Ionnis said gently, the sorrow on his face making him look three times his age.

The rebuke irritated Conrad; the bishop crossed to us and, looking put out, began to lecture: "Young man —"

The young man calmly interrupted. "I have seen bad things. You say pilgrims, but it is not pilgrimage. It is something else. And now you reward the leader of them all. Understand me."

"*I* understand you," I said, "and now I *really* don't want to attend." I gestured toward the Latin Quarter, where I knew Jamila was. "I'll see you back at camp, I want—"

"No," Ionnis said, wagging a finger at me. "Not safe alone. Not for you Franks."

"Why wouldn't he be safe?" Conrad asked. "We're welcome everywhere!"

The youth gave him a sad, weary look. "Sir," he said. "I show you something. Come." He gestured down the thoroughfare we were on and led us south along it a hundred paces. We were looked at uncomfortably, otherwise ignored, by all the locals in the street; not at all as it had been a fortnight earlier. Finally, we reached a market square against the harbor wall. It smelled like fish. Today was a Friday, but the fishmongers had scattered to other climes, for a large group of sweaty, long-haired Greek soldiers—looking displeased about their task—were destroying their own defenses. A three-hundred-foot section of wall, many centuries old and still strong, was being torn out stone by stone, and it was exhausting work, especially in the August heat. The Greeks were watched over by some French soldiers, all wearing the pilgrim cross prominently on their shoulders. A tall scaffold supported the men in their disassembling process. At the foot of it, a couple hundred Constantinopolitans stared up at the razing of the wall, enraged but not daring to speak to armed Frankish soldiers.

"They take down the wall because your Marquis Boniface asked it," said Ionnis. "So that we will be more vulnerable to you. You make us dependent on you for our safety. And people do not like it. So they do not like you. So you must not wander alone around the city, especially on Coronation Day. Understand me?"

Gregor shook his head. "But we were here less than a fortnight ago and we were welcomed everywhere. You saw it yourself!"

"We always welcome victors," young Ionnis explained wearily, as if he himself had weathered generations of such behavior. "It is our way. Understand me. We don't care who is in charge, but we prefer they leave us alone. It takes something like this wall, or your plundering churches, it takes a large arrogance to disenchant the whole entire city, and so quickly. I speak with no anger myself, I only want you to understand why it is not safe for him to go off alone now. Understand me? He cannot do it."

Conrad was appalled. "Young man, did you say plundering churches?"

As if in response to his query, a shout of protest turned us all in the direction of armed guards leading a procession. Following after them came two men carrying a silver casket with gold geometrical designs framing a fleur-de-lis. Gregor made a horrified sound in the back of his throat, and I found my fists clenching: we both recognized the casket. It was the outer casing of the Virgin Mary's gown, from the first church we'd been to on our pilgrimage two weeks earlier. It was being carried in the direction of the Great Palace, south of Hagia Sophia. More guards used lances to fend off enraged merchants, artisans, and several priests, all of whom were grabbing for the casket.

A protester threw a stone at the guards, and a rearguard soldier broke formation to grab the offender, shoving him to the side of the street, out of sight. The rest of the crowd shouted and backed away—for a moment. Then like a wave they rushed toward the guards, and a brawl broke out. Two of the Varangians grabbed the casket protectively for safety and rushed down the street with it, sans processional.

We stood there stupidly, watching as if it were a performance. Ionnis waved us toward the square where the wall was being dismantled. "Step back," he said, sounding urgent but not panicked. "Look away. Step back!"

"That's from the church where we met you!" Gregor said.

"It will be melted down for coins to pay you," said Ionnis. "It happens every day now."

"*What?*" Conrad demanded, horrified.

"I misspoke," Ionnis said. "Usually it is altarpieces melted down. This is worse, because it contains a holy relic. So maybe it will not be melted down, but it still becomes a commodity. This means things are getting worse. Understand me?"

Conrad looked beseechingly at Gregor. "Someone must warn Boniface —"

"Boniface *ordered* me not to care about such things," the knight said, cutting him off.

Conrad looked as if he'd been punched in the stomach. "I'm going to speak with him about this!" he announced.

"Oh, *that'll* be effective," I muttered. Gregor cuffed me on the side of the head.

Moving south of the brawl, we approached a high wall protecting the back of Hagia Sophia, the Church of Holy Wisdom, as Ionnis dutifully cascaded information upon the retinue.

This wall behind Hagia Sophia, the Church of Holy Wisdom (Ionnis always said these phrases together to emphasize the church's spiritual heft—this place was named for no mere piddling saint, this was a church consecrated to Wisdom herself), was merely one end of

an enormous palace compound. The compound included the minis-
tries and offices required to run an empire like Byzantium and a city
like Constantinople; it included also city lodgings for ministers and
officers who otherwise dwelt in the hinterlands. This was very different from what we in the West thought of as the means to rule; both
my king and Gregor's were often on the road to the far reaches of
their realms. In Byzantium, the far reaches came to the ruler. At the
other end of this same compound, over half a mile away facing down
onto the Sea of Marmara, sat old Bukoleon Palace—at one time the
domestic hearth of the decrepit Roman Empire and now the domestic hearth of the decrepit Emperor Isaac.

The compound also included, however, things of interest and
delight to the masses, who were (under controlled conditions) allowed through the gates. In particular there was the Hippodrome—a
huge stadium but such a narrow ovoid that at least one fatal accident
could be presumed per month as the chariots careened around the
tight curves at either end. Consequently, it was a wildly popular attraction with the citizenry.

Even more astonishing than the size of the thing itself were the
large bronze statues that literally ringed the top of it. There were
horses, deer, cattle, dragons, fawns and satyrs, centaurs, demigods
and demons—all of them so lifelike, even from this distance, I expected them to move.

"Some of those are real!" Otto insisted, sounding endearingly like
a dolt.

"No, no," Ionnis said. "Not real. Metal." He rapped on Otto's helmet, tucked under Otto's arm. "Bronze. Understand me? First time,
everyone thinks they are real."

"Who is the artist God has blessed with the skill to so replicate
his own designs?" Conrad asked softly, in a tone of genuine awe I'd
never before heard from the bishop.

Ionnis shrugged. While he was tickled by our responses, he was
as blasé about the statues as he'd been about the aqueduct a fort-

night earlier. "Nobody knows. They've been there for centuries."
He pointed to the Hippodrome's gateway, where four large stallions
seemed about to leap off, pulling a chariot behind them. "You see
them? Their leather harnesses rot away and we give them new ones,
and those rot away, and we give them new ones, and so on, forever."
He shrugged. "It is just like Stanpoli: The thing that controls them
is impermanent, it will rot away, but they remain forever unchanged.
And anyhow the harness is just a trapping. It does not make them
what they are, or give them their power or beauty, or even really control them. *Understand me.*"

Gregor and I exchanged looks. We understood him. There was
more to our little guide than met the eye.

Ionnis—in no hurry to arrive at the coronation—let us gawk for
a few moments at the four horses of the Hippodrome and their myth-
ological and bestial cousins. Then he grimly turned our attention to
our left, where we would finally enter Hagia-Sophia-the-Church-of-
Holy-Wisdom for the crowning of Alexios-the-Snot-Nosed-Boy.

From the outside, what we saw was clearly not *a* building but an
entire small city covering a hill, although there was no hill—obviously a *group* of buildings with nice solid internal walls that just happened to be built all on top of one another. They were all graceful, I'll
grant that—round and soft and warm-toned, whereas most fortresses
of comparable size bristled with cold, masculine grimness—but the
compound was not as visually thrilling as any church I'd seen traveling through France or Italy. It was just *big.*

Then I went inside. Somehow, it was much, *much* bigger on the
inside than it was on the outside.

There was a foyer, wonderfully cool after the heat outside. This
alone was as large as any church I'd ever been in, and far more expen-
sively decorated, with intricately inlaid stones of maroon porphyry
and green serpentine. There were so many carvings and mosaics and
tiles, I grew dizzy craning my neck to see it all.

And that was just the entrance hall. Then, skirting the thirty-foot-high Emperor's Door (only for use by snot-nosed boys and their daddies), we went through one of the lowly fifteen-foot side doors, and into the lap of Wisdom. Because we were with a bishop's party, we were given a brief fanfare by the heralds on duty, and swarms of Greek citizens (who appeared, uniformly, to be wearing pearls) stood aside to make room for us. Ionnis's mood improved a little; he had no intention of staying, but he liked his fellow citizens making way for the party that he led.

There were already thousands of people waiting, all standing, in the central nave of the church, and floods more entering. Churches here were set up differently from the ones back home: beside the lack of seats, everything was open, with galleries above that looked down onto us. These were already full of people, mostly men and all well-dressed, like the nobles in Blachernae—these were probably, in fact, those same nobles. Our brief fanfare echoed high above, and for a moment the loud hum of voices softened, as thousands and thousands of heads turned in the muted light to see who had entered; the voices returned to gossip when they realized we were nobody special after all.

Remembering the lovely Blessing Christ on the domes of the other churches we'd seen, Gregor and I glanced up at the same moment. Panic overcame me and on rubbery legs, I tried to run outside, for the vast expanse of universe above—Blessing Christ and all—was collapsing onto us. Gregor grabbed me by the collar and held me back.

"It's falling!" I shouted, my voice muted into the hubbub of the crowd. "The roof is falling!" I held my arms up and out and shook them hysterically at the humongous stone dome that hovered over a room larger than the dome itself was, with no columns or other form of support to take its weight—what looked like a city outside was a single, impossibly large space in here. "Look! Look! *Nothing is holding up the roof!*" I grabbed Gregor's hand at my collar and tugged desperately to get away from him.

Ionnis, although still not smiling, laughed at me. "Illusion," he said smugly. "This is a great work for God. It has stood for nearly seven hundred years. God will not let it fall on us today." With Gregor's hand still on my neck and my stomach turning over, I tried to nod.

But then, of its own accord, my head changed direction to say no. My eyes flickered toward the dome, and involuntarily I cringed with a new wave of panic. I felt like I was drowning. "I don't want to stay in here."

Ionnis grimaced understandingly. "Neither do I." He glanced at His Eminence. "Holy sir, I deliver you. Now, I take the little man to the ferry to return to the camp."

"You don't want to stay for the coronation?" Gregor asked me, disappointed. "After all we've done—" He lowered his voice. "All *you've* done to bring it about?"

I shook my head, shamed but in thrall to my terror that the roof was about to fall on us—which it obviously was, if one only really looked at it.

We were excused; I raced toward the well-dressed artisans gathering hopefully near the door. Ionnis grabbed my wrist to keep from losing me in the crowd.

It was amazing how long we kept moving while remaining under the same floating roof, but eventually, *finally*, we were outside, in the garden, still buffeted by streams of people but out of the worst of the throng. Ionnis released me. I took a shaky breath and looked back at the perilous building. From out here, it looked huge but benign, almost motherly, and obviously not about to fall apart at all. I was embarrassed, but frankly glad to avoid the coronation.

"People go in there and they feel the grandeur of God," Ionnis said, with a gesture toward the church. I wasn't sure if this was meant as rebuke or exposition.

"God is terror?" I asked in amazement and then, recovering: "Don't answer that."

Ionnis shrugged, glanced about at the darkening sky, as if contemplating all possible future destinations. "Back to the ferry for you then?"

"I have a choice? I thought I wasn't allowed to go off on my own."

He shrugged again. "Not on your own. But with me, if there is anything you want to see. You and your friend, I like you, although you are grumpy. Not bad, just grumpy. What was the word—*duress?* You are duressed? Preoccupied, at least. Understand me?"

"I'm preoccupied about a woman. Understand *me*?"

"I am preoccupied too," the young man said. "About a city."

"You win," I said, both sarcastic and genuine, and loathing myself. "Your unhappiness is more serious than mine."

He was disturbed by the sarcasm (being, like Gregor, not spiritually constructed for irony) and responded with concern. "This is a big city, with many people and many holy things. We are attacked so many times in history we don't count them, but we have never had an army *here*, like this, before. We thought everything that could ever happen had already happened, and so when it happens again, we know how to respond—we look at how the problem was handled *before*, and we do the same thing *now*, and it works, and we go on. Understand me? We remember the past, we learn from it, we use it. But this . . ." He made a general, hopeless gesture toward the east, where the army was camped on the other side of the harbor. "This *has no past*. So nobody knows what to do."

His face shone with anxiety in the twilight. His eyes were even darker than Jamila's, with a frightening luminosity. He was pleading with me to fix the problem, or at least to reassure him. I wanted to say something calming, but it would have been a lie.

"I wish I could help you," I said.

Ionnis continued to stare at me a moment. He nodded, then shrugged with resignation.

Then his gaze flickered past me, and a look of astonishment animated his face. He swung his arms up and waved them wildly at somebody approaching from behind me. And then to my astonishment, Ionnis, the unsmiling little Greek, actually *grinned*.

I turned. Rushing toward us through the crowd, well-dressed, well-coiffed, was Otto's cell mate Eyebrow from Blachernae, with two servants scurrying behind. I thought he was running toward me, but no, it was Ionnis he wanted: the two men shouted and embraced each other fiercely, actually leaping around in a circle as they slapped each other on the back and kissed each other's cheeks. It looked like a family reunion.

Perhaps it was. I could make out enough Greek to grasp the two of them had some familial connection, although Mourtzouphlos was much older and obviously of higher rank. Ionnis used a term of address toward Mourtzouphlos that employed the word for "uncle" but included other words I didn't know. Once they stopped hopping around happily together, and Mourtzouphlos stopped squeezing Ionnis's cheeks like a cook squeezing a piece of fruit, Ionnis remembered me and hastily made a gesture of introduction.

Mourtzouphlos's face lit up again, and he embraced me, but without half the hysterical delight he'd displayed about young Ionnis. "The Madman of Genoa!" he hollered, almost winding me with the intensity of his hug. He smelled of exotic spices—especially his magnificent and now carefully curled auburn beard. He was as understated in his dress as he was ebullient in his manner: what he wore now, although newer and better-fitting than his prison togs, was hardly fancier. "My deliverer!" He turned to Ionnis and explained something rapidly, in Greek. Ionnis's face took on a tinge of awe; he fell to his feet and kissed the hem of my tunic.

"Don't do that!" I said, alarmed. "Please! Eyebrow, how do you know this fellow? Why is he kissing my tunic?"

"He was in my household as a boy," Mourtzouphlos said and signaled Ionnis, like a hunting dog, to let me be. The young man, already back to his silent gravity, scrambled to his feet, but his eyes stayed on me. "I told him how you saw to it I was released. He is the orphan of my oldest friend, so I raised him in my home to be a rascal like me, eh, until I was thrown in jail eight years ago, and it has only been by letters and gossip we hear from each other, until this moment! He looks like his papa or I would hardly recognize him! Now he is on his own, a good boy, a student, eh?" he said, swatting Ionnis affectionately on the head. Ionnis smiled sheepishly. "And practicing languages with real foreigners!" He patted Ionnis's arm. "You are coming to the coronation?"

Ionnis's face clouded, and he shook his head, responding in Greek.

"Eh eh eh," said Mourtzouphlos with a gesture. "So our friend understands."

"I do not go to a coronation I do not approve of," Ionnis said in French.

"And I tell you," said Mourtzouphlos, also in French, "that this coronation is better than no coronation. Because of this coronation, I—your benefactor—am out of prison. And that Usurper is gone. He was very bad for Stanpoli."

"Will this usurper be any better?" asked Ionnis.

"We will know soon," said Mourtzouphlos. I felt a little as if they were showing off by speaking so brazenly in front of a member (as I must have seemed to be) of the occupying army. "He is Isaac's son, and Isaac was a weak ruler but a good soldier, and meant well, so there are possibilities. And the more we know, the better. So you will march into that church with me, and sit with me in my little corner, with all the other little courtiers, and you will learn what you can by watching this prince. You will form your opinions by your own perceptions and experiences, and not by listening to hearsay. Yes? You will not believe something even if you hear it from me. You must decide for yourself. Yes? This is the only way to be certain of anything in this world. Eh? What do they teach you at this university anyhow?" He laughed and gave Ionnis an affectionate thwack on the arm. "We go now. Madman, join us? We celebrate together afterward!"

I shook my head. "But you go ahead, and enjoy the coronation."

"We will try to."

"You are not safe to be alone in the city," Ionnis warned me.

"Of course he is! He is *wily*," Mourtzouphlos announced happily. "All right, now I must pay attention to a stupid boy. Not you, Ionnis, the prince. He's what we have, so let us hope he will be good enough." He grinned and whacked me on the shoulder. "It is good to see you, Madman! Where is your woman?"

I winced. "She's not my woman."

"Eh?" He was shocked. "What happened to her? She wanted your hand up her skirt, I can tell this in a woman. Did you insult her? You are the insulting sort."

I shook my head. "It's a long story, for another time." I gave him a feeble smile. "It's good to see you, Eyebrow."

Mourtzouphlos was suddenly giving me all of his attention, piercingly. "We must get her back for you," he decided. "Before the army leaves us, which will be soon, thank God, no offense—you and I must find each other and drink a lot, and I'll tell you how to woo any woman in the world to your bed." I gave him a grim, polite smile, which he knew was disbelieving. "No, I mean it!" he said. "Not now, we have a coronation to attend, but tomorrow or the next day, I'll find you and we'll speak of this . . . and other matters," he added, with a sobering of tone. "In the meantime, Madman . . ." He wagged a meaningful finger at me. "Do not sulk because of some woman, especially one I *know* wants you between her thighs. You will have her back soon enough. She is a wise lady, she knows you are her mate."

Despite Ionnis's concerns, I was left alone to walk back to the ferries—or the Venetian Quarter, which was where I actually wanted to go, hoping to stumble across Jamila. Nothing real would be gained from stumbling across Jamila, but of course obsession does not concern itself with reality much.

But I became hopelessly lost getting back the harbor. The urban congestion stymied my sense of direction, and I have no idea where I went, but I had a protracted tour of poorer neighborhoods—where a foreigner felt truly like a foreigner and not a sightseer. I righted my way when I found I had wandered into the valley of the aqueduct, but I'd drifted farther north by the time I found the harbor and opted for a ferry ride straight back to the army camp rather than risk further misadventure in a bootless attempt to hunt down one woman amidst hundreds of thousands.

Feast of St. Stephen, 2 August

This first morning in the reign of His Majesty Alexios IV, I took myself to Milord Boniface's to ask when we would board the ships.

Milord Boniface said: "The emperor hasn't presented the second half of what he owes us, Gregor."

I asked: "Will he present it today? You said he'd present it right after the coronation. It's after the coronation, milord. When will he present it?"

Milord Boniface: "I do not know, Gregor."

Myself: "You don't seem to be in a hurry to move on, milord."

Milord Boniface: "The emperor is coming here today to meet with me, and I shall broach the subject."

I pressed on: "You have heard that Isaac took a relic of the Virgin Mary's robe from a church near Blachernae? There was a riot. Inciting riots is no way to stabilize a city."

Milord Boniface: "Conrad mentioned it. I will discuss that too with His Majesty."

Myself: "May I be present?"

Milord Boniface: "I fear your admirable German bluntness would not find favor with a sovereign of the Byzantine persuasion."

*   *   *

"ALL RIGHT, *all right*," I said crossly when Gregor repeated their conversation to me. I set aside my pressing need to curl up on the floor and think about Jamila, at least enough to present myself as a musician again at Boniface's tent.

That day—and the next, and the next, and every day for a week— Alexios ferried across the harbor on the royal barque and spent the afternoon in Boniface's tent, where I can tell you with authority that His Newly Crowned Imperial Snot-nosed Majesty spent most of his time (in his purple shoes and purple robes) playing betting games, getting drunk, and flirting clumsily with a stream of women . . . including Liliana (who, dressed in increasingly bejeweled outfits and smiling stiffly, avoided me and left the tent the one time I leered at her). We sang His Majesty's favorite song several times each afternoon. He was delighted that I could play tunes Byzantine and Arabesque. Otherwise his tastes tended bizarrely toward the German, but I had some repertoire there too—rhythmic allegorical ditties about falcons, linden trees, thorns, pagans, the usual.

The marquis himself was never inebriated and seemed to find Alexios's behavior increasingly appalling, but he continued to play the supportive father figure. That first day, as he'd promised Gregor, he did ask about the remainder of the money. But seeing how distressed the query made His Majesty, he never broached it again—which was oddly weak for Boniface. I began to suspect that he was *allowing* things to remain in limbo; on Gregor's behalf, I wanted to know why.

I doubted Liliana was remaining here entirely of her own free will, but I also doubted she was miserable being pampered. I was by now a regular among the sycophants who infested the marquis's tent, so I had leave to wander the compound. A few days after the coronation, with the excuse that I had to relieve myself, I drifted toward the sound of female voices, and finally, near an open-air section that was used as kitchen and scullery, I found myself face-to-face with Liliana.

She was emerging from the darkest tent in the compound, a make-shift butlery, with a new jug of wine for the drunkards around Alexios. Her outfit was sumptuous but very revealing, vaguely Arab—bright blue, pearl-studded, and sleeveless, the skirt three large, leaf-shaped pieces of cloth that barely covered her knees and threatened to reveal everything up to the waist in a brisk breeze. "What a lovely tunic," I said quietly, in greeting. "Couldn't Fazio afford the rest of it?"

"Oh!" she said and stopped abruptly.

"Are the pearls from His Majesty? The goodies of one oyster in exchange for the goodies of another?"

Aware of others around us, she collected herself and said, in full voice, "What do you want, little lute player? Have you saved up your pennies to buy an hour of my time?" She smiled with those full, delicious lips, but the effect was artificial, almost smarmy.

"What is your price these days, milady?" I asked. Lowering my voice slightly: "I know a fellow who'll give his liver just to—"

"Let him save his liver for someone younger," she said, her smile wavering.

I stepped close and risked a whisper. "Do you want me to get you out of here?"

"It would be a waste of time," she whispered back, with a nervous glance around. "The marquis would simply . . . collect me again."

"Can't you make him lose interest?" I said. "Make yourself repellent to him?"

She gave me a complicated look consisting mostly of sarcasm. She did not respond verbally at all, which I took to mean that the suggestion was ridiculous.

"Then what should I tell Otto? He's driving us all to madness."

Her expression changed. She looked like the Liliana I knew, for a flicker; then she pulled herself back to the moment and said, "Tell

him to find another woman. My days with him were numbered anyhow. I'll soon cross a threshold, be too old to warrant his attention.
It's happening sooner than I'd hoped, that's all. The amount of effort
he'd have to put into getting back a whore is not worth the little
time we'd have left together. Boniface is twenty years my senior, so
with him, there is a different equation."

"Let me get this right," I said. "You're in love with Otto, Otto's in
love with you, but you're staying with Boniface for reasons that are
stupid. Have I missed anything?"

She looked at me for a moment, and then, that old smile—half-
sympathetic, half-amused. "You're seeing your own story when you
look at mine. If I go back to Otto, you think that means that Jamila
would go back to you."

I blinked and dropped my voice to an anxious whisper. "What do
you know about Jamila? Boniface was told she died in the Pera fire."

Liliana looked horrified; I shook my head, and she relaxed, voic-
ing a nervous little sigh. "No, he never told me that—but he doesn't
tell me much." A pause. "To answer your question, I can tell she left
you by looking at your face."

"Imagine the same look on Otto's face."

"You know lots of whores, can't you find him someone his own
age?" she asked, almost impatiently. "Someone whose presence in his
tent won't make his leader angry at him?" She brushed past me and
was gone. From then on, whenever I entered the tent to play, she'd
find an excuse to leave.

During that week of limbo, Boniface never invited Gregor to his
compound, nor would he admit Gregor when Gregor sought an audience—which Gregor did loudly every morning. So he tried leading
martial exercises, as he had in the past—an efficient way of dissemi-
nating his opinions (or, in the past, opinions he affected to have).
But here too he was stymied: the men he usually trained with, finally
well-victualed and recently battle-tested, considered themselves on
furlough, and most could not be bothered to leave their tents in the

August heat. His failure to incite his fellows against the lack of forward movement would daily propel Gregor to try a second time at Boniface's, where he would daily be deflected a second time.

On the fourth day that he was refused admittance to the marquis, Gregor stood just outside the perimeter of the pavilion, in full view of Boniface (since the pavilion's sides were always open to allow the breeze) and demanded an audience so loudly that Otto claimed he could hear it a hilltop away exercising the horses. This interrupted my one thousandth recitation of "Kalenda Maya," for which I was grateful. Boniface responded by immediately closing up the sides of the pavilion to keep Gregor's eyes off of him; moments later, when Alexios departed for Blachernae, Boniface went with him.

Feast of St. Sixtus, 6 August

I have recently noted within these pages my attempts to return this pilgrimage to its appointed course. Lest I be accused of lacking detail, following is one particular example of my efforts. I write this in the joyful hope of certain victory from those efforts, the celebration of which I have anticipated tonight by a rare indulgence in spirits, which Otto procured. My penmanship may be unduly influenced by this.

Upon Milord Marquis's abrupt removal to Blachernae, I retreated in agitation to my tent and began to express my dissatisfaction loudly to my brother, in these terms:

"By St. John's head, I'll speak to somebody! Milord Baldwin, His Eminence Conrad, somebody! Or even Milord Dandolo of Venice! We'll spend the winter living in tents and twiddling our thumbs if this keeps up, while Alexios plays dice games and his father plunders churches of their holy relics! There are only two months left to our contract with the Venetians, and we haven't even reached the Holy Land!"

My brother calmed me down, and I sent the Richardim with requests to all three of the men I mentioned above—Milord the count Baldwin, His Eminence Bishop Conrad, and Milord the doge

Dandolo—and not an hour ago, to my amazement, I received answers
back from all three that at some time tomorrow I might take an audience with each. The esteemed Count Baldwin has actually invited me
to approach his private compound first thing in the morning, after mass.

In celebration whereof, my brother Otto and I have been imbibing.
For surely all of these men know me and my business, and their very
willingness to meet with me suggests they are already determined to
press Milord Boniface in a way that I may not. With our imaginations
stimulated by our refreshment, Otto and I have planned out exactly
what I shall say on the morrow. The Briton, who is in an exceptionally
bitter mood this evening, mocks us, but I think his sourness is mostly a
guilty conscience that he himself has stopped trying to accomplish anything, combined with jealousy that he knows tomorrow I will
accomplish much.

46

IN THE MORNING, Gregor went off to have a moment
of private contemplation before meeting with Baldwin of
Flanders. I grumpily took myself to Boniface's tent to offer
my services for the day, mostly because there was nothing else to do,
and I had no instruments of my own now (having destroyed them), so
if I wanted to play, I had to subject myself to those who owned some.

But Boniface wasn't in. His steward took me across the hillside,
to Baldwin of Flanders's compound—the very site where Gregor was
due to arrive for his private meeting. I was told a meeting with Emperor Alexios had been called (phrased in the passive voice, as if the
meeting had spontaneously generated itself). Dandolo of Venice,
who hated sitting through meetings with Alexios, had asked espe-

cially for me to play music in the background, as a palatable distraction. I was flattered.

The bishops, Alexios, Dandolo, Boniface, and some fifty barons—including Baldwin—were assembled, waiting for something. Moments after I'd started playing, Gregor was ushered in, dressed for effect only in his pilgrim's garb of long shirt and sandals.

He gawked when he saw the crowd: this was to be a private audience with Baldwin about moving on quickly to the Holy Land—hence his outfit, which suddenly looked ridiculous in front of all the lords. It looked especially ridiculous in front of Alexios, who was dressed more grandly than usual (with a *new* pair of purple boots) and who fidgeted with his crown in a way that seemed less about nerves and more about wanting to make sure that everybody noticed it.

Apparently they'd been awaiting none other than *Gregor*—for as he arrived, Baldwin gave him a nod, and the meeting was called to order. Gregor was stunned.

"I have a proposition to make," His Majesty announced, to get things started.

"Is it about paying us?" asked Dandolo.

"Yes, in fact, it *is*," Alexios said loftily, as if he had somehow turned an insult back against the doge. "In fact, I shall pay you far more than I originally promised."

"How? In relics?" I called out, as if I were making a stupid joke.

Alexios glared at me. "Shut up," he said. "You don't have leave to speak in my presence. Fazio, if he does that again, have him whipped."

Barons glanced at one another; some suspiciously, some hopefully. "Perhaps you should clarify how you intend to pay what you already owe us before planning to go further into debt on our account," Baldwin said in a reasonable tone. "We have heard rumors that your treasury is empty."

"We have just paid you a large amount of money," Alexios said. "Naturally, our immediate means are limited. But our needs and yours fit well together, so here is my offer: We shall pay the Venetians for another year of service to your campaign, provided you remain with us here in Byzantium through the autumn and winter, until March."

"Absolutely not!" said several voices at once; other voices were less articulate but just as angry. Gregor said nothing but glared at Boniface, who knew he was being glared at and ignored it. So this was the egg the marquis had patiently been hatching. The man had a confounding lack of urgency about reaching his destination. As back in Zara, he must have wanted Gregor present so he could rein him in before the other leaders. I suspected he'd have a harder time of it this time.

Alexios held up his hand in a temperamental gesture, the most imperious thing I'd ever seen him do. "Do not interrupt!" he ordered them. "Listen to the offer before refusing it! From now until March, you will go with us inland to Thrace, to chase our uncle the Usurper further out of power, and to inform and reclaim provinces that might be indifferent to our ascension. And—more important—to demand tribute from those outlying areas as proof that they accept us as their emperor. Such tribute will provide the revenue not only to pay all of you what we still owe but, further, to cover another year of Venetian service. Some of you will stay behind to oversee repairs to the city and to receive payments from my father, Emperor Isaac, on the outstanding debt, as he is able to collect it from the city."

"How will he do that, Your Majesty; by plundering the churches?" demanded Bishop Conrad.

Alexios looked in the direction of the voice without bothering to specify who had spoken. "I do not see how our means matter to you, as we are not yet Roman Catholics. Once we have converted the patriarch, you may make noise on his behalf. Until then, really the Christians of this town are heretics to you, and your care for their holy places seems inappropriate. Would you protest such treatment of a synagogue or mosque?"

"Christian relics are holy no matter who is holding them, Your Majesty," Conrad retorted.

"Holy—and valuable," Alexios retorted in turn.

"Milord, they are *priceless*," Conrad corrected. "As are the reliquaries that house them. The Church will not abide—"

"The Church won't have to abide anything," Alexios interrupted. "We have an entire *empire* from which to extract homage. There will be no further need to strip churches. By March, we will have paid everything we owe you. And then it will be time for you to sail to the Holy Land, and continue your mission with riches in your coffers and additional men at your back. Tell me how this pleases you."

"It does not please us *at all*, milord," boomed the German-accented baritone from the middle of the crowd. "We do not want to add another seven *days* to this stymied campaign, let alone seven *months*. We want to be bound for the Holy Land *now*."

"Gregor—" Boniface said sharply, as murmured agreement rose under the pavilion roof. I idly wondered how much trouble Gregor was about to get himself into. I didn't care what the army did, but I preferred Gregor's outlook to any other, so I decided not to interfere. Better to let him explode than fester under Boniface's repression.

"Your Majesty, we came here with the belief that we were performing an act of heroism by ridding a land of a tyrant, but we know we are not welcome here," Gregor continued. "Spending an entire winter in our tents as unwanted guests of Byzantium has *nothing* to do with our true mission, or our crusading vows."

"Gregor," Boniface said again and stood up. "We have no choice." He seemed about to begin a soliloquy, the public delivery of which no doubt accounted for his son-in-law's presence at this summit—but Gregor did not give him the chance.

"Your Lordship!" Gregor shouted. Men, even those who'd voiced their agreement, moved away from him with wary looks. "We are in the same position! Again! For the third time! You said this about the diversion to Zara, *and* about the diversion to Byzantium, and now you say it about *loitering* here for seven *months*! Why is there *never* a choice? How can God be testing us so sorely that he requires us to do these shameful things? Why can we not contemplate instead that this is God expressing his displeasure at what we've done—especially when *the pope himself* voices the same displeasure?" He looked around the room, eyes wild. "Do you all realize the pope forbade any attack on Byzantium?"

He believed me! At last, he believed me!

"For the third time," Boniface said stonily. "Yes, Gregor, for the third time—there is no alternative. Tell me how we can get the army to Jerusalem by the end of next month, when the Venetian contract will end. Tell me how I may lead such a campaign." Again he assumed the attitude of a man about to hold forth in a suasive manner to an underling—again, Gregor interfered by actually responding to him.

"Easily. Just go to the Holy Land. Go to Egypt, as planned. God will be on our side, and we will take so much booty there, we can at that time pay the Venetians for their continued service."

"The Venetians should take that on faith?" Boniface asked sarcastically.

"It's a *pilgrimage*, milord!" Gregor said with exasperation. "*Everything* is taken on faith! That is the *meaning* of a pilgrimage! Anyhow," he added quickly, "you're already taking it on faith that Emperor Alexios will provide! Between God and Alexios, I do not see why Alexios should be the more trusted."

I liked that retort; Alexios did not. "How dare you!" he cried.

"Young Gregor has just hit the very reason we must *stay*," said Dandolo. "Alexios does not inspire trust—not in us or in his subjects."

"You will rescind that statement!" snapped Alexios.

The doge's tone was withering. "No, I won't. If we leave now, you will be toppled before our sails are out of the harbor—"

"That's not true!" Alexios shouted.

"That's not our *concern*!" Gregor corrected.

"Yes, it is!" countered Dandolo. "Because if that happens, God alone knows what will happen to the Venetians and other Latins living here. God alone knows what will happen to the trading relationships I have labored so hard to stabilize these past decades, and all of the concessions I've won for Venice with this victory. We took on the responsibility of changing the leadership—and now it is our responsibility to see that the new leadership is stable and safe, or we ourselves, and those we're responsible for, will suffer for it."

"We never vowed to take on so much!" Gregor said angrily. "We said we'd *place* him on the throne, milord, we never said we'd *steward* him there indefinitely. That is far beyond the scope of our treaty."

"Boy," the doge said, with unusual patience, "if we do not do it, we destroy ourselves. The Greeks expelled the Venetian residents here some thirty years ago. In one single day—the twelfth of March, Anno Domini 1171—every Venetian in the Byzantine Empire was arrested and all their goods confiscated. Some were never released. The Byzantines turned on other foreigners a decade after that. When things get very bad here, it is easier for the populace to blame foreigners than to blame their own rulers—and it's easier for the rulers to blame the foreigners too. I am responsible for the well-being of the Venetians within these walls, and I cannot leave until I believe that things are stable. The best sign of stability, to me, is a leader capable of honoring his promises in a manner that does not provoke his people to insurrection." He turned his blind face in the direction of Alexios's chair. "That puts responsibility on you, *royal child*," he said tersely. "We shall have to see what you are made of. Lead the men to Thrace, if you are able. If you are not able, do not forget that we are waiting here beside your city, more than ready to pick up the pieces of your empire and put them back together ourselves. You have already seen what we are capable of." Almost in a fatherly tone to Gregor, he concluded, "We must stay through the winter. We must provide His Majesty with soldiers to stabilize his rule. The local forces cannot do it, and the Varangian Guard is only large enough to guard the city, not the entire empire."

"Agreed," said Boniface, and from the grim expressions on the other leaders' faces, it was clear that no argument would be tolerated.

Especially not from Gregor, who looked as if steam might start shooting out of his nostrils.

Feast of St. Laurence, 10 August

An hour after the shameful meeting with Emperor Alexios, I found myself in my father-in-law's tent, staring at him in disbelief at the newest outrage he'd just spoken.

"You're leaving me behind?" I echoed. Otto stood beside me, equally amazed.

"You really think I can allow you within ten leagues of Alexios? He believes that I'm having you whipped for insubordination. He wanted to watch it personally. You have me to thank for talking him out of that," he responded.

I ground my teeth and said, very sore, "Have I not proven that I do what is demanded of me? I am one of the best soldiers in the army, milord, and you will need your best soldiers for the task before you. You do this to insult me, but you harm yourself in making the insult."

"It's not an insult, it's a strategy," Milord Boniface said, in a gentler voice, and seemed truly to want to make peace with me. "Of all my knights, you are most in the public eye. I won't drag you along on a mission that is a revolting necessity to you, as I gain nothing from your fellow soldiers sensing your revulsion, and I suffer mightily for Alexios knowing your revulsion. Instead you will accomplish something for me that you, the renowned Gregor of Mainz and my son-in-law, are in a unique position to do: You will keep peace here in the city while we are away. This helps me and should please you. I do not bother trying to please many members of this army, Gregor, especially those I've saved from a well-deserved flogging, so I suggest you adopt a more reasonable demeanor with me."

I took a deep breath and tried to adopt a more reasonable demeanor. I failed.

Milord Boniface continued thus: "There is, clearly, a growing ten-

sion between the city and the army. Our women are afraid to go over there and even the soldiers now hesitate. As Milord Dandolo insisted, we cannot leave until the treaty has been fulfilled in a climate of stability and peace. I would have you do whatever is necessary or possible to foster such a relationship between the citizenry and the soldiers who remain here."

Said I: "The best thing would be to coax Isaac to return the relic of the Virgin."

Said Boniface: "Then do so."

This surprised me. I asked if he were serious. He said he was, and said further:"Go to Isaac—you still have my seal—and tell him it is my wish that the relic be restored to the church."

I asked, "What if he won't do it?" for it seemed to me that great man would not listen to a mere deputy like myself.

"Then the shame is on him, not on us. Make your plea very publicly; make sure the Greeks know you have asked this of him." And with a smile at me: "You are my son, after all; I cannot imagine a better person to stay behind to represent me and, by extension, my army."

"Milord Dandolo is staying behind," I said immediately.

"Dandolo represents the Venetians, not the army. He and the other Venetians are still under excommunication from Zara and will have nothing to do with the army unless it's unavoidable. He will hardly set foot off his galley. He does not speak for me."

"Baldwin of Flanders is staying behind," I said. I was unwilling to present myself to the emperor if there were others of higher rank more equal to the task. "He is a count, and your immediate subordinate. He represents the army far better than I could."

"Baldwin of Flanders is a very good man," agreed Milord Boniface. "However, Baldwin is suspect in the eyes of the Greeks because he led the charge at Blachernae. You did nothing on the field that day, so you are known only by stories of your other exploits, all of which sound very good to Greek ears—very Christian, very peaceful."

I was perplexed by this assertion and asked him what he meant.

To which he replied: "Your and Simon of Montfort's ludicrous attempt to spare the Zarans? They like that. Your being the first man during the scuffle with the Venetians, in Zara, to drop your arms and embrace a peace? They like that too. Your willingness to break up the army on Corfu to avoid coming here at all?"

"How would the Greeks know these things about me, milord?" I asked, amazed.

Boniface shrugged. "Word gets around." (Later the Briton insisted Boniface himself made sure such words got around.) "The important thing, my son, is that you are already their unlikely folk hero. You will stay behind and help the city love us, and by extension love Alexios, whom they associate with us. Then when spring comes, it will be safe for us to leave for the Holy Land. And as for you, Otto," he said, without pausing, shifting his gaze to my brother, "it is a mutual benefit for you to come with me. You are not known as a peacemaker, so keeping you here with Gregor accomplishes nothing. On the other hand, you're an excellent soldier, and famous at the moment for surviving capture. It's good morale to have famous knights on the front lines; their exploits get exaggerated in a manner that strikes fear into the hearts of enemies."

Now I must mark here that my brother is not yet belted, and not for lacking virtue or valiance. His demeanor made me rightly proud of him:

"I'm not a knight, milord," said Otto.

Said Milord Boniface: "So I've been told. It is high time you were knighted."

"I made a vow to St. George that I would not be knighted until we were within the walls of Jerusalem itself, as victors," said Otto.

"If you are knighted now, as well as being of greater use to the army, you will get a greater share of the spoils of victory," Milord Boniface said. "You now receive a sergeant's share, which we both know is far below what you deserve."

I know my brother well; it would be a lie to say he was not sorely tempted by this. But: "I am deeply honored by the offer, milord, but

I took a solemn vow," he said. "I am a man of my word. So I thank you, gracious lord, but I must decline."

Milord Boniface looked displeased. "I have never in my life before this had to convince somebody to accept knighthood," he said with mild exasperation.

Said Otto: "Neither before, nor now, milord, for you won't convince me."

"If you will let yourself be knighted, you'll have Liliana back," Milord Boniface said. I must admit once again that, knowing Otto as I do, it would be a lie to pretend he was not sorely tempted by this too.

But he said, in a voice of great politeness: "That reeks of bribery, milord. Even if I'd been willing to accept knighthood, I would now have to reject it, as that offer is insulting both to her and to me. I will go with you if you order it, but only as a sergeant."

Milord Boniface blinked in surprise. So did I. So did the Briton, when I told him this story an hour later. We were both proud of Otto, and we both told him so. I am sure that Liliana, had she heard it, would have blushed with pride.

A FEW DAYS LATER, in the middle of August, Alexios rode out with Boniface and the vast majority of infantry and cavalry. Otto of Frankfurt, whose warrior star was rising, had the honor of riding with Boniface's guard. The tent—indeed, our whole section of the camp, in long-term residence now on the hill around Galata Tower—was immediately quieter, calmer, and duller without Otto's company.

I sought out Liliana and learned she'd accompanied Boniface. She had been given her very own veiled litter, overflowing with silks, with furs, with jewelry. Otto would know exactly where she was, but he'd never be able to actually get near her. I knew how that felt—daily I stared at Jamila's temporary new home from across the harbor.

Gregor, the pragmatic German, adjusted himself to his new role with resigned determination, wanting to excel at his assignment. Immediately he went to speak to Emperor Isaac, to request His Majesty return the relic of the Virgin's robe to the church from whence it had been taken. Isaac—to everyone's astonishment—agreed to his request, and already by the next day, songs in Greek praising the righteous heart of Gregor of Mainz began to float about the city. Heartened, Gregor then petitioned Count Baldwin to host camp feasts to which could be invited the influential members of Byzantine society. I found this charmingly naive of him; it came to nothing. As Baldwin pointed out, the army had no money for staples, much less a feast—that was why we were stuck here in the first place. If Gregor wanted to win over the people of the city, he'd have to find another way.

Unfortunately, he found one. Or rather, it found him—and me.

47

IT WAS DRY as bone now, but those who knew warned that winters were wet here. So all the lords who had stayed behind, and the knights who could afford it, built simple green wood structures, optimistically called cabins, in place of their tents. The raising required the labor of everyone in camp—even me, once Gregor pressed me into service. I was reminded of the peculiar little skills that Wulfstan had made sure I'd mastered: tying of ropes and using of pulleys, balancing on precarious perches while using heavy tools. I was, to my surprise, genuinely helpful putting up our roof and the roofs of several of our neighbors, but I took no pleasure in my helpfulness. When I look back on this period, I am belatedly humbled that Gregor didn't throw me out on my arse. I must have made appallingly unpleasant company.

A few mornings after the bulk of the army left with Boniface and Alexios, we awoke to the smell of smoke and the traumatized cries of women and children in an Italian dialect. The older Richard had already dressed and gone out to investigate. He returned with disturbing news: there had been a violent anti-Latin riot in the city the night before; several hundred expatriate Genoese had seen their homes go up in smoke, and they'd fled with their families here to the crusader camp for safety.

The fire was less than half the size of the one that had claimed the Jewish settlement of Pera, a tenth the size of the one that had devoured the nobles' homes near Blachernae. But it was to have consequences that dwarfed both those infernos together.

Because the following night, the nineteenth of August, a number of these homeless refugees got roaring drunk and rowed back across the harbor with a few unidentified pilgrims (the Franks blamed the Venetians; the Venetians blamed the Franks). In a somewhat off-point act of vengeance, they set on fire Constantinople's only mosque, perched small and unprotected on a thin protrusion of land between the city walls and the harbor near the Venetian Quarter. They were finally smiting infidels!

This small act of vandalism led to unprecedented devastation.

For the fire leapt over the wall around the mosque and engulfed the little wooden houses near it, which fueled it to acts of greater ambition. By the time the sun rose, a thousand homes were ashes and the fire was growing. From the army camp, in the dawn light, Gregor and I watched huge, menacing clouds of grey and black smoke move with alarming speed deep into the center of Constantinople. Latin traders and their families rushed out of the harbor gates and waved frantically at us across the Golden Horn.

"Jamila's somewhere in that fire," I said, horrified. "I have to get her out." I began elbowing my way through the crowd of spectators to head down the hill.

Gregor grabbed my arm to hold me back. He pointed to where

the Venetians were already casting off their longboats from the main galleys. "Let them take care of it, they know what they're doing. We'll have enough to do when the victims arrive here."

Across the harbor, some of the besieged stole or commandeered ferries or rafts and began to row over toward us. Within an hour there were thousands of Venetians, Pisans, Genoese, and Amalfians crowded at the harbor, waving their arms and screaming in terror across the water to the army, shoving one another to get closer to the landing sites.

From where we perched, we could hear the sounds of buildings creaking and collapsing, small explosions. We could make out dozens of squiggling lines of movement—brigades, thousands of citizens running about frantically with buckets and oiled sacks of water. Nothing quenched the flames. Orange tongues of fire darted above the city walls as the inferno worked its way straight across the center of the peninsula toward the Sea of Marmara, cutting a swath of destruction through the lower section of the city, burning half of the Latin Quarter and probably half of the poorer Greek homes too—it consumed an entire hillock in the densest part of town and moved on southward, where it would range until it literally ran out of city to burn: a gruesomely seductive spectacle. The fire might have spread to the eastern tip, except the stone buildings of the imperial properties—the Hippodrome, the Great Palace of Bukoleon where blind, demented Emperor Isaac lurked, and the Church of Holy Wisdom—turned it back.

For three days that fire raged out of control as people streamed into our camp. There were thousands and thousands of refugees, all of them Latins by race but many completely assimilated into Greek life. They were packed into extra tents, given winter blankets to make shelters; some huddled around the edges of the army camp, or even squatted near the ruins of the burned-out Jewish settlement, although most were too superstitious to go through its iron gates into heathen territory. Few were hurt, but many were hungry, and all were frightened and angry. They weren't all homeless; the fire had spared half the Latin sector. But they knew they'd be persecuted for this destruction done to the city by their fellow Latins. Desperate to be sheltered by the army, they were well-behaved and obedient; within a day, extra latrines had been dug and foraging parties set up to secure food enough for all of them. Those who'd brought money or tradable goods were sent for food from the closest villages—and from Emperor Isaac, who was quick to double the army's rations in order to minimize pillaging.

Gregor and I helped the settling in of all these frightened people. Gregor in particular was in his element, overseeing and protecting the downtrodden, all of his golden-boy energy for several days in full force, bent wholly toward Good Samaritanism. I took occasional vacations from that role and roamed the throngs of strangers frantically seeking one familiar face.

The day after the flames stopped, I took a break from drawing water for the new refugees. My fingers were stiff and wrapped with bandages to protect a sprouting of blisters. I'd pulled muscles in both arms. Now I was kneeling outside the hut, gingerly trying to teach the younger Richard how to juggle hardwood blocks. Seeing a look of amazement on the boy's face, I turned to follow his gaze and dropped the blocks.

In tow behind Jamila was a small crowd: Samuel and a dozen others, from children to an old man. I leapt up. My impulse was to embrace her, but I checked it.

"Jamila," I said stupidly. Her hair escaped raggedly from beneath her veil; her face was smeared with sooty grime. Staring at her, I told Richard to get Gregor. She did not quite look at me.

"Will you take us in?" Samuel asked, pushing ahead of her, equally sooty. "Now that you have made us refugees twice over?"

48

GREGOR ARRIVED BREATHLESSLY a few moments later. He was pleased to see Jamila but looked leery of her entourage, especially Samuel. He finally decided, with the concerned frown of an older brother (although Samuel was the elder by a decade), "I cannot promise your safety if you are known to be Jews, but you're welcome to stay as long as you are willing to pose as Gentiles—which would include participating in all masses and suppressing your own religious rituals."

Samuel was displeased about this caveat but accepted it; hundreds of other Jews, scattered amidst these refugees, were doing likewise. We reerected Gregor's tent in a small gap between our little cabin and a neighboring German knight's, and the Jews crowded into it to set up sleeping mats, which Jamila had made sure came with them.

I was ecstatic she'd been restored to me, but she had not spoken a word, and made eye contact with neither Gregor nor me. There was no room for an extra body in the tent; Gregor, myself, and the younger Richard all hovered in the doorway watching the Hebrews settle in. Jamila coughed a dry cough, winced slightly, and licked her lips once; even as Samuel opened his mouth to ask for water, I was off with an empty bucket, desperate to be useful. But when I returned, eagerly playing Aquarius, Jamila was not there. Samuel informed me tersely that she and Gregor were speaking alone in the cabin.

I stepped out of the stifling tent, into the almost-as-stifling air, and paused at the door to the cabin.

". . . don't seem yourself," Gregor was saying within, sounding awkward.

"On the contrary, I am very much myself," I heard her reply promptly. "I would hardly say you knew me under circumstances where I might be my real self."

"I would hardly say *these* are circumstances where you might be your real self."

There was a pause, as if she were taken aback by the retort. "How do I not seem myself?" she asked at last.

"You seem squelched. When we've seen you in the company of certain others—"

"Samuel," she clarified. "This is only the second time you've seen me in his company, sir."

"All right, yes, Samuel. Although I suppose I'm wrong. You are no doubt now in company equal to your intellect, and admittedly none of us are scholars worthy of your—"

"Samuel is unused to such discourse with a woman," she said; through the door, I imagined I could hear bitterness in her voice. "I had more satisfaction debating Bishop Conrad on the *Venus*. It is a small price to pay. Sir, I know that Christians face east to pray, but here the Holy Land is more to the south, if you want to adjust your altar—"

"I thank you, but do not change the subject. It occurs to me that you are only in your present circumstances because of happenstance—"

"I would not call it happenstance, I'd call it the Frankish army," she replied. "Three times over—the diversion to the city, burning Pera, and now this anger caused by the occupation. *You* are responsible for my present circumstances, sir. I wouldn't call it happenstance at all."

Another pause, as if he were the one now taken aback. "How can I help you?"

"You're doing a lot, letting us stay here. We thank you."

"*You. Jamila,*" he clarified. "How can I help you not to be . . . squelched?"

Another pause. "You can't," she said. She stepped to the door and threw it open so hard it smacked me in the nose. "Stop lurking and come inside," she said.

Embarrassed, I entered, holding the bucket out before me, my free hand rubbing my nose.

"Forever taking care of me," Jamila said warmly, suddenly her old self. She took the bucket from me and gulped down several mouthfuls. "Thank you," she said, lowering it to her hip. "You need a haircut or you're going to look like a Greek soon. I have a message for you from Eyebrow. That's the real reason we've come over here."

"Who?" Gregor asked, as I, with a double take, said, "What?"

Jamila took another sip, then set the bucket down. "A fellow called Mourtzouphlos was Otto's cell mate in Blachernae," she explained to Gregor. "He was released, at our urging, when the Usurper fled, and he's now a minor official in the imperial court. Very minor, but he quite prefers it to prison. He's had scouts looking for us both since the morning after the coronation, and they found me the day the fire broke out. He wanted me to give the Madman of Genoa a message. That's why we came. There were Greeks we might have stayed with in the city, but Samuel agreed that I should get this message to you, and fleeing the fire was a good excuse for coming over here."

"What are you talking about?" I demanded, still fidgeting with my nose to make sure it wasn't broken.

"It's not broken," Jamila said. "It isn't even bleeding." She glanced toward the door; I pushed it closed. She gestured the two of us to move closer to her and whispered. "Isaac's running out of easy sources of gold and silver to refill the treasury. He's taken money from most of the nobility, and he's already plundered many of the churches for altarpieces and decorations. Obviously the nobles have more money, but they're very good at hiding it. Mourtzouphlos is afraid that Emperor Isaac will start taking the holy reliquaries, and he wants your assistance to prevent that, for everybody's sake."

"He already started taking them," Gregor said. "There was a riot over that. At my request, Isaac returned what he'd taken. He knows better now."

"Mourtzouphlos is afraid it's only a matter of time before it happens again."

I grimaced. "Well, the containers *are* gold and silver, with pretty rocks on them, but they're hardly—"

"They have meaning that is worth more to the soul of the city than the value of the gold and jewels combined," Jamila said impatiently. "Stanpoli without its relics would be like . . ." She shrugged, unable to think of a worthy simile. "It would be just another city."

Gregor nodded, arms crossed over his chest, looking grim. "The relics have meaning to the pilgrims too. When we were seeing the city in July, I felt the sharpest covetousness I've ever known, merely being in their presence. They have a value infinitely greater than could ever be assayed by material measure. But given a chance, the army would take their material measure."

"But what does Mourtzouphlos want from *me?*" I asked.

"That is something he'll explain in person," Jamila said. "He asks you and me to meet him in a week, at the monastery of John of Studious, in the western corner of the city by the Golden Gate. There is a holy mass there, attended by Emperor Isaac, on the feast day of the beheading of John the Baptist."

"So you'll be staying here right next to us, in the extra tent, for the next week?" I asked; it was of infinitely more significance than relics or even a reunion with Mourtzouphlos. "All the time?"

The look Jamila gave me made me feel that I was approximately seven years old.

"I meant to say, of course I'll help," I corrected myself hurriedly.

"John the Baptist is my family saint," Gregor said, which struck me as suspiciously irrelevant—until he continued, "So I shall attend as well."

49

IT WAS A MORNING'S JOURNEY to the far western reaches of the city; Mourtzouphlos sent Ionnis as a guide. Jamila came, which delighted me; and Samuel didn't, which delighted me even more. Samuel was a physician, as his brother had been. He and Jamila had spent much of the past week attending to refugees who'd been wounded, either in the fire itself or in the exodus to escape it. I made myself as useful as I could—which wasn't very useful, compared with either of them, but children preferred me to Samuel, and I felt that proved something good about me.

I had never been within a walled enclosure so enormous one could ride for an hour and not see the end of it; even now, two months after I'd first seen the size of the city, its vastness was almost incomprehensible to me, like a story I'd invent for children back home.

Much of our trip took us straight through the rubble, all that remained of what the fire had destroyed. The burned smells lingered thickly in the air. Between this fire and the one near Blachernae during the battle, nearly a quarter of the city's land was scorched—and nearly half the houses. Families had swept up the ashes, the ruins of their lives, and spread mats for sleeping where their homes had been. It would have been a miserable sight to see even a village living so, but street after street after street of it, in every direction, up and down a hill, up and down another, up and down a third . . . it was appalling, and Ionnis made it worse by pointing out the sooty foundations of once beautiful, now extinct structures. It was a huge relief to finally move beyond the fire's scar, into a wooded area in the west, where gardens and orchards and farms and the odd outlying home had been spared.

Here, where all was still peaceful and sylvan in the heat, we arrived finally at a large, walled monastic community, with a flourishing village around it. Many of the people bustling about the small central square whispering political gossip were probably refugees from the fire. Ionnis delivered us to a smiling Mourtzouphlos in the monastery's courtyard, then disappeared into the church to stand in the back with the commoners.

I've never been much interested in or impressed by ceremony, so forgive my lack of detail about the Feast of the Beheading of St. John the Baptist. I'd been under the impression that His Majesty would ritually reenact the beheading, which I was looking forward to; I felt cheated when that turned out not to be the case at all. There was an elaborate holy mass, in which things were done behind a large golden screen. This screen featured molded images of Jesus's life, of his pretty mother, and of John the Baptist, sporting angel wings. Following that, the holy relic was brought out for Isaac to feel—he could not see it, being blind—and then the congregation stood in a long line to view the relic up close, too. We had beside us jovial Mourtzouphlos, who threw around his weight as a minor member of the imperial train, and thus we were given a place near the front of the line. We waited perhaps as long as it would take to string a fiddle before we were close enough to the relic to nearly touch it.

The relic was larger than many, literally the entire top of a skull. The reliquary covering it was elaborate; when I really looked at it, I was amazed by the detail of the work, despite the usual gaudy Byzantine jewelry: gold, with large globs of gemstones on it. One large carmeline glob was centered near the top, circled by turquoise and pearls, with a pink ruby and an emerald below. The underlying gold was the most interesting part: there was text on it, in Greek letters raised right out of the skullcap. Impressed despite myself, I glanced up toward Gregor, intending to admit that I could see the attraction. I was stopped from speaking by the extraordinary expression on his face.

Gregor believed this was the actual skull of the actual John, the actual Baptist. I was prepared to believe this was a possibility, but it did not hold me in thrall. There was a look of wonderment in his eyes, a solemnity upon his face, that even for him was extreme. He was enraptured. The world could have disintegrated around him, and he would not have minded, now that he had seen *this*. I've never experienced that feeling, but seeing it on the face of a man I respected and knew well, I could not doubt the profundity, the sincerity, of . . . *it*. I was not changed by seeing the relic. Gregor was. When we moved away from it, he radiated a silent, profound contentment that I could only remember feeling immediately after making love to a woman I adored. I envied him. The diversion from the pilgrimage, Boniface's multihued perfidy, the tragedy of the fire—none of this had a hold on him now. He continued to radiate contentment through the rest of the mass. I was envious, although I did not know of what.

With a final blessing by the patriarch, the ceremony was finished, and a processional removed us from the church. A few pious stragglers lingered just outside the door, in the walled-in front yard of the monastic grounds. Stragglers such as, for example, one slight Briton, one bushy-eyebrowed redhead and his one unsmiling acolyte, one Titan-size German pilgrim, and a veiled Jewess passing as a Christian widow.

When Ionnis explained that the large, blond stranger was actually here with us, Mourtzouphlos looked suspiciously at Gregor and asked, in Greek, who he was.

"This is Otto of Frankfurt's brother," I said in French.

"Another German? What does he do here?"

"I am a friend," Gregor said.

"Of whom?" asked Mourtzouphlos.

"Of the city," said Gregor.

Mourtzouphlos considered him a moment, then finally nodded, almost as if to himself. "You are called what?" he prompted.

"Gregor of Mainz."

Mourtzouphlos's eyes widened; he had heard the name, as most of the city had by now. But the effect on Mourtzouphlos was unexpected. "Eh! You are that damned marquis's son-in-law!" He spat at Gregor's feet.

Gregor tensed, but he was too disciplined a soldier to respond out of anger. Ionnis said something quickly in Greek; I recognized phrases like "in dispute with . . . wants to fix . . . relic of the Virgin's robe."

"That is different! Then you will join us," Mourtzouphlos announced, instantly converted. "Sorry about the spitting, eh? But I blame Boniface for all of this nonsense."

"What nonsense?" Gregor asked, reflexively defensive.

"Emperors are weak and stupid men, they almost never do what is attributed to them, it is their handlers who are nefarious, and we all know Boniface is Alexios's handler," Mourtzouphlos announced. And then, without a pause, he was all smiles again. "How is my friend Otto? Did he get his woman back?" He glanced at Jamila, glanced at me, and winked meaningfully: I see you got *yours* back!

"Why did you summon us?" Gregor demanded.

"I didn't summon *you*," Mourtzouphlos said, with playful, familiar sarcasm, as if they were old chums. There was no way to judge his status relative to Gregor's, but since this was his city, and his summoning, he wasn't going to grovel. "But I will talk to you anyhow, as I said. My Emperor Isaac is badly counseled. He's plundering the churches, to pay the army what stupid Alexios promised to pay."

Gregor shook his head. "He *was* plundering them. That has stopped now"—he said and, bristling from being spat at, emphasized—"because of *my* intervention."

"Really?" Mourtzouphlos asked sarcastically. "Allow me to tell you otherwise. When he leaves, Isaac will take with him the very reliquary we were just admiring."

Gregor's brow creased. "What?"

"Oh, yes," Mourtzouphlos said, with an expansive shrug. "I heard him give the order to his men before we left Bukoleon Palace. In fact, I heard him decide to do it many days ago, which is why I set about to find this little vagabond, so he could stop it."

"But . . ." Gregor objected. "I petitioned him to return the other relic, the Virgin's robe, and he did so without a fuss."

Mourtzouphlos shrugged again. "He's thought better of it since then. If he's not stopped, there'll be nothing left of value in any house of worship in the city. He's already taking the decorations, and now he intends to take the relics. So I want to stop him."

"How?" asked Gregor.

Mourtzouphlos shrugged, a gesture I was starting to think of as the essence of Greek (or at least, Mourtzouphlean) self-expression. "We can't *talk* him out of taking all the reliquaries, or *threaten* him, so obviously, we have to *hide* them all, so he cannot *find* them to *abscond* with them."

Gregor and I exchanged wide-eyed looks; we had not expected such a ridiculous proposition. Jamila raised her brows in silence.

Gregor spoke first. "It is my assignment to prevent any activity that would provoke further outrage between the Greeks and Latins," he said. "I would not see holy places plundered, but if Isaac cannot pay us—"

"But he can," said Mourtzouphlos. "He can find the money another way."

"How?" I asked. "By taxing all the citizens beyond reason?"

"Oh, no, that takes too long," Mourtzouphlos said dismissively. "No, he'll plunder the nobles first. One thorough purloin of a noble's treasury will give him as much as months of taxation on the merchants."

"Isn't *yours* a noble's treasury?" I asked. "Won't *you* be plundered?"

Mourtzouphlos grimaced, and shrugged. "I survived years of imprisonment, and I can survive my coffers being emptied. It is less grievous than my *city* being emptied. My personal material loss is less tragic than the loss of the city's spiritual wealth. I love Stanpoli with my *soul*," he said, thumping his expansive chest. "All its people love it so. Eh, you ask any of them if they would rather lose their own right eye or the wonders of Stanpoli, and although half of them never go to church, they'll pluck out their eye and offer it to you. This is the greatest city in the world, and we must keep it that way. Isaac looks at the relics and sees only commodities; I see the past and the future of Byzantium."

Gregor, still in the haze of contentment from viewing the skull of his favorite dead mortal, was moved by this. He frowned thoughtfully. He was actually considering Mourtzouphlos's request. "So you are saying all the city's reliquaries would be *hidden* somewhere, until the debt has been paid, and then they'd be returned to their churches?" Mourtzouphlos nodded. "Where will they be hidden?" Gregor asked. "And how?"

Before Mourtzouphlos could reply, there was a wail from within the building, and an enraged older man, humbly dressed but dignified, walked very fast out of the church, both hands raised before him as if he were about to strangle an invisible opponent. It took me a moment to realize that he was chasing somebody who had exited the church before him without attracting our attention: one of Emperor Isaac's Varangian Guard, who held a red satchel. The guard was a head taller than his elderly accoster and simply ignored him. Without pausing or glancing to either side, the Varangian carried his small burden out the front gate of the courtyard, where he was joined by four others who surrounded him protectively; they disappeared. The older man kept up a sharp diatribe in very precise Greek, so clearly enunciated despite his anger that I could understand about every fifth word, most of which were curses.

Jamila, Ionnis, and Mourtzouphlos, understanding all of it, exchanged grim looks. Once the Varangians had disappeared, the elderly fellow reined in his verbal diatribe and turned, muttering to himself, back in to the courtyard. Where he saw Gregor.

Gregor, blond, short-haired, and wearing the cross on his back, was obviously a member of the invading army, even though he wore neither mail nor sword within the churchyard. Furious hatred animated the old man's dignified features, and he resumed his ghost-strangling deportment as he crossed quickly back toward us, then began haranguing Gregor in Greek so foul even Mourtzouphlos blushed. Gregor stood there staring down at him in bemused discomfort, until Mourtzouphlos interjected something, got the man's attention, and then, with a calming hand on the man's arm, led him away, speaking in soothing, compassionate tones.

"What in the name of Abel was that all about?" Gregor asked.

"That was the head of John the Baptist that the guard was confiscating," Jamila whispered. "Emperor Isaac has taken it. The old man is angry at Isaac, but he is angrier *by far* at the army whose demands for payment have led Isaac to take it."

Gregor looked miserable. "That army restored his anointed emperor," he objected dutifully. "That deserves reward."

"Isaac's restoration matters more to Isaac than it does to the old man," Ionnis interjected. "He cares more about the relic than about the emperor. Understand me? He has lived through maybe seven emperors, and he only ever sees them when they come here to venerate the relic, once a year. But the relic itself, its proximity benefits him every day."

Mourtzouphlos, having calmed the elder, returned to us. He said nothing.

"What will happen to that relic now?" Gregor asked.

Mourtzouphlos shrugged with bitter resignation. "It will probably go with your accursed Boniface back to Lombardy, and you can worship it at his court." He gave Gregor a piercing look. "Doesn't that make you feel better about the theft? That you prosper by it?" He patted the back of his hand against Gregor's chest, with the St. John's wort emblazoned on the shirt. "You seem attached to this particular saint."

"I am, but I will not prosper by any theft," Gregor said. "In fact, I'll do all I can to see the relic returned. I was successful last time, I should be successful now. And I will help you protect the rest of the relics too. But where will you hide them? And *how?*"

Mourtzouphlos gestured grandly to me. "This is why I summon the Madman. I cannot think of how to do it myself. I know only that it must be done. I have access to manpower, and to a little money, if necessary, to finance a plan. But this crazy foreigner"—here he grinned at me—"he is clever, and he is lucky. *He* will think of something."

I opened my mouth to speak. Gregor gestured me to wait. "If we do this, the army must get credit for it too," he said to Mourtzouphlos. "When the relics are taken out of hiding, you must announce to all the grateful citizens of the city that this plan was the brainchild of Greeks and Latins working together—not just any Latins but specifically members of the pilgrim army, who have no desire to bring any harm to this city."

"I'm not the pilgrim army," I objected. Gregor looked at me sternly. "Oh, all right," I said. I glanced at Jamila. "What exactly do you Israelites get out of this?"

"We have already discussed that," Mourtzouphlos said.

"The Jews will be protected," Jamila said. "The treasures of the Pera synagogue will be hidden with the relics, safe from Isaac's clutches, until the imperial debt is paid by other means. The Jews are always the first ones plundered. Samuel speaks for the community, and he endorses my participation in whatever is to be undertaken."

"So the only question that remains," Mourtzouphlos said, looking hopefully toward me, "what *is* to be undertaken?"

"Oh, that's obvious," I said. "Does anybody have a boat?"

It took more than a month to prepare it—the greatest beneficent heist in the history of Christendom. Should I live to be one hundred, and my deeds become immortalized in song, please know that there is nothing in my life of which I'm prouder than the preemptive abduction of those relics.

Even though it all went horribly wrong.

50

WE COMMUNICATED FURTIVELY, through Greek messages in Roman script, or French messages in Greek script. Jamila and I would ferry over to the city and meet Mourtzouphlos, or Ionnis, on the edge of the burned area, or behind Hagia Sophia, or at the entrance of the Hippodrome. I spent a fortnight learning what I needed to, and then nearly three weeks preparing all the others involved. During that month, Emperor Isaac continued to enrage the pious of the city by further stripping the churches of their gold and silver decorations. He would not receive Gregor, or respond to Gregor's request to return the head of John the Baptist to its church. That removal had set off citywide riots, with most of the anger aimed at resident Latins; there were several deaths. Isaac would not return the relic, but he did not, for now, try to confiscate another one; the more Latins fled in terror to the army camp, the larger the army camp became—and it was Isaac's responsibility to feed that camp. This made him wary of inflaming anti-immigrant sentiment within the city.

Gregor, during this month of preparation, went daily as a pilgrim to the holy places of worship around the city; he befriended priests and novices, although they spoke no language in common. With his reputation for having reclaimed the Virgin's relic for its church, Boniface's seal to give him secular prestige, and his own obvious piety resonating from him like spiritual tintinnabulation, he learned every major church's most beloved, valued relics, and he promised every priest and monk he met, in elaborate sign language, that he would never let Emperor Isaac remove them. Half the clergymen of Constantinople wanted to adopt him within an hour of meeting him. His old golden glow began to shimmer through again: this was not the crusade he had set out to accomplish, but he was still safeguarding the veneration of the Christ.

On his third day out, his timing was fortuitous and he fended off a Varangian guard who had come on a raid to abscond with the hem of the robe of St. Andrew from one of the several hilltop monasteries.

Gregor was displeased to learn that evening that the Varangian was actually one of Mourtzouphlos's servants in a stolen uniform—my idea. But the monastery he'd defended sang his praises widely, as I'd hoped. His reputation preceded him to his next clutch of churches. I was so pleased, I wanted to send a Varangian daily for him to fend off after that, but Jamila counseled caution, and so we staged only a mock attack once again.

It was enough to give him exactly the reputation that was required, however. Ten days before our actual escapade, he shifted tactic and returned to each church he had visited, this time with Mourtzouphlos and Ionnis (who seemed to know every cleric in every church), and they shared our secret intentions with the clergy Gregor had already befriended. Mourtzouphlos had doubted this part of the plan would work; he was sure the Orthodox clergy would never trust a Catholic, but Gregor's genuine piety combined with Mourtzouphlos's hearty patriotism proved a potent mix.

Jamila and I were together for hours every day, even through the Jewish high holidays (Samuel taxed Gregor's patience in his attempts to honor Yahweh in stealth within the tent). She and I saw to the technical details of the plan: measuring distances, calculating probable bribes, collecting supplies (lamp oil, rope, extra wicks), estimating the needed manpower, guessing how much bulk we'd have to hide, deciding what to wrap things in, trying to anticipate every hitch and plan against it. Unsurprisingly, Jamila was more practical than I was and thought of things that would not have occurred to me—securing extra supplies, considering not only the weather (which I as a Briton do on reflex) but cosmopolitan exigencies, like the state of the streets, or what to do if we encountered unexpected public processions, the night watch, et cetera. In all our plotting and planning, we never had any kind of privacy. That hardly mattered. Her presence was my sunlight. I flirted with her shamelessly, sometimes right in front of Samuel, who found me distasteful, even boorish. I was a wit; I bantered in three languages at once; I played the lute in the evenings (having bought a new one in the city with my accumulated doge money), and made eyes at her in front of all her people in the doorway of the tent; I kissed her hand in public when we went over to the city. It was an unprecedented indulgence to have such access to a woman I so enjoyed. The younger Richard had decided (in the absence of Liliana, and the growing sway of his own ability to grow a beard) that Jamila was the most sensual creature in Byzantium, and he behaved atrociously toward her, which allowed me to be her chivalrous protector. (Samuel was protective too, but never in a way that seemed remotely chivalrous.) I awoke every morning on the floor of the cabin, aching to make love to her, but once I was up and about and my blood was flowing, simply being in her presence made me float with joy. I was stupid with quiet happiness, and so was she. Too stupid.

At last our night of effort arrived. It was early October now—a year since we'd departed Venice. We would have about a dozen hours of darkness, under a moonless sky.

My plan sounded much simpler than it really was: We would use the city's water system to spirit the relics out of harm's reach.

Clerics at each of the churches Gregor and Mourtzouphlos had readied brought their most precious relics in their most precious reliquaries to an unremarkable garden near the Hippodrome. The elders of the Jewish community brought the treasures of the synagogue—all sorts of cumbersome, odd-shaped silver things, some with little pointing hands attached to the edges, some resembling funnels or pointed hats. There was a tree we appointed as the meeting place. The relics were delivered here from churches all over the city. Then they were spirited—sometimes by the clerics themselves, if they were afraid to let go of them quite yet, otherwise in hay carts steered by Mourtzouphlos's men, under Ionnis's direction—a bowshot away, to a discreet entrance to one of the cisterns.

I had not been down to any of the cisterns yet, but I'd learned enough, with the aid of Ionnis and Jamila, to implement my plan. I knew there were a series of these huge stone holding tanks underneath this part of the city, a series of artificial underground ponds, connected by tunnels; I knew that the largest ones all were fed by the aqueduct; most important, I knew the aqueduct, in turn, was fed by channels that came from (and therefore, went back to) routes outside the city walls, if one had the perseverance to go against the very feeble current of a minute slope. There was a channel off this waterway to another cistern, up near Blachernae Palace; Blachernae was a few miles northwest of here, in the direction we'd be traveling, so we'd arranged for some of Mourtzouphlos's men to receive relics directly from the city's northernmost churches there, and then connect with us at Blachernae.

I am not fond of water, but I was personally overseeing the project, alpha to omega. Approaching midnight, all of the bundles and boxes and crates that we were expecting had been brought to us; Gregor and Mourtzouphlos did much bowing and saluting, oath taking and signing of formal receipts promising to return St. Agnes's toenail and St. Bartholomew's beard and St. George's testicle—all in jewel-encrusted gold or silver caskets and boxes and jars—just exactly as we had received them. Jamila's presence was not required now, but Gregor had coaxed Samuel into allowing her to come with us, mostly because he knew I wanted her there, and he was relieved by how my mood had improved over the past weeks.

When all the bundles had been brought, and then taken below to the cistern, I grabbed Jamila's hand and went down the damp stone steps with her, entering the largest cistern of the lot. Gregor and Mourtzouphlos would travel separately aboveground, Gregor following the route of the aqueduct with some of Mourtzouphlos's men, and Mourtzouphlos rushing ahead to the Blachernae diversion to keep an eye on things there. We would all meet up at Mourtzouphlos's home, near Blachernae.

Everything around Jamila and me changed subtly as we descended. The slight breeze from above vanished, replaced by very still, moist air. The shapes of sounds changed somehow. The cold pinpoints of starlight above gave way to a spill of amber summoning us from below.

I knew there was some eight feet of water in the cistern. Eight feet is easily the height of a tall room. So I had expected to see a large chamber, nearly filled, with just enough room beneath the ceiling for the longboats (which we'd pilfered from the Greek navy which sat rotting in the upper harbor—that had been Mourtzouphlos's special project). I thought the rowers would have to crouch to keep from being tonsured by the ceiling, in fact.

Nothing in the world could have prepared me for the cistern we descended into. It was a man-made stone cavern, *enormous*, and it was filled with columns, spaced regularly in rows at about eight paces apart. And despite the eight feet of water, the columns rose above the surface and continued upward for fully the height of three men before reaching the ceiling, which we caught a glimpse of by lantern as we descended: it was all graceful vaulted arches, as you would find in a large, expensive church in France—what was a crowning architectural flourish in the West was here no more than the roof of a water pit, condemned to perpetual darkness, not considered worth looking at. It was naturally black as ink down here, but the four small long-boats, each with lanterns fore and aft, threw enough light for us to see the forest of stone columns. We could not see down into the depths, but Jamila remembered from childhood stories that it was teeming with blind freshwater fish. Here was an environment made entirely of water and stone, far more than Venice ever was—everything both softer and harder than the ordinary, sounds both muted and echoing. In the midst of our hurried anxiety, there was a moment of inexplicable and utter calm.

"These pillars are all stolen from pagan temples throughout Anatolia and Greece," Jamila whispered to me. "I heard a story when I was a child that two heads of Medusa rest underneath two of these columns, condemned never to see light for all eternity. They've been there nearly a thousand years. And it will never be empty, so there will never be any way to learn if this is true."

"At least they'll get their beauty sleep," I whispered back.

We got into the final boat, which had just enough room for us among all the bales of relics. I unrolled the diagram of cisterns and tunnels that Jamila and I had spent a month constructing. "I hope we've gotten this right," I whispered. "Or we'll end up in Bulgaria." I kissed her on the lips and hugged her to me, feeling for a moment like a king about to circuit his kingdom with his queen and all his riches.

Mourtzouphlos's men rowed us between two columns of marble arches, and so began the journey.

It was damp hours later, nearing a damp dawn, that we had been pulled, rowed, and sometimes paddled up through the cisterns, tunnels, the aqueduct, more tunnels, and finally the Blachernae cistern, where we were reunited with Mourtzouphlos and Ionnis, just as the lanterns were running low of oil. I'd been looking forward to a view of the city from up on the aqueduct, but sky and ground were equally dark. Jamila and I, although enjoying having been practically stuck to each other by the ribs, were wet and shivering; Mourtzouphlos invited us at once to step out of the boat and join him and Gregor for refreshment at his home, which he had been granted when Isaac reinstated him to court. It was near Blachernae, on the edge of the huge section that had been burned in the Venetian attack.

Mourtzouphlos's men, who had done all that upstream rowing, were not yet finished with their work. They refilled their lamps, ate something quickly, and then continued on in the blackness; they would have to get the relics beyond the walls of Blachernae, up a channel through the hills, before daybreak. Once out in the country, they could rest, before continuing the journey north the next day toward the forest where the water originated. A distant kinsman of Mourtzouphlos's who lived up there had agreed to hold our cargo for us, without even asking what it was; we had the impression he was used to doing things illicitly. My plan called for Mourtzouphlos and me to ride out from the northern gates of the city at dawn, intercept the boatmen, and then remain as guards over the relics until we saw them safely delivered to Mourtzouphlos's kinsman with our own eyes.

Mourtzouphlos was waiting for us with dry cloaks; he offered one to me and gently draped the other around Jamila's quivering shoulders, stealing a kiss on her forehead as he tied it closed for her. Still damp and shivering, we followed him along a broad avenue for a few hundred paces until he stopped before an extremely plain stone building—the front was flat, undecorated, with less character than a fortress. High up to either side was a small domed window that looked bored. The whole front of the house presented bleakly to the street—it threatened to be even bleaker than the prison Mourtzouphlos had spent so many years in. With a smile, he gestured us through the large wooden door, which was already standing open to receive us. He grabbed a torch near the door and followed behind us.

His torch was unnecessary, and my concerns groundless. Lights were everywhere, anticipating the master's return—for this was a minor palace, almost as grand within as Ca' Barzizza back in Venice,

and it was all Mourtzouphlos's. We entered a shallow, broad vestibule, which opened at once onto a small atrium. The whole building
was constructed from pale stone and decorated almost as relentlessly
as a church interior; I was glad that in the dim light of the torches we
couldn't see all the details, for I guessed Mourtzouphlos's house was
as boisterous as he was.

In the middle of the atrium was a small pool, open to the sky. The
water level was low; autumn had been dry so far. To our right were
doorways opening into several smaller rooms, but these were dark.
To the left, through a huge, open set of double doors, was an outdoor
covered gallery and then an open courtyard full of coiffed trees. This
too was lit, perhaps to show it off to us; it seemed to extend back
along that whole length of the building. I could hear the tinkling
water of a fountain within.

Directly across the pool from where we stood, on the far side of
the atrium, was a doorway opening into a brightly lit room. "Come!"
Mourtzouphlos said. He didn't seem to notice that Jamila and I were
both struck dumb by the unexpected opulence of our surroundings: the walls were covered with paintings and mosaics, many of
them featuring voluptuous nudes. Cheerfully, he led us around the
pool and into the lit room on the far side. This was the heart of
Mourtzouphlos's new home: a large room, with mosaics on the wall,
a few pieces of massive carved furniture, and an enormous couch
of sorts against the far wall. It seemed to be both his office and his
sleeping quarters. In one corner was an array of religious icons, which
Mourtzouphlos crossed to directly and kissed.

The most notable thing in the room to me, however, was Gregor.
He was pacing the left-hand wall, full of large open windows looking
out onto the gallery. He was anxious and almost jumped when we
entered.

"So?" he said, crossing to us, his outstretched hands looking as if
they were waiting to fend off a charging bull.

"Everything went very smoothly," I said. I even yawned to show him how incredibly blasé I was about what we'd just accomplished.

Mourtzouphlos, however, grimaced slightly. "There has been a very little problem," he confessed. "But I have handled it," he went on, reassuringly, seeing the immediate alarm on all our faces. He gestured us to sit on cushions around a low table near the center of the room. We did not move. He gestured again. "It is no cause for panic, please be at your ease." He waited until the three of us had settled around the table with him. Then he called a servant to pour us wine into glazed earthenware cups. Finally, when he felt he'd demonstrated how calm we could be about it, he continued. "As you know, the plan was to send the relics all the way out to the forest. Today I received intelligence to doubt the trustworthiness of my associate up there, although he is a kinsman. So I have decided not to send the relics out of the city at all. I am going to hide them in plain sight—I have told my men to keep them hidden in the Blachernae cistern."

"What?" Gregor said, looking unhappy.

Mourtzouphlos smiled at us like a young boy who had just performed a trick for doting relatives. "The boats will stay in the cistern at Blachernae, and the relics will stay in the boats. Clever, eh? Nobody ever goes down there, unless on business they should not be engaged in to start with. I will post a guard. And this way, we can return them immediately once the debt has been paid. I think it is even better than the original plan."

"I don't like knowing they're still in the city," Gregor said.

"If you can think of somewhere else to hide them, let me know," said Mourtzouphlos, with his Greek shrug. "Otherwise, I will report to you regularly about them." He grinned happily at all of us. Sitting beside Gregor, he slapped the knight's knee. "Eh, my friend, we are truly allies now!"

Gregor frowned. "There is one relic not with the rest," he said.

Mourtzouphlos nodded. "The head of John the Baptist, as you call the Precursor. This has been on my mind too."

"You have Isaac's trust," Gregor said, in a meaningful tone.

Mourtzouphlos shrugged. "I am a nobody in his court, but yes, he trusts me well enough. But if I were to steal it from him now, he would then start looking for it—and then looking for all the others too."

"So the most precious relic of all must be sacrificed to protect the others?"

Mourtzouphlos made a soothing gesture. "Calm yourself, my friend, of course not. I will find the head and keep an eye on it, and at least make sure nothing evil comes to it. If nothing else, I will *certainly* see to it that your accursed imperial puppeteer Boniface doesn't get it."

51

BY THE TIME we returned to camp, it was midmorning, and we were, all three of us, exhausted and bedraggled.

"Well," Jamila said wearily as we hesitated between the tent and the cabin.

With a jolt I realized I'd just lost my excuse for spending most of my waking hours with her. Panic washed over me, and at that moment, to make it worse, Samuel came out of the tent.

Jamila, seeing him, transformed immediately into the silent woman with eyes averted that she always was in his presence. It was plain he hadn't slept all night either. He nodded gruffly to us. "We will move back into Pera, now that Jamila is not needed with you," he announced. "I met with the elders last night, and it is decided."

"Pera . . . is charcoal," Gregor said.

"We begin today. We must take wood from the forests while they are still standing, before rebuilding of the burned sections of the city depletes all supplies." He shifted with stiff discomfort. This was a man who did not like asking favors, especially of the very soldiers who had put him in need of favors. "But we are still discussing what to do about the women. While we get the timber."

I almost fell onto my knees in prayer. "They're welcome to remain here in the tent," Gregor offered. "As long as they continue the masquerade—no religious rituals, and they must attend mass daily, and speak only Greek or French."

"We accept," said Samuel. "And thank you." He managed to say this without expressing any sense of gratitude.

I nearly started *humming*. The corners of Jamila's mouth pushed up a little.

So another month passed, while Boniface and Alexios chased after the Usurper in Thrace.

Jamila and the other women remained in the tent, and I found excuses to be in there during daylight hours. My languages grew much improved, and I learned to play the lute almost perfectly imitating Jamila's style. In fact, I even wrote a song for her:

> What ails the lady,
> That first she'd steal my soul with her eyes,
> And then, having stolen it, forsakes it?
> Swords are unleashed from the scabbards of her eyes,
> And she flashes lightning from her cheeks!

The women in the tent fell all over themselves with mirth when I performed it and pinched my cheek and told me it was such a shame I was uncircumcised. One of them even offered me something called a *bris*, which caused Jamila to cover her face and laugh so hard I thought she might do herself injury. Whatever a *bris* is, they never gave me one. I mended the tent roof for them, the first time it rained; with specie I made from playing for Dandolo and around the fires at night, I bought them extra blankets, so that as the nights grew cold they would not suffer. It seems shameful to admit to joy when there

was much unjoyful going on around me, but emotions are not rational. I was happy to be in Jamila's presence, to do what I could for her
and others. For me it was a good month; for Gregor too, I think.

Feast of St. Callístus, 14 October

After a hiatus I unroll this scroll, to bear witness to the stasis we are in.

*I attempt daily to carry out Milord Boniface's orders: I grasp every
opportunity to promote goodwill between the city and the army remaining in camp, but there are few opportunities to do so formally. Emperor
Isaac deflects my requests for audience and, further, remains derelict
in paying the remainder of the debt, despite his infamous plundering
of certain aristocratic families, including one called Doukas—that is,
Mourtzouphlos. Mourtzouphlos remains cheered despite these woes.*

*The Briton and I (and Jamila) accept Mourtzouphlos's frequent
offers to visit him in his home. He serves us the best wine I have ever
tasted, and he makes us laugh with his warm spirit and his jokes and
songs, although he is often very rude. He has given the Briton an excellent new fiddle, cedar above and sycamore below, decorated along the
fingerboard, with a variety of bows for different kinds of playing. It is
remarkable to me that, in a time of great unrest and tension, there is always this place full of light and laughter, and that we may be a part of it.*

*More important than selfish pleasure, however, these evenings of
fellowship accomplish more good through subtle means than any of my
official embassies. For Mourtzouphlos, although a minor official at the
court, seems to know everyone in the city's broader society. Arriving at
his house, we are equally likely to find ourselves dining with a bishop
of the Orthodox Church, a high-ranking aging eunuch, a famous musician, the emperor's Jewish physician, a wealthy Genoese trader, or a
well-respected wood-carver. These men speak with us (through Jamila,
who interprets) frankly of their lives and concerns. It is remarkable
to me how similar we are, despite their unusual religious habits, daily
customs, and alien tongues.*

For an example, if I may wax personal: my wife's confinement, and my distance from it, have been much on my mind of late, for by now she must have delivered and I do not know the result of it. Here are men who will speak to me of their own experiences with frankness, telling me I should be glad to miss her swollen appearance anyhow; or that the best marriages are formed from a tie of friendship more than passion, so truly ours is model; or that it is better not to be close to her, that I may not mourn her overmuch should she die in childbirth; or assuring me that, however distant she seems now, when I am reunited with her and see our flesh united in a child, she shall be as dear to me as Christ himself is to the angels. These comments lead to conversations such as I usually only have with my own kin and confidants.

These people talk as much as women, and yet there is nothing womanly about their discourse; in fact, they are to be commended for their intelligence and insight. Mourtzouphlos and the Briton spend more time than I deem seemly lambasting the evils of those who would conquer others, and put as if in the same camp any army that has ever raised a sword to overwhelm any other army. They do it only to bait me, and to laugh at my discomfort, but even this is done in good spirit.

Such teasing is minor compared with other discourse, such as the citizenry's anguish regarding what the army has accomplished. These men blame Milord Boniface, and suspect his motives for putting such a puppet on the throne. Indeed, Mourtzouphlos in particular delights in testing my devotion to the marquis by calling him by foul (but clever) names, giving me a conspiratorial grin. These men tell me also that they admire me personally but that the army I am with is a faceless, nameless mass of alien force, and if we would have the city love us, we must all be kinder. I do not know how to manifest this request. Because I feel unequal to that task myself, I now make it a habit of bringing to these dinners—with Mourtzouphlos's permission—my fellow pilgrims. I hope to increase amity between city and army. Bishop Conrad has gone with Boniface to Thrace, but other clerics join us, although this leads to difficulty sometimes. For example, a cleric of each side argued theology, and the Greek cleric quoted a recent patriarch (that is like the pope) who said that he would rather be ruled by Moslems than by Catholics, for the Moslem will not force him to convert but the Catholic would make him follow the Roman customs. And I remain shocked at the doctrinal differences between the churches. For example, the Greeks rarely take communion, for it strikes them as an act of awesome power requiring weeks of preparation. These people speak of death as Hades, personified as Charos—a pagan figure! The Church does not correct them, for the Church itself seems hardly concerned with immediate afterlife, saying we cannot know the state of the soul between death and Judgment Day, and therefore the earthbound Church cannot have jurisdiction over it. Jamila and the Briton both applaud this reasoning, and I do see the sense of it, but still it strikes me as passing strange to follow a religion that does not tell you exactly what happens when you die, and how a priest can help you control it.

A happier tiding: Last week Baldwin of Flanders's own steward came along to one of Mourtzouphlos's feasts and reported to his master good things about the Greek character and, in particular, sang praises of our host Mourtzouphlos and his mistress. These are small triumphs, but perhaps they will lend themselves toward something large.

There is one other triumph, not small but not yet accomplished, which is: Mourtzouphlos tries daily to learn where Emperor Isaac keeps the head of John the Baptist. Surely if we find this head and I, or Milord Baldwin, return it to its rightful home in the monastery called St. John of Studious, the army will be hailed as the protector of the city's sacred things. Mourtzouphlos may yet succeed in this. Meanwhile, I am grateful for the companionship, for Mourtzouphlos is the only man alive I know as boisterous as my brother, whose company I sorely miss while he fights in Thrace.

GREGOR, JAMILA, AND I enjoyed those weeks, but we were living in a bubble. The relationship between the army and the Greeks was disintegrating. For example: the section of the seawall facing the harbor, torn down at Boniface's order on Coronation Day, was now being rebuilt by civilian vigilantes, and Emperor Isaac never made a move to stop them. Gregor tried meeting with the rebuilders; his efforts came to nothing. He even asked Mourtzouphlos to help him with it, but Mourtzouphlos didn't know who was behind it, and could not find out. He was nervous about anything that would put him officially in the public eye. "I do better when I am working quietly away from notice," he said. And with a wink at me, "You know what I mean, don't you, Briton? Eh, you and I, we're like twin souls. More freedom to enjoy and less bullshit to endure!"

Near the end of this month, deep into the autumn now, the Jewish men returned from the hills with timber to rebuild Pera; Jamila would soon have a home to go to and would no longer sleep where I could find her first thing in the morning and last thing at night. I rejoiced for her but mourned for myself, and punished myself for that selfishness by offering to help the Jews to build, as much as Samuel would trust me with a hammer.

But crusading pilgrims, and refugees from the fire, liked the idea of easy lumber and absconded with the Jews' supply of it by force. Gregor and some other knights tried to prevent them—likewise, by force—and fights broke out between groups of soldiers.

That's when our Gregor showed himself artful, making a suggestion worthy of Otto, Jamila, and myself combined. He implemented a trial by might, a sophisticated means of justice wherein whichever party bashes up the other is legally and morally superior. The appropriated timber became the goods of whoever won a sets of jousts, or a duel, or a boxing match. Gregor's "team" returned whatever they won to Pera (where, unsurprisingly, it was often absconded with again by the other "team").

The clergy who'd remained behind were unnerved by this double heresy—first that there was a mini-tournament held by pilgrims (tournaments were off-limits to pilgrims), second that it was in defense of the property of Jews. But then they saw the wisdom of it: it allowed the soldiers to keep battle-ready and yet contain their violence within regulated limits. I suggested the team opposing Gregor donate their "winnings" to building winter cabins for the bishops, and that ended the clergy's final moral squeaking on the subject. All of this put the Jews in the odd position of being minor celebrities, as they were offering (albeit against their will) the local equivalent of a fair lady's kerchief at a tourney. In the end, this did not really *help* Pera, but it kept the residents from further harm and at least passed the time until the bulk of the army came back.

And then the bulk of the army did come back. Months earlier than we were expecting them.

52

NO OFFICIAL REASON WAS GIVEN, but it was whispered by the heralds that Emperor Alexios returned home early in response to reports that things were getting worse between the army and the Greeks. This, despite Gregor's best attempts to grease the social machinery between the two.

Heralds announced that the return was imminent. Gregor was put on alert for summons to the border of the camp to salute his father-in-law's triumphant return. All scheduled tourneys were canceled; the Jews—including Jamila—retreated into the as-yet-unrebuilt Pera and locked the gates; the refugees from the fire threw themselves into neatening the camp to show the returning army they were worthy of continued shelter.

For a day or two we all hovered in anxious anticipation. Neither

Gregor nor I wanted to see Boniface, but we heartily missed Otto. I wondered too how Liliana had survived the excursion. Having (some) access to the woman I desired made me feel for Otto.

Then a herald came by the cabin and told Gregor the approaching army (somewhat ragtag in formation, but still in formation) had been sighted. Gregor dressed in his best ceremonial tunic and sat himself on the largest trunk as the Richardim each laced up a boot. I (ruefully) practiced "Kalenda Maya," that vapid May Day song I had not even had to think about for nearly three blessed months.

There was a rap on the door. I put down the lute and went to unbolt it, expecting it to be Gregor's anticipated summons from Boniface.

It was Jamila, looking sober. Not grim exactly; this was more of a somber resignation.

"What does Samuel want now?" I asked, in lieu of greeting.

She shook her head. "You degrade yourself by indulging in such simplistic cynicism," she said. "This was *my* idea."

"What was your idea?" said Gregor, from inside. He flexed his feet experimentally, nodded at the tightness of the boot lacing, and gestured at the Richardim, which meant they could go about their own affairs. They returned to a game of chess.

She held out her hand, and I took it, as if to help her in; we never passed up an opportunity to touch, although we hadn't had a single opportunity to touch in private since she'd been reunited with her tribe. "I've been far too free while Boniface has been away," she said.

"Not free enough," I murmured. She didn't acknowledge the comment. I took the hint and abandoned all hope of playful banter for the rest of the visit.

"I'm sure I've been recognized around camp over the past few months," she told Gregor. "Boniface has probably learned I didn't really die in the Pera fire, or he'll hear it soon. I don't want to resume a pointless game of hide-and-seek with him now he's come back. Instead, Samuel and I will go to him as representatives of the

Jewish community and ask him to protect Pera, in exchange for my offering my services as a guide when the army moves on to Egypt." Seeing us both about to protest, she held a shushing hand out toward each but spoke directly to Gregor. "Sir, you've been very noble in your attempts to safeguard our lumber, but it's become a game for the soldiers. We don't dare actually build anything with it, in case it becomes forfeit to your opposing team a few days later. You have regulated the plundering by means of the tournaments, but you haven't stopped it. Boniface can—or at least, he can more than you can."

"But if you—" I began to protest.

"If I go to him in a public forum, as a member of the Jewish community, he can no longer insist that I'm a Saracen princess. And he can no longer claim that Gregor is harboring me. All of my old value as a pawn disappears. Then I'll immediately make myself valuable again, by offering my services as a guide. Pera gets protection if I do that." Gregor and I both began to voice objections; she pivoted slightly toward me and, speaking over us, concluded, "And I will *stay with you* and go on to the Holy Land."

That silenced my objection. Gregor made a few mumbled sounds of concern, then shrugged. "I cannot dictate your actions," he finally said. "But I think it's riskier than you're presenting it. For both of us, Jamila." He stood, reached for his sword belt, began to buckle it on. "Boniface's entourage is expected, so I'm going to the edge of camp to greet them. I assume you are not asking me to tell him anything."

She shook her head. "I'll do it myself. I wanted to let you know, so you will not be surprised by it. We will do it tonight at the homecoming feast."

With a gesture toward the door, Gregor said, "Let us hope that's not the only happy revelation of the evening. God willing, we will also hear that the debt is paid and there is nothing to further retard our progress. I'm off."

Seeing the Richardim make no move to accompany him, I whis-

tled at them and coaxed, "Don't you want to go with your master to
see the troops come back?"

They exchanged glances, shrugged indifferently, and shook their
heads.

Gregor examined the human geometry of the cabin. "Ah," he
said, drily. He was suppressing amusement, which involved expressions unfamiliar to his facial muscles. "Richardim, come along with
me and show respect to our leaders," he said.

The two servants leapt up, and the grandson, who was losing,
pretended to accidentally knock into the chessboard, jarring all the
pieces from their positions and effectively ending the game. "Sorry,"
he said with mock apology to his grandfather and gave him one of
the cloaks. As he was pulling on his own wrap, he paused, examined
the cabin as Gregor had a moment before, and lifted his head to express a deep, vocal breath of insight. "Ohhhhh," he said, sniggering.
"He's finally going to fuck her. When's my turn, Jamila?"

I veered from embarrassment to indignation. "She's not a common woman."

"Shame," said Richard, giving her a ludicrous expression of lust.
Unfortunately, he had hurtled into full-on adolescence around the
same time Liliana had ended up with Boniface. He was irritating all
of us.

Jamila just smiled. "I'm old enough to be your mother," she informed him.

"You're the one told us about Oedipus," he retorted.

"Richard," Gregor said sharply, and the boy's face went blank; he
fell into line behind his grandfather and followed Gregor out of the
cabin, slamming the door.

Then there was a pause. Jamila and I were alone, standing within
inches of each other. She reached up and casually pulled off her head
band, let it fall to the floor. I reached without looking and grabbed
her other hand.

"This isn't why I came," she said softly, not looking at me.

"I know."

"I only came to tell Gregor—"

"Came to tell Gregor you're staying with this tribe, not that one. And now here we are. A mere hundred and sixteen days since the last time we were alone in private."

"Hundred and seventeen," Jamila corrected.

She moved in toward me as if to begin a dance, casually, as if we did this all the time, her free arm slipping between my elbow and my side, and stretching behind me, her fingertips coaxing my spine closer to her. I dropped her hand, and we embraced, clutched each other, her face buried in my shoulder. Without lifting her cheek from my body, she pivoted her face up toward mine, and I lowered my own head to kiss her on the lips. "This time we won't be interrupted for hours, by anyone," I whispered.

"Don't tempt fate by saying such a thing," she warned, but she smiled.

I led her to Gregor's camp bed, our one attempt at domestic civility, on the far side of the cabin. Lacking a resident female, the space had few creature comforts, but the Richardim had hung dividing curtains near this end of the room, to keep the heat in around the master's bed; they and I still slept on the mats on the floor of the main part of the room. Untied and pulled across, these curtains offered privacy and darkness. I gently pushed her down on top of the bed, then closed the curtains and knelt over her on all fours, like a protective she-bear over a wounded cub. Jamila reached up to clasp her hands behind my neck.

I collapsed on top of her and spent a moment kissing her face. I felt her hands all over me, trying to lift my tunic to get at my belt. "No, first I'm undressing you," I whispered. "That's where we were interrupted last summer, remember?"

"You're certainly taking your time about it," she said.

"I'm trying to be courtly," I said, as if insulted. "It calls for a certain etiquette."

"Yes, first you unlace the back of my tunic, then you tug—"

"No!" I pulled both of us up to sitting and reached behind her. "I'd never be so rude as to simply unlace your tunic," I said, unlacing her tunic. "First I must write you eighty-seven love poems, each one with a reference to the corn growing in the field, the sun rising, every part of your anatomy being more valuable than gold, and my own prowess, which I shall refer to entirely with sexual imagery while claiming that I'd never sully you with my own sexual urges. Then, I will set these poems to the music of 'Kalenda Maya' and sing them outside your window in a whisper under cover of night. Then, if they please you, you must throw me your sleeve out the window."

"My *sleeve*? Why am I not wearing my sleeve? Did some other wooer already relieve me of my clothes, while you were busy serenading me?"

"That's right," I said, continuing to unlace her. "It was young Richard."

"Did I enjoy it?"

"Not as much as you enjoyed listening to my love songs."

She made a face. "I was afraid you'd say that."

"After you throw me your sleeve, I fight in a tournament, with your sleeve wrapped around the end of my lance."

"No! Really?" She erupted into peals of laughter. "Gentile poetry is excruciatingly unsubtle. Just out of curiosity," she went on, as I finished unlacing her tunic, "*if* you were to simply take my clothes off to ravish me, what's the next step after unlacing my tunic?"

Her simply saying the phrase "take my clothes off to ravish me" made me so hard I was instantly too clumsy to continue to undress her, as if my intelligence could reside in only one part of my body at once, and it was no longer my fingers. "Um. It depends on how quickly you want me to see you naked."

She grabbed my head and nearly jerked my face into hers. "I wanted you to see me naked last year," she whispered and kissed me. "And I still want you to see me naked immediately."

I was so thrilled I almost fainted. "If the laces were truly loosened enough . . ." I began nervously. I slid my hand and arm down the back of her tunic to demonstrate how very loose I'd made them. I hoisted her to standing. "Then I think perhaps allowing the subject to stand and lifting the dress from the hem of the skirt straight over the head would be an efficient— And so it is!" I was already peeling the tunic off. Kneeling upright on the camp bed, I threw the tunic up and to the ground and grinned hungrily at her, as she stood before me in just her long chemise.

"But of course I'd never subject you to such crude behavior as just tearing your tunic off. We'll do it properly, in the courtly manner. First, I shall win the tournament," I said, watching what I could of her flesh move beneath the thin linen shift. I got the impression that her breasts were a little larger, her waist a little smaller, than they appeared when she was fully dressed. Not that it would influence my desire for her, but I was hungry with curiosity to see the details for myself. How strange that I knew her so well without ever having seen something as much a part of her as her belly. "And then you must somehow send word that we might meet in private for a chaste kiss."

"How send word?" she asked. She sat beside me on the bed, reached up under her chemise, and began to untie her hose. "Shall I send you one of my stockings?" She'd gotten her shoes off without my noticing; now she pulled off the knee-length stockings and offered them to me, garters and all.

I took the offering with trembling hands but gave her a disapproving look as I tossed it aside. "That will suffice for now, if it must, but in the future, I beg you, a more genteel symbol of interest, please. Something as coarse as an actual undergarment suggests a lack of refinement. We are courtly, after all; it's not as if we were planning to— Oh good Lord, oh dear—" For she had taken one of my hands and guided it up under her chemise, all the way to the top of her lap, where she pressed it, palm down, into the soft crevice between her leg and torso. "I can't think clearly enough to comment any more on the topic," I said, plaintively.

"Thank *God*," she whispered and pushed closer to me. The warmth of her body was its own scent. I yanked the chemise over her head with my free hand, and then there she was for me to look at, completely unclothed, my hand already very near to where other parts of me were drumming to go. Her skin was darker than any woman's I'd seen naked, but even in this dim light it had a brilliance to it.

"It's hardly a perfect body," she said, matter-of-factly.

"It's yours, and it's naked, and it's next to mine," I answered. "It's more than perfect, it's miraculous."

"Nakedness is more useful when it occurs in pairs," she said and reached for my belt.

I grabbed her hand before she could touch it and kissed every knuckle in turn. "I'll do it," I said. "You better just lie back and try to resign yourself to your fate."

"Is there any danger my fate might involve your actual flesh?" she asked, a hint of real impatience tingeing the playfulness. "Or do you intend to *talk* me into a sexual climax?"

I let go of my belt and gave her a look of complete shock. "Are you under the delusion *you're* going to enjoy this? I'm so sorry, that's not how we do things in Christianity."

She sat up, resting her weight on one elbow in a way that flexed one ample breast into an unnaturally perky, inviting position. "If you don't take your clothes off immediately, I'm going to wrap up in a blanket and go offer myself to young Richard," she said. The perkily positioned breast looked like it was begging to be suckled, so instead of answering, I clamped my lips over her nipple and ran my tongue around it. She sagged back onto the bed. "That's a start," she said in a strange voice, and lying supine, her back arched slightly under my weight, she groped around blindly for my belt.

"Hey!" cried a familiar voice from the front room. "Where is everybody?"

I buried my face into her breast to smother my shout of frustration; I felt her torso shudder a little with repressed amusement as she raised her head to kiss me on the temple. "Someday, someday," she promised in my ear. "I'll get you unclothed someday."

"Gregor, oh, you brave young knight?" sang out a hearty, accented voice to the tune of a German drinking song. "Crazy Briton? Sturdy servants, old or young? Ah, there's one of you anyhow! Big Brother!" And then Otto's laughter, interrupted by Gregor's voice, muffled but happy.

By now I had already shoved Jamila's chemise back over her head; she smoothed it down, stepped into the tunic, and I managed to tighten some of the laces. "Here," I called out regretfully, as soon as Jamila had nodded to me in the darkness. I swept the curtain out of the way.

53

 CROWDED IN THE DOORWAY as the setting sun loomed behind them were Gregor and the Richardim. With Otto. And Liliana.

Even backlit in a dim room, Liliana's face was rosy, and she seemed buoyant with health, and remarkably happier than when I'd accosted her in Boniface's compound in her whorish outfit. Gregor had met them outside and was finishing mutual embraces.

"Liliana! You look beautiful!" I cried.

"That's just your concupiscence speaking," she said with a fetching smile, pointing first toward the feminine head band lying in the middle of the room and then toward my groin (my tunic skirt was not lying flat). "To whom do you owe— *Jamila!*" She was delighted when she realized who had been in the back section of the cabin with me, now sheepishly collecting her stockings. A second later the two women were in each other's arms, kissing and nearly giggling. The Richardim leered at me in a way that almost made me feel as if I'd been caught committing incest.

Jamila stepped back, looked Liliana up and down hard for a moment, and her eyes got very round. "Liliana—" she began, but Liliana shushed her.

"Wait," she said in a conspiratorial voice. "First we have important and very belated news for the master of the house."

"I wouldn't quite call this a house," said Otto, slinging down his leather satchel. He grunted cheerfully. "Better than the tent, though. It will be good to get back to Germany, where they know how to provide creature comforts! Brother," he continued and gestured to Gregor, "have the boy light a lamp and let me show you important news from home."

As Richard struggled with the lantern, his grandfather and I pushed a chest across the floor. Richard put the lantern on the chest, and we all clustered about it: Jamila and I close together; Gregor alone; Liliana and Otto, practically in each other's laps. He wrapped himself around her, and they moved almost like one body, the outsides of her arms couched within the insides of his, him pushing back her hair from her face as if they were his eyes that it was falling over. Both of them—especially he—looked so stupendously in love, it made my recent behavior toward Jamila appear decorous.

"We have a lot to tell you," said Liliana.

"Begin at once," Gregor ordered.

The lovers glanced at each other in that annoying way lovers will, holding an entire conversation with their eyes and proud of the fact that they have no need of speech. Otto reached for a pouch on his belt, but Liliana was in the way of his accessing it easily, so she reached for it instead. She untied it and pulled out a smaller leather bag, which she handed to Otto. As we all watched, Otto unknotted the bag, drew out a small bit of vellum folded into quarters, and handed this in turn to Gregor. It was sealed on the fold with wax, and then one side had been waxed as well to take the imprint of a seal: a five-pointed blossom of St. John's wort.

"When our King Philip sent a courier from Germany for news of the campaign, the courier won an extra fee for bringing along this very private message in addition to his master's charge."

"This is my seal," Gregor said unnecessarily. Otto gestured him to open it. He used the tip of his dagger to break the seal, unfolded the parchment once and then again, so that it lay like a tulip in his large palm. It was old, and thin, and soft. Nestled in it was a bit of colorless fluff, tied off in the middle with blue thread. Gregor stared at it.

"Shall I tell you what it is?" Otto asked in an eager voice.

"I can see what it is. It's fluff," Gregor said, bemused, peering through the lamplight into the parchment.

"It's hair," Liliana corrected. "The baby's hair."

"Your son's hair, Gregor." Otto grinned. "You have made me an uncle."

Gregor breathed in sharply and almost dropped the parchment. Liliana rescued it from his grasp; Jamila and I cheered automatically in our respective native tongues, creating a brief auditory cacophony as Gregor stood abruptly and turned away from us, overcome. Otto jumped up, smacked him on the back, embraced him.

"Open my satchel, Brit," he called out heartily, gesturing toward the leather sack near the door. "Take out the skin you find in there. I brought back the finest juice of the vine in all of Thrace, saved especially to drink to this occasion. Let's put it around the table now!" He clapped his hands and began a very buoyant-sounding song in German.

If this were anyone but Otto, I would have thought he was exaggerating his excitement, out of either politeness or mockery. But Otto wasted no time on politeness and was too artless to feign interest for his own amusement. This was genuine delight for another man's good fortune. It was touching to see him so entirely unselfish.

"Ten fingers and ten toes, I assume?" Jamila asked, as we passed the wineskin around. Otto finished the verse—which involved a silly bit of hopping about and rolling his hips—and Gregor collected himself enough to rejoin us. There were tears in the corners of his eyes.

I took a swig of the wine. It was good, but not as good as the stuff we'd had at Mourtzouphlos's. "The little fellow already has hair, eh? A sure sign of healthy balls," I announced approvingly.

"It's not *facial* hair," Jamila said. "How is the mother?"

"The lady mother is very well, says the courier, but sent a message by word of mouth that, if Gregor wants another one, he'll have to sire a bastard."

"A toast to Marguerite," said Gregor warmly. We drank Marguerite's health, and then drank Gregor's health, and then the health of the baby, who'd been named for both of his grandsires: Gerhard Boniface. We even drank the health of one of the grandsires.

"*Mazel tov*, sir," Jamila said, then her eyes swiveled firmly to the returnees. "Now. There is more going on."

"Not for Gregor," Otto said cheerfully, smacking his brother affectionately on the shoulder. "The rest will only be so much noise to Gregor."

"No, no," his brother insisted. "I'm recovered. I'm not the one who had to birth him, after all. Tell us all the rest of your story." With a gesture to Liliana: "Obviously there are developments we want to hear about."

The two lovers cooed silently at each other a moment, having another of those annoying, silent lover conversations.

"Well," Otto said at last, smug, "to put it crassly, I outlanced the marquis, so I got to have the lady."

"Bollocks!" Liliana laughed. She's the only woman I know who could say "Bollocks" and still sound feminine. "You'd best let me explain."

"Start from the beginning, before we even left here for the Thrace campaign," Otto said, as if this were an old favorite they both knew by heart.

Liliana shrugged agreeably. "Boniface wanted to keep me, as you know, and I saw no reason to protest."

"We are insulted and chagrined," I said.

"Why? Jamila was gone, I assumed you would follow her, and I assumed that Otto would find himself another woman, because he does like regularity."

"But you missed me," Otto prompted, lest she forget that part.

"Of course I missed you," Liliana said, as if it were so obvious it was silly to have to mention it. She patted his wrist. "I missed everyone, but especially you." Turning her attention back to us, she continued, "I really thought he must find himself another woman, you know that. Our unlikely tribe, I thought, was dispersing. If I tried to leave, Fazio would just find an excuse to come and scoop me up again, either for intelligence or just for pleasure. I did less harm to all of you by staying with him."

I snorted. "You really called the Marquis of Montferrat *Fazio*? To his face?"

"He liked it. I did what he liked. I was rewarded for it. It was a workable arrangement except . . ." She laughed that winsome laugh that made every man within hearing want to lift her skirt, even if he'd just been staring at Jamila's naked belly.

Otto preened, wrapping his arms around her. "She missed me. She missed me so much she whispered *my* name into Boniface's ear when *he* was mounting her. Twice!"

Gregor smacked his head into his palm and laughed ruefully.

"That's brilliant!" I declared, falling against Jamila with amusement.

"That was before we even left for Thrace!" Otto added. "Boniface was so unnerved about it, he almost didn't want me along, but he knew he needed me, especially once Gregor made himself loathsome to Alexios. Gregor, remember when he offered to give me Liliana if I'd just agree to be knighted? She'd called him by my name just the night before—he was actually trying to get rid of her without losing face." He was tickled by that. "And then once we were on the road—" His eyes twinkled, and he lowered his voice with conspiratorial decorousness. "He couldn't perform."

"Oh, *stop* that, you are such a *child*," Liliana laughed, pretending to elbow him in the nose. "One night, there was *one night*—"

"One night when he couldn't perform!" Otto squealed triumphantly, grinning at us from behind her elbow.

"When you are a man of fifty, with the welfare of an entire military campaign on your shoulders, some horny little brat in the bloom of youth will sneer about *you* that way," Liliana scolded. "But it is true, by then I was not encouraging to him. So let us say, courteously, only that the marquis and I had some differences. But he was still jealous of me, and assumed we would recommence at some point. So I was sequestered during part of the campaign—it was by far the longest time since I grew breasts that I've actually been left alone by men! Until Otto figured out in which tent I was being held, and snuck in one night and we had a reunion—"

"We had six reunions," Otto corrected triumphantly. "And that was just the first night."

"That must have been around the last week of August," Jamila said, looking Liliana up and down.

Liliana blushed; Otto said, "Yes, it was! How would you know that?"

"Full moon," said Jamila. "That's when she would have been most fertile."

"*What?*" I'm not even sure if it was Gregor or I who spoke it.

Otto beamed at Gregor. "You're not the only one condemned to fatherhood," he announced. "*I'm* making *you* an uncle too."

I gaped at Liliana; Gregor likewise. "You're with child?" one of us whispered. I am the one who thought to ask, "Are we pleased about this?"

"Boniface wasn't," Liliana said blithely. "Especially since it was so unlikely to be his. But there was nothing he could do without seeming adolescent, so he just threw me out of the tent."

"That's not quite it," Otto said, sobering and hugging his arms around her from behind. "He offered to keep her, even send her back to his palace in Piedmont, if she'd get rid of it or let him claim it as his own."

"Idiotic offer, but there is no accounting for male pride," she said.

"And Liliana said no," Otto concluded.

"That's not quite it either," she interjected. "Liliana almost said yes, because Liliana was overwhelmed and not sure what to do, and an ancient thirty, and did not trust downy-cheeked Otto of Frankfurt to be good for much."

"And downy-cheeked Otto of Frankfurt," continued Otto of Frankfurt, "went to the Bishop of Halberstadt, who was of course in Thrace with us, and drew up a contract promising Liliana and the child a house on his estate back home in Germany. And Liliana swore in exchange to give up her loose ways and know nobody but Jesus and the father of her child."

"And then Otto threw himself at Liliana's feet and said he'd take good care of her, and wouldn't care if it were somebody else's child; as long as it was her child, he would love it as his own," Liliana said, genuinely touched. Her face wrinkled with amusement. "He did all this in private, but he did it right in front of Boniface."

"And Boniface was a real ass to me for a few weeks, but I'm an excellent sergeant and he needed me too dearly," Otto said with satisfaction. "And so here we are."

There was, so to speak, a pregnant pause.

It was broken by a herald calling from outside, with the summons

Gregor had been expecting: Boniface had diverted straight to Blach-ernae Palace with Alexios; now he wanted Gregor to join him there as his bodyguard at the homecoming feast.

Otto, unsurprisingly, had not been invited to attend the feast. This proved to be to his benefit: it meant Boniface could not blame him for what happened next.

54

MOURTZOUPHLOS, AS PART OF his duties in his lowly courtier position, had been responsible for planning the entertainment for the great homecoming festivity and had arranged for me to play the lute. So I was going with Gregor.

Neither of us was looking forward to seeing either Boniface or Alexios again, but I at least would probably be able to spend part of the evening with Mourtzouphlos. (Besides our being of a mind about the situation overall, he did a brilliant impersonation of His Majesty the Snot-Nosed Boy. He'd not yet met Boniface, but I was confident he'd develop a nasty imitation of the marquis too, since he had already made up his mind to detest the fellow.) So after Jamila returned to Pera, and Otto and Liliana had trundled their belongings into the little cabin, I'd hastily put on the best red-and-white tunic I had—something Jamila had just recently sewn for me, with a dis-tinctly Greek flair to the embellishments even though the cut itself was snug and French. I wanted to stop by Samuel's house in Pera on our way down to the ferry and show it to her (and to see her again, and to look at her lap and remember what it felt like to have my hand against her skin there), but Gregor wouldn't detour.

We ferried over, watching the campfires of the city nervously spring up in the dusk: fifty thousand little points of light; before the inferno, it would have been smoke coming from fifty thousand roofs.

Boniface's seal allowed us into the water gate of the palace, and then eventually up into the great, gold-ceilinged, nymph-festooned hall. Gregor was recognized at the door and immediately escorted toward Boniface to join his bodyguard; I was shepherded to the musicians' stand. Mourtzouphlos had been made a deputy steward for the night, his sphere of responsibility one segment of the hall floor. He saw me, winked, and grinned. I nodded once in response.

He winked again and pointed to the ground: *Now*, he was telling me. *Tonight.*

Amazed, I repeated the gesture from across the room, with a questioning expression: *Tonight?* Meaning: *We are going to reveal the relics scheme tonight?*

He grinned, nodded—and then playfully blew me a kiss and turned his attention to an approaching servant. I felt my pulse quicken. Mourtzouphlos's role at court had some connection to financial administration; he must have already determined that Alexios had brought home enough plunder or tribute to pay off the debt to the army—which meant it was now safe to take the relics out of hiding. And here he was, acting at the first possible moment, just as he had promised weeks earlier. Gregor would be ecstatic. We would *definitely* have much to celebrate later on. With pleasant anticipation, I began to tune the palace lute and watched what was happening in the hall.

Marquis Boniface was, as ever, handsome and well-polished. He embraced Gregor with all apparent affection, as if they'd parted on the best of terms three months ago, as if Gregor's brother hadn't virtually cuckolded Boniface in the interim. There was genuine warmth on both faces, and I gathered they were discussing the birth of little Gerhard Boniface. Then the marquis turned his attention back to the royal family, whose thrones he stood beside. Gregor, with one other guard, stood slightly behind them.

Emperor Alexios looked a little seasoned by his time in the saddle, but hardly more imperial for all that. His father, Isaac, surrounded even here by his astrologers, seemed almost glum to have him back, no doubt because he would now have to scoot over on the throne to make room for another royal derriere.

Isaac looked far the worse for the stress of the last few months. He'd seemed older than his years even when released from prison; now he was frail and sunken into himself. This was especially notable beside his lovely young wife, Margaret—to whom Boniface was exceptionally gallant. So gallant that I racked my brain trying to remember if the marquis were currently married (Isaac did not look like he'd survive much longer). The quartet was receiving formal greetings from members of the court and army leaders; Boniface regularly gave Margaret words of compliment, praising her coiffure and her wit (she had not spoken once), bending over her as near as decorum would allow. She smiled politely while her hand gripped her husband's arm so tightly that her knuckles went grey. Ah, court intrigue. How I hadn't missed it.

Near this cluster were two men probably more powerful than all of them combined: Doge Enrico Dandolo of Venice and Constantine Philoxenites, the tall, reedy eunuch who controlled the treasury— and more formidably, who virtually commanded the Varangian Guard. Dandolo had made occasional visits to Philoxenites during the army's absence, to make sure the eunuch wasn't overlooking some vital little silver stash that might rest more comfortably across the harbor in the crusading camp. The two of them were adversaries, yet alike in nature. They were entirely more at ease together than were any of the courtiers; they spoke each other's language in more ways than one.

Mourtzouphlos was stepping up to the thrones now, his thick mane of auburn hair tied neatly back. He bowed deeply, received barely a nod from all of them in return. Nothing remarkable in that; he was a virtual nobody in the court. He murmured something into the empty space between Alexios and Boniface, eyes averted. I'd never seen him act with such constraint before.

He glanced up and winked at Gregor. Gregor tensed in anticipation.

"To whom do you address yourself?" Boniface was asking him.

"To you both, milords," said Mourtzouphlos. "If you might kindly spare the time tonight." He was unused to groveling, and I could tell that it was hard for him.

Boniface and Alexios exchanged glances.

"Who is this man?" Boniface sniffed.

A pause, as Mourtzouphlos recovered from being sniffed at. "I was in prison with Emperor Isaac, milord," he said. "And released when His Majesty was released. I promise you, His Majesty Alexios will want to hear my news."

"You may approach us after supper," Boniface decided. He glanced behind him to Gregor. "Allow this man to approach us," he ordered. Gregor nodded.

DINNER SEEMED TO LAST forever. To Boniface's right sat a man of about fifty years I'd never seen before. One of the other musicians, a pilgrim fiddler, whispered to me in an awed tone that this was none other than the great Raimbaut de Vacqueiras, Marquis Boniface's longtime friend, who had traveled overland from Piedmont and joined the army in Thrace. The fiddler told me, wide-eyed, that Raimbaut was the most popular, most famous, most talented troubadour who'd ever lived.

"What's he famous for?" I asked.

"Why," the fellow said, his eyes opening with surprise toward me and reverence toward the master lyricist, "he wrote 'Kalenda Maya,' of course!"

I decided to avoid him at all costs.

Gregor remained standing behind the marquis and did not touch the food, although he was occasionally offered a horn of weak wine. The opulence of the hall's inhabitants was staggering. All of these courtiers had been robbed of at least a little of their patrimony in Isaac's frantic attempts to raise money. But they were sycophantically polite to both Their Imperial Majesties, and to Her Majesty, and even to Boniface. The smiles might have frozen fire, but the smiles never wavered.

At one point during the meal, Mourtzouphlos was able to swing close to the musicians' dais, and I announced to the fiddler that I wanted to sit out for one tune. I carried the lute with me and held it up toward Mourtzouphlos.

"Some of the inlaid wood is loose and it's causing a rattle," I said loudly. "May I knock it out?"

"Absolutely not," Mourtzouphlos said sharply. "Do not defile imperial property. Let me see it in better light, I am sure we can find a solution." We marched off across the crowded, noisy hall together. Huddling over the belly of the lute near the brightest wall lamp in the room, I elbowed him slightly. "So all is well?"

"Eh! Better than you could possibly imagine," he whispered back, with a grin. "I hate these stuffy court affairs, though. I would we could do this over an intimate supper in my little hall."

"Gregor will want to know what's what with the head of John the Baptist—"

Mourtzouphlos winked. "It rests now with the other relics in the cistern at Blachernae." He grinned. "If Gregor would like to keep it, he's more than earned it."

I was surprised. "Of course not. He'd want it returned to where it came from."

Mourtzouphlos shrugged. "Very well, as long as it doesn't go to that prick Boniface." Sobering a little, he said, "You realize that when I begin to explain to His Majesty and Boniface that the relics have all been absconded with, they will be so alarmed they will order me jailed."

"Of course. But Gregor won't trundle you out of the room while he knows you've more to say."

Mourtzouphlos grinned, chuckled, almost giggled. "Yes, my friend. Much more. This will be a performance you will not forget." His eyes wandered toward the high table, and he blinked once in surprise. "Isn't that your woman?" he said, elbowing me.

I turned. Arm in arm, Jamila and Samuel stood at the foot of the dais where Alexios and Boniface ate saffron duck. Boniface dropped his knife and gaped at Jamila. So he really had believed her dead. He didn't look distressed so much as utterly confused—even more confused than Bishop Conrad, who had believed, through all of this, that Jamila of Alexandria was an infidel princess. She was dressed modestly in blue and white, the colors of the Hebrew tribe, and Samuel wore a prayer shawl and a skullcap. They wanted to make sure every person present knew that she was a Jewess—not Egyptian royalty.

Instinctively I tried to hand the lute to Mourtzouphlos and run toward them; he grabbed my shoulder firmly and pulled me back. "Let them do whatever they are planning," he said. "I know this Jew; he's a physician and he tended to the prisoners in Blachernae. He is an intelligent and good man, even if his sense of humor is so small it could be crushed by a pebble. Your woman is in good hands. Trust him."

Because Mourtzouphlos did not know the history of Jamila's role with Boniface, what happened next appeared quite unremarkable to him, but my heart was in my throat: Samuel presented her as a member of the local Jewish community who happened to know an unusual amount about the language, geography, and culture of the land the Frankish army was next bound for. Samuel then lamented that the army had stolen lumber for rebuilding Pera and requested that Boniface and Alexios together protect the Jews, on the ground that the Jews were the best, most industrious textile makers in the empire, and paid a heavy imperial tax on exports, and surely the emperor required that steady income and would want to keep it safe; as for the army, its self-restraint would be rewarded by the Jewess's willingness to share her extensive knowledge of the environs to which they were planning to depart come spring.

Alexios and Boniface glanced at each other, and each of them said "Yes" at once. The two suppliants nodded gratitude—the Hebrews never bow to earthly authority, which often gets them into trouble—and left the hall.

And that was the end of it. I could breathe again. In fact, with a dizzied sense of delight, I realized she had just promised to stay with me.

Mourtzouphlos, sensing that I'd calmed, released my shoulder, slapped me fraternally on the back, and said, "Eh, you see? No danger to your darling, and now she has announced she goes with you when your army leaves! Now all you have to do is get up her skirt when Samuel isn't looking, not that he's much of a threat. Probably hung longer—Did you see the size of his feet?—but I bet you know how to cast your rod better." He clapped me on the shoulder. "This is a happy, happy night for all of us!"

Feast of St. Martin of Tours, 11 November

When I want to do the right, only the wrong is within my reach.
—Romans 7:19

It is with horror and sorrow that I must report the exposure of the most damnable villain I have ever known, and the beginning of my deepest humiliation. For surely all is ruined now. And on this day, the day I have learned of the birth of my son, the day that kith and kin have been restored to me.

Supper was finally over at the end of the homecoming feast, and Mourtzouphlos made his way to the high table. I stepped forward to meet him to go through the ritual of patting him down for weapons. I was, I confess, almost trembling with anxious expectancy. We—

Mourtzouphlos, the Briton, and myself—had often discussed how this moment would unfold. If Mourtzouphlos's revelation (of hiding the relics) went as expected, there would be an unpleasant response from Emperor Alexios, but it would be followed by desirable action: The army would be promptly paid and, until March, could devote itself entirely to spiritual and physical preparation for the campaign's real pilgrimage at last. At last! There would be no more excuse for a delay. Never had I felt so close to seeing us returned to our true purpose. I could not know how mistaken I was.

Mourtzouphlos was allowed to approach Milord Boniface and Alexios. He spoke in a low voice, and I could not hear the initial exchange. But I could see Alexios's face grow alarmed, and Milord Boniface tense. I had expected that. A few people started to watch. I stepped in closer, to appear to be the attentive bodyguard, until I was breathing onto Mourtzouphlos's neck. Mourtzouphlos continued to speak softly, but I could hear him now. He was speaking in Greek to make sure he was completely clear to Emperor Alexios; Emperor Alexios was translating to Milord Boniface.

"He vows," Emperor Alexios was explaining, in a frightened voice, "that he will not reveal the whereabouts of the relics until their safety is guaranteed by an oath that I will not use them to pay the debt to the army."

So it had started. And so far, it was going as we planned.

Milord Boniface looked away. "Blackguard," he muttered in disgust, as Mourtzouphlos continued speaking softly to Emperor Alexios. "Accursed upstart—"

"But more than that," Emperor Alexios interrupted nervously. "His men are positioned around the city, and they are going to tell everyone that you and I conspired together to steal the relics for our personal benefit."

I was amazed to hear this, for that was not part of the plan. The threat we had agreed to was simply this: if Alexios did not immediately pay the army from whatever plunder he had brought back from Thrace, it would become known that the relics were missing. Nothing more for now. That would create trouble enough for the emperor. I did not see the need for Mourtzouphlos to have added further intrigue. For now Milord Boniface was under threat, which was not to have been a part of it at all.

"There is only one way to prevent this from happening," Alexios continued nervously, translating. If Mourtzouphlos was holding a knife to his throat, he could not have looked more fearful. "And I must act on it immediately. This man wants to be promoted to protovestiarios. Royal Chamberlain. Tonight. At once."

I shuddered, then grabbed at Mourtzouphlos's arm; he spun around, eyes flashing triumphant fire, and demanded loudly in French, as if he had never seen me before, "Foreign toad! Who are you to lay violent hands on a member of the imperial court?"

Now people were staring at all of us, and I was loath to make matters more spectacular. Milord Boniface gestured me to release Mourtzouphlos and back away, and I obeyed him. Then Milord Boniface shook his head toward Emperor Alexios. "Absolutely not. Tell him no. You and I agreed that I was to be chamberlain."

Emperor Alexios had a false-looking smile on his face, so that no one staring at us should know he was distressed. He spoke in a neutral tone to Mourtzouphlos, who replied with a congenial-sounding growl. I looked quickly at the musicians' platform for the Briton and was anxious to see he was not there. He must have snuck closer to us, to hear better what was happening, but I did not dare take my attention from Mourtzouphlos long enough to scan the crowd.

"He says that he is doing this only for the good of Byzantium," Alexios continued translating in a hollow voice. "He is the only true-hearted civil servant in all of the empire, he has no personal interest in public office but he feels he must have some official credibility, in order to use the stock of relics in the best interest of the city. He says the only way I can be sure to profit from their rescue is if the person who has rescued them is a significant figure in my court." With the sickly smile still on his lips, he muttered to Boniface, "He assures me that half of Stanpoli already knows something strange has happened to the relics, and that if I do not do this, he will signal his men to spread word around the city tonight that it was I who stole them, at your insistence, with the intention of their being used to pay the debt. I assure you, Fazio"—his voice wavered—"I am as good as dead if the people of this city believe I would do that."

Before the end of the feast, to much pomp and circumstance, a highly decorated pair of green leather shoes were brought out to the high table, held high on a plump cushion for all to see. These signified the currently unfilled office of royal chamberlain, a post usually reserved for the most trusted of eunuchs. To polite applause and much gossip (for he had been a relative nobody), Alexios Doukas, known as Mourtzouphlos, was held up off the steps by two huge Varangian guards, as the steward of the palace knelt and tied the green shoes onto Mourtzouphlos's feet. The new royal chamberlain graciously received the adoration of the court.

Milord Boniface kept a smile on his face, but he was almost rigid with rage. I stood behind him at my post, horrified by what was happening but unable to do anything to prevent it without bringing disaster upon my own head. I thought perhaps that Mourtzouphlos was still of the mind he had always seemed to be, and that he had done this suddenly, merely to prevent Milord Boniface, whom he hates, from taking the office of chamberlain. Even now I did not think there could be any evil in his heart.

Then, as Milord Mourtzouphlos received the final congratulation, he turned around to face Boniface a final time. "And by the way," he said loudly, in French, so that all lords of the army could understand him plainly, "please thank Gregor of Mainz for helping me to collect them all."

55

Continuation

In the chivalric tradition, when a young man receives the belt and sword of knighthood, he is knocked hard on the side of head, the intention being to shock him into clearly remembering the life-altering event forever. My treatment at Milord Boniface's hands later that evening had a similar effect. It even began with an actual cuff to the side of the head, and surely I deserved it.

The Briton was there for it, in Boniface's private tent. Milord Dandolo had demanded to be present for the confrontation and insisted he required soothing music for his extreme irritability. Even his own men regarded this demand as peculiar, but Milord Dandolo nearly had steam coming out of his ears, and all feared to cross him.

"Are you treasonous, insane, or stupid?" Boniface shouted at me.

As calmly as I could, I explained to Milord Marquis and Milord Doge what the original plan was for the relics. I said the intention was not only to protect the relics but to use them as collateral to force Alexios to pay the rest of the money, lest he face the wrath of his own people if the relics weren't returned. I explained that my error and folly had been to trust Mourtzouphlos; the scheme itself was sound. I attempted to remain vague about my connection to the Greek, but under furious questioning it came out that both Otto and Jamila had been instrumental. This did nothing to improve Milord Boniface's mood, but rather had him uttering unkind oaths about my lance,

*which he called "an accursed entourage." He declared that I may have
committed treason.*

"I admit I erred," I said. "But please understand, milord, I was
trying to follow the spirit of your orders to me. Accuse me of incompetence, if you must, but never treason. I was acting in the interest of the
army."

"The interest of the army lies in getting paid, you idiot!" Milord
Boniface shouted. "You did something to prevent that!"

Myself: "Milord, Emperor Isaac would have performed a heinous
sin—"

Milord Boniface: "That is not your concern, Gregor."

"My concern was the city's perception of the army," said I. "That
was my assignment from you. The army was being blamed for what
Emperor Isaac was doing. I had to stop him from doing it."

"But Isaac was paying us!" Milord Dandolo shouted.

"Milord Boniface," I said, "you condoned my asking Emperor Isaac
to return the Virgin's relic to its church. Surely you would not have
done that if all that mattered was what we could materially obtain."

"You completely misunderstood the point of that exercise," said Milord
Boniface. "It was to publicly demonstrate our piety. If Isaac had refused
to return the relic to the church, that would have been the end of the
matter, but we would still have appeared virtuous to the citizens. What
you've done here is not similar. You have, by your example, encouraged the
Greeks to defy us. That does not promote harmony. That promotes insurrection. When word spreads, as it will before the sun rises, that Mourtzouphlos won advancement by sabotaging the army's expectations—"

"The army's expectations never included plundered churches," I
argued.

"The army's expectations included getting paid!" said Milord Dandolo. "If the emperor decides to pay in melted-down reliquaries, then he
pays in melted-down reliquaries, and nobody protests. If you protest,
you put others' interests ahead of ours."

"Milord!" I protested. "I don't! It was the interest of devout Christians—"

Milord Boniface's face, already scarlet, began to turn a strange shade of violet. "You put the interests of devout commoners ahead of the interests of the nobles, who were robbed in lieu of the churches. How is that a good thing?" He was so angry, he threw a stool. "I need the nobles on my side, Gregor! They are the ones whose goodwill you should have courted, and you have wasted all your time and chance on rabble!"

I was amazed. "The Christians of the city—"

"The only Christians of this city who matter are the noblemen, for the love of God!" said milord Boniface. "Better the gold should come from some empty building where it is merely being gazed upon by simpletons than from the coffers of actual, worthy noblemen who will feel the pinch of it in their daily lives!"

I was too horrified to speak, then stammered, "The spiritual value of the relics—"

"Why do we not deserve their value as much as a crowd of ignorant Greek merchants?" Milord Boniface shouted. "We require recompense, and if I take it from the nobles, I'll lose favor with them."

"You'll lose favor with them?" Milord Dandolo snapped. Suddenly the discussion felt even more fraught. "Do you not mean the emperors will lose favor with them, milord?"

"Yes, milord," Milord Boniface said, but he looked flustered.

"That better have been what you meant, milord," Milord Dandolo warned.

"Why care what the nobles think of you, milord, when we're about to depart?" I asked.

"We are not about to depart," Milord Boniface corrected brusquely. "We cannot sail in winter. This is November, we don't leave until March."

I asked, "Is it so important to have the goodwill of an enfeebled aristocracy for four months that you'd sacrifice the spiritual heritage of one of Christ's greatest cities to secure that?" I looked at both the noblemen; Milord Dandolo felt the scrutiny and appeared uncomfortable. But Milord Boniface was the one I needed an answer from, and so to him, I pressed, "As the leader of a pilgrimage, you would make that choice, milord?"

Milord Boniface ground his teeth so that the muscles rippled all the way down his jaw. "You must not phrase things that way, Gregor," he said tightly.

"Of course not, milord," I said, for I had no heart to argue with something so villainous. "You are angry. Give me my punishment, and let us be through with this."

"There is nothing to be gained in his punishing you!" said Milord Dandolo. "What matters is to rectify the situation that you've allowed to happen."

"How?" I asked. I had been trying to think of an answer to this question myself from the very moment I realized Mourtzouphlos had used us for his own ends.

"I don't know!" shouted Milord Boniface.

"But Gregor of Mainz, you cannot be part of the solution," said Milord Dandolo. "Whatever guardian angel you might have watching over you, let him keep your hands bound and your mouth gagged. Save yourself for soldiering."

"We are entirely in agreement on that much," said Milord Boniface. "Every time I place trust in you, Gregor, you betray or disappoint me. I had such hopes for you. But this is desperate, what you've allowed to happen. We do not even know this man, and he's made himself Alexios's highest-ranking domestic officer after Constantine Philoxenites!"

"Befriend Mourtzouphlos," I urged. Milord Dandolo mocked this, but I continued: "Find common ground. You are still Alexios's hero, it's not as if Mourtzouphlos is going to steal that—they hardly know each other. I know the man well enough to believe he acts not for himself but for his city. His villainy is only his clumsy attempt to do what he believes is right." In saying these words, I thought of the Briton, who has so often performed in like manner. I did not glance toward the lute player as he strummed quietly near Milord Dandolo. I finished by saying, "I counsel you to give him a chance, in private, to explain himself."

"How can I trust a man who has done what Mourtzouphlos did?" Milord Boniface demanded. "Because of him, we will not be paid, unless the money is forced from the coffers of noble families whose goodwill we require to keep Alexios in power. And Mourtzouphlos accomplished that villainy only by duping you. I shall never deal with such a man, and when Alexios comes to see me tomorrow for our daily conference, I shall counsel him to somehow discredit the rascal."

"What if he brings the rascal with him?" I asked.

Milord Boniface shrugged. "So much the better. We may have a frank encounter away from the hungry ears of the Byzantine court fops."

"I will be a part of that conversation," Milord Dandolo announced. "And of every conversation involving Emperor Alexios hereafter."

Milord Boniface grimaced unhappily but could not deny Milord Doge's right to intercede when his own son-in-law had fouled things up so shamefully. "Very well, milord. But until this is resolved"—he gave me a look of bitter disappointment—"I cannot have you near me, Gregor, or ask anyone with authority to trust you. Count Baldwin of Flanders is horrified that this happened right under his nose."

"And mine!" Milord Dandolo shouted.

"You were not in charge of my men in my absence, Dandolo," Milord Boniface corrected him and turned his attention back to me. "I hear you even convinced one of Baldwin's men to dine at Mourtzouphlos's house! Any commander less indulgent than I am would have you hanged as a traitor—you've been conspiring with the enemy."

"He's not the enemy!" I said. "He is a rascal, I agree, but he is not our enemy."

"Not yet," corrected Milord Dandolo grimly.

Milord Boniface made a contemptuous gesture. "You're dismissed. I shall resolve this tomorrow when Alexios comes to see me."

"We shall resolve it when Alexios comes to see us," Milord Dandolo corrected.

ALEXIOS DID NOT COME to see them on the morrow. Or the next day. Or the next.

Emperor Alexios never set foot in the army camp again.

56

WHENCE" IS A TUTOR'S GAME for budding scholars, strategists, and politicians. The premise is simple: Given an initial scenario, A suggests the likeliest (or most outrageous, tragic, et cetera) outcome, which becomes the scenario for which B must suggest an outcome, which in turn becomes the scenario necessitating A's next outcome, and so on until it stops raining and the pupils are allowed to go outside and roughhouse or chase girls. Unlike chess, there is no winner to the game, which is, in a way, the point.

The events of the next eleven wintry weeks were a prolonged, oblique game of Whence, from which all emerged older but largely unevolved. Each player, for his own reasons, was waiting for spring to arrive, and it often seemed as if it never would. For those among you who require greater anecdote, following are abbreviated glimpses from that dark period, for I don't care to revisit it in detail:

From the day Mourtzouphlos rose to chamberlain, Emperor Alexios never once had audience with Marquis Boniface—who'd been, until that moment, his greatest friend and comfort. He still fed the army, to keep it from ravaging surrounding villages, but he stopped sending money in fulfillment of the treaty and ignored all of Boniface's written pleas, as did Isaac. Mourtzouphlos likewise rebuffed my and Gregor's epistolary efforts.

Whence:

Gregor, determined to salvage what he could of a project he'd thought of as his Christian duty, went with me to the city, to the cistern near Blachernae—where we discovered (as we'd feared) that the relics were no longer in their hiding place.

Whence:

We went to Mourtzouphlos's to confront him but found only Ionnis, who told us somberly that Mourtzouphlos was gone: he dwelt in Blachernae Palace now, at the emperor's right hand. So we went to Blachernae but were not admitted, although Mourtzouphlos certainly heard that we had been inquiring after him.

Whence:

Mourtzouphlos, with great fanfare, returned the relics to their churches—with the exception of the silver from the Jewish synagogue and the head of John the Baptist, which he insisted the army had stolen. Then he publicly (and falsely) proclaimed that the debt to the army had been paid, the hardship was over, the danger past . . . and *then*, a few days later, he made the alarmed claim that the Latins were planning to pillage the churches of their relics *anyhow*, just because that is the sort of thing Latins *would* do.

Whence:

Anti-Latin riots at once tore up the city. Resident foreigners—men, women, children—were kidnapped, thrown into boiling oil or onto open flames, mutilated, torn apart. Horrified, survivors of these ravagings scrambled across the harbor to the army camp. (Many had only recently *left* the army camp, where they'd fled after the fire.) Boniface largely ignored them.

Whence:

Gregor of Mainz once again organized the pitching of tents and rationing and foraging of food, exhorting his fellow knights that it was their Christian and chivalric duty to care for the weak and downtrodden. His chief allies in this, besides myself, were Bishop Conrad of Halberstadt (who spent a lot of time wringing his hands) and Dandolo of Venice (who wanted to be sure that Venetian expatriates, at least, were fed and sheltered). Rumors sprang up that there would be armed retribution; here too Gregor shone, calming the martial impulse, exhorting all to turn the other cheek in the name of Christ, and to trust that the army leaders would find a nonmartial solution.

Whence:

The army leaders called a parliament to dream up a nonmartial solution. Gregor petitioned to attend, for he understood Mourtzouphlos better than any lord in the army. He was rebuffed by Boniface on the grounds that they were dealing not with Mourtzouphlos but with Alexios, whom Gregor understood not a whit. Thus, no Gregor. (At this point, Gregor began to spend much of his spare time before his altar, praying.) However, Dandolo requested his favorite lutenist, so I had the odious privilege of witnessing this parliament. The lords, inexplicably believing that Alexios actually had control over his subjects (Isaac was now dismissed as demented), sent a personal envoy to chastise the emperor for the riots. As if this would accomplish something.

In a way, it did. When the French envoy dared to criticize His Majesty in front of all his courtiers, those courtiers (who actually did not much like Alexios but liked the French envoy even less) took matters into their own hands, hurling indignant insults at the envoy with such unremitting anger that the emperor himself was spared from speaking.

Whence:

Alexios cut off all contact—and far worse, cut off the army's rations.

It was early December; we now had no food, nor any means to purchase any.

Whence:

Boniface immediately formed foraging parties, and for some weeks, the army and its new refugees dined well on the spoils of local aristo-cratic summer palaces. Otto of Frankfurt proved himself exception-ally keen at ferreting out hidden stores in the palace cellars; news of his ability reached Boniface's ears.

Whence:

The marquis grudgingly appointed Otto one of the chief organizers of such raids.

I had reinserted myself into Boniface's tent as occasional musi-cian, to keep an eye on what was happening; in a time of watchful waiting, one wants to be watchfully waiting at the heart of things. With that smarmy troubadour Raimbaut in residence, there was less call for me, but I played a better lute than he did. As I softly strummed and hummed Bertran de Born's "Praise and Admonitions" ("I love watching knights chase people from their homes with their possessions clutched desperately in their arms" and so on), Boniface wrote Alexios and warned him the army would soon deplete its diet of abandoned-palace fare and would have to begin ravaging nearby populated towns in search of sustenance. It was Alexios's duty as em-peror to protect those towns, he wrote, and the best way to do it would be for Alexios to feed the army.

Alexios did not respond.

Whence:

At the disparate urgings of both myself and Boniface, Gregor put down his rosary long enough to dictate a new letter for Mourtzouphlos, begging him to intervene, to prevent what would surely become a rampaging spree of unprecedented magnitude.

Mourtzouphlos did not respond.

Whence:

Gregor returned to his prayers at the travel altar.

In fact, every moment he was not training, assisting his brother, or tending to the refugees with me, Gregor could be found kneeling before his altar in penitential prayer. He told me in a shaky voice that he was terrified he was starting to lose his faith.

Whence:

He confessed his fears to His Eminence Bishop Ineffectuality-Made-Manifest Conrad—whose responses did not satisfy.

Whence:

Gregor took it upon himself to correct his own soul with yet more prayers and now almost constant fasting.

Whence:

He came to the likelier conclusion that *his* faith was fine; it was Boniface's that was wanting, and by association, the entire campaign was tainted, and so, in short, Gregor endangered his own immortal soul by remaining with the army. However, because he had taken an oath to serve, he could not desert.

Whence:

He considered himself imperiled for being true to his sworn word.

This was an overture to melancholic madness. Gregor believed he'd spend the rest of his days atoning for the sins he and the army had already committed, and the rest of eternity atoning for whatever the army might yet do. (Why he felt personally responsible for the sins of an entire military campaign is a spiritual tick of the faithful which I am completely unqualified to explain.) I was sorry to see him in such a saddened state, but I thought it was good for him: he *needed* to be disillusioned. Just as I, the winter before, had been wrenched from my own peculiar ethic of minstrel-assassin, so now he was being wrenched from the simplistic certainty of Christian knighthood.

Meanwhile, the rest of us made better use of our leisure time. One would think Otto had invented pregnancy, he so fawned on Liliana. They were more amorous than ever. It is said a woman with child has a greater carnal appetite than any other woman, for she has no monthly chance to purge herself of her female essence. I've no idea if this is true in general, but it was true for Liliana. It is also said such a woman has limbs and joints more limber than those of other women; I do not know if this is true either, but Otto decided that it was, and chose to experiment accordingly. I will omit details. Imagine what you will, you have not imagined the half of it. Eventually we were all bored by it, even young Richard, which is saying a lot.

I never had a moment alone with Jamila; still, I was in her company for hours at a time. Under Boniface's protection, the Jews were finally rebuilding their settlement. It was rising again on its original footprint, but top priority was reestablishing the textile industry; workshops were completed first, and people crowded together until actual homes could be rebuilt. Samuel, one of the most prominent here, was among the first to have his house completed, and he was sheltering as many of his kith and kin as could squeeze under the roof, including Jamila. The house, although the largest, was not big. Built so that one side nearly hugged the protective wall around the settlement, it was just four rooms: a large main chamber, where families arrayed themselves for sleeping; to the right, an eventual study that was now a dormitory for unmarried or widowed women (Jamila's domain); to the left, close to the perimeter wall, the kitchen; then a ladder up to Samuel's private chamber, with the house's one great bed; but at first, this was also crowded with elderly rabbis in need of shelter, and Samuel himself slept on the floor.

Jamila never left the walls of Pera, but I was allowed to enter them; several times a week, I did. We played music together, practiced languages, debated the political situation with Samuel and his menagerie of guests (although I got the impression that, when I wasn't there, Jamila was not included in such discussions). I was allowed to witness the Chanukah candelabrum on its final blazing night. I cannot say I ever felt actually *welcomed*, but they knew I was at Boniface's elbow, and they wanted to know what I knew. Remembering what was under that tunic and knowing I'd have a chance to caress it once she'd left with us for the Holy Land—this was the most extended, most erotic foreplay in the history of sex, far more erotic than Otto's and Liliana's exertions. The world was falling apart around us, and I knew it, and it concerned me—I even did my part to help it—but when I was near Jamila, I could keep all that at bay.

Until the army raided Pera.

This defied Boniface's protection of the settlement, a protection that consisted mostly of some sergeants stationed by the Pera Gate who spent a lot of time playing dice. The raid was originally just to find wheat, but then a hidden chicken clucked too loudly in someone's bathhouse. Amazingly, no Jews were hurt in the ensuing rampage, but none were left with food or fowl either.

The pillagers fed the entire army camp that night; despite a tepid official rebuke from Boniface, they were treated like heroes. Gregor and I were appalled; he sought audience with Boniface but was refused; Jamila and Samuel, likewise. In my general state of stubborn, stupid hopefulness, I thought I knew how to fix the problem; but of course, I was merely having my own turn in this winter game of Whence. To wit:

I went to the gates of Pera, where a group of armed men anxiously watched against further pilgrim incursions. They recognized me.

"Jamila," I said.

"Samuel," they corrected. Grudgingly, they let me through. One of them, with a blade the length of my forearm, followed me to Samuel's house.

I rapped hard on the door. Voices within argued mysteriously; I heard over and over again an Arabic term I recognized: *Dalalat al-Ha'irin*—"The Guide for the Perplexed." This was the title of a book by the sage Maimonides, a favorite of Jamila's; she sometimes explained bits of it, and I found it interesting, but I never had the patience for philosophy. Her voice was not among those raised in the debate.

Samuel's servant opened the door. He saw me, looked unhappily over his shoulder, and made a plaintive expression in the direction of his employer, huddled in a group with some of the elders of Pera; these were the ones handling their impending starvation by debating the finer points of Jewish philosophy. The place was almost starting to look lived in. Samuel rose from the cushioned stool where he sat, came to the door, excused the servant. He looked appalled that I had the temerity to exist.

"Do you really expect us to speak to *any* Latins, after what you did to us today?"

"I need Jamila's help," I said. "To translate for me. To Isaac."

"Isaac?" he frowned. "Isaac ben Moses? Why do you need to speak to—"

"Isaac Angelos," I corrected. "The elder emperor. Remember him?"

Samuel blinked at me. "Are you mad?"

I said nothing. My stomach suddenly growled, loudly.

"What right has your stomach to growl? I'm the one who did not eat tonight," Samuel snapped.

"I didn't eat either," I retorted. "I would not eat stolen food."

Samuel, without a smile, laughed bitterly. "Well, unless you brought it back to us, you'll get no commendations from me. If no measurable good came of your not eating it, then you're just a fool for going hungry when you didn't have to."

I was stung but could think of nothing to say. It was the kind of comment Jamila might have made. Samuel glanced back at a noise, then frowned and spoke in Arabic.

"Don't be ridiculous," Jamila said mildly, coming up behind him. "What is it?" she asked me. "Samuel, please let him into the house."

"I require Jamila's assistance," I said and added, choking on it, "Sir."

"Samuel," Jamila said in a voice of appeal and then vented rapidly to him in words I couldn't understand. He retorted; she retorted. They were both polite, but they were obviously arguing. The men in the room all looked astounded: Jamila was hardly displaying her customary backbone, but she was standing up to Samuel in a way that I—and apparently Samuel himself, and the rest of Pera—had never witnessed.

Finally Samuel made a small but angry gesture, and turned back to me. He gestured me into the house and pointed to a cushion, the only seat left. I sat. Everyone was staring at me, and none with friendly looks.

"I heard you talking about *Moreh Nevuchim*," I said, using the Hebrew name of the book just to show off, in a failed attempt to bring the social climate of the room above freezing. "Have you heard Jamila's thoughts on Maimonides? Very interesting."

If I had been speaking to moss, I would have gotten more of a response.

"If any harm comes to her, or if she in is any way coaxed into embarrassing us, you will pay for it with your blood," Samuel announced.

"An eye for an eye," I said quickly.

"That phrase is always misused," Samuel said. "It refers to righteousness, not revenge. It means that if I pluck out your eye, I shall volunteer to you my eye in payment for it. Do you understand?"

I nodded. "An eye for an eye. I swear to you."

I was delighted by how quickly she agreed to go with me. There was still ferry service across the harbor, although it was expensive now. By the time the church bells rang compline in the darkened cold, we'd entered the old palace compound, gone past the Hippodrome with its lifelike menagerie, past Hagia Sophia, past the many gardens, past the entrance to the cistern, and all the way to the gates of Bukoleon Palace, Isaac's home on the southern shore. It was a long journey for two on foot and hungry.

"Are you ready?" I said, before the gate.

"I think so. This is hardly as dangerous as last time."

"Well, then," I said and gestured broadly. "Let us begin."

The Madman of Genoa was announced, with the polite reminder that His Imperial Majesty had met the seer and his lovely interpreter on the day of His Imperial Majesty's deliverance from prison—deliverance that was in no small part a result of the Madman's efforts. We did not have to wait long before we were invited in.

Isaac's palace was modest compared with Blachernae (where his son resided), but it was still bedazzling. His Elder Majesty received us in a small room, entirely of dark marble. He wore his purple shoes, his gold-and-purple gown, even a crown, as he sat at a private supper table (made of a dozen kinds of inlaid wood); here he had just finished entertaining four devout astrologers, of different ages and girths, all wearing pearl-studded red gowns and all soporific from overeating. What looked like the remains of fully half a cow lay heaped on a tray. One stargazer plucked off bits of meat and tossed them to some happy dogs at Isaac's feet. I swayed with hunger and grabbed Jamila's hand. She squeezed mine back.

"Sit!" Isaac said. I held out a chair for Jamila; I knew he couldn't see me, but Isaac sensed this was my action and informed me, barking, "Not the woman, she can stand. This is a mutual honor. Nobody sits in the presence of the emperor, but I respect the men who really understand power, and I make exceptions. Sit!" And he waited until I sat. Jamila remained standing, leaning slightly into my shoulder. "I remember you," Isaac continued. "You convinced my usurping brother to abdicate. You're the one who talks directly to God."

"When he sees fit that I should do so," I concluded. Jamila was translating, with a nervous, apologetic smile at the astrologers. They did not look happy to see competition.

"Well, he is obviously willing to speak to you now, or I would not have let you in," Isaac announced. Jamila translated this charmingly circular observation, and then added softly and desperately, "Say something to make him give us food."

"Tell him my channel to God is cleared by the passage of meat down my gullet."

Jamila said as much, sounding slightly sheepish. The astrologers, realizing we were in their same category of bald self-interest, warmed to us and sliced us rump meat.

"Honor among thieves," I observed.

"I won't translate that," Jamila said with a gracious smile, not looking at me.

Once we had been fed, and given some excellent wine, Isaac demanded to know what words of God the Genoese eccentric could impart to him. "Shall I banish my sodomite son? Or shall we kill all the Venetians?" he asked eagerly. "I can do it, you know. I have only to lift my finger and the ground beneath them shall split open and they'll fall into the earth. My astrologers have told me as much." This, from the man who'd once outwitted the legendary Emperor Frederick Barbarossa.

"Ask him to show me how he does that," I demanded. "The refugee children back at camp will *love* that trick." She glared. "Never mind then. Tell him no harm to the Venetians—in fact, he should keep them safe, so they can take the icky French and Flemish away come springtime." When this missive from the Almighty was delivered, I came to the heart of my message. "He must feed the army."

Jamila hesitated.

"Go on," I urged. "Don't let the charlatans intimidate you. I'm a greater charlatan than the four of them put together, you've seen my handiwork." She smiled a little, nervously. "So tell him: to remain king of the known world, he needs the Jews."

"Why?" Isaac wanted to know.

I had an answer ready, but Jamila had a better one and substituted it promptly: "Because the Jews make the best textiles and pay the highest taxes and have no buffer from religious persecution except the emperor's goodwill and patronage, so they're your most loyal subjects. But they're in danger because of the hunger of the horrible pilgrims."

"So," I concluded, taking over, "Isaac must place armed guards around the gates of Pera. And send a thousand head of cattle to the army."

She blinked nervously. "Whoever's expecting to eat those cattle will retaliate—"

"They'll retaliate against him, and he can handle it—he's an emperor."

She translated my command. Isaac was unconvinced. "He thinks if he just killed all the pilgrims, that would be easier," Jamila explained. "Frankly, I agree with him."

"No, no, he mustn't do that," I said and raised my voice a little so Isaac would hear my gravity. "He must take care of them all through the winter, so that they may leave in March for the Holy Land, where they will kill off the infidel enemies of Christ while conveniently extinguishing themselves on the battlefield at the same time. Both of his enemies, east and west, gone." I snapped my fingers. "In a single battle. If the Franks die now, the Mohammedans will rise up against him within a year. Tell him God said so!" I raised my voice dramatically and made a few flourishing hand gestures. Then I remembered

Isaac couldn't see me and stopped bothering. I had no need to make an impression on the astrologers, who were already dozing off with their heads on the table.

My pronouncement did not have the effect I was anticipating. Isaac, it turned out, did not really want to hear the Word of God; he wanted to hear that all would be well, that without his doing anything, he would outshine his sodomite son and be ruler of the world for the rest of his life, which—he had been promised four times over—would last at least another eighty years. He was extremely irritated God had the temerity to tell Isaac himself to make an effort. While too frightened to defy the Madman who had helped restore him to his throne, he wanted no more news that was disheartening. So he promised he'd do the best he could to accomplish these requirements, paid generously for services rendered, and then banished the Genoese Madman from his presence forever.

I thought I'd attained something benign. But all I'd really done was play my turn.

Whence:

The following day, a thousand head of cattle on their way to slaughter were collected against their drivers' wishes by imperial troops and delivered across the harbor to the army camp without a word of official explanation.

Whence:

That evening, a week before Christmas, a mob of beefless Constantinopolitans slunk down to the harbor under a glorious full moon, filled a clutch of small boats with pitch and tinder, and set them aflame. They steered them in the direction of the Venetian fleet (because of course the best way to make an army *leave* is to *destroy* their only means of doing so). The sailors on watch, who had clearly seen the hubbub form in the moonlight, repelled them with grappling hooks, far enough out of the harbor mouth that they were caught up in the Bosporus current and sailed, terrible but harmless, down into the Sea of Marmara. (It was at this point that my hopefulness began to abate.)

Whence:

Undeterred, and despite the solemn Christmas observations on both sides of the harbor, the Greeks tried again on New Year's Day. This is the Calends of January, the most festive day in the Byzantine calendar, traditionally given over to forgiveness and renewed good fellowship—but also to disorderly pranks.

It was very dark; the sliver of the waning moon had sunk below the horizon. The mob was more organized this time, tying seventeen timber ships together so that a wall of fire erupted from the harbor toward the fleet. Thousands of Greeks climbed up onto the harbor walls, in the dark, to watch what they heartily hoped would be a conflagration even greater than the damage to their city. The Venetians, still vigilant, again deflected the attack, again with grappling hooks and the help of the Bosporus current.

Whence:

From that day on, endless minor scuffles between Greeks and Latins were blamed on all manner of pretenses, when pretenses were bothered with. I was now convinced that anything I did only made things worse—even with Jamila's assistance—and consigned myself to the role of witness for the while. In truth, it was hard to do much useful in a constant state of hunger. Food was getting scarcer. Some enterprising Greeks still made the sojourn over the harbor, but their prices were prohibitive, with two-penny bread becoming twenty-three-penny bread, and that once it was stale. A rumor began that knights were killing and eating their own horses, which by the ethos of knighthood was nearly cannibalism. Pera was pillaged again; after it turned out there was nothing left to steal, Boniface issued a furious condemnation against such pillaging and sent his most profuse apologies to the elders of the settlement, claiming to have flogged the perpetrators and begging the elders to still allow Jamila of Alexandria to accompany the army when it departed in early March. That much was no subterfuge: Jamila as a guide was a genuine and unexpected boon.

Everyone went to bed hungry. Soldiers began to desert.

Whence:

Boniface decided that there would have to be a direct confrontation with his former lapdog, Emperor Alexios. He needed good soldiers.

Feast of St. Lucían, 8 January A.D. 1204

I write now of a victory, but I feel defeated.

The Marquis Boniface, who has had naught to do with me since the shameful event of Mourtzouphlos, commanded me to leave off my prayers and fasting long enough to be a member of his honor guard as he rode to Blachernae. I obeyed him because I must. My brother Otto was beside me.

With no armor but our shields, we approached the palace walls, from the same angle as the army last July. The marquis's intention was to demand a parley with Alexios. I do not know if Alexios would have condescended to speak to the marquis; we never had the opportunity to learn. We were attacked before we'd even reached the walls—ambushed, by a large and violent raiding party led by none other than Mourtzouphlos himself. He'd been waiting with his men behind the rise of the hill before which the army had encamped last summer. He learned from spies that we were coming, that we wore no armor, that we had no bloodthirsty intentions, yet he fell upon us with bloodthirstiness, in full armor. I think he did so so that his name would resound through his beloved Stanpoli and he would be hailed a hero of the people, for the people hate us now, and admire anyone who does us harm. We, who came as pilgrims, seeking only to do a favor to an empire. And yet, we deserve every mouthful of spit, every curse, every invective that has been hurled at us since then.

Without any attempt to parley or warn us away from the walls, Mourtzouphlos and his men let loose war cries and a spate of arrows toward us from behind. Indeed, it strikes me as miraculous that none in the rear guard was struck off his horse, for we were overtaken so abruptly that our lances were useless. Only then did he sound a shrill horn to alert archers on the walls of Blachernae.

Half a year ago, I would have delighted in describing the brief struggle that followed, but I lack the heart for details now. It is enough to say this: when the Greeks meet us on an open field, we will best them. We will always best them, that will never change, for we are better soldiers. Once, I believed this meant that God was on our side somehow, but now I know it means nothing but that we are better trained at fighting and killing, and I am not sure how that shows that we have the favor of the Christ. All the same, we are the better soldiers, both individually and as a unit, and as soon as we were recovered, it was clear that we would be the victors of this skirmish.

But then the favor seemed to shift toward the Greeks. We'd dropped our lances, for the enemy was in too close. I shouted for the soldiers to form a line between the marquis Boniface and the oncoming mass, which outnumbered us by four to one at least—that is, we were a dozen and they were perhaps fifty. But then archers on Blachernae behind us began to shoot, so that we were caught between two hazards. Mourtzouphlos and his men were bearing down upon us with shortened lances (although the Greeks are poor with lance). I sent two archers to fend off the archers; this left four archers and six horses, and I placed the horses in front of Boniface, with myself in the center and Otto to my right. But the horse to my left shied at an arrow with a large, red scarf attached to it; this was surely planned ahead of time, for once there was a break between myself and the shying horse to the left,

Mourtzouphlos spurred his mount forward into the breech and swung an ax to take off Boniface's head.

There was little I could do in that moment—my sword was in my right hand, and Mourtzouphlos was to my left. So I urged Summa to sidestep left very fast, and then I shook my foot out of my right stirrup and pushed myself out of my saddle and right at Mourtzouphlos, so that, despite the deep seat of his saddle, we both fell over his horse and landed together on the ground hard, he with his ax above his head; I pinned the ax to the ground by slicing my sword down into the handle as we landed.

Mourtzouphlos is large for a Greek, but not so large as I am. He was startled to be blindsided that way, and his face was red with anger when he realized he could not lift his ax. And yet when he looked up and recognized me, he began to laugh so that I could feel his body shaking beneath his scaled breastplate. He made a mad comment: "I hope when you go whoring you are gentler with the ladies, German!" Then he struggled to get out from under me. Beyond us, Otto moved in front of Boniface to protect him. I could hear him shouting at me to kill Mourtzouphlos. Mourtzouphlos heard him too and released the handle of the ax. He said, "Now I am unarmed! Would you murder an unarmed man? Is that not accounted evil in your code of chivalry?" (For in the days when I would dine at his home, we spoke of chivalry, and he had affected interest in it.)

I pressed the side of my sword hard to his throat. "You have done me great wrong," I said. "You are a man of no honor, and you do not deserve to be treated with any honor in your turn." I raised my sword to strike him clear through the throat, my own throat filled with bitterness that I should kill a man who once was a friend. But before I'd swung the blade, Otto cried out a warning and I looked up: the archers on Blachernae were about to release a cloud of arrows at me, and I had to roll off Mourtzouphlos lest I be hit; indeed, I am amazed he was not felled by those arrows himself. They continued to rain down, but *now he was on the other side of their arc of travel, so that (leaving his damaged ax behind) he could run back in through the gate. His men, as soon as they'd seen him unhorsed, had already fled, for they were cowards.*

Boniface abandoned his intentions to parley with Alexios, and we returned in haste to the camp. The marquis made it widely known to the army that his loyal son-in-law had saved his life against the nefarious Mourtzouphlos, but he has said nothing to me directly and done nothing privately to encourage any love again between us. I therefore resume my more important work, which is my prayers and supplications.

WHENCE:

Gregor returned to the private purification of his own disillusioned soul.

Meanwhile, back in the city, Mourtzouphlos made it known that he, although a mere palace official, had dared to raise arms against the hated foreign army. This did not actually make him more popular— but it certainly made Alexios even less so.

Whence:

As I warned, we were all eventually eleven weeks older, and generally in straits more dire, but otherwise largely unevolved.

And then, on the twenty-seventh of January, everything and everyone began to change.

57

I'D SPENT THE EARLY AFTERNOON that day in Pera with Jamila. It had been a good day, largely because Samuel was not at home. Most of his lodgers had relocated into their own, newly roofed houses, and the only other woman still in the house was conspicuously absent, although she made significant noise from other chambers just to remind me she was there. I'd wrapped myself around Jamila and plastered her face with kisses. It had been seventy-seven days since I'd undressed her, to be interrupted by Otto's homecoming. In a mere thirty-three days more, Boniface would depart for the Holy Land, with a Jewess as his guide and a Briton as his occasional musician.

But at this moment, thirty-three days was an impossibly long time.

"We can't keep this up this much longer," I warned her.

"No," she agreed and hugged me even closer against her. "We can't."

She meant something different, but I didn't know that yet.

The door began to open, and I hastily unwrapped myself from Jamila, falling off the cushions onto my arse in my haste not to be too close to her when Samuel entered.

But it wasn't Samuel. It was the old man, the rabbi to whom I'd recited the children's rhyme the summer before—and with him, to my confusion, was Ionnis, our former guide and Mourtzouphlos's former ward. They didn't seem to know each other, but they were jabbering in Greek—or rather, Ionnis was and the rabbi was listening with anxiety. They looked toward Jamila as they entered, as if they'd come specifically to find her, but they were both urgently relieved to see me. "The one I wanted!" Ionnis said.

Jamila rattled off a feeble-sounding excuse in Arabic to the rabbi, to explain why she was alone with me. He ignored this display of decorum, grabbed Ionnis by the arm, and dragged him to my side. The two men, old and young, then began to hold forth to Jamila in agitated Greek, delivered so fast that I couldn't grasp it, although it sounded like they said "Hagia Sophia" at least a dozen times. I decided that I must be mistaken and that anything Greek sounds like "Hagia Sophia" if you say it fast enough.

Jamila looked horrified but held up her hand to stop them, and nodded in my direction. "He cannot understand," she said in French. "One of us must explain."

"I will," Ionnis said with a desperate significance. "Madman, understand me."

The situation they were so upset about was about the most bizarre political crisis I've ever heard of. In short, Emperor Alexios had a rival claimant for the imperial crown. That in itself was not bizarre (the Byzantine throne seemed eternally up for grabs), but details of the situation defied belief: A mob of thousands had formed in Hagia Sophia a few days earlier, apparently spontaneously. They were disgusted that Alexios refused to attack the evil foreigners who were pillaging their kinsmen's villages (this was exacerbated by the fact that it was Mourtzouphlos, not Alexios, who had faced off with Boniface); they were enraged that the city's most priceless relic, the head of John the Baptist, was still in unknown (but presumably foreign) hands; in short, they were fed up and demanded that Patriarch Ionnis Kamateros (the pope's equivalent) anoint a new ruler—even though nobody wanted the position. When it became clear that there would be no volunteer for the post of pretender emperor, the mob had spent days seeking out an acceptable nobleman upon whom to foist the honor; their first two choices for this dubious distinction had fled the city, knowing the Varangian Guard would immediately slaughter such a claimant as a traitor; then at last the mob had cornered one Nikolas Kanavos at knifepoint in Hagia Sophia and demanded he be crowned; the patriarch had refused to crown Kanavos against his will, and so the crowd had somehow *performed this office themselves* ("Understand me?" Ionnis demanded, himself incredulous); then this mob of thousands, with their reluctant pretender emperor forcibly laced into imperial purple shoes, locked themselves in the church, demanding that Alexios abdicate and that the Varangian Guard swear its loyalty to Kanavos. (Isaac was by now forgotten.)

"I came to tell you this, Madman, so you can do something," Ionnis concluded.

I blinked. "What you're describing is lunacy. I can't play at being Madman of Genoa and mend something of this magnitude, Ionnis. This is far too serious." I almost told him I could actually mend *nothing at all*, but he would not have believed me.

Ionnis looked as if I'd betrayed him. "You made a usurping emperor abdicate, I heard about it from Mourtzouphlos! If you could do it with that one, do it with this one."

I suddenly felt like I was drowning. "Ionnis, the Usurper was almost on his way out anyhow—like a loose tooth that just needed one final yank. I did very little, really."

"You were the mastermind of the relics! I know my uncle shamefully undermined you, but still you thought up *how*. So just think up how, *now*," Ionnis begged. "Go to Hagia Sophia and convince the crowd and their emperor to go away. Otherwise, very bad things will happen." To Jamila, as if this would solve the only possible objection I might have: "You go with him as interpreter."

The old rabbi guessed the meaning of this final thought and erupted into a panicked speech against her doing any such thing. Samuel was invoked in almost every sentence; Jamila began to look resentful at the very syllables of his name.

"Lad," I said, wincing with apology, "I have no idea how to handle that situation. The very thought of it frightens me." He began to protest; I shook my head. "I am only successful when I can confuse people's sense of what is reasonable. A mob—especially the mob you're describing—*has* no sense of reason. I cannot outwit something witless."

"What does great Mourtzouphlos wish to do about the problem?" Jamila asked.

The youth shrugged his shoulders in that profoundly Greek way, but he looked tormented. "He is like a different man since he put on those green shoes. He wants what is good for the people, but I don't know if he really understands the people anymore now that he is surrounded by courtiers. I think this turns even his head. I never see him. So, Madman, you must do something. There is nobody else!" There was a tremor in his voice, his eyes glistened—he was terrified. He'd been there and seen it for himself, and the unflappable young man was deeply flapped.

"I can do nothing myself," I insisted. "But maybe Gregor can." Gregor was sunk in prayer before his altar, and my pestering him would accomplish nothing—but seeing Ionnis's haunted face might catalyze him. "Will you come with me to speak to him?"

Ionnis shook his head. "If this destroys the city, I want to be with my friends when everyone dies."

"Nobody is going to die," I said, not sounding or feeling very convincing.

"I go to the city," Ionnis said. "This is the beginning of the end of everything."

I ran back toward the camp, wondering if there were any way to use this crisis to exhort Gregor out of his inactivity. I was cresting the spine of hill that separated the army from the walls of Pera when I glanced back and saw the imperial barque pulling across the harbor. From where I was, I could just make out the central figure standing arrogantly on the deck, surrounded by Varangians.

It was not Emperor Alexios. Or even Emperor Isaac.

I broke into a run again, arriving breathless at the cabin, threw open the door, and shouted, before my eyes had adjusted to the dim light, "Mourtzouphlos is coming!"

Liliana, noticeably round of belly now, was resting in a corner; otherwise, the cabin was empty. "We know," she said.

"Where's Gregor?" I demanded.

"Boniface summoned him as an extra bodyguard when Mourtzouphlos was seen ferrying over." She gave me a nervous smile. "Things are about to get interesting." Now there was less smile and more nervousness. "Since Jamila isn't here to do it, let me be the one to insist you do not meddle now. Please." She put an almost apologetic hand on her abdomen. "*Please.*"

"Done," I said.

Feast of St. Gilduin, 27 January

What I write now is a recording of the lowest extreme of the lowest abyss to which this campaign can possible fall.

It begins with myself, Milord Boniface, and Mourtzouphlos, in the outer chamber of the marquis's pavilion. For a moment the three of us just stared at one another. Mourtzouphlos was wearing a white turban and tunic, and the green shoes of his office. He gave me a smile like a boy pleased with himself for getting away with mischief. I almost expected him to take me aside to ask that there be no ill will between us two.

"What is your business?" Boniface asked sharply.

"His Majesty sent me," Mourtzouphlos said, growing equally sharp. "He begs you to come with me to Blachernae at once, to meet with him in private. The situation in Hagia Sophia is very grave. His Majesty is frantic. He has exhausted the skills of three different physicians trying to contain his anxiety, but he says only a conference with you will calm him. I disagree, but I am the only man in Blachernae whom Alexios trusts, and I have been sent to summon you, the only other man alive he trusts."

I wanted to ask Mourtzouphlos what he had ever done that Alexios should trust him, but I did not think it wise to speak. And when I think of Alexios—so weak and frightened, ever seeking counsel of an older man—and Mourtzouphlos—so charismatic and full of strong opinions—I can almost believe it, if the youth is desperate enough.

"You must understand," Boniface said, "that given our last encounter, I am not inclined to trust my safety to you."

Mourtzouphlos nodded. "Yes. Please bring anyone you wish for protection. What happened between us was the unfortunate result of each of us doing what we needed to. Tonight we have the same goal, which is simply to offer succor to His Majesty."

"Come, Gregor," Boniface said, with the sort of gesture one might make to call a hunting hound to heel. He signaled also to Claudio, his chief bodyguard.

We ferried over as the sun dipped down toward the horizon. Mourtzouphlos kept up a stream of conversation but only with me, not with Boniface or anyone else. He spoke of all his Greek friends whom I had met at his home last fall, offered news of them and other such ridiculous manner of discourse. Of course I did not answer, but that didn't stop Mourtzouphlos from chatting with his accustomed humor. This disturbed me for several reasons, the most significant being that it does not reflect well when a treacherous enemy insists on treating you as a friendly confidant in front of your superior. I was disturbed also to see how convincingly friendly he still appears, even now I know his villainy. The fellow must be mad. Every Byzantine I've met seems a little mad.

As darkness fell, we were admitted through the water gate straight into Blachernae. Here, we had direct passage all the way up to the emperor's chambers—these must have been the same chambers, although not the same emperor, where the Briton and Jamila found themselves last summer.

Emperor Alexios was pacing his bedroom looking pale and feverish, his newest physician near him. We were admitted with a flourish and then were told, like all attendants, to stand around the sides of the room. The first thing I noticed was not Alexios himself but his physician—who was the Jew named Samuel. Then the flurry of introductions began, and I bowed to His Majesty and had a chance to look him over.

Emperor Alexios is unwell. He has not blossomed, and will not blossom, into an imperial presence. He looks as if he has not been eating, and he claimed that people are trying to poison him. He told us a remarkable story about a mob forming in Hagia Sophia to choose another emperor, although the Varangian Guard will attack anyone who threatens him. "I need you, Fazio, I need you," he sobbed, grabbing Milord Boniface's hand. "I'll give you anything you want if you'll just bring your men across and get rid of the mob! Send them right into the church! Anything you want!"

"I want you to give us what you have sworn to give us," Milord Boniface said calmly. "Especially food. You must send food to the camp at once."

"We cannot afford so much food right now," Mourtzouphlos interrupted. "His Majesty is in distress and requires your council. He does not require your army. We are able to take care of our own leader. As I told His Majesty, the Varangian Guard can handle the mob if it does not disperse on its own."

"The guard is not big enough for a mob that size," Alexios insisted.

"If Your Majesty allows a foreign army into the city right now, Your Majesty will have worse problems than that mob," Mourtzouphlos warned.

"We'll find a way to get you food," Alexios said to Milord Boniface.

"And the money you owe us," Milord Boniface continued. "All of it. Tomorrow. Once we're in the city, we will not leave until you've paid in full, and presented us with enough livestock and grain for a month."

"That is impossible!" Mourtzouphlos said angrily, stamping his foot. "This is deep winter! You will starve half the city with such a demand!"

"Then good luck sorting out the excess of emperors on your own," Milord Boniface said. He raised his hand as if signaling to Claudio and me it was time to go, but Emperor Alexios, looking panicked, grabbed the marquis's arm and pulled it down.

"No! I'll do it! I'll find the money!" he insisted.

"Physician, something to soothe the emperor?" Mourtzouphlos said, irked.

Samuel had been mixing a concoction at a table by the window. "I am almost ready here," he said.

"Are you trying to poison me?" Alexios demanded.

"No, Your Majesty," Samuel said in a patient voice, not looking up at him.

"Alexios," Milord Boniface said, with paternal strictness. The young man turned his frenzied glance back toward him. "You've said before that you would pay us, and then you haven't done so. I need surety. Right now. Before I leave this room, I need collateral. Something solid. Tonight. Or I will not bring the men tomorrow."

Emperor Alexios looked pained and cried, "But I have nothing! For the love of God, Fazio, I've already given you Crete."

"What?" I gasped, amazed.

Alexios, still clutching Milord Boniface's arm, turned to me. "Yes, I gave him Crete," he said. "For helping me achieve the throne. What more do you want, Fazio?"

Milord Boniface gave Mourtzouphlos a knowing look. "I would not mind the head of John the Baptist, to begin with. Despite the rumors you have tried to spread to encourage hatred of the army, you know we do not have it."

"It is lost," Mourtzouphlos said. "But even if we had it, we would not give it to you." And then, with an expansive gesture I did not care for, aimed at me: "To Gregor of Mainz, who deserves such a treasure, perhaps. But not to such a man as you."

Milord Boniface refused to be baited. He glanced around the room thoughtfully, then smiled and said, "In that case, I want this palace."

The Greeks all gasped when this was translated; Mourtzouphlos turned purple with rage, but he held his tongue.

"Blachernae?" Emperor Alexios said. "You want to own Blachernae?"

"If you do not pay the army what you owe us, then you open the doors of Blachernae to the army as soon as we've dispersed the mob," Boniface announced. "I will leave a group of knights inside the gate, on our way to the church."

Mourtzouphlos, nearly frothing at the mouth, and with many large gestures, spewed forth in angry Greek. He was interpreted like this by a very cowed interpreter: "Milord Mourtzouphlos doesn't think you should have come to Stanpoli at all."

There was a pause as we waited to hear the rest of the translation. The interpreter elected not to go into detail.

"You were released from prison thanks to us!" Milord Boniface said indignantly.

The interpreter hesitated. "Milord Mourtzouphlos doesn't see it that way," he replied at last. He turned to His Majesty, who looked distressed but gave a gesture of permission. Samuel crossed the room and handed Emperor Alexios something to drink.

His Majesty took the cup, which was carved of ivory, and looked at it mournfully. "I hope you are not poisoning me, Jew," he said.

"Of course I am not, Your Majesty," Samuel said. He took the emperor's free wrist and spent a long time feeling his pulse as conversation continued.

The interpreter smiled apologetically and said to Milord Boniface, and to me, "Milord Mourtzouphlos says that the imperial court of Constantinople has been in shambles for decades, that the system is collapsing from within, the mobs are getting more powerful, the highest-ranking families are making all the decisions without thinking about the empire as a whole, just their own desires and interests.

Some twenty years ago, the royal family was so enfeebled that, when Manuel died, they could not even bring themselves to oust the hated foreign woman and her young son who were left in charge, and at the same moment Hungary took over Dalmatia and everybody made a fuss but nobody did anything about that either. Milord Mourtzouphlos says the nobles of the empire are their own worst enemies. The Usurper was hardly more than a puppet for an entire rotting oligarchy. Milord Mourtzouphlos thinks it all would have imploded within a few years anyhow, and we'd be free without the humiliation of being indebted to an outside occupying force. Milord Mourtzouphlos thinks you are taking credit for something that would have happened anyhow."

Milord Boniface was enraged by this depiction, but he kept himself in control. "I have given you my terms, Alexios," he said. "They are nonnegotiable."

"I accept them," Emperor Alexios said desperately. He pulled his wrist free from Samuel's grasp, flung the empty medicine cup across the room, and fell on his knees, still grasping Milord Boniface's hand, which he now began to kiss. "Thank you, Fazio. God bless you for giving me another chance. Bring your army right away."

58

GREGOR GRIMLY DESCRIBED the situation to us in the lamplit cabin as the Richardim and I were helping both him and Otto get into their full battle armor—only the fifth time in a year that either soldier had had to do so. It was the dead of night. Liliana, bleary-eyed, hands resting protectively around her taut belly full of five months of growing life, watched this gearing-up ritual. She was terrified of Otto going off to battle, and angry at herself for being terrified. Otto was fiercely delighted to do something besides foraging and did not understand why his brother (or the mother of his unborn child) was so unhappy about it.

"The entire army is about to be admitted into the city"—Gregor began to explain.

"The city can take care of itself," said Otto. "All those winding streets and overhangs and blind alleys? And half a million citizens? I'm more concerned about the *army*. Nobody can *take* Constantinople."

"I was thinking about our destination, actually," Gregor said wearily. "We will be marching, armed, into the largest temple of Christ ever built. Six months ago we were there as pilgrims, and now, to enter by force as soldiers"—he shuddered—"Whatever happens, it is going to be ugly."

"Not as ugly as starvation," Otto assured him. "And finally we're going to get everything that's due to us! You want to resume the pilgrimage? Now we'll do so by the first of March!" He winked at Liliana. "We'll land a month before your time, and there are abbeys aplenty in the Holy Land for your lying-in. This is the best of all worlds." Liliana forced herself to smile. Nobody, not even Otto, believed her; he signaled the Richardim to hold off putting on his helmet, and clanked across to her, to kiss her forehead. "I'll be careful," he said, his lips nuzzling her temple. "For both your sakes."

Now grooms held horses' heads, squires helped their burdened masters to mount up, and camp followers clustered around watching in excited, frightened huddles. I was coaxed into playing some crusader songs for Boniface's household. An hour before dawn, the cavalry was mounted, the army in formation and listening to a hurried mass. The mood was shortsightedly hopeful. They were about to march inland up the harbor, cross the bridge, then head back along the other shore toward Blachernae, where they'd be admitted by Alexios. Then this foreign occupation army would march through the city, into the greatest church in the world . . . and before they left, they would have done a good deed, and in return received food and gold and the means to complete their pilgrimage come spring-time. Finally, finally, *finally*, the standoff would be over. Byzantium's internal crisis was the army's panacea. They would get to be heroes all over again.

Before they had begun, however, a ferry came careening across the still, dark harbor, oars slapping. "Milords! Milords! Milord Mar-quis!" a voice screamed out.

The screamer scrambled up the steep slope from the harbor all the way to Boniface, who had a grim-faced Gregor beside him—and that dim-witted little dark-haired minstrel just paces away from the horses' heads, where I'd been leading the crusader songs ("God is be-ing besieged in his holy kingdom, so let's see who actually goes to his aid," and so on.) The screamer was one of Boniface's spies, making an appallingly dramatic appearance. "Milord!" The fellow gasped for breath, looking hysterical. "The Emperor Alexios has been thrown in prison by Chamberlain Mourtzouphlos, and Mourtzouphlos has declared himself the new emperor!"

Boniface was horrified. "When did this happen?" he demanded.

"As soon as you'd left," the man said. "Treachery incarnate. He claims Alexios is a traitor because he would have allowed a foreign army to overrun the city. His Majesty had gone to sleep with drugs from his physician, and Mourtzouphlos woke him, warned him there was a crowd massed against him come from Hagia Sophia, and got him to go quietly, in disguise—straight down to the prisons, then clamped him in irons and took the purple for himself."

"Well then, we'll ride to get him out," Boniface said, furious. "We'll do that first and kill Mourtzouphlos, and then go right on to Hagia Sophia."

I dropped the fiddle from knee-height so that it made a resonat-ing *thwack* at my feet. Gregor agreed with me.

"Milord," he said in a private, urgent voice, "I counsel against that. It's too chaotic there to keep a starving army focused when you don't even know what to focus on. Wiser to tell the army to stand down and give the situation a day or two, until we understand what Mourtzouphlos really wants."

"It's obvious what he *wants*!" Boniface snapped. "He wants Alexios's throne!"

"Milord, I disagree with you," ventured Gregor. "There are now *four* emperors within the city walls, and Mourtzouphlos is by far the least legitimate, the only one not actually crowned. It is almost a parody that he calls himself emperor—I say that knowing the man's character. I do not believe he intends or even hopes to actually become the real emperor. This is a strategy to achieve some other end—he wants to make sure that he is *listened to*, for he considers himself the city's truest spokesman."

"And what does he want us to hear him say?" Boniface demanded sarcastically.

"Exactly what he said tonight: keep the army out of the city. He is afraid of the damage it will do. It is his response to an emergency. Let him try to disperse the Hagia Sophia mob himself. He'll fail, and then he'll realize he needs our aid. Then we can negotiate with him for Alexios's release, and everything else we require."

Boniface grimaced at young Baldwin of Flanders, who was a stone's throw away on his stallion, his helmet off and his face straining in the torchlight to overhear. Baldwin came closer; Hugh of St.-Pol and Louis of Blois, his cohorts, moved closer too. Boniface summarized Gregor's argument for them, making it clear he was not convinced by it.

"What if Mourtzouphlos really means to make himself emperor?" Baldwin asked.

"One cannot *make oneself* emperor," Boniface said, which was a grudging acknowledgment of Gregor. "It is in the hands of the Varangian Guard, which means the hands of the eunuch Constantine Philoxenites." And then, a challenge to Gregor's theory: "The most alarming thing about this development is that the Varangians have

not already killed Mourtzouphlos for this attempt. It suggests Philoxenites has been wooed by Mourtzouphlos."

One of the other counts shook his head. "Philoxenites?"

"The eunuch who controls the treasury," said Boniface. "He, of
course, can be manipulated by everyone else in the court, but ulti-
mately, he is the voice who tells the guard to whom they owe their
loyalty whenever there's a deposition or an abdication. There's been
a lot of that in his lifetime, so I imagine he has become quite astute at
guessing which way the wind will blow."

"*If* Constantine Philoxenites has told the Varangians to consider
Mourtzouphlos their emperor, milords, the Varangians will fight us
when we try to enter," Gregor added. "We need preparation before
meeting them."

Baldwin, who'd led the force that never managed to storm Blachernae, nodded grimly. Boniface glanced at Hugh of St.-Pol and Louis
of Blois. They nodded too.

The marquis voiced a sigh of aggravation so extreme it was nearly
a shout. "Stand down," he growled in frustration to his herald, and
the order was echoed in voice—*stand down, stand down*—as well as
by drum code, trumpet, and horn across the night to the whole of the
army. Gregor and I, for the first time ever, risked exchanging direct
looks in front of Boniface. I could feel my heart thudding against my
rib cage.

WITHIN A WEEK, the situation had simplified, but nowhere near the
way Gregor had predicted. Through the mysterious forces that control a mob's emotions, the reluctant emperor Nikolas Kanavos in Hagia Sophia lost all support and was assassinated by the same people
who had forced the crown onto his head just six days earlier. Alexios
and his father were reported alive, but imprisoned and thoroughly
deposed. It was impossible to reach them, just as it was impossible
to reach Alexios's Jewish physician Samuel, who was kept at Blach-

ernae all week to tend to His ex-Majesty's health. The Jews of Pera, increasingly frightened by this rising madness among the Gentiles, barred their gates to everyone, including me. ("You promised me you wouldn't meddle," Liliana said, panicked, when I tried to figure how to get in to see Jamila anyhow. "With anything. Just sit still and agonize with the rest of us.")

Mourtzouphlos was crowned at Hagia Sophia, as soon as the last of Kanavos's supporters-cum-executioners had been chased out. Whatever mysterious force it is that controls the passions of eunuchs had inspired Constantine Philoxenites to hand the Varangian Guard over to Mourtzouphlos.

Still there were three anointed emperors in the city; even now, Boniface and Dandolo remained hopeful of a diplomatic resolution. The day of Mourtzouphlos's coronation, they sent word to Blachernae seeking parley with Mourtzouphlos but received only the message that His Majesty Alexios V Doukas was otherwise engaged.

That night, Baldwin of Flanders's brother Henry led an expedition north toward the small town of Philia, where it had been reported by scouts that there were still edibles to pillage. The shortage of food was so severe that even Boniface was personally affected. People slept when they were not required to do something for survival, just to conserve their energy. I tried fishing, but winter waters were not as generous as those of summer. I tried to visit Pera to see how they were managing, but with Samuel still absent, nobody would let me in—and neither would anyone let Jamila out. I could have climbed the wall near Samuel's house and entered in through an upstairs window, but Pera was full of too many watchful eyes—all of them keeping their watchfulness especially trained on the physician's house. I couldn't even stand outside the gate and *ask* to enter without half the settlement rushing over to glare at me. So I went back to Gregor's cabin, to try to calm an anxious Liliana—now convinced she'd be a war widow without the benefit of ever having been a wife.

The group under Henry was not his regular company but which-ever riders had stamina enough to stay on horseback for the twenty-mile trek that began in total darkness, later to be lit by a waxing moon. Otto volunteered to go, determined to make sure the mother of his child would not lack for nourishment—although the mother of his child much preferred he just stay at home. Gregor remained behind, again anchored at the knee to his altar with its nasty lit-tle crucifix. He blamed himself for Mourtzouphlos's rise to power. I pointed out that Mourtzouphlos was *my* fault, since I had gotten him out of prison to start with; ah, reasoned Gregor, but *my* being here to do that in the first place was *Gregor's* fault.

At that point, I stopped trying. I'd thought, once, that Gregor's disillusionment with all things crusaderish was the best thing that could happen to him. Disillusion is to be embraced; it lightens the soul's load a great deal, for *illusions*—especially the lofty ones that Gregor always clung to—can be such a very heavy burden. So I'd decided to let him wallow in it awhile, certain that, when he grew bored of wallowing, he would be ready to return to action, rising like the phoenix from the flames, his golden-glowing certainty and cha-risma returned and refitted for better action. I'd had cheery little fan-tasies of him wresting control of the army from Boniface and leading it to Jerusalem himself—there he would negotiate some Saladin-like arrangement with the current rulers and everyone would beat their swords into plowshares.

But now it was clear that Gregor's disillusion would lead to noth-ing but further disillusion, a cancer growing upon itself. I kept hop-ing that things with him were now as bad as they could get, and that eventually they'd of their own start getting better, because he was *Gregor*, after all, and even if it was at the last moment and under ex-treme duress, Gregor always managed to get his head on straight and do, or at least attempt, the right thing.

But not this time.

*   *   *

I CAN DESCRIBE the raid on Philia, and Otto's role in it, for so many men were full of stories afterward I could have written twenty ballads just from their accounts; it reached the point that Liliana could no longer bear to *hear* the name of Philia.

Nobody on the raid wore full protective gear—getting in and out of armor without a squire's help is nearly impossible, and they wanted to be light on their feet. The rout was easily accomplished: the inhabitants fled into the wilderness rather than face armed and mounted warriors; without bloodshed, the entire town was the crusaders'. And it was, indeed, fat with staples and livestock and dried fruits and root vegetables and bread and butter and cheese . . . the company allowed themselves the rest of that day and the whole of a second to feast and relax, having sent word back to the main camp that they were bringing back enough for the army to gorge for a fortnight.

The next morning, they began a slow but happy return trek with all the food. Much of it was put on barges sent up after them, but there were cattle to herd, and cattle are slower than horses. Thirty knights and more numerous mounted sergeants—perhaps a hundred in all—settled into a plodding pace, the peace of the empty countryside around them lulling them to calm. They were singing rounds of crusader songs and playing guessing games among themselves in the drowsy, cloudy afternoon—

—when they were ambushed by four thousand mounted Byzantines.

Mourtzouphlos must have flung himself and his new purple shoes onto his horse outside Hagia Sophia as soon as his coronation ceremony was over, and never gotten off again: he'd raised a mounted army forty times the size of the company they hunted, then set out toward Philia carrying a gem-studded gold icon of the Virgin.

Soldiers and horses screamed out in alarm, but these were hardened fighters, accustomed from tournament training to rude surprises.

Even as they cried out to Jesus for deliverance, the Franks dropped their lances—their ambushers were too close for lances to do much good—and pulled out swords and daggers to fend off the attackers.

When various men described this later, they were too excited to speak clearly of the details, but in very little time, it was obvious that the tiny pilgrim force was routing the Byzantines entirely. The Greeks turned and fled, many dying as they went, without a single pilgrim suffering the indignity of even falling from his saddle.

Emperor Alexios V and his bodyguard galloped back toward the city in a panic, but Otto and a few others were determined to ride them down—this was personal for Otto, because *he* blamed himself for Mourtzouphlos, too. As Otto raced after his former prison mate, Mourtzouphlos's aide threw down the royal standard; Otto's stallion shied but leapt on still at the Greek's heels. Then Mourtzouphlos hurled the icon back over his left shoulder and raced on toward safety.

Otto took the bait, turning Oro so sharply that he was never more than four horse lengths from the icon. Had Oro been slightly faster, Otto might have even caught the holy image while he was still in the saddle. As it was, he was on his feet and threw himself over the Virgin protectively so that none of the other riders could rob him of this prize. He clutched Our Lady to his chest and uttered prayers and hallelujahs in her name all the way back to the army camp, where he gave the icon to Liliana as a gift and announced that if they had a daughter, her name must be Maria.

At this point Liliana finally let go of my hand, to which she had clung so ferociously for the past two days I wasn't sure if I could ever hold a bow again.

Boniface promptly summoned Otto and explained, in dulcet tones, why a mere sergeant (let alone his whore) could not personally keep a priceless icon of the Virgin. Otto resented the condescension, but he agreed to relinquish the Virgin to the chief Cistercian monastery in France, as long as he was widely credited with having

liberated her from the heretical clutches of the Orthodox Church—
and as long as all the bishops, and Boniface himself, thanked him
publicly.

The real triumph of the day was all the food, and there was feasting and relieved celebrations around the camp that night—except of
course for Gregor, who stayed in the cabin on his knees to atone for
Otto's successes. I was paid to play for dances until the early hours of
the morning, but it was hard to keep my own cheer up, thinking of
Gregor's state of torment. Otto had no patience for it.

The next day, rumor reached the camp that Mourtzouphlos had
returned to Constantinople and had the gall to tell the citizens that,
far from suffering an ignominious rout, he had *bested* the crusader
troops in the ambush, with the help of the miraculous icon of the
Virgin. When the obvious question was asked of him—where, exactly, *is* the icon of the Virgin? Is it perhaps with the famously missing head of John the Baptist?—he claimed it had been immediately
put into safekeeping in a vault somewhere.

I'd promised Liliana (and myself) not to meddle, but as soon
as I heard this rumor, I knew what had to be done. I also knew I
couldn't do it myself and maintain my status as dimwit in Boniface's
eyes. Gregor wouldn't help me—Gregor wouldn't leave the cabin
now, except for guard rotation. Otto, however, loved my plan and
carried it out energetically: he borrowed back the sacred icon from
Boniface (who himself liked the idea enough to take credit for it)
and displayed it up and down the harbor in a Venetian longboat.
In a second boat, a loud percussion band drew insistent attention
to the treasure. One huge banner in Greek proclaimed the truth of
what had happened outside Philia and denounced Mourtzouphlos as
a coward and a liar; another called for the return of Alexios IV, the
rightful emperor.

The escapade was satisfying, but the truth is, it didn't make much
of an impression on anybody.

Except Mourtzouphlos. Who realized that Boniface, Dandolo,

and the other leaders would never take him seriously as long as Alexios IV was still alive.

The following morning, as the army was breaking its fast, an arrow landed in the middle of Boniface's compound with a parchment tied to it. Nobody knew where it came from; the harbor was more than a crossbow shot wide at its narrowest point. The message was brought to Boniface, who opened it.

In French, it read:

> *It was Mourtzouphlos, and it was murder.*

An hour later an official envoy arrived from the palace of Blachernae with the shocking news that Alexios IV—prince, pretender, emperor, breaker of promises, and snot-nosed boy—had died of natural causes in his sleep.

The news flew around the camp, where it was met by horrified silence.

Later in the day a second envoy came to announce that Isaac II, when he heard about the death of his beloved son, had immediately died of shock.

There were no longer four emperors in the capital. There was only one.

Mourtzouphlos.

59

WE HAVE NO TREATY with Mourtzouphlos," Boniface re-
iterated later that morning.

The army leadership had been called to emergency parliament, with Dandolo and the bishops. Besides concern about the
growing crisis, I was panicked for selfish reasons: a guard at the Pera
Gate told me the elders were preparing to relocate the settlement en
masse, away from Constantinople, at the first sign of renewed martial
activity. The only mouthpiece I had against such activity was Gregor,
who would do nothing on his own. So I committed a minor forgery,
as a result of which Boniface thought Gregor had petitioned to attend the emergency parliament. When his response arrived *allowing*
Gregor's presence, I'd convinced Gregor (who did not bother to read
it, because he was too busy praying) that it was *ordering* his presence.

So Gregor was present now—and so was I, in my usual position of
stupid lutenist, at Dandolo's request—but seeing him in situ, I wondered why I'd bothered. His beard needed trimming, his hair needed
combing, and his clothes needed putting on: he was still dressed as
a pilgrim, in cross-bearing undershirt and nothing else, despite the
winter cold. The skin around his eyes was the color of lead; he was so
exhausted and undernourished he appeared to be drunk or drugged.
John the Baptist would have looked debonair in comparison, even
after Salome got her prize. I was afraid Gregor might fall over, into
either a stupor from which he'd never recover or a seizure of speaking
in tongues. Torn between concern, disgust, and guilt, I was almost
curious to see which it would be.

"The treaty was with Alexios," Boniface was explaining. "If he *is* dead, there is no more treaty. We no longer even have the right to *expect* the rest of what was owed to us. And we'll be out of staples by the end of the month."

"By then it will be March," said Baldwin of Flanders. "And we will leave here anyhow. That was the agreement." This reassured me; I hoped it really was so simple. "Clearly this entire diversion has profited us nothing. Let us admit our error, leave Constantinople behind, and turn our faces toward the Holy Land at last."

Dandolo was glaring; his blindness allowed him to glare in all directions at once. "How do you propose to do that, milord?" he asked with a sarcastic politesse.

"In the ships waiting in the harbor, milord," said Baldwin, imitating his tone.

"And how do you propose to pay us for them, milord?" Dandolo asked. "The agreement to go to Jerusalem in March rested on Alexios's funds, which he neglected to provide before his expiration and is *very* unlikely to provide now."

"Are you Venetians not our fellow pilgrims, milord?" Gregor spoke without permission, hoarsely, his eyes unfocused. Stupor or seizure? I still wasn't sure. "Did you not all take the cross before you left?"

"What does that have to do with it?" Dandolo demanded—in a tone suggesting Gregor should stop pursuing the matter instantly.

"If you took the cross, you're honor-bound to complete this pilgrimage anyhow, milord. Your entire navy's been excommunicated, your souls are more in need of pilgrimage than the regular pilgrims' are. And if you are going to make this pilgrimage, then for the love of God, milord, simply *take us with you*." He was a little agitated; my money was leaning toward seizure.

"We're not going anywhere unless we're paid," said Dandolo.

"Milord," Gregor said with frustration. Now his eyes were finally focusing, but with poignant futility, they were glaring at somebody who couldn't see him. "No other pilgrims expect to be *paid* for concluding their pilgrimage, why should you? You have, finally, been paid for the ships themselves, and for your year of contracted service to us. You have received *all* the money *we* ever promised to pay you. Those debts are canceled, that business is concluded. All is even. Now we are all here together, as a unit, far from home, grievously besieged, with a shared oath to honor. We must stand together and do what we've sworn to God and the Holy Father that we would do—liberate the Holy Land. There will be loot in plenty there; you will be more than rewarded for your goodness. Why are you refusing to go where you're guaranteed to benefit materially and spiritually? Why instead insist on staying someplace where you are no longer likely to benefit at all? What kind of stubbornness is that, milord?"

"German boor," Dandolo spat as Boniface leapt up, enraged, to shout, "*Gregor!* Enough! Beg the doge's pardon and leave at once."

"Milord," said Bishop Conrad, standing, placating hand outheld. "I must speak."

I don't think I'd heard Conrad speak, much less take a stand on anything, since just after the coronation of Alexios IV, early last August. This was turning out to be an entertaining parliament; I could hardly wait to learn what vacuity His Eminence wanted to explore today. I prayed it would not be in support of hostilities.

"Another sanctimonious German," the doge said dismissively.

"Gregor of Mainz's reasoning, whether sound or not," clarified Conrad, seeing Boniface and Dandolo both about to protest, "will strike a chord with every soldier in this army, and if you throw him out now, he will see to it they all hear about it. And frankly, milords, and I hope I speak for all my brethren," he added meaningfully, glancing at the other bishops, "his reasoning *is* sound, in the eyes of the Church."

"The Church is not *funding* this expedition!" Dandolo snarled.

"Who funded Christ's ministry, milord?" Gregor asked. "Or St. Paul's?" Some of that old glorious righteousness was returning to his face. He stood up a little straighter.

"This is not a theological debate!" Dandolo shrieked, incredulous that he should even be expected to respond to this. "I am responsible for the wealth of my people."

"So come to Jerusalem with us, milord, and bring back riches!" Gregor shouted back, suddenly looking a foot taller. "And save your men's imperiled souls while you do it!" For a moment, he looked so glorious, if the army could have seen and heard him, they'd've all been off toward the Holy Land by dinner.

But: "Gregor! Silence!" Boniface yelled. "Dandolo, milord, I beg your pardon."

"I've handled worse than him," Dandolo said with a harsh laugh. "As long as we agree he is not to be listened to."

Gregor opened his mouth to speak; Boniface glared, and the knight sat, hard, on the stool he'd been assigned. Even seated, he looked taller than he had in weeks.

"Of course he is to be listened to," said the Bishop of Soissons severely. Good heavens—*two* prelates were rising to the occasion. Possibly unprecedented. "His Eminence Conrad is correct. Gregor of Mainz has made an argument I can easily imagine every sergeant and foot soldier in this army giving voice to. My guess is that half the common mariners, if they were actually *informed* of their own ex-communication, would likely take it up as well and sail the dissenters straight to Syria—"

"With all the clergy," the Bishop of Troyes—*a third prelate!*—added. This was remarkable: the clergy, after more than half a year of spiritual slumber, had woken up and remembered that they were on a pilgrimage! Gregor looked as if a vise around his chest was suddenly loosened; I felt that way myself.

There was a deeply uncomfortable silence in the pavilion. Dandolo would have to bend; I was eager to see him do it without losing face, because I liked the spirit of the man even when I violently disagreed with him. He was enraged but waiting to see how the church-men's declaration would be received by the lords before he made his next gambit; the lords in turn were waiting to see what Boniface would say; Boniface was upset but inscrutable.

He had risen to chastise Gregor. Now he sat again and rested his fingertips together, tapping them slowly and watching the tapping with apparent fascination. "Let us adjourn until tempers have cooled," he suggested. "Let us take a few days to contemplate the situation, and our alternatives, and to grieve the murder of an ally and onetime friend. In the meantime, let us all keep our own counsel." He did not look at Gregor as he said this. "I will call another parliament in a few days. We must remember that fulfilling our crusading vow outweighs all other considerations. As Gregor of Mainz has so ably *demonstrated*, if we don't do that, we risk internal insurrection."

Dandolo frowned but did not object. The lords and bishops filed out. Boniface signaled Gregor to stay a moment longer. When they were alone—or relatively alone, with only some of Boniface's servants and lackeys and the one lute player huddling around the edge of the tent—the marquis finally looked at his son-in-law.

"I am tempted to have you flogged," Boniface declared, angry but contained. "I know you won't apologize, but may I ask if there is some extenuating situation in your life that can justify this outrage? You look appalling. Do you need to stage a tournament and release a little battle lust? Do you need a new woman, since the Jews have taken one of yours and your brother has rendered the other so unattractive? Is there some vice to which you're addicted, the absence of which might account for your craziness?"

"The only thing missing from my life is movement toward Jerusalem, milord," said Gregor quietly. "I've spent years preparing for a pilgrimage, and I will see my vows fulfilled." He turned his back on the marquis and walked out of the tent.

And then, for over a fortnight, Boniface did nothing—and neither did Gregor. Gregor had acted most satisfactorily once I pushed him onstage, so to speak, but of his own volition he clutched himself to his altar with its crucifix, and to his private prayers. Reports reached camp of a grand state funeral, of Emperor Alexios V (Eye-brow) publicly prostrate with grief before the casket of Emperor Alexios IV (Snot-Nosed Boy).

Latin expatriates, who'd already sought temporary shelter with the army after the summer fire and then after the December riots, began to reappear at camp a third time, frightened for their safety in the increasingly xenophobic city. They were taken in, but not as easily this time; Gregor of Mainz, the golden knight who'd been their patron twice before, was nowhere to be seen now. He was in his tent bewailing the evil actions of his superiors, despairing of returning the pilgrimage to its right course. By now—seeing him too mired in un-happiness even to accomplish some little good when the chance for it came to his door—I'd evolved beyond annoyed impatience and was concerned about him. I and others did what we could to help settle in the new floods of refugees, but Gregor, perhaps from his years on the tournament circuit, had a way of coaxing large groups of people to cooperate for a common good, a knack I've never had.

The food supplies from Philia were gone; most refugees brought food with them, but not enough to feed an army. More foraging par-ties went out, but they had to go farther and farther away, since they'd already wreaked devastation on all the towns and countryside within two days' ride in all directions. Otto remained one of the captains of this industry and sometimes managed to drag his brother with him; their increasingly long forays agitated Liliana no end.

I was still not allowed into Pera. The locked gates were guarded by grim, unspeaking youths hovering behind them; the community kept itself silent to the outside world, and I couldn't even discover if Samuel had returned from Blachernae. I understood the caution, but I tried to get word to Jamila to meet me somewhere, even if we had to speak through a chink in the wall, like Pyramus and Thisbe. I spent whole days waiting at the entrance for a response to my messages; none ever came. Otto accompanied me sometimes. Knowing Jamila might not now come with the army as a guide (upon its March de-

parture for the Holy Land), Otto was determined to convince her at
least to rejoin our little tribe as Liliana's midwife; his self-centered-
ness was almost endearing, and almost justified my own selfish impulses. We tried to coax gossip, even rumors, from the Jews guarding
the Pera Gate, but they were so incommunicative they seemed inhuman. I knew Jamila could take care of herself, and it felt to me as
if the price she paid for rejoining her community was to have been
promptly placed in prison.

March was approaching, and the army itching to be gone. Various rumors spread around the camp, none of them helpful to morale:
It was said the army would be left here, deserted, on the shores of the
Bosporus come March, when the Venetians would instantly sail for
home; it was said the leaders would revert to the original plan to sail
first to Egypt for money and resources, which would extend the pilgrimage by months and might trap the army in the Levant over yet
another winter; it was said that even then, they would owe all their
booty to the Venetians for taking them there; it was said that even if
the Venetians didn't take the booty, the leaders would. Sometimes it
was whispered that there might be a direct assault on the impregnable, holy city of Constantinople itself. This evoked more dread than
all the other rumors combined.

Food grew dangerously scarce, knights began again to eye their
horses ravenously, and now we had more mouths to feed as expatriates kept flooding into camp. The refugees earned their keep by helping to collect and load small boulders into the ships. These were to
be ballast, as well as fodder for the catapults when they approached
the shores of the Levant.

But the mariners were never actually instructed to prepare the
ships to sail away.

It alarmed me that the all-important meeting about what must
happen next—adjourned by Boniface just as it was about to lead to
forward movement—was never reconvened. I tried to keep a daily
eye on both Boniface and Dandolo, but each seemed to be waiting

either on the other or on some external force to prompt his next move. I turned my attention then to the bishops, who were doing *nothing* to follow up on their grand display of pilgrim righteousness. They spent hours huddled together in the pavilion of the Bishop of Soissons, but they wouldn't let me near. They spoke to no one, did nothing. So, as a precaution, I quickly shifted my energy into spreading rumors. Gradually, thanks to me and my fellow gossipmongers (whores, minstrels, bored servants), the men became aware that, all the way back at Zara, the pope had directly prohibited an attack on Constantinople. Surely, then, such an attack could *not* be in the works—for if it were (went the rumors), *surely* the clergy would take all possible steps to prevent it.

The clergy suddenly made themselves scarce.

"You promised not to meddle," Liliana reminded me for the hundredth time, trying to pretend it was a game between us. "You're meddling. You're going to get us all killed. Teach me to play chess or something."

I still could not get into Pera. Dandolo, Boniface, and the counts began to meet in private (total private for a change—no clergy, not even any stupid lute players), and new rumors (not mine) of an attack on Constantinople ricocheted around the camp. Knowing now the danger this would place on their souls, the rank and file were profoundly disturbed, and the clergy grew even more invisible. There was an unbearable sense of waiting. The rumors of an attack even made it through the fog of Gregor's penitential practice; he continued his fasting and prayers until he seemed to grow physically smaller, a sort of tired insect infecting one corner of the cabin.

By early March, the Venetians had made no gesture to prepare the ships for sailing, and the last of the Latins were expelled from the city, swelling the size of the army camp almost beyond capacity and prompting the Jewish community to strew broken glass atop the settlement walls for extra protection. No official declaration had been made, but everybody knew there would be war—indeed, in a sense there already was war, for every few days a foraging party or outlying watch would have to fend off Greeks. The Greek bands were small, badly armed, and pathetically ineffectual. Few of the pilgrim soldiers were ever wounded, but news of each attack still made Liliana shake with fear.

Liliana was big now and did not like to go out unless she had to. She had feminized the hut almost beyond recognition. I kept protesting (mostly to cheer Gregor up) that we were just about to leave it; she would smile bravely and say, "Well, let's keep it nice until then, anyhow," and continue to shakily embroider rags to hang as curtains over windows we did not have. I loved her for it—she was the only one among us preoccupied with something more than impending battle. Otto, ironically, was one of the loudest voices against an attack, trying to start rumors that the army would decamp quickly so it would have landed safely before Liliana's time came. But he'd never had Gregor's clout with either the leadership or the rank and file, so his efforts were in vain. He sought audiences that he (a mere sergeant) was never granted with the barons; he tried to fill his brother's large boots on the training field but was always outranked by Boniface's knights, who threatened him to silence if he started debates about what they, the army, ought to do next.

I say "they" not "we" because I didn't know what I myself would do if by some miracle they suddenly *did* sail for Egypt. Jamila going along as a guide, in exchange for Boniface's protection of Pera, was unlikely now—but perhaps, as Otto fantasized, *perhaps* she might come with us anyhow as Liliana's midwife. Surely she could find no satisfaction in her present circumstances. But I couldn't reach her to coax or ask, although I still tried every day.

Otto was almost as desperate for her to come with us as I was. In fact, he was so determined to convince Jamila to stay with us, he would occasionally go on his own to Pera, to try talking his way through the gates after I'd endured my daily rebuff. I knew he'd never be successful, but whenever he went trotting off to try, I'd wait for his return on the off chance he might have Jamila with him. I would catch myself anticipating and lecture myself until I had abandoned hope. It was the sort of cheerful repetition that made our cabin the homey little place it was, those days.

So I was amazed one day, just after dinner, to hear Jamila's voice intermingling with Otto's down the avenue between the cabins.

She was coming back to me.

I hurled the door open so fast I almost ripped it off its leather hinges.

60

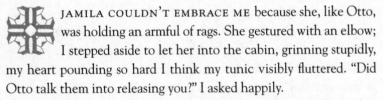 JAMILA COULDN'T EMBRACE ME because she, like Otto, was holding an armful of rags. She gestured with an elbow; I stepped aside to let her into the cabin, grinning stupidly, my heart pounding so hard I think my tunic visibly fluttered. "Did Otto talk them into releasing you?" I asked happily.

Jamila shook her head, trying to determine where to deposit her burden. "I ran into him as he was adding to his"—she glanced at her holdings—"collection."

Liliana smiled and started to rise to her feet. Otto was proving himself a provider, and during this period of limbo and deprivation, his pillaging tendencies had been partially redirected toward rags. There was now a pile of elegant swaddling materials (brocade burp cloths, silken diapers, scraps of chased leather to make baby boots) large enough to sleep on, although the child was still two months away. Otto took Jamila's bundle and tossed it onto the heap. He was preening.

"Never mind war booty, you are every expectant lady's hero,

milord," Liliana said. She reached out toward Jamila in welcome. Jamila put her arms around Liliana without much energy, an automatic response to show regard—and Liliana, noticing immediately, pulled away to study her. I moved closer to Jamila, for my own embrace.

But Jamila avoided looking at me and did not move toward me, which was awkward. Otto and Liliana exchanged glances; I pretended not to see them doing this.

"Gregor's just back from a foraging party," Otto announced, kissing Liliana's cheek. "I have an overnight sortie—rumor says the head of John the Baptist's in a village north of here, and Boniface wants his best retriever for the job."

Liliana muttered her usual Otto-leaving-camp mutters. "Give me a cloak," she said finally, holding out an arm. "I'll go with you to meet Gregor." She did not add: *because these two seem to need to talk in private.*

When we were alone, Jamila finally looked at me.

"We're going," she said, sounding hoarse.

"We are?" I asked, wary. "Where?"

She shook her head. "You cannot come."

"Then who is we?" I demanded.

"You know who it is," she said, looking down. "I want to say something to you because I don't know when I'll see you again—"

"Stop it, stop it right now," I said, shaking my head. "Stop talking nonsense. I don't know where the Jews are going, but you and I are—"

"My heart has three parts to it," Jamila said, ignoring me. Oh shit, this sounded rehearsed. "One part has just my two dead children in it, and nobody else. Another is where I hold most of the people whom I have ever known or loved—my parents, my husband, everyone." A pause. This was definitely rehearsed. "The third part just has you. And this will always be true. I want you to know that." She took in a ragged breath. "Samuel and I are married."

I have no idea what my body did for the next several moments. I had never been so dumbfounded in my life.

"Jamila—" I finally managed to breathe, incredulous.

"It is an obvious and desirable match; it is good for the whole community."

She may as well have been speaking Norwegian. "What *community?*" I breathed. "Pera is about to be destroyed again, you *know* that—"

"That is why we're leaving. Immediately. We will never be safe here with Mourtzouphlos on the throne. And we certainly can't sit and starve in the crusaders' shadows. We will rebuild as soon as we find haven. There must be families, and Samuel and I can make a family. So it *is* good for the community," she said again.

"But is it good for *you?*" An inane question, but I was trying to put my senses back in order.

"Better than being a parasite Jew among an army of crusading Christians. Better than being a parasite among the Jews as well. It is a good match," she said, sounding like she was trying to convince herself. "I am his brother's widow, and that's a common and desirable remarriage. We are both skilled in healing. We'll do well together. But he's being questioned in Alexios's death, so we have to leave."

There was a silence. I still could not think clearly.

"I said married, but it is not quite that straightforward. We're be-trothed as of this morning, but the wedding is not for a year," she said, as if this could possibly make it better. "It's a custom among Jews in this part of the world. To have a betrothal with cohabitation, for a year, before the *chuppah*. It allows time to make sure it is a good match, it guards against divorces."

"You've been completely dishonest with me," I said.

"No, I—"

"Stop!" I grabbed her shoulders and shook her, and she cowered; the moment made me furious at both of us. "I've fallen more in love with you every passing day, and you've known that, and you've let it happen, and you've never warned me that, in the end, you would go to someone else."

"What exactly are you accusing me of?" she demanded nervously. "Other than being Jewish, I mean? You said you would return me to my people, and you did so. How have I wronged you in that equation?"

I growled with frustration and let go of her, but I hit the wall so hard with the heel of my hand that I actually hurt myself, and yelled in anger.

"There's nothing profound about what you're feeling," she said quietly. Again, it sounded rehearsed. Maybe she herself had heard this speech from Samuel. "Do you know how often people almost get what they want and then don't? There is nothing remarkable or noble about such suffering." She turned away, but I grabbed one side of her collar and pivoted her back toward me. "Let go of me," she said. "Just over the hill, within those walls, is a man whose life and mine make sense together. There is so little in this world right now that makes any sense, how can you fault me for taking what is offered to me? Let go of my collar or I'll cry out and get us both in trouble."

"I like getting in trouble with you," I said in a broken voice. "I think we do it very well together." But I let her go and turned away, pressing the heel of my hand against my eyes, cursing to myself.

She watched me for a moment. "Samuel realizes—"

"He can't possibly," I snapped. "Does he realize I have my own *compartment?*"

"Yes," Jamila said. "He does. How can he not, when he indulges your trying to make love to me under his own roof? He understands me better than you do. I had a regular life, and then it was irregular, and now it can perhaps be regular again—"

"I've never had a regular life, whatever that means, so I cannot begin to understand the value of it."

"I know that," she said. "I hope someday you have the opportunity to know the blessings of it. Then perhaps you won't judge me so

harshly for having chosen it. If I could have you *and* a regular life . . ."
She let her thought trail off. "And Samuel knows that. He had a
wife. He lost her in childbirth. He will not love like that again, he
doesn't even *want* to, but he desires the regularity of such a life. And
the community desires it for him, and for all of us. There is nothing
wrong with that, it's how God made man to be."

"Not all men."

She smiled a little but looked pained. "That's true. Sometimes
God is feeling playful, and makes a man like you instead."

"Thank you for explaining my existence. I'd been wondering
about it."

"I envy you. I envy your freedom to think about only what you
want. You don't have the burden of *your people*."

"That's because my people are dead," I said harshly. "It's really
rather liberating."

"Do you have anything to say to me that isn't selfish?" Jamila
asked. "Or aren't you capable of that?"

That stung a little. "I hope he grows to cherish you as you deserve," I tried, almost choking on the words.

"It won't happen," she said, without emotion.

"I loved somebody very much once, and still hold her memory as
deep in my heart as anyone has ever been. But there is room for you
there too."

"Samuel is not like you," she said simply. "If I were in love with
him, that might devastate me. As things are, it doesn't. He and I
have no illusions about any of this."

"I didn't realize disillusion was a prerequisite for domesticity. Is
that what you call a regular life? Then spare me from it. You may as
well leave now, Jamila. Liliana hopes we'll end up trysting, and I'd
hate for her to come back here and catch us disappointing her."

"There's still time for a tryst," she whispered.

"What?" I said in a hollow voice.

She rubbed her fingertips against the back of my hand and wrist.

I took a sharp breath and made a weak sound of yearning; I could feel that touch all over my body.

I pushed her away. "I don't want a consolation prize," I said angrily.

"I do," she said and started sobbing.

We grabbed each other, sank to our knees, and stayed clenched together.

After what seemed a very long time, her tears stopped, leaving a damp patch on my tunic. I kept holding her, feeling her gasp a little for breath beside me, wanting to do more but not daring to. Until she tipped her head up to look at me, with such sad longing on her face. I kissed her, and she pressed against me with an intensity I'd never felt before from her, until she had pushed me over and was lying on top of me, trying to reach between us to untie my belt. The playfulness of our two previous, aborted attempts was gone: She was not leaving until we'd managed, just once, to be lovers in the proper sense.

"Samuel?" I said in weak protest, looking up at her.

"He knows I'm here, and he knows why."

"And he allows it?" I asked in amazement.

"He allows more than you seem willing to," she said with exasperation. "I think he would like us to finally get it over with."

I grabbed her and rolled on top of her, pulling my belt from out of her hands to untie it myself. I don't think my hands have ever moved so fast before: I had completely undressed myself in the time it takes to draw three breaths, and had Jamila's tunic off and was about to remove her shift when—

"Hello?" said a voice from outside, with a sharp rap on the door.

"*No!*" I shouted furiously, leapt to my feet, and scrambled naked for the door. Jamila, at the same moment, uttered a pained laugh. I hurled the door open, snapping "*What?*" before I'd even seen who stood there.

It was a boy, a servant who had the luck (as a youth that age would consider it) to work for the whore pavilion running errands.

His eyes widened when he saw me naked in the doorway; he glanced into the cabin, but it was too dark to see. "Excuse me, sir," he said—embarrassed, amused, and startled all at once. "They've been asking after you, that's all. Dandolo's men. Asked could you come and play a—"

"*No*," I said and slammed the door shut, bolting it. Feeling like an ass, I unbolted it, opened it a crack, said, "Thank you, lad. But no," closed it again, then ran back to Jamila. She was completely naked by now and chuckling softly at my explosion.

I nearly threw myself on top of her, and suddenly I was inside her, as if our coupling was an old, familiar habit. Words like *lust* and *passion* are almost irrelevant. It was as natural and necessary as breathing, as voluble as music. Our bodies simply imitated what all the rest of us had been doing for more than a year.

We were alone for a while; we even drifted into brief sleep. Finally we dressed and sat up, holding each other as we had when she'd first dissolved into tears. It seemed impossible to believe we'd never do that again; it seemed almost as impossible to believe we hadn't done it a thousand times before. I have no idea how long we stayed there, clutching each other as if we'd drown in letting go.

Liliana eventually waddled back to the cabin, and Gregor came with her, just off guard duty. They were talking about something as they approached—perhaps something about Otto, or babies, for there was warmth in both their voices, and Gregor had not spoken warmly about anything for weeks.

Gregor swung open the door, saw us in our miserable clutch, and froze.

"This looks dire," he said with brotherly concern, stepping into the cabin.

Liliana moved her bulk past him, gave us a questioning look. She breathed in deeply through her nose, smelled the sex, and winked at Jamila, looking very pleased.

Then she realized, from our attitudes, that ours was not a happy embrace; her smile vanished, and she rested a sympathetic hand on each of our heads. Jamila gave her an appreciative expression that wasn't quite a smile, then buried her face against my arm.

"I'd better go," she whispered.

I was staring at the floor, but I sensed Gregor and Liliana exchange looks. They understood. Liliana took a few steps away from us.

Jamila, using my arm to steady herself, stood up. She sighed heavily, and I glanced up to look at her as sunlight from the doorway fell on her. She rested her hand on my head, tousled my hair.

"Walk me to the gate of Pera?" she asked.

"Stay," Liliana said, urgent yet so softly it was almost whispered.

Jamila shook her head but looked like she might dissolve again. She tapped my head. "Walk me to the gate?" she repeated, almost voiceless now. She held out her other hand to help me up. I took it and pulled myself to standing.

"Come on then," I said grimly.

But as we approached the cabin door, I was blocked by a small, brown-haired figure. Boniface's youngest page, a boy of ten years, appeared, standing shy and proper with his hands behind him. I pulled back.

"Oh, good," Gregor muttered. "I'm about to get rebuked for something new. What is it this time, lad?"

The boy had bright, wide-open eyes. He looked terrified of whatever his mission was. "Your brother, milord?"

"You want Otto? You just missed him, he went out with a scouting party at the last bell, past the northern perimeter. He won't be back until tomorrow evening." A pause. The boy said nothing. "What do you need to tell him?" Gregor asked.

The boy glanced uncertainly around the three of us. "I was told to . . ." He hesitated.

"Speak, lad, we don't bite," Gregor said impatiently. We were all staring at the boy, which only made him fidget more.

He brought his hands forward from behind his back—gripped in his right hand was a sword in its familiar scabbard, nearly as large as he was. "I was told to return this to you, milord."

Gregor exchanged concerned looks with Liliana and me. "That's Otto's sword. Why are you bringing it here? Who gave it to you? He needs it. Take it back to him." The boy stared at him. He took a tentative step into the cabin and laid the sheathed sword on the floor before Gregor's feet, then withdrew back outside as if one of us might sting him.

"I was told to return the sword here," he said again.

I moved toward Liliana and held out my hand; she grabbed it and squeezed it so hard I almost pulled it away again. Gregor gaped at the boy with agitated confusion. "Don't leave it here. Take it to Otto, lad!" he ordered, gesturing. "Give him . . . give him back the sword. Where is Otto? Lad! Tell me, where is Otto?"

The child looked as if he might start crying. "They . . . they just sent me to return the sword. They said somebody else would bring the news."

"What news?" Gregor demanded, grey eyes bulging.

"They said I wouldn't have to tell you!" the boy insisted.

I broke free from Liliana and leapt toward the door, grabbed the boy's wrist more harshly than I meant to, and dragged him back up into the room, shouting, "Tell us what? What's happened to Otto? Is he wounded?"

The boy stared at me in terror and shook his head.

"Captured?" I pressed.

The boy shook his head.

Suddenly my throat was too dry to speak. "What, then?" I managed to asked.

"They said I wouldn't have to tell you," the boy croaked. "Let me go."

In the stunned silence, I released the boy's hand. The child craned his neck around me and said fearfully to Gregor, "I'm very sorry, milord."

Gregor, stupefied, could not respond.

"Can you give us any details, lad?" Jamila said quietly beside Liliana.

"I heard it was Mourtzouphlos himself," the boy said. "Just here, just north of the camp, an ambush, just as they were setting out. That's something, isn't it? That it would take an emperor to strike you down."

"Thank you, lad," Jamila said very quietly. "You may go."

Liliana broke first, dissolving into gasping, frightened tears. Jamila wrapped her arms around her at once, and I leapt toward them, rocking her, shushing her, controlling her collapse to the floor.

Gregor just kept staring at his brother's sword.

Act V

PILGRIMAGE

Mourtzouphlos summoned his people and said,
"Behold! Am I not a good emperor? You've never had
an emperor so good! Have I not done right? Now we've
nothing to worry about."

—ROBERT OF CLARI'S *Chronicle of the Fourth Crusade*

61

I SEARCHED FOR the Richardim while Jamila tended to Liliana; Gregor did not move from the spot where he'd received the news. He seemed unable to wrest his eyes from Otto's sword.

I sent the Richardim to Bishop Conrad, to retrieve Otto's contract from months earlier, giving a parcel of his German estate to Liliana and the child. It was probably unenforceable, but Jamila and I hoped a letter of endorsement from Boniface might give it some added heft in Otto's family. This meant, of course, that we had to somehow *obtain* such a letter from Boniface.

As we debated how to do this, I sat with Liliana, my arms around her bulk, rocking her. Her face was splotched red, but the sobs were finally subsiding—Jamila had given her a sedative and she grew stuporous. Jamila herself set about preparing Gregor to meet Boniface. She stood over him like a cross mother as he washed, trimmed his beard, put on fresh clothes for the first time in weeks. It reminded me of the ritual Liliana had put me through in Venice. I hugged her closer to me.

Having been made presentable, Gregor returned his attention to the sword on the floor. Jamila turned to me. "You can't go with him, speak for him, can you?"

"Then Boniface learns his imbecilic musician is not so imbecilic, and is actually a part of Gregor's lance. I don't care, but that insight will not put him in a generous mood."

"So we'll have to convince Conrad to do it. Gregor's in no state to be convincing." A pause. "Let's get Liliana to an abbey. Samuel may have heard of such places within riding distance. You'll have to leave right away. Before the fighting."

"Can you and Samuel take her when you go?"

She shook her head. "Samuel would not allow it, for her sake as well as ours."

BISHOP CONRAD CAME to the cabin just after dark. He left his servants outside and was slightly uneasy to find Jamila not only present but apparently in charge of everything; in a Christian house of mourning, that should have been a Christian's job.

"Don't fret, Your Eminence, I've not been telling them heresies about where the soul goes after death," she said, to greet him. "Have you brought Otto's contract?"

"You know this is hardly binding," said Conrad, holding it out to her. She took it and placed it in Gregor's hand. He looked at it without interest, the way an animal slowly bleeding to death might look at a passing bug. Then he looked back at Otto's sword.

"It may not be binding, sir, but if Boniface adds his endorsement, Otto's family will be in less of a rush to contest it."

Gregor raised his head and finally contributed to the discussion. "Otto and I had different mothers, and it's through his mother he has the estate he intended for Liliana. The family's kindhearted but very pious. A marriage would make all the difference."

"Or the appearance of a marriage," I amended.

"I will not assist in such deception," Conrad huffed.

"I will," I announced placidly. "And I'm the one taking her back there."

"He wanted to marry me, and I would not because it was not in his interest to marry a whore," Liliana said, sounding apologetic. This being needy sat uncomfortably upon her. "If the child is all that's left of him, surely they will not turn us out. They know about me. His mother allowed me at her table once."

"They'll take the child and turn *you* out," I said. "We'll say you were married."

"I will not allow that to pass," Conrad announced.

"Want to come back to Germany with us to argue it before the family?"

"I *will* be back in Germany in time," he warned. "And I will tell the truth."

"You would do that to her?"

"If she would mock a sacrament that way, of course I would."

Jamila, usually more practical than I, tried the rarely conceived of posthumous approach: "Your Eminence, is it too late to marry them?"

Conrad made a disgusted face and declared, "She cannot marry a *corpse*," which made Liliana start to weep quietly again.

"You're being *very* helpful, Your Eminence, thank you," I said. "Why do we have the pleasure of your person here, anyhow? All we requested from you was the contract."

"I came to offer comfort—" Conrad began, but the rest of it was drowned out by the bark of Jamila's mocking laughter. Jamila did not laugh much, and never mockingly; it made an impression. Even Gregor glanced up to glare incredulously at Conrad.

"—And to tell you things you need to hear," the bishop continued. "But first: If you want to help her, I agree you should ask Boniface to intervene on her behalf."

"Then please, I beg you, sir," said Jamila, "do a kind thing and approach Boniface in this matter. For obvious reasons, the rest of us are dreadful candidates."

A pause, then: "I'm not a good candidate either," said Conrad.

"Why?"

"He . . . is pressuring the clergy to do things that we are not comfortable doing."

"Such as?" asked Gregor.

Conrad shook his head. "What he wants will never happen. But until it's resolved, I cannot approach him." He looked us over. "The Jewess is the best choice."

"No," I insisted, arms protectively still around Liliana. "She has obligations here, and he'll try to take her along to the Holy Land."

"But nobody is going to the Holy Land," said Conrad.

A dumbfounded pause.

"Excuse me?" Gregor said.

"That's what I'm here to tell you. I was on my way with the news when I heard about Otto. I just came from a parliament of the leaders." He gestured to me. "I was surprised not to see you; it was the sort of thing Dandolo would ask for you to play at."

"He did," I said, remembering the boy who'd knocked. "I was engaged."

"It was a war council," said Conrad. "No longer to determine *if* we'll fight but precisely *when* and *how*."

A moment as we all took that in. It was not a huge surprise.

"And what is our rallying cry?" asked Gregor wearily. "The treaty with Alexios died when he did, so we cannot legally say we have a right to anything from the city."

"Mourtzouphlos murdered Alexios, and Alexios was our ally. That is the excuse." Conrad grimaced. "The real reason is that we've no money, and the only way to get any is to take the city."

"And this . . ." Gregor looked almost too tired to speak. "This is acceptable to the barons? This is excuse enough for a pilgrim army to go to war against Christians? Given we only came here because we wanted to *help* these Christians?"

Conrad grimaced again. "It is a problem," he admitted. "They'll fight, but only with great reluctance. And as of today the reluctance grows much greater—because assuming we take the city, the army is staying here. Intact. For at least a year."

Gregor surprised me by letting out a string of curses, livelier and louder than had come out of those lips in many weeks. He even sat upright. "On what excuse is *that* being demanded of us?" he asked at the end of it.

"The leaders have decided it," Conrad said. "Once the city is taken, it must be stewarded. Anything less than the entire army to protect it, and it will be lost all over again. So a treaty was signed today, between the lords and Dandolo."

"*Dandolo*," Gregor muttered.

"It is easy to blame Dandolo, but he is the least eager for it," Conrad said. "And I must say that, except for the siege of Zara, he has been truer to the pope than most pilgrim leaders have been. So. The treaty says that the army is staying here, to oversee the transfer of the city into pilgrim hands."

"Whose hands, *exactly*, will those be?" I asked.

"They all pledged themselves to a treaty on that very issue," Conrad said. "Assuming we win, one of our own must become the new emperor, as there are no acceptable native candidates remaining."

"Boniface of Montferrat," said Gregor, like someone who's just realized he's been swindled.

"No, no," Conrad said quickly, soothingly. "It's to be decided by election."

"It will be Boniface," Gregor said.

"Maybe not," Conrad insisted. "I have the honor of being an elector. There are twelve of us, six pilgrims, six Venetians. The pilgrims are clergy, to avoid partisanship."

I laughed. "You're a crony of Boniface's, how can you claim no partisanship?"

"Boniface runs unopposed, so there's nothing to be partisan *about*," Jamila hypothesized.

"Son of a whore," I muttered. "*Emperor Boniface*. I wonder how long he's—"

"You're far too cynical," said Jamila. "I am sure right up until the *moment* of Alexios's death, Boniface was *perfectly* content to be imperial puppeteer."

"Milord Boniface has serious competition for the crown," Conrad informed us.

"Of course," I said. "He'll be up against everyone's favorite blind octogenarian."

"No, Dandolo has made it clear he does not wish to be considered. From today's parliament, however, there is much to support Baldwin of Flanders."

This surprised all of us. "Baldwin's younger than *I* am," I said.

"Do *you* want consideration?" Jamila asked me drily.

"You'd need Jamila as your chancellor," Liliana muttered into my ear, in a game attempt to join the conversation.

"Baldwin is a goodly, chaste man," Conrad said, ignoring us.

"He's also a vassal to the King of France," Gregor pointed out wearily, "and so the French clerics will vote for him."

"And there are more of them than there are of me," said the German cleric, "so Boniface will have no unfair advantage, even if I wished to give him one."

"It will still be Boniface," Gregor said. "Let us, none of us, pretend otherwise."

"Son of a whore," I muttered again.

"Actually, sir," said Jamila, drumming her fingers on the nearest chest, "think about this for a moment. Half of the electors will be Venetians, correct? The Venetians make their policies not as individuals but as a collective unit that always puts the interest of their republic first. Boniface is allied with Genoa, Venice's trading rival. Venice will want the new emperor to favor Venice over Genoa—"

"—So none of the Venetians will vote for Boniface," I said, getting it. "If Baldwin is the only option, they'll vote for Baldwin. So Baldwin starts with half the votes, merely for not being Boniface.

If a single cleric votes for Baldwin, Baldwin wins." I smiled. "Then Boniface will *not* become the emperor. There *is* a little justice in the world."

"*Surely* he has already figured that out himself," Liliana said, shifting her bulk uncomfortably in my arms. "I'll wager he's got some plan in place already, to rig the election." Gregor made a disgusted sound, an all-vowel expression of agreement.

Conrad looked nervous about the direction the conversation was suddenly going. "Boniface, as commander of the army, directs all his thoughts on the battle before him."

"So," said Gregor, "to conclude, the pope's army, assembled expressly to protect Christendom, shall sack the largest Christian city of the world and then become a mercenary force to keep a conqueror upon the throne there. Thank you for this news, Father. It makes my course of action clear." He finally stood up, looking unsteady. "Liliana, I'll take you back to Germany myself. I quit this travesty as of this moment."

Conrad crossed to Gregor, took his hand, and stared into his eyes, unctuous with concern. "Gregor, you must stay and fight," he said. "If you don't, it will reflect badly on you, and it will affect not only your own future but the future of your son."

Gregor gave Conrad a look of open disgust, so bald the clergyman released him and took a step away. "You've just come from Boniface yourself," Gregor declared. "He told you to work on me."

Conrad fluttered his hands anxiously. "I am not here as Boniface's agent. He and I are at odds right now, I told you that." Soothingly again, reaching again for Gregor's arm. "But I know how the world works, lad, and I would see you prosper, that you may do God's work the rest of your life. You have a child to consider now."

"I have more than one," said Gregor. He pointed to Liliana's swollen belly. "I know her better than I know the woman I'm married to. How can I not be concerned about my brother's child too?"

"All the more reason to secure your own glory as a soldier," said

Conrad. "Let the British vagabond take Liliana to safety for you, and you stay here to do your duty."

"My duty is to be a pilgrim," Gregor said.

"And a soldier," Conrad amended, but he sounded very tired as he said it.

"While on pilgrimage, I am first and foremost a pilgrim. I've tried being a soldier first, and it impedes the pilgrimage. I took a *vow* to be a pilgrim, I took no actual vow to fight. Where is my brother's body?" he demanded, with an abruptness that is the prerogative of the bereaved.

"He's lying in the chapel by my lodging," Conrad said.

"We have a tradition, before burial—" Jamila began, but Conrad cut her off saying, "Absolutely not. There shall be no unchristian rites."

"It's not a rite, it's just a custom," Jamila said defensively. "Of washing the—"

"The last thing you need is rumors spreading that a Jewess was performing oblations on the corpse," said Conrad.

"Please don't use that word," Liliana said, with labored breathing. I rubbed her shoulder again, feeling ineffectual.

"We have a burial ground, it has been sanctified. You may have his effects, I'll send the rest of them to you." He gestured awkwardly to the sword, which had not been moved since the boy set it on the ground. Gregor picked it up, almost as if he were afraid Conrad would make a lunge for it; he carried it to his travel altar and laid it beside the crucifix.

"Your Eminence, Liliana doesn't need effects, she needs a *legacy*," Jamila pressed. "Will you help us, *please*, with Boniface?"

"We don't need Boniface," said Gregor from the candlelit altar. He reached beneath the altar cloth for something. "Your Eminence, if I may tax your indulgence, I have a quill and ink and even parchment, if you will take dictation, for I write too slowly. I'm adopting

Liliana and her child into my house. I'll sign my name to it with blood."

Liliana, still cradled in my arms, suddenly released a sigh and shuddered with relief. "God bless you, milord," she said in a quiet voice.

62

O wearied brethren, weighted down with grief,
turn your hearts to this eternal truth from the dawn of creation:
Many have drunk, many will drink,
and the last shall drink as the first ever drank.
O Brethren, may the Lord of Comfort comfort you.

—JEWISH BLESSING OF THE MOURNERS

THE NEXT DAY, too, was like a bad dream. There was a funeral mass, with the body lying strangely calm and restful, more restful than it had ever been, even in sleep. The wound was in his chest and was disguised by a burial robe; his face was almost white. I wish that I had not attended; the chill of others' deaths, still crying out for retribution, hovered too close, reminding me, chastising me.

Liliana, at Jamila's order, did not attend. We brought her a lock of Otto's hair, and his dagger; Gregor gave me Otto's chain-mail coif. The other armor was dispersed to sergeants Otto had befriended, or to the Richardim. Gregor kept his brother's sword and shield.

Very late that night, Liliana was asleep or dozing; Jamila and I huddled upright and facing each other under a blanket, fully clothed, arms and legs folded around each other for warmth and comfort. I wanted to spend the rest of my life holding her like this.

"I don't know what to do now," I whispered into her hair—we were so interlaced that our mouths were at each other's ears. "After I've gotten Liliana to safety."

"Whatever you want," she said. "It is a blessed freedom few will ever know."

I shook my head, felt her hair brush against my face. "I have no freedom at all. I took a vow once, a death pact with my own conscience. I was reminded of it there in the chapel—I have unfinished business. I haven't carried out a bit of it—"

"Because you had an excellent deferral," Jamila argued. "You swore to do a good deed first. And you've done it: I'm back with my people—"

I tensed; she, thinking I was about to pull away from her, clutched me harder. "You are about to enter a loveless marriage. Forgive me if I don't think of that as quite *triumphant.*"

"That's not the point I was after," she said. "Samuel came for me seven months ago. You've lived that long with your good deed completed but without returning to a pursuit of vengeance. Why return to vengeance now? Have you learned *nothing?* Do you still think the best response to violence is more violence?"

"Isn't that how your God works?"

She shrugged. "I know stories of a God who works that way. I have never had the hubris to *imitate* his methods, but I don't think my life would have come out any better if I had." She lowered her voice further, brought her face even closer against the side of my head, and concluded, sounding both plaintive and seductive, "For we fragile mortals, there are more useful impulses than vengeance."

"The only impulse stronger than revenge is love, or the hope of it, and you're taking that away from me." Under my hands I felt her draw in a breath to retort, so I raised my voice a little and kept talking. "It was a glorious distraction, those seven months or so, and I do thank you for it, Jamila, but that's all it was: distraction. I'm ashamed it took me so long to see it. Wulfstan would be *appalled* if he knew how I wasted those months—I could have gotten back to England and *accomplished* it by now."

"Actually," she said, in an even more intimate tone, "I think you've been doing exactly what Wulfstan hoped you would."

I pulled my head back away from her so I could stare at her. "How can you say that? He taught me to plan a murder-suicide, and I'm no closer to doing that than I was when I last saw him."

She shook her head. "I've been meditating on this Wulfstan. I think that was just a feint of his."

I barked with sarcasm: "How do you figure?"

She gave me a knowing smile that sent tingles down my spine and made me even more desperate to spend the rest of my life sitting this close to her. Releasing me, she sat up a little so that I had to release her too; she retracted her hands so they were in the small space between our bodies. Then she began to count off on her fingers: "He made sure you learned everything a man like you would need to learn to survive on the continent: languages, music styles, certain basic skills, such as recognizing plants and reading the directions and winds and weather. He tried to teach you, as much as a landsman could, the skills a sailor needs: climbing, balancing, ropes, knots, and one you never mastered—swimming, which a lot of sailors can't do anyhow. Then, having done all that, he sent you toward Venice on a false pretext—"

"The entire monastery heard that the Englishman had gone to Venice."

"Or maybe the entire monastery simply repeated what they'd heard from Wulfstan," said Jamila. "I think he invented your Englishman's destination. And I think he'd intended to deceive you *from the start.* He sent you exactly opposite from where your Eng-lishman really was—but in the right direction to learn how wide the world is. He gave you a set of skills and then sent you to the place you could best use them, and where your lack of piety would not stand out: Venice. He was not preparing you to die, he was pre-paring you to *live.* Perhaps he even hoped that you'd go along on this crusade and become a pilgrim in your own fashion. As you ar-guably have."

I wanted to disagree with her, but here's the crazy truth of it: half the skills that Wulfstan had insisted I learn truly did have nothing at all to do with subterfuge or murder; and all of these had come in handy in my stint as a reluctant seafaring crusader.

She took my silence as concurrence. "So do you understand what that means?" she continued, grabbing my hands in hers. "You must go forth and live—and you must pass the skill for living on to Gregor."

"I'll be very busy, making sure that everyone I know stays alive and healthy."

"It is a good antidote to your former life," she said. "I wish I had a better antidote to my own." She took my chin in her hands and looked at me very seriously. I loved the feel of her hands on my face. "I mean that about Gregor. I hadn't seen him in a few weeks, and he frightens me. He's lost too much weight, and his face is the color of death. The light is gone from his eyes."

"I cannot stay here to keep an eye on him *and* take Liliana to safety," I argued.

"Then stay here with Liliana, until you both know that Gregor's safe," she said.

"I could use a little help."

She shook her head—and to my disappointment, released my chin. "I told you, there's already a dissenting faction within Blacher-nae claiming Alexios was murdered. Mourtzouphlos will try to shift suspicion to Samuel, so we must leave. I'm surprised Samuel hasn't come here himself to drag me off."

I threw my arms around her again and buried my face against her neck. "Don't go with him. I beg you not to leave me."

"I beg you not to beg me."

"I have *nothing* if you leave."

"You have yourself," she answered. "Not a bad thing to be stuck with, I think."

"A wasteland."

"A wasteland's just a useful field in need of reclamation," she said and gently shrugged my arms from off her. She kissed me, leaned her head against my cheek a moment, then disentangled her legs from around me and rose to her feet. She tugged at my hand.

I didn't move.

"Walk me to the gate of Pera. After all we've been through, be the one who delivers me at last."

"Delivers you to *what?*" I demanded in a surly voice.

But I walked her toward the gate. We held hands but didn't speak: each time one of us drew breath to say something, the other one would tense in uncomfortable anticipation, and the would-be speaker would stop short. We wove our way through an acre of anxious, milling infantry, along a path I knew by heart now, and then for the length of a bowshot we were in a stretch of wooded, rocky hillside. Then the Pera Gate. It was locked, patrolled from within by two armed Jewish youths.

I felt my entire body tense. I stopped a few paces from the gate and turned to Jamila, taking her hands in mine. I was trembling. "I've failed," I said. "I can't do this."

"You've done it before," she said hoarsely, attempting a sympathetic smile, looking at my collarbone to avoid eye contact.

"No, that's the thing, you see. I haven't." Her eyes glanced up to mine; I had to look away, over her head. "You've left, and others have taken you away. I've even told others I would deliver you to them. But I've never had to actually *do* it." I could hardly get the words out. "And I can't do it now, Jamila. I'm failing to fulfill my oath, and

I don't care. Tell me what impossibility needs to be achieved that we can stay together, and I'll make it possible."

"I can't," she said woodenly. "I cannot do that to my people or to Samuel."

"You owe me far more than you owe Samuel."

I said it without thinking, out of desperation, but it was a mistake. She stiffened, pulled her hands out of mine. "I owe you?" she said, as if sounding out a foreign phrase. "I'm not denying you did great things, but did you do them so there would be a debt?" She gave me a surprised, hurt look. "I really did not think you were that kind of man."

"I'm not," I stammered. I reached for her hands again; she pulled them away and kept looking at me in that awful, reappraising way. "I didn't rescue you or try to feed your people or any of that *so that* you'd be indebted to me, but look at what I've done for you compared with what he's done!" She only looked more appalled, but I couldn't stop. "I've been a worthier companion! I *deserve* you. Even though I don't know half as much as he does and am not pious and have no skills or money or community or— *Dammit.*" I clenched my teeth and rushed toward the gate, not even waiting to see if she would follow me. My throat was so constricted I didn't know if I was about to sob or to vomit.

Jamila said nothing, followed a few paces behind me. I stopped when I got to the gate, and Jamila walked up to me. I couldn't look at her. "I'm glad you said it," she said in a voice that sounded like it was about to crack. "It was unpleasant to hear, but it makes it a little easier to part. You have delivered me—so you've fulfilled your word, even if you've abused your will. Do you hear? *You have fulfilled your word.* Do not use me as some tortured excuse to punish yourself." Seeing I would not turn to her, she turned her back on me too and said, now really sounding on the verge of tears, "I pray that contentment, or at least unselfishness, will wrestle its way into your life somehow, someday. Go with God." She walked through the gate and signaled the guard to close it again. She disappeared into Pera without looking back, leaving me with the bitterest parting blessing I've ever received.

63

THE ATTACK WOULD BE by boat. The Venetians had great success during the first attack on the city, while the army had survived solely because the Usurper had turned tail and run away. So the galleys were once again covered in vinegar-laden hides and nets of grapevines once again woven to throw over them.

Mourtzouphlos, seeing the army prepare for a harbor siege, ordered the harbor walls built higher with wooden parapets, rising too high for the Venetians to throw grappling hooks and set up assault bridges.

When Dandolo realized what Mourtzouphlos was up to, he rigged the ships to support higher assault bridges.

When Mourtzouphlos realized what Dandolo was up to, he built the amendments even higher.

When Dandolo realized what Mourtzouphlos was up to, he rigged the ships to support yet even higher assault bridges.

And thus it went throughout the rest of March and into April, while Liliana, Gregor, and I all mourned in our different ways, and the Richardim grew skilled at chess, and Pera was deserted by the Jews, who fled to places unrecorded.

Eventually some of the added wooden towers were seven stories above the city walls. If I'd stood atop there, no doubt, I could have seen Jamila wherever she had gone with Samuel. I smarted, remembering our final moment. I wondered how they were together now, if she laughed or groaned under his touch. Such thoughts tormented me, but not as fiercely as thoughts of the two of them enjoying each other's company. And yet I doubted that was happening, and the doubting was further torment—Jamila was not easily joyful, but I could make her smile. That was one small *mitzvah* left undone, every day, and few were the good deeds I could do in its place. I was glad Gregor was not among the forces preparing to wage war, but I desperately wished I could bring him back to himself.

The evening of Thursday, the eighth of April, the army (except for Gregor of Mainz) armored itself. Collectively, it looked toward the city, and its seven hills. On the tallest, the hill of Christ the All-Seeing, were Mourtzouphlos's large vermilion tents. With the swath of burned-out city at his feet, he watched the enemy army lead its horses onto transports, seal the doors closed for the harbor crossing, board the ships being blessed by priests.

At dawn the next morning, he was still on that hill, watching the ships slowly move the short distance across the harbor. Mourtzouphlos and a hundred thousand others watched the crossing, while trumpets were sounded and large drums beaten. From outside the walls of empty Pera, my hair slapping my cheeks in the morning wind, I watched Mourtzouphlos watching. He treated the day as if it were a picnic, a celebration of the inability of the Franks to even touch his shores. I wondered, as I did every day, where Jamila and Samuel were at this very moment, and thought it was a pity that Samuel hadn't poisoned Mourtzouphlos. Then I thought about it a little more and decided it was almost as much a pity that he hadn't poisoned *me*.

The wooden parapets added to the walls had more than height to aid them: they had been buttressed out over the harbor, so any ship that landed would be directly beneath them, and vulnerable to attack. Tons of broken stone waited to be dumped upon anyone who succeeded in making it ashore. A few of the small ships were able to beach, and their men began to set up a siege machine . . . only to have it, and those men, smashed to pieces by attacks from above. Dandolo, when told this was happening, screamed to his men that, in that case, they must stop trying to attack from the shore and try putting the assault bridges into place above. I swear I could hear that shrill voice all the way across the harbor. I wondered what Boniface was doing. I wondered where Jamila was. I'd probably spent every moment of that month wondering where Jamila was. My imagination went to dangerous places. I'd been inside her—what if she carried my child? No child of mine could ever pass as Samuel's. Everyone would know, she would be shamed, unless I could find her and marry her . . . I, the greatest mocker of romantic tales, lost hours of my life to such reverie. Even now, as I stood watching an actual *naval battle*, my mucking up our last goodbye seemed at least as detrimental to the well-being of the world as Dandolo's hollered orders.

What the doge had demanded was tricky work, for it required the larger boats—those with sufficient ballast to counterbalance the top-heavy weight of the bridges—to get in close enough that the sailors could fling out grappling hooks and latch on to the walls. The Venetians were skilled at this, and seasoned; it was how they'd rapidly captured two dozen towers in one morning last July. The wind was usually from the north, which helped to push the boats toward the walls. But today, they faced an obstacle: the wind shifted, not merely away from the north but entirely around so that it came up from the south, moist and unrelenting—so strong that the ships suddenly could not, even with oars, get close enough to throw out any grappling hooks. The watching emperor himself seemed amazed by this boreal aberration: there was no southern wind in the harbor; the locals did not have a phrase to describe such a thing. Even the ships that had already landed were pushed back, leaving men stranded at the walls, where they were crushed by showers of stones from above.

The doge shouted out in that distinctive yap of his that this freak wind would soon die down. But hours went by and there was no letup. By the middle of the afternoon, a hundred men had died in the attempt to make contact with the walls. The undertaking was a disaster. When the order was called for a retreat, jubilant Greeks watching from the walls—many of them mere yards from the bulk of the invading army—dropped their breeches and exposed their backsides to the failed conquerors.

By the time the horses were unloaded, the sun was setting, the air felt feverish, and the entire army was ready to burrow itself under the rocks from shame and hopelessness. The rising of the south wind had convinced the sailors, and half the soldiers (good Christians all), that an ancient sea god was against them. The deaths of so many men in a single afternoon with nothing gained convinced even most of the leaders that this attack had been a monstrous, possibly sinful mistake. Only Dandolo and Boniface had any stomach to continue it. It was one week shy of Good Friday and the pilgrims had their Lord much on their minds.

That evening, Boniface summoned the bishops and other clergy to his pavilion. Nobody else was present; I tried to talk my way in as musician, but Claudio the bodyguard would not allow me. So I hovered within spitting distance until the meeting adjourned and then, leaping out of the darkness, tried to strike up a casual conversation with Bishop Conrad on his trek back to his tent. "As I told you several weeks ago," he said blandly, "Boniface wants something from the clergy that the clergy will not give him. Don't trouble yourself about it."

"What happens next?" I demanded. "What should I tell Gregor?" This was just a feint; Gregor was long past caring about anything but his soul and God.

"I don't know, my son," Conrad said, sounding tired. "That will be up to the army leaders to decide tomorrow. Our Orthodox brethren may be misguided, but I begin to agree with them that the Church should take no part in warfare."

I was pleasantly surprised by this statement, but Conrad hurried off before I could ask him if he were planning to convert.

AFTER A MOST DEPRESSING NIGHT for everyone—during which a hundred men deserted—Dandolo and Boniface met the other leaders to try to rally them. I was, as always, called in by the doge to play for them. As always, nobody listened to me; even when I literally stopped playing and just sat there plainly eavesdropping, I was ignored.

At the start of this meeting, I was convinced there would be no further attempts at aggression. The most common comment from the group, repeated approximately every moment somewhere in the pavilion, was always a variant of this: "Surely this is a sign from God that we are wrong to be attacking New Rome/ New Jerusalem/ the Queen of Cities!"

But eventually they were all bored with this and moved on to discuss alternative battle plans. Dandolo refused to attack from the Bosporus or Marmara—the seawalls were too strong, but more than that, the current and the wind were impossible to combat.

"But the wind came from the south yesterday," somebody argued. "If we were south of the city, it would push us back *toward* the walls."

"The current is a stronger consideration than the wind," Dandolo said, dripping contempt for the landsmen who did not know basic facts of navigation. "And that current would send us all the way south to the Hellespont. Anyhow, if the wind sprang up to prevent us by some ancient god, the god will not *continue* blowing when it would be to our *advantage*. We must attack within the harbor."

"We can't land the boats because the wind's too strong!" somebody argued.

"What if we tied boats together?" Baldwin of Flanders suggested. "Lashed them somehow, to stabilize them. It would make them heavier against the wind and more stable against counterattacks from the walls. Since there's no current in the harbor . . ."

Boniface ridiculed this, perhaps because the idea was coming from his rival for the throne. Dandolo ridiculed Boniface's ridiculing and announced that Baldwin's idea was the only way to do it. I wondered—idiotically—what Jamila might suggest if she were here. Really that was just my soul's pathetic need to think about her whenever possible, and to further chastise myself for how ungallantly I'd parted from her.

Heralds went out around the camp announcing a day of rest for the Sabbath. On Monday, the twelfth of April, they would try a final assault, with the boats lashed together.

The soldiers were not happy. They were all convinced the defeat—their first actual *defeat*—was a sign from God that this was not his Plan. Many disheartened men pulled together and collectively asked permission to sail immediately to the Holy Land, there to ask forgiveness from the Lord for their digressions from the original pilgrimage.

Loud and unrelenting in this group was Gregor of Mainz.

Unseen by almost anyone for weeks, Gregor had gained mythical status within the ranks. His refusal to fight was heralded everywhere; his gaunt, pious features widely discussed. His suddenly taking action galvanized the army. This could easily turn into a repeat of Corfu.

To say that Boniface was displeased would be a massive understatement.

Before he did anything about Gregor, however, Boniface once again called the clergy into his tent and kept the pavilion surrounded by such a wide swath of guards that there was no way to get close enough to hear. I was wildly curious by now. Especially because this time, when they exited, the clergy were all dour-faced. I meandered up to Conrad, pretending again that I'd just happened to run into him, wanting him to be reassuringly mysterious, as he'd been each time before. Instead, he looked distant, sad, defeated. But he still wouldn't tell me what the matter was.

"I went on this pilgrimage because I myself was under excommunication," he said quietly, almost talking to himself. I had no interest in his autobiography; still, this was an intriguing detail. "I decided I'd rather be in the hands of God than in the hands of man." He gave me a look almost as sad as anything I'd ever seen on Gregor's face. "I fooled myself to think so. As long as we tread the earth, the hand of man will always be closer to us than the hand of God." He sighed heavily. "At least I know that now."

Palm Sunday, 11 April A.D. 1204

I begin now what shall be the last entry I ever make in this chronicle, a writing that has failed in its intended goals as much as the campaign it attempts to chronicle.

After the crushing but deserved defeat of Friday, it is clear to the entire army that we are committing a sin so grave God himself inter-vened with warning winds and severe humiliation. Many men bonded together to return to the path of righteousness. Many knew I had not fought that day and came flocking to my lodgings to ask why and to beg me to speak to the marquis about returning to our sworn duties as the pope's army.

I went to the marquis this afternoon to represent these men, for it does my heart good they are so outspoken, especially as the clergy has again fallen silent. Boniface anticipated my arrival and had with him Dandolo of Venice. (It is queer to me that the Briton was summoned to play for us again, even for this matter; I have never encountered a leader so incapable of counsel without distraction as Dandolo.) We met in private, just after Boniface's private meeting with the bishops, and they berated me soundly for wanting to press on with our pilgrimage. They angrily informed me how things must be. In truth I did not listen to the first long stretch of their soliloquies, but I do remember details that appalled me. Among these was that all statues of the city, including the many dozens that adorn the Hippodrome, shall be melted down into coin. Because they know I am loath to assist in harming Christians,

they asked that, upon their victory, I oversee the process of tearing
down these statues, so that money can be made of them; that money
may be used toward a future pilgrimage, where indeed I may at last see
the Holy Land, and so I should be glad of this. I told them it is useless
to discuss what would happen after a battle when that battle must never
happen to begin with. We must set out now, with what we have. We
must make our way in the wilderness as Moses and his flock did, for
surely we are no less hardy than they were.

I would have walked out then, but Dandolo spoke something dreadful, and I saw the effect it had upon the Briton, and felt the effect it had
on my own soul and I was stopped by it: "Know that if you leave now
for the Holy Land," said the doge, "you shall only survive along the
way by pillaging villages and innocents. There shall be no manna from
heaven, no water from a rock. You must get sustenance yourself, and
you have no means to get it but the sword. You may use that sword in
battle against soldiers or in the desert against women and children.
Which makes you a better man?"

I agreed then not to leave but said that neither would I fight a battle
I know is sinful.

This was not well-received by either man. Boniface threatened to
ruin my good name, to rob me of my estates, to alienate me from my
wife and child if I failed to fight when battle resumed. Here is something
I have decided: Either I do my duty out of honor, and because I know it
is the right, or what I do cannot be called duty but only enslavement. In
any case, it is no longer the work of a pilgrim.

My way became bitterly clear to me.

I told them that I shall fight, and that I shall even tell others to stay
and fight as well.

I did not tell them what else I shall do.

GREGOR FINALLY AGREED to fight, but I wondered how he could
be fit for it. He'd done little to train for weeks, gotten no exercise,

hardly eaten. The army was full of men ready to desert; if Boniface's intention was for Gregor to rally them back to the cause (whatever the cause was supposed to be these days), he would be disappointed. In my opinion, the man could barely stand on his own.

But he'd promised Boniface to make a circuit of the camp and exhort others to stay. I knew he wouldn't actually *exhort*; the most he managed was to tell men what he was doing himself. As soon as Dandolo dismissed me, I sought out Gregor to accompany him on this perambulation.

We wandered through the camp as it began to grow dark. It was cool, barely warmer than Britain this time of year, but drier. The place was full of men anxiously huddled around campfires, praying, singing, playing musical instruments (badly, most of them). For perhaps an hour, as night crept in, I bit my tongue and allowed Gregor to explain to his chivalric acolytes that he had chosen to stay and fight. When pressed for an explanation, he usually chose Dandolo's (that he'd rather use his sword against soldiers than against innocents), but it was a depressingly small number who even questioned him: most, upon hearing his decision, simply switched their own position to match it, trusting him to do the right thing. He looked nauseated by his sway.

On the other hand, only a few hundred sought him out at all, and it was clear that most of the would-be deserters were still planning to desert. Gregor, the longtime proponent of keeping the army whole, truly did not give a damn.

The conclusion of our wanderings brought us back to the German quarter, and we passed near Conrad's pavilion. Before it, in a large open space where morning mass was celebrated, stood the bishop, and he was preaching. He was preaching in German, to a rapt and happy audience of soldiers. Yes, *happy*—they kept exchanging looks of relieved, cheerful astonishment, as if they'd just been told "No, don't worry about what St. Paul said, lots of fornication will actually get you to heaven faster!" The men we'd seen skulking about with long faces for weeks, not quite as bad as Gregor but hardly eager, suddenly these same men were radiant with certainty. They looked, for the first time since last summer, like real soldiers. The transformation was abrupt, astonishing—and affected nearly every soldier present. I felt afraid of them. More disturbing, I almost felt *uplifted* just witnessing their vigor.

We paused on the outskirts. Gregor listened to His Eminence's lecture, and what happened to Gregor's face as he listened is hard to put in words. He grew so still, a moth might have landed on his lower lip, laid eggs, and tended them until they hatched. But his eyes blazed with a dozen different inner fires.

"What is he saying?" I finally demanded, growing impatient.

"This has Boniface's stamp all over it."

"What does? What is he *saying*?"

Gregor swallowed, cleared his throat, and in a hesitating voice, he began to translate the phrases that were coming out of Conrad's mouth. "*Not* a sin . . . a *good deed* . . . the Greeks are worse than Jews . . . they say that we are all dogs because we follow the law of Rome . . . they do not revere the Holy Father . . . worse than Jews, worse than Mohammedans . . . heretics, all heretics, what you are doing is a holy duty . . . and now," he concluded, as the entire mass of listening soldiers (including all the ones who'd been about to desert) suddenly shuffled to their feet, "he invites them to take communion and says absolution is offered to all who fight in the holy war tomorrow."

"What holy war? They're attacking fellow Christians."

"An hour ago they were attacking fellow Christians. *Now*, they are attacking heretics. This is the new Jerusalem. The clergy have just made *this* the pilgrimage."

I almost vomited. "This is what Boniface has been asking the clergy to do. But Conrad said they'd never give in."

"Conrad stopped resisting. I guess they all did." Gregor seemed to be very far away. "He knows the pope's against it, and not only is he letting it happen but he's telling them the pope *wants* it."

"Well, let's tell them the truth!" I shouted and lunged in the direction of the flock.

Despite his apparent weakness, Gregor was much stronger than I was. He grabbed my arm and pulled me back. "You'll be trampled underfoot," he said. "This is a stampede of piety, and it is many thousands strong. You won't be heard, and if you are, they'll strike you down as a blasphemer. I've seen you show intelligence. Try to do so now."

"But don't they understand the priests are *lying* to them?"

"Why should they? I would have believed this, once." He glanced at me. "I might have believed it even now, I think, if you had not stumbled into my life."

"Should I apologize for that, or accept your gratitude?"

"It doesn't matter," Gregor said distractedly.

"Why would Conrad *do* that?" I spat.

Gregor gave me a look that, more animated, might have been droll. "Is this the first time you're noticing the clergy lacking moral rectitude?" he said. "Boniface or Dandolo must have scared them again. They're good at it. At least it's almost over now."

The camp felt, sounded, and almost *smelled* different, with waves of sudden conversion to the cause, as company after company of soldiers succumbed to the soothing news that they were miraculously back on the pilgrim track, that this Heinous Sin they'd fretted about for months was actually the Will of God. Never mind what Gregor of Mainz was up to; there was no longer any need for anyone to even think about deserting.

I watched Gregor watching these men, as they reclaimed their own pale versions of his long-lost golden glow. I was angrier than he was, but I suspected there was a deeper grief for him. He was losing something I had never had; my loss of Jamila paled beside it.

"Indulge me," I said, as we began a slow walk to the cabin. "Pretend—just for the novelty of it—that I am ignorant. These soldiers suddenly believe they are about to see their pilgrimage fulfilled.

You know that's a lie. But *why*, exactly, is it a lie? Don't cite the Holy Father, please," I added hurriedly, as he opened his mouth. "I know the army's disobeying his orders, but for all we know he secretly wants them to do this. Anyhow, there was always more to *your* pilgrimage than just doing what the pope expected. What was it?" A pause; I hesitated, feeling almost childish to add the most important thing: "And can I help you get it back?"

He stared at me for a moment and then said quietly, "That is the most generous question anyone has asked me for a year or more."

Continuation

I was moved by the Briton tonight. Usually he is a man with little piety, and no patience for mine. We had a most peculiar conversation, a layman's catechism, in which I was expected to be the minister. For brevity I will write the words only, but in the speaking of those words, there were many hesitations and false beginnings on my part, and mysterious, thoughtful pauses on his.

Myself (because he asked): A pilgrimage is a voyage taken to a holy place.

Him: We've done that. We are at a holy place, one of the holiest in Christendom. And a journey brought us to it! So it is a pilgrimage! So be joyful—we accomplished it!

Myself: It must be more than a journey, and even more than the destination. It is what you do at the destination. It is the culmination of a holy intention.

Him: Your original pilgrimage would have culminated in attacking people who don't share your beliefs. You will be doing that tomorrow. Why then is tomorrow not a culmination of your pilgrimage?

Myself: Because I do not believe that tomorrow's attack is in defense of my religion, as it would be in Jerusalem. For this to be a pilgrimage, I must accomplish something about which I might say to myself, "I strove for this because I am devoted; I attained this because

I am devoted. I return from such a journey forever changed, because I have attained something I would not have even tried to attain if my faith were not so dear to me." If I die in the attempt, I know my soul goes to heaven, because what I was doing when I died made me worthier of heaven. That's not true of tomorrow's attack.

Him (after a long silence): So this notion of "I got something because I'm so devoted to my faith"—is this why relics obtained on pilgrimage are so sought after? I cannot understand the fuss over the relics, when your own lands are already lousy with relics that can be bought from any priest.

Myself: That is a part of it—

Him (hastily, conclusively): So relics can turn a journey into a pilgrimage.

Myself: Do not misunderstand me, a relic is not required for a pilgrimage. Any relic is sacred, for it helps the saint to hear your prayers; but a relic from a pilgrimage reminds you of your actions long after the pilgrimage is completed. However, the memory of an Action does the same. An action is in fact better than a relic—for an action, once accomplished, is always a part of you, it can't be taken away.

Him (as if working out a riddle): But is there any action you can undertake tomorrow about which you might say, "I do this because I am devoted"?

Myself: No.

Him (as if having solved the riddle): Aha. Then what we need is a nice little relic to transform this into a pilgrimage for you.

This was such an irrelevant and hypothetical musing, I did not respond to it. He is not made of pilgrim stuff. He walked with me back to the cabin, and then he disappeared.

I return now to my prayers and to my preparations.

I'D NEVER TRIED to sneak about the city without Jamila. I would never pass as a native, and the city had expelled all its foreign residents. Thanks to Dandolo's obsessions with my lute playing, I had coins enough for a ferry, but the ferries had stopped running, and sentries outside the harbor walls forbade a boat from crossing anyhow.

These factors meant it was better not to enter or even approach the city itself. So I walked under a waxing moon a mile inland up the harbor, crossed the bridge, and then walked back a mile south, until I was outside the walls of the city, facing Blachernae.

When people have a natural talent, it can be hard for them to describe to others exactly how they do it. Suffice to say: I climbed the wall of Blachernae in the dark without a single Varangian guard noticing my presence. I've done this sort of thing since I was a small boy, evading the *teulu* (my king's royal soldiers)—and the *teulu* were more alert than Varangians, for the *teulu* knew to expect my particular mischief and were ever on the lookout for it. True, I knew my native castle far better than Blachernae, but Blachernae is better stone. Here I could trust the smallest natural bulge or mason's groove to hold my weight; also, walls that size often sport scaffold holes from their construction, which makes such climbing unexpectedly easy.

I landed breathless and nervous on the parapet. It took a marriage of memory and common sense to move around the palace compound without being stopped. Stealth played almost no part in it: as the last time I was here, in daylight with Jamila, I was astonished at the general disorder in the running of the palace grounds. I was actually glimpsed a few times, by people who looked like their jobs should have been to stop me, but I carried myself as if I belonged there and I was never questioned. It was too dark to see my clothing clearly; a few weeks earlier (in a bootless effort to make Gregor attend to his appearance) I had returned to my native custom of wearing no beard, so perhaps in the dark I was mistaken for a eunuch.

Across a huge courtyard and through one half-shuttered window, I recognized the imperial bedchamber. Some short time later, through that same window, I entered it and settled myself upon the bed, awaiting His Majesty's entrance.

I sat there, callused fingertips snagging on the gold thread embroidered into the red silk of the coverlet. It occurred to me—now, and only now, with a pause to reflect—that this was probably folly, that I had botched it before I began, and that I would probably be summarily executed as soon as His Majesty entered the room. And that even if I was not, I was unlikely to obtain what I had come for. And that even if I did obtain it, I was unlikely to return alive. My plan *could* work, but I'd grown dependent on Jamila; she was always the one who attempted to be at least a little sensible, and I wished she'd been available to tell me what I was about to do wrong.

I looked around the room, wanting something to distract myself while I waited for His Majesty to retire from the celebratory banquets below. There was a harp, and a lute, and a few other instruments leaning in one corner. I went to them. The harp has always been my instrument, but this was different from the one I knew from home. The strings had a familiar texture, the hair of some animal (back home we used horsehair, but almost everyone else, except the Irish, uses gut). I hadn't strummed a hair-strung harp in nearly four years, and the particular feel of the strings filled me with nostalgia. But there were no other similarities: there were three times as many strings on this harp as I was used to, and the sound box had one open side, covered with skin, which gave the entire instrument a strange plunking tone—too alien for me.

So I picked up the lute instead, tuned it, sat back on the bed, and played the very first piece Jamila had taught me. I played it worse than any other lute tune, because my fingers stubbornly clung to their early sense memories of not knowing how to work the thing yet. But I liked the melody, and it reminded me of her, which soothed me.

And more than that—it was the tune I'd played most often at a certain house not far from here, all through last autumn. It would be recognized by His Majesty, even through the closed door.

Footsteps finally approach the room and stopped abruptly. I kept playing.

After a moment, the door was pushed open fast, and two Varangian guards rushed in. These men made Gregor look petite. They moved straight to the bed; one yanked the lute out of my grasp; the second grabbed me; the first, having set the lute down on the floor by the bed, began to frisk me for concealed weapons. I had none.

They released me and exited the room, leaving a large, purple-clad Emperor Mourtzouphlos standing alone in the doorway.

"I see you changed your shoe color," I said. "You looked much better in the green."

He threw back his head and laughed. "I *knew* that you would come," he said, delighted.

64

 MOURTZOUPHLOS STEPPED into the room alone; guards outside pushed the door closed behind him.

"You knew I'd come? *I* didn't know I'd come," I protested.

Mourtzouphlos shrugged happily. "I know you better than you know yourself. I will even tell you why you are here."

"You will?" I said, confused.

He waggled his huge eyebrows at me. "You do not want either side to win, because you love Gregor but you hate his army."

"Not to mention his commander—"

Mourtzouphlos spat. "*Especially* his commander. However, you want to be on whichever side *does* win, and you know it will be my side, so you have chosen me."

"I have?"

"Don't bother playing coy with me. I'm glad to see you, Madman! In your heart, you are glad too, because you know that the well-being of a nation is better than the well-being of a single knight. You are sad for Gregor that he will lose, but not so sad that you would try to help him win."

"Well, helping him win would be helping *Boniface*," I said, as if the name were nauseating. "But I'm not throwing in my lot with you, Mourtzouphlos."

He gave me an ironic look. "I don't need your help, of course, for as you saw two days ago, those foreign pigs will never defeat us."

"Especially not with Boniface leading them—"

Mourtzouphlos spat a second time. "Don't mention that man's name again! This is *all* his fault. Do you think I *enjoy* all this nonsense? I'd much rather be in my little home bouncing on top of Eudocea and getting drunk. But, Madman, if you're not here to help me, then you must be here because you want something from me and you believe that you can make it worth my while. This is also pleasing to me. I even know what it is you want, speaking of bouncing on pretty women. Tell me your offer."

"I have nothing to offer you."

He expressed mock surprise. "She is worth so little to you?"

A confused moment. "What?" I asked, with a sinking feeling.

"Jamila," he said. "I've been waiting for you to go claim her. Have you already lost interest in her, then? Eh! Fickle boy. No eyebrows for you. Let Samuel have it all."

"What are you talking about?" I asked, fighting off sudden panic.

Mourtzouphlos frowned. "You don't know? My men are not so good at spreading rumors as you and I were in our heyday. It is hard to get the right kind of help these days—"

"Where's Jamila?" I demanded sharply and suddenly wished I had a knife. "She fled. They all fled."

"She's in Pera, just around the hillside from your camp," said Mourtzouphlos.

"Pera is completely empty," I insisted. "All the Jews fled."

"All the Jews fled, *except* for Samuel and his household,"

Mourtzouphlos corrected in a jovial tone. "Despite their efforts to flee. He is being held under suspicion of having poisoned my beloved and lamented predecessor, Alexios, God rest his soul. With all these preparations for war, which that damned pestilential, accursed marquis has foisted upon me, we have not the time or the means to attend to Samuel's possible treason. Out of gratitude for his good works in the palace, we have elected to keep him confined not here but in his own home in Pera, with his entire household, including his intended bride, in place. They are under guard, and they are quite alone, but they are there." He gave me a careful look, saw how flummoxed I was. "You did not know about this? I *meant* for you to hear about it. I *thought* it accounted for your presence here."

"That's the problem with rumor," I said, trying to regain the appearance of calm. "It is never a reliable medium. What are you planning to do with them?"

He shrugged. "I believe my reputation will be hallowed, after tomorrow's victory against that scum-sucking marquis, but in case it is not, and unfortunate questions continue to be asked about my predecessor's death, there must be someone other than myself to have to answer to them. His Majesty's physician is the obvious choice."

"And Ja—"

"Jamila is free to leave the house at any time, but of course, you are the only person with whom she would feel safe leaving it, especially now that the entire community has been dispersed again."

I took a moment to make sense of this but couldn't. "What is the benefit to you, in that? In allowing her to leave?"

"I was only doing you a favor! To send you a message, to let you know that I want to continue our agreeable association of the past, which has been rudely interrupted only by this army we both hate so much. It is not sensible for you to continue with that accursed campaign, and you have nowhere else to go. So the solution is obvious: stay with me. You and Jamila both. The army will give up and wander off to Jerusalem with pretty Gregor, or back to Europe with the marquis of villainy, and you can help me restore this empire to its former glory."

"I didn't come here with any intention of joining forces with you, and I still have no intention of doing so," I stammered. I was so worried about Jamila, for a moment I forgot what my mission actually was.

"But you have come anyhow." He hummed with a knowing smile, as if he were about to unmask me as his secret acolyte.

"I'm here for Gregor's sake. You owe him something. I've come to collect the debt. That's all."

He grimaced a little, disappointed. "Really? Then I overestimated you. You only want revenge?" His eyes blazed suddenly. "You blab for months to me about hating conquerors, about a vow that you took to bring down those men who conquered your home. I think, Here is my brother! Another smart and clever man like me who will not sit idly by while tyrants act! And now you have such an easy opportunity to join with me against this damnable would-be conqueror, this man who used an entire religious undertaking to put a puppet on a throne that he might pull the strings—and instead all you want is vengeance for an act that is utterly unremarkable in wartime. Do you have the word *hypocrite* in your tongue?"

"We have a word, *galanas*," I said, "Restitution for murder."

"This is a war, idiot. We all kill each other, and it isn't murder."

I hate it when people get legalistic. "You wronged Gregor when you killed his brother," I insisted. "You owe him something, even if it wasn't murder."

"Is that British law? We are not in Britain, my friend." Mourtzouphlos laughed. "Here we have other rules."

"All right then. Not an eye for an eye, but a head for a head. For Otto's head, give me John the Baptist's."

He considered me and looked mockingly amused. "I am very fond of Gregor, as I hope you know. But are you really saying you have come all the way here, and put your life into my hands, merely for a bit of bone to cheer up a grumpy soldier?"

At least he wasn't denying that he had the relic—but that made it sound less heroic than I wished it to. "Yes," I said.

He looked now slightly irritated with me. "You do understand," he said, "that if this truly is your only reason for coming here, and you have nothing to offer me, and no wish to join me or support me—if you're nothing but a man from the enemy side who has breached my defenses and snuck into my private sanctum to make a silly demand of me, then my inclination is to kill you. But I suspect you've something else in mind."

"I have in mind that you give me the relic, and let me go in peace."

He thought this was the start of a jest. "And why should I do that?"

"Because it is the right thing to do. Even without Otto's blood on your hands, there is a debt. I helped deliver you from bondage; Gregor and I together rendered the relics of this city unto you, and look what you've leveraged from that little prank! All I'm asking is that you render one single relic unto him. It has no meaning to *you*, does it?"

"What, the head of John the Baptist? Of course it does, it's sacred."

"We gave you a city full of sacred relics. This one has special meaning to him. He desperately needs special meaning now. It has nothing to do with what happens tomorrow—you will not be endangered by his having it, Mourtzouphlos, but it will save his life."

"Why should I care about his life?" He laughed. "He's my enemy!"

"He never raised his arm against you except to protect Bo—"

"Don't say that man's name in my presence," Mourtzouphlos said sharply.

"Except to protect his cowardly, villainous father-in-law from your ambush."

Mourtzouphlos gave me a sardonic look. "You are forgetting Gregor and nearly twenty thousand others tried to *sack my city* Friday—"

"Gregor didn't fight," I said. "He would not do it. He defied the marquis because to him it was evil." Mourtzouphlos was startled by this, so I pressed on where I thought I saw an opening. I wanted to settle this quickly and deal with Jamila's situation. "You have a rare quality in a leader, which is that you know how to cherish men by their pure mettle and not just by their convenience. You know that Gregor is a good man. He deserves some recompense from you. Think what it would mean to him to have the head of John the Baptist."

Mourtouzphlos grimaced thoughtfully. "Yes, my friend, admittedly that would be very *nice*, but still, the *safer* course of action is to kill you." In response to my look of outrage: "I thought I understood you, but clearly I don't, so it is not safe to have you out and about. It is regrettable you felt the need to come here for such pathetic purposes. I cannot believe you of all men would do something so *stupid*." He sighed with genuine—but insultingly casual—regret and drew a curving knife from a scabbard that was tied beneath his sash.

"Will you be able to you live with yourself if you do that?"

"I have had Otto's blood on my hands for a month, and I have been managing quite well, thank you for your concern."

"You only ever *met* Otto in prison and then twice under arms. You and I were comrades for many *weeks*."

"We can still be comrades now, if you would only agree to it. I would welcome Gregor too. His loathsome, nefarious leader has been even more of a disappointment to him than mine was to me, and he would be justified in moving on to something better. Let that something better be Byzantium. I would gladly offer him a place in my court. He would be quite a—what is the term—quite a catch. That whoreson Boniface would be beside himself." He grinned. "That would be the single most satisfying development of the year, in fact." He raised the sword questioningly. "I can send across the harbor for

Jamila, and she will be here in under an hour. Will you join me? Or shall I sheathe this knife in your guts? It is your choice."

"I make it a habit to refuse when my life is offered to me under those terms."

He lowered the knife a little, looked at me as if I were pleasing him. "I must say, you are talking like a man who believes he will be alive to see the sun rise. So I think all this behavior is a ploy. I think there is more to your presence here."

"There really isn't," I apologized. "I'm just here to make a reasonable demand, and I hope you will be reasonable in granting it."

"And if I am not?"

"Well, I guess you'll have to kill me then," I said. "It's getting late, and you have a big day ahead of you tomorrow, so we might as well get it over with." I grabbed a low ivory stool, glanced around the ornate room, and pointed to a spot in the center. "Shall I kneel here for the beheading? Is it to be a beheading, or just a stabbing? Or a throat-slitting?" I looked around. "I've seen this sort of thing before; there tends to be a lot of blood. Do you want something to soak it up?" I asked, as I took my self-appointed place kneeling. I positioned the stool in front of me. "Shame to make a mess of the place." And pointing: "Mind the lute. The blood will ruin the strings."

He was giving me a warily amused look.

"This is entertaining, but I have *not* decided *not* to kill you," he warned.

"Well, obviously," I said and gestured to the altar I'd set up. "At this point it's just a matter of who does it first, you or Boniface. I'd rather keep it between friends."

"You don't believe me?" he said, getting annoyed.

"Oh, I do," I assured him.

"You don't seem very *distressed* about it."

"Is the point of killing me for me to end up dead, or for you to get some satisfaction out of seeing me distressed?"

He laughed. "I have *far* more interesting forms of satisfaction."

"Yes, you do—for example, imagining what it will do to Boniface, once his army is utterly repulsed by you, when every one of them goes home completely empty-handed, *except* for Gregor of Mainz."

Continuation

The preparations referred to above were interrupted by the Briton's returning very late with a most remarkable thing: the head of John the Baptist, which he presented to me. He will say only that Mourtzouphlos's hatred of Boniface accounts for it, which makes no sense to me. He was distracted by thoughts of his own, even as he gave it to me.

I am of course moved almost beyond words by this. It is the most extraordinary object I have ever held, in the most exquisite and finely labored reliquary, with more jewels than I have ever owned in my life. I was conflicted as to what to do with it. It ought to be returned to the monastery from which it was stolen, but if I take it there, it will simply be stolen again tomorrow, if God for some reason smiles on this benighted campaign and the city is taken.

So I gave it to the Briton as a gift. He was taken aback and protested that he had given it to me so that I would have a relic and therefore a pilgrimage, and therefore something to be joyful of.

"It is your antidote," he said.

This required a second brief discourse on the nature of a pilgrimage, which in the end I still do not think he quite understood. In truth, his confusion breeds with my own. I tried to explain to him that a pilgrimage is not about what one obtains but what one does. It must be a transforming experience. My sitting in my cabin and being given a relic as a gift through no effort of my own, this is not transforming.

To which the Briton said: "Once you were a wide-eyed innocent, and now you're not—you don't consider that a transformation?"

To which I said: "The transformation must bring you closer to knowing God."

To which he said: "But you do know God a little better now.

God doesn't reward you for mindless submission. God expects you to
perform right action, even if there is no hope of the outcome being what
you want. In truth, I have learned that myself. If you will excuse me, I
have my own pilgrimage to complete."

He shoved the head of John the Baptist into his tunic. Then he did
something most peculiar, which I hope does not bode ill, considering
his state of mind: he took a length of rope we had in the corner of the
room, perhaps five fathoms long, which we had gotten once to mark
off a boxing ring for training squires. He wrapped this around his body
as if he were bandaging his torso with it. Then he went to the clothes-
peg and took Otto's extra winter tunic, which is too large for him, and
placed it over all so the rope was not visible. He left once again.

If he has gone to hang himself, as I suspect, I envy him the freedom
to do so.

Now that I have written this, I shall conclude my preparations for
tomorrow.

SAMUEL'S HOUSE had six Varangian guards around it in their neat
scale armor, each with a sword and a two-handed ax. This seemed
excessive in an otherwise abandoned settlement. There was a man at
the door, one at each corner, and one up on the roof. They spoke to
one another in a speech I recognized but could not speak myself; they
were from England and spoke as Wulfstan did. I shared something
with these men—their people, like mine, had been oppressed by the
Norman lords who now ruled England, many months' journey from
here. Our similarities ended there.

Now, at night, the house was literally surrounded by torches. A
small handcart beside the door suggested that food and supplies were
being brought in by the guards.

One side of the house was barely a pace from the settlement's
perimeter wall, although it rose a floor above it. This meant that
somebody on the roof, or climbing out the window on the upper

floor, theoretically could jump out of Pera into denuded wilderness. This would have been very foolhardy even for someone like me—the jumper would land upon a very steep, rocky slope—but it was possible; hence the guard on the roof.

I walked toward the window I knew opened into a room intended eventually to be a study; now it was (or had been recently) where Jamila slept. I did not enter it but stood beside it and spoke, with unbridled, sophomoric expressions of affection. I said things an adolescent might think about his first love, but so syrupy that even the adolescent would know better than to say them aloud. I said them anyhow, because this really was my last chance to do so, ever.

My soliloquy placed me between two of the guards; I used no Greek, but my message was obvious, especially since (I now knew) these men had been waiting about a month for me to do this. I told Jamila that people are seldom given second chances in life and that when they are, it is a sin of stupidity to take the *wrong* second chance. I said not one abusive thing about Samuel, although Lord knows it would have been easy and I was in a mood to do it. But I did tell her that I knew she was free to walk out of the house to join me, and I begged her to abandon him. I was, in other words, both genuine enough to unburden myself and horrible enough that she would never respond.

The window was only an opening cut out of the wall, fitted with wooden shutters on leather hinges. One of these was closed, the other open just enough for me to speak into it. "How many times must one man rescue the woman he loves from tyrannical captivity?" I bemoaned and now raised my voice to make sure I was being heard. "From those who would keep her under their dominion, for false reasons? For here I am to do it a third time! I escorted you to freedom from Barzizza's house and then again from Boniface's clutches, and now once again I am here for you, to—"

Heavy footsteps had begun to move across the beaten-earth floor inside. The window shutter was flung open from within the house; I leapt back and stopped speaking. Standing there with a lantern was pale-eyed Samuel, his height exceeding mine by even more than usual, for the house was slightly elevated. He was quietly enraged.

"Will you stop that?" he demanded. "Your words are tearing her apart. What would you have her do?"

"I already said it plainly—I'm here to rescue her from the wrong life!" I said loudly and tried to call over his shoulder. "Jamila! Come out here! I have to take Liliana away to the abbey tonight, and I want you to come with us! It's no good to make sacrifices merely from a sense of duty and not from faith or love! You yourself have watched Gregor learn that very lesson!" I stepped up to the window and cocked an eye at Samuel, asking snidely, "Is it asking too much to request you call my woman over?" His face hosted an extraordinary range of emotions, very quickly in succession; I heard the soldiers behind me snicker a little. This was a boring post and had been going on for weeks now; they were hopeful of distraction.

My comment, which Jamila could hear plainly, brought her running to the window. She had been sobbing; her face was still livid. "What are you up to?" she whispered fiercely, sounding nasal.

"You are permitted to leave," I said, loudly. "These guards all know that."

"I can't do that. And if you really think I would, then you're a beast."

"Shall I come in and claim you by force, like a barbarian? Shall I emulate the great crusaders and fight for what I want? Samuel ben David, I challenge you to a duel!" This line was delivered with great physical bravura so the guards would understand that something dramatic was afoot. They were very pleased.

"Don't be ridiculous," said Samuel.

"Aha! You accept!" I said. "Come out here and fight me!"

Samuel glanced down at Jamila. "What the devil is he doing?" he asked—or something like that, in Arabic.

Her response, also in Arabic, probably meant: "Only the devil knows."

Samuel glanced farther out the window now, at the nearest guard. "Am I allowed to step outside?" he asked, then repeated the question in Greek.

The guard grunted unsurely and called for his superior at the front door, who had been inching his way over to see what the commotion was about.

"Then I will come inside and defeat you in your own home!" I announced and, reaching up, began to climb in through the window. Jamila and Samuel pulled back into the room, startled.

The guards immediately grabbed me to haul me back out, amused but chastising. I made a great show of trying to push them off. "This man has taken my woman!" I stormed at them, as they carried me, one by the ankles and one under the arms, and dumped me on the ground a few yards off. I leapt to my feet immediately and ran back for the window. "I demand satisfaction from him before I go! Jamila, translate!"

This, the delighted guards could understand without translation. They prevented me from going back in through the window, but they were already placing wagers on which of us would win a fistfight. Samuel was growing more disgusted; Jamila muttered to him warningly in Arabic, and he settled into stony silence as the guards and I agreed that Samuel and I were to have at each other, fists only, and only within the house. The first injury that drew blood or broke a bone would end the match. Jamila would go with the winner. (Jamila's *willingness* to go with the winner did not factor into the discussion, even when she, as translator, brought it up.)

The guards were invited inside to watch the sport, so we waited a moment until the fellow on the roof descended from his post. I saw with relief that Samuel's "household" now consisted only of Samuel and Jamila—he must have dismissed his servants, for their own safety, when the rest of Pera fled. That would make this easier.

Samuel and I stood in the middle of his nearly empty main room, two paces apart, facing each other. Torches were brought in so everyone could see the violence. I made a great show of preparing for these fisticuffs; Samuel did not. With withering superiority he looked, literally, down his nose at me as I rolled up my tattered sleeves, hopped around a little, spat into my palms, and rubbed my hands together. He was my senior by only a few years, but he seemed ancient in demeanor. The six guards had pushed the cushions and few pieces of furniture to the sides of the room and were surrounding us, standing but bent over slightly to bring their heads closer to the spectacle. They were arrhythmically clapping their hands in anticipation. Four wagered on me, two on Samuel. Of my four, one bet the others that Jamila would not go with me even if I won, because she'd have to stay and tend to Samuel's wounds—plus, I was obviously mad.

I appointed Jamila herald and ordered her to stay close to us, no matter how rough the match became, so that she could call out for a cessation if she saw damage done. It would also be her honor to begin the fight by dropping a kerchief or a scarf "or your sleeve, or something like that," I said to her, my eyes fixed on Samuel.

"I appreciate your . . . chivalry," she said uncertainly. "But I do not trust it, and I will not condone your fighting. If you wait for me, you will be waiting for years."

"Not for years, for*ever*," I muttered. I kept myself from looking at her directly, but my eyes glanced vaguely in her direction.

One of the guards spoke a little French and realized she was balking, so he volunteered to start in her place. He lifted his arm and lowered it with a shout, and then the others began shouting too.

I leapt at Samuel and shoved him hard on one shoulder, pushing him toward the side of the room where a ladder leaned against the wall; he stumbled, astonished and frightened that I had actually struck him.

"C'mon," I said. "Hit me. If you dare! Hit me hard!"

He looked at me in disgust. "I am a physician. I took an oath to cause no harm."

"Hit me!" I shouted and moved closer to him; I reached up and struck him across the face. Reflexively he held his hands up, in a nervous, almost girlish way, to ward me off; I hovered too near to him and pretended I was going to smack him again, and he angrily grabbed both of my wrists and began to shove me backward.

"You arsehole!" I shouted. "Let go!" I shook my wrists as if trying very hard to get away from him; he clung on tightly to prevent my slapping him again. Relying on his grip to keep the connection, I leaned toward him and then pivoted around to reverse our direction. We approached the ladder looking as if he were pushing me back toward it.

At the foot of the ladder, I feared an awkward moment. But Samuel—although utterly confused by my intention—understood that we had to reach the upper floor. After a hesitation, he released my wrists and managed an impressive punch to my midriff. But I had unexpected armor there—not only was the length of rope coiled around me, but the head of John the Baptist, which Gregor had not had the graciousness to accept, was in its red bag, tucked beneath all into my shirt. So Samuel hurt his own fist more than he hurt me. We both managed to pretend this wasn't so; I bent over with a breathless gasp of agony, and he pulled his arm back to attack me again—at which point, with a look of pained panic, I turned around and scrambled up the ladder. He scrambled after me, grabbing at my boots and shouting. I screamed in alarm. The Varangians were clapping, hollering, delighted that they were going to get their money's worth. The guards themselves gave Jamila a lamp and gestured her up the ladder after us, cheerfully warning her to keep close watch on us both. From the moment of my first strike, they had begun to raise their wagers. We were now worth five *stamenon* apiece, about the cost of a set of new fiddle strings.

The ladder opened directly into Samuel's bedchamber, with a window facing the Golden Horn, over Pera's perimeter wall. I reached for the collar of the overtunic I'd worn, and with a shout I ripped the whole thing down the front, moving to the far side of the room; be-

fore Samuel was fully upright in the space with me, I'd thrown myself
into a chest so hard that the chest, although heavy, moved a full foot
across the floor back toward him. "Take that!" I shouted and began
to uncoil the rope from around me. Samuel, uncertain, made a move
to attack me again; I shook my head and handed him the end of the
rope, gesturing him to pull it as I turned away from him, so that I un-
wound like a top. He pulled at it, looking dumbfounded. As I came to
the end of my unwinding pirouette, I threw myself against the wall,
stomping as hard as I could as I went. "Ouf!" I groaned. "You whoreson!" I squatted low and then shimmied my hip against the chest,
causing it to shriek across the wooden planks for another hand span;
now it loomed over one end of the ladder hole and bumped Jamila's
shin; she squealed a little, which delighted all the men below who
were trying to look up her skirt as she ascended.

Jamila was up now. She looked at me in the lantern light and
grew very still for a moment. "I finally remembered to bring a rope," I
whispered loudly. She sat the lantern on the windowsill, grabbed the
line from Samuel's distracted grip, and began to tie one end of it to a
leg of the heavy wooden bed.

"No, I will not yield her!" I shouted as she did this and threw
myself directly over the ladder hatchway, dropping the torn tunic
down the hatch onto the heads of the men who were about to mount
the ladder themselves. They began to cheer over the tunic and were
distracted briefly. "*Never!*" Urgently, I gestured to Samuel and then
to the chest. I grabbed a handle at one end of it; Samuel, finally understanding, grabbed the other handle, and we shuffled it over the
rest of the opening, in halting fits and starts, with mutual groans and
shouts and curses in a cascade of languages. Just as one guard's head
was about to extend up through the hatch, Samuel and I shot the
chest diagonally across the rest of the opening, blocking entry to the
second floor. The guard, peripherally seeing a large object moving
toward his head, shouted with alarm and ducked down the ladder,
collapsing onto his comrades, who guffawed at him.

Jamila jerked at the rope to test her knot, then turned to the window and threw the rest out. It smacked against the inner side of the perimeter wall and fell down the side into the alley. She cursed nervously under her breath and began to haul it back in.

I gestured toward the window. "Gregor's packhorse is down the slope," I whispered, then threw myself to the ground and turned the clumsiest, loudest somersault I could. A riot of laughter from below, although a man on the ladder tried to move the chest out of the way. Samuel pointed in the lamplight to a second chest. I nodded and scrambled up, and all three of us struggled to hoist this chest high enough to set it on top of the first as I continued to thump the floor and utter curses.

"One horse for three people?" Jamila grunted in a whisper as we hefted it.

I wanted so badly to that say the horse was just for Samuel, and that she'd have to stay with me to assure he got to safety. But that wasn't true, and it wasn't why I'd come.

"Two people," I grunted back. "Not me." It was too dark to see Jamila's reaction to this, but I could *feel* it—there was a change in the air, almost in the temperature of the room, that tickled the hair up and down my arms, burst moths out of waiting cocoons in my belly. She muffled a sob. "What the devil's *in* this?" I demanded loudly and furiously, as if I were swearing. The chest felt like solid iron.

"The Holy Scriptures," Samuel responded.

"*Finally* they're good for something!" I shouted. Once we had them in place, I flipped myself over both chests, landing on my side with an arm outstretched to make the loudest possible noise for the fellows downstairs. I jumped up and looked over the chests, saw Jamila, fretting, trembling, back at the window. She had finally figured out that she needed to *coil* the rope to throw it, but she hadn't succeeded yet in lobbing it over the wall; she was trembling almost too much to hold it.

I scrambled to my feet, stomped across the room, took the rope from her, and hurled it out across the narrow gap between house and perimeter wall. It went over easily. She was shaking so badly now she seemed to have trouble breathing. I leaned in close enough to say quietly, "Don't worry about me, I can get out of here. You get far away fast, before the men downstairs can sound an alarm." I leaned over and kissed her on the lips. "Now I really have delivered you, and willingly."

She kissed me back and nearly collapsed against me with a sob, which I decided (for my own sanity) was an expression of gratitude for my saving her man. Any other meaning of that sob and I couldn't have kept this up. I pushed her away gently, threw myself against the other wall, smashing into the stacked chests. Samuel stood near me; I grabbed his right hand, shook it courteously, and then threw myself to the floor again with a loud and angry curse.

"Despite the symbolic redundancy of what I'm doing, I can't keep this up much longer," I grunted softly. "So *please* get the hell out of here."

Continuation

At last I finished the preparations, with the help of my servants. All the money and valuables I had about me were put into packs across one sumpter horse; the other horse had disappeared, and after threats, young Richard confessed the Briton had taken it. I thought he'd abandoned me, but I was mistaken, as you shall see. The money is for Liliana's transport, and safety during such, in the months to come. Also on the pack went Otto's sword and the few effects left to him, including some of the outlandish things he had collected for Liliana and the child. There also, a letter to my wife and son, although these may not reach Germany for a year or more. Otto's horse, Oro, has been saddled and the stirrups adjusted to Liliana, although her belly barely fits behind the pommel. To Liliana I have given a letter, addressed to a monastery lying to the north of Pera: His Eminence Bishop Conrad knows some-

body who knows somebody who knows the abbot there, who has agreed to take Liliana in until she and the child may travel safely. To Liliana, I have given also a purse with an offering for the abbot.

To each of the Richardim, I gave silver statues from my travel altar and bade them relish them and not sell them. I unrolled the maps to the abbey that Conrad had sent us with the letter and reviewed them with the Richardim, and in the middle of our doing this, the Briton returned. He was limping, extremely disheveled, and bruised around the face. Liliana cried out in alarm and asked him what had befallen him. His reply was cryptic: "My pilgrimage is well-concluded, although I've no relic to show for it."

I instructed him to travel with Liliana to the abbey. He is to be her guardian until she is safely home in Germany. He did not object to this.

He began to object, however, when he realized I had ordered the squires to accompany them. He protested that a knight in battle needs his squires, or he simply cannot manage, he has no way even to get out of his armor.

Of course I did not respond to this. Instead I took from my own private parcel of most treasured goods the marquis's wax seal. Those few soldiers who don't know me by sight know me by the seal. With the end of my dagger, I stabbed a hole in the lower corner of the contract I had dictated to Conrad, the one making Liliana and her child wards of my estate. I dragged the leather thong of the seal through the hole in the document, affixing it to the seal. I handed this to Liliana, saying, "Now you have Boniface's endorsement to protect you."

Rather than expressing relief or gratitude, she looked disturbed and went a little pale. "How can you part with that?" she asked me, referring to the seal. It has always been my talisman of privilege.

I told her, and this is true, that I do not need it anymore.

LILIANA AND I exchanged looks, shocked. I limped over to her, and she whispered urgently, "Stay with him. We can get to the monastery without you. Don't leave him here alone. What in the name of St. John happened to you, anyhow?"

"What about *after* the monastery?" I asked. "Can you get back to Germany without me, if you need to?"

With a sheepish smile, she whispered, "Before Germany, the Holy Land."

"*What?*"

She took my hand and placed it on her belly. "I would like some part of Otto to have made it there," she said. "To him this was, more than anything, a great adventure. The greatest adventure of his life. It seems a shame not to see it through for him."

Somehow, more than any of Gregor's fine and noble words, *that* struck me as a pilgrimage. I hugged her and started sobbing.

Gregor was aware that they left, and that I did not go with them. He didn't even comment, didn't spare me a look. He went back to his altar, knelt, prayed briefly, and then began writing in his little German book. When he finished with that, he returned to praying.

I picked up the case of every instrument I owned and walked out of the cabin.

Over the next hour, limping about the anxious, darkened camp, my mind fixated on that last kiss from Jamila, I managed to concoct something like armor for myself. The chain-mail coif of Otto's would cover my head. With squires who had gone through growth spurts, or graduated to full armor, I traded my instruments for a padded *acheton* (a sort of quilted hauberk), leather britches, a wooden training shield, and a dagger fashioned from a broken Rhineland sword.

By the time I returned to the cabin, Gregor had fallen asleep by the altar. I arranged my own pathetic suit of armor near his, pulled a blanket over him, and then crawled beneath it myself. I noticed he was using Otto's shield.

We woke at dawn to the reveille of trumpets.

65

How shall I begin to tell the deeds wrought by these nefarious men!

—NIKETAS CHONIATES, *O City of Byzantium*

HERE IS SOMETHING nobody ever says about participating in a battle: long, long stretches of it are very boring. Except for the heightened awareness that any moment might bring death, of course, if you care about that sort of thing.

In the dark of the morning, we dressed. I was so sore from my self-inflicted thrashing, I could hardly move. Gregor was appalled when he realized I meant to follow him into battle. I ignored his protests.

We then spent all morning sitting in a boat.

We were on the *San Giorgio*, Boniface's ship, which had been lashed to the *Innocent*. There were twenty such pairs of transports tied together for stability, as Baldwin had suggested. Each pair had high siege ladders with grappling hooks protruding from the perilously high-built castles fore and aft. Most of the ships would sail as close as they could toward the harbor walls and throw out the hooks to try to latch on to the walls, thus allowing soldiers to leap onto the towers; Dandolo and Boniface had offered a high reward to whoever first landed on the city walls.

But the wind was high, and against the ships, and so for hours this was an exercise in futility. Meanwhile, however, archers and crossbowmen from both sides were filling the air with pointed death; there was a constant exchange of catapulted rocks and mortar. Most horrifying and damaging was Greek fire, which the Greeks would glob onto their arrows and shoot at us. The magical horror of this substance is that *water* makes it burst into flame. Short of suffocating it with sand (we had none), either dousing it with vinegar (in short supply) or pissing on it seemed the only ways to contain it. Every ship in the fleet, including ours, was slippery, damp, and fetid by midmorning. Many of the soldiers—especially the infantry, who lacked chain armor or decent helmets—withdrew into the holds of the ships in response to the barrage of flying hazards. Gregor didn't, so neither did I. It was fine if I died now, I decided, because it would no longer be suicide—I felt a calm sense of acceptance that finally I'd done something completely right, and so my earthly labors might end soon. I would be remembered well, at last. Perhaps, despite three years of grandiose posturing and preparation, that was all I'd ever really wanted.

An arrow bounced off Gregor's helmet, another sank into my pathetic wooden shield with such force the shield split in two, and I tossed it over the side. I looked at my equally-pathetic dagger, and tossed that overboard as well. I knew I'd never use it.

Boniface called Gregor to the bow for a conference. From the moment we'd set foot on the boat (right foot first, at the insistence of the mariners), it was clear that Gregor would, as long as battle lasted, operate like the brilliant soldier that he was trained to be. Through the worst of their disagreements, this was one thing Boniface never doubted, and now I too realized it was a trait that would not falter, even here. But still I wanted to keep an eye on him, so I trailed at a distance, and then gradually, as they conferred with several other barons, I moved closer to try to hear. Gregor, with the calm confidence of a man in his element, pointed to various spots along the harbor wall—not the towers but the base of the walls. He pointed inland, toward a northern gate near Blachernae, made expert little gestures explaining something to Boniface, and then looked around the crowded deck, apparently getting a measure of the manpower available.

I drew closer, desperate to hear. "Hello, milord," I shouted over the thunder of bellowing sails, creaking rigging, screaming of fire arrows, and general cacophony of men shouting orders at one another. I grinned stupidly at Boniface.

It took the marquis a moment to grasp whom he was looking at, between the coif on my head and the unexpected context. "Is that the lute player?" he shouted back, frowning. "What in the name of all things holy are you doing on a battleship?"

"I need to see things close up, for real, so I can sing about them," I said earnestly and pointed to another armored figure in the stern, who was probably humming "Kalenda Maya" to himself. "Just like my hero there, Raimbaut of Vaqueiras."

"Raimbaut is a knight, a trained soldier," Boniface said impatiently. "Stupid ass, you're going to get yourself killed. I don't care, but stay out of the way of the soldiers or I'll skin you alive. War is no place for simpletons."

I wanted to argue this point but didn't. Instead I bowed and withdrew, but kept an eye on Gregor so that I could speak to him as soon as possible.

Gregor, still near the foremast, gave directions to several waiting sergeants, and they in turn began to move back through the ship, delegating orders. It was amazing how, despite the chaos, the men were very sharp and quick about responding to their commands: weapons were collected from belowdecks and dispersed to waiting sergeants above. No, not weapons: instruments, implements. Picks and axes, heavy, unwieldy but very strong, like weapons from hundreds of years ago. They looked more like they were designed to attack inert material than living enemies.

We were sailing up near Blachernae, in part because the expanse of rocks at the base of the walls there gave the opportunity for a second type of approach: landing at a now bricked-up gate and breaking through it, to let troops in on street level. This, it turned out, was Gregor's plan. When I was able to get close to him again, he

was amidships and watching two of the other bound-together sailing transports making yet another attempt to latch on to the walls,
farther down the harbor.

"Ten knights and sixty sergeants," Gregor explained, when I was
near. We squinted into the late-morning sun. He pointed to a gate.
"That gate there. Petrion."

"I'm coming," I said.

"No, you're not."

"When do we start?"

"*I* start as soon as the *Lady Pilgrim* and the *Paradise* secure a tower.
We'll get the Greeks' attention on that, and then my men and I
will head to shore." He pointed to the two largest ships in the fleet,
lashed together to create an unwieldy but huge and strangely stable
conglomerate. Its few oars were straining now against the wind, to
press it right up to the walls.

As we watched, the wind suddenly shifted east; in the lurching of
the ships and mortars landing in the water, a wave was generated that
pushed the twinned vessels landward. The soldiers and mariners on
the *Lady Pilgrim* who were operating the siege ladders and grappling
hooks scrambled to latch on to a high, projecting wooden tower. But
a Venetian sergeant on the top of the tallest mast was nimble, and
cocky: as the mast tipped close enough, he actually grabbed the city
wall with his bare hands and leapt from off the mast right onto it.
Every member of the crusading army not actively engaged in handling the boats had his eyes on this man, and as his feet landed on
the battlement, a cheer broke out from thousands and thousands of
throats all across the waters of the Golden Horn.

But that cheer instantly mutated into cries of outrage, for no
sooner had the sergeant gotten his bearings than did half a dozen
Greek soldiers hack him to bits; he had probably not had a chance to
draw breath before he had been quartered and his body parts unceremoniously hurled off the tower onto the rocks below. The Greeks,
many of whom could see this clearly from where they were, cheered

now in their turn. The Latin voices had been fewer than twenty thousand; the Greeks, many hundreds of thousands.

Mourtzouphlos had a good view of it as well, lolling as he was on the hillside where he had lolled through the last failed assault, three days before. A moment later I could hear, even over the fury of battle, faint echoes of the trumpets and drums he had with him, celebrating this thwarted attempt to breach the city.

But as all of this was going on, a knight in proper armor (which the sergeant hadn't had) was climbing up the ladder that had been nailed to the mast. Despite the bulk of his protective layering, he too managed to get to the top of the mast, and when the boat next heeled landward, he defiantly imitated the sergeant's actions—landing on his feet and breathless but armed and armored. The group of Varangian Guards who had just dispatched the sergeant turned their weapons now on the knight but were rudely surprised to find those weapons less effective. The knight killed one with a thrash of his sword, and the others hesitated, glanced at one another.

As the knight had leapt out to grasp the tower, the mariners in the forecastle had thrown their grappling hooks to secure the siege ladders, and already several soldiers were clattering their way across the small chasm from boat to tower—and then they were on the tower. About a dozen of them made this perilous journey before the heeling of the boat reversed and the ladder broke away from the city walls, slamming two knights to their deaths on the rocks below.

As I watched this, rapt with horrified fascination, Gregor had seen his moment and rushed to give the order for our own twinned vessels to move in to the Petrion Gate. I tore my eyes away from the swordplay a hundred feet above the water's edge and looked around the ship. I could not see Gregor in the armored press of bodies, but I could tell where he must have gone: he was summoning the men who would disembark with him. There was, within the solid mass of soldiers on the deck now, a current of flesh and armor moving toward the port side near the stern, near me. We were turning so that the port side really was the *port* side: a wide gangplank was being pulled up from the deck and made ready to allow the knights and sergeants to race down it onto the rocks.

Gregor had chosen a small gate, bricked closed, near the area that had been burned by Venetians the summer before. The towers here had been built up with wood palisades as high as the rest of the harborside, but these towers had been damaged seriously in that earlier battle. The guard on them was not so heavy because there was less room for men among the rubble; there would be less resistance as the mining operation proceeded below.

Besides the ten knights and sixty sergeants, there were several dozen servants, carrying extra shields, hatchets, stones, and large pieces of board covered on one side with (by the stink of it) vinegar-soaked hide. It was simple for me to add myself to their number; I went over the rail and down the splintery plank, landing in ankle-deep water a few yards before the gate.

The gate itself was a large wooden structure, six paces across and more than twice the height of a man. In less time than your average early-morning piss, this had been completely destroyed by swords, axes, picks, and hatchets.

But behind it was revealed a wall of rocks, which had been built weeks earlier. It was made of smaller stones than the city walls but engineered so that it seemed to be a continuation of them. Gregor gestured to the servants, who raised the covered boards up into an interlocking grid, moving with a synchronicity suggesting they had practiced this. The weave of boards became a roof over the heads of the sergeants, who immediately went to work trying to break down the wall.

What followed was another short period like the morning, both harrowing and dull. Hacking through stone is not accomplished quickly, and the wall could not be undermined, built as it was on solid rock. We had only a few yards of rock ourselves—much of it slippery wet and sometimes slimy. So there was no choice but to strike away at the wall, under the cover of the makeshift protective roof. Beneath the hide, I finally realized, the boards were wrapped with iron; they were very heavy, but they deflected fire arrows from the towers above.

As the sergeants went at the wall with picks and hatchets, the knights (and the extraneous sergeants, since not all of them would even fit before the gate) kept watch for attacks from other directions, especially down in the harbor, where the tower had been taken. I glanced that way myself; the swordplay above continued. I dared not allow my attention to be distracted, so I turned my back on it and focused entirely on Gregor.

The sun was coming from our left, but as it moved, the shadow of the wall inched over us; this made it colder but easier to see. I don't know how long it took before one of the miners finally broke through and let in daylight through the wall; there was a cheer, and the dozen or so men who had been hacking away all crowded to look. Gregor had been standing with his back to the work, protected only by his own shield, which he carried over his head against debris and arrows from above. He was shouting out to the boat, which was trying to hold steady beside us. Boniface was shouting back at him from the deck. The wind, still largely from the north, kept sending his words toward us but not Gregor's toward him; as a result, the marquis was mostly shouting out to Gregor that he could not hear what Gregor was saying.

When the cry of triumph came from the wall, Gregor interrupted the bootless conversation to spin around and see. He rushed back to the wall and began to grab the sergeants by the shoulder, shoving them roughly out of the way. I took a step toward him on instinct, protectively.

Boniface pointed at me, eyebrows raised, and shouted something about idiocy, but I wasn't listening. My focus was on Gregor now; he was at the wall and pushed aside the last of the sergeants to kneel down and gaze through the little chink. It was suddenly much quieter than it had been, with the stoppage of stonework—but it wasn't actually *quiet*. The chink was about knee-level. Everyone who had peered through it was somber.

I grabbed the elbow of one of the tossed-aside sergeants. "What is it?" I demanded.

"There's a whole company of Greeks massed in the street on the other side," he said. "Archers and swordsmen both."

Gregor rose and pointed to the rock. "Keep going," he ordered.

"Milord," said a sergeant, "if we take down the wall, they'll just attack us—"

"Ten of you," Gregor said and gestured sharply for the roof to move back over the spot where the chink was. Everybody scrambled back into place. "Keep it hidden from the towers. Here's what you do—" As he gave the orders, he demonstrated expansively with his arms, too abstract for it to mean anything to the Greeks above. "*Weaken* an area large enough for six men abreast, standing. Don't break all the way through. Once you have that, then down here, where the chink is, actually break through the stone just large enough to fit one knight."

He stepped back from the mining operation, again his shield raised over his head. I tried to intercept him but he pushed me aside—he didn't even see who I was, he was so focused on his efforts—and ran back toward the ship.

"Milord!" he bellowed out to Boniface. "The gate is about to fall! Arm the knights and have them ready to go through. Archers first. There are at least three hundred Greeks waiting on the other side." The wind had shifted, and the words reached Boniface; the marquis turned and began to holler orders to his men. Immediately the archers on both ship and tower increased their volleys at each other. Gregor turned again and marched back toward the wall. I followed him.

"Why only large enough for one man?" I demanded. Even standing next to him, I had to shout, nearly scream, to be heard over the renewed pummeling of metal on rock.

"Safer that way," Gregor shouted back brusquely. "Take 'em by surprise."

"But whoever goes through first—"

"Whoever goes through first will always be remembered as a war hero," said Gregor, "and those he leaves behind cannot be shamed." Then he crowded under the protective roof, where there was no room for me. An arrow nearly took my ear off; I retreated beneath the shield of another knight.

The two sergeants lowest down began to clear away rubble to see how large a hole they'd made. Gregor, noticing the shift in activity, pushed them aside again and checked the size of the hole against his own shoulders.

Three arrows zinged through the hole at angles and glanced off the rocks. Gregor instinctively drew back. A pause. No more arrows. Gregor pointed to another low spot on the other end of the blockading wall. "Now start to break through a small section there, to distract them. But be ready to bring down the whole thing." He dropped his shield by the hole, got to his knees, and filled the opening with his bulk.

"No!" I shouted and pulled away from the protection of the knight's shield. The sergeants had leapt to their feet in alarm and were gawking at Gregor as he began to push himself through the narrow hole. "No! No!" I kept shouting. "Stop him!" Blazing arrows sailed past me thickly; I could not dodge them, there were too many, so I could only run straight ahead and hope that God was on Gregor's side. I reached the safety of the roof without being hit, collapsed onto my knees at the hole, and grabbed at Gregor's shins. "Don't! Don't do it!" I looked up at the waiting sergeants, and at the knights who were worriedly adjusting their armor. "Stop him!" I shrieked. "Pull down the rest of it now and everyone go through at once! With shields, for the love of God!"

Gregor pushed back with one leg to disengage me. "Let go," he shouted. "I have to do this."

"No! Wait until the rest of the wall is down!"

"That's what they're *expecting* us to do," he said. "I'm going now."

My fingers clamped around the edge of his shield, and I dragged it closer to myself. "Then take this at least."

"It will get in my way."

"Take the shield!" I screamed and shoved it at him. He grabbed it from me and impatiently flung it out of my reach, rattling over the stones, then turned, gave me a final kick to force me from him, and began to crawl through the hole.

"Gregor!" I shrieked. I reached in after him. He kicked back again, the hard heel of his boot slamming me in the forehead. For a moment I could see nothing, feel nothing but a blackness that was hot and cold at once. Blinking spastically, I tried to open my eyes, instinctively reaching forward through the hole to grab again at his feet.

It was too late. He had gone through.

Behind me men were shouting, some trying to pull me out so that they could get through themselves. Above us, others were knocking down the rest of the tottering wall. In a moment there would be a large opening, and the two companies would meet.

But right now the Greeks had none to face but Gregor. I kicked furiously at those trying to draw me to safety, reached out to grab Gregor's shield, and then scrambled, dragging the shield, in padded leather and Otto's coif, through the gap and into the city.

66

A MAN DRAPED IN chain mail cannot rise quickly from his stomach. Gregor had erupted from the hole headfirst, but I was close behind him, and although burdened by the shield, I had more dexterity than he did. I climbed on his back and sat upright, legs forward, and dug my heels into the fronts of his armpits so that when he stood, he lifted me with him on his shoulders—the long Italian shield hanging from my arms and covering his face and shoulders, so that we might have appeared to the startled soldiers before us like a British-headed German giant.

As Gregor rose, his fist closed around his sword hilt. For the briefest moment, we stood in a face-off with a company of Greek soldiers, their scaled armor this time made of iron. One face (for Gregor's was covered) against three hundred, a hundred of them attached to archers, and all the archers with arrows on their strings. So this is what my death would finally look like.

A solid wall of arrows flew in our direction. I cowered and dropped my head onto Gregor's left shoulder, by my own left knee; doubled over, I was behind the shield, but most of Gregor wasn't, and he couldn't see around the shield. He was hit at least two dozen times and staggered backward from the percussive impact.

Every arrow bounced, deflected harmlessly off the shield or his armor. Arrows don't bounce. Those arrows bounced. Not one of them pierced his armor, but he shuddered and stumbled under me. While our faces were close, he grabbed the shield from me with his left hand and shouted, "Get off of me!" He'd drawn his sword now, so he couldn't use his right arm; he tossed the shield in the air and caught the hand-grip at a better angle but could not get his arm through the strap.

Now holding the shield, he brought his left arm high to knock me off his shoulders. Overcome by a ridiculous and desperate impulse, I reached into my tunic, ripping down the front, grabbed the red bag, leaned forward, and shoved the reliquary down the front of Gregor's chain-mail hauberk. The relic—at least in my fevered mind, at that moment—accounted for the bouncing arrows. Leaning forward put me in the path of Gregor's shield, and I turned my head so that the iron-ringed edge of the shield smacked hard into Otto's coif on my head; with the harshest wrench I've ever felt, my body was shoved headfirst right into the ground behind Gregor's feet. I lay dazed.

Above me, Gregor lowered the shield, raised the sword, and roared like a crazed pagan barbarian. The Greek soldiers, as a unit, cringed into a collective backward step. I scrambled to my feet, my head throbbing. I looked desperately around for a place to flee—a window or door in whatever buildings lined the street—but Gregor was running directly *at* the Greeks, as if he himself, a single man, could overwhelm them all.

At that moment, the wall behind me shuddered as the soldiers brought it down. There was a violent crash, and a cloud of sprawling stone chips erupted, on its own so spectacular it might have stopped an army. Gregor did not turn to look; he kept screaming and charging at the Greeks.

The pilgrims had lined up in a block—six across, six back—and when the wall fell, three dozen of them created the impression of a crowd disappearing out of view. Nothing human but their pale eyes glinting through the slats beside the noseguards, they looked inhuman, terrifying. They'd heard Gregor scream and imitated him, a howl picked up by the sergeants huddled behind them. All of them thought he'd be dead by now. When they realized what he was doing, they sprang after him, picking their way over jumbled rocks and drawing their swords, screams overlapping like plated armor.

The Greek company turned and fled. They did this with grace and precision that would have made a dance troupe proud. I leapt to the side of the avenue and barely avoided being trampled by the knights and then the sergeants who came after them.

The road curved sharply south just up ahead. The frightened Greeks, Gregor on their heels, disappeared around the curve faster than the small company of Franks could rush through the gate.

Despite my throbbing head, I'd done the one thing I do easily in such a situation: climbed straight up a wall, using cracks in stone and lumber to get off the ground for safety, but not so high that I'd attract the attention of the archers above. From where I was, I could easily see Gregor.

When he reached the southward curve in the avenue, he stopped abruptly. Just stopped. He was quickly joined by his fellow knights; they waited for orders, but he gave them none. He just stood there, his face invisible behind the helmet but his body stance suggesting he was stupefied to be alive.

Another knight pulled off his helmet to holler, "Tell the others to come ashore!"

This snapped Gregor to attention. Instantly efficient, he shouted orders to the sergeants, set one to guard the curve; others broke down the barred entrances to the tower steps to assault the tower guards. This cut short a new rain of arrows from above.

Gregor looked around at the hubbub, still agog to find himself alive. He gestured sharply out the gate to the harbor, where more soldiers were disembarking from Boniface's boat. Foot soldiers shoved away debris from the opening of the gate. "Hurry!" Gregor shouted several times. He gestured out.

Rapid percussion from the other direction caught everyone's attention. I climbed down from my perch to stay close to Gregor. The guards up by the curve in the road began to point and shout excitedly, and I recognized the word *Mourtzouphlos*. Then I recognized the clattering as horses' feet, shod, upon the paved avenue: Mourtzouphlos, seeing from his hill that somebody at the gate had frightened off a whole battalion, had come riding down to investigate. He rounded the bend with a dozen mounted Varangians.

Gregor stood alone in the street, near the bend, as the men he commanded cleared away rubble from the toppled wall. Actually, he was alone except for me, but I stayed close to a building, a fistful of rock in my right hand, foolishly thinking I could offer him protection.

Gregor pulled his helmet off and hurled it defiantly aside. Mourtzouphlos recognized him, pulled up his horse abruptly, and raised a hand for the Varangians to remain where they were. Having just survived three emperors in rapid succession, all of whom could hardly hold a sword, they looked alarmed at the prospect of one who might try to defend himself. Alone, Mourtzouphlos reined his horse, at a nervous walk, closer to Gregor. He had the sun behind him, and Gregor and I both squinted to look up at him.

"Get down from that horse and fight," Gregor said in a harsh voice. He gestured furiously with his sword. "Get down! Now!"

Mourtzouphlos gave him his signature cheeky-sheepish laugh, although it sounded very fake now. "My guards will be upset with me if I do that."

Gregor ran toward the horse as if to spook it, arms flailing, sword jerking over his head. The horse tossed its head almost contemptuously and didn't move. "Down!" Gregor shouted. "Get down here, you son of a whore, or I'll run your horse through."

Mourtzouphlos didn't move.

"You owe me too much not to give me satisfaction," Gregor said—or something like that; he was so angry now it was hard to understand his words. His face was red and wet with tears. He grabbed the horse's bridle and jabbed the sword up at Mourtzouphlos.

Mourtzouphlos, with a gloved hand, swatted it away. The guard lunged, but Mourtzouphlos held up his hand again. "No," he called out calmly, eyes on Gregor. "German, you're the only one of this foreign invasion not made entirely of manure and hypocrisy. I know you are disturbed by all of it. Put up your sword and go to Jerusalem."

"Get down here and fight me!" Gregor shrieked, so loudly that Mourtzouphlos's horse flattened back its ears.

"I can't do that, my friend. Why? For the simple reason that you'll win, and then where will Stanpoli be? Without an emperor, just so that you may have vengeance? As much as I'd like to indulge your baser instincts, I must put my city first. So"—and here he shrugged—"I decline your invitation." Eyes on Gregor, he shouted over his shoulder in Greek to the mounted Varangians; two of them reined their horses around and trotted off back to the curve. I had understood enough to grasp that they were going for reinforcements. Gregor understood it too.

He hurled some choice expletives at Mourtzouphlos, then spun around in the paved avenue to call out orders to the men, preparing the company for an assault in which the crusaders would now be the ones on the defensive.

But he was interrupted by a new percussive noise, this time from beyond the gate, and this time actual percussion: a report of drums. Then a series of staccato trumpet bleats. With this fanfare—which seemed silly in its specificity, in the midst of such a day of chaos— Boniface of Montferrat and his bodyguards entered through the gate on foot.

Marquis and Emperor looked at each other. Everyone paused, as if something could be decided by parley in this moment. Actual quiet settled over the open space.

"Ten thousand men are about to storm in through this gate," Boniface announced; in the sudden stillness, he didn't need to shout it to be heard. "And there will be ten thousand mariners behind them. That is twice the size of the Varangian Guard, and you and I both know the rest of the Greek army, however massive, is completely useless. Surrender now and your life will be spared, although you don't deserve it."

A pause.

Then Mourtzouphlos shouted, "Ha!" with a scorn that wasn't entirely convincing.

Gregor, enraged, ran at Mourtzouphlos as if he'd pull him off the horse.

Mourtzouphlos drew his sword almost too fast to see, then just held it out casually at his knee, straight at Gregor, so that if Gregor kept running he would impale himself. Mourtzouphlos made no other attempt to defend himself. In fact, he looked smug, and his smugness was aimed right at Boniface: *Watch me destroy your greatest weapon.*

I shrieked as Gregor's chest slammed into contact with the tip of the sword. Gregor jerked backward, as if kicked in the sternum; his arms flailed in front of him as shield and sword both fell out of his grip. He staggered back and collapsed onto the pavement stones, a dreadful rasp squeezing from his lungs.

His chain mail was cloven through—but there was no blood, either on him or on Mourtzouphlos's sword. He rolled onto his side, his arms protectively clasped over his chest. He was breathless but otherwise unhurt.

Mourtzouphlos gawked in shock, examined the end of his sword as if he'd never seen it before, then looked up nervously at Boniface, who was equally astonished.

And then Gregor—who absolutely should have been dead by this point, several times over—reached across, grabbed his own sword, and started to get up.

"Get down here and fight me," he ordered, in a voice three octaves lower than his normal speaking voice, and barely human, struggling to draw breath.

Before Gregor was fully up, Mourtzouphlos wheeled his horse and galloped off around the curve in the avenue, the Varangians closing rank behind him.

Gregor staggered to the side of the road, a hand pressed to his chest. With the other hand he waved off attempts by fellow soldiers to come near him. Boniface, in the gateway, gaped at him. There was a moment of relative silence, and then somebody on the ship called out; Boniface's attention went back out to the harbor; the crash and chaos of a battle returned, although there was no enemy in sight here.

I ran across to Gregor. He was quiet now, his hand over his chest. There was a strange, somber radiance on his face. He was still sobbing, but he didn't seem upset.

"I know what this is," he said softly, when I reached him, his hand on his chest.

I shoved my hand down the front of his tunic and pulled out what I'd put there. I untied the red velvet bag and drew out a curving disk of bone the size of my outspread hand. The delicate gold clasps that held the reliquary to the relic had been shattered—but nothing else was hurt. Impossible, but still true. Gregor reached into the bag and drew out the relic-less reliquary. It too was miraculously undamaged, every pearl in place, the priceless pink ruby whole and secure, the soft gold undented. I took it from him with my other hand, and for a moment we just stared at relic and reliquary, asunder.

"This," I said at length, "is what I would have to call a metaphor." I offered him the skull. "This must be yours." I closed his fingers over the edge of it. "The fruit of your pilgrimage. But I'll take the rest back if you don't mind, it might come in handy." I shoved the bejeweled reliquary back into the bag, then shoved the bag back down my tunic.

Gregor, still sobbing and still radiant, kissed the skull with great reverence and slipped it into his own tunic—actually, under his shirt, so that it was against his skin. He tried to watch it even as it disappeared into the fabric.

WITHIN TWO HOURS, most of the Frankish army had disembarked and marched in through the Petrion Gate. Gregor remained dazed but continued to command the men who'd been entrusted to him.

Except for Galata Tower, I'd never seen him in his element before, and despite my hatred of armed force, I was in awe. He was extraordinarily hardy, stronger than I'd thought a man could be, especially one so in need of food and exercise; he wielded his sword with terrifying gracefulness, disarming foes more often than he struck them; he threw himself into circumstances where he would be killed and yet always emerged the victor; he was good at organizing groups of men to attack other groups of men and send them fleeing every time. I hated that a man I had such regard for possessed those skills, but I was still astonished by them. Running after them like the pitiable camp follower I was, I saw them turn back every company of Greeks, even the Varangian Guard. They fanned out across the hill where Mourtzouphlos had been watching the army's earlier attempts. Word of Gregor's inexplicable survival had spread like Greek fire among the enemy; battalions fled at his approach. I doubt he drew blood all day.

I lost sight of Boniface, who was trying to communicate with Dandolo and the other leaders. As the sun sagged toward the horizon, trumpets rang out from the top of the hill, signaling the army to regroup close to the shore. Gregor called his men together and headed up the hill toward the main pavilion.

The rest of that afternoon, and much of that evening, was full of meetings and conferences, as everyone tried to figure out what had been accomplished and what must happen next. At sunset, a general parliament was called in the flat section of the city burned last summer. Torches were lit, and hundreds of lords and barons sat on the ground, or on their horses, gathered around a hastily erected platform upon which sat Boniface, Dandolo, Baldwin of Flanders, and a few other leaders. On the steps to the dais sat Gregor of Mainz, hero of the army, looking dazed. Not far off was the ubiquitous musician. I'd not been summoned this time, but I was so familiar to both Dandolo's and Boniface's men, that (having doffed my makeshift armor) settling within earshot was no great difficulty.

It seemed that the army had taken the city, but the meaning of this was unclear. They certainly had not taken the *entire* city, or even *most* of it; they'd been called to heel overnight because the place would be too treacherous after dark. There had not been a surrender, or even a defeat; there had merely been an extremely effective *breach*. Mourtzouphlos had fled to Bukoleon, the Great Palace, where Isaac had once resided. He would regroup overnight, Boniface warned, and so without question, the army would be attacked at dawn by an unfathomably huge counterattack of enraged, defensive citizens.

"We have accomplished something extraordinary, something un-precedented," he assured them. "But we have not accomplished all, yet. For safety's sake, tonight, we must bivouac close together with the wall directly at our back, just within the gates wherever possible, with an alert watch. God has smiled on us today, and I pray he will do so tomorrow, but tomorrow we will be in their streets and their neighborhoods. It may be the hardest day of your lives. It is not yet time to celebrate. There is still much to fear."

Having struck this solemn note, he gave loud and lengthy praise to the men who had been particularly useful to the cause, the list climaxing with his beloved son-in-law, Gregor of Mainz, father of his latest grandchild and arguably the most important hero of the campaign, who had magically defied death twice in the time it takes to fletch an arrow. After this was a tedious meal, made up of food purloined from local residences. This was followed by a solemn mass of thanksgiving for the victory thus far, and *this* was followed by further exhortations of the clergy that the crusade was only half-accomplished, and that these pseudo-Christians were even worse than infidels. Then came further exhortation from Boniface, then Baldwin, each trying to get the last word in (no competition there, of course), until I wondered if the army would be allowed to sleep at *all* before sunup. It was almost as if Boniface was trying to exhaust his own men.

Throughout, I could not manage to get close to Gregor, but I watched him. His strange glow never dissipated. He sat quite still, his hand resting on his middle, just above the belt, on the relic, in his own private meditation with John the Baptist, the Precursor of Christ. The hypocrisies of the priests washed over his head. The exhortations of the army leaders, likewise. He was a man apart. I was humble enough to realize that he'd been saved in some way I could never understand.

"Is it true, what I heard today?" a voice asked in my ear. I glanced over and saw the wide-eyed face of Bishop Conrad. "That Gregor tried to impale himself on Mourtzouphlos's sword but was saved by an angel of the Lord?"

I looked at him for a moment—this man of God, this servant of the Holy Father, this spineless collaborator in the army's final push. "Yes," I said. He did not express concern for why Gregor would try to impale himself, and so, peevishly, I added, "It was an angel from the Orthodox Church, and he's coming back to torture you for encouraging all these numskulls to hurt his minions."

Conrad winced, an expression I was tired of seeing on his jowly face. "My son," he said, "we had no choice. If the army did not try again, wholeheartedly, the campaign would have imploded. We'll never get to Jerusalem, but at least this way the men can feel the past eighteen months have led to *something* worthy of their suffering."

I did not know until that moment that I could hold this man in any more contempt. "You defied the pope's wishes and encouraged slaughter under a false pretext, so that a bunch of soldiers would *feel better*?"

"They have toiled and suffered much in the name of the Church," Conrad said steadily, but he didn't meet my eye. "The Church must reassure them they have been right to do so, or—"

"Or they might turn on the Church instead," I concluded.

"Turn *from* the Church, rather," Conrad said. "To reject our teachings would be to imperil their souls and cast them into darkness."

"Would it really?" I pointed across the crowded open square, to the most radiant soldier in the army. "Do you call that darkness?"

67

FINALLY, AFTER MIDNIGHT, I was able to have a moment alone with Gregor. He'd been invited to Boniface's tent but hadn't headed there yet and showed no look of wanting to.

We met somehow in the crowd that was wearily dispersing at the close of Boniface's final campaign speech and just looked at each other.

"Is it a pilgrimage yet?" I asked.

"It will be when I turn the other cheek," Gregor answered. He had that almost postcoital expression on his face that I remembered from last summer, when he'd first seen the head of John the Baptist.

A pause.

"There will be a massacre tomorrow," I said.

"I will not participate in it."

"Can we stop it?"

"No," he said. "But we can minimize the damage. God spared me from myself today, and there must be a reason for it. It is *not* so that I can fight tomorrow—far from it. I think it must be to spare as many others as I can, in turn."

A thoughtful pause.

"I suppose we may as well start at the top," I said.

"That's just what I think too. I hear he has fled to Bukoleon."

Moving out into the city was oddly easy. The troops had been called in hours earlier, but Gregor was well-known to the guard and still in full armor. To walk openly into enemy territory at night without a backup suggested the walker was either mad or divinely protected, and whichever they thought was true for us, we were allowed to go.

The camp flanked a steep hill just above the Venetian Quarter. A straight line to Bukoleon (if there could be such a thing as a straight line in this city) would take us past the Hippodrome, with its statuary—all of which, we now knew, was destined to be downgraded from art to commerce by being melted into money. As the kite flies, we would have skirted the southern end of the Hippodrome, but the layout of the compound swung us north around it, so that we were within a bowshot of Hagia Sophia.

When we saw Hagia Sophia, we both froze. The huge church was lit by torches, within and without; I'm surprised we didn't notice it from farther away. It had a hum around it: thousands of liveried servants milling about outside suggested that inside, some great congress was forming. We both changed stride for that direction, assuming Mourtzouphlos must, for some horrific reason, be calling a war council in the world's most lavish church.

I stopped first. "We can't just walk in and ask to chat with the emperor."

"We couldn't have done that at Bukoleon either. What is your plan?"

I shot him an impatient look. "Having a coherent plan is *not* my modus operandi. Haven't you learned that yet? Plans calcify far too quickly to keep up with reality."

"All right then," Gregor said, sounding like a sarcastic younger brother, which used to be my role. "What shall we do when we get there?"

I twinged, remembering a similar argument with Jamila. It was about this time last night I'd helped her escape me. Her counsel would have been helpful now, but I'd probably have ignored it were she actually here. "Let's get there first and see what the options are."

"We'll be shot before we get close enough for that."

He had a point. At the palace, at least, there'd be a wall, and guards, and *order*. Here, a space open to the public, with lots of nervous, armed servants scuttling about, anything could happen. I know how to subvert order. Subverting chaos is much harder, and I'm not sure what I'd've done about it, but fortune smiled on us and I did not have to make the choice, because Ionnis appeared.

Out of the darkness, an unsmiling cherub. He did not greet us; he just appeared and stood there as if awaiting commands. I couldn't tell from what direction he'd come.

"Were you tailing us?" I demanded, spooked, and he gave me the classic Greek shrug, which in this case I took to mean yes.

"I have a message from Mourtzouphlos," he said. "He welcomes you to dinner if you find yourselves in Anatolia."

Gregor blinked. So did I. "What?" I finally said.

"He's gone," Ionnis said, again with the shrug. He pointed vaguely in the direction of Asia. "There. Or maybe there." Another jab in the air, this one to the west. "He was so frightened by what happened in the street, German. He is not superstitious, but he understands it was the relic and he took it as an omen of his fall. He took some of the royal women with him, and money. This is not news," he added, seeing our astonishment. "Your Boniface knows it by now, I think. Understand me? He went out earlier and tried to raise an army, but nobody was interested, so he lost heart and fled."

"Nobody was *interested*? He can't raise an army of city dwellers when their own city is under attack?" Gregor asked incredulously.

Ionnis gave him a curious look. "The city was not under attack, *he* was. Why should regular citizens put themselves at risk for him? The worst that would happen is he'd lose, we'd get another emperor. We are seasoned at that. Understand me? He had no support, and so he fled."

Gregor and I exchanged looks of alarm. "Lad, the city *is* under attack," I said. "It needs to defend itself."

"The leaders wondered about that, so they chose a new emperor." Ionnis gestured toward the church. "They went in there to crown Constantine Laskaris."

It suddenly felt as if we had wandered into somebody else's war. "Who in the name of God is Constantine Laskaris?" demanded Gregor.

"He is Isaac's niece's husband's brother," Ionnis said, bored. "Once he was crowned, the Varangians would do his bidding, and he could raise an army like Mourtzouphlos tried."

"Might he be more successful?" Gregor asked, still looking dumbfounded.

Ionnis shrugged. "Perhaps he might have been, but he won't be now."

"Lad, you're talking in riddles. Please explain yourself," I said.

"Just before he was to have taken the crown, Laskaris fled from Hagia Sophia straight to Asia. So we are, for the second time in one evening, without an emperor." He seemed completely undisturbed by this.

"So you're saying that no army will be raised at all," Gregor clarified.

Ionnis nodded peaceably, glad we finally understood him.

"In other words," I tried, "given that the Varangian Guard obeys only an emperor, and there is no emperor, the city now has absolutely no organized protection."

Ionnis shrugged, a gesture of relieved finality. "The Varangian Guard are back in their barracks and will remain there until the emperor summons them tomorrow for his coronation. The fighting is over. This is the best thing that could happen for the city."

A very confused pause. "What emperor?" Gregor finally asked. "I thought you said Laskaris had fled."

"Not *Laskaris*, milord," said Ionnis, as if this were a tasteless joke. "He was never crowned. He will never come to anything."

Another confused pause.

"Do you mean Mourtzouphlos?" Gregor tried, warily, as if it were a trick.

"He is fled too," Ionnis said impatiently.

"Then which emperor, lad?" Gregor demanded. I did not ask this question because I had already figured out the answer and was trying to regain my balance.

Ionnis gave Gregor an incredulous look. "The *victor*," he said, as if to a slow child. "Bo-ni-fa-ce."

"You can't crown him as *your* emperor, he's *our* leader," Gregor said, now treating Ionnis as if Ionnis were the slow one. "We're still at *war*."

"No we're *not*," Ionnis corrected him. If circumstances hadn't been so horrifying, it would have been almost amusing to see them trying to outcondescend each other. "Understand me: Mourtzouphlos was at war with Boniface. Boniface won. That's it, it's over. Now Boniface is the emperor. So we'll crown him, and that is it. The city doesn't like that it's a Latin, but at least the matter's over."

Gregor finally understood too, and spoke while I was trying to find words. "Lad, that is *not* what this war is about. There is an enormous army camped within your walls that believes it is here to conquer you. *You*. The *city*. No matter who is emperor."

"Why?" Ionnis sounded incredulous; this concept truly had not occurred to him.

"Because you're heretics and infidels," I said, "who happen to be rich."

Something unpleasant animated Ionnis's face, from some well deep within: he'd heard stories of what the crusaders did a hundred years ago to the infidels in Jerusalem. "How . . . how can we be *infidels*? We're *Christians*."

"But not Roman Catholics," I said.

"But . . . you . . . the army has already come here to replace the ruler once, and has been here for so long, nine months, and you have never called us infidels. The argument was with the *ruler*! You came to *help* us! Why would you come to the aid of infidels? You were pilgrims to our city! You worshiped in our churches and revered our relics!"

"How many people think as you think, Ionnis?" I demanded. "Do your elders understand that the city will be pillaged tomorrow, no matter who is emperor, if there is no resistance?"

"Even if there is," Gregor said in a soft, miserable voice. "I don't think *creating* resistance is the best strategy."

Ionnis was openly frightened now. "*Everyone* thinks as I do," he said, barely breathing. "The entire city. There are thousands in Hagia Sophia right now, decorating it for a coronation. People are putting on their best clothes, polishing their jewelry, to welcome the new *basileus*. The woman I am to marry is staying awake all night to sew a new gown. She thought it was for greeting Laskaris, but now it will be for Boniface."

"Not Boniface," Gregor said. "If the army wins tomorrow, it will take possession of the city, but there will be an election later to decide who the emperor will be. Tomorrow there is no emperor."

"Who could it possibly ever be but Boniface?" Ionnis said, desperate for his version of reality to prevail. "So he'll be crowned a little earlier than expected. Let him be crowned tomorrow, and everything will be just as we expect it."

"Ionnis!" I grabbed his shoulders and shook him. "The city will not be fine. No matter who the emperor is, the city is going to be *sacked* first. You must get out of here tonight. Take your family, tell your friends. Tell *everyone*. Tell people they must leave—tonight. *Right now*. Whether or not there is an army to fight the pilgrims tomorrow, the pilgrims will come in here and destroy everything."

"But for as long as Boniface has been here, the fight has been about who is the *leader*. Now *he* is the leader. Why is that suddenly not enough?" Ionnis demanded.

"I wish I could explain this," I said. "But I can't. It's a Catholic thing. Just please trust me. Make people understand they need to leave the city."

"They'll think I'm mad—"

"Try anyway," I said. "Gregor and I don't speak Greek, and they wouldn't trust us anyhow."

"But we'll work on the problem from the other side," Gregor said. He spoke in a firm, bright tone I hadn't heard him use in months, and it got my full attention. "While you do that, we'll stop Boniface from taking the crown."

"That won't prevent the sack," I objected. "And besides we won't have to stop him, he doesn't even know he's up for it. Let's not make unnecessary work for ourselves. He spent all evening warning the army that the Greeks will attack at dawn—why for a moment would he suspect they are about to offer him a *crown*?"

"Maybe because his two elder brothers came very close to being crowned, at different times over the last few decades?" Ionnis said, his voice still shrill.

"What?" I gasped.

"Didn't you know that?" Gregor asked me with mild surprise.

"He is very familiar with our ways. I even heard Mourtzouphlos say so," said Ionnis. "Surely he is spending the night preparing for the dawn reception that will take him to Hagia Sophia to be crowned. If he said to expect an attack, he is either mistaken or lying. Are you *sure* that's what he said?"

I glared at Gregor, incredulous. "He has a family legacy of reaching for *this throne* and you never *mentioned* it to me?"

"It was never relevant. We were never trying to crown *him*, just Alexios."

I shook my head to clear it. "We don't have enough time to deal with all of this," I said. "Ionnis, do you understand what you need to do?" The young man nodded a real nod, not a shrug. "Then go and do it."

He grabbed my hand. His was trembling. "You will be remembered in my prayers." He offered the same tentative benediction to Gregor, then ran off.

A pause. Then: "The question is," said Gregor, "if the crown is offered to him, will Boniface be fool enough to take it?"

"That's not a question. Of *course* he will." I spat.

"But he signed the treaty agreeing the emperor must be chosen by election," Gregor said. "If he breaks that, total chaos follows. The army will suddenly be at war *with its own leader*. Right here in the streets of the city. Boniface knows that." He was trying to convince himself. "It's better for him to win the election—then he'd be honorably proclaimed emperor and have the army under his sway."

"So you think he'll wait for the election?" I asked.

"Yes?" Gregor said—just like that, so hesitant it was a question.

"Knowing perfectly well that he will *lose* the election?"

Gregor winced. "It's not a given—"

"Gregor! Jamila saw it clearly—half of the electors are Venetian! They'll vote against him on principle, because he's allied with Genoa. All it takes is *one bishop* to vote for Flanders over Montferrat—think about that! Baldwin of Flanders, the only pure-hearted pilgrim on this crusade other than you. It would take some perverse, sinister miracle for Boniface to be elected emperor. He *knows* that. So if he knows they're going to offer him the crown tomorrow morning, don't you think he'll *take* it?"

"But the chaos—"

"The Varangian Guard will take care of the chaos. It's their city, and they're almost the size of your army—and he's kept the army *awake* half the night. Deliberately. Tomorrow morning they'll be no match for the Varangians. Tomorrow will be dreadful anyhow; this will make it worse. Ambition is blinding, Gregor. If Boniface knows that crown is being prepared for him, he'll convince himself he can take it and defend it."

"Then we must make sure it's never offered to him."

I smacked him on the arm. "Good lad! Now you're thinking. Let's go."

"To Hagia Sophia?" Gregor protested. "That's a mob, and we don't speak Greek! What can we accomplish there?"

"Nothing. Let's go."

Gregor blinked a few times. "Go *where?*"

"To find Constantine Philoxenites, the eunuch who controls the Varangian Guard by controlling their purses."

Gregor considered this a moment, then said grimly, "I think I know where he is."

"He must be in Bukoleon Palace tonight, that's where the Guard is barracked—"

"No." Gregor cut me off grimly, shaking his head. "If we are right about any of this, then Constantine Philoxenites is in Boniface's tent. *Right now.*"

I drew in a breath of pained admiration. Gregor reached out for my arm, already pivoting back toward camp.

"Wait a minute," I said. "For once, let me think through a project." It was pity Jamila was busy fleeing to some backwater village to be somebody else's docile helpmeet for the rest of her life . . . "You and I can't order anyone else to do or not do anything. We don't have that power ourselves."

"So we alert Dandolo and let him take care of it," Gregor said.

"I agree. But . . ." Jamila would already know how to finish that sentence. "To level an accusation against Boniface, we must have evidence," I warned. "Or at least, we must be able to bear witness, and not simply tell Dandolo that we're suspicious. Even if Dandolo shares our suspicion, I doubt he can do much in response to a mere suspicion. Boniface is still the leader of the army."

"So we'll spy on Boniface's conversation with the eunuch—"

"Better yet. Boniface trusts you again, thinks you're back in the fold, you're Miracle Man. Let him try to lure you into helping him— and I wager all you need to do is show up at his pavilion and he'll start right in on you—and *then* we'll go to Dandolo."

"But once Boniface tells me his plans—even if he trusts me—he'll keep me on a short leash," Gregor said. "I won't have the freedom to *get* to Dandolo. And *your* getting to Dandolo accomplishes nothing—you're perceived as an imbecile by all of them."

"You're right," I said. "So I guess we'd better *use* that."

I SENT GREGOR IN ahead and loitered on the outskirts of Boniface's compound. I had a heavy feeling in my gut that I had planned this badly, but I could not determine how.

Before long, I saw what I was waiting for, the final confirmation that we were not inventing any of this: a tall, hairless, reedlike man flanked by two enormous, fair-haired soldiers. All of them wore long, Frankish-style cloaks concealing their Greek clothing and armor; the two Varangians were groomed like the pilgrims, hair short and beards trimmed. So the trio did not stand out as Greek, and they moved unnoticed away from Boniface's tent, where Philoxenites the eunuch had just offered up the Varangian Guard—and therefore, his city's future—to the Marquis of Montferrat. I allowed a few more moments, and then I headed to the tent myself.

It was almost routine by now, my having access to Boniface. Always Claudio, the leader of his personal bodyguard (who never seemed to leave his post even to defecate), would check me for weapons, but then I'd simply enter; Claudio assumed somebody else had summoned me to play, and even when Boniface himself was not expecting me, he assumed somebody else had summoned me and would assign me to the corner and tell me what he felt like hearing. Tonight was no different, except he made no request, for he was in the middle of explaining to his disarmed son-in-law what a good and thoughtful usurper he would make.

"I'd never have planned it this way myself, but it's now out of my hands. Thousands of innocent people and hundreds of soldiers will die if the events of tomorrow are not managed properly," he was saying as I settled in the corner. "You and I must work in concert to prevent meaningless deaths. Tomorrow will be very confusing."

Gregor looked dismayed. "Please explain again, milord."

Boniface nodded solemnly—the kind of solemnity that barely masks unbridled glee. "The people of this city believe that I should be their new emperor."

"Does their belief matter, when they are heretics?"

Boniface deflated somewhat; perhaps he'd been hoping Gregor might comment on their excellent taste in emperors, or at least admit that he thought Boniface was deserving of it. "We are speaking not of religious matters but of civic ones, my son," he said. "It is their city, and they would offer it to me."

"What of the election?"

"I'll win the election." He said this with such offhand confidence, I was thrown.

"You will?" Gregor asked, equally amazed by the declaration.

"Gregor, don't look so astonished! Baldwin is a boy. Virtuous, almost to a fault, and very brave, and good in battle, but far too young and far too pious for any Venetian to trust him. The Venetians will vote as a block, for me. So I need but one more voice, and obviously Conrad will provide that. It is as good as given that I will win the election. Do you follow me so far?"

Gregor dutifully nodded.

"Would you therefore agree with me that I am, essentially, the new emperor?"

Gregor nodded again, looking chagrined. If Boniface were seeking congratulations, he did not get them.

"And what is the emperor's greatest strength?"

Gregor looked lost, then said tentatively, "The Guard? The Varangian Guard?"

"That's right. They are a fierce and extremely destructive force. I would not call them bright. But they are as loyal to the emperor as dogs."

"So they will become your men."

"Yes. But only if I am crowned at dawn in Hagia Sophia—and that is why I need your help with this."

I couldn't wait to hear his reasoning. Gregor merely looked morose.

"Why?" he asked obediently, sounding bored.

"I know the ways of this city. Tomorrow morning, a procession will come to this very tent from the Greeks, proclaiming me their emperor and wanting to escort me to Hagia Sophia to crown me. What do you think is the correct response to that?"

I made a contribution here: "Perhaps to say Thank you, but let's wait until the election, since I'll win it anyhow?"

Boniface gave me a sour look. "You are not invited to participate in this discussion."

"I admit, milord," Gregor said, doleful, "I would agree with your musician there."

Now Boniface nodded. "That's what I thought at first too. And of course I would do that if I thought it wisest. But do you know what will happen if I do that? If there is no emperor to crown, the Guard will be directionless, and may even be dispersed. Those men, without a leader, in this city, are extremely dangerous, especially to native civilians. They will do more damage than the invading army in its victory looting. They will rape and kill without compunction—and worse than that, because they know where all the treasure is, they will take it all and leave the city, and we will find ourselves stewarding a bankrupt empire."

Gregor looked tormented. "What are you asking of me, milord?"

"I'm asking not as your lord but as your father."

"Yes . . . Father. Please tell me what you would of me."

"It is a given that I will be elected emperor. It is also a given that the best way to keep the Varangian Guard under control is to point them immediately at a man and say, 'He is the emperor.' Tomorrow morning, that man must be me. Then they will listen to me and help to control and limit the pillaging, rather than making it worse by contributing to it. This is not about ambition, it is about the simple facts of what must be done to help control the damage to the city. Do you follow me so far?"

Gregor nodded. Boniface sounded so rational, and Gregor looked so miserable, I began to worry that the knight was actually believing the marquis's seductive lies.

"Good. So. The election is not rigged, but we all know it is essentially for show, and for the good of the city and the army both, I must be crowned tomorrow morning in Hagia Sophia. Many will understand this, but many won't. We must reassure people that this is not a stolen crown. Things will happen too fast, there will be no opportunity to explain it all to everyone. Men will respond with emotion, on instinct. If they believe that I am trying to do something wrong, they will misbelieve, and that will lead to catastrophe—the Varangian Guard will attack them. If they sense and believe—even if they do not understand why—that I am doing something benign and necessary, they will allow the coronation and all will be well. So some impressions must be made now, immediately, before dawn. I, because I am the interested party, cannot try to sound disinterested about my need to take the throne. You, however, can. You have done a thorough job of making it absolutely clear that you are not my partisan, that you will never support me just for the sake of supporting me. You will always do what you consider right as a soldier. While this has caused problems between us in the past, I see now it has been God's way of preparing you for your greatest contribution to this entire campaign: you must help me to convince the others that my taking the throne tomorrow is acceptable. Will you do that? I think we must begin with Baldwin of Flanders."

"Why not Dandolo?" I said.

Boniface glanced over his shoulder and gave me a nasty, patronizing smile. "Are you trying to follow along?"

I shrugged. "I thought Dandolo was important."

"He is," Boniface said offhandedly. "But he has retired to his galley for the night; he probably won't be aware of any of this until after it's happened anyhow. The ones I am concerned about are the troops on the ground, especially the man who would be most personally affronted by my accepting the offer, and that's young Baldwin. Will you help us, Gregor? Will you help to keep the peace? Gregor, are you all right?"

Gregor looked as if all the life force had been pressed out of him.

"I swear on my own life," he said in a hollow voice. He didn't actually specify what he was swearing to do, but this detail was lost on Boniface.

There followed a few moments of Boniface thanking him, telling him which guards would go with Gregor on his rounds, giving him instruction on how best to approach Baldwin. Neither Gregor nor I heard a word of Boniface's instructions, since we both knew they would never be carried out. I pretended to be bored by all of it; Gregor radiated a growing depression as he nodded and looked increasingly distracted. Several times, Boniface stopped and asked him if he were unwell; Gregor insisted he was fine but was less convincing every time he said it.

Now he was bowing to take his leave, his eyes glancing occasionally toward the door, where Claudio remained with his sword and dagger. Gregor's eyes fastened onto his sword with a terrible, desolate longing.

I dropped the harp onto the ground and clambered up.

"Milord," I said in a desperate voice, "don't let him go."

Gregor froze.

Boniface blinked at me. "What?"

"It's all a lie, milord; he'll undo you if he goes out there," I said. "Please forgive me for not speaking sooner, I was trying to see what he was up to. He's in the pay of Dandolo, milord; Dandolo's been suspecting you of late, and he told Gregor there was a fat estate in it for Gregor if he kept an eye on you and reported to him. If you let him leave now, he'll go straight to Dandolo and set him wise about your plan."

Gregor looked so horrified by this announcement that Boniface was immediately convinced it was the truth.

"Gregor?" he said, appalled.

"My lord, it is a lie," Gregor said, weakly and too late to be convincing.

"It's not," I insisted. "As God is my witness, this man will not do what he's promised to when he walks out of here. Shall we go to Dandolo and ask him directly if I got it right?" I added helpfully.

"Of course not, you imbecile," Boniface snapped, then turned his anger back to Gregor. "Gregor, disprove this at once."

"I cannot," Gregor stammered, red-faced. "Except to give you my word."

"That won't suffice," Boniface said. "As Dandolo seems to have the prior claim."

"He does not, milord; this knave is the liar."

"I am not," I hissed. "Come on, let's go ask Dandolo." I took a step for the door.

"Stop, idiot," Boniface said sharply, and I stopped. I was close enough to Gregor for him to grab me round the neck.

"Traitor!" I sneered.

He lunged; I ducked. Claudio, outside, dropped Gregor's sword and dagger and leapt into the room to land on top of Gregor. Gregor didn't even struggle.

Boniface looked back and forth between us, suspiciously. "Claudio, keep Gregor isolated for a moment. Don't let anybody near, even the other guards. I want to interrogate this fellow in private."

And then it was just the two of us. And Gregor's weapons lying in the doorway.

"Sit," Boniface said, meaning on the ground, exactly where I was. I sat. "Tell me everything you know."

I tried to look terrified and flummoxed by this order. "Everything?

I know you're the leader of the army," I began tentatively, in my most stupid voice. "I know Christ is the savior. I know Venice is an island. I know—"

"Stop it!" Boniface snapped impatiently. "Tell me what you know about Gregor's supposed betrayal. And why you waited so long to say anything about it."

"Oh," I said. I thought about this a long time. "Which should I answer first?"

"The first question first. Quickly."

"Right," I said. "Well. Gregor knew already that the city would want to make you emperor, and he had already decided that he would have to stop you. He wanted to assassinate you, but I talked him out of it."

"How did he come to know of it? And why were you having such a discussion with him in the first place?"

"I don't want to tell you those things, milord," I said. "They'll ruin the surprise."

"What surprise?"

"The surprise about Dandolo," I said.

"What surprise about Dandolo, you stupid wretch?" Boniface snapped. "Answer immediately or I will break your neck."

"The surprise about Dandolo," I said, "is that even with Gregor indisposed, Dandolo's about to learn that you've negotiated with the Varangian Guard."

Boniface went a little pale. "How is he going to learn that?" he demanded.

"I'm going to tell him myself," I said, grinning, and stood up. "Right now."

68

I RAN OUT of the tent, grabbing Gregor's dagger as I went. Not that it would do much good, but grabbing a weapon seemed a sensible thing for a sudden fugitive to do.

By the time Boniface had shouted "Guards!" I was outside. But I did not want to disappear entirely. Even as I ran, I thought of Jamila, for it occurred to me I'd overlooked two things in planning this scheme, both of which she would have noticed. The first was my assumption that Boniface would pursue me himself—this was unlikely, so I was hugely relieved to see I was correct. He had his own sword with him and, despite my relative youth and agility, never had me out of his sight.

"Who are you?" he shouted as we stumbled down an alley of tents, where soldiers were too antsy now to fall asleep, having been alerted to the fear of attack overnight.

"Just a friend," I said over my shoulder.

"Whose man are you?" he tried next.

He didn't actually want to kill me—he wanted to own me. In the midst of his shock, some part of him had assessed that somebody had a damn clever little spy, and he wanted that spy for himself. And then, the question that I needed him to ask:

"Why did you want me to imprison Gregor?"

I didn't answer yet. We were at the edge of the Lombard compound now; and now, it changed to German; here, the small compound of Count Berthold of Katzenellenbogen. This would be a good place to do it.

I didn't know any of these knights personally, but they all recognized me from when I'd played around the campfires; they also
recognized Boniface. And, most important, they recognized that I
was fleeing from him. Germans are good soldiers. Every single one
of them tried to grab at me; I let three of them tackle me and pin me
down on some dusty straw near a building as I wriggled like a worm
cut into pieces. Boniface was hovering over me a moment later.

But of course, he could not speak freely, given that we now had
an audience.

"Who is this knave?" he demanded.

An awkward pause. Then somebody offered, "He follows Gregor
of Mainz, milord."

The marquis was astonished by this revelation—a detail I found
surprisingly satisfying. I had, in fact, fooled this man for well over a
year now.

"How long has he done so?" Boniface stammered. "He's not even
German."

Another pause, then somebody offered, "Since Venice, milord.
He was some vagrant whom Bishop Conrad entrusted to Gregor's
care."

Boniface blinked and finally looked at me directly. "The madman
who pretended to try to kill me?" he demanded.

"At your service," I grunted. I couldn't get enough air in my lungs
with the blond thug sitting on my chest to say more than that.

The Count of Katzenellenbogen had emerged importantly from
his tent, seen he was severely outranked, and retreated back inside.

Boniface considered me with curious satisfaction. "So you are a
friend of Gregor's," he said softly. "Yet you wanted him in chains.
Why?" He signaled the soldier to raise his rump so I could draw air.

"I just wanted him unarmed," I grunted urgently. "Can't you see
he's wrong in the head? He tried to get himself killed today, and
surely you could see his great despondency when you told him of your
schemes tonight. You've robbed him of the will to live." I imagined

Jamila telling me not to lay it on too thick. I stopped abruptly, as if choked up.

"There's been a mistake," Boniface said calmly to the glowering Germans, in German. Then he pointed to one knight at random and repeated it in Italian—which meant he wanted me to understand what he was saying. "Here is my glove," he said, removing it and tossing it with casual elegance to the man. "Take it to my tent, and show it to Claudio. Give him the order that he is to release Gregor of Mainz, with my apologies—and he is especially to give Gregor back his sword. He is not to allow Gregor near the harbor, but otherwise he is not to interfere in anything Gregor attempts. Anything." He smiled at me with bitter triumph and signaled the rump to descend onto my lungs again.

I struggled wildly under the weight. "Whoreson," I tried to growl, with hardly enough air. "Villain! What are you up to? Would you kill your own son?"

"I am not responsible for Gregor's actions," the marquis said loftily. "I shall be grieved to lose him to his own crushing sorrow, but happily his son remains among us, and I will raise him in my image, and he will be far less of a sanctimonious headache." I writhed and tried feebly to curse again, under five hundred pounds of German youths. Boniface, feeling in control of the situation now, gestured up and down with one lazy finger to the man whose buttocks crushed my rib cage. "Give him another chance to breathe, and then descend again." The lazy finger moved to me. "Don't be a fool about it," he suggested. "You'll gain nothing with this crowd by shouting out lies, especially since most of them speak only German."

He drew his sword. This move, as was true of all he did, had an elegance and suavity to it that was infuriating: I did not care to believe somebody so loathsome could be so debonair. Now the sword was out, and at my throat. He gestured with his head for the trio to get off my chest and various limbs. "*Danke*," he said and then something about next day, and his tent, and a reward.

"I assume you'd like to speak to me in private," I said loudly from my supine position, glancing about. "You can tell these men to scatter, but they will all keep an eye and ear peeled—and some of them do understand us."

"We can speak softly," Boniface said. "Or I might just kill you now. But I want to know what motivates you."

I started laughing. "I cannot be useful to you, milord."

"Were you responsible for Gregor's actions?"

"Now *that* is a complex question," I said, rolling my eyes and trying to sound cocky, which is hard to do while lying supine with a sword at one's throat.

"Give it a simple answer," suggested Boniface.

"I'm not good at simple. Gregor is the captain of his own soul, but sometimes I have played his navigator."

"In what directions did you navigate him?"

"Away from the shoals of mindless piety and perhaps toward craftiness."

Boniface laughed ruefully. "He was never seaworthy for those waters, was he?" He was already thinking of Gregor in the past tense; I was touched by his attachment.

"I did what I could," I said. "Today, it hasn't helped *at all.*"

"If I take you into custody until after my coronation," he said, "if I prevent you from preventing me but keep you alive—might *we* have waters to navigate together?"

"I'm flattered by your interest, milord, really I am," I said. "But I'd have to say that no, we don't. Unless you take Gregor into custody as well, so he can't hurt himself."

"Give me the dagger," said Boniface. I didn't move. He pressed the sword a little harder to my throat. "*The dagger,*" he repeated. "*Now.*"

"Is that so you can murder an unarmed man, instead of an armed man?" I asked. "You're going to disengage my head from my neck anyhow, I don't see how either of us gains much by my giving you the dagger."

"My reasons are immaterial," Boniface said.

"Then so are my reactions," I said. "*Imagine* that I am giving you the dagger. The actual giving, and the actual dagger, are immaterial. Would you like something else from the immaterial realm? Some barley perhaps?"

"You are a madman," Boniface decided.

"Yes, it's true, the Madman of Genoa, that's me. Constantine Philoxenites knows me well and will sing my praises if you ask him. I gave your poor little Alexios his throne, you know—or helped him to it, anyhow."

The sword released a little from my throat. "What?"

"Did you hear about me?" I asked in a hopeful voice.

Marquis Boniface frowned in the torchlight. "Isaac said something about a madman of Genoa, but I assumed he was ranting."

"You may ask his pretty widow about me. I was also the mastermind of the relics scheme, and the one who brought Jamila to Gregor." He stared at me in bald astonishment. "And, oh yes, you saw my handiwork in Zara too—the tiff with Simon of Montfort, and the rumor that you'd reward the soldiers with gold."

"I confess I am amazed at what I'm hearing," Boniface said. "I suspect you are worth having in one's thrall."

"I'm a little large for the average thrall, actually," I said, rolling my eyes again. "For most people it is too much to have me in their *kingdom*."

"Get up," Boniface said, decisively. The sword did not move.

"Am I to rise *into* the sword?" I asked. "Impale myself from below? A sort of enforced suicide, to make up for our first encounter?"

"Get up. I am not interested in killing you. "

I lifted my head and neck, and the sword retracted to my movements, although Boniface did not move away from me. I rose on my elbows, sat upright, tucked my legs beneath me, rose to my knees. The sword stayed at my throat. I glanced around.

"Do not even contemplate escape," Boniface advised.

I obliged him now, as I had already contemplated it during my silly prattling, when I'd had a better view of our surroundings (looking up) than he had (looking down). Directly behind where I now knelt was a torch that was secured to an actual building—a wooden structure, possibly somebody's house, although that person and family must have long since fled. Viewing it from my supine position by rolling my eyes, I had already worked out (although my view was upside down) exactly how to climb it.

I got to my feet by jumping not only up but back and slightly to the side, hands out; I grabbed the torch and threw it in Boniface's face; he leapt back in alarm. He shouted aloud as the torch dropped into the straw I had just been lying on; both of these details drew attention, and I had a moment to clamber up the wall of the house, something no muscle-bound knight would be able to do nearly as fast as I could.

On the roof, I tried to get my bearings. With my backside to Boniface, the harbor was to my left—quite close, but on the far side of the precariously amended city wall. The doge's galley would be moored near the Venetian Quarter, which happily was the northernmost of the Latin neighborhoods; I was near the edge of it.

Shouting behind me caught my attention, and I turned around to look down at Boniface. He was screaming at some squires to follow me up, although it meant passing close to the growing flames. Starting a fire had not been part of my plan, so I had to handle this carefully now. I walked along the edge of the roof, glancing down at Boniface and remaining visible, moving fast enough that the boys would not quite reach me before the far end. Boniface stalked from below, shouting and gesturing, as if he wanted me to leap into his arms.

I came to the far end of the building. Before me, the harbor wall; behind, the squires; below, Boniface; and somewhere behind him, the spreading fire. Boniface, with a soldier beside him brandishing a torch, still clearly wanted to negotiate; he wanted to make *use* of me somehow, wanted to know of what else I was capable.

"Look!" I shouted down to him and pulled out the red velvet bag, and then the reliquary of the Baptist. He could not see it clearly from the street, but the torch threw enough light that he could tell it was something gold and jewel-encrusted. I explained to him, helpfully, what it was, and how I'd gotten it. "This is the source of Gregor's miraculous survival earlier today!" I concluded grandly. "The loss of it is what sent Mourtzouphlos fleeing! Would you like it?"

I'd spoken only to tease, but he took me seriously. "Come down here and we'll discuss it," he said and signaled the boys to stand away, although they had reached me now.

I glanced around the rooftop. The long building I'd just traversed defined one side of a rectangular courtyard; this dead-ended against the high harbor wall; the two remaining sides were other buildings— in other words, the courtyard was the interior of a long city block. I looked down at Boniface. "Your boys may shadow me to see I don't run off. I'll meet you in the next street over."

"Why?" Boniface demanded impatiently.

"Because I *say* so," I responded cheerfully and waved the reliquary. "I'm the one with all the power here, remember? I'll meet you over there."

And then I took my time about it. I shuffled, hopped, danced, turned in circles, acted like I'd no care in the world. This was hard, as the fire was now the size of a horse, and I had to walk right back past it as it climbed up the side of the building; Boniface detoured to skirt the fire on his way around the block below. Soldiers had already formed a brigade to douse it, but flames had leapt onto the roof, and a new generation of them was licking away at debris scattered on the tiles.

It took as long as it would take to jog a mile for me to simply circumambulate the three contiguous rooftops to the opposite corner. Boniface, shadowing my progress from below in the streets, was almost apoplectic. I made most of the trip perilously close to the eaves, and the boys were too wobbly to get near. Boniface yelled demands and questions the entire time; I kept forgetting to respond to him.

Finally, we were both on the far side, I on the roof and he in the street. I waved gaily down to him, as if just noticing a friend in a crowd. "Shall I come down, or would you like to come up?" I gestured. "Lovely view of the fire from here, just marvelous silhouettes of soldiers in the dark."

"Throw me down the relic," he said.

"What, so that your little friends can then take out their daggers and stab me to death? I don't think so."

"Throw down the relic and then come down yourself."

"What's in this arrangement for me?" I asked.

"Your life will be spared."

"I seem to be sparing my own life just fine without your help, thanks," I pointed out cheerfully.

"Have you noticed that you're *cornered?*" Boniface shouted with frustration.

I was up against the harbor wall on this, the far side of the courtyard; the fire was earnestly consuming the far building and roof I'd just traveled. By its light, I could see the texture of the stone wall, against which I was now, in fact, cornered.

This was the second moment of the evening Jamila might have warned me of, my personal blind spot in all my mischief: having done my deed, what was I to do next? For my plan ended here, having distracted Boniface and taken him as far from the harbor gate as I could manage. And so here I was, cornered by flames, with an empty reliquary and an enraged, homicidal marquis at my feet.

But no, it would be easy to climb up the rock wall—and atop it loomed Mourtzouphlos's wooden towers. Within moments, I could be the highest person in the city, with a thick layer of stone between myself and the fire.

Boniface saw what I intended.

He barked orders in German to guards he had collected as he'd stalked me. Four of them divided into pairs; they laced their hands together like slings so that other guards could climb onto their shoulders and then scramble up onto the roof near the squires. No, not other guards—one other guard, and Boniface himself. "I'm flattered," I called down, watching him, "if that's how badly you want me!"

I turned to climb the stone face of the harbor wall. The stone was cold but almost chalk-dry. I pressed my fingertips into two small cavities, pulled my weight up against the wall, lifted one foot, toes groping in the darkness for a bulge or crevice lip to light upon. I lifted my other foot to seek more purchase, but a noise alerted me that Boniface had scrambled onto the roof. My weight still pitched and pressed against the rock, I turned my head as far as I dared to look behind me.

Boniface wasted no time going after me. He ran instead toward a circular stone protrusion bulging out of the wall. I hadn't registered its presence, but of course, it was a guard tower—and within would be a stairwell. I can climb a wall fast, but not as fast as an unencumbered man can mount steps. When I saw that he was heading for the tower, I took a breath, jumped back down onto the roof, and sprinted to the open tower door myself, beating Boniface there by perhaps two heartbeats. Now it really was just a matter of who could run up stairs the faster.

I raced in blackness, Boniface an arm's length behind; up and up and up and up and now it was no longer stone, it was wood, we were in the amendment, it was rickety, it was sticky with oh God that must have been blood, there were discarded weapons to trip over, and oh no that was someone's arm, I tripped but righted myself, heard him do the same, up further, another round, and another, and now the whole thing swaying—how did they have armored knights in here without the damned thing falling over—and now suddenly—

—suddenly out under the stars, and a fat moon slung low in the western sky behind me. We were higher off the ground than I'd ever been in my life, as high as the blessing Christ in the dome of Hagia Sophia. The wind slapped my face. I remembered, more than saw or sensed, the shape of these new parapets: built to jut out over the water to dump rocks onto the tall ships below. I grabbed for a railing,

found it, and followed it a dozen long paces out over the shallows.
Then it stopped and I was cornered.

Boniface had fallen behind—he was twenty years my senior and
bore more weight than I did. But there was nowhere for me to go,
and he was on me in a moment.

"Surrender the relic," he said, between gasps of breath. "And surrender yourself."

"Look," I said, also breathing hard, and pointed down into the
harbor.

One ship below was brightly lit, every lantern glowing from bow
to stern, important-looking men crowding onto the deck. The ship
was enormous, and its sides bristled with the paddles of dozens of
vermilion oars peeking out of their locks.

It was the doge's galley. Soldiers covered the upper deck, except
for one canopied space in the center. We were too near to it, too high
up, to see beneath that canopy. We could see only the boots of the
man on the nearer side.

"Those are Gregor's boots," I explained in a sympathetic voice.
"He has given your man Claudio a bloody nose now, I'm afraid, and
is at this moment telling Dandolo exactly what you're up to. No, I
stand corrected. He has already done so, for look "—this, pointing to
a longboat that was pulling across the small stretch of water between
harborside and galley—"that's Constantine Philoxenites, who has
had *quite* an exhausting night with all you crusader types and your
political intrigues. Dandolo has summoned him, to explain in no uncertain terms that Philoxenites will not do what you bribed him to
do." Seeing the look on Boniface's face, I added, "I doubt you'll be
letting me go now, even if I did give you this lovely reliquary." Then
I pushed the gem-encrusted gold skullcap back into its red bag and
hurled it as hard as I could out over the harbor. It arced gracefully as
Boniface shouted, and it landed with a gentle *thwap*, cradled in the
canopy on the galley.

Before it had landed, the marquis's gloved hands were already around my neck. I kneed him in the crotch and felt his grip loosen, and then I used his arm for leverage to clamber up onto the swaying wooden railing. I'm not afraid of heights, but I am a little leery of hurling myself to my death. Directly below me, a hundred feet distant, were the rocks out of which the city rose. If I went straight down, I would die there. I could not throw myself as far out into the harbor as I'd thrown the reliquary. The ships were all moored tightly together for security, deeper into the harbor; the doge's was the closest one to shore. I had a chance of landing in water deep enough, if I could only make the leap.

Climbing I can do; even climbing down. Jumping is much harder. I closed my eyes and leapt as I felt Boniface reach out to grab at my leg. The cold night wind rushed over me. Time slowed. I felt myself move up and out, and then I seemed to hang in space in buffeting eddies of air for too long to believe; and then I was overwhelmed by the absolute absence of anything under me at all. I began to fall, and did not know where or even if I'd land. In that moment, I realized with gratitude that all need of vengeance was completely washed away; all I wanted was to hold Jamila one last time.

69

THE IMPORTANT CONFERENCE HAD already been disturbed, by something landing on the canopy above; before a mariner could be dispatched to climb the ratline and retrieve the mysterious projectile, there was my larger interruption to deal with. I'd fallen about a hundred feet away from the galley. The galley master sent a longboat to retrieve me and tried to keep anyone important from having to think about me.

I'd never been on Dandolo's galley, or any ship near to it in stature; it was beautiful, magnificent, unlike any of the pilgrim transports. Everything was painted a rich, warm red, with gold-leaf embellishments, all the details of bulwarks and trim carved with curving, flowing decorations. I tried to take it in as I coughed the Golden Horn out of my lungs. The doge's steward wrapped a blanket around me; I'd been recognized as the stupid lute player, so they knew this was no enemy attack gone awry; they wanted to question me but were willing to wait until I had my voice back. Meanwhile, I was left where I'd been bundled on deck, behind Gregor, so I heard the end of the conference.

The conversation between Philoxenites and Dandolo was pointed and brief; as soon as he'd been summoned to the doge's galley, the eunuch had known how this would go. I heard only Dandolo's winning argument: "Regardless of who's emperor, I will have the heaviest hand in the city's trading contracts. If you must determine where to place your loyalty, ask: Is your treasury kept full by the activities of the court or of the wharf?"

"I see your point, milord," Philoxenites said quietly. "We enter a new era. You may decide to whom the Varangian Guard should pledge its loyalty."

"You miss my point entirely, sir," Dandolo said sharply. "I don't demand such power. I demand that the Varangians pledge themselves to whomever is properly elected. I demand until that time, they pledge themselves to nobody *at all*, but remain in their barracks. Do not offer *me* the taste of tyranny, the aroma is far too tempting. You control the Varangians, Philoxenites. I ask only that you *do* control them, and not hand them over to the highest bidder."

"It shall be done, milord," said Philoxenites, looking grateful he'd be keeping what little remained of his manhood.

"Excellent. You may go," said Dandolo. Philoxenites practically leapt into the longboat waiting to return him to the docks.

Dandolo turned his attention toward where he knew Gregor was sitting. "So we have come full circle, lad, you and I. In Zara we were enemies, and now we work to the same purpose. Meditate upon what that might teach you of the nature of the world." Before Gregor could answer, he continued, louder, to the deck in general, "And that goes double for the human projectile, whom I presume to be your musician friend."

"My musician friend?" Gregor said in a garbled voice.

"The lute player, who pretends to be stupid," said Dandolo. "I know you're here, fellow. Approach and speak."

Gregor glanced back at me, and we exchanged amazed looks. "Yes, Your Grace," I said at last. Folding the blanket around myself, I moved closer to him and bowed, although he couldn't see it. "How . . . but how do you know who I am?"

Dandolo laughed. "I am Enrico Dandolo," he said, as if that explained everything. "I don't know who you are, but I know how you work, and have from the first moment you presented yourself to play back in Zara. I knew you were keeping an eye on something. Within days I knew that something was Gregor of Mainz, and within a few days of that, I knew you had a better head on your shoulders than he did, even when you and I had different aims. That's why I insisted on your attending nearly every vital meeting the army leadership has ever had. Do you think I have music playing in the background for *war councils* at home? Don't be ridiculous. I hoped the more you understood what was going on, the more you could keep Gregor in line. You did a miserable job, by the way, but I suspect he'd've been even more wrongheaded left entirely on his own."

For a moment I couldn't speak. "Your Grace," I finally stammered. "If I may say so, I am overwhelmed by your perspicacity."

"You may say so," Dandolo said. "I am not convinced I put it to good use, but I am grateful it has at least allowed us to reach this necessary moment of cooperation."

"Yes," I said heartily. Glancing up, I noticed that the awning still sagged above him—the red bag had been forgotten. "Your Lordship,

I'd like to express my admiration with a heavenly offering. If I may have leave to climb the ratline?"

I was allowed to do so. I collected the bag, clambered back down, untied the bag, and with permission, laid the reliquary on the doge's lap.

"John the Baptist," I announced. Dandolo drew in a sharp breath; his fingers reached for it, and he began to feel the worked gold and inlaid jewels. "Like yourself, milord, he knew what was going on better than the general public," I added. Gregor gave me an appalled look; I grinned and shrugged it off. As Dandolo's fingers grazed each stone, I told him what he was feeling: pearl, pink ruby, turquoise, emerald. His smile grew until I thought he might pull a muscle in his leathern face.

However, satisfied by the decorative abundance, he did the obvious thing and turned it over, to feel the sacred skull itself. His smile vanished instantly.

"It is a reliquary without a relic," he observed sharply.

"Oh, dear," I said. "Must have gotten lost in the scrape with Boniface." I glanced up to the deserted battlements and wondered fleetingly where Boniface was now. "I'd offer to retrace my steps, Your Grace, but in this case, I did not actually take any."

Gregor had turned red. "Your Grace," he said, his tone already so confessional that it was obvious he was the current holder of the skull.

The anger on Dandolo's face evaporated. "Ah," he said, interrupting Gregor's confession. "I understand. There can be only one solution, then." He signaled his steward. The man stepped up to us and took the reliquary from the doge. "Find a skull for this," said Dandolo offhandedly. "It's the head of John the Baptist." The steward, expressionless, nodded and vanished into the aftercastle. Gregor looked horrified. I chuckled and pulled the blanket tight around me against a gust of predawn wind.

"It is a pity we haven't worked more congruently," I decided.

"Yes," said Dandolo, not nearly as amused as I was. "It is." A pause. Philoxenites was gone. There were guards around, but otherwise it was just us three. It was nearly dawn, a huge tragedy lay ahead, and I could not imagine what else we had to discuss, but Dandolo's expression suggested he had more to say. "I think you understand what happens at dawn."

"The city falls," Gregor said grimly.

"The *nation* falls," I amended.

"Yes."

"And we can't stop it."

"That's correct," said Dandolo. "Nor should you want to, for this will be a day long celebrated in history."

"Celebrated in *some* people's history," I corrected.

"And lamented in others," Dandolo said comfortably. "It is the way of the world. Nobody *enjoys* it, but nobody has engineered a workable alternative. Do you know where my people come from?" he demanded suddenly, turning his full attention to Gregor.

"Venice," Gregor said with caution.

"One of the greatest and most violent maritime powers the world has ever known," I clarified, without caution.

"Venice," corrected Dandolo. "A cluster of swampy islands to which a small group of desperate refugees fled when they were being persecuted, centuries ago. They did not whine about their situation; they took control of it and prospered."

"And went on to persecute others in their turn," I shot back.

"Occasionally," Dandolo acknowledged, comfortably. "When their well-being required it. If you knew our history in detail, perhaps you'd point out the precise moment we went from the underdogs you approve of on principle to the empire builders you seem on principle to despise. Even if you could isolate that pivotal moment, however, you cannot freeze it in time and keep us so. Civilizations do not work that way. It is a burden God has given man. Venice has always sown what she's reaped, and shall continue to do so until she falls as well.

Yes," he said, sensing my stare. "Even Venice will fall. Every power does. Our star shall be eclipsed, eventually, and we'll even deserve it when it happens. Likewise the empire that falls today deserves to fall—or it would not be doing so."

"Thank you for explaining that to me," I said. "It would break my heart for us to part company if I felt that we were truly in accord about the nature of the world. Thank you for reminding me we aren't."

Dandolo smiled. "We aren't *yet.* When you are fifty years advanced from where you are now, remember me and see how the world looks to you then."

"I seriously doubt I'll live that long."

"Well then," concluded Dandolo, "you'll never have to learn."

"ALL RIGHT, YES, he *probably* had a point, but I wasn't going to give him the satisfaction of admitting it," I muttered, and then, wanting to change the direction of the discussion, "Very convincing suicidal behavior, by the way."

"Learned from the best," Gregor muttered back.

It was almost dawn now, grey, cold, and windy; we were in a longboat, spitting distance from the harbor docks. We both knew what tragedy would begin in the next hour. Our only balm was knowing we'd prevented it from being worse.

"I hope people listened to Ionnis," Gregor said.

Not surprisingly, Boniface's guards had been waiting for us at the wharf, wrapped in cloaks against the chilling gusts. Dandolo's men, forewarned, would not deliver us into their custody. So there was a standoff at the Venetian Gate; we remained on the longboat with well-armed mariners, leaning against each other for warmth. My tunic was still damp, and the blanket hardly helped. "At least you block more of the wind than Jamila would've," I said with a resigned sigh.

Finally, just before the sun rose, Boniface himself, agitated, came

to the harborside to see us—or rather to see Gregor. He did not acknowledge me. His last attempt was one of shameless sentiment. "My
son," he said in a wearied voice, looking every inch the martyred father, "what have you done?"

Gregor said nothing. He gestured for the mariners to row, and we
pushed away, leaving Boniface behind us as we slid through the water
to the inland harbor.

Epilogue

If rumor is to be believed, in two days' time will be the coronation of
Emperor Baldwin. Of Boniface, we heard little, only that he was offered the crown that morning but did not dare take it. The Varangian
Guard, leaderless, fled without inflicting damage—but what we heard
of the destruction of the city by the so-called pilgrims is ghastly. Greeks
fleeing faster than we ourselves traveled passed us and horrified us with
their tales. Thousands fled and were saved from savagery, so Ionnis did
his job well.

The monastery where Liliana sought refuge was so besieged with
refugees the Briton and I did not try to stay there, just let her know
that we were near and then set up camp on their foraging land. Yesterday she was safely delivered of a baby girl, and once she is recovered,
she and the squires will join me in pilgrimage. A real pilgrimage.

Days ago, the Briton and I went into the forest for fuel, but of
course there were many others there as well—there are thousands and
thousands of refugees everywhere; the city must be nearly empty. And
among these many thousands, we caught a glimpse of a woman with
her back to us, her head veiled, but we both recognized her gestures
and the way she stood. The Briton made a strange noise and looked as
if he would collapse.

"If you're going to be like that, go after her," I said.

He shook his head. But then he stood there staring for fully as long
as it takes the Richardim to put me in my armor. "Go after her," I
repeated.

"She chose another way."

"Sometimes our choices are meant to be mistakes we learn from." (Who could once have imagined my saying such a thing?) "Give her a chance to tell you if she made a mistake."

He looked at me nervously. "Maybe it isn't her. Maybe it is her but she doesn't want to see me."

I pointed back in the direction we had come. "If that's so, you still have a home and company. You know where to find me. I'll be there at least another fortnight."

He glanced at her, at me, at her again. She was moving away now, almost out of sight. "I'll do it, but we both know it's for nothing. I'll see you at the tent by sundown."

"I'll be there another fortnight even if you're not back by sundown. Except my wife and I, I cannot think of two people more due for time alone together. Take it."

A nervous laugh. "A nice thought, but I'll be back by sundown."

Suddenly he was no longer beside me but running toward her. I watched him approach. At the moment he reached her, and put a careful hand on her shoulder, I turned away. I think I even covered my eyes. I did not want to know, it felt too private. I found what kindling I could and came back to the tent.

That was two days ago. He has not returned.

Author's Note

For those curious about the history-fiction ratio, in what you have just read, I offer the following:

The foiled attempt (by Abbot Guy, Simon of Montfort, Robert of Boves, et al.) to "save" the Zarans is historically true, but it did not require the assistance of a British heretic. Simon left the army shortly thereafter and eventually went on to give us the Albigensian Crusade. (What was Zara is, in present-day Croatia, Zadar.)

A dramatic splitting of the army on Corfu, and its emotional reunion, really happened. Gregor and Jamila, being fictional, had absolutely nothing to do with it.

Alexios III, "the Usurper," rode out with a massive army to meet the Franks on 17 July 1203—then turned around, rode back inside the city walls, and fled Constantinople a few hours later (as per chapters 39 and 40). His army outnumbered his attackers' by at least ten to one (one eyewitness claimed by one hundred to one), plus he had a geographical advantage. Much conjecture has gone into why he did not actually engage in battle. The most convincing argument (which is still not entirely convincing) is that he never meant to attack the army at all; his presence was simply a feint to draw the Venetians away from their attack on the harbor.

Alexios III's mental instability, like that of his brother Isaac II, is not my invention.

Mourtzouphlos had been a prisoner for years and was released when Isaac was. He went from relative obscurity to the powerful position of *protovestiarios* within days of the army returning from Thrace—and immediately after Mourtzouphlos's accession, Alexios stopped behaving like Boniface's lapdog, which catalyzed a severe disintegration of relations be- teen Alexios and the army. But the device of smuggling relics via the aq- ueduct and cisterns is an invention (although those cisterns were used for smuggling other things, including people, for centuries).

The army's decisive final entrance into Constantinople in April 1204 began with a tower being taken, followed by a single soldier pushing his way through a tiny hole in a bricked-up gate—an act all his fellow soldiers believed was certain death. The soldier's brother, fighting beside him, tried to prevent him from going through. (The brother was Robert of Clari, one of the three primary contemporary chroniclers of the crusade.)

Ionnis's understanding of what the crusaders' victory meant (and, more important, didn't mean) seems to have been the understanding of the city overall. The actual sack of Constantinople, which I chose not to write about directly, was so devastating in large part because the people of the city did not understand they were going to be attacked and pillaged. They believed that accepting Boniface as their conquering hero–emperor meant that all the acrimony was finally behind them. They thought it was just yet another argument over who would be sitting on the throne.

FOLLOWING THE HISTORICAL events used as a backdrop for this novel, this is what occurred:

At dawn on April 13, Boniface of Montferrat was offered the crown of Byzantium by high-ranking Byzantine officials, who came to escort him to Hagia Sophia for what they assumed would be his coronation. While he did not technically accept the crown, he went with these officials on a processional, during which the army began to sack the city.

The sack lasted three days. In addition to the usual pillaging associ- ated with martial victories, the sack is remembered largely because of the innumerable relics that were taken from the city's churches and sent back to western Europe. (The treasury of San Marco in Venice displays a num- ber of these; more famously displayed on that church are the Four Horses of San Marco, which were originally the Four Horses of the Hippodrome in Constantinople.)

In May 1204, Baldwin of Flanders was unanimously elected Emperor of Constantinople by the twelve electors (six Venetians, six clergy).

After Mourtzouphlos fled the city, he sought out Alexios III (a.k.a. the Usurper in this novel), who blinded him and took him captive. Mourtzouphlos managed to escape but was caught in the autumn of 1204 and brought back to Constantinople, where he was sentenced to death. At Dandolo's suggestion, Mourtzouphlos was pushed from the top of the Column of Theodosius to his death. Shortly after this, Boniface captured "the Usurper," who was not executed; some sources have him being sent to Boniface's own territories in Northern Italy, others, spending the rest of his life in a monastery in Nicaea.

Bishop Conrad of Halberstadt (laden with relics) sailed from Constantinople to the Holy Land in August 1204, returned to Venice in the spring of 1205, then, after a blessing from the pope in Rome, returned home to great acclaim.

Enrico Dandolo, the Doge of Venice, died in June 1205, in his nineties. He was buried in Hagia Sophia, where a small memorial to him can be found on the upper gallery.

Boniface (who had married Emperor Isaac's widow, Margaret, to shore up his imperial prospects) survived a severe falling-out with Emperor Baldwin, was made ruler of Thessaloniki, and was killed in battle with the Bulgarians in September 1207. His friend and troubadour Raimbaut of Vaqueiras (author of "Kalenda Maya") was probably killed at the same time.

In July 1261, Greek-Byzantine forces overran Constantinople and reclaimed it from the Catholic Latins. The Latin Empire had lasted less than sixty years.

The reliquary head of John the Baptist, as described in this book, resided in the Monastery of St. John of Studious before the sack and remained somewhere in Constantinople even after that (it is now on display in the treasury of Topkapi Palace); another head of John the Baptist, however, made its way back to Venice, and another one to France. There is also one in Damascus.

THE NARRATIVE OF THE Fourth Crusade is known to us today through the chronicles of Geoffrey of Villehardouin, Robert of Clari, Nicetas Choniates, and various others (often anonymous), as well as the many historians who've helped to bring the primary sources into focus. If you're interested in learning more about "what actually happened," there are three excellent books, all called *The Fourth Crusade*. The one by Donald Queller and Thomas Madden is the most comprehensive; Michael Angold's looks primarily at Byzantium; Jonathan Phillips's is more a work for general readers, and it's a page-turner.

THE HISTORY

BEHIND

THE STORY

SARAH MAYHEW

Meet Nicole Galland

Award-winning screenwriter NICOLE GALLAND is working on her fourth novel, set in Leominster, England, in 1046. Raised on Martha's Vineyard, she has been an itinerant gypsy for much of her adult life, dividing her time between East and West coasts. However, she has recently married and rumor has it she may even settle down soon.

Galland, a Harvard graduate with a degree in comparative religion, personally retraced the Fourth Crusade's entire bloody path while researching the book. The result is a rich and riveting tale replete with exotic settings, full-blooded and complex characters, and sparkling wit.

About *Crossed*, she says, "If Monty Python made a movie of the infamous Fourth Crusade, surely the tagline would be: 'No infidels were hurt in the making of this crusade.' The parallels to contemporary events are almost as eerie: a western military coalition invites itself to liberate a rich eastern land from a usurping tyrant, then finds itself an occupying force fighting insurrectionists. Sound familiar? Well, it happened in the early thirteenth century—and it's happening today. What better timing for a novel about this pivotal event in world history?" Visit her Web site for future developments: www.nicolegalland.com.

The Story Behind
Crossed: A Tale of the Fourth Crusade

IN THE SPRING OF 2003, I was one of (I'm sure) many people who felt as if the zeitgeist of the planet was coming to resemble the Dark Ages or, at best, medieval Europe. "Somebody who knows something about the Middle Ages and writes fiction really ought to write a novel about the Crusades," I concluded. Exactly four minutes later, when I'd turned my attention to other things, I abruptly remembered that *I* know something about the Middle Ages, and *I* write fiction. Overwhelmed by a sense of dreadful obligation, and being by nature rather lazy, I made a pact with myself: Since my first two novels and all my medieval research were circa A.D. 1200, I'd write a crusade book *if* there had been a crusade circa A.D. 1200.

There was. At first glance, the Fourth Crusade did not seem like promising material for a novel meant to reflect today's troubles, as its tagline was, in essence, "No infidels were hurt in the making of this crusade." But I became intrigued by the Fourth Crusade, for two reasons. First, although the religious strife turned out to be Christians against Christians, the overall shape of the campaign was startlingly similar to what was going on in the contemporary world (and as I wrote it, developments in Iraq continued to mirror Byzantine history). Second, it was a heck of a narrative all on its own. If Monty Python had made a movie about one of the crusades, this is the one they would have chosen, and they'd hardly have to alter anything.

Here's one thing I can't change about myself as a novelist: I don't really write *about* history; I write about *characters* who happen to be trapped somewhere in history. I let my *Crossed* characters evolve over time, while I did more in-depth research (including retracing the steps of the whole Fourth Crusade—Venice to Zadar to Corfu to Istanbul). As usual when writing, I became obsessed with the project and talked to everyone I met about it. And I was fascinated by people's responses, which often began with, "Oh, the Fourth Crusade! I remember learning about *that* one! The *real* story was . . ." And then they would enthusiastically tell me what they'd been taught in school or history books. Interestingly, most interpretations blame the diversion to Constantinople on one of three parties:

1.   the Pope (who wanted Church reunification);

2.   the rank and file of the crusading army (who wanted loot);

3.   the Venetians (who wanted to be the supreme trading power in the Mediterranean).*

While all these folks did indeed want these specifics (and obtained them thanks to the diversion) that doesn't make them responsible for *causing* the diversion. It took me a while to realize that; I myself began researching *Crossed* certain the Venetians were behind it all. I no longer believe that. As the story reflects, I think the people who *were* really behind the diversion—a cabal of the ruling elite in

---

* For ages there was a (now disproved) conspiracy theory, claiming that the Venetians had just concluded a trade agreement with the Egyptians, and that they had engineered the diversion to Constantinople to avoid attacking their new allies in Egypt. The trading agreement in question actually came years later, and played no part in Venice's role in the Fourth Crusade.

Byzantium and the Holy Roman Empire, all related by marriage or blood—are the ones who escape blame in the common view. (People who are really behind things tend to be very good at that.)

I was so intrigued by this *Rashomon*-like (or in modern parlance, spin-doctor) phenomenon, that by the time I finished *Crossed*, I decided to explore multiple/conflicting interpretations for my next novel. Set in England in 1046, it gives four possible interpretations of a real-life event—a minor historical footnote that seldom makes it into general-interest books, but indirectly altered the course of European history . . . depending on whose version you believe.

A Conversation with Nicole Galland

You've said that you don't really write about history, but, rather, you write about characters who happen to be trapped somewhere in history. That's an interesting distinction; can you elaborate a bit?

I'm fascinated by how character and setting influence each other, but between the two, I love character more than setting. Lots of people who don't like historical drama *love* James Goldman's *The Lion in Winter* because even though it's about a medieval dynastic dispute (yawn), it's *really* about a dysfunctional family who deserve their own HBO reality series. They *happen* to be the royal family of medieval England, but you don't have to care about medieval England to care about them. You don't come away from the play feeling as if you "know" medieval England—but you definitely know *them*. Compare that to Dorothy Dunnett (I'm a huge fan of hers, too), who submerges her readers in a world full of characters who wouldn't work in any other setting. I love her Lymond as long as he stays in the sixteenth century; if I met him at a dinner party next Tuesday, he'd alienate me. So I'm more of a Goldman than a Dunnett— I aim for characters who resonate regardless of their setting. I don't know if I succeed at it, but it's what I aim for. In *Crossed*, my main passion was to tell the story of my characters and their evolution. Primarily, the Fourth Crusade is there to help me tell their story; secondarily, they are there to help me tell the story of the Fourth Crusade.

Are there any real-life historical characters in Crossed?

Except for Gregor and his entourage, all major characters in *Crossed* are bona fide real-life historical figures, and pretty important ones to boot. Dandolo, the Doge of Venice, would easily make the Top 5 list of Eye-Poppingly Impressive Medieval Personages. In depicting the real-life people (all men), I stayed as true as I could to the historical impressions of most of them. The less I respected somebody, the more creative license I gave myself in depicting him.

Why did you choose the disastrous Fourth Crusade as the setting for this novel?

I'd promised myself that I would write "a crusade novel" only about whatever campaign was set in the era I already knew well. This turned out to be the Fourth Crusade—and when I read a synopsis of it, I almost fell out of my chair, because it reminded me so much of what was happening in Iraq. A western military coalition, supplied and led by the leading capitalist power in the world (in their case, Venice), decides (uninvited) to "liberate" a rich eastern land (in their case, Constantinople) from a tyrant. This coalition's purported intention had been, originally, a crusade against dangerous Islamic extremists farther to the east (in their case, the Holy Land), but they decide it is more important to take down this tyrant first, even though his is a secular government. Why? Well, the highest-ranking member of the coalition (Prince Alexios Angelos) bears a personal grudge against the tyrant—because the tyrant had it out for his father. When the western military coalition attacks, the tyrant—an unscrupulous man whose path to power was a bloody one—turns and flees without a real fight, leaving his land in the hands of these western "liberators." Mission accomplished! There is (briefly) great rejoicing on all sides. However, the "liberating" military gets stuck there as an occupation force with no exit strategy, fighting a growing force of insurrectionists who do not care for the puppet regime the westerners try to set up. As I worked on the story, contemporary circumstances continued to mirror history: the puppet regime faces increasing resistance from the natives, while hostility against the western occupation forces grows so severe the military suffers guerilla attacks from insurgents on a daily basis. And so on.

As well as the parallels to modern events, I was drawn to the Fourth Crusade because it's just a heck of a story. As I'm fond of saying, it's the Crusade Monty Python would have picked, because they'd hardly have to change anything about it to turn it into very dark farce.

Are there lessons to be learned from the events of the Fourth Crusade that might be applied to a current-day situation?

Oh, yes, but we're not likely to learn them. The biggest one is, of course, that those who do not remember the past are condemned to repeat it. The final disaster, what led to the fall of Constantinople and the destruction of the Byzantine Empire, was not a clash between two religions, but between two long-conflicting sects of one religion: Roman Catholicism and Eastern Orthodoxy, the two principal faces of Christianity.

Originally I thought, well, at least that's *one* problem that won't come up this time around. So I got a queasy feeling in the pit of my stomach as the Sunni-Shia conflict overshadowed all other problems in Iraq. As of this writing (mid-2007), it seems likely that the future of Iraq hangs on this issue. In 1204 the Catholic soldiers wanted to throw in the towel, convinced it was sinful to attack their fellow Christians, but then the Catholic priests convinced them it was the will of God to destroy the hated Orthodox heretics who had persecuted their Catholic brethren. This incited the Catholics to capture and pillage the city, making their religion dominant. Once again: Mission accomplished! Except that their new world order lasted not quite as long as the USSR did, and then their old enemies came back and reclaimed their territories, in the name of God, before eventually losing the same territory themselves to the Moslems, who also took it in the name of God. The lesson everyone needs to learn is leave God out of it.

Jamila is a fascinating character; in many ways, a woman ahead of her time. Can you tell us a little bit about how you developed her character?

Developing characters is often a murky process; I don't fully understand it myself. Sometimes—as with Jamila—it's like making gazpacho: I knew what ingredients I wanted to include, so I threw them all together and let them season each other. In her case, there were five basic ingredients. First, I wanted a Jewish character, because that's an underrepresented subculture of the era. Second, I wanted an outsider who could comment intelligently, wittily, and informedly on the crusader zeitgeist. Third, I wanted a chance to display elements of the Arab world that otherwise wouldn't have made it into the story—since, after all, they never even *reach* the Arab world. Fourth, I wanted my narrator to have a worthy love-interest who could match his wit and attitude, and inspire him to evolve out of his own morbid self-absorption. Finally, and most important: I wanted to create a strong female whose strength was independent of her gender. I love all of my female characters, but they are usually so defined by *gender*—even my one heroine who passes as a man is preoccupied with making sure she's not perceived as female or feminine. I wanted to create a strong, capable, admirable, likeable, worldly character—who *happens* to be female. That aspect, more than anything, may be why Jamila is "a woman ahead of her time"—in that era, not many women had the luxury of being valued for their soul first, their sex second.

Questions for Discussion of *Crossed*

1. Discuss the title of the book. What are the possible applications of the word *crossed* to the events and characters of the story?

2. Whom do you consider the most sympathetic character in the story? Why?

3. Which character behaves the most honorably throughout? Why?

4. If you were to find yourself in this story, which of the five main characters would you most resemble in outlook and action? (This might be a different response than the ones given for questions 2 or 3.)

5. Discuss the differences of the two narrators—in their character and background; their morality, values, and belief-systems; and their story-telling styles.

6. Discuss Dandolo's comments near the end of the book about the fall of empires. Does this seem like a purely

historical observation, or are there possible implications about today's world as well?

7. Discuss Jamila's dilemma in having to choose whether she will remain with a man she loves or return to her community. What do you think of the choice she makes, and what choice would you make in her position?

8. What do you think is implied by the end of the epilogue: that the Briton has found a way to join the Jewish community, or that he and Jamila have gone off on their own?

9. Who is a better ruler, Dandolo or Boniface? Why?

10. There are strong parallels between the Fourth Crusade and the current situation in Iraq, but the author emphasizes these parallels infrequently in the text itself. How often, if ever, did such parallels occur to you as you were reading?

The lighter side of HISTORY

PORTRAIT OF AN UNKNOWN WOMAN
A Novel
by Vanora Bennett
978-0-06-125256-3 (paperback)

Meg, adopted daughter of Sir Thomas More, narrates the tale of a famous Holbein painting and the secrets it holds.

THE SIXTH WIFE
She Survived Henry VIII to be Betrayed by Love...
by Suzannah Dunn
978-0-06-143156-2 (paperback)

Kate Parr survived four years of marriage to King Henry VIII, but a new love may undo a lifetime of caution.

A POISONED SEASON
A Novel of Suspense
by Tasha Alexander   978-0-06-117421-6 (paperback)

As a cat-burglar torments Victorian London, a mysterious gentleman fascinates high society.

THE KING'S GOLD
A Novel
by Yxta Maya Murray   978-0-06-089108-4 (paperback)

A journey through Renaissance Italy, ripe with ancient maps, riddles, and treasure hunters. Book Two of the Red Lion Series.

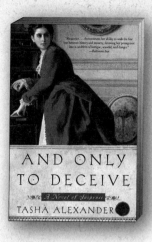

AND ONLY TO DECEIVE
A Novel of Suspense
by Tasha Alexander
978-0-06-114844-6 (paperback)
Discover the dangerous secrets kept by the strait-laced English of the Victorian era.

TO THE TOWER BORN
A Novel of the Lost Princes
by Robin Maxwell
978-0-06-058052-0 (paperback)

Join Nell Caxton in the search for the lost heirs to the throne of Tudor England.

CROSSED
A Tale of the Fourth Crusade
by Nicole Galland   978-0-06-084180-5 (paperback)
Under the banner of the Crusades, a pious knight and a British vagabond attempt a daring rescue.

THE SCROLL OF SEDUCTION
A Novel of Power, Madness, and Royalty
by Gioconda Belli   978-0-06-083313-8 (paperback)
A dual narrative of love, obsession, madness, and betrayal surrounding one of history's most controversial monarchs, Juana the Mad.

PILATE'S WIFE
A Novel of the Roman Empire
by Antoinette May   978-0-06-112866-0 (paperback)
Claudia foresaw the Romans' persecution of Christians, but even she could not stop the crucifixion.

ELIZABETH: THE GOLDEN AGE
by Tasha Alexander   978-0-06-143123-4 (paperback)
This novelization of the film starring Cate Blanchett is an eloquent exploration of the relationship between Queen Elizabeth I and Sir Walter Raleigh at the height of her power.

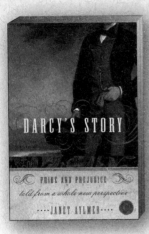

DARCY'S STORY
by Janet Aylmer
978-0-06-114870-5 (paperback)
Read Mr. Darcy's side of the story—*Pride and Prejudice* from a new perspective.

THE CANTERBURY PAPERS
A Novel
by Judith Healey
978-0-06-077332-8 (paperback)
Follow Princess Alais on a secret mission as she unlocks a long-held and dangerous secret.

THE FOOL'S TALE
A Novel
by Nicole Galland   978-0-06-072151-0 (paperback)
Travel back to Wales, 1198, a time of treachery, political unrest...and passion.

THE QUEEN OF SUBTLETIES
A Novel of Anne Boleyn
by Suzannah Dunn   978-0-06-059158-8 (paperback)
Untangle the web of fate surrounding Anne Boleyn in a tale narrated by the King's Confectioner.

REBECCA
The Classic Tale of Romantic Suspense
by Daphne Du Maurier   978-0-380-73040-7 (paperback)
Follow the second Mrs. Maxim de Winter down the lonely drive to Manderley, where Rebecca once ruled.

REBECCA'S TALE
A Novel
by Sally Beauman   978-0-06-117467-4 (paperback)
Unlock the dark secrets and old worlds of Rebecca de Winter's life with investigator Colonel Julyan.

REVENGE OF THE ROSE
A Novel
by Nicole Galland
978-0-06-084179-9 (paperback)
In the court of the Holy Roman Emperor, not
even a knight is safe from gossip, schemes, and
secrets.

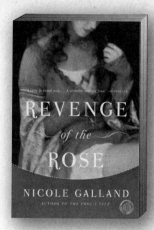

A SUNDIAL IN A GRAVE: 1610
**A Novel of Intrigue, Secret Societies, and
the Race to Save History**
by Mary Gentle
978-0-380-82041-2 (paperback)
Renaissance Europe comes alive in this dazzling
tale of love, murder, and blackmail.

THORNFIELD HALL
Jane Eyre's Hidden Story
by Emma Tennant   978-0-06-000455-2 (paperback)
Watch the romance of Jane Eyre and Mr. Rochester unfold in this breathtaking
sequel.

THE WIDOW'S WAR
A Novel
by Sally Gunning   978-0-06-079158-2 (paperback)
Tread the shores of colonial Cape Cod with a lonely whaler's widow as she tries
to build a new life.

THE WILD IRISH
A Novel of Elizabeth I & the Pirate O'Malley
by Robin Maxwell   978-0-06-009143-9 (paperback)
Hoist a sail with the Irish pirate and clan chief Grace O'Malley.